The Nine Inheritors

The Extraordinary Odyssey of a Family and
Their Ancient Torah Scroll

PRAISE FOR

THE NINE INHERITORS

The Nine Inheritors will entertain and engross you—and linger. Richly drawn and authentic characters face a common challenge: how each will inherit the family Torah: a treasure, yet, to some, a burden. Tied together by bloodlines and Jewish tradition, each inheritor gains personal insight by ownership of the Torah. With her lyrical prose and unexpected twists and turns of plot, Ms. Datnow has created an unforgettable family story that will surprise and delight the reader.

Elizabeth Kohn, attorney

Like all good Yiddish epics, The Nine Inheritors: The Extraordinary Odyssey of a Family and Their Ancient Torah Scroll *begins with a vision. And that vision propels us on an unforgettable journey through generations of the Rosen family, accompanied by their sacred Torah Scroll and everything it represents. Claire Datnow has written an instant classic and a book, I believe, that will become a mainstay of contemporary Jewish literature. From the moment that Shmuel Rosen commissions his "magnificent sefer Torah from Jerusalem" (for many good reasons and a few wrong ones) until that same Torah lands battered and bruised – and in a way, far more magnificent – in a far-off land, I found myself holding my breath. I've often said, "I don't read Fiction." I'm an historian, a scholar. And then, a rare book comes along that lulls you into embracing the story of it all. I used to have three favorite works of Fiction:* The Last of the Just, East of Eden, *and* The Plague *and I. Now, thanks to Ms. Datnow, I have four. Today,*The Nine Inheritors *quietly took its place beside the other three.*

Kyla Rigney, free-lance writer and reviewer

2

Books by Claire Datnow

NONFICTION

Behind the Walled Garden of Apartheid: Growing Up White in Segregated South Africa

The Final Diagnosis: What the Autopsy Reveals About Life and Death, coauthored with Dr. Boris Datnow

FICTION

Young Adult Eco Mystery Series:

The Adventures of The Sizzling Six: The Lone Tree

The Adventures of The Sizzling Six: Who Stole the Cahaba Lily?

The Adventures of The Sizzling Six: The Living Treasure

The Adventures of The Sizzling Six: Who Kidnapped the Koala?

YOUNG ADULT BIOGRAPHIES

Edwin Hubble: Discoverer of Galaxies

American Fantasy and Science Fiction Writers

The Nine Inheritors

The Extraordinary Odyssey of a Family and Their Ancient Torah Scroll

A Novel

Claire Datnow

Media Mint Publishing
Birmingham, Alabama USA

FIRST MEDIA MINT BOOK EDITION 2011

For information:
Media Mint Publishing
2021 Brae Trail,
Birmingham, Alabama 35242
www.mediamint.net

Library of Congress Cataloging-in-Publication Data
Datnow, Claire
The Nine Inheritors:The Extraordinary Odyssey of a Family and Their Ancient Torah Scroll/Claire Datnow
1.Jews—Lithuania—shtetl—religion—culture—Fiction
2.Jewish diaspora—1780-2021—Fiction
3.Torah—Torah scribe—Torah study—Fiction
4.Jews in America—religion—culture—Fiction
5.Judaism—Fiction

LCCN: 2011935903
ISBN 978-0-9842778-5-8

Book and cover design by Boris Datnow

Printed in the United States of America

Dedication

Dedicated to the 250 Jews from the village of Linkuva, Lithuania, killed in July 1941 by the Nazis and their Lithuanian collaborators, among them my grandmother Blume Klein, and my aunts Dora and Toibe Klein. In loving memory of my parents Cecil and Gertrude Klein. And to my children, their spouses, and my grandchildren, Allen, Margarita, Sonia, and Claudia; Steve, Jacie, Emily, and Lilly; Stuart, Robyn, Madeline, and Elise.

Sources and Acknowledgments

While it is too daunting to cite every book and article that provided background information for what I have written, I do wish to list the most useful sources. *There Once Was a World*, by Yaffa Yiliach; *A Historical Atlas of the Jewish People*, edited by Eli Barnavi; *Atlas of the Jewish World*, by Nicholas de Lange; *A Century of Jewish Life in Dixie: The Birmingham Experience*, by Mark H. Elovitz; *The World of Sholom Aleichem*, by Maurice Samuel; *The Jew Store*, by Stella Suberman; *From the Ends of the Earth: Judaic Treasures of the Library of Congress*, by Abraham J. Karp; *The Old Country: The Lost World of East European Jews*, by Abraham Shulman, foreword by Isaac Bashevis Singer; *Kabbalah: The Way of the Jewish Mystic*, by Perle Besserman; *The Nine Questions People Ask About Judaism*, by Dennis Prager and Joseph Telushkin; *Jazz: The First Century*, edited by John Edward Hasse; *The Making of the Atomic Bomb*, by Richard Rhodes; *Treasury of Jewish Quotations*, by Leo Rosten; and *Salvation on Sand Mountain*, by Dennis Covington. Thanks to David Kleiner for permission to use his original lyrics. Thanks also to AskMoses.com for permission to quote from Rabbi Mendy Hecht. My sincere gratitude to Jamie Reinhardt for his dedicated shaping of the first draft. Thanks also to Judith Shulamith Langer-Surnamer Caplan for her sensitive feedback. I am grateful to Jane Hinds, Helen Forman, Evelyn and Charles Felice, Shirley Aaron, Ree Morin, Aubrey and Joan Lurie, the late Martha Bazzell, Ellen Bruck, and to Rabbi Scott Hausman-Weiss for their helpful comments. My sincere appreciation to Ada Elgavish and George Henshell who generously took the time to critique the final proof. Thanks to Gaby Elgavish for feedback on esoteric religious questions. Thanks to my daughter, Robyn Usdan, my sons Allen and Steve for their loving and enthusiastic support. My appreciation to Elizabeth and Robert Kohn for their judicious guidance and belief in me as a storyteller. To Boris, my husband and loving companion, my heartfelt thanks for your expert technical assistance, wise counsel, and, above all, your unfailing devotion.

Descendants of Shmuel Rosen

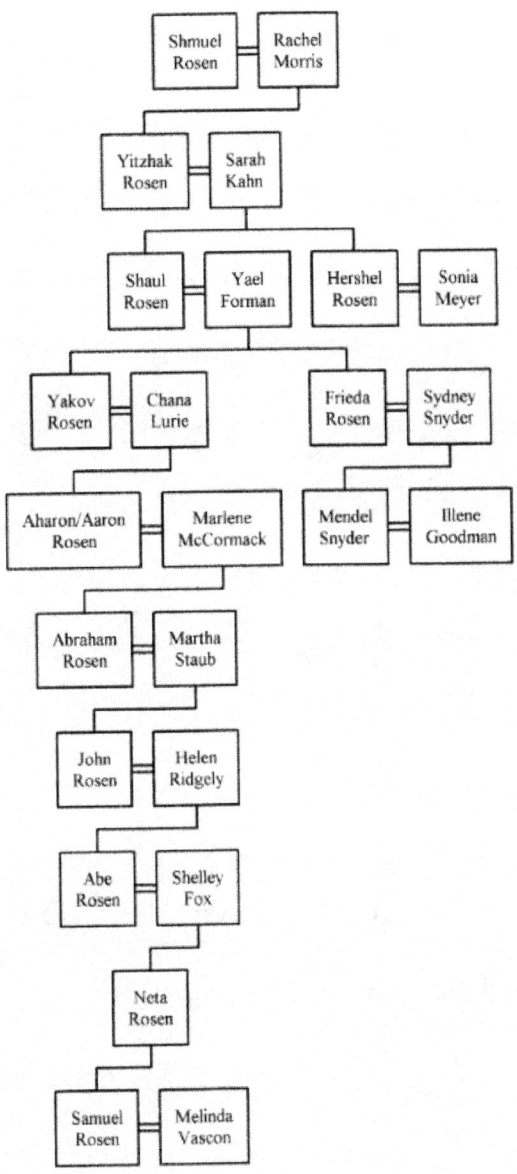

The photo was taken at the wedding of Cecil Klein's first cousin, Freda Kapuler and her groom Meier Blumsohn, in Linkuva, Lithuania, the shtetl where my father was born in 1912, just before he immigrated to South Africa with my grandfather, Sydney Klein, in 1928.

Table of Contents

Table of Contents (continued)

Prologue

The story of the Rosen family and their Torah is a kaleidoscope of the past, present, and future—shards of history picked out of the dust of time like multicolored gems captured in a translucent holding chamber and reflected in mirrors. Twist it this way and that against the light, and ever-changing patterns appear. Notice, however, that one gem remains fixed and gleaming at the center, like the North Star, their sacred family legacy, the Rosen Torah.

Observe the *sofer*, or trained scribe, as he dips his elegant goose quill into the raven-black ink and reverently, meticulously creates their Torah, letter by letter on special soft parchment in strict accordance with prescribed laws. Appreciate that it took over a year to complete; that a single error of the precisely 304,805 stylized Hebrew letters that make up the scroll will render it unfit for use.

Understand that Orthodox Jews revere the Torah as the literal word of God, revealed to Moses on Mount Sinai, embodying the wisdom of the ages collected in the first five books of the Hebrew Bible and containing the origin, history, and religious laws of Judaism; that it delineates a complete system of 613 commandments, or *mitzvot*. Imagine that, in order to lead a moral life, Orthodox Jews must fulfill these commandments, some daily, because the Torah is a living document whose teachings and traditions unfold over generations and millennia, the central guide to the relationship between God and man. Embedded in the sometimes monotonous and sometimes upsetting narratives are the highest ethical imperatives that still speak to us today as universal truths.

For all these reasons, to its inheritors—the Rosen Torah whether devoted to the Torah or indifferent to or even ignorant

13

of its teachings—was never just a possession; in a sense it became their possessor, a potent, sacred entity wielding its own power.

Remember all this as the Torah and its nine inheritors are swept along the fast-moving, treacherous tides of history.

❧1❧

The Patriarch: Shmuel Rosen's Vision

True dreams come from angels; false dreams come from demons.
                                                                Talmud

Before daybreak, Shmuel Rosen of Valinsk, Lithuania, owner of the town's thriving tavern, and his niece Tsiporah, hovered in the shadows of a half-open door, to bid farewell to her groom, Tevya Moriva, as he set out on a long and dangerous journey to the Land of Israel. Only they and a lone gypsy peddler witnessed the barrel-chested, powerfully built fiddler as he led his long-eared donkey across the deserted market square enclosed by rows of narrow two-story gabled shops, and beneath the church with the tall steeple and low clock tower that caused him to flinch uneasily as it chimed the lonely dawn hour. At the well on the west end of the cobbled square, he halted briefly to fill a leather flagon with fresh water, turned to wave a last goodbye to his bride, then strode up the hill toward the wooden *shul*, or synagogue, its triple-tiered roof glinting dimly on the summit.

Patting the donkey smartly on the rump to keep it moving at a brisk pace, Tevya grumbled, "Shmuel talked me into sneaking away like a common thief, when a klezmer band, fiddling its heart out followed by a procession of village people should be cheering me on and wishing me Godspeed. But when I return, it'll be a different story."

At the top of the hill, Tevya paused to look back at the *shtetl*, or town, he would not see again for many months. In the murky light he could just distinguish the main road leading to the marketplace and the steep roofs of the shops surrounding it. His eyes followed the jumble of streets as they oozed off sideways from the market to become lanes and backyards where humble shoemakers and tailors, bakers and butchers, blacksmiths and candlestick makers dreamed of tumultuous and profitable market days. On the outskirts of the shtetl, the headstones of the Jewish cemetery appeared to float in an amber sea of grain gradually giving way to wild meadows and dense forests.

As he gazed, the sun rose above the hill, transforming the shtetl with its ruddy glow into a mysterious silhouette that floated before his mesmerized eyes like the great city of Constantinople where he was born.

A chill ran down Tevya's spine, and he closed his eyes and sent up a prayer: "May it be Your will, Hashem, our God, that You lead me toward my desired destination. And please, Hashem, King of the Universe, may I return to Valinsk to find my wife Tsiporah, now carrying our child, both waiting for me in good health." For good measure he could not resist adding, "And, Hashem, if it's not too much to ask, may I return a rich man. Blessed are You, Hashem, our God, King of the Universe. And, one more thing please, Hashem may my child be . . ." The strident wake-up call of a rooster pierced the silence, interrupting his litany and provoking his donkey into discordant braying. Hurriedly opening his eyes, Tevya saw that the morning sun had washed his illusion away; in its place stood the humble shtetl he had come to think of as home. With his prayers ringing in his ears, Tevya urged the donkey across the rickety wooden bridge spanning the cold, clear Wilja River, and down the road that snaked toward the eerie forest.

The train of events that set Tevya Moriva's historic journey in motion, began just a few months earlier, on the seventh of August 1790, or according to the Hebrew calendar that starts with the creation of Adam and Eve, the twenty-seventh of Av 5555, the day on which Shmuel celebrated his fifty-seventh birthday.

On that day Shmuel awoke, shivering with desire. Propping himself on one elbow, he gazed at his wife, Rachel, as if seeing her for the first time. She lay beside him, sprawled on her stomach, her eyes darting rapidly to and fro beneath the delicate skin of her eyelids as she dreamed one of her many strange dreams. If he had been looking at her critically, he might have noted that her features were too irregular, her nose too thin, her lips too full, her eyes too far apart. But Shmuel saw only the sheen on her hair, the delicate blush of her cheeks, the softness of her skin, and the strength of her long limbs.

She was his third wife, and had produced his seventh child and only son, the apple of his eye, Yitzhak. His previous two wives had died in childbirth, leaving behind six daughters. And although Rachel was not as beautiful as his first wife, Blume, or as capable as his second wife, Ida, she responded to him with a passion that they had never achieved; and she treated him with the proper respect and consideration a husband deserved.

Awakening leisurely, Rachel watched through half-closed eyelids as her spouse flexed his muscles and pushed out his chest; her nostrils flared with delight as he rolled over and took her warm body under him. When he cried out at the peak of his pleasure, she was suffused with a sense of her own power, letting her hand stray into the thicket of his black beard with its early streaks of gray.

As Shmuel threw back the sheets and swung his feet onto the floor, she stretched, and opened her wide, gray eyes. She was about to wish him a happy birthday when he bellowed, "Woman, you have defiled me!"

Rachel turned pale and began to tremble. Her tongue felt thick in her mouth as she swore that this was not her time to bleed, that she had been clean for seven days and had purified herself in the *mikvah*, or ritual bath, as prescribed in the Torah.

Nonetheless, Shmuel's face flushed with anger; how could she deny the stains on the sheets? Despite the pleasure she had just given him, despite her protestations, he backed away, for a man is forbidden by the commandments of the Torah from having sexual intercourse with a *niddah*, or menstruating woman.

Rachel watched Shmuel dress hastily, with his back to her, like a man escaping from a fire. His shoulders looked so broad, his profile so strong and proud, that she cried out, "Please, Shmuelke, don't be angry with me, it was an accident!"

She saw his back stiffen before he half turned to her and said sternly, "I must do what is prescribed in the Torah—I must go to the bathhouse to purify myself." He shrugged on his overcoat, forcing the buttons into the wrong holes in his haste to be gone. Without thinking Rachel reached out to button it properly.

Shmuel reared back in alarm crying, "Do not touch me; you are niddah," leaving Rachel's hands suspended in the air as if beseeching him to stay, hands in supplication against the pain of rejection. As he turned and retreated, Rachel's arms dropped heavily to her sides, and she sobbed, "I'm sorry!"

Shmuel closed the door with a thud, leaving his wife bewildered and sobbing with shame.

After a while she rose quietly. Taking care not to touch and thereby defile any object, she dressed and hurried to consult Rabbi Ben Levi's wife, Rebbetzin Feigel, who like her husband, was a respected leader in her own right. Over glasses of scalding-hot lemon tea, she listened calmly to what Rachel had to say.

"Rebbetzin Feigel, I swear it was an accident. I took all the precautions, I ritually washed myself, and wore clean white underclothing and slept on clean white sheets for seven consecutive days after bleeding."

"I'm sure you did, Rachel, but at your time of life menstrual cycles are uncertain," she said. "You must take extra care to observe the special rules." Rachel nodded her acquiescence.

"Examine yourself internally twice, once at sunrise and once at nightfall. If you find blood, or a bloodstain on your clothing or bedding, you must once again check that your bleeding has stopped and then restart the count of seven clean days."

"I will take extra care, but Shmuel is so unforgiving even though it was an accident."

Seeing the hurt in Rachel's eyes and knowing that Shmuel could be harsh, the rebbetzin said, "I understand you are suffering because your husband is angry, but he is rightly so. It is not for us to question Hashem's laws, but to obey them. You must put your personal feelings aside and find peace in doing what is right."

Rachel nodded, still her eyes filled with tears.

"Do not be disturbed by these changes in your body. Remember, Hashem has made you according to His will—aging body and all. Thank Him that you are alive to grow old."

Rachel was grateful to the rebbetzin for being gentle with her, but she felt her heart collapse, and began sobbing, "Now my womb can no longer nourish the daughter I have yearned for all these years."

"Rachel, you have taken care of your stepdaughters lovingly, and have provided Shmuel with the son he longed for. These are *mitzvot*, good deeds, according to God's Torah."

Rachel took a deep breath and started to protest, "But Shmuel doesn't appreciate . . . "

"Go home, Rachel. Wash the sheets, cook Shmuel's dinner, make your specialty, chopped liver with goose fat. Maybe uncork a bottle of wine. Follow the examples of your mother and grandmother." Rebbetzin Feigel put her glass down on the table with a soft clink and stood, signaling to Rachel that she was being dismissed, if ever so gently.

As Rachel got up to leave, the rebbetzin took her hand and pressing it firmly, said with a gleam in her eye, "After dinner when your husband is feeling content, don't be afraid to speak your mind!"

Although there was a hard lump in Rachel's throat, she smiled and kissed the rebbetzin's cheek, for she understood what it meant to be a woman of the shtetl.

Shmuel was experiencing turmoil of quite a different nature from that of his wife—a turmoil not born of confusion and anxiety, but more akin to excitement that only added to the commotion of his fifty-seventh birthday.

That morning, to his astonishment the household cat Simcha, a fine mouser, bore a litter of seven kittens, all males, who would undoubtedly help their mother decimate the vermin overrunning the barn. Shortly before lunch, the good news came that the authorities had granted him an exclusive concession to sell alcoholic drinks, which he had been scheming for months to obtain. Minutes after that came the joyous message that his niece Miriam had announced her engagement to Isaac, seventh son of the revered scholar Rabbi Meier Berk, bringing immense honor to the Rosen family. In the midst of congratulations, a maid rushed in to tell them that his oldest daughter, Mina, had prematurely given birth to his seventh grandchild, a tiny boy with a fuzz of red hair—his six previous grandchildren were all girls. On hearing this, Shmuel clapped his hands crying, "Congratulations, Mazel Tov, may this grandson, Hashem willing, grow up to be a *talmid chochom*, an outstanding scholar and religious leader!"

After all that uproar, Shmuel was glad to find a moment of peace at *mincha*, the short afternoon service. While reciting Psalm 145, "One generation shall praise thy works to another, and shall declare Thy mighty acts," his mind drifted to the unusual events of the day. *I'm a practical man, I don't give in to superstitious nonsense like some fools,* he muttered to himself, *and yet it seems to me that so many male births all in one day, and on the day of my birth no less, must mean something. And so many sevens maybe could be a sign of something, too.* Shmuel continued to sway back and forth in prayer, and to mouth the rest of the psalm, but his thoughts were elsewhere.

My dear grandmother Roche Leibe, may she rest in peace, he mused with a shudder, secretly dabbled in kabbalistic mysticism and the gematria, searching for meaning in the numbers assigned to Hebrew letters, although it is frowned upon by traditional Orthodox Jews. Shmuel tried to reason with himself, but he could not shake the feeling that someone more learned, a man like Rabbi Ben Levi, might find meaning behind the strange and wonderful happenings of the day. *If I consult the rabbi I will have to be careful not to offend him. It's a sore point with him that his sister and brother-in-law recently defected to the*

Chassidim — a shocking event almost unheard of in our congregation. Since Chassidim have introduced questionable occult practices and ideas to our traditions, our rabbi, with good reason, fears we will judge him guilty by association. On the other hand, if I don't consult him, these thoughts will keep spinning in my head and drive me crazy, Shmuel continued to debate with himself. By the time he said the final prayer of mincha, God is one, Shmuel had made up his mind to consult the shtetl's sage, even at the risk of incurring his wrath.

Rebbetzin Feigel ushered Shmuel into her husband's small study, where he found him seated in a straight-backed wooden chair with his head bent over a religious text. Shmuel stood in the doorway, raking his fingers through his luxuriant beard, his deep-set eyes glittering like black diamonds. A hefty mass of flesh, he filled the space between the doorjambs. He took a moment to look around the room while he waited for the rabbi to notice him. With envy, Shmuel observed the signs of scholarship, the clutter of papers and books scattered over the desk, the multitude of tomes lining the walls, the table piled high with rolls of parchment and writing implements, and the imposing grandfather clock with a brass pendulum.

Finally, the rabbi looked up. He was not entirely comfortable with Shmuel's outsized presence and his legendary reputation for violence. In his mind he quickly reviewed the man's colorful history:

A drunken Cossack had once threatened to shoot Shmuel, and, without hesitating, the tavern keeper had knocked the gun out of the man's hand. The enraged Cossack had then grabbed a glass of hot tea and flung it into Shmuel's ear. Despite the excruciating pain, Shmuel did not loosen his grip until he had hurled the man, with a great bellow, out the door and into the street. And then there was the questionable way in which he conducted his grain business; it gave the Jewish community a bad reputation. Shmuel frequently waylaid peasant farmers on the road to market by seizing the horse's reins in his huge hands as the loaded cart rattled by. With brute strength he led the spooked horse and unnerved farmer into the stable attached to the back of his house. There he haggled over the price of grain until the farmer gave in; more often he took off muttering curses under his breath. Undaunted, Shmuel would chase after the retreating cart, seize the horse's reins, and begin the haggling all over again.

Eventually these rough tactics began to backfire. When the farmers caught sight of his massive bulk straddling the road, they spurred their horses on to a frantic pace. Undeterred, Shmuel quit chasing carts and instead began to lease fields directly from the farmers. When the harvesting began he rushed sacks of flax, wheat, and barley to the large centers of Vilna or Kovna, where he sold the grain at a tidy profit. In this way Shmuel had become one of the wealthiest men in a shtetl where most of its inhabitants teetered on the edge of poverty.

Despite these flaws, Rabbi Ben Levi thought with grudging admiration, *Shmuel is strong and courageous, a shrewd businessman, and a fellow Jew. To fulfill my obligations as a good rabbi and a decent human being who cares for the people of my shtetl through all their tribulations, it is my duty to listen to what Shmuel has to say.*

Realizing that he had left Shmuel standing in the doorway too long, the rabbi rose and, gesturing toward a narrow sofa stuffed with horsehair, said, "Come in, Shmuel, come in! Sit down. Make yourself comfortable. Tell me what's on your mind."

Thrusting himself though the doorframe, Shmuel sat down. When the little sofa groaned under his weight, he rose in alarm and remained on his feet while he related the puzzle of the males and the sevens, with lively gestures and just a little exaggeration. As he finished, he mopped the sweat from his face with a worn cotton handkerchief and eased himself back on the couch. "Rabbi, you know I am a practical man. I don't believe in superstition any more than you do; but please, tell me what am I to make of all these fortunate events on the day of my birth, and what can all these sevens mean?"

As was his custom, the rabbi leaned back in his chair, adjusted his *yarmulke,* or skullcap, and closed his eyes to think things over.

Then he sat upright abruptly, and lectured Shmuel, "What you have just related smacks of Chassidism. I have made it known that I completely disapprove of their movement. They say that their spiritual leader, the tzadik, has supernatural powers. And they spread propaganda that certain kabbalistic rituals together with gematria will enable a man to establish a direct link to God! The study of the Torah is the foremost obligation of a Jew, and even to suggest something like *that* is comparable to Torah study is a blasphemy."

Shmuel had braced himself for the rabbi's outrage, so he said meekly, "I understand."

Not to be appeased, the rabbi leaned forward and waved his index finger in indignation. "In my opinion, Chassidim dangerously undermine tradition!" He itched to dismiss Shmuel without further discussion, but the man before him was a *macher*—someone with connections, who had a way of imposing his will on the people of the shtetl. It was rumored that he made bribes to Lithuanian officials, but he also gave to the Valinsk burial society and to the synagogue. It wasn't easy to get Shmuel to give charity, and when he did you could be sure that he had a hidden agenda having to do with false pride and the need to elevate himself in the eyes of the community. Still, it would be wise to keep Shmuel's goodwill.

After this silent deliberation, the rabbi proceeded to list some allusions in the Torah to the number seven, ticking each one off on his long fingers. "Since you mentioned sevens . . . First, seven is the number which symbolizes many gifts or blessings from Hashem. There are seven benedictions recited at the wedding of a virgin. When they arrived in the Promised Land, the Israelites found seven crops, which stood for seven blessings, wheat, barley, figs, grapes, olives, pomegranates, and dates." He paused to take a sip of strong, hot tea before going on. "In Psalm 29, there is a description of the seven voices of God. There are seven days of the autumn festival known as Sukkot, when we make seven circuits around the shul." Here the sage raised an eyebrow, inviting Shmuel's acknowledgment. Not wanting to interrupt, he only nodded vigorously, so the rabbi gave him some more. "Moreover, the Holy City of Jerusalem has been destroyed and rebuilt seven times." Another sip of tea. "Also, do not forget that after God created the world in six days, on the seventh He rested, giving us the Sabbath, our most important holy day. The Talmud states 'All agree that the Torah was given to Israel on the Sabbath Day,' the seventh day of the week."

The rabbi's bushy eyebrows now jumped up and down in scholarly excitement. Suddenly a strange passage from the Babylonian Talmud, the basis for all codes of rabbinic law, popped into his head. It advised a troubled dreamer to transform a dream from evil to good by intoning, *"It is good and may it become good. May the merciful One transform it to good. May heaven decree upon it seven times that it become good and always will be good."* But not wanting to encourage Shmuel to give more weight to irrational beliefs, or to open the door to rumors he decided against divulging it.

"So many references to seven in the Torah!" Shmuel exclaimed, "Still, Rabbi, what am I to make of it?"

The sage lifted his hands and shrugged. "I repeat that I don't have a direct link to God. I am a humble rabbi and devoted scholar." Shaking his head, the rabbi warned, "The Torah says, 'Do not act on the basis of auspicious omens. Do not act on the basis of auspicious times.'"

"Rabbi Ben Levi, I understand. Still," Shmuel pressed on, "you are steeped in the wisdom of the Torah and the Talmud. Perhaps you can give me some idea of what all this good fortune might mean to me personally?"

Again the rabbi sat tugging on his long sideburns, silently willing himself to stay calm and think rationally. Shmuel, he now realized, had just presented him with a golden opportunity, Hashem willing, to make much needed repairs to the shul—at a time when his good standing in the community was in question after his sister's disgraceful defection to the Chassidim. He decided to goad Shmuel into giving money for the renovations, but he would have to proceed carefully, because Shmuel was no fool. So he proclaimed, "I suggest that you put the nonsense of sevens out of your mind. Consider instead the importance of males in the story you have just related. Think of your son, Yitzhak, and your newborn grandson, may Hashem bless them.

Think of an act that will bestow blessings on them and on future generations of Rosens."

"Yes, an act that will bestow blessings on them! So, what should it be?"

"A rich man like you can do a great deal. Just think of our shul—its roof is leaking, there's a crack in the window on the south side, the Torah is worn and is continually in need of repair, and I could go on. Think of those things. " The rabbi glanced at the clock. "I advise you to go home, to pray, and to immerse yourself in the study of the Torah and the Talmud, which explain the importance of charity as a mitzvah or blessing."

"Wonderful advice! But with due respect, Rabbi Ben Levi, I came to you with one puzzle and I'm leaving with another." Shmuel spread out his palms and pushed out his lower lip to emphasize his point. Although he pretended not to have understood, he knew he was being dunned for a sizeable charitable contribution.

The rabbi recognized the source of Shmuel's resistance: the man was arrogant; he wanted something more than to give his hard-earned money away; he wanted to do something that would confer honor and recognition on him. He yearned for prestige and would use his wealth to buy it if he could find a way that suited him.

The rabbi shifted in his seat and cleared his throat. "Shmuel, the sages say that a man should combine Torah study with charitable actions; in this way a father can serve as a personal example to his son, and at the same time earn the respect and honor of the community." He could tell from the way Shmuel was leaning forward to catch every word that he had finally snared the macher. Now was the time to drive his point home:

"The most respected men of our congregation, whose places are reserved for them by the shul's eastern wall nearest the Holy Ark, have earned this honor because they are *shayne yidden*, or beautiful people, which as you know has nothing to do with looks and everything to do with being a *mensch*, a person of integrity."

From the way Shmuel knotted his hands over his ample belly, the rabbi felt that he had indeed touched a raw nerve. A man like Shmuel, despite his wealth, was lacking in scholarship and could not hope to become a shayne yid, unless he showed great piety or, lacking that, gave generously to charity.

Shmuel knew that the rabbi was manipulating him, and he resented it; but he had tested the rabbi's patience enough for one day, so he stood, thanked him politely, and left.

On the way home he began mulling over what the rabbi had said, so preoccupied with colliding thoughts that he failed to make his customary stop in the marketplace to buy a pinch of snuff, even when Gitke Lutz, the shopkeeper, called out to him to step inside.

That evening, after the delicious meal Rachel had prepared, Shmuel gave her a detailed account of the conversation between himself and Rabbi Ben Levi. Rachel listened with rising alarm, and when her husband had finished she was tempted to question him — what did he really want from the rabbi, what did the rabbi want from him? But to signal that she was still upset with the way he had treated her that morning, she withheld her comments — for the moment.

Shmuel could tell from his wife's silence that he had offended her. Yet what right had she to complain, he rationalized, for weren't they both bound to the laws of the Torah? And didn't they both enjoy sex? And why shouldn't they? The process by which procreating gets done is regarded as a mitzvah, a divine command. And, since God had chosen an especially private part of the male to carry the sign of His covenant with the Jewish people, there was no shame in sexual intercourse between husband and wife.

Downing glasses of tea poured from the steaming samovar, husband and wife sat mute, each nursing his and her grudges and ruminating over the cat-and-mouse game between Shmuel and the rabbi.

That night the couple tossed and turned under the quilt of eiderdown, taking great care not to touch each other. But the angel of sleep was slow to come, and when it did, it brought only fitful rest shredded by haunting dreams. At dawn Rachel awoke with a start and told Shmuel she had dreamed of herself as a young bride on her wedding day.

"I swear to you, Shmuelke, we were standing under the canopy just as we did so many years ago. I wore my silk bridal gown and the beautiful string of fine Baltic amber my mother and father gave me for my dowry — the one with six small beads and a large one in the center." Sitting on the edge of the bed, Shmuel wondered foggily if this dream had anything to do with the blessing of charity the rabbi had spoken about.

"Suddenly the string broke and seven amber beads rolled away, scattering like chickens fleeing a wolf," Rachel went on, closing her eyes and stroking the soft skin on her eyelids with her fingertips as if to see the dream more clearly. "You got down on your knees and began scratching for the beads like a rooster in a barnyard scratching for worms."

"Get on with it, woman!" Shmuel didn't appreciate the image she had conjured of him crawling on the floor, his rear end raised in view of the entire congregation.

"As you found each bead, you placed it in the palms of my hands. Then the rabbi poured wine as dark as blood into my cupped hands, making the beads float like babies in a womb."

"Babies in a womb, no less!" Shmuel sighed at the extravagance of his wife's imagination.

Rachel's eyes had the glazed look of someone seeing beyond this world. "Then I heard the rabbi say, 'The blood of our children will be spilled, but the Torah will endure; it is to the soul of our children what rain is to the soil.' He scooped the beads from my palms and scattered them onto the Torah unrolled on the lectern. I watched, frozen to the spot like a pillar of salt, terrified that the rabbi had defiled the Torah with wine that dripped from the amber. But, miracle of miracles, they knotted themselves back into a perfect strand around my neck, and the Torah had not a stain upon it!" Rachel spat three times, "Tooh, tooh, tooh!" to avoid the evil eye, before going on.

"Woman, stop ranting!" Shmuel admonished, trying to ignore the shiver that ran down his spine. Then a bit more gently,

"Such a dream calls for a hot cup of tea with cherry preserves. You can think and think, and study the Torah and the Talmud until your eyes blur, and not solve the problems of life; still a good cup of tea always helps," Shmuel reflected.

After tea, Shmuel found that he was late for the daily *shacharit*, or morning services. As he neared the synagogue, he heard the familiar singsong cadence of men at prayer wafting down to him. He quickened his lumbering pace uphill, inwardly berating Rachel for delaying him with the account of her weird dream.

On reaching the summit, Shmuel paused to catch his breath and look down at the shtetl. His eyes followed the cramped streets of the artisans, and beyond them the muddy lanes of wagon drivers, butchers, and the teachers who ruled by the whip. *I was born in this shtetl and here I shall die, leaving my children to carry on the traditions of our forefathers.* He waited for another thought to come; but none did, so he mopped the sweat trickling down his face and into his beard with his worn handkerchief, and hurried into the synagogue.

In the sanctuary, he squeezed past men, already deep in prayer, covered in *tallises*, or fringed prayer shawls. Upon reaching his accustomed seat, he wrapped his tallis around his shoulders and wound his phylacteries onto his arm and forehead with the appropriate benedictions. Opening the *siddur*, the prayer book, he began to sway back and forth: "Give thanks unto the Lord and call His name." When he came to the Shema—the declaration of faith in one God that he had recited a thousand times as a faithful Jew—he raised his voice and cried, "Hear O Israel, the Lord is our God, the Lord is One."

Shmuel continued to follow the time-honored order of morning services without skipping any of the required blessings or prayers. He would no more alter their order than attempt to rearrange the universe. Nevertheless, trying to catch up to the rest of the congregation, he recited the prayers too rapidly, causing his tongue to slur over the words; and when he looked up, he caught the disapproving eye of Rabbi Ben Levi. Shmuel quickly covered his eyes with the palm of his hand to show he was concentrating on the meaning of the words. At the same time he inwardly pleaded, *Rabbi, slow down, you are going too fast for those among us whose tongues are not so nimble.*

After introductory prayers, it was time for the Torah reading as today was a Thursday. Itsik Bernstein, the *shochet*, or ritual slaughterer, on being called up to *aliyah*, or accorded the honor of saying the blessing over the Torah, proudly ascended the platform and opened the handsomely carved wooden doors of the Holy Ark to reveal the scroll bedecked in all its finery. As he did so the congregation rose and remained standing out of respect for the Torah, while reciting verses of praise. The shochet lifted the Torah out of the ark, and as Shmuel joined in the chanting of the Shema, a sudden rush of *kavanah*, or devotion, stirred in his veins at the thought of God's Torah and the countless generations who had died to keep it alive.

Next a synagogue official called upon Moishe Hirsch, who owned the village mill, to carry the Torah around the sanctuary. A stab of envy momentarily dampened the flame flickering within Shmuel, for once again he had not been chosen for aliyah. Men lined the aisle, reaching out to touch the Torah with their prayer books or the fringes of their prayer shawls and then pressing it to their lips as a sign of love and reverence.

After circling the sanctuary, Moishe brought the Torah to rest on the reading table on the *bima*, or raised platform. He sat as the cantor slowly, deliberately, reverentially undressed the Torah, removing its silver breastplate, the crowns on the handles, the mantle and the binding cord. Then the cantor took it from Moishe, and unrolled it on the lectern to the Torah portion for that day. Never touching the delicate parchment, he followed the text with a silver *yad*, or pointer, in the shape of a closed hand with an extended index finger. Shmuel listened with admiration to the cantor's easy diction as he chanted the verses without vowels or musical notations to guide him; one had to memorize them from a special book.

At the conclusion of the reading, yet another honoree raised the open Torah on high, turning it to the left and right to display the Hebrew text before all the congregation, who

29

chanted, "This is the Torah that Moses set before the people of Israel." As Shmuel intoned the words, a persistent, muffled coughing and wheezing distracted him. He half-turned and saw that it was Mendel the schoolteacher, choking on his own phlegm. He had lost weight, his beard was a scraggly mess, and his hands shook. *Mendel has never overcome his grief at the loss of his wife and newborn son, but he continues to keep the Torah's eternal laws,* Shmuel thought approvingly.

With a sigh, Shmuel turned back to face the ark, and saw that Rabbi Ben Levi's eyes were again upon him. The Rabbi wants my very being, he thought. He doesn't get angry and he doesn't nag; he just wants me to follow him in performing every mitzvah — that's tradition and I am just a cog in God's wheel, or maybe that wheel is crushing me — an errant thought he quickly banished.

Another honoree rolled up the scroll, bound it, and replaced the cover and adornments. Then with fitting ceremony, blessings, and prayers the rabbi returned the Torah to the ark; and as Shmuel lifted his voice to join the congregation singing with great devotion, "It is a Tree of Life to those who hold fast to it, and all of its supporters are happy," the meaning of Rachel's dream broke over him. In that instant a vision of a magnificent *sefer Torah,* seemed to shimmer before his eyes. A handwritten scroll of fine, golden-hued calfskin inscribed by a *sofer* with expertly fashioned Hebrew lettering as dark as ebony. The scroll was securely fitted to finely polished and sturdy olive wood posts. Ornate silver finials, with crowns and tinkling bells set with gleaming semiprecious stones, adorned the top of the posts. A burgundy mantle of precious Damascus silk, embroidered with a golden border of twisting grape leaves, covered the Torah. Over the mantle a breastplate of solid silver and gold, engraved with the lion of Judah, hung from a chain, and also a slim, delicate silver yad dangled from the poles. Oh! Oh! A marvelous Torah clothed in silk and jewels, crowned in silver to be perpetually read and interpreted. The flicker of deep religious zeal that he had felt moments ago, again burst spontaneously into flame, leaving him weak and trembling. He had been wrong to feel crushed by tradition; it was carrying him upward.

"I will commission a magnificent sefer Torah from Jerusalem, in honor of my beloved grandfather, who found his last resting place there. It will be the Rosen family's sacred legacy, binding the generations together through the God-given traditions of my people, reminding them to honor and observe them," Shmuel cried, overcome by the magnitude of his vision.

Those seated nearest to Shmuel gaped in astonishment at his outburst. As soon as prayer services were over, Shmuel hurried to tell the rabbi of his extraordinary vision.

When he had finished, the rabbi sat gazing at Shmuel in amazement, thoughtfully stroking his beard. It was his duty to guide these people, his fellow Jews, to the Torah; but he had hoped to steer Shmuel into giving a considerable donation to the shul. Instead this *macher* had interpreted him quite differently, choosing to commission a Torah—from Jerusalem, no less. Yet why should he be surprised? He had lectured Shmuel on the importance of the Torah and its commandments and, given Shmuel's arrogance and his need to elevate his status in the eyes of the community, he should have foreseen this possibility. The ingrained traditional shtetl hierarchy that placed some on top and others at the bottom of the rung was not a good thing and had nothing to do with the teaching of the Torah, but he could not change what had become an entrenched way of life; he could only lessen its worst consequences.

The rabbi could see from the fervor shining in Shmuel's eyes that he would not easily be dissuaded, as owning a Torah would undoubtedly place him higher on the shtetl's pecking order, closer to the scholars on the top, and above the property owners, shopkeepers, artisans, laborers, and paupers at the bottom.

"This is indeed a worthy mission! As you know, of 613 mitzvahs incumbent upon all Jews, the final one is to write a Torah. But what led you to make this momentous decision?"

"My wife's dream, of course!"

31

Levi's eyes narrowed. Could it be possible that this hardheaded businessman had made a weighty resolution based on nothing more substantial then a woman's dream?

"The making of a Torah is no small undertaking, Shmuel. I would advise you to think carefully before you act, consider the enormous cost and risks involved," he cautioned. "But for now, please relate this dream to me."

Shmuel launched into his wife's vision, adding a few embellishments of his own, before concluding, "And now do you see, Rabbi, that's how I realized what blessing I should confer upon my family?"

The rabbi failed to follow Shmuel's leap from a woman's dream about beads and chickens to commissioning a Torah. In order to avoid anything that might hint of his approval of Chassidim, he said, "It would be best for you to explain your interpretation of her dream, because it is not customary for a rabbi to interpret dreams."

Believing that Ben Levi was testing him, Shmuel gave a smile so broad that his eyes retreated into the fleshy pouches of his face. "You want *me* to interpret it?" he inquired, wondering if the rabbi could be trying to expose his lack of scholarship.

The rabbi did not return his smile. "The Talmud advises us that a dream not interpreted is like a letter not read. Therefore I will listen to your interpretation."

Shmuel shifted his considerable weight onto the balls of his feet, put his hands behind his back, and poked out his bottom lip. "Rabbi, the seven amber beads are my offspring, right? After all, don't I regard my family as precious jewels? The broken strand and scattered beads signify the persecution of the Jews and their scattering in the Diaspora. Am I correct?"

Ben Levi put the tips of his bony fingers together and held Shmuel in a steady gaze.

Recalling the many times he had been beaten with a long cane for "being as ignorant as a donkey," Shmuel felt like a schoolboy being quizzed before the entire class. Once, in a fit of anger, he had grabbed the end of the cane and twisted it out of the teacher's hand. But the schoolteacher wrested it back and beat him so hard that it broke in half.

"Have you more to tell me?" the rabbi prompted, waking Shmuel from his disagreeable train of thought.

Shmuel silently chided himself, I am a successful businessman, and I hope soon to be a man respected for my magnificent Torah. No need for me to be so meek.

With a circular motion, the rabbi was gesturing impatiently for him to go on.

"Where was I? Oh yes, the wine and blood and the babies Rachel saw in her dream. Could they stand for life, for the cycle of birth and rebirth?" Shmuel paused to discern if the rabbi approved, but the man just sat with his arms folded. So he went on, "The Torah, of course, represents God's eternal laws commanding us to keep our traditions alive from generation to generation."

"Yes, it represents God's laws." The rabbi adjusted his prayer shawl and skullcap, struggling to regain control of the situation. "And you understand that the Torah is the Tree of Life, and the study of the Torah leads to good deeds, and good deeds lead to a good life," Rabbi Ben Levi advised, realizing now that although things had taken an unexpected direction, he needed to turn Shmuel's decision to his own advantage.

"Yes, I fully understand, Rabbi."

"Also, consider that according to the Torah when male offspring exist, they are invariably the exclusive heirs of their father's estate. However, it is not necessary to own a Torah, if your heirs faithfully learn the Torah and follow its commandments, its teachings will be passed down through the generations, ensuring a blessing on them all."

"Yes, Rabbi."

"And I would suggest that in addition you make a . . ." the rabbi broke off, and cleared his throat so loudly that Shmuel thought a herringbone had lodged there. He had started to ask the macher for a generous donation, but decided it would be wiser to wait until the Rosen Torah became a reality. Instead, he said, "I would suggest that you house your Torah—when and if it finally arrives from Jerusalem—in the shul. In that way you can ensure that it is safe, that it is properly protected, and that it can be read in front of the congregation."

Upon hearing these pronouncements, Shmuel felt a glow of satisfaction settle in his stomach like Rachel's fine chicken soup and dumplings. For a moment he imagined himself carrying the Rosen Torah, and Yitzhak, his only son, chanting from it in front of the congregation; and he shivered with awe and pride. His increased stature as owner of a magnificent scroll would ensure that the Rosens would be called upon almost as often as the Talmud scholars to take the Torah from the Holy Ark. With a Torah of his own, he would gain a jump on those who saw fit to exclude him from their Saturday tea-drinking and discussion sessions just because he had not graduated from the *yeshiva,* the Jewish academy of higher learning. Now he would be just as good as they were.

Realizing that he had been outmaneuvered, Rabbi Ben Levi stood, shook Shmuel's huge hand with his bird-like one, and said, "A blessing on your family. May good fortune follow you and your Torah!"

"Thank you, Rabbi." Shmuel said, surprised to feel tears prickling his eyes.

As he prepared to leave, the rabbi added a caution: "You should understand that, while a family inheritance of such importance can inspire your descendants' highest aspirations, such an inheritance can also cause grudges and rivalry within the family, and arouse the envy of others in the community. It is also a great responsibility, for what is the burden of inheritance when one is bequeathed a Torah?"

Shmuel was too consumed by his vision to pay attention to the rabbi's warning. As he lumbered out the door and down the hill, his heart swelled with exhilaration so overpowering that he began to clap his hands, stamp his feet and sing out loud, "*Oi, Oi, Oi, un mir zainmen ale brider, un mir zingen freieche lider, Oi, Oi, Oi!*" Oh, we are all brothers, and we sing happy songs, Oh!

❦2❧

Shmuel's Emissary: Tevya Moriva Journeys to the Holy Land

May you rescue us from the hand of every foe, ambush, bandits and evil animals along the way, and from all manner of punishments that assemble to come to Earth.

The Traveler's Prayer

After his vision of the Rosen Torah, Shmuel had conferred with two of the shrewdest men in the shtetl, Yankel Klein and Moishe Hoch. Klein pointed out that qualified Torah scribes could be found in Lithuania, making it unnecessary to send a courier all the way to Jerusalem. Hoch added that the journey would take months, would be extremely dangerous, and very costly. He advised Shmuel not to throw money away on such a venture. In the first place, where would he find the right man for this undertaking, one that would keep him from home for many months and from which he might never return? If he found such a man, the risk of being attacked by robbers and left for dead on the roadside would be hard to surmount; even if he managed to escape with his life, the chances of the Torah being stolen or destroyed were too great. In short, the odds were against such an undertaking.

Undeterred, the macher poked out his lower lip and explained, "After my grandmother died, my grandfather, Zaide

Lazar Rosen, bid farewell to all that was familiar to him and made *aliyah*, the ascent, to the Holy Land, even though by then he was in poor health. At the time I was a small boy and didn't understand how courageous he was to leave all those who loved and cared for him behind. This mission is to honor him."

"Yes, I recall that your zaide's younger son, David, accompanied him, Hoch reminisced. "And when he died, just a few years afterwards, David returned with many wondrous tales."

"I remember the grand procession that came out to bid your zaide farewell," Klein sighed, "as if it were yesterday."

Shmuel could still picture his grandfather, seated on high like a sage, looking down on the people of the shtetl as they crowded around his carriage. How they had wept when he promised to offer up prayers for them once he reached Jerusalem. As the carriage started to roll, Shmuel had jumped onto the running board screaming, "Zaide, Zaide, take me with you!" His mother had to pry him loose, kicking and protesting. As he watched the carriage cross the wooden bridge and disappear around a bend carrying his beloved grandfather away, he had burst into uncontrollable hiccupping and sniveling, wiping tears and mucus from his face on the back of his clenched hands. The older boys had jeered at him, and it had taken years of fist fighting to rid himself of the nickname "Crybaby."

The night after he had consulted with Klein and Hoch, Shmuel told Rachel, "A Lithuanian Torah would be very fine, but still it would be created by a local scribe. I've made up my mind that our Torah will come from holy ground, from Jerusalem."

When Rachel suggested that the money to finance this particular project might be better spent on the family's immediate needs, and also to repair the shul, Shmuel rebuffed her, declaring that the Rosen Torah *was* meant for the family and the shul. Didn't she understand how such a magnificent Torah would confer prestige on their congregation? More importantly, couldn't she see that by inheriting such a Torah his descendants would become guardians of the family's legacy and of their faith and heritage? So solemn a responsibility would elevate them from not just any family, but a family with pedigree that counted for something, a family with *yichus,* or prestige.

However, there still remained one major obstacle: where to find the right man for the mission. At first, this proved to be difficult. Men who were trustworthy were not willing to go, and those who were willing to go were not trustworthy. But then fate presented him with Tevya Moriva, the cross-eyed fiddler.

One stormy night, roused by the discordant squawking of the chickens in the opening under the oven where they roosted in the winter, Chava Beilis, Shmuel Rosen's widowed sister, had discovered her daughter, Tsiporah, and Tevya coupling on the kitchen floor. Chava had turned and rushed from the house, running through the downpour, stumbling and sniveling like a drunken peasant, to her brother Shmuel's house. In her misery she did not stop to consider that she was delivering Tevya Moriva into her brother's hands.

Teyva had honestly earned the nickname *der shtarke,* the strong one. Though short in stature, he had a wrestler's barrel chest and powerful arms, and was not afraid to break up a brawl. Shmuel hired Tevya to help at the Rosen Tavern, where his pugnacious reputation—underscored by the thrust of his chin and the odd angle of his left eye—was enough to warn ruffians away and keep the drinkers quiet. Tevya was especially useful on market days when crowds of peasants came to the tavern for a glass of pure grain whiskey, and hearty food, drinking away the profits they had just made selling their goods.

Shmuel also learned that Tevya was a man of some experience with languages. He had been raised in a Sephardic Jewish community under Ottoman rule, near Constantinople, and could speak Turkish and some Arabic, as well as Hebrew and Yiddish. Shmuel knew that this improved his chances of getting through the foreign lands that lay between the shtetl and Holy Jerusalem.

For these reasons Shmuel was convinced that Tevya was his man, but he needed to think of a scheme that would convince him to undertake such a long and dangerous journey.

When confronted by Shmuel about his amorous tryst, Tevya quickly proclaimed his love for Tsiporah. He swore that he wanted to marry her but did not have a shekel to his name. Tsiporah also pleaded with her uncle to allow her to marry Tevya, declaring she loved him. Shmuel scoffed at the very notion of love. After all, parents whose judgment was based on practical matters like property and status should be the ones to arrange marriages.

Shmuel weighed the pros and cons of giving his permission for them to marry. On the positive side, he had a soft spot for his niece, who had tenderly nursed his wife, Rachel, back to health during a severe bout of pneumonia. But a fiddler without even a common trade to his name was a less-than-appealing prospect. Also on the negative side, Tevya's family *yichus* was obscure, as he had been orphaned at an early age. He came from a family of klezmerim, an itinerant band of folk musicians, thus placing him far down the ladder of respectability. These musicians were poor and uneducated, and had a reputation for preferring alcohol and women to the study of the Torah. Even worse, Tevya's lust—clearly demonstrated by his behavior with Tsiporah—could spell trouble in the future.

On the positive side, Tevya's physical strength, courage, and cheerful disposition were excellent attributes. Besides, his fatherless niece could hardly be considered a great catch. With a dark moustache on her upper lip and a figure like a sack of potatoes, she was not likely to attract the most eligible young men. Such a pity! How he would like to have married her off to a brilliant scholar, preferably from a wealthy family.

Over the next few weeks, Shmuel continued mulling over the advantages and disadvantages of this particular union, until his sister confessed hysterically that Tsiporah was pregnant. Upon hearing this shocking news, Shmuel could not restrain his anger. Grabbing the hapless Chava by the arm and shaking her back and forth so that she cried out in protest, he yelled, "My God! This will destroy the reputation of our family forever! Now the whole community will . . ." He stopped in midsentence and looked up at the rafters for a moment. The vein throbbing in his forehead gradually subsided and, prodding his sister out the door, he said in a more conciliatory tone, "Go home, Chava. Don't worry, I've thought of a brilliant plan to take care of the situation."

As soon as she closed the door, he did a little jig and rubbed his hands together, delighted that he had seized on a way to turn this shameful affair to his advantage. He would approach Tevya with an offer he could not refuse.

That afternoon, Shmuel put his enticing proposition before Tevya. "If you are willing to undertake a journey to Jerusalem," he told him, "and return with a sefer Torah intact, then I will personally provide a generous dowry for my niece, a beautiful fox fur coat for you, as well as kest, or room and board for you and Tsiporah." Tevya tapped his index finger on his lips. "And after your first son is born — if it's a son — twelve pieces of gold. As for the journey, I will provide everything needed: a donkey, money, basic provisions." To clinch the deal, Shmuel ended by saying, "And then, of course, there is the prestige a luftmensch like you, will gain from marrying into a family like ours."

Tevya felt a hot stab of anger at Shmuel's calling him a foolish dreamer, but he knew that he had no leverage. He would be a fool not to grab this golden opportunity. He started to speak, but Shmuel was already pounding his back with a heavy hand. "No need to thank me. Just get the job done!" Tevya swallowed his pride, now determined to carry out the task no matter how difficult it might prove to be. After all, he thought, what did a man like him have to lose?

As Tevya made his way back to his lodgings at Chava Beilis, running long fingers through his bush of curly hair, he muttered to himself, "No need to ask permission from my bride-to-be for a woman is subordinate to a man. Still, to sooth her fears and get her blessing, I must plead my case. But that will be no easy task for Tsiporah will be extremely upset to part from me for such a lengthy and uncertain trip — and especially with our baby on the way." A rain shower had just passed and Tevya halted to watch barefooted children splashing and pigeons bathing in the puddles, while continuing to mumble to himself, "First, I will assure her that I can take care of any dangers I might meet along the way. Next, I will put forward my most forceful argument that with the money and prestige earned from this mission our future will be secure, and we could start a business of our own." He distractedly shooed away a pigeon hovering overhead, "Also, how can she deny that if I turn her Uncle Shmuel down it will cause ill will, even jeopardize our future livelihood in the shtetl. If I succeed in this mission I will bring something of inestimable value to the Rosens and to the whole shtetl." With that, he thumped his fist into his palm and marched on.

Chava Beilis was grateful to her brother for solving her predicament and saving face before the community. Before Tevya's departure, she hastily arranged a wedding for the unruly couple. Given the circumstances, the affair was not as elaborate as might be expected for a family of the Rosens' standing, but it was nonetheless a joyful celebration. Chickens and geese were butchered, preserves and wines brought up from cellars. Chava and Tsiporah, with the help of family and friends, prepared braided breads, fish cakes, pickled herrings, and a fine assortment of cakes, cookies, and dried fruit.

On Saturday night, following the service signifying the end of the Jewish Sabbath after sundown, a candlelit procession moved through the streets toward the courtyard in front of the shul. The bride and her mother held long, twisted candles as they followed the musicians; in the rear, young men brandished burning torches as they danced. Summoned by the music, the inhabitants of the shtetl, dressed in their finest Sabbath attire, joined the parade.

The rabbi performed the marriage, held in the courtyard under the *chuppah,* or wedding canopy. After the ceremony, which sanctified the union before God, the happy throng, again led by joyful musicians, made its way to Shmuel's house. As they danced along the children showered the couple with wheat to enhance fertility — a welcome if perhaps superfluous gesture.

Since the town lacked a wedding hall, the reception took place in the big stable attached to Shmuel's house. For the occasion the animals were put out to pasture, the barn cleaned, the floor spread with fresh sand, and the rafters decorated with chains of bright paper lanterns. Long tables covered in coarse white linen were set up for feasting. Planks placed on large barrels provided a makeshift stage for the klezmer band. Between performances a master of ceremonies told jokes and kept things lively, while the guests ate their fill and then washed everything down with mead, wine or whiskey.

Shmuel was in his element, wolfing down a loaf of bread with a heaping platter of fish cakes, consuming slices of honey cake, and downing shots of whiskey. Satiated, at last, he belched loudly and began to sing and dance, encouraging others to join him, a happy mountain of flesh, the rolls under his chin quivering and his heavy paunch gyrating in time to the beat.

Two days later, just before Tevya's departure, Shmuel requested a favor from him. Pressing a stone from the shtetl's cemetery into Tevya's hand, he said, "Please place this on the grave of my dear Zaide, Lazar Rosen, who lies buried in Jerusalem, to show that I have not forgotten him."

"It will be my honor to do so," Tevya said, aware of this custom to accord respect for the dead. "But how will I find his grave?"

"I have already told you where to find Manasseh Ben Israel, the Torah scribe. He will know where Zaide lies. You see, Zaide and his son David, lived with the scribe's family until Zaide passed away." Pulling a faded and folded paper from his coat pocket, he handed it to Tevya. "Here also is a map David gave me many years ago, showing the section of the cemetery in which you can find my Zaide's tombstone."

And so it came to pass, just weeks after Shmuel's vision, Tevya set out on his journey to distant Jerusalem. Sometimes walking, sometimes riding the donkey, heading always southward toward the Bosphorus, he traveled through Poland toward the Land of Abraham, Isaac and Jacob, many months away. Having no map or compass to guide him, the emissary had to rely on the locals who were not always trustworthy.

To make matters more difficult, bands of escaped serfs, Cossacks, and even renegade Jews terrorized travelers through these regions of southern and eastern Europe. For safety he banded together with others journeying his way, whenever he could, entertaining them with music and song, bawdy jokes, and clever riddles. And before night fell, Tevya made for a village where the locals were acquainted with other Jews; there he could be assured of food and shelter, no matter how humble.

After weeks of travel to the slow and steady clip-clop of his donkey, Tevya reached the Carpathian Mountains demarcating the northern border of the Ottoman Empire, the Turkish state spanning Southeastern Europe, the Middle East and North Africa. Minarets and mosques began to dot the land more profusely, clear signs of the domination of the Ottoman Turks. As he pushed doggedly on, heading southeast, his spirits lifted at the thought that he was nearing the halfway point of his journey to Jerusalem. Finally he reached the great city of Constantinople on the fast-flowing waters of the Bosphorus, connecting the Mediterranean Sea with the Black Sea like a sinuous eel. Wearied by months of travel, he rested for a few days in the shadows of the soaring minarets and shining domes.

Awakened before dawn by the cries of the muezzin calling his faithful to prayers, he commented groggily before murmuring his own morning prayer, "The muezzin wakes his flock like a rooster crowing, but Jews don't need a reminder to say prayers to God."

On his way to the souk for a light breakfast of freshly baked flat bread, honey and dates, he paused to watch the caiques and feluccas skimming over the Bosphorus with sails full; the oil lamps in the stern still glowing like fireflies. The scene evoked delightful memories from his childhood in this place. He stood there in a trance, gazing at the great circular towers and white walls of a fortress on the hill, reflected in the water below, emerging in the translucent dawn light. And he dreamed of breaking free of his obligations, to rove the world unfettered — forever! Then he thought of the Torah he was duty-bound to bring back to Valinsk, and turned away from his foolish desires.

On his last day in Constantinople, he sold his worn-out donkey and bought a fresh one. If his luck held, he would soon be in Jerusalem.

❧ 3 ❧

The Birth of the Rosen Torah

You can't drive away darkness with sticks or weapons. The only way is to light a candle and the darkness will disappear by itself. Our candle is the Torah.

Talmud

After six months of hard travel, Tevya reached his final destination. From atop the Judean hills, he looked down on the ancient city walls of white limestone suffused in the bronze light of the lowering sun. Dizzy with awe that he, of all people, should be in the place that Jews had venerated for thousands of years as their Promised Land, he whispered, "If I forget thee, O Jerusalem, let my right hand forget her skill." The ground he stood upon, the air he breathed seemed charged with splendor, with the eternal bond between his people and God. Through eyes glazed with tears the city wavered on the horizon; a sob rose in his throat as he offered up fervent thanks for his safe passage.

Then he hastened down a stony road to hunt down his quarry, the *sofer*, or scribe, Manasseh Ben Israel, who resided in the vicinity of the Western Wall in the Jewish quarter of Old Jerusalem.

As Shmuel had instructed he made the necessary down payment of gold coins to Manasseh, with a promise to pay the remainder on completion of the Torah.

The scribe hefted the coins in his hand and said frowning, "It's a good thing I have other sources of income—repairing

44

Torahs, teaching at the boy's Hebrew school and performing circumcisions—to cover the cost of raising a large family." Then he commented with a resigned chuckle, "The rabbinical sages of ancient times so highly valued their sofer that they observed fast days in his honor, praying that he would not become rich and therefore unwilling to stick with the task of writing scrolls. Their prayers must have been heard, because taking up the sofer's profession is the equivalent of taking a vow of poverty."

Knowing that he would live in Jerusalem for many months while the sofer labored over the Torah, in exchange for board and lodging in the Ben Israel's house, Tevya offered to help with household chores and to give fiddle lessons to the older children. A handshake, sufficient between honorable men, served as the contract.

The scribe's house, tucked away at the end of an alley overlooking a common courtyard, was a narrow two-story structure of weathered Jerusalem limestone. Tevya's little room on the rooftop afforded barely enough space for a bed and his scanty belongings, but it led out onto a terrace with a grape trellis and pots of bright flowers. To catch the breeze, on hot nights he slept in the roof garden where he lulled himself to sleep fiddling melancholy love songs to Tsiporah. At dawn he awoke to the muffled, deliberate tread and tinkling bells of a camel train passing along the dusty road in the valley below. Through sleepy eyes he saw, silhouetted against the pale light, a graceful stork balanced on one leg beside her nest, and a surge of delight coursed through him to have arrived safely in Jerusalem at last.

In the dwelling below, Manasseh, his wife Shula, and their five children made for a noisy, unruly and cramped household, causing the fiddler to reflect silently that although the scribe was required to totally immerse himself in the sanctity of his calling, he apparently had energy left for the fulfillment of his sexual desires. When he craved solitude, Tevya escaped into the maze of streets surrounding Ben Israel's home hemmed in by walls and ancient doors.

Over the following months, Tevya rambled through the old city freighted with layer upon layer of history and culture. He discovered the mosaic of people inhabiting Jerusalem—Muslims, Christians, and Jews—had segregated themselves by different sectors, living there as if they had always had the right to them. Tevya, who had developed the habit of talking to himself, mused aloud, "It's the same way in the shtetls, Christians and Jews don't trust one another."

Many nights the emissary sat in the dusty court, beneath two twisted olive trees, listening with half an ear to the scribe's discourse. The distant focus in his eyes and the deep timbre of Manasseh's voice revealed that he spoke not only to Tevya, but also to the world at large.

"The Ben Israels are Sephardic Jews with roots going back to the thirteenth century, to a time when Jews, Christians, and even Muslims lived together in relative peace and prosperity in a land called Castile, the land of castles; and its glorious capital of Toledo, now all part of Spain."

Tevya became impatient with this conciliatory tone and growled, "May we outlive our enemies, and may they rot . . ."

Manasseh hastily interjected, "But all that changed. To make a long story short, Jews were expelled from Castile, in 1492. Together with thousands of others my family became homeless. The Catholic Church had no mercy. They burned and hanged and tortured without compassion those they declared heretics, the overwhelming number of whom were converted Jews and Muslims. Thank God, my family fled to Jerusalem where they found refuge.

"You see the Ottoman rulers were more tolerant of Jews." The scribe stood up and paced round the courtyard with his hands clasped behind his back, a black silhouette against the arched windows covered by filigree screens. After a few more turns he looked up at the stars as if interceding with the Almighty. "I make a living, thank God, but business is not so good anymore. The once glorious Ottoman Empire is becoming a backwater beset by beggars and flies."

Manasseh had steeped himself not only in the complex history of his family but also of Jerusalem, a subject he was just as eager to expound on. At this juncture the wine was making

46

Tevya drowsy, and he found it hard to follow the scribe's story. "Jerusalem has been under Muslim control since the Ottoman Turks defeated the Mamelukes in 1517. Under Ottoman rule it was divided into districts administered by native Palestinians."

Tevya swatted a fly trying to drink moisture from his eyes, and mumbled, "It's getting late . . ."

"I'll leave you with this thought, Tevya: You can't drive away darkness with sticks. The only way is to light a candle. Our candle is the Torah."

A loud snore from Tevya told him he had lost his audience of one.

As talkative as Manasseh was by night, he said little during the day as he set about preparing to create the sefer Torah. Painstakingly, reverently, he followed every detail of law and custom in its preparation.

For the parchment he tanned the skin of a kosher animal—in this case a calf—killed by a ritual slaughterer. He soaked it in lime for nine days, then dried, scraped, sanded, and stretched it on a frame until it became a smooth sheet on which he could write. After that he cut it into neat rectangles.

The scribe made the ink and pen without using metal, which can be forged into weapons that take life; a Torah gives life. For the ink he blended foul-smelling gallnuts made from oak leaves formed into hard balls by wasps to build their nests. He ground them into a powder and mixed it with water, then added copper sulfate, and also gum Arabic to give elasticity to the dried ink so that when the scroll is rolled up the letters will not crack. To ensure that the ink remained fresh he made only two teaspoonfuls at a time. For the quill he chose large goose feathers and whittled them till they were sharpened enough to make perfect letters.

Turning to Tevya, observing him with mouth agape, he said, "I must create a slit in the quill to hold just enough ink to write God's name, as the Torah commands us to write His name with one dip into the ink well."

Now the writing materials were ready, the scribe could begin. In preparation he immersed himself in the waters of the *mikvah*, and prayed that his work would be empowered by holiness.

The scribe engraved 42 faint horizontal grooves into the parchment, marking the rows for the Hebrew words, and two vertical lines for the margins that by tradition are five fingers wide. The placement of each character and the style of the text had to be done strictly according to tradition. He examined a completed text, never trusting his memory before writing a word lest he change it even by one iota from the way it had been handed down from God to Moses. Only when the scribe had pronounced the word out loud would he allow the quill to touch the pure vellum. Keeping his hand steady he meticulously created perfectly formed letters with sufficient space between them so that an ordinary schoolboy could easily distinguish between similar characters.

Each time he wrote the name of God, the scribe intoned, "My intention is now to write the Holy Name," then immediately inscribed it without pause, mindful of Rabbi Ishmael's instructions, "Be careful in thy work, as it is heavenly work, lest thou err in omitting or adding one iota, and so cause the destruction of the whole world."

From time to time, Tevya observed the scribe — mesmerized by his graceful rhythm — as he dipped the quill into the ink, bent over like a tree swaying in a gentle breeze, then steadying his hand, formed the letters stroke by measured stroke. Manasseh ended each day's labor on a joyous sentence, as prescribed by Jewish law, then waited for the ink to dry before covering the parchment with a cloth to protect it from the dust.

Finally, the *hamsin*, the hot desert winds of summer, subsided, and as they did the scribe completed the scroll he had been working on for nearly a year. As he examined the finished parchment pages, Manasseh stroked his beard, grateful, proud and confident that he had not erred once in writing the name of the Almighty, for His name cannot be erased. If he had made that mistake, the whole sheet of parchment on which it occurred would be put aside to await reverent interment in consecrated earth.

Manasseh's eyes swept over the work, noting how he had crafted each letter to the exact same size with crowns like crows' footprints on the upper points, nice broad horizontal strokes, and fine vertical ones. Neither instructions, nor commentary, nor illustrations, nor illuminations, adorned the Torah, as they were not permitted, but in its craftsmanship it was a work of art.

"Tomorrow," Manasseh told Tevya, "I will begin reading through the entire Torah with the scholar Mendel Peretz — word-by-word, line-by-line, from the first sentence to the last, as it has been done since the first Torah was created. This is the only way I can be sure that no mistakes have been committed."

Tevya nodded, joining in Manasseh's satisfaction with a hearty, "It's magnificent. Mazel Tov!"

"When that is done, then I can sew the separate sheets of parchment together with thread made from the sinews of an ox's leg. After that I will attach each end of the scroll to olive wood posts."

Tevya rubbed his hands together and clapped the scribe on the shoulders, "And thanks to you, I can then finally return to Valinsk with the wonderful Torah."

The scribe took a step backward to admire his work from another angle.

"When I have delivered the Torah safely to Valinsk, Shmuel Rosen will attach silver finials to the poles and dress the Torah with a red silk cover and breastplate that he said he would commission." *And then I will be the hero of Valinsk*, he thought. As if he were being swept down a treacherous river toward a brighter shore, the emissary felt lightheaded and giddy at this triumphant prospect.

Now that his sojourn in Jerusalem was drawing to a close, Tevya had one more urgent task to fulfill — his promise to Shmuel to place the stone on Lazar Rosen's grave. Manasseh provided directions to the cemetery near the Old City's Jewish Quarter above the Shiloah wellspring, atop the Mount of Olives. One of the oldest and holiest of Jewish cemeteries dating back to Biblical times, a host of prophets and sages lie buried there awaiting the coming of the Messiah.

With these instructions and the map in hand that Shmuel had given him, Tevya found the section without difficulty and tethered his donkey to an olive tree near the gates. Then he wandered amidst the dusty and crowded rows of graves built of stone and mortar and capped with inscribed marble lids. He was surprised that they sat above ground on the steep, rocky slopes. Neither flowers nor sculptures embellished them, instead mounds of small stones, placed by visitors, indicated that the living had not forgotten their dead. It distressed him that vandals had smashed many of the covers, making the inscriptions difficult to read.

As ominous storm clouds began to gather over the mount he realized, too late, that it would not be easy to distinguish Lazar Rosen's grave from hundreds of others. He hastened his search, and soon his back began to ache from stooping over. When Tevya at last identified his grave from the inscription, he started chanting Kaddish, the prayer for the dead, just as the rain came pelting down. Swaying back and forth with eyes closed, intoning the hallowed words from memory, thoughts of his own father and mother stirred a wave of melancholy deep inside him, mingling the tears running down his face with the rain.

Before leaving, he placed the stone that Shmuel had given him on Lazar's tomb as a reminder that they had not forgotten him. Then he picked up a pebble that had rolled onto the path and shoved it into his pocket.

A month later, the scribe and the scholar, Mendel Peretz, summoned Tevya to his workroom. As Manasseh pronounced the last letter of the last word, the sun burst free from a bank of clouds pouring a golden shaft of light onto the open scroll. Tevya's heart soared, and he thought: *The eye of God Himself is illuminating this Torah with His special benediction.*

Now the emissary could make final preparations to retrace his journey and bring the Torah, Hashem willing, safely back to Shmuel Rosen, who no doubt had been waiting with anxious anticipation all these months in Valinsk. Under the critical eye of the scribe, Tevya packed the heavy Torah into a leather pouch made especially for the purpose and secured it to a fresh donkey.

Satisfied that all was in order, Tevya gave Manasseh the remainder of the gold coins owed him. Then Manasseh embraced him and wished him a safe and speedy journey. The children said their goodbyes, the little ones with a shy hug, and the older ones with a solemn handshake. Shula pressed something into his hands with a demure smile and a finger to her lips, and said, "Go in peace, Tevya." Opening his hand, a shiver ran down his spine at the sight of the gleaming silver amulet in the shape of a hand with the palm facing out, an eye drawn in the center, the fingers spread for protection. She had given him a hamsa hand to ward off the evil eye. His lips moved as he sought to find words to express his gratitude, but when he looked up she had disappeared.

Tevya journeyed north toward Valinsk, leaving behind the desert sands and dusty camel trains, the palm trees, orange groves, and alien people. On this homeward leg of the journey he traveled alone, quietly, almost invisibly, avoiding whenever possible the areas he knew to be infested with robbers. He stopped for the night at homes where he had stayed before and, having spent most of his money, relied on the generosity of those who wished to share in the mitzvah of bringing the precious Torah safely to Valinsk, for without their hospitality he might have starved.

When, months later, he skirted the familiar fields of barley, wheat, and rye, Tevya experienced a surge of delight, knowing that he was just days away from Valinsk. With victory so close, he was too seasoned to let his guard down, becoming more vigilant than ever.

He was making his way through an isolated stretch of forest, the sun low on the horizon, when the donkey went into a fit of twitching and shivering. Alarmed, Tevya quickly halted and looked around. The trees were so dense that they obstructed his view and slowed his passage. Mingling with the pounding of his heart he heard the howling of wolves, distant at first, but growing closer. He hastily untied the Torah from the donkey;

51

freed of the load he had been carrying, the beast immediately broke into a panicky trot and ran off. Cursing under his breath, Tevya ran a distance from the path and climbed into a tree, wedging the Torah between the forked branches as he waited and prayed for deliverance.

Wolves! He tugged at the hamsa hand around his neck and sent up more prayers. These animals were not the stuff of nightmares but a real and potentially fatal danger in this part of the world. A pack had once attacked Shmuel Rosen's nephew, Berel Pincus, reducing him to a scattering of bloodied bones. The memory so frightened Tevya that his bowels let loose.

"I can outwit a man more easily than a wild animal," he growled miserably. If he were to lose the Torah, he thought, how could he return to Valinsk without shame? No, he had to save it no matter what! He clung to his perch throughout the black night, his muscles cramping with cold and fatigue. Once he dozed off and woke to feel the leather bag slipping from his grasp. With a fearful yelp, he regained a hold on his precious cargo. After that he kept himself awake singing klezmer folksongs, laughing and weeping to the lyrics, until his throat hurt.

Not until shafts of sunlight pierced the dense canopy, did he dare to inch his way stiffly toward the ground. Warming his aching body in the sun's rays, Tevya reviewed the situation. He had saved his life and the precious Torah, but gone were his fiddle and donkey, and he smelled worse than a wild boar. He had no choice but to resign himself to making the remainder of his journey on foot. Removing a dagger from his boot, Tevya cut a branch from the lower limbs of a birch, and carved it into a sturdy walking stick.

As he stumbled on, with the sefer Torah in its pouch safely strapped to his back, swinging his staff to propel him along, he cheered himself with thoughts of modest fame: "Surely the people of the shtetl will hail me as a hero. I have traveled so far, and survived so many dangers."

Even happier thoughts occurred to him as he made his footsore way. "Then there is the little matter of the dowry to collect from Shmuel. And I will be reunited with Tsiporah and my child. Be it a girl or boy, I will love the baby with all my heart." He wiped the tears from his eyes on a tattered sleeve before pressing on in silence.

After a time he was greeted by yet another joyful vision. "And how I will enjoy the festivities for the dedication of the Rosen Torah! There will be plentiful food, wine will flow, and I will eat and drink until my sunken belly is as round as a ripe melon." But perhaps it was too soon to rejoice. Willing himself into a more sober and dignified frame of mind, he admonished, "But I won't become big headed. I won't strut about like a rich man!" Nevertheless, he could not restrain himself from letting out a whoop of joy, and when he heard his victorious cry echoing through the forest he slapped his thigh and cackled out loud.

⤙4⤚

Tevya Returns a Hero Unsung

The words of the Torah are compared to water, wine, and milk, because just as these are kept in the simplest of vessels, so the Holy Words are preserved in the humblest of men.

Talmud

At the dawn of a new day, Tevya reached the outskirts of Valinsk. The sun floated just below the horizon, illuminating the sky in its tangerine glow. A flock of crows, startled from their roost, cawed angrily as they rose and circled above fields of early flax and rye. The Wilja River, swollen with spring rains and melting snow, roared a turbulent welcome to him. On the riverbanks, quivering stands of willow and birch, festooned in a delicate green lacework of nascent buds, beckoned him home.

"Is it possible that almost two summers have come and gone since I last set foot in Valinsk?" Tevya reflected, scratching his beard and shaking his head. Shivering with anticipation, he trudged on, tattered and weary, lightheaded with excitement.

Only when he reached the old cemetery on the hill did he feel truly at home. "Home at last, or as close as a wandering Jew can call home!" Tevya exclaimed.

His heart missed a beat at the sight of the familiar black basalt and red brick gravestones. The mute monuments engraved with special symbols—menorahs, shofars, hands raised in blessing, lions, ewers, and bowls—greeted him like the faces of long-lost friends. Tevya bowed his head and thanked God to be alive after all the ordeals he had survived. Then he whispered a blessing to Reb Szulkin, resting below a handsome gravestone with the Ten Commandments. And to Beile Asner, who had left behind three small children and lay beneath doves in flight above a nest of chicks, he murmured, "May your dear soul rest in peace."

Leaving the burial ground behind, he walked on dizzy with hunger and exhaustion, through orchards flush with fruiting blossoms and vegetable gardens planted in leafy rows of spinach and cool-weather lettuce. Just before entering the town, he came upon an encampment of Gypsies, dressed in bright rags, cooking breakfast over a campfire in the center of an irregular circle of covered wagons. As soon as they sighted him, they beckoned to him and shouted ribald wisecracks.

"Looks like Lady Luck trampled all over you! Come, I'll tell your fortune!"

"Don't pay attention to her! Come to me! I'll read your cards or your palms. Maybe there's a beautiful woman in your future! She'll swell your love stick! And her belly!"

Tevya attempted to move on, but a young woman with a sensuous body danced around him, fingers snapping, hips swaying, eyes flashing. Even with tender feet, Tevya could feel them itching to dance.

"I'll come back one day, and you can train me to dance like a Gypsy!" Tevya promised.

"People who aren't Gypsies can never learn to dance the way we do!" she retorted.

The brave fiddler loved their wild dance and music and always attended their performance on market days in Valinsk. Once, lured by the compelling beauty of the music and dance, he had hidden in the woods near their encampment, listening to the passionate, erotic playing by Polgar, the King of the Gypsies that ignited desires so intense he almost fainted. Now Tevya waved temptation away, but vowed to return soon.

Preoccupied with these forbidden feelings, Tevya suddenly found himself standing at the entrance to the main street of Valinsk. For a moment he felt disoriented, and it occurred to him that he did not know what day it was. The dusty streets were quiet, and even the houses seemed asleep. After his long sojourn in foreign lands, everything was as homely and comforting as warm bread, yet at the same time strange and new. Tevya mused aloud, "It can't be Thursday; that's market day. The place would be a madhouse, people running everywhere.

All at once he saw, in his mind's eye, farmers riding to market, their wagons brimming with produce; peasants from the nearby villages carrying crates of honking geese and baskets of juicy fruit and vegetables. His ears seemed to fill with a cacophony of sounds: clucking chickens, whinnying horses, grunting hogs, mooing cows, bleating goats, all mingling with the clattering of wheels on cobblestones. And rising above the din, calls of vendors, shrill or melodious, luring customers to their stalls. The illusion fired his imagination so intensely that he could smell the powerful mix of odors emanating from clods of steaming dung, hoops of ripe cheese, cuts of fresh meat, barrels of pickled fish, mounds of warm yeast bread.

As if a curtain had gone up, the town awoke; the momentary hush broken by the buzz of people setting in motion their daily business. Tevya's mouth watered as he passed a barefooted boy selling bagels stacked on a stick, but he didn't have a single coin left having spent all on the last leg of his travels. Rubin the peddler with bags of old clothes tossed over his hunched shoulders completely ignored him, but Manny the butcher, leading a calf to be ritually slaughtered by the town's *shochet*, slapped Tevya on the back and cried, "Tevya is it you? Are you alive?"

"Praise to God!" Tevya said, slapping him back.

"Hey! What's in the bag?" Manny inquired, burning with curiosity to find out if this was the long-anticipated Rosen Torah.

Tevya made no reply but winked and plodded on. Despite his fatigue he observed everything as keenly as if seeing Valinsk for the first time. Passing a row of one-story wooden houses, he remarked to no one in particular, "Nothing seems to have changed in this poor section, except that it has become a mite shabbier."

Farther on the cottages gave way to more substantial whitewashed homes with attached stables, and vegetable gardens that ran to the cultivated fields beyond. Surrounding the marketplace on all four sides, were two-story brick houses with stores on the ground floor, and, on the western end loomed the church, its steeple towering over the square. On the opposite side, he spied the tavern's squat brick structure pierced by narrow windows and a heavy wooden door, and its painted sign, "Rosen's Tavern," flapping in the brisk spring breeze. He hesitated, his heart pounding, steeling himself to go to the tavern then it occurred to him that Shmuel would not be there this early in the morning, so he limped on to the Rosens' house near the shul.

In the middle of the square, he halted to draw water from the well. *Ahh, cool well water with its special taste of home*, he thought. He washed his face and dried it with a dirty rag then turned left onto the steep thoroughfare ascending to the shul.

At the top he paused to orient himself. Fluttering his hands in a gesture of pleasure he saw that the usually bare *shulhoyf*, the space in the front of the synagogue, was covered in meadow grass and wild flowers after the warm spring rains. His eyes swept around the area taking in the bathhouse half way down the hill, where married women immersed in the *mikvah*, and men enjoyed the steam room or washed before the Sabbath; the homeless shelter and the shack where the shochet slaughtered animals for the kosher meat market; the *cheder*, a primary school for the youngest children; the *yeshiva*, or school of higher learning. Tears pooled in his eyes as they came to rest on the wooden synagogue, on higher ground, in the heart of the complex; a bastion of faith crowned by its dignified tiered roof. *Soon*, he thought, *the Torah I have carried back with my sweat and tears will be safely housed there, bringing* mazel *to the people of the town, and honor to the Rosen family and to me.* A shuddering sigh of sheer relief and deep satisfaction escaped his cracked lips.

Schoolboys were beginning to gather outside in the break between morning prayers and the start of classes. The sight of Tevya, dazed, tattered, spattered with mud, stinking of stale

57

urine and excrement, a bulky leather pouch strapped to his back, brought too inviting a target.

"What have you got in the bag? A corpse?"

"Have you been traveling with the Gypsies?"

"Hey, cross-eyes, been sleeping with the pigs?"

"Need to go to the bathhouse?"

To the boys' chagrin and astonishment, Tevya struck out and hit one smartly on the shoulder with his stick, causing the others to scramble for safety. He hobbled doggedly on toward Shmuel Rosen's house, inwardly returning their mockery: *What do you stupid schoolboys know! I am a hero now, a man of courage, and a man to be respected! Soon you will beg me to tell of my adventures. How you will listen with eyes glowing and mouths agape. How you will revere me for bringing this wonderful Torah from the Holy Land to your poor shtetl!*

On his way to prayers Shmuel, the shtetl's *macher*, caught sight of this man coming into view. The top of the man's head bobbed toward him then dropped out of sight, rising a little larger each time. The sunlight streamed over his round face and massive shoulders. Shmuel froze—his right foot planted ahead, the left lifted off the ground—straining forward to be certain who was coming toward him. With a start that set his heart racing he recognized Tevya.

Identifying Shmuel at the same time, Tevya let out a loud whoop. Shmuel shouted a reply, and they rushed toward one another, arms extended wide.

"Miracle of miracles, you made it back to Valinsk!" Shmuel cried, extricating himself from Tevya's malodorous squeeze, then noticing Tevya's sorry state, he commented, "But not without a struggle I see!"

"Thank God, thank God, I survived the journey."

"And you have my Torah in that bag!" Shmuel yelled.

"Yes, it is your Torah," Tevya roared back.

"I must see it, now!"

"What, here, in the street?"

With an impatient gesture, Shmuel pointed to his house. "No, let's go inside."

Tevya followed him into the gloom of the house, his pupils dilating in the dim light as he grappled to remove the bag from his back. He washed his calloused travel-worn hands in a bowl of water Rachel kept in the kitchen, as thoroughly as he could and dried them on a clean rag, before removing the scroll, unadorned and as yet bare of its silk mantel and silver trappings. Then with shaking hands he placed it—naked and pure as a newborn babe, yet saturated with the weight of tradition—on the kitchen table, and with a flourish invited Shmuel to examine it.

Shmuel gazed at his Torah, amazed that the vision, which had haunted his dreams for so long, was real, an actual physical presence before him. His heart hammered in his chest and his breath came so rapidly that the air whistled between his teeth, yet he was reluctant to touch his Torah. Finally, he untied the silk cord and unfurled the scroll with trembling hands.

Even more magnificent than he had pictured it, an unsullied scroll of soft, golden-hued calfskin inscribed with perfectly fashioned letters, shimmered before his eyes. Clapping his hands together in wonder, he cried, "What a beautiful sight!" Then he threw back his head and crowed, "Oh, how they will respect me, and bow themselves before me when they see my magnificent Torah! Oh, what a grand ceremony I'll give . . ."

Tevya banged his fist on the table, making the Torah quiver, "Be quiet!" he shouted. "*Haken mir nicht in tcheynick!*" Stop annoying me!

"What's got into you, Tevya?" said Shmuel, taken aback. "This is a time for celebration!"

"It's also a time to thank God for His benevolence."

"Of course! Blessed are You, Hashem, our God, King of the Universe." Shmuel said, bowing his head, just for a moment, before letting his eyes sweep over the Torah to make sure it was still there.

Tevya quivered with frustration. "And it wouldn't hurt to thank me either!"

Without taking his eyes off the scroll, Shmuel patted Tevya's filthy arm, trying to hide his revulsion. "I understand.

You're tired from your long journey. Go to the bathhouse and wash up, you'll feel better then."

"No! I need to see Tsiporah and my child right now."

Shmuel tried to meet Tevya's impassioned gaze, then quickly let his eyes drop to hide the pity in them. The man had no way of knowing that his child had been stillborn, and he hated to be the bearer of bad news at this moment of triumph. Shmuel opened his mouth to say something, but Tevya looked so weary that he could not find the words or the courage to tell him. Instead he simply stuck out his meaty hand. "Mazel Tov, Tevya. You accomplished your mission!"

Tevya ignored the proffered hand. "We'll talk about the dowry, the money, the kest, the fur coat you promised me later." Then he turned his back on Shmuel and stumbled out the door trembling with a feverish urgency to hold his wife and child close.

⮜5⮞

A Dedication and a Defection

In the Torah, it is justice, and justice alone, that receives the double imperative: "Justice, justice you shall pursue."

Torah

On the seventh Saturday following Tevya's return, the entire shtetl formed a joyful street procession that accompanied the Torah with the same affection and respect it might show a bride from the most prestigious family. The scholars and wealthy householders, puffed with prestige, had the honor of carrying the Torah from Shumel's house to the shul. Only Tevya failed to join the merriment. Still grieving for his lost child, and mortified by Shmuel's arrogance in failing to honor him in any way, or recognize his achievement in bringing the Torah to Valinsk, he pushed his way forward and managed to lock eyes with the object of his fury, pointing his finger meaningfully at Shmuel — a long work-roughened shaft of a finger — the offensive attempt of a poor man to assert his will over a wealthy one. But Shmuel, on his day of honor, ignored him, barely masking his indifference, even dislike, as his eyelids drooped and eyes glazed over.

As the procession reached the shul everyone crowded into the pews of the sanctuary. The most prominent and honored men of the congregation, the *shayne yiden,* took the places reserved for them in front nearest the Holy Ark. Behind them came the householders, while the poor and uneducated, the *proste yiden,* sat in the back. The women and children were relegated to the upstairs gallery where they sat behind a filigreed screen.

61

When all had taken their places, the heavy doors to the sanctuary reopened with a muffled creak, and the congregation came to their feet and craned their necks to see the proud and massive Shmuel with his arms wrapped around the marvelous Rosen Torah that had come all the way from holy Jerusalem. Behind him, wearing a *kittel* or white robe as on the High Holy Days, strode the cantor, followed by the rabbi in his own white robe. Officers of the temple followed, wearing silk *tallises* and *yarmulkes*. As they proceeded down the aisle all eyes feasted on the tops of the Torah's poles now adorned with finely wrought silver finials, small crowns gleaming with semiprecious stones, and tinkling bells that swayed gently above Shmuel's shoulder, on the elegant yad suspended from a fine chain, the solid silver breastplate engraved with the lion of Judah, and on the handsome red silk mantle embroidered with gold thread.

The solemn procession advanced down the aisle then mounted the steps to the *bima*. When they reached the lectern, the rabbi halted and turned to the congregation. The officer just behind the rabbi collided into him, and there was a moment of confusion as he, too, turned and faced the assembly while the others scrambled to follow suit.

"Oh God of our Fathers, we of the Valinsk congregation accept this sacred scroll, the magnificent legacy of the Rosen family. Each time we read from this special Torah, we should remember that we are partners with God through the continual process of creation." He paused and raised a trembling finger above his head as a caution to his listeners: "You must study and observe the divine commandments or mitzvot of the Torah. By following these you will be guided to perform more mitzvot, or more good deeds. Therefore, remember do not esteem a beautiful object, even one as fine as the Rosen Torah, more than a beautiful deed."

Even the most ignorant understood what their rabbi was telling them: a show of wealth is nothing more than vanity if it is not translated into virtuous actions. All eyes now turned to Shmuel, who felt at once empowered and yet burdened with the many new obligations that he would be expected to fulfill.

"May we be worthy of this sacred Torah." The rabbi's voice trembled with emotion, but his gaze remained fixed on Shmuel, now seated, as the officers removed the ornaments, then he signaled to him to place the Rosen Torah on the reading table.

Looking out at the congregation, Shmuel said with shining eyes, "This is a momentous occasion. It is the culmination of my deepest wishes. I hope our family legacy, this beautiful scroll, will bring blessings to all of us." He might have continued, but the rabbi cut him short by unfurling it and reciting the first blessing, the *Birkhot Ha-Torah*.

> *Praised is Hashem, who is praised forever and ever*
> *Praised are You, Hashem our God, Ruler of the world,*
> Who chose us from all the nations,
> And gave us the Torah.

After that the Sabbath service continued when seven members of the Rosen family, as a special honor, were called on to read from the Torah. When they had finished, the congregation joined in reciting:

Praised are You, Hashem our God, Ruler of the world, who gave us the Torah of truth, and implanted within us eternal life.

Then the rabbi held up the open scroll for the congregation to view, and a gasp rippled through the sanctuary. It was as if their sacred text had been opened before the eyes of God. Their daily struggle for bread and ever-present fear of the hostile world surrounding them were sublimated by a feeling of connection to eternity. They did not see the Torah's physical beauty as distinct and separate from its content. In their minds its beauty derived from what it stood for — the perpetuation of God's commandment to do justice in this world.

The flock longed to bask in that sublime moment forever, but too soon the cantor rolled the halves of the Torah together and girded it with a strip of silk. With help he slipped it into its red cover, replaced the ornaments then handed it to the rabbi. Holding it vertically in his arms, he turned toward the Ark where the glow from the Eternal Light, suspended above, bathed him in an amber halo. Shmuel had the honor of opening the Ark doors, and he began to sob in a hot flood of emotion as the rabbi placed the Rosen Torah beside the Valinsk Torah. He felt as though he were drowning in a torrent of raw emotions: joy, pride, reverence, and deep satisfaction. The congregants, also overcome by exaltation at the splendor of the Torah, wept along with him.

The most prominent scholars of the congregation wept with pleasure tinged with envy that one such as Shmuel had momentarily outshone them. Shmuel's blatant exhibit of power added fuel to the smoldering rivalry between the learned and the wealthy. They also wept out of vanity: their synagogue now housed a Torah finer than any other. Behind them, the householders glowed with pride and self-satisfaction that one of their own had so visibly elevated his status. Sitting among them, Shmuel's only son, seventeen-year-old Yitzhak, overcome with esteem for his father and with religious fervor, sobbed audibly.

The poor and uneducated basked in reflected glory, yet once again they were reminded that even in God's house respect and dignity fell upon the learned and wealthy, while they were ignored. Among them Tevya, seated in the very last row, seethed with hostility. He who risked his life among bandits and murderers to bring the Torah from Jerusalem, had been denied the honor of carrying the Torah or reading from it. Neither Shmuel nor the rabbi had mentioned his name, not even once. He turned to Isaac the candlemaker seated next to him and sneered, "A rich man carries his brain in his wallet."

The candlemaker tried to comfort him with a quip of his own: "God is an honest repayer—but he is in no hurry."

Tevya, not to be outdone, replied: "God loves the poor but helps the rich."

Someone nearby got into the spirit: "May his teeth fall out—except one, so he can suffer from toothache—and also let onions grow in his navel."

Likewise in the women's gallery upstairs pressing her hands between her knees to still their trembling, Tsiporah whispered, "Shrouds have no pockets," she said. Then more loudly, "The rich man's foolishness is more admired than the poor man's wisdom!"

In the front row Rachel, who was oblivious to the distant hiss of wisecracks, gripped the pew to stop herself from twitching with pleasure. She was sure that Shmuel's increased status would now pave the way for their son, Yitzhak, to become a scholar and for the youngest of the Rosen daughters, Lena, to become the wife of a scholar.

Just as Shmuel had anticipated, the magnificent Torah in no small measure helped him to get elected to the *kahal*, the self-governing body of the community. Shmuel boasted to Rachel that election to the kahal was no minor achievement among the Jews where one's social ranking was fixed. The constant reminders of his place in the shtetl's hierarchy—seating arrangements in the synagogue, honors in shul, invitations to attend Torah sessions with the scholars, burial sites in the cemetery—would no longer be a source of irritation to him. And as a member of the kahal, he had leapt upward into the "Jewish aristocracy" that controlled the shtetl's finances, its social leadership, and served as its court of final appeals.

Soon after the acquisition of the Rosen Torah, just when everything seemed to be going so well, Catherine the Great seized what was left of Polish Lithuania, bringing Valinsk under Russian rule. Czarist Russia's history of anti-Jewish policies gave the people of the shtetl good reason to fear pogroms, conscription, and economic sanctions bearing down on them like wolves on their quarry. At the next meeting of the kahal, during a discussion of financial aid for the shtetl's needy, Meir Koppleman, the intellectual, rose abruptly and began to pace back and forth in front of the window.

Shmuel, newly confident, broke the ice. "What's on your mind?" he asked.

Koppleman came to a halt, and said through clenched teeth, "Catherine the Great has decided what's to be done with Jews living within Russia's borders."

The men shook their heads and pulled on their beards. "Trouble's never far from us," Shmuel growled.

"Let's first have some refreshments. Then we can discuss this with cool heads," Koppleman counseled. After his wife had poured wine and served cake, he went on, "From the experience of the sovereigns who annexed parts of Poland, Catherine knows all too well that the Jewish population will not be easily integrated."

"So, what does this mean for us?" Nathan the butcher said, sniffing for danger.

"Catherine has decreed a territory within the borders of czarist Russia where Jews will have authorization to live, and our shtetl of Valinsk is to be included." An apprehensive silence followed this news. Koppleman closed his eyes, letting the silence grow. It was a frigid winter day, and outside they could hear the sharp snap of branches breaking under the weight of snow and the crunch of cartwheels moving over ice glazing the streets.

Shmuel's tongue ferreted between his teeth as if something nasty were stuck there. Suddenly, he struck his fist on the table and cried, "Catherine the Great and her warmongers can go to hell! Valinsk will survive within the Russian Empire. I feel it in my bones."

"Brave words don't stop us from being no more than horse manure to Catherine the Great," one elder observed.

"Mark my words," Koppleman said, "The borders are uncertain, and will expand and contract at Catherine's whim. We Jews can never be sure when a decree will come down ordering us to leave our homes!"

Shmuel, still emboldened by his new eminence, retorted: "Our people will carry on as before, celebrating births, Bar Mitzvahs, marriages, and Holy Days."

Tevya and Tsiporah knew no such confidence, as the humiliation of being ignored by Shmuel was compounded by a string of heartbreaks and disappointments. After weeks of procrastination Shmuel told Tevya that since their baby had been stillborn, he felt justified in reducing the twelve gold coins he had promised to only two. Suppressing his pain, Tevya had stooped

66

to a final attempt to ingratiate himself, presenting Shmuel with the stone from the Jerusalem cemetery he had collected while saying Kaddish at Lazar Rosen's grave. Unexpectedly overwhelmed with emotion, Shmuel thanked him profusely then pressed four gold pieces into Tevya's hand from a bulging purse, saying, "This should more than repay you for your trouble."

Tevya glared at Shmuel but rage choked off the words he wanted to say. Unable to communicate, he switched to action, lunging forward and delivering a crushing blow to Shmuel's jaw that sent the huge man reeling backward onto the ground. Before Shmuel could recover, Tevya spat in his face and walked out of his house, swearing aloud never to return.

That night Tevya told Tsiporah he could no longer tolerate Shmuel or the people of the shtetl and had decided to cast his lot in with the Gypsies. He said that he loved her but would not force her to come with him. If she chose to go it would be a chance for her to see and to experience the amazing world outside the narrow confines of Valinsk. At first Tsiporah vehemently resisted. Just the thought of cutting herself off from her family and venturing beyond what was now being called the Pale of Settlement, where there was no Jewish community, terrified her. It would mean breaking with the only way of life she had ever known.

In the end Tsiporah's love for Tevya prevailed over her fear. Tevya was her soul mate and her solace through grief at the loss of the child. Without him her life would be emptied of joy or meaning.

The next day, the Gypsies returned to Valinsk, to trade horses at the fair. When the fair ended, the couple slipped away with them, absconding for good, leaving behind nothing but the hamsa hand Tevya had brought from Jerusalem — perhaps because it had failed to bring them luck — and a note saying they had gone to "seek their fortune."

Shmuel and his sister Chava could not accept that Tsiporah would willingly abandon her family. Hastening to the rabbi's house for advice they blurted out the tragic turn of events, declaring that they suspected Tevya had abducted Tsiporah and decamped with the Gypsies. Outraged, Shmuel concluded that he would call upon the men of the shtetl to rescue his niece.

Fearing an ugly confrontation with the Gypsies, Rebbetzin Feigel tried to reason with him. "First, we cannot be sure they followed the Gypsies. Second, perhaps Tsiporah went with her husband of her own free will."

Chava put her hand to her mouth, the blood draining from her face. "How can you say such a thing!"

"Tsiporah's love for Tevya may have overcome her sense of right and wrong," the rebbetzin continued with compassion. "For true love is not governed by rational thinking but springs from deep and hidden passions we cannot always control."

The rebbetzin's reasoning shocked Chava and Shmuel. What was this talk of love? The business of marriage, children, and the perpetuation of a Jewish home came first, affection would grow out of that—how could the rebbetzin suggest otherwise?

Rabbi Ben Levi noted with silent satisfaction Shmuel's bruised and swollen face; the result of Tevya's assault the night before, he surmised. Looking directly at the macher he said, "I warned you to approach the Torah with proper humility, for arrogance causes ill will."

Shmuel shook his head in confusion, his words muffled by his swollen lips. "Rabbi, I'm not sure I understand."

"Let me speak plainly. You did not honor Tevya in the way he deserved. He risked his life to go to Jerusalem and to carry the Torah safely back to Valinsk, to bring prestige to you and your family. In return you have all but ignored him, and even demeaned him. That may be the real reason he left with your niece."

Shmuel reared back as if the rabbi had slapped him. "Excuse me Rabbi, but I did my best for Tevya."

"It's time for you to be honest with yourself," the rabbi pressed on. "Your actions drove Tevya and your niece out of the community."

Shmuel's eyes narrowed, "Rabbi, I made a beautiful wedding for my niece and Tevya, I paid for Tevya's room and board at my sister to help to cover her expenses, and I gave him a coat even better than the one I promised, a full-length one made of the finest pelts. And I've given generously to charity." Only last week he had made contributions to the building fund to repair the shul's leaking roof, and to the Chevrah Kaddishah, or burial society, so that the poor peddler, Abba Lev, could be buried according to the proper rites.

"But charity is not the same as *tzedakah*, Shmuel. Charity is a voluntary act motivated by your feeling another's pain and finding in yourself the desire to help. Tzedakah does not invoke feelings at all. Tzedakah is a matter of justice and therefore an obligation, whether or not you feel like it. One who does not give tzedakah to the needy is not simply uncharitable of heart, but in violation of the Torah."

Now Shmuel's sister pressed the rabbi's point. "I begged you to give Tevya the twelve gold coins you promised him, and to start him in business. And now look!" Chava began to weep again.

Shmuel folded his arms across his chest and lifted his massive chin. "We've been over that issue too many times. I promised to give him the gold when his first son was born. If you hadn't sided with the fiddler against me, this wouldn't have happened."

"We're talking about family not a business deal with strangers. Enough, arguing, Shmuel!" scolded the rabbi.

"But an agreement is an agreement," Shmuel insisted.

Ben Levi growled, "Mr. Rosen, the Torah exists only among those who humble themselves on her behalf and are not arrogant!" Then he turned to Rebbetzin Feigel, "Please, show Shmuel and Chava out!"

Shmuel's chin fell to his chest. Once again he had been found wanting. The rabbi had made it all too clear that the while the Torah had elevated his status it had also obligated him to live up to a higher standard than those less fortunate than himself.

After they left, the rabbi sat in the kitchen while Feigel prepared dinner, brooding over what had just taken place. He hadn't meant to be disrespectful to Shmuel, only to make him more aware of his obligations to others—but perhaps he had been too harsh. After acquiring the Rosen Torah, Shmuel had given more to charitable causes than before, and had served the kahal well. Perhaps his Torah had exerted a good influence on him after all.

As if reading her husband's concern, Feigel said, as she placed a bowl of steaming cabbage soup in front of him, "There's nothing wrong with being ambitious, its got Shmuel where he is today. He's a wheeler-dealer, but he would never knowingly do something dishonest for personal gain. His problem is arrogance." The rebbetizin added thoughtfully, "Unfortunately, he also likes to flaunt his wealth."

"You're right Feigel, his behavior doesn't win him the respect he desires, instead it causes resentment and envy." He swallowed a spoonful of the flavorful broth with an audible slurp to show his appreciation for his wife's cooking.

Feigel ladled some soup into her bowl, and then joined her husband at the dinner table. "People are in awe of Shmuel's achievements, but behind his back they run him down, which makes him more determined than ever to prove himself superior."

"I'll try to be more polite to him next time, but the man tries my patience." Dabbing at the liquid dribbling down his beard he, added, "His Torah may yet teach him to be more of a mensch."

What hurt Shmuel most was the loss of his sister's love and respect. No matter how he tried to make it up to her with generous gifts, Chava blamed him for the loss of her only child. She left a lamp burning in the window every night; she never gave up hope that one day Tsiporah would return. Seeing her lamp flickering from dusk to daybreak, the shtetl people shed tears for Chava's anguish.

From time to time, news of Tevya and Tsiporah reached the shtetl, but most of it turned out to be only fanciful rumors. Travelers said that the couple had been seen as far away as Jerusalem. Others reported that that they had become king and queen of the Gypsies; that they had watched Tsiporah dancing with grace and abandon, and Tevya fiddling with marvelous virtuosity. Among the wilder rumors were that they had converted to tragic Christian pilgrims who testified for the man from Nazareth, and that they earned their way as frauds who extracted money from the gullible with bogus tales of miracles and herbal concoctions. These stories were told, retold, and greatly embellished, but never substantiated.

While the rumors were hard to believe, the Jews of Valinsk kept on speculating among themselves. Was it possible that the couple *had* converted? What option was there for a Jew who wanted to walk away from his community to stay being a Jew? How could a Jew practice Judaism without belonging to a community of Jews? Where would they find a shul, a *minyan*, or ten men, to conduct services from the Torah—if they even possessed a Torah? Where would they find kosher meat without a *shochet*? Where would Tsiporah find a *mikvah*, outside of a shtetl? And what would happen if something went wrong? As a Jew it would be impossible to survive without the support of a community in times of need. That is why the Torah commands Jews to take care of less fortunate fellow Jews. To survive Tevya and Tspiorah would have had to take on a new identity, perhaps Christian or Muslim, they whispered, cringing at the thought.

After many years without any sign of the couple, the discussions decreased yet the gossip still persisted. One evening, after the Sabbath meal, when Shmuel Rosen was fast approaching the venerable age of ninety, he gathered his family around the bed where he lay. "I commissioned our Torah to bind generations of Rosens to one another, and to ensure that our traditions will be observed," he said, his voice trembling with fervor.

With tears in his eyes, his son, Yitzhak, said, "Don't worry, Papa, we will take good care of our Torah."

"Yitzhak, remember you must approach the Torah with humility." He motioned for his granddaughter to prop him up on the pillows.

"Yes, Papa, I will."

"If only I had listened to the rabbi's warning, and to Chava." The family gathered around him, pressed forward to

71

hear his words. "My dear departed sister, forgive me for Tsiporah . . ." Shmuel's jaw fell open, and he closed his eyes.

"What's the matter, Papa?" Yitzhak said, shaking his father gently.

"Shush! He's dozed off," Rachel admonished. She could tell from Shmuel's heavy breathing he was still alive.

"He said something about the rabbi and about Tsiporah."

"Let him sleep. You can talk about it later." Yitzhak frowned and shook his head, knowing there might not be a later. Something was weighing on his father's conscience that, until this moment, he had been too proud to voice.

❧6❧

The First Inheritor: Yitzhak Rosen, the Cantor Who Sang Too Much

A cantor is a fool: he stands on a platform but thinks he's on a pedestal.
Joseph ben Me'ir ibn Zabara, Book of Delight

The Jewish community of Valinsk took great pride in their cantor, Chazzan Yitzhak Rosen, a God-fearing man of blameless character, and the son of Shmuel Rosen. He possessed a magnificent tenor voice of extraordinary range, and his characteristic "sob" inspired and thrilled his congregants They boasted that he could recite liturgy by heart, had perfect pitch, and spoke with diction clear as a pure-bronze bell.

He was born to be a chazzan, they proclaimed, as truly as a wild goose is born to fly and a canary to sing. His singing was so melodious, and he prayed with such devotion, that he moved the congregation to tears. In addition, he was more than a chazzan; he was a *chazzan-payton*, a cantor and poet.

With a full red beard, wavy red hair that escaped the confines of his cantor's black silk hat, and luminous green eyes, with a slight oriental slant, and full lips, he was strikingly good looking. Women secretly wanted to cover his mouth with kisses, to drink in the beauty of his voice, to hold the feeling he inspired deep inside them forever. The men honored him as the *shaliach tzibur*, their leader in prayer.

On a more prosaic level, Chazzan Rosen had qualified as a *shochet*, and a *mohel*, or one who performs circumcisions. Since

73

the cantor's position alone did not adequately provide for his growing family, these occupations supplemented his income satisfactorily. It also helped that he had married Sarah Kahn, daughter of a prominent family from Krakow.

Two years earlier, Yitzhak had studied in Krakow, since the market town of Valinsk did not offer the advanced training needed to meet the requirements for a shochet, mohel and cantor. There his time was consumed by studying under the renowned and demanding Chazzan Seftel Klein. In his meager free time, Yitzhak explored the city, and was amazed by its fine buildings and vibrant cultural life; he especially loved to attend the opera, a form of entertainment novel to him. The dramatic, passionate music inspired him to begin composing songs of his own. Soon after he arrived in Krakow, he met Sarah Kahn at her uncle Moses Orenstein's home, a respected teacher at the yeshiva. For her it was love at first sight. She could not take her eyes off Yitzhak as he talked of his new experiences in Krakow, gesturing with fluid graceful motions to emphasize a point. What captured her attention most were his dark green eyes, sparkling with intelligence yet deeply compassionate.

Listening with mounting admiration to the dashing young man, Sarah's heart began to flutter in a strange new way. When she heard him sing in shul for the first time she swooned, and the women rushed to revive her with smelling salts. Seeing her pale face and enlarged eyes, her uncle became sufficiently alarmed to call a doctor, happily unaware that she was suffering from her first infatuation. From that day forward her heart belonged to Yitzhak, but wisely she allowed him to play the traditional role of the bold suitor in order not to scare him away.

Approving of the budding romance, the Kahns invited the young man to Sabbath, where seated around the table, the family loved to hear his pure voice join theirs in song. After a year of ardent courtship, the dashing Yitzhak proposed to his beloved, and she joyfully accepted. Then the couple announced their intentions to both sets of parents, and immediately afterward negotiations bounced between the Kahns and Rosens. Only when

74

both sides had agreed upon the dowry, were they free to go ahead with the marriage plans.

The night of their honeymoon the couple made love for the first time, in the dark. Sarah wore the soft cotton nightdress her mother had embroidered with delicate rosebuds; Yitzhak wore nothing. They found it to be a strange, exotic experience different from any other, which seemed to suspend time, and released a deep-seated instinct to meld with another human being. Their passionate lovemaking became a lasting bond between them.

Although it was the custom for a son-in-law to be taken into the home of his wife's parents, where a space was partitioned off for them, Yitzhak persuaded Sarah to come to Valinsk to live with his parents pointing out that they would at least have a room to themselves in the Rosens' house. While Yitzhak found life in Krakow stimulating, he had more to offer in his shtetl where his talents were truly needed, Krakow already having attracted more than its share of chazzans.

Sarah tried to make a good home for her husband, but it wasn't easy. She had to accommodate to being the underling daughter-in-law in Shmuel and Rachel's home. Her mother-in-law made it clear that she was in charge of the household, and her father-in-law was domineering. In Krakow the Jewish community were a close-knit group, but they minded their own business — most of the time. In Valinsk, to Sarah's dismay, people were shamelessly nosey and gossipy. At night she cried herself to sleep for the life she had left behind — until their first son, Shaul, emerged into the world, with a lusty cry; then everything changed. A year later, Sarah gave birth to their second son, a tiny feisty boy they named Hershel. After that, with her duties as mother added to those of a cantor, shochet, and mohel's wife she was too busy to miss Krakow.

When Shmuel passed away at the too ripe age of ninety, Yitzhak was by then a solid citizen with married sons and grandchildren. The community expectantly awaited the announcement sure to follow, as a second shoe must drop after the first, that Rosen had bequeathed the Torah to his only son. Seven days after *shiva*, or the formal mourning period, their expectations were confirmed, and all enthusiastically supported Chazzan Yitzhak saying that he richly deserved to be the inheritor of the precious Rosen Torah—all with the exception of Rabbi Ben Levi's successor, Rabbi Benjamin Asner. Having continued to nurse the hope that the Rosens would donate their Torah to the shul—as he had strongly advised over the years— Rabbi Asner could barely mask his disappointment when Yitzhak categorically refused to do so.

As befitted his status as the owner of the Rosen Torah for more than three decades, and a member of the kahal, Shmuel Rosen's burial plot was in the most prestigious part of the cemetery, on the higher ground of rabbis and scholars. The artisans and pious men rested in the center of the cemetery, and the paupers and uneducated were buried in the low-lying muddy ground near the fence. Still, the patriarch rested in a simple pine casket without nails since the Bible says, "dust you are and to dust you will return," nothing should inhibit its natural decomposition.

Rabbi Asner delivered a carefully worded eulogy. He began by praising Shmuel for the fine legacy he had bequeathed to his son—far superior to merchandise, property, precious stones or gold—which would be passed down to his progeny in a long line stretching into the distant future. And surely Shmuel's children would honor him, the rabbi said, not just as their progenitor as it is commanded in the Torah, but as keepers and transmitters of the teachings of Judaism.

And yet, even as he praised Shmuel, standing by the open grave, the rabbi appeared to be holding a more complex interior monologue with himself. As the mourners listened, his words seemed to expand, not by design or rancor, but merely by implication, into a gentle reprimand. To be worthy of the Rosen Torah, he said, Yitzhak and each succeeding inheritor should strive to fulfill the mitzvot—all 613 of them listed in the Torah— and in particular to be considerate and kind to others, be they rich or poor, members of the family or strangers from afar, and to give not only from charity but from tzedakah.

He paused, and Yitzhak, who had been listening with closed eyes, looked around as if waking from a nightmare. Even in his grief he could not fail to notice the contradictory responses the rabbi's eulogy had evoked. The scholars were stroking their beards and shaking their heads, the balebatim, or people of high standing, were shifting from foot to foot as if there were stones in their shoes. The backbenchers were divided; some were smirking behind their hands, while others were shedding tears. Some orphans and paupers, who lived in shacks on the edge of the shtetl, to whom Shmuel had given charity in his lifetime through the burial society, were dabbing at the tears brimming from their eyes. The others who had done favors for Shmuel Rosen without reward, what were they thinking now? *Despite the special milk I gave from my prize cow when your child was ill while my own child went hungry, you totally ignored the invitation to my daughter's wedding; although I got badly hurt when I took your side against the drunken Cossack, you turned me away when my house burned down; though I risked my life to guide you home in a blizzard when you were lost in the forest, you refused to help with my daughter's dowry.* And if Shmuel could hear their accusations would they flood his heart with regret and shame that he had turned them away?

To Yitzhak's overly sensitive ear, the rabbi's tribute had disparaged more than honored his father. The more he listened to the rabbi's words, the more perplexed and upset he became. At the conclusion of the eulogy, Yitzhak was convinced that his father had not been praised so much as criticized and found wanting. Not once had the rabbi exalted his father for his leadership of the kahal, or for his generous charity; not once had he exhorted his son to follow in his footsteps. Instead Asner had subtly drawn a picture of a man who did what he could to elevate his status in the community—and little more; a man whose heart was not really behind his deeds of charity, a man who had not fully absorbed the meaning of the obligation of tzedakah.

Upon leaving the burial ground, Yitzhak plucked a few blades of grass from an untended grave, chewing them to release the bittersweet juice to comfort himself. Growing up as the only, most privileged son, Yitzhak was constantly reminded, *"du shtamst fun yichus,"* you come from a prestigious lineage. Yes, in life Shmuel Rosen had been an overly proud man, still he could not see why the rabbi had demeaned him in front of the whole community.

As the only son and heir to the Torah, he had always basked in his father's adulation. From childhood he had aspired to do what he could to justify his father's pride in him. Now he expressed his sorrow in the way that brought him comfort, the language of song: "Just as the plucked grass will grow again, so will my father live once more," he intoned to himself. But he found no solace, feeling instead a terrible loss. An involuntary cry rose from his throat as he jammed his knuckles into his eye sockets, as if to staunch the flood of tears. Then he hunched over and wept.

Yitzhak kept this simmering resentment about the eulogy to himself. This only fueled his misery, and led the community to assume, mistakenly, that the loss of the chazzan's father was the sole cause of the depression that noticeably impaired his singing.

Reciting Kaddish for his father, which makes no reference to death but extols the Greatness of Adonai, our God, and calls for peace, helped to ease Yitzhak's anguish. To lead the daily prayers in front of a *minyan*, and reaffirm his faith in God despite this loss, was *his* responsibility as the only son. And he would do it as prescribed, for eleven months and a day, because according to tradition, his father's soul must spend time purifying itself before it could enter heaven.

"Each time I recite the Kaddish, your grandfather's soul "earns points" in its heavenly quest," he told his son Hershel.

"Why did our sages decree that it be said for only eleven months?" Hershel asked somewhat rhetorically, having studied the rabbinical commentaries in the Talmud.

The chazzan knew his son was testing him, "For the most evil person the maximum time required for purification is twelve months. Your grandfather was an honorable man, and needs no more than eleven months."

Musing on what his father had just said, a burst of insight opened in Hershel's mind; the three stages of mourning supported the grieving family, gently guiding them and the community through the loss and pain, and easing them back into the world. Immediately after the funeral the Rosens sat *shiva*, or mourning, for seven days. They lit a memorial candle, as a soul is compared to a flame. Mirrors were covered with sheets for it is considered idolatrous to look at a representation of a human being during prayer when our thoughts should be directed only to God. The family sat down, on low chairs, to a "meal of condolence" provided by the community, symbolically affirming that the living must go on. During this time relatives and friends paid calls to Shmuel's house to remember him and to comfort his family. Then for a month after Shmuel's death, by tradition the immediate family did not attend weddings or festivities where music was played. The men did not shave or cut their hair during this phase. After that they remained in mourning for a year. The unveiling of the tombstone ceremony, which could take place at any time within that period, brought a sense of closure to their grieving.

At the unveiling attended by the family and close friends, Yitzhak himself chanted selected Psalms, gave a brief but glowing eulogy honoring his father, then removed the cloth covering the headstone, and movingly recited the El Malei Rachamim—"God full of compassion," prayer—the Mourner's Kaddish. Seeing the name of their beloved chazzan etched in stone, the bereaved experienced a moment of stark realization about the awful finality of death. The impact was jarring yet opened a pathway to accepting the reality of the loss, and the return to normal life.

When the long, sad months of grieving had passed, Sarah asked permission of Rabbi Asner to hold a ceremony in honor of the passing of the Torah to Yitzhak, and to rededicate it to the synagogue.

As custodian of the Torah, Yitzhak felt both pride and a weighty responsibility for its preservation. He remembered how his father had glowed with satisfaction each time a male member of the family had been called to remove the scroll from the Holy Ark, or to read a designated passage. His father had bequeathed the Torah to him not as a gift but as a sacred trust to be passed on from generation to generation. In the fullness of time, Hashem willing, he would bequeath it to his oldest son, Shaul, named after his paternal grandfather, Shmuel.

To celebrate the dedication of the Torah, Sarah, the family, and friends prepared food for the special lunch they would host after Saturday morning service. Each woman made her specialty: braided egg bread, chopped liver, pickled herring, beet salad, savory fish balls, cakes and cookies. Sarah felt like a queen when Yitzhak, still remarkably handsome, stepped forward to read and chant from the Rosen Torah. After services, everyone crowded around the family to congratulate them and wish them Mazel Tov. Sarah happily acknowledged their good wishes and then urged them to eat their fill.

There was a more practical matter for Yitzhak and Sarah to consider—how to manage the Rosen Tavern he had also inherited, for the chazzan and his wife had too many other obligations. After some debate they chose Yitzhak's half-sister, Tovah, and her husband Rubin Shor, who labored as a tailor for pittance. Rubin was hard working and trustworthy, and Tovah practical and thrifty—though not miserly as she always gave to charity.

Despite all his merits, the chazzan exhibited a minor character flaw: a tendency to showmanship. On more than one occasion, he repeated and embellished the prayers and chants so that the congregation became restless, openly fidgeting and frowning because it delayed them from their daily chores. Even the worshippers who so admired Yitzhak eventually complained that he kept on chanting for the sole purpose of displaying the beauty of his voice. Rabbi Asner himself, the same rabbi who had brought the chazzan such grief delivering his father's eulogy, conveyed the general uneasiness in the form of an edict.

"The official council has set down restrictions concerning the number of prayers the chazzan can chant during Sabbath services. In future you need to limit yourself to that number. After all, you are a man of God, not His messenger, and certainly not a klezmer musician or a traveling actor. Don't try to aggrandize yourself." The rabbi carefully observed Yitzhak's reaction, hoping that his response would indicate that he had learned from his father's example that a life devoted to glorifying oneself rarely brought true contentment.

Yitzhak's face reddened, "Rabbi, there's no need to needle me about my vanity, Sarah already does a good job of that. I'll follow what the council rules, as I'm obliged to do. But," the chazzan said, shaking his head, "I won't accept the opinion that I show off. I sing because of feelings that well up inside me," he paused to search for the right words. "I'll limit the number of prayers but not the way I sing them. It's a spiritual passion that spills over like water from a deep underground spring."

The rabbi didn't truly empathize with the chazzan's response; however, he had pressed his advantage far enough. Still, he couldn't help feeling disappointed that his chazzan was too headstrong to admit to his craving for adulation.

And although the cantor dared not challenge his rabbi's ruling, he privately complained to Sarah, as he had many times before, "Why am I always under scrutiny? Do they question my piety?"

"No, they don't question your piety, maybe it's more that they envy your talent. By flaunting your voice in front of the congregation so shamelessly, you are inviting the *ayin hora*, the evil eye, to bring misfortune down on our heads." Then she hastened to spit three times and uttered, *"Kenna hora,* may the evil eye stay away from us!"

"Woman, that's senseless talk! For God runs the world and has *not* given it over to jealous people."

"Yes," Sarah said, "if we live modestly, give to charity, and don't parade ourselves before others, we do not have to worry about the evil eye."

One night as they lay in bed, Sarah grew tired of Yitzhak's protesting and grumbling. So far the community, awed by his musical gifts, had continued to tolerate Yitzhak's excesses, but she feared that they would one day call him to account. Although it was late, Sarah sat up in bed, plumped the pillows around her and began to lecture her husband. "Let me recount the tale of Chazzan Moshe Apirion."

"I know his story well," the chazzan said.

"Maybe, maybe not."

"What do you mean by that?"

"Maybe you were told the story of what happened to Moshe, but you weren't listening. You certainly haven't applied it to yourself." Then, without pausing to hear his objections, she went on, "You see Moshe was only sixteen when his father died. And, of course, by tradition a chazzan must be a married man, so he was married off at sixteen." Sarah sighed as if recalling a personal tragedy. "Moshe's voice was so beautiful, so powerful, that he was invited to perform in the Warsaw Opera, no less!" At this point, although Yitzhak made a show of opening his prayer book, she continued her story. He didn't wish to argue with his dear Sarah, but he did love opera. It was its mesmerizing enchantment that had drawn the cantor ever farther in his quest for virtuosity and fame.

"In Warsaw he fell in love with a famous Polish opera singer. A woman as white-skinned as a corpse and as heavy as our milk cow. Can you imagine! He lost his mind and abandoned his poor wife and children." She looked accusingly at Yitzhak, who was ostensibly swaying back and forth in prayers. "But all sinners come to a bad end!" she proclaimed to get his attention.

His head snapped up. "I'm not a sinner!"

She kept on, "He lived with the opera singer for many years. They even had an illegitimate child, a huge disgrace! But in middle age he was overcome by guilt. To punish himself for the sins he committed, he swore never to sing again." Sarah glanced sideways at Yitzhak and noticed that once more he seemed not to be paying attention. *My husband is too proud to admit his shortcomings just as his late father was,* she thought, *but for Yitzhak's own good I'm not going to stand for it.* To bring him back to her story, she got up, removed the prayer book from Yitzhak's hands, and poured a cup of tea from the copper samovar.

"Moshe wanted to redeem himself in the eyes of God. So he wandered from shtetl to shtetl, sleeping in the village *hekdesh,* the homeless shelter, or in fields and barns like a stray animal. In the end . . ." her voice dropped to a whisper, "he froze to death in the streets." She wiped tears from her eyes with the corner of her nightdress, observing him carefully.

On hearing this story for the seemingly hundredth time, Yitzhak shrugged his shoulders and raised one eyebrow, as if to imply, *how does this relate to me?* He could not heed her warning, for he was not merely a chazzan, but a *chazzan-payton,* a cantor-poet. Sometimes *piyyutim,* or hymns, even came to him unbidden, in dreams or when his emotions overwhelmed him. When Shaul, his first-born son, came into the world, a beautiful song for blessing the occasion seemed to pour out of his very soul. He insisted on singing it at the newborn's circumcision, and when the last notes died away, the guests spontaneously applauded. After that he received requests to sing at other circumcisions, even Bar Mitzvahs and weddings.

When his younger son recovered from a serious illness, he composed a hymn thanking God for His mercy. Yitzhak sang it so movingly at the Sabbath service that when he had finished, after a moment of entranced silence, the congregation erupted into loud clapping, and kept on until the rabbi rose and banged on the lectern to quiet them. And the rush of burning devotion Yitzhak felt reading from the Rosen Torah often gave birth to new melodies.

When he sang *piyyutim* of his own creation he felt as if the Almighty Himself touched him. He dared tell no one of his transcendental experiences, especially the rabbi who regarded the growing importance of music in the synagogue with suspicion. Had not the Council of Rabbis prohibited the playing of instruments in the synagogue as an unholy imitation of foreign rites? In moments of despair Yitzhak experienced a wild impulse to leave Valinsk and join the Chassidic movement where joyful music infused every aspect of life. With them he would be free to sing and compose until he ascended to higher levels of spiritual release and ecstasy.

And so the uneasy truce between the chazzan, the rabbi and the community continued — until a great fire roared through the shtetl.

❦ 7 ❧

Yitzhak and the Crimson Devil

The ideal chazzan is a prayer, not a performer. He doesn't sing to entertain the congregation — he humbly uses his God-given gifts to uplift and inspire himself and whoever happens to be listening.

Rabbi Mendy Hecht

For five years the Torah remained safe in the Holy Ark where Yitzhak's father, Shmuel Rosen, had first placed it. Then came the terrible night of the Crimson Devil that would live on in memory as the worst fire in the history of Valinsk. Chazzan Rosen would forever recall exactly where he was and what he was doing when cries of alarm rang out in the marketplace. He was with Mottle the shoemaker, getting his boots resoled. He would later recount that maybe it was his own soul that needed mending!

He rushed outside and saw a dark column spiraling into the air from the direction of the synagogue complex. Fanned by a stiff wind, a dense cloud of fiery sparks and hot ash whirled toward the marketplace threatening to engulf the entire shtetl. Yitzhak's first impulse was to run up the hill toward the shul, even without his boots. He pushed and shoved his way through the marketplace, elbowing the vendors frantically trying to save whatever they could.

As he ran barefooted he sent up a prayer, "Please God, keep the Rosen Torah from being destroyed in the fire." He could see a pillar of smoke, shot through with flickering tongues of flame, billowing from the crest of the hill. More alarmed with every stride he repeated his prayer, "Please God, keep the Rosen Torah safe". This time he added, "I promise to be more restrained if only the Torah is saved. May Your Name be praised forever and ever."

As he drew near, an explosion from the direction of the synagogue flung him to the ground. Convinced of God's wrath, remembering his wife's warnings, he asked, "Hashem is this my punishment for singing too much?" Then he pledged the unthinkable: "Please, Lord God if our Torah survives this fire, I vow never to sing in the shul again!"

By the time he reached the top of the hill, a distraught crowd had gathered. The chazzan pushed through the wailing throng and, despite the cries of warning, rushed headlong through the doors of the synagogue. Burning splinters rained down on him as he stumbled through the foyer. Frantic with the need to save the Torah, he ran toward the sanctuary and kicked open the heavy wooden doors. A cloud of acrid smoke enveloped him, and still he staggered forward in a fit of coughing. With a fearful crash, the windows blew out hurling missiles of needle-sharp glass everywhere. Fresh air, pouring into the main sanctuary through the broken windows, now fed the ravenous inferno and a wall of fire rushed toward him. Yitzhak screamed and began beating at the flames licking at his coat. Somehow he managed to claw his way outside. Helping hands pushed him down, rolled him in the dirt to smother the fiery clothes and carried him half-conscious to the river below. They plunged him into the icy water then applied salve to his burns and covered them with strips of cloth torn from a woman's apron.

All night he shifted uneasily between restless sleep and fearful awakening. When he fully regained consciousness, the emotional pain of losing the Torah was more excruciating than the burns and blisters on Yitzhak's flesh. He had betrayed his sacred promise to keep the Rosen Torah from harm. God had punished him for his pride. Black despair descended upon him, blotting out his desire to live.

After the fire had spent itself, the villagers dared make their way back to Valinsk. A cloud of ash and soot covered everything, and the stench of singed hair and burnt animal flesh fouled the air. Many homes had been destroyed and all that remained of the Valinsk shul was a blackened shell. Thankfully no lives had been lost.

The next day, Jews from nearby villages came by horse and wagon to offer shelter to the homeless. As soon as Sarah, their sons, and their sons' families were settled in the homes of relatives, Yitzhak returned to the ruins of the synagogue. With bandaged hands he sifted through the smoldering rubble, hoping to find one semi-precious gem, a scrap of melted silver, a shred of red silk, a thread of gold embroidery — any fragment that might serve as a reminder of the scroll. When the blisters on his hands became too painful, he poked through the embers with a stick, finding nothing. The Torah had vanished. He stood where the Holy Ark had sheltered it for so many years, and tears as bitter and salty as the Dead Sea coursed down his face smeared with black ash. Sarah had warned him to be more humble, but he had not heeded her, and this was his punishment.

In his grief and remorse at the loss of the Torah, he tore what was left of his scorched coat, as was the custom for those in mourning for the dead. Then, without making a conscious decision, he wandered into the woods. Two days later a search party, urged on by a frantic Sarah, found Yitzhak in a willow tree overhanging a bend in the river some miles from the town. Peering up through the branches, they could see his bandaged hands and feet, his blistered face and his burned left cheek bore a rough imprint where it had pressed against the bark. His eyelids were swollen from weeping, and the skin under his eyes was bruised. His clothing hung in shreds. Yitzhak's wife and sons were immediately summoned, but even their pleading could not bring him down or induce him to accept food or drink.

The shtetl's elders tried to dislodge Yitzhak from his tree: "I understand your distress chazzan," the chief rabbi said, searching for a way to bring him to his senses. "But please bear in mind that we do not pay honor to the physical scroll itself, but to God's laws inscribed in it." He peered up into the tree to discern the impact of his words, hoping for a response. The ominous creaking of a branch overhead accompanied by a low groan, urged the rabbi on. "Without question we feel a deep spiritual connection to the actual Torah itself that is why we revere it, house it in the Holy Ark, and cannot hold services in the shul without it. Yet the destruction of one Torah—even the extraordinary Rosen Torah—does not destroy God's commandments. What is more, you can commission a new Torah, as your father did. That is a true mitzvah. "

Yitzhak remained deaf to their arguments. Even to Sarah's persistent entreaties. "Your father, may his soul rest in peace, wouldn't have wanted you to starve to death for his Torah!" Eventually, she sent the rabbi and their sons back but insisted that she remain under the tree and join her husband in his fast.

Trapped in the depths of despair, Yitzhak no longer cared if he lived or died. Biting insects ceased to bother him; he did not feel them feeding on his raw flesh. He did not hear the birds chirping, the cold wind sighing in the branches, or even the sound of his dear wife's voice. He had withdrawn from the world, adrift on a sea of guilt and remorse, having broken a sacred promise to his father, and robbed his sons and his sons' sons of their legacy.

Sarah feared for his sanity. After all, did not *halacha*, Jewish law, define an insane person as one who walks alone at night, sleeps in the cemetery, tears his garments, and loses everything that is given to him? Gripped by anxiety, Sarah stood guard beneath him, shivering with hunger, cold and fatigue, scratching at insect bites until blood oozed from them. In her misery she muttered under her breath, *perhaps it would have been better if our patriarch, Shmuel Rosen, had never commissioned the Torah.* Still, she mourned that her father-in-law's grand vision had died with the loss of the Torah. She had respected more than loved him, and it frightened her to think that even in death he still held tremendous power over Yitzhak. In a moment of clarity brought on by hunger and deprivation, Sarah grasped the true significance of Shmuel's legacy. By bequeathing the Torah to Yitzhak, and his progeny, Shmuel Rosen had hoped to gain eternal life, for to be revered and remembered for generations to come is a way of achieving immortality.

Suddenly she raised her voice in protest in the silent night, "Shmuel you should have foreseen that such a legacy is also a great burden. If you can see Yitzhak's suffering now, please help him!"

In time, fatigue overcame her and she fell into a troubled sleep. In a dream a vision came to her, terrible in its lurid details. She saw Yitzhak walking the streets under cover of night, his mouth agape in a soundless scream. In his hand a dagger dripping with blood. He plunged it into his throat over and over again. She tried to wrench it from him, but the bloody handle slipped from her grasp. When she awoke, she could not banish the awful nightmare; and she knew that if they did not get help soon, both of them would go mad.

Four days after the inferno, Dov Meir, the *shammash*, or sexton, who had, mysteriously disappeared after the fire, trudged back into town, filthy and exhausted, pulling a rickety cart behind him. Search parties combing the area had all but given up, when he rematerialized like a phantom, but stinking like a beggar. As soon as news reached Sarah, she sent a message begging Dov, Yitzhak's closest friend, to intervene before her husband died of exposure and starvation. Even in his deplorable state, Dov did not stop to cleanse himself at the public bathhouse before hastening to the woods. Mottle the shoemaker led the sexton to Yitzhak, where he climbed up into the tree and perched on a branch opposite his poor friend. They spoke quietly while those below strained to hear above the babble of the river.

It emerged that Dov had been inside the synagogue decking the reading table in white silk for the High Holidays known as Rosh Hashanah, the New Year, and Yom Kippur, the Day of Atonement, when he saw flames shooting from the sanctuary. In moments, the intense heat and suffocating smoke sent him reeling outside.

"Once I reached the woods, I kept on running like a goose with its head cut off," he told his friend, who appeared not to hear, still clutching the tree, eyes shut tight. "As I ran I felt waves

89

of heat pursuing me, as if the devil wanted to possess me. I ran on until I came out on a dirt road which I followed until I came to a farmhouse.

"He saw Yitzhak's swollen eyes open to slits. "I begged the farmer for a little water and a crust of bread, but they took me for a Gypsy beggar and set their dogs on me." At the memory, Dov Meir began to weep silently, and covered his face with his hands. Yitzhak, too, began to wail; the two perched on their lofty roost cawing like bedraggled old crows.

When he regained control of himself, Shammash Meir continued his tale. "Because I escaped in a panic, I lost my sense of direction. It took four days to get back to Valinsk. On the second night a great storm split the skies, turning the river into a raging torrent that I could not cross for another a day."

"Oh may God forgive me!" Yitzhak moaned.

"Forgive you? For what?" Dov Meir almost lost his grip on the branch.

"For the loss of my family Torah!"

Dov opened and shut his mouth and blinked his eyes. "Oh, you misunderstand me, my friend! I came to tell you that I carried both Torahs home safely!"

Yitzhak slapped the side of his head as if trying to clear it.

"You see, when I saw the sanctuary on fire I immediately threw open the doors of the Holy Ark, removed the Torahs, both the original Valinsk Torah and the Rosen Torah. Then I fought my way out of the shul, and made for the safety of the woods behind the synagogue. As I just said, I lost my way and when I thought I couldn't go on, I came to a farm. I dared not show the farmer our holy scrolls, so I hid them in a pile of freshly mowed hay. After the farmer chased me off, I crept back at night and retrieved the Torahs. Then I trudged on in the dark until I came to a cow pasture. An old cart filled with hay stood by the fence, and I hurriedly placed the Torahs in it. I pulled the cart back to Valinsk like a mule—a very wet, old and tired one."

Yitzhak blinked and rubbed his sore eyes.

"And now, thanks to Hashem, I sit with you, my dearest friend."

Finally comprehending this incredible news, Yitzhak nearly lost his grip on the tree, then righting himself he cried: "The Torahs have been saved! Dov removed them to safety before the shul was engulfed. *Praised are You, Adonai our God, Ruler of the world, who gave us the Torah of truth, and implanted us with eternal life."*

Those below began to rejoice with him, raising their voices to thank God for His mercy. In their euphoria, Shaul and Hershel now scaled the tree to embrace their father. As they attempted to bring him down safely, the branch on which he had perched for days finally snapped, dropping all four into the river. This turned out to be its own blessing, as no one had needed a bath more urgently than Yitzhak and Dov, at least not since Tevya returned from Jerusalem.

Long after his burns had healed and new skin had grown over them, Yitzhak realized that he had forgotten to ask the shammash, who was no longer sprightly, how he alone could have carried two heavy Torah scrolls through a storm without damaging them. Then again, he was glad he had not asked; after all, miracles cannot be explained. As for the townsfolk they repeated the tale so often that it took on a life of its own.

After this occurrence, more than ever, the chazzan longed to lift up his voice in song, but in his agony at the loss of the Torah he had made a promise to the Almighty never to sing in the synagogue again. God had heeded his plea, and the Rosen Torah had escaped the fearful Crimson Devil unscathed, and when the Valinsk shul was rebuilt it would be housed in the Holy Ark.

The near-destruction of the family Torah convinced Yitzhak to acknowledge his sin of self-adulation and to keep the vow he made. When he revealed to Sarah the pact he had made with Hashem, She cried out, "It's my fault, I should never have nagged you about singing too much."

"No, I should have listened to your warning. I will go to the rabbi and tell him why I can no longer serve as chazzan."

Rabbi Asner questioned Yitzhak closely. Exactly what had he promised Hashem? Yitzhak explained he had sworn never to sing in the shul as retribution for being arrogant. The rabbi immediately pointed out that it would be even more arrogant to make the assumption that God had sent the great fire, which had destroyed much of Valinsk, just to teach the chazzan a lesson. The rabbi's argument startled Yitzhak, and he replied that he would think it over carefully.

Cradling the tips of his fingers and frowning, Rabbi Asner advised, "Yitzhak, you know *Teshuva*, in other words repentance, is a way of atoning for sin."

"Yes, off course."

To drive the point home, he went on, "If you cease doing what is forbidden, regret what you have done, and resolve never to repeat those actions, then God forgives you, and you can forgive yourself."

Yitzhak looked doubtful. "Still, I must keep the promise I made."

"Just for once listen to my advice!" the rabbi admonished. Once he had time to think things over, the rabbi felt certain that the chazzan would change his mind, if not he would have to think of a way to entice him back.

Without song, Yitzhak lost the zest for life that Sarah had so loved since she first met him. The spring in his step, the sparkle in his eyes, the quick laughter, and the flow of fresh ideas were replaced by melancholy inertia. Often, in the middle of some task, Yitzhak would stop and stare into the distance, lost to what was going on around him. Sarah became so distraught that she begged her husband to return to singing and to composing music.

In the end, she gently persuaded him, as only a loving wife can do, that he would not be breaking his promise to God if he sang for her alone. He had promised Hashem not to sing in the shul, but had said nothing about singing at home. After all, she pleaded what good had this act of contrition done; what was the use of him pining away?

In this way the chazzan was able to express the creative spirit that burned within—without violating his vow. Late at night, Sarah would draw the curtains tight, seat herself by the fire and give all her attention to Yitzhak. When he lifted his voice in song for Sarah, the despondency that pressed down on him lifted, reigniting his sense of wonder and joy at being alive. No longer constrained by the critical ears of the congregation, his compositions became more inventive and powerful.

He did not know, however, that the people of the shtetl had discovered his new practice. At night they gathered silently in the woods behind his house. As they listened to his beloved voice, their pent-up frustrations and despair were washed away on the swelling tide of his ardent arias. When the "recital" was over, they dispersed without a word, cleansed and exalted, willing to face their poor, uncertain lives in the shtetl. And yet their exaltation was tinged with sadness. Listening to Yitzhak in the confines of his home, no matter how beautiful, was like hearing a caged bird sing.

Months later, the Valinsk shul was finally rebuilt with the volunteer labor of the community, and contributions from rich and poor alike. Moshe, the shtetl's revered Torah scholar, commented that while slaves in Egypt they had been forced to build the pyramids, but for the shul the Valinskers gave their sweat and tears willingly. Now the congregation wanted their cantor back in the new Valinsk synagogue where he belonged. A delegation approached Rabbi Asner requesting that he speak to Yitzhak about taking up his old post as chazzan.

The rabbi had foreseen this, and had worked out a strategy in advance: He did not want a confrontation with Yitzhak; he wanted a reconciliation that would persuade him to resume being their chazzan. As a peace offering, he brought a bottle of wine and yeast buns that his wife had baked early that morning, full of cranberries from the nearby bog. He and Yitzhak sipped wine, enjoyed the buns, talked about the daily affairs of the shtetl, and weightier matters like the increasing pressure of the czarist government to get Jews to speak and write in Russian. Finally, discussion came around to the question of Yitzhak returning to his post.

"Did you give up being chazzan because I was too harsh with your father, and with you? If so I sincerely apologize." For the rabbi to confess what had been weighing on his conscience, ever since Yitzhak had renounced being a chazzan, wasn't easy.

Yitzhak stifled the involuntary chuckle of surprise bordering on derision that escaped his lips. "Rabbi, you astonish me!"

"Will you accept my apology?"

Yitzhak took time to contemplate his situation. After harboring a grudge against the rabbi for so many years, it was difficult to let it go. Yet it would be the right thing to do. "I accept your apology," he said, forcing a smile.

"Thank you."

"But I didn't give up being a chazzan because of the way you treated my father or me. It's more complicated than that," Yitzhak explained. "I failed my father when I almost lost his Torah, and I've failed to live up to the shtetl's expectations of me."

"Listen, whatever is on your conscience can be settled between you and God. Now it's time for you to think about your duty to the community instead of retreating like a man defeated. Take up your post, get on with your life!"

Taken aback by the rabbi's intensity, Yitzhak rose from his seat and paced round the room muttering to himself. Finally, he came to a halt, sat down and locked eyes with the rabbi. For a breathless moment the rabbi and the chazzan felt themselves bound to one another, as though on a seesaw that could tip either way.

Without dropping his gaze, Yitzhak spoke, "If I agree to resume my duties, will I be free to create hymns and to sing them at services and celebrations when I am moved to do so?"

The rabbi snorted in surprise. It was on the tip of his tongue to tell Yitzhak that he was asking for too much, but he could see that the balance had shifted. This time the chazzan wasn't going to bow to his authority so easily; he had no choice but to concede. Lifting his glass Asner forced a smile, and said "Of course," and the two men clinked glasses, "L'Chaim! To life! To health, to music!"

That night after Yitzhak had snuffed out the lamp, burrowed under the eiderdown, and wrapped himself around Sarah, savoring her smell and her warmth, he told her that he had accepted the rabbi's offer to be reinstated as the chazzan of Valinsk. Sarah turned to kiss him, "At last, we can be happy again," she murmured into his beard.

Before Yitzhak fell asleep one final soliloquy ran through his head: Everyday I study a portion of the Torah to anchor myself to my people, to God, and to honor the promise I made to my father. But now I find myself in a strange position: I who believe in holding strictly to tradition have brought about change. I am now free to break with tradition, to create new music. And I am happy, yet also afraid of where it will lead. Then he drifted into the blissful oblivion of sleep.

⇜8⇝

The Second Inheritor: Hershel Rosen, The Righteous

Troubles no one wants to steal from you; good deeds no one can.

Yiddish folk saying

Yitzhak Rosen liked to say that his younger son, Hershel, conservative and down-to-earth, fit shtetl life like a lid fits its pot. But his older son, Shaul, was a frustrating enigma to him.

"Our oldest is suited to shtetl life no more than a silk coat to a pig," Yitzhak mused to his wife Sarah.

"Are you telling me that my son is a silk coat, or a pig?"

"What do you think? Of course a silk coat! Would I compare my own flesh and blood to a pig?" Yitzhak retorted. "Shaul could be a brilliant Talmudic scholar, but instead he dreams of . . . of what?" Pride shone in his eyes, but behind the pride was a sadness that seemed to reflect the ancient and tragic history of his people.

"Maybe becoming a great philosopher like Spinoza?" said his wife.

"Spinoza no less!" Yitzhak dismissed her with an exasperated sigh. "Even with my reprimands and the teacher's punishment, Shaul won't apply himself to learning the Talmud or Torah."

"At the gymnasium he is an outstanding student, and you are proud of the praise the teachers heap upon our son, so don't *kvetch*, so much."

From the age of five, Shaul had attended *cheder* where classes were taught in Yiddish and Hebrew. After turning seven, he attended twice weekly the Russian language gymnasium, or secular school. There he excelled in literature and languages including Hebrew, Russian and French. Yitzhak hoped that Shaul's fascination with non-religious studies would pass and he would go on to yeshiva to get a proper religious education.

His father had every reason to fear secular education, for a Russian gymnasium exposed his son to ideas that could easily lead to a loss of faith. Yitzhak mustered his strongest arguments in a desperate attempt to persuade Shaul that there was little future for him after graduating from the gymnasium. He would find only insignificant jobs: tutoring the children of the wealthy, writing letters for Jewish patrons, and completing official forms for the illiterate. But to possibly advance in a Christian society, he would need to enter a university. Since Jews were excluded from the university, to be accepted, many chose to discard Judaism. If he chose the unthinkable he would become an outcast with his own family and the community—surely he didn't want such a terrible fate? If he converted, even with a university degree the chances of being hired as a civil servant or engineer in Russian society were limited. Just the shadow of Jewish ancestry would degrade him. With tears spilling over, Yitzhak declared that just the thought that this could be his son's fate, made him ill.

With these burning issues in mind, his father adamantly refused to allow Shaul to continue to study at the gymnasium for high school students, insisting that he go to the yeshiva, as a result Shaul rebelled and went to work in the tavern at fifteen, secretly continuing his secular studies on his own. Over the years he built up an excellent library ranging from literature to philosophy, medicine to law, mathematics to astronomy. Sometimes, when the young men found a moment to rest from their religious studies, they came, covertly, to hear Shaul explain the latest scientific developments, or talk of events in the outside world that, in comparison to his contemporaries, he knew a great deal about.

When, belatedly, the Haskalah or Enlightenment, proclaiming universal equality of man and the supremacy of reason, reached Valinsk in the 1860s, Shaul eagerly joined the conflict that erupted between the rabbis and the yeshiva students, siding with those who dared defy the ban on all books except those of a religious nature, even at the risk of expulsion.

Rumors began to circulate that Shaul was a dangerous firebrand, but the ardent young man captured Yael Forman's attention. She and her mother, Luba Forman, recently arrived from the shtetl of Pikeli, had rented a room in the widow Davidson's house on the same street as the Rosens.

Shaul had first seen Yael, accompanied by her friends, standing on the fringe of a group of young men in the marketplace. Some of the men had carefully trimmed whiskers and skullcaps, some had rampant beards, some wore the traditional round hats, and a few wore more sporty caps. In the center of the group stood Shaul, gesticulating wildly to make a point with a young Chassid. When he stormed off, Shaul immediately noticed Yael with her head cocked to one side as if considering the merits of the debate about the need for learning Russian, French and German—all infused with the potentially dangerous ideas of the Enlightenment. She wore a loosely fitted dark green dress of soft cotton that allowed her to move freely, yet when she walked it caressed her revealing her supple curves. Their eyes met, and beneath her intense scrutiny he felt himself being judged. Did she approve of his lanky frame, his narrow fine-featured, pale face with its bright eyes?

The wry smile playing around her mouth, the way she tossed back her luxuriant black hair, which curled softly around her high forehead, was a direct appeal to him to approach her. He introduced himself, and when she shyly posed a question about the right of girls to attend school, he became as tongued-tied and vulnerable as only a young man in love for the first time can be.

Observing the intense relationship that was growing between his son and Yael, Yitzhak began objecting to Shaul's possible choice of a marriage partner. Mother and daughter were talented seamstresses with a reputation for making fine garments that lasted for years. Yael's family on her mother's side, the Lemans, hailed from Pikeli, Lithuania; they were devout and well respected, but very poor. Yael's late father, Elijah Forman, had been a simple coachman and horse-trader, who traveled with horse and wagon over the dirt roads connecting the shtetls, through summer storms and winter blizzards. In the markets he would stop to feed his horses, exchange news, and to inquire if someone had a horse to sell or trade. When Yael was just four years old, her father came to a tragic end; he died at the hands of a band of forest robbers after getting stuck in the mud during an early spring thaw. After that, the four sons helped their widowed mother and little sister eke out a living until Yael was old enough to work as a seamstress.

"Yael is hardworking," Yitzhak conceded, "but her family, although pious, lives in poverty."

"Don't they say a beautiful girl is half the dowry?" Shaul parried.

"A decent dowry would make life easier for you."

"Yael is of greater value than any dowry," Shaul retorted. "Her kindness, intelligence and talent are worth more than riches."

"You've got a point," Yitzhak said, adding with a sigh, "If rich people could hire other people to die for them, the poor could make a wonderful living."

After months of deliberation, Yitzhak finally conceded. "Shaul, you have always chosen to follow your own path, even when it is difficult and unfamiliar. Although I am not filled with pleasure at the prospect of your marriage, Yael *will* make a good wife, and in your mother-law you will acquire a pious and honorable though impoverished woman."

To Yitzhak's relief, his younger son Hershel was the exact opposite of his older brother. He was conservative, compliant and sweet natured. Slight of build, standing a little over five feet four tall, with a sparse beard, always fastidiously dressed in the traditional black gown and round black hat, there was something vulnerable about him, conveyed by of his diminutive stature, and the melancholy expression in his large brown eyes. Unlike Shaul,

Hershel readily agreed to study at the yeshiva and to follow in his father's footsteps as chazzan of Valinsk. Although Hershel displayed none of his father's brilliance, his voice had a pleasant timbre to it that projected his kind disposition. A tender, honorable and pious soul, Hershel was well liked in the community.

In due course, Hershel married Sonia Meyer, daughter of the *shochet* — the woman his parents had chosen for him. Sonia was an excellent homemaker and a shrewd businesswoman, a good match for Hershel who tended to be impractical. To Hershel's disappointment, they produced three daughters but no sons to carry on the family name. His daughters were talented and hardworking, but as females they could never hope to become cantors or scholars.

While Sonia wished that she could have borne a son, she was grateful for her three loving daughters. Unlike boys, who had to attend school or apprentice themselves to a trade, her girls stayed home to help with the endless, exhausting chores and with the family general store. Their work began before dawn when the cocks crowed and continued until the owls went hunting after dark.

Only visits to the bathhouse — on the eve of the Sabbath, and before Holy Days — provided the women respite from the drudgery of their lives. In the steam room they would wash their hair and soap themselves clean while an attendant tossed buckets of hot water over their tired bodies. Then they would stretch out on the wooden benches around the room and doze as the vapor rose from a pile of hot stones on to which water, perfumed with fresh birch wood, had been poured. As the steam swirled around them, a wonderful sense of peace veiled their worries for a time.

The two older Rosen girls, Ida and Miriam now in their mid teens, accepted their traditional roles as women of the shtetl and worked hard to provide an income. Together with their mother they helped in the family store that allowed their father to devote the necessary time to studying the Torah and Talmud. Ida, soft-spoken, plump, and pretty, took pleasure in cooking and helping her mother run a kosher home. Miriam, tall, big-boned,

100

and energetic, enjoyed tending the garden and the chickens, the geese, and the milk cow. Under her care, their vegetable garden flourished and kept the household and the store well stocked with fresh lettuce, chard, spinach, cabbage, peas, beets, and tomatoes. In addition, Miriam arranged for the lease of a small fruit orchard that provided fresh apples and cherries, which she made into flavorful preserves.

Leah, the youngest daughter, was the tomboy and rebel of the family. Diminutive and outspoken, she was not pretty in a conventional way; her nose was beaky and her lips were too thin. But she had a silky complexion, a radiant smile and smoldering dark eyes that reflected her passionate nature. When Leah was little, and her next-door playmate, David Zuk, turned four, she cried with envy as he was taken to school by his proud parents, knowing that there he would be given a writing tablet and showered with fruits, coins, and candy. She begged to start school with him, and could not understand why this was out of the question for a girl.

Leah shunned household chores and preferred to help her mother in the shop, which could be entered from a side door of their home. The family store was a necessary source of income, but unfortunately, taxes, license fees, and bribes demanded by the local Lithuanian officials cut deeply into the profits, so the income had to be supplemented by the sale of homemade goods. The business would have shown little profit without the excellent yeast buns that Sonia and Ida prepared before dawn five days a week, fresh vegetables from Miriam's garden, and cottage cheese made with milk from their cow, and preserves from the orchard.

Leah proved to have her own entrepreneurial drive. She devised a plan to start the town's first lending library. Her Uncle Shaul's library provided the inspiration for her idea and the core of her collection. When Shaul discovered that his little niece loved books as much as he did, he began inviting her into his home to read to her. She would sit with her eyes closed, breathing in the smells of leather, parchment, and ink, and let her uncle's voice, rich and warm as melted honey, carry her away to other worlds.

Shaul's heart ached for this innocent child, who did not fit neatly into the narrow mold of the shtetl any more than he did.

To start her own library in the family store, Leah scrounged, traded items from the store for books, and even wrote her own stories for the children. For one grosz, customers could borrow a book, and soon the mothers were returning for another book, then another and another. In the winter Leah gathered the youngsters around the stove, and in summer they sat under the shade of an apple tree near Miriam's vegetable garden.

Even before Leah began, the children sat quietly, their eyes bright with anticipation. Her surprisingly resonant voice, dramatic gestures, and flashing eyes transfixed even the most boisterous children. Their genuine delight so exhilarated her that as she recounted her tales her eyes began to sparkle and an intense blush spread across her cheeks and throat as if she had swallowed too much wine. Listening to her daughter, Sonia shook her head and lamented to herself: *In a world of ordinary people, my daughter's passionate temperament will cause her much pain.* As each story reached its climax, the children involuntarily held their breath or exclaimed out loud at an unexpected twist. And when the tale ended, they let out an audible sigh and begged for just one more.

On Saturdays, when the learned men came to the house to study, Leah served glasses of scalding tea while listening to their discussions of Jewish philosophy, history, and customs. At first Hershel wanted to exclude his precocious daughter from these sessions, but his wife prevailed. "It couldn't do any harm to let Leah listen quietly if she promises not to disturb the men with questions," she pleaded. Hershel conceded as he found it difficult to impose discipline upon his girls, usually leaving his wife to make decisions concerning them.

As Leah grew older, she observed that although the discussions were heated, the men never expressed skepticism about the basic tenets of Judaism. For fear that they would forbid her to attend the sessions, Leah often choked back the words that would interject her doubts and uncertainties: Why men say a prayer that loosely translates to "Thank God I wasn't born a woman." Why women can't women be part of a minyan? Why can't they study the Torah in the way men do? Why do they have to sit apart from men in shul? Only with Uncle Shaul and Aunt Yael did she feel free to question without being censured.

The winter that Leah turned twelve, a deadly dysentery epidemic erupted in the region of their shtetl. Its first victim was the rabbi's daughter, after that the Valinskers would wake up to hear of others that had passed away during the night.

Shaul, Yael, and their two children, Yakov and Frieda, became extremely ill with high fevers and stomach cramps, with Shaul the most critical. Sonia cared for them throughout their illness, and fearing for Shaul's life called in the *feldsher*, or folk doctor. He prescribed a potion for pain, and instructed her to fill a calf's bladder with ice and apply it to the patient's forehead to bring down the fever.

Although Leah had been forbidden to visit her uncle during his illness, she crept over to his house early one morning and peeked through the window. She saw her mother dozing in a chair and Uncle Shaul curled on the bed in a fetal position, his eyes swollen shut and his face bruised from the cold burns caused by icy water leaking from the calf's bladder. Leah's piercing scream jerked Sonia awake in time to see her daughter crumple to the ground outside.

Two weeks after contracting the illness, Shaul succumbed. Sonia sent for Gimpl the undertaker and his son Yossel, but they were overwhelmed with preparing the many who had died, and did not arrive for several hours. Leah watched horrified as they loaded her beloved uncle's corpse onto a sled for transport over the snow to the building near the cemetery where it would be ritually cleansed and guarded overnight for burial the next day. At a safe distance, she followed, ducking behind cover to be sure no one observed her. When they reached the building, Gimpl and Yossel carried Shaul inside. Outside, Leah remained rooted to the spot until the very marrow in her bones seemed to solidify. Finally she collapsed onto the icy ground and sobbed uncontrollably.

For weeks afterward, Leah felt utterly abandoned by her uncle and confidante. Shaul had been the one person who had encouraged her to read, to ask questions, who laughed at her sly observations about the goings on in the shtetl, without censoring her. She barely ate, falling prey to an irrational fear that human-shaped devils with chicken feet were pursuing her. Convinced that these devils would drag her off to the mountains where they lived, Leah suffered terrifying nightmares and moved from one bed to another, unsettling everyone already exhausted from the illness and the death raging through their families.

As deeply as Leah suffered, Shaul's children, Yakov and Frieda, sustained the worst blow. On one of the most miserable days of his boyhood, Yakov sat in the corner of the darkened bedroom in a big chair by his mother's bedside. She had been sleeping for a long time, and even in her sleep she shivered. The boy hardly recognized her, with skin yellow as tallow, and dark hair dry and matted as frostbitten weeds. When she awoke, she opened her sunken eyes and stared at him without moving or acknowledging his existence, then a flicker of recognition came into her eyes and she tried to smile despite her labored breathing. Her cracked and trembling lips drew back into a frightening grimace. The boy obeyed the unsteady hands motioning him to come nearer, to put his ear close to her mouth. Terrified, he strained to hear what his mother was saying as the smell of death, bitter and foul, filled his nostrils. Then he burst into tears and could not stop himself from rushing out of the room to where his Uncle Hershel waited in the kitchen. He felt strong arms lifting him, holding him tight, and the deep voice whispering in his ears, soothing him.

"Mother wanted to tell me something, but I couldn't understand," the boy sobbed. "Is she going to die?" Hershel did not reply, but Yakov felt his uncle's tears falling into his hair and wetting his scalp, only exacerbating his dread.

When his mother died hours later, Yakov mourned together with his uncle and the Rosen clan. The epidemic had carried his father away just weeks before. Numb with shock, and a white-hot rage that withered his sorrow, the boy understood: Now and forever more he would be an orphan.

Loving and righteous Uncle Hershel and his kindly but formidable wife, Sonia, took the orphans into their home. It had three small bedrooms and a kitchen with two ovens: one for cooking and the other for baking. In the winter the bedrooms were frigid, and everyone huddled round the kitchen stoves.

The children would be an added burden, but Hershel and Sonia had solemnly promised Yael on her deathbed to care for them. In any case, there was no orphanage in Valinsk because the kahal had decreed that orphans be taken care of by their relatives. Hershel and Sonia were kind to the children; it was a mitzvah written in the Torah. Even so, deep inside the orphans never felt wholly drawn into the family's innermost circle of love. They watched the parents spontaneously praise, hug, or kiss their own three girls Ida, Miriam, and Leah—and felt excluded and alone.

The girl cousins accommodated in their own way to this new family structure. Frieda was pliant and shy, and the sisters found it easy to boss her around or to ignore her as they pleased. Yakov, on the other hand, was strong-willed and quick-tempered, and when Ida and Miriam tried to cajole him into joining their girlish games, he resisted, and soon learned to stay out of their way. However, Leah, the family tomboy, became his surrogate "brother." Together they roamed the woods and hatched practical jokes to annoy the older sisters.

With two more mouths to feed, the meager family income barely covered their needs. While they lived, Shaul and Yael had managed to keep the family tavern afloat, but with a steep increase in the tax on the Jews, they found it increasingly difficult to turn a profit. After Yael and Shaul's early demise, Hershel inherited the tavern. Unfortunately, he hadn't the nose for commerce, the aggressive drive to survive rough times; as a result profits dwindled under his aegis. His decision to sell proved to be a wise one, because shortly afterward the government took over the alcohol industry, prohibiting all sales of spirits to Jewish proprietors of taverns and inns. With that capricious, spiteful decree, this spring from which the Rosens,

105

and other Jewish tavern owners had drawn their livelihood, dried up. Still, the money from the sale was just enough to defray the cost of raising the orphans.

Finally that terrible epidemic ended as spring thawed the ice and snow. The children's melancholy waned, and as the summer reached its peak, they could no longer resist joining the shtetl children in raiding the orchards for tart green pears, ripe purple plums, and sticky yellow gooseberries. They stuffed their pockets with the stolen fruit, then fled, holding their sides to suppress shouts of glee. In the muddy area behind the cemetery, out of sight of the farmer, they devoured the treats all the sweeter for being pilfered.

Then Yitzhak began complaining of chest pains. The local midwife, who also served as the shtetl's feldsher, prescribed various concoctions, which did little to alleviate his discomfort. He lingered through the summer and into the late fall, until one evening after services Yitzhak became violently ill, and died in his wife's arms. Sarah held him tightly to her breasts and thanked him for his love, for allowing her to serve him as a loving wife. Then she wept as an eternity of darkness descended upon her.

The Rosens buried their own cantor-poet in the ancient Valinsk cemetery, known as the "House of Eternity," under a birch tree next to his mother Rachel, and father Shmuel. Above his right shoulder lay Shaul, his beloved son, and his daughter-in-law Yael. At the funeral, Hershel stood apart from everyone, close to the grave's edge, with his head bowed, his body swaying ceaselessly in the ageless chants. The rabbi's prayers mingled eerily with the sighing of the wind. Sonia hovered protectively behind Hershel, her arms linked to her daughters.

The mourners huddled together in the chill fall wind blowing across the old burial ground on the hill. The melancholy autumnal smells of cut hay and rotting manure from the fields surrounding the cemetery mingled with the odors of dead leaves and wet dirt freshly piled at the grave.

Through a blur of tears they gazed down on Valinsk, at once familiar and strange, a shtetl inhabited by the living and haunted by the dead. Their eyes strayed over the muddy path meandering downward through boggy meadows, across the rickety wooden bridge to the huddle of gabled cottages with their backyard vegetable gardens and orchards, the lanes converging on the cobbled square, and, on the opposite hill, the wooden synagogue flanked by the houses of learning.

Hershel's utter calm even as his father's coffin was lowered into the grave, caused a tremor of foreboding to pass through the mourners. When the first shovel of dirt splattered onto the coffin, a frightening shriek rent the air. Everyone turned to see Leah collapse; roll slowly over onto her side with her knees pulled to her chest and her face buried in her hands. Before Sonia could react, Hershel stepped back, and bent down to raise his daughter tenderly to her feet. Sonia saw their fingers entwine as they stood at the maw of the grave, cleaving to one another, until the coffin had disappeared beneath the earth, and the Mourner's Kaddish said. Behind them the women clutched each other for support, their mouths twisted in anguish.

Six months later, Yitzhak's tombstone was erected at the unveiling ceremony. Hershel had ordered two tablets, symbols for the Ten Commandments, to be engraved upon the monument, representing his father's reverence for the Torah, and to watch over the members of the family buried nearby. In composing the inscribed dedication Hershel had made a great effort to find the exact words that would express his reverence. It read:

Here lies Yitzhak Rosen, son of Shmuel Rosen.
Pious and loved by all he observed the Torah
with humility.
He trained his children to walk in the path of justice.
May his soul be bound up in the bond of eternal life.
Born 10 Cheshvan 5529. Died 20 Kislev 5599.

Although justifiably proud to have inherited the Torah, guilt tormented Hershel. He regretted that he had not talked to his father about his inheritance, but by nature Yitzhak Rosen had been a private man pouring all his feelings into his music. Now Hershel told himself that he could not be blamed for his brother Shaul's untimely death. Yet Shaul had been the more talented and brilliant of the two, and he felt that his father had been too harsh in his judgment of his brother for not attending the yeshiva. He tried to put his guilt aside: even if Shaul had lived, his father might not have chosen his first-born son as the next inheritor because he had spurned tradition and religion. Still he could not rid himself of the feeling of being a usurper, who had inherited the Torah by chance.

Hershel's immediate problem, however, clearly was his daughter Leah. Yitzhak's funeral had taken place just a few months before Leah turned thirteen, and on the brink of womanhood, she openly rebelled against customs that limited a woman's participation in religious ritual. One day on the steps of the synagogue, where others could hear, she declared, "If I were a boy, I would have been accorded the honor of reading from the Rosen Torah!" Her shrill voice made her father cringe with shame,

As others listened, Hershel wagged his finger warningly at his daughter, but she would not be silenced.

"I am as learned, even more learned than many of the young men attending the yeshiva. Is it right to ban me from our Torah?"

"Don't talk like that. You must put a stop to these crazy ideas."

"Why is it crazy?"

"It's not for us to question. Men and women have different obligations. We must respect tradition!"

"God sees me studying the Torah daily." Choked by rage, her voice sounded high and childish. "He knows what is in my heart."

"Your uncle and your grandfather, may they rest in peace, raised your expectations too high!" her father snapped.

"Grandfather Yitzhak respected my desire to learn!" Leah countered, with justification. She had begged Yitzhak to teach her the Torah. At first he had done so reluctantly, as an Orthodox woman is not required to study, and is exempted from the daily services as well as the performance of those mitzvot that had to be performed at specific times throughout the day when mothers needed to take care of the children and the household. Although Yitzhak had his reservations, his granddaughter's thirst for knowledge so impressed him that gradually he set aside many hours to give her the scholarly education a grandson would have received.

Hershel did not relent. "Yes, your grandfather taught you well, but he feared your hot temper."

"My grandfather adored me!"

"You'll never find a husband with that sharp tongue," Hershel lashed back.

Her father's rejection of her wishes, and the death of her uncle followed far too rapidly by her grandfather's demise, triggered an emotional outburst that the people of Valinsk would never forget.

It took place during the festival called *Simchat Torah,* or rejoicing in the Torah, which marks the end of the annual cycle of Torah readings and the immediate beginning of a new cycle. For years she had fantasized that one day she would be accorded the great honor of being called upon during Simchat Torah to read the final portion of the five books of Moses. Rationally, she knew that this could never come to pass, as only a man could be chosen as the *Hatan Torah,* or the bridegroom of the Torah.

The festivities, so like a joyous wedding, made Leah itch to dance and sing. The "bridegroom," followed by the most important members of the congregation, headed a happy procession. As a child, Leah and the other small children were swept up onto their fathers' shoulders to wave flags and hold lighted candles. But now, Leah was too old to join the dancing throng. Watching from the women's upstairs gallery, she felt imprisoned behind the carved screen. The cloying odors of perspiration, lavender water, and camphor closed her throat.

She observed mesmerized, as men in the sanctuary leaned forward like reeds driven in the wind, to touch the Torah with the fringes of their prayer shawls; a river of bobbing heads;

children waving flags; candles burning brightly; red apples being tossed into the air; drumming of feet; clapping of hands; voices rising in song echoing off the domed ceiling. Without premeditation, she jumped to her feet and ran down the steps to where her father danced with the Rosen Torah.

She shoved her way through the throng, unaware of heavy heels crushing her toes or sharp elbows jabbing into her ribs. When she reached her father, she tried to seize the Torah from him. With a strangled exclamation, Hershel twisted sharply away from her outstretched hands, lost his grip on the Torah, and fell to his knees in the aisle.

The women in the upstairs gallery moaned in horror, some swooned away. Downstairs in the main sanctuary, the men gaped in dismay at the sight of the Torah on the floor. Hershel remained crouched over it, the cover still dangling from his daughter's clenched fists like a carcass without bones. The voices of noisy celebration gave way to utter silence. Men turned white with fear, then purple with anger. Overcome by shock and humiliation, Hershel refused to stand. His shoulders shook with silent weeping. The rabbi tried to escort Leah outside, but she put her head between her knees and wailed. She wept and wept, until she could hardly breathe, and had to be revived with smelling salts.

Fortunately, Hershel had the presence of mind to curl around the Torah at the very moment the scroll began to slip from his grasp, thus preventing the parchment from being torn. The scroll was minutely examined for the slightest damage, and found to be kosher, or fit for services in the shul. The rabbi then decreed that the entire congregation present at the time, except for the children, would be required to fast on a chosen day, the eighth day following the mishap, and to give generously to charity.

Amid the resulting trauma, no one gave a thought to Leah's own suffering, or the emotional damage inflicted on her. Instead they castigated her for simpleminded foolishness and outrageous behavior.

Leah tried to explain what had happened to her mother, "I wanted only to be free to become one with God's joyous spirit. Why has He punished me?"

"My darling daughter, in time you will be happy as a wife and mother!"

"If only I had been born as a boy! Then the Rosen Torah might have been mine!" Leah declared, almost fainting at the thought.

Sonia's heart ached to see her daughter in such distress. She did what she could to comfort her, but she could do nothing to stop the malicious gossip. People branded the ardent, headstrong young woman as *meshugga,* or crazy. They whispered that the dybbuk—the dislocated soul of a dead person escaped from Gehenna, the place of purgatory—had possessed her. They could not accept that a woman raised in so pious a family would dare enter the male section of the shul to grab the Torah. Out of pity for the Rosen family, the adults of the shtetl attempted to treat Leah as before, publicly at least, although she often caught them staring at her with a cold, suspicious gleam in their eyes. Their sons and daughters shunned her completely. Leah felt like soiled underwear left hanging on the line where every passerby could see it.

It hurt Sonia and Hershel deeply to see their youngest daughter's high spirits crushed and to watch her go about her daily tasks brooding and silent as a shadow. But their greatest concern was now practical: how to restore the sullied reputation of their daughter, so that a suitable husband could be found.

"Our daughter has many good qualities," Sonia reassured her husband. "She's pious, hard working and intelligent."

"But what self-respecting male would want to live with a woman that tries to act like a man?"

"Let's not rush our daughter into marriage. She's young. In time she will mature."

"But what's to be done with her? Her will is too strong!" Hershel moaned.

After intense discussions with the rebbetzin, the Rosens made the decision to send Leah to her older sister, Ida, now married to a wealthy fur dealer, Boris Krantz. Ida and Boris lived in a fine home in Riga, about 190 kilometers away, and generously agreed to come to Leah's aid. Compared to the village of Valinsk, Riga had much to offer, and Leah didn't protest too long or too loudly at being sent there.

As soon as she had settled in the Krantz's home, Leah begged her sister for permission to enroll at the fledgling government-sponsored school on Lacplesa Street, where secular subjects were being taught. At first Ida absolutely refused to go along with her younger sister's scheme. She was reluctant to upset her family or her status in the community, and knew that her father would oppose it. On a recent visit to Riga, Hershel had vehemently denounced the Russian government's campaign to revamp the system of Jewish education with secular schools. To Boris's consternation, his father-in-law declared that the government's *real* intention was to eliminate Jewish studies, uproot the study of the Torah and the Talmud, and eventually merge Jews with Christians — in other words, to obliterate Jewish identity.

Nevertheless, Leah continued to plead, and even threaten to run away disguised as a boy. After much soul-searching, and against her better judgment Ida gave in to Leah's request in the fervent hope that this new interest might calm her, and help to draw her out of her depression. Knowing full well what their parents would think, she swore Leah to secrecy.

The sisters somehow managed to guard their secret for months before word reached their father via the shtetl's primary rumormonger, Shlomo Wolf the retired butcher.

"Leah was seen walking, unescorted mind you, in the company of a handsome Russian *shegetz*! Because this young gentile is the son of a military official, it will cause serious problems for your family," Wolf warned.

"What's to be done!" Hershel groaned, holding his head in his hands, indecisive as usual.

"There is nothing to be done but bring Leah back home and marry her off to anyone halfway acceptable," Sonia snapped.

Over her protests, they ordered Leah to return to Valinsk the following Friday before sunset. To celebrate her daughter's homecoming, Sonia lovingly prepared the Sabbath supper — golden chicken soup, glistening fish cakes, and honeyed carrots — and told her husband that after such a fine meal Leah might be more receptive to the idea of marriage.

Hershel dreaded having to confront his daughter about the necessity for marriage. When the dishes were cleared, he downed a shot of brandy, kept only for special occasions, and tried to concentrate on a religious text. Finally, Sonia said impatiently, "Hershel it's getting late, go to Leah, she's sitting in the kitchen."

"If I were a wealthy man like my grandfather Shmuel Rosen, may his soul rest in peace, a scholar would be glad to marry my daughter," he sighed.

"Stop putting off what cannot be avoided," Sonia reprimanded. Despite his wife's prodding, Hershel could not summon the nerve to bring up the subject of marriage with his headstrong daughter.

That night he slept restlessly, and the next morning he left earlier than usual for the synagogue, where he twice lost his place in the service to the astonishment of those he led in prayer. Back from the shul he sat down to enjoy a Sabbath lunch of chopped radishes and onions, and jellied calf's foot with just the right tang of garlic. Although he pretended not to notice Sonia's anxious glances, he did not enjoy the meal as much as usual.

After his customary Sabbath afternoon nap, Hershel woke with a sour stomach and a dry mouth, and called for Leah to bring him a jug of cider. When he had poured a glass for both of them, he asked her to sit with him at the kitchen table.

"Leah, you must understand that we have survived persecution for thousands of years only because we have kept our faith and our traditions strong. We live side by side with people different from us — Lithuanians, Tartars, Belarussians, Russians, Germans, Poles, and Gypsies." Hershel leaned forward and took his daughter's hands in his. "And although many have tried to convert us to their religions, we have stood fast in the face of intimidation, persecution and even murder."

He was well aware that Leah knew all this, and his lecture did little to assuage his daughter's fears. "Papa, what are you trying to tell me?"

"That it's time for you to take a husband."

"Papa! Please, I'm not ready!" In her distress Leah got down on her knees and beseeched him, "Send me to Palestine, or even to America! There I can start a new life. I won't be a source of disgrace to you any longer." Her pleas truly terrified him. God forbid she should consider leaving home! Who ever heard of a young girl traveling by herself!

"My darling daughter, it is out of the question. Rest assured that once you are married and have a husband and children of your own, you will settle down."

To Leah, marriage sounded like being thrown into a well and left to drown. "I beg you, don't marry me off to a stooped-backed *yeshiva bocher* with greasy side-whiskers, who sits all day over his books while his wife slaves to put bread in his mouth."

"Please Leah, don't talk like that!" He could hardly believe that his daughter had insulted him. Any promising yeshiva student would make a most prestigious match, greasy whiskers or not, and he would quickly have endorsed it. "You're in enough trouble already," her father said, turning pale.

With Leah's reputation, they would have to rely on the skills of a good *shadchan* or matchmaker. They chose Clara Bernstein who kept a well-researched list of young people in the surrounding shtetls, and did her best to match couples most suited to one another.

At the urging of the Rosens the matchmaker began searching for a husband for Leah. She warned the Rosens that it would be no easy mission because of their daughter's reputation as a *meshuggana*. After prolonged and complicated negotiations, the matchmaker found someone, Dovid Goodman, in a distant shtetl. "He's a pious Jew, a carpenter who makes a living from his trade, of good character, and in good health. What more can you want for a son-in-law?" Clara's full lower lip quivered with satisfaction.

"So he is perfect. Wonderful!" Hershel noted that the matchmaker avoided his direct gaze. "But tell me, does he perhaps have just one little fault?"

"Well, I would not call it a fault. Maybe he's a little shy, a little high-strung."

"Shy is not so bad. High-strung could be a problem."

"Forgive me, but Leah is a little on the excitable side herself."

"So? She'll make a wonderful mother. You yourself praised her gift for inspiring children. Before we can make a deal, I beg you to be honest with me."

"Would I lie to you?'"

"Well?"

"So he stutters a little. Maybe a lot."

Hershel tried to mask his laughter by clearing his throat and blowing his nose. "He stutters? You mean he talks with difficulty?"

"So? A carpenter needs to be an orator? Your daughter loves to talk, nonstop, and Dovid can't talk even when he tries! They make a perfect match." And with that they shook hands.

Hershel did not spend much time haggling over the shadchan's fees. Once the matchmaker was satisfied, arrangements could proceed for the signing of an engagement contract in the presence of Leah and Dovid, and their immediate families.

The rabbi drew up the contract strictly according to Jewish law, including details of the dowry, the specifics of the marriage ceremony, which party would be responsible for payment of various expenses, and the date of the wedding. The cantor then read the contract aloud for the families to hear, and to tacitly approve—although now and then a raised eyebrow or a frown betrayed a particular member's disapproval. After that the groom's mother and the bride's mother vigorously threw a plate to the floor and broke it while the guests cried "Mazel Tov!" To celebrate the propitious occasion, and to reward their patience, they all enjoyed the hearty banquet, while the cantor said prayers for the well being of the couple. No one appeared to notice the unsmiling face and red-rimmed eyes of the bride to be.

The weeks before her marriage, Leah continued to beg her parents to let her go free, but to no avail. At fifteen she became what she had most dreaded: a married woman burdened with the thankless, endless responsibilities of a shtetl wife.

⤜ 9 ⤛

Leah Rosen: the *Agunah,*
or Chained Woman

And if she does not find favor in his eyes he shall write her a bill of divorce and put it in her hand and send her out of his house.

Torah

Leah discovered to her astonishment that there were two Dovid Goodmans. By day, he was silent and solemn, growling and stuttering when she approached his carpentry bench. Night revealed a different, hidden Dovid. She had feared their marriage bed, but to her delight her husband was a lover of considerable patience and tact.

By the time Leah gave birth to their first child a year later—a healthy boy they named Sholem in honor of his great-great-grandfather Shmuel Rosen—she had learned to cope with the two Dovids. She stayed out of the way of the first Dovid by day, and enjoyed the attentions of the second at night.

In years following, she gave birth to another boy, Lazar, followed by two girls, Bessie and Shayne. She took good care of the children and the household and continued to work in her mother's store to supplement their income. Soon after the birth of Shayne, Sholem became ill with dysentery.

Mad with anguish and grief, Leah crept into the synagogue late at night. Although it was forbidden, she opened the doors of the Holy Ark. Trembling like a new bride, hesitantly, reverently, she touched the red silk mantle of the Rosen Torah then bringing her fingers to her lips she kissed them. Prostrating herself before the Holy Ark, she sent up a prayer, "Almighty God, Creator of the Universe, please save my son Sholem. You must have made a mistake, surely it is not written in Your Book that it is Sholem's time to die."

But God did not spare her son.

Leah walked the streets in the darkness throwing her head back, howling at the heavens, and rebuking Hashem for forsaking her. People shook their heads and shivered in fear: "There goes poor Leah the meshuggana. But then, can you expect otherwise of a woman who has lost a child?"

In time she came back to the world for she saw without her care and compassion her three surviving children and her husband were becoming unhinged.

In their tenth year of marriage, with no apparent reason, Dovid developed odd behaviors. He washed his hands repeatedly, pulled out chunks of his hair, one corner of his mouth twitched, he awoke at night screaming and complaining that he heard strange voices calling him. His stuttering worsened until even Leah could make no sense of what he said. Overwhelmed by the urgency to find a cure, Leah tried an increasingly drastic series of remedies. First she asked Rabbi Berel Sandler, the young rabbi now presiding over the Valinsk shul, for special permission to invoke a blessing for her husband, so gravely in need of divine intervention. She consulted Rivka Beker the *feldsher*, a respected local practitioner of folk medicine, who dispensed her services at the public baths on Fridays. The feldsher recommended bleeding with leeches and cupping glasses for Dovid's illness; in fact anyone with a pain — the poor, the wealthy, and even the healthy — believed that cupping was the best possible cure. The only results were large, circular, bleeding welts on the hapless carpenter's back from the suction cups. Sick with foreboding, Leah traveled with her husband to Vilna to consult with a licensed medical doctor, who prescribed enemas and medicines formulated by a pharmacist. Still, the carpenter's condition continued to deteriorate.

Finally, she petitioned Rabbi Zalman Segal, a renowned Chassidic sage, to perform an exorcism. The rabbi solemnly declared that a dybbuk had possessed Dovid. For a few weeks after the exorcism to sever the bond between her husband and the dybbuk, his nervous tics abated, only to return in full force.

Nothing could prevent Dovid's steady descent into madness. He began wandering the streets at night, and slept all day like a man in a coma. Leah had to face the awful truth—she could do nothing to save him. She fought off the waves of guilt that caused her terrible nightmares. Her children shared their mother's anguish, but in the end they convinced her that it would be a mercy to send Dovid to the only communal farm far from the shtetl where others like him were fed and sheltered.

When her younger daughter, Shayne, married, Leah took stock of her life. Lazar had become a scholar, and had married well; Ziva Lux, the butcher's daughter, brought him a fine dowry and made a good wife. Her beloved daughters, unfortunately, had married men far below them in education and ability because of their father's station in life as a lowly carpenter and a madman.

Alone in her bed, reviewing the marriages of her children, Leah felt that a chapter in her life had come to an end. Uninvited, a vision of the kosher slaughterer, Max Stein, hovered behind her eyelids. She squeezed her eyes tight to banish his image, but the lines of his face—the horizontals of silky black hair, trim mustache, and straight eyebrows, bisected by the strong nose, and full, moist lips—circled like a hora folk dance faster and faster in her head. She sat up and tried to think calmly.

It had started with the illness of Max's wife, Toby, whose heart condition made it impossible for her to walk but a few steps without wheezing and turning blue. Out of compassion, Leah agreed to help the Steins with the household chores. To her pleasure, Max invited her to borrow books from his collection, and even donated some to her library. Soon they were spending long hours discussing literature and looking into each others eyes while Toby lay in the bedroom asleep. Since the death of her Uncle Shaul, many years ago, Leah hadn't known that joy.

One Friday afternoon as Max was preparing for the Sabbath, Leah stopped by the Steins with a loaf of freshly baked *challah*. He invited her in and, without warning, began kissing and caressing her, opening for them both the floodgates of untapped desire. Just that easily, though not without guilt, they become lovers. They tried to be discreet, but lust overcame them, and they had sex whenever they could—even on the floor of his slaughterer's shack. Afterwards, the remorse she felt at having transgressed the Torah's teachings pervaded her with despair. Her visits to Dovid at the communal farm only aggravated her misery. She could not deny that she was betraying her husband, abandoning him to a useless life, sneaking away to the excitement of her trysts with Max.

She sat on the edge of the bed and sent up a prayer for her deliverance from the deceptive life she was leading. Toby Stein's condition was weakening; the poor woman had little time left on earth. She needed to divorce Dovid, the sooner the better, so that she would be free to marry Max when the time came. In desperation she consulted Rabbi Sandler.

"Rabbi, I beg you to help me to obtain a *get*, an official divorce from my husband."

"My dear Leah, I cannot help you. Jewish law forbids it. Your husband, being insane, is unfit to grant a divorce, and his consent is crucial to the divorce process."

"Surely a compassionate God would not want me to suffer like this. Please help me to find a way."

"I understand your anguish," the rabbi said, offering a glass of sweet wine to calm her. "Now that you are an *agunah*, the only thing that can release you from your chains is your husband's death."

"This torment is driving me crazy!"

"Leah, it's not easy for a husband in your situation either," the rabbi said searching for something that might console her. "Did you know that if a *woman* were to become insane, her sane husband could divorce her only if he obtained the permission of a hundred rabbis?"

"You are condemning me to a life of misery!"

"My dear Leah, who would God judge most harshly, a bigamist or an adulterer?" he growled, alluding to the rumors that were circulating about her and Max. Leah's temper exploded. In one swift movement she rose and dashed the wine into the rabbi's face.

Outraged, the rabbi wiped the red liquid from his face.

There was nothing more she could do but break off the conversation and walk out of the room with her head held high. But Leah's heaving chest, white face, and trembling lips confirmed the rabbi's suspicions.

Thus it was that Leah became an *agunah*, unable to marry until her husband divorced her or died. To add to her suffering, her father tormented her with his refusal to make a firm promise to bequeath the Torah to her son Lazar. In an attempt to persuade him that his grandson deserved to be the heir, Leah bragged about his achievements.

"Lazar is an outstanding rabbi and scholar. Did you know that people are already talking about him as their next *gaon*, their spiritual and intellectual leader?" So what if she exaggerated a little. "Papa, people trust Lazar not only for spiritual advice but with their money. Do you know that the widow Davidoff asked him to keep her accounts and money safe?"

"Would I expect otherwise of a grandson of mine?" Then becoming impatient with his daughter's boasting, he groused, "What is it you want of me, Leah? Remember, the Torah says, 'Thou shall not covet.'"

"Papa, for me I want nothing. For Lazar I want the Rosen Torah."

"So weighty a decision cannot be made hastily. Still, I will consider Lazar," he said. And with a flick of his hand Hershel dismissed her, having made no promise concerning the Torah. This was how it always went. She could not understand why her gentle father taunted her that way. Since no one knew for certain who would become the inheritor of the Rosen Torah, the uncertainty ignited rivalry between Leah and her sister Ida, and between Lazar and Ida's oldest son, Moses, seven years his senior, who insisted that he was the rightful heir to the Rosen legacy.

Relegated to the lowly status of woman chained to her marriage, Leah recklessly continued to meet her lover in secret. But the shtetl was no place for such trysts. One morning the milkman on his early rounds discovered them in the barn making love in a fresh pile of hay. Inevitably, Max lost his living as the town's shochet. Anticipating this disaster, Leah had secretly made plans for their escape. The couple in charge of the communal farm, where Dovid lived, had grown too old to manage it, and begged Leah to come to their aid. Dovid's condition had deteriorated so badly he no longer recognized his wife or his children. So the lovers retreated to this remote place, where they were sorely needed. The irony of her situation did not escape Leah. She, who had been branded as crazy, was now caring for the truly insane. In an insensitive and cruel world, the line between the sane and insane seemed as thin as that between life and death.

To their surprise, Leah and Max found life on the farm peaceful enough, a sanctuary away from the ugly prejudices and restrictions of conventional society. Having no preconceptions the residents took a special liking to Leah. To them, her wonderful tales shone a light into the dark cave their souls inhabited. As a storyteller, Leah perceived that her words held the power to entertain, to teach, and to heal. Over the years she had honed her storytelling to do just that, and now she used her gift to help those most in need. As for Max, he held religious services for the Jews among them, as if he were the cantor and chief rabbi. And so Leah at last found a measure of happiness and fulfillment away from the judging eyes of the shtetl.

❧10❧

The Third Inheritor: Yakov Rosen, the Orphan

Whoever brings up an orphan in his home is regarded as though the child has been born to him.

Talmud

If misfortune had beset Leah, it dogged her orphaned cousin in equal measure. Yakov was not born with a silver spoon in his mouth. His was made of tin and filled with a bitter tincture. Although Yakov's parents, Shaul and Yael, named him after his gifted grandfather, Yitzhak Rosen, he had inherited neither his good looks, nor musical genius, or the good fortune to be nurtured to adulthood by his own loving parents. However, Yakov was a bright child, and had his parents lived, he would surely have received a good education, but Uncle Hershel simply could not afford it.

On Yakov's tenth birthday, Hershel apprenticed him to the baker, Louis Weltz. Although the young novice was quick to learn and toiled without complaint, Weltz was leery of his hot temper. Once, when fighting between Poles and Lithuanians broke out in the marketplace, Yakov grabbed a pistol from Weltz's desk drawer, and slipped outside to join the melee. In the heat of the rowdy confusion, out of sheer bravado, he fired it over the heads of the rioters and dove for cover. Weltz, terrified that they would turn on him because of Yakov's wild behavior, boarded up the shop and hid in the oven all night.

Another time a Lithuanian student taunted Yakov, calling him anti-Semitic names and chalking a cross on his back. Yakov settled the matter to his satisfaction by giving the boy a good *potch,* or smack, in the face. This time it was Yakov who ran to hide; just a few men who studied in the shul at night knew he was in the shul's attic.

Uncle Hershel felt guilty about having to apprentice his bright and determined nephew to a baker. He rationalized that although the work was menial, Yakov would learn a useful trade. To alleviate his conscience, Hershel personally prepared his nephew for his Bar Mitzvah. The boy was an eager student, and he continued supervising Yakov's studies for several years after his thirteenth birthday. In this way, with little formal schooling, Yakov learned the Hebrew text of the prayers together with the melodies that traditionally accompany them.

At sixteen — shortly after his cousin Leah had been married off — the orphan met Chana Lurie. Like a child drawn to sweets, Yakov fancied Chana the first time he saw her. She was just fifteen when she came into Louis Weltz's bakery to buy challah for the Sabbath. Wearing a white blouse, and a long, navy-blue skirt that swished around her ankles as she walked briskly into the bakery, she immediately captivated his attention. The beam of light coming in through the store window caught the blaze in her dark eyes, the delicate arch of her high cheekbones, the smooth skin on her forehead, the shell pink of her ears, and the sheen of her golden brown hair woven into two long braids. She seemed both heartbreakingly desirable and yet unattainable to a boy of his status. A strange, powerful, unfamiliar longing tugged at Yakov, compelling him to quickly learn what he could about her.

He discovered that she was the daughter of Aharon Lurie, a wealthy timber merchant, that she hailed from Kovna, and that she had come to help her sister who had just given birth to a baby three weeks prematurely. He kept watch for her and tried to strike up a conversation whenever she came into the bakery. As

124

for Chana, at first she scorned this lowly baker boy. Still, she conceded that while he was not exactly handsome, he had a radiant smile, fierce green eyes, and an arresting shock of red hair, and although he was short in stature, there was a sinewy strength to him. They exchanged only a few words at the bakery, yet his confident, forthright demeanor intrigued her.

When Chana returned home, Yakov began a letter-writing campaign. For two years he wrote to her every day. Once, well after midnight, his uncle discovered him hunched over the kitchen table. From the trembling quill and luminous expression on Yakov's face he divined that his nephew was composing a love letter. Squeezing his nephew affectionately on the shoulder, he said gently, "Love is the most precious gift, but one that is too easily broken. Be careful, Yakov."

Taken aback by his ardor, Chana read the letters at first for amusement and sent only cursory replies. Gradually, however, she began to look forward to his missives overflowing with sweet compliments, youthful passion, and with quotations from the Torah and the Talmud. Instilled with the shtetl's reverence for erudition, Chana did not regard Yakov's liberal use of quotations as pedantic or insincere; she admired his skilful use of them. In one of her favorite letters Yakov invented a playful skit in which she featured as Esther. Then gradually, and with unaccustomed tact, Yakov worked up the courage to send her a written proposal of marriage, quoting loosely from the *Song of Solomon*: 'Behold, thou art fair, my love; behold, thou art fair; thou hast doves' eyes; thy lips are like a thread of scarlet, and thy speech is comely. Thou hast ravished my heart with thine eyes.'

Like a man condemned, he waited miserably, anxiously, and with trepidation for Chana's reply. To his enormous joy, she accepted — with the proviso that she would need time to convince her father.

Whenever she dared to bring up the question of a possible marriage to a young man who worked in a bakery, her father rolled his eyes and sighed deeply, then admonished her to leave the responsibility of finding a suitable spouse to him. Despite his disapproval, Chana pestered her father until he consented to make his own inquiries. To his surprise he learned that Yakov came from a good family but his parents had died when he was a young boy. Reluctantly, Mr. Lurie agreed to meet with his Chana's suitor, who eagerly hastened to undertake the journey to Kovna to ask for permission to marry his daughter.

The young man's square jaw, piercing eyes, prominent nose, and especially his straightforward responses, lent him an air of command that impressed Chana's father. After engaging Yakov in a scholarly discussion, Lurie was pleased to find that the suitor was as learned in the Talmud and the Torah as his daughter had boasted. While Mr. Lurie was favorably impressed with Yakov, Mrs. Lurie, who ruled the roost at home, had reservations. She wanted to know what her daughter saw in this young man. He was a poor orphan, he was short, he had a long nose, and, most worrisome of all, rumor had it that he had a violent temper.

"You say that Yakov is from a good family, and a scholar. But we must not forget that he is a poor baker's assistant," she objected to her husband.

"Poor he is. But he is not afraid of hard work. I'll offer to take Yakov into the timber business."

While her parents sat in the kitchen and argued about his suitability as a husband for their precious daughter, Chana showed Yakov the sights of Kovna to calm him.

Chana's father finally won the heated argument by quoting from the Torah that marrying one's offspring to an orphan is a special form of charity and an act of atonement for sins. When her mother still looked doubtful, he cited the Torah, again: "Do not mistreat widows and orphans," and, "If you mistreat them, and they cry out to Me, I will hear their cry."

"So, do what you have to," Mrs. Lurie said, throwing her hands into the air. "All I want is for my daughter to be happy." Mr. Lurie beamed with relief, for without her agreement there could be no marriage.

On returning to the house Chana's father informed Yakov that he would consider a proposal. The young suitor was so overjoyed that he paid little heed to Lurie's caution that he would first need to meet with his uncle and aunt before any arrangements could be formalized.

Before departing, Yakov gazed into Chana's adoring eyes, his very own Chana with her lovely thick braids, and the blush rising on her cheeks. He could hear her rapid breathing, and feel his own heart racing with desire. Unbidden, the image of Chana with her head arched back to reveal her long, white neck, and her lustrous hair fanning over the pillow, floated before him, and he cried out with joy, knowing that his life would be changed forever.

As soon as he returned form Kovna, Yakov came rushing into the Rosens' home shouting, "Wish me Mazel Tov! I'm getting married," causing his startled uncle to spill the hot tea he was sipping onto his lap. After they had mopped up the mess, and applied ointment to his burns, Hershel demanded that his nephew repeat the announcement just to be sure he had understood — secretly he had been afraid that Chana would reject the lovelorn Yakov leaving him hurt and depressed. Reassured, the chazzan hurried to the store to tell Sonia the happy news.

He found his wife working at a table in the back, hidden behind sacks of flour and sugar and barrels of herring and pickled cucumbers, making a thick, malodorous salve she had concocted for mangy cats, which sold well. "Wish me Mazel Tov! Yakov and Chana are getting married!" Hershel cried clapping his hands together in happiness. "Yakov's chosen a wife from a better family than even I could have hoped for, given that he is an orphan and a humble baker."

"Please excuse me if I don't agree that the Lurie family is equal in *yichus*, to ours," Sonia said, lifting one eyebrow before going on. "The Luries may be good business people, but scholars they're not." It was Sonia's way of fanning her ego, for while her husband was nowhere near as wealthy as Mr. Lurie, he was more learned, and everyone in the shtetl agreed there was nothing more prestigious than a life devoted to religious study. With a flourish, Sonia added, "And what's more, you have taught Yakov so well that he too is well-versed in the Torah and the Talmud."

127

"True, but yichus is like potatoes; the best ones are in the ground. And although the Talmud sages advise that one should not marry for money, I say why marry into a poor family if you can marry into a wealthy one?"

Sonia nodded. "Even a poor orphan has to get married."

"And I thank God for Yakov's good fortune to be marrying the woman he loves."

Sonia wiped her hands on the stained apron she wore in the shop. "So, what should be included in the dowry?"

"Yakov said that his future father-in-law offered to take him into his lumber business, which is excellent!"

"Yes, but it's not enough. It was wrong of Yakov to start negotiating without first consulting us."

"I'll wait for Mr. Lurie to arrange a formal meeting with me. That's the way it's done."

"Don't wait, go now! Go to Lurie on Yakov's behalf. Get him to offer him at least two years of kest."

"Yes, yes, room and board would help," Yakov agreed.

"I'm telling you be bold. Insist on a copper samovar, covers and pillows of eiderdown, linen tablecloths, and brass candlesticks. Also a good bed and mattress."

"What if Lurie doesn't accept our terms? Yakov will never forgive us."

"It's in your hands. You must find a way, or it will be on your conscience until the day you die." Sonia washed her hands with carbolic soap and wiped them on her apron. Then adjusting her headscarf, she said, "I will wish the couple all the happiness in the world — after you have arranged for a decent dowry."

Sonia had no inkling that the command she had so cavalierly uttered would drastically alter Yakov's life. She called after her husband's retreating back, "Be firm! Don't let Lurie bully you into taking less than your nephew deserves!"

128

৵11৶

The Secret Pact

Selling a Torah scroll is permitted to enable marriage or Torah study.

Megillah, or Book of Esther

After Chana had served her potential uncle-in-law, Hershel Rosen, with tea and homemade cakes and in return he had effusively complimented her on their excellence, only then, with much nervous clearing of his throat, did he deem it proper to bring up the subject of the dowry with Mr. and Mrs. Lurie.

In response, Mr. Lurie tilted his head to one side and pulled down his mouth. "Contrary to what some may say I am not a rich man. But Mr. Rosen, perhaps you have something of value you could provide for Yakov?"

"Yakov is a poor orphan, yet a rich man could not exceed him in piousness. My wife and I took him in and gave him a home and brought him up to be a mensch."

"You will be rewarded for your good deeds when the time comes to depart this Earth. Remember, when you help one such as Yakov, you should imagine that there is no God to help him, that you alone must meet his needs. That is the true meaning of tzedakah, charity with justice."

Dumbfounded by Lurie's scholarship, the chazzan stuttered, "Eh, very true. Still, I do not understand what more I can do for Yakov."

"According to the Talmud, a man in financial distress may go so far as to sell a Torah scroll in order to get married.

129

Even objects that have been set aside to be donated to a *shul* or even a *sefer Torah* can be converted into money to bring an orphan to the *chuppah*," Lurie goaded him.

Hershel's heart thumped against his chest. "But what has that got to do with me," he said making a pretense that he had not understood the implications of Lurie's words.

Chana's father discarded all attempts to be tactful. "I'll come straight to the point. If you will agree to bequeath the Rosen Torah to Yakov, I will provide a generous dowry, including kest and a livelihood at the lumber mill."

Hershel felt lightheaded. "This is too much to ask. You have no right to it."

"Rosen, I want my grandson — God willing I should have a grandson — to inherit that Torah. You can reject or accept my offer, but before you make up your mind, consider the consequences to your nephew."

A cold sensation tingled down his spine; his brother Shaul's hands were reaching out to him from the grave. It would be a mitzvah to return the Torah to Shaul's son, and in doing so he would lessen his life-long guilt that the scroll by birthright should have gone to his gifted older brother. Perhaps God had forewarned him that Yakov should be the Torah's next inheritor by providing him with three daughters and no sons. Yet Leah, his youngest daughter, coveted the Rosen Torah for her brilliant son, Lazar. If he passed on the family inheritance to his nephew it would be certain to stir up jealousy. Still, Lurie had made it clear that he desired the Rosen Torah. But his nephew, already punished more than anyone deserved by losing his dear parents, should not lose the woman he loved. He didn't want to inflict pain on anyone. What should he do? The hapless cantor sat opposite Lurie, raking nervous fingers through his beard, trying to come to a decision; then shaking his head reluctantly, he stood up.

Seeing that his quarry was about to depart, Lurie put up his hand, and to drive home his advantage quoted from the Torah. "Not so fast chazzan. The Torah commands: 'You shall not ill-treat any widow or orphan. If you do mistreat them, I will heed their outcry as soon as they cry out to Me, and My anger shall blaze forth and I will put you to the sword, and your own wives shall become widows and your children orphans.'"

Stifling a groan, Herschel sat down again. "Please stop! You have convinced me that bequeathing the Rosen Torah to my nephew will be the most just and righteous thing to do."

Before leaving Kovna, the cantor made a pact with Lurie: to avoid provoking acrimonious disputes within the family, he swore Lurie to secrecy about their transaction. Satisfied that Lurie would not breach the confidentiality between the two of them, the chazzan signed the *tenaim,* or formal document, stipulating the date of the wedding, the kest and items to be included in the dowry: a copper samovar, comforters and pillows stuffed with goose down, brass candlesticks, and a hand-crocheted tablecloth for the Sabbath; also a bed and mattress. Although Yakov was not a yeshiva bocher, since he had not studied at the yeshiva, Mr. Lurie conceded to add a room to their house for the newly weds, to sweeten the deal in "exchange" for the Rosen Torah.

Early the next morning the chazzan made the tedious journey home in a creaking stagecoach pulled by two sturdy horses. The passengers, for the most part Jews, were wrapped in fur coats with lamb's wool hats on their heads to ward off the cold. The narrow highway wound between cultivated fields and gloomy forests, and the occasional isolated shtetl. Wedged tightly between a yeshiva student with a huge basket of food packed by his mother, and a burly merchant with a bundle of silver fox furs. Hershel soon felt stifled for lack of fresh air. Bouncing over roads mired by the spring thaw, he grumbled into his beard, "My wife ordered me to act as a *shadchan,* and I have granted her wish in a way she never expected. Now I'll have to come up with an explanation on how I struck such an excellent bargain without revealing the secret pact I made with Lurie! But it won't be easy."

After a poignant wedding where tears of sorrow were shed for Yakov's dear parents who had passed away before they could share their son's joy, the couple moved in with the Luries as planned. In the first years of marriage, Yakov was, for the most part, content. He suffered the belittling remarks of his mother-in-

131

law, but thankfully the birth of her grandsons blunted her sharp tongue. In quick succession, Chana had given birth to three healthy boys — Berel, Chaim, and Aharon.

The Luries made a good living from the sale of lumber since government restrictions on Jewish ownership of forestland were not strictly enforced. Yakov liked accompanying his father-in-law into the depths of the woods and watching the immense rafts of logs, marked with Lurie's personal insignia, float down the river toward their sawmill plant. Soon he learned how to grade lumber: the best grade to be used for fine furniture, the next for construction, and the poorest for firewood. However, the young man's good fortune soon ran out.

The czarist government began to impose new regulations on logging, severely eroding profits. Shortly after this setback, Mr. Lurie's health declined. A serious heart ailment sapped his strength. Within a few months he died, leaving the timber business to his oldest son, Banesh.

Just weeks after his father's funeral, Banesh informed Yakov that he could not keep him on. "We'll all end up eating nothing but stale radishes and onions, and drinking weak tea like the poor if we have to support your growing family."

Yakov and Chana now had to make a weighty decision about their future. Working as a baker's assistant offered a meager living as he well knew from past experience; to improve their income they needed to open their own bakery. The only good baker in Valinsk, Louis Weltz, to whom Yakov had been apprenticed, had recently passed away and the family was unable to carry on. Although Kovna was a larger center, and a railroad hub, there were already four excellent bakeries in the Old Town where most Jews resided. For all these reasons, their prospects would be better in Valinsk.

For capital they turned to Ida's husband, Boris Krantz, the prosperous fur dealer in Riga. Ida, who had grown up in the same household with her orphaned cousin Yakov, successfully pleaded their case with her husband to provide start-up capital for their bakery. However, the baker and his wife had to make do with a rented place on a side street near the market as the best locations around the square were tightly held by families who passed them down to their kin. Chana, the once-pampered daughter of a wealthy merchant, now found herself working long hours.

The labor was grueling. Yakov arose long before dawn to stoke the ovens and start the yeast rising. Determined to make the finest dough, instead of using a big dose of yeast, he chose to get up even earlier than most bakers to allow a tiny amount of yeast the hours needed to multiply into a spongy leavening agent. This slow process gave Yakov's ryes and pumpernickels their complex flavors. When the shtetl housewives tried to pry out Yakov's secret, he replied cryptically, "There is no secret. Remember, if dough had eight fingers and two thumbs, it would be sitting on them."

No matter the weather, at daybreak Chana dressed and walked to the bakery, still heavy with sleep. Even so, the familiar clatter of boots against cobblestones as the men made their way to the shul for early morning prayers, and the steady splatter of milk flowing into wooden pails as the shtetl women milked their family cows in the barns attached to the house, soothed her. These other early risers, in turn, found comfort in the first fragrant whiff of fresh dough, and the jaunty ribbon of smoke from Rosen's Bakery spiraling up the chimney into the dewy morning air. Once at the bakery, Chana kneaded the dough that Yakov had started earlier until her back ached.

Although Yakov took for granted his wife's hard work, he was extremely sensitive to the fact that people praised her for the success of the business. He hated to admit that without her the bakery would not have survived. He rationalized that he was as industrious as his wife, and that it was customary for women to run the shtetl's shops and market stalls, manage the home and take care of the children. Indeed, the domains of men were those of religion and the larger worlds of trade and public affairs. The wife of a scholar or religious leader had an especially important role in making a good living in order to free her husband to pursue his spiritual vocation; to attract a good rabbi, a shtetl often granted his wife exclusive rights to sell yeast, candles, or ceremonial wine.

Yet Yakov shared the men's conflicted feelings about these strong-willed, outspoken women. Despite their prominent role in the marketplace and the household, their names rarely appeared on any official document as the proprietors of their businesses, even when they owned them outright and ran them single-handedly. This tradition was so deeply entrenched that woman like Chana seldom received due credit from their husbands.

At the end of a long day Chana would return home to prepare dinner and do the household chores while Yakov went off to the synagogue to pray and to chat, to study at the *beth midrash*, house of learning, or to the bathhouse to relax with the men of the shtetl. Chana resented his relative freedom. When she complained about her husband's lack of appreciation, Yakov retorted, "If I was a respected scholar or rabbi, instead of a lowly baker, you would proudly accept the time I find to study and pray." Without admitting it, Chana knew this to be true.

The reputation of the Rosens' Bakery grew steadily. Just when the bakery was becoming profitable, tragedy struck. First their oldest son, Berel, developed a high fever and a hacking cough. Chana tried all the known remedies, including leeches, which sucked on the boy's tender flesh to no avail. She held him day and night in her arms, crooning to him and praying desperately for relief. The boy improved for a few days, then his condition worsened rapidly, and he died.

A year later, the second son, Chaim, sustained severe burns. While helping to stoke the bakery's huge ovens for the Sabbath challahs, a load of hot coals fell onto his feet. Despite applications of various salves and herbs, the burns turned gangrenous. The child lingered on for weeks writhing in pain, finally succumbing to infection. Now only Aharon, their youngest son, remained; named after Chana's father, Aharon Lurie, she prayed that he would bring pleasure and pride to them.

Heartbroken and embittered, the couple no longer believed that the shtetl was a place to raise their child safely. It was time for them to seek a new life in The Holy Land or America.

Yakov tried to convince Chana that America offered all comers a chance to start afresh. At first Chana resisted—she had heard that even in America some were hostile to Jews. To counter her fears, her husband filled her head with stories of those who had made fortunes there. A smooth-talking agent of a Hamburg shipping company, traveling through the shtetl in search of business, made their dream of emigration burn even brighter. The salesman's colorful poster showed a sturdy steamship carrying passengers toward the amazingly impressive New York skyline, their eyes shining with hope. He assured the couple that his company had just built four fine ships and new and improved facilities to house and feed families waiting in Hamburg to sail to America.

Chana wrestled with the temptation to leave the country of her birth in order to raise their surviving son in a happier land. Most nights, exhausted from work, she slept soundly for a few hours then she awoke with a start to an uneasy sense of something gone wrong. She would strain to hear Aharon's regular breathing, and listen intently in case he cried out in his sleep. She lay next to Yakov, the corners of her mind harboring frightful dream-images of her departed sons. Lifting her hands to heaven, she whispered, "Oh, God, please let me leave my sorrows behind in this shtetl. Let me raise my only son to manhood." No matter how daunting, they had to go to America to find peace, she told herself.

Yakov suffered his own powerful fears. From childhood, terrifying tales of the *chapers*, or kidnappers, who snatched boys from their families to be conscripted into the army, obsessed him. These were not imaginary fears. If the notorious chapers didn't get you, then the kahal might; strict quotas imposed on the kahal to provide a certain percentage of the town's inhabitants for the army, forced their leaders to hand over the sons from the poorest families and also orphans.

Once in the Russian army, Yakov knew full well that Jews were treated with particular contempt and brutality. According to a law issued in 1827, conscripts could be required to serve up to a 25-year term in the czar's army. Like all the other conscripts, Jews were placed in military schools to learn academic and military skills. They they were also coerced through "re-education," harassment, and cruel punishment to renounce Judaism in favor of the state religion, Orthodox Christianity. The baker had witnessed the disastrous results of such brainwashing on a man from Valinsk, Bentsel Leib, one of the few Jewish conscripts who survived the army. He returned with a disfigured face, an amputated leg, and stuttered unintelligibly. He was emotionally and psychologically scarred, unable to live a normal Jewish life. Eventually Bentsel banded together with other released soldiers to live in a remote little village, exiled from friends and family.

To avert this terrible fate, many young men chose to run away rather than submit to the horrors of life in the army; others inflicted injuries and illnesses upon themselves rendering them unfit to serve in the army. Yakov's third cousin had swallowed a "medication" that ruined his lungs and left him ailing and wheezing for the rest of his life. Another man had rubbed ashes into his eyes, causing blindness in one eye.

Yakov would never forget the day the army came to Valinsk. As soon as the soldiers arrived they went on a drunken binge, looting stores and beating every Jew who had the misfortune to cross their paths. The Russians were particularly vicious to the recent Jewish recruits drafted into their company. Eli Zundel and David Peretz were beaten almost senseless while their parents stood by helplessly weeping and wringing their hands. If he or his son Aharon were conscripted into the Russian army, he knew what horrors they would suffer. They had to leave before their luck ran out.

It would take months to save enough from their meager income to buy rail and steamship tickets. Certain that no one would approve of their decision, the baker urged his wife to keep their plans secret until they were ready to leave. When his wife objected, Yakov reminded her of the uproar that had followed when Morris Berman, the shtetl's tailor, announced that he was immigrating to America. The family felt that Morris had somehow shamed them in the eyes of the entire community and for months slunk around the shtetl like pariahs.

After a year of hard labor and self-denial, saving every kopeck and ruble for the passage to America, the baker, and his wife and child, were ready to depart. They were just about to reveal their plans that Friday night after the Sabbath meal, when Uncle Hershel, complaining of indigestion, excused himself. Suddenly the company heard a shout from the bedroom, and everyone rose from the table and rushed to his room.

Hershel lay stretched out on the bed, his head thrown back, and his eyes cold as stones.

"What's wrong? What's happening?" they screamed.

"Fainted? Water! Hurry!"

"Water! Water!" Sonia shrieked.

Ida scurried back with a bowl and a dipper; Sonia scooped water into the dipper and splashed it on the chazzan's frozen face.

"Get the doctor!" Leah screamed.

"'The doctor! The doctor!" they all shouted.

Miriam dashed out of the house, not stopping to put on her coat.

"Squeeze his nose!"

"His nose! His nose!" they all shrieked.

Sonia rubbed Hershel's hands, squeezed his nose, pulled on his eyelids, and drenched her prostrate husband with water.

When Hershel could not be revived, hot tears flowed for the loss of their loving husband and father, the virtuous chazzan of Valinsk; even the most righteous could not escape death.

Only Yakov did not weep. He wore the wooden expression of one made numb by the death of too many he had loved. He thought of his uncle, who had cared for him, and of his own mother and father, and his two small sons, all irrevocably and forever departed from the Earth. As he stood at the foot of his uncle's deathbed, a painful sense of loneliness and

137

inexplicable shame, which only an orphan can feel, pervaded his soul.

On the night before the funeral, Yakov awoke before dawn, put on his long fur coat, mittens and boots, pulled his well-worn fur hat down over his ears, and made his way by the pale light of a horned moon toward the cemetery. Without any clear intention, he tramped over the bridge and up the path through fields and meadows. Once this walk had been peaceful, but since the czarist edict a decade ago, their land had been confiscated and redistributed to gentiles, who harassed weeping Jews as they trudged to the cemetery. Yakov ignored the biting wind that numbed him to the bone despite his heavy coat and hat, the icy slush that seeped into his boots, and the blood that oozed from a deep wound in his leg where a peasant's dog had attacked him.

At the cemetery, he paced between the tombstones, his moon-cast gray shadow trailing behind or skipping ahead, the chill wind lamenting its sorrow, until he stumbled upon his uncle's freshly dug open grave that seemed to draw him into its maw. Without hesitating, he lowered himself to the bottom and stretched out on his back, his eyes wide open. He lay motionless, watching the snow swirling like sparkling white flour from the sky, gripped by powerful memories . . .

He stands under the chuppah, and his happiness is complete. Close beside him his radiant bride; around him the family that cares for him; behind him the wedding guests. He has difficulty concentrating on what the rabbi is saying he is so intoxicated with the wonder of the moment.

"Righteous and just is the man who raises an orphan and enables him to marry. Such a man is Hershel Rosen," the rabbi proclaims.

"Uncle Hershel, did you care for me out of pity, or because you loved me like a son?" His uncle shakes his head, and there are tears in his eyes. The rabbi intones, "The sages teach us that kindness is greater than charity. Charity is giving money to those in need. Kindness can be given with one's heart. Charity is for the poor; kindness can be done for

either the poor or the rich. Charity is for the living; kindness can be done for the living or the dead."

"Uncle, just answer my question. Did you love me as your own son?"

"You will have my reply to that question soon," Hershel's ghost admonishes him . . .

Yakov did not know how long he remained in the grave, communing with his departed uncle. The sound of the gravedigger's boots crunching into the frozen earth shattered his trance. With a startled groan he rolled over, stiff with cold, struggled to his feet, as the soft blanket of snow covering him like a shroud fell away. The terrified gravedigger dropped his spade, and fled howling like a madman.

The orphan stumbled home, torn, bleeding, bruised, and blue with cold. When he lurched through the door, the blood drained from Chana's face. "What happened to you?" she cried as she removed his clothes and poured hot water from an iron kettle into a tub.

"I visited the cemetery."

"Alone? At night? Are you crazy?"

"I wanted to pay my last respects to Uncle."

"You're an educated man; you know it is written in the Talmud that the cemetery is the dwelling place of defiled spirits who can transform themselves into sorcerers!"

"That's just simple-minded folklore," he retorted, wincing as Chana swabbed the dog bite with some homemade concoction, then moved on to the gash in his forehead. "It was very peaceful in the grave."

"What? You were in your uncle's grave?"

"Yes, it was peaceful there."

"Oh, Yakov, you are crazy! You could have frozen to death. The evil spirits could have taken hold of you," she berated him trembling with anguish.

A week after the funeral, Yakov learned to his astonishment that his Uncle Herschel had bequeathed the Rosen

Torah to him. The chazzan had answered him from the grave, washing away any lingering doubts that he had loved him like a son. With this wonderful revelation came a new perception of himself and his mission in life. As the Torah's custodian, Yakov committed himself to doing all in his power to protect it, to follow its commandments, and to pass on its teaching to his son.

Chana could scarcely believe that Hershel had chosen her husband in place of his own brilliant grandson, Leah's son Lazar. Neither her father-in-law or her father had revealed their secret pact, and she could find no explanation for the good chazzan's decision other than that he had loved and trusted her husband to take care of the family's holy legacy. She reveled in the satisfaction and pride of knowing that Yakov had been chosen, above everyone, as the inheritor of the family's precious Torah. Best of all, their son Aharon, would one day inherit it from his father.

Yakov took the inheritance as an omen that his years of bad luck were over. "I believe that Hashem has chosen me to bring our Torah to the New World, and to pass on the sacred teachings of Judaism to the next generation," he declared.

"True, Yakov, but Hashem has also placed a great weight on you."

Seeing the intense light blazing in his eyes, she shuddered, suddenly fearing that his fervor, his complete dedication, might turn into an obsession.

When the identity of the inheritor was at last revealed to all members of the Rosen family, confusion and then anger ran rampant. Choking back bitter tears, Leah vehemently objected, declaring that her father's decision had been based on misguided pity for an orphan. Clearly, she said, her son Lazar was the most worthy. Ida then resentfully accused her sister of poisoning Hershel against her own sons. In less time than it takes to don a prayer shawl, the husbands had joined in the battle and the chazzan's house echoed with impossible questions and spiteful accusations. Eventually Ida's husband, Boris, rose to his feet and roared, "Be quiet! Be quiet! It's time to go to the rabbi to get the matter resolved."

Still muttering and shaking their heads, the family made their way to Rabbi Zelig Shimon's house, just behind the Valinsk shul. After they had seated themselves around the dining room table, Rabbi Shimon listened to each sister justify why their cousin Yakov should not inherit the Rosen Torah. Finally, turning to Yakov, who sat with his hands clenched in his lap, the rabbi asked if he had anything to say.

"I cannot go against my Uncle Hershel's wishes," he declared, "and that is all I have to say."

The rabbi observed the firm tilt of the baker's jaw, his pursed lips, his fierce gaze. He nodded, stroked his beard and deliberated the matter. The laws of inheritance set out in the Torah, state that male offspring are the exclusive heirs of their father's estate, and that only in the absence of sons can daughters become the heirs. But considering that this was a Torah—which women are banned from touching or reading from publicly—Hershel's daughters were not suitable inheritors. The chazzan could have named one of his grandsons as the inheritor. Instead he had made the decision to bequeath the Torah to Yakov. Being an orphan gave him special status in the eyes of the Torah, which commands us not to mistreat widows and orphans.

After explaining all these considerations to the family, the rabbi concluded that Yakov should keep the Torah. The Rosen sisters did not want to appear disrespectful by openly contradicting the rabbi; still they furrowed their brows, and drew their lips into a thin line to show their displeasure.

With great solemnity the rabbi said, "Thousands of years ago our ancestors, after fleeing from Egypt, received the Torah at the foot of Mount Sinai, in which it is written 'Thou shalt love thy neighbor as thyself.' Ah, what a Torah God gave us! And shall we honor it with foolish quarrels and false pride?" To their discomfort, the sage continued to expound on the meaning of the Torah, and when he had finished they thanked him and left for home, subdued, and ashamed.

141

Despite the rabbi's decision, Leah could not curtail her displeasure for long. Leah came to Yakov, her dark eyes overflowing with tears, she begged him to remember their childhood friendship; how they had bonded together as brother and sister; how she still grieved for her lost son; how her husband had descended into madness; how she was now a chained woman; how much she had suffered only because she had the misfortune to be a woman. When she had finished the bitter litany she sat with her head bowed, waiting for her cousin's response. After a moment of silence, Yakov inclined his head sympathetically, and said that he was sorry for her *tsores*, her troubles, but they all have their own tsores. To give up the Rosen Torah to her son Lazar would not undo her misfortunes. "Hershel Rosen was sound in body and mind when he bequeathed the Torah to me. I will not go against my uncle's wishes," he declared, and refused to discuss the matter further.

Hurt and rejected by her childhood friend, Leah stormed out of the house. The Rosen women, their husbands, and offspring, continued to proclaim that Hershel had made a foolish decision. And Yakov remained steadfast in his determination to honor the humbling responsibility the chazzan had placed upon him.

Yakov and Chana at last broke the news of their impending departure for America on Sukkot, the joyous harvest festival. The whole family was seated in their temporary shelter of pine and willow branches, decorated with fruit and vegetables, where they took their meals for seven days to commemorate when the Israelites lived in huts, or *sukkot,* during their forty years of wandering in the wilderness after the Exodus from Egypt. As the couple had feared, their announcement was received with incredulity and dismay. One yelled that by going to America, Yakov would be making off with their family Torah, forever depriving them of their legacy. Another pleaded that surely he would not take the Torah away from them to a distant, foreign land, to an uncertain fate? A third decreed that he had no right to abscond with the Torah, thereby sundering the branch of the Rosen family remaining in Valinsk from their inheritance.

Surely if Hershel had foreseen such a terrible event, he would never have bequeathed the Torah to Yakov.

Throughout their outburst, Yakov sat stony eyed and silent. When they had finished he thundered, "Enough! How dare you accuse me of making off with the Torah like a *gonif*, a thief! Our *Yiddishkeit*, our identity, our traditions, our way of life, are rooted here in Valinsk, they are part of our very existence. I will carry the Torah to America where our heritage is in danger of being lost. There I will keep the teachings of the Torah alive, no matter how difficult."

The news of the couple's impending immigration to America, and the loss of the scroll roused the community at large. A delegation of shtetl elders came to Yakov's home to plead with him.

"Surely you understand that your great-grandfather, Shmuel Rosen, placed his Torah in our synagogue for safekeeping almost a hundred years ago. He would not want you to jeopardize its safety by taking it on so long and dangerous a journey," one elder argued.

Another said, "It would be a huge mitzvah to leave it here."

A third added, "Think of the Rosen Torah as a way of redeeming yourself. Let the Torah remain here in peace, here in Valinsk."

"Redeem myself from what, from whom?" Yakov growled, bunching up his fists.

The elders shrank back, intimidated by the inheritor's outburst.

The senior elder, said in a conciliatory manner, "Well, perhaps I should have said it's your duty to the people of our shtetl. Don't you agree?"

Rebuffing their invitation to a moral debate, Yakov placed his hands on his hips and said with finality, "I'm not going to argue with you. You have no right to the Rosen Torah. God has given *me* the responsibility of bringing the scroll to the New World. It's no use; you won't change my mind."

In their eagerness to persuade him to give up the Torah, they had insulted him, and betrayed their greed. Did they think a simple baker wasn't good enough to inherit the Torah? Yakov was glad that he would be rid of these ingrates. Soon he would be off to America with his son and wife who had staunchly supported him in his determination to keep the Rosen Torah.

When all attempts to dissuade Yakov and Chana failed, a cloud of despondency settled over the shtetl, as if someone had died. To make matters worse the couple had chosen to go to the New World instead of the Holy Land. Yakov's mother-in-law begged them to consider going to the Promised Land instead of America — if they had to go.

"Settling in Jerusalem will strengthen your spiritual commitment to the Jewish people," she declared. Then squeezing her daughter's hand, to emphasize her point she added, "Respectable Jews don't go to America. It's a *wilde triefe medine.* Who in their right mind would willingly go to such an wild and non-kosher place?"

Yakov had heard that it could be difficult to find kosher food in America, but he wasn't going to admit it. "Haven't you heard the streets are lined with gold?" he retorted. He could tell by the steely glint in Mrs. Lurie's eyes that she would do her best to undermine her daughter's decision.

In place of the happy celebration they would have received had they chosen to emigrate from Lithuania to the Holy Land, everyone came to weep and to lament their departure. This so unnerved Chana that she began to sob as if her heart would break. Fearing that it was all too much for his wife, and that she might loose her courage, Yakov plied her with glasses of wine. Instead of soothing her, the wine made Chana giddy and melancholy. She laughed and cried in turns until Yakov carried her to bed in a stupor.

The baker's most difficult task was saying goodbye to his sister Frieda. After services at the synagogue on Friday, Yakov, Chana, little Aharon and Frieda sat around the family table for Sabbath dinner. As the steaming soup was being ladled into bowls, Yakov felt Frieda's eyes on him and glanced up. There

144

was a sudden connection between the misery in her eyes and the guilt in his heart: *Your place at this table will be empty from now on,* Frieda reflected. Unable to contain her tears, she rushed into the kitchen where he heard her weeping miserably. To comfort his sister, he invited her to take a walk with him.

The evening was mild. A warm wind, harbinger of spring, melted the blanket of snow to ragged patches on the roofs, and slushy puddles in the streets. Arm in arm, sister and brother began walking toward the cemetery where their dear great-grandparents, grandparents, and his children rested beneath the earth. Crossing the bridge over the river, Yakov saw himself reflected in the thin layer of ice still glazing the deep pool he and his friends used as a swimming hole. *Next summer I won't swim in this pool,* he thought. Clouds scudding over the moon dimmed his reflection, and he felt himself hovering on the brink of a mysterious new life.

They trudged on, too downhearted to speak, listening to the crunch of their footsteps on the path. Yakov thought of the many happy times he had foraged in the forest for mushrooms and berries with his friends. Finally, Frieda broke the silence, "Yakov, will you promise to send for me as soon as you can?"

He promised that he would, unless death overtook him first.

The following Saturday night, at the conclusion of Havdalah, the service that ends the Sabbath, Yakov removed the Rosen Torah from the Holy Ark. Then, with the blessing of the rabbi, he placed it on his shoulder and stepped proudly off the bima. He could feel the eyes of the congregation boring into him as he made his way down the aisle—and caught the parting imprecations being whispered. As the solid wooden doors shut behind him with a thud, he heard women grumbling. But Yakov felt only an urge to shout out loud, "At last, I'm on my way! At last, I'm free!"

❧12☙

The Torah's Odyssey to the New World

Little is more extraordinary than the decision of a family to migrate, to say farewell to the community where it has lived for centuries, to abandon old ties and familiar landmarks, and to sail across dark seas to a strange land.

John F. Kennedy, A Nation of Immigrants

Yakov, Chana, and five-year-old Aharon had little to pack: comforters and pillows stuffed with goose down, brass candlesticks and a hand-crocheted tablecloth for the Sabbath from Chana's trousseau. She had bestowed their few pieces of furniture and the copper samovar upon a poor book peddler with six children who had recently lost his wife. They also brought a change of clothes, blankets, and Yakov's blue velvet bag with his *teffillin,* or phylacteries and prayer shawl, also a sack of brown bread for the journey. Yakov wrapped his cherished Rosen Torah securely in a woolen blanket to carry in his arms.

After a tiring journey by stagecoach to Kovna, approximately 100 kilometers to the west of Valinsk, they arrived just in time to board the steam train, for the forty-eight-hour journey to Hamburg. As the locomotive gathered speed, Yakov's eyes fixed on the glistening tracks, and his hopes and dreams soared. Chana's teeth were chattering and a pounding headache made her wish that she were back in the familiar shtetl.

The train ride was the first of many discomforts they were to experience on that long trek to a new life. They sat awkwardly on hard wooden benches fitted into freight wagons, choked by

146

sulfurous smoke, and stung by cinders that flew in through the windows and clogged their eyes and throats. To relieve themselves they had to join the line of women, children, and men who shared a common hole hacked into the floor in a corner of the boxcar.

Determined to protect his Torah from harm, Yakov seemed impervious to these inconveniences, cradling the scroll in his arms, while Chana embraced her child as if he might evaporate into the acrid air, both unyieldingly bound to their separate treasures as day dropped into night and night ascended to day. They finally reached Berlin, where they were to change trains, exhausted from lack of sleep, anxiety, and overexcitement. Only Aharon, who had rested in his mother's arms, responded with amazement and delight to the grand station. They had never seen a place as enormous and imposing, with its sweeping arches, the cacophony of hissing steam, clattering luggage carts, throbbing engines, shrilling whistles, and shouting crowds.

From Berlin the train traveled on for another twenty-four bone-rattling hours to Hamburg, the great North Sea port teeming with those like themselves who risked all for a chance at better lives; part of a vast throng swept up on the rising tide of history, leaving the tired Old World for the beckoning promise of the New World.

The Rosens boarded in the facility built to house and feed families in Hamburg prior to sailing to America. To their disappointment the place proved to be overcrowded, shoddy and makeshift, far from the glowing picture the smooth-talking shipping agent had depicted. After three long days the call came that their ship had docked, releasing them from the frustration of waiting around with nothing to do.

As the family approached the gangplank to board the *Deutschland* for the trans-Atlantic voyage, they paused to gawk at the ship towering above them. The Rosens had never seen anything so impressive. In her fresh coat of black and red paint and gleaming rows of portholes, the vessel appeared to be a luxury hotel.

147

Once aboard, the favorable perceptions were replaced by dismay. Their below-deck accommodations were packed with other emigrants — Poles, Lithuanians, Ukrainians, Russians, Latvians, Czechs, Slovaks and Hungarians. It was a hellhole of foul smells — sweat-and-urine-soaked straw mattresses, stale air, and putrid vomit, and the relentless throb of engines always in their ears. Steerage had no bathing facilities or dining rooms; the passengers washed in buckets of cold seawater and ate in their bunks. The Rosens were grateful that before boarding, Chana had purchased a small barrel of salted herring to supplement what they correctly guessed would be the meager shipboard fare of watery cabbage soup and coarse brown bread.

The mother feared for her child's well being, but the boy never complained. He laughed at the ceaseless bucking of the ship, and marveled at the great rolling waves. Yakov and Chana could only grimace as they compared their nasty surroundings with the glossy pictures and perfidious descriptions of the agent from the steamship company.

Through all these hardships Yakov only relinquished the Torah when he needed to eat, to wash or relieve himself. Then he asked a pious Jew — one of the faithful who joined him for morning, afternoon, and evening prayers — to keep it safe for him. "It's your sacred duty," Yakov commanded, intense jade eyes flashing with conviction and his bright red hair vibrating with emotion.

After days of misery, Chana and Yakov found that they could prevent the worst seasickness by remaining on deck where the fresh sea air made her feel better. This relatively calm spell came to an abrupt end when a ferocious Atlantic storm swept down on them.

At one moment the ocean was placid, at the next they raised their eyes to behold armies of churning, bruise-green clouds with pitch-black underbellies. Hurricane force winds piled the sea into walls that advanced toward the ship like the battalions of an avenging army. The crew ordered everyone below deck, where they sat shivering in the dark, terrified by the rising crescendo of the storm.

The tempest raged all night. Again and again, the vessel climbed to the crest of a monster wave, only to plummet downward with sickening force, twisting like a cork in a vortex. The *Deutschland* floundered in the trough of the waves, shuddered and groaned and rocked from side to side, throwing passengers from their bunks. The fearsome sounds of goods crashing and breaking around them mingled with the roaring of the wind and the waves, and the terrified shrieks of passengers imploring God to save them from drowning in a watery grave.

The ocean rose higher and higher, until the deluge poured water down the smokestacks and put out the fire that drove the ship's engines. Left to drift at the mercy of the sea; men, women, and children felt a cold, wet death stalking them. Overcome by dread, Chana passed out while holding Aharon in her arms.

When she came to, she called out for Yakov, but heard no reply. Frantically she groped in the dark, cutting her hands on debris as the storm ceaselessly vented its cruel, pitiless anger. Toward dawn, the winds subsided to a steady gale, and darkness gave way to murky light. Still weak and trembling Chana willed herself to leave her bunk in search of Yakov. She implored other passengers for help, but most were too weary and ill to respond. She searched the corridors, cabins and passageways, with her frightened child clinging to her skirt.

Staggering through galleys reeking of stale and greasy food and up to the islands of prohibited luxury, the domain of the upper-class cabins and dining rooms, she called out to Yakov like a woman possessed. Ignoring the signs barring entrance, she made her way down to the engine room, where half-naked men, streaked with sweat and oil, worked frantically to start the engines. On beyond the engine room she descended, braving her fear of rats, into the dank hold, all the while howling for her husband while Aharon cried, "Papa, Papa!"

For hours she hunted for Yakov, once dozing fitfully from sheer exhaustion, to awake with a terrified start to the rumble of the ship's engines. She recited a prayer of thanks for the ship's revival, and for safe passage across the Atlantic. She roused Aharon then lurched to her feet with a moan. Ignoring her chattering teeth and aching joints, she resumed her search, this time out on the open deck as the force of the wind had abated somewhat. Passengers shook their heads and whispered that the unfortunate woman had gone mad with grief.

Chana would always remember the icy shiver that chilled her blood when a bright spot of color caught her eye. She froze, focusing intently on a fragment of burgundy silk shot through with gold thread, glinting like a coin thrown her way, beckoning to her like a text written in cipher. In a daze she stumbled toward a large, sturdy, watertight box that housed the ship's spare fire hoses. Clawing at the lid she forced it open, and saw her husband wedged inside, curled around the Torah. Falling to her knees she cried out in anguish at the sight of his ashen face and mouth twisted into an awful grimace.

Seeing his father lifeless, Aharon balled his fists into the air then threw himself on top of the corpse, wailing "Papa, Papa, don't leave me!" He kept up his childish piping barely audible above the mighty clash of wind and waves, scraping his small fingers through his father's matted beard. When Chana tried to pry the boy off he held on, repeating "Papa, Papa, get up!" In the wake of the storm, the seas still churned, smashing salty shards onto the deck that stung the boy's skin and blinded his eyes. Squeezing them shut, he sat up to rub them on his sleeve. Quick as the flash of a shark's tail, a tremendous gust lifted the boy aloft, ballooning the loose sleeves of his shirt out like wings, parting his red lips in a beatific smile. Chana gaped in utter incredulity. Before she could gather her rattled wits the wind dropped Aharon down onto his father's chest with a thump that forced the air from his lungs.

At last, Yakov's eyes fluttered open and he whispered through cracked lips, "Water, water . . ."

The boy chortled, "Papa, I saved you! Mama did you see me flying like an angel?" From that moment on Aharon believed that he single-handedly had magically brought his father back to life.

Sobbing with relief, Chana bent to embrace her husband, while a deckhand made the sign of the cross, and whispered "In the name of the Father and the Son and the Holy Spirit," with an awed expression in his eyes. Someone brought water. Yakov gulped it down, and groaned as he stepped stiffly out on to the deck still clasping the Torah.

The passengers in steerage were the first to hear that Chana had found Yakov—dehydrated but still alive and safe. At the height of the storm, thinking only to protect the Torah, Yakov had found the safest of hideaways and crammed himself and his scroll into it. They concluded that a blow to the head had rendered him semi-conscious for many hours, but it was clear that through his ordeal he had never let go of the holy scroll. The news quickly spread throughout the lowest decks where a mood of elation raised despondent spirits, banishing the terror engendered by the storm. Word of Yakov and his sacred scroll soon spread to the captain and his crew and the first-class passengers.

Everyone aboard felt cheered and comforted by Yakov's endurance—even those who doubted that it was God Himself who had watched over him. The happy news made it easier for the immigrants to bear the last grinding days of discomfort, and many saw in the Torah's survival an omen for their good fortune in America. Those who had heard rumors of Aharon's amazing levitation, which brought his father back from the dead, came to ask Yakov's permission to touch the Torah, cocooned in its red mantle, in the hope of receiving a blessing. Leery of this unwanted attention, Yakov protested, "I'm not a rabbi, just a humble baker. Our Torah's fate is uncertain as the fate of our people, but with God's help I will protect it with my dying breath."

After three interminable weeks at sea, the Rosens stepped onto firm ground at Castle Clinton, the brownstone fort on the tip of Manhattan that served as the immigration center. They sent up prayers for their safe arrival in the New World, and for the fulfillment of the secure and prosperous life they had yearned for as they toiled in their modest little shtetl of Valinsk.

Yakov and Chana conferred all their love and all their hopes on Aharon, their last and only surviving son. It was

Yakov's fervent wish that the boy keep the family tradition alive by becoming a chazzan.

"May it please You Hashem, that Aharon grow up to be a pious and righteous man, worthy of inheriting our Torah. And Hashem, if it's not too much to ask, may he also inherit the musical gifts of his grandfather Yitzhak."

"Amen," his mother said, smiling through her tears and kissing her son tenderly.

The soft warmth of her body comforted the boy, still he whispered, "But I haven't decided what I want to be when I grow up."

"What did you say?" his father asked.

The boy didn't answer. He was too enthralled by the massive circular fort, and the teeming, sprawling city beckoning to him beyond.

❧13❧

Life as an Immigrant

Fathers are always trying to make their sons good Jews: when will they try to be good Jews instead of leaving the task to their sons?
Yiddish folk saying

In New York City, Yakov, who spoke no English, barely scraped by as a peddler with a pushcart. However, he was determined not to remain a lowly hawker in this noisy, congested metropolis. In place of the shtetl surrounded by fields and forests, he found himself in a crowded city where block after block of five-and six-story tenements shut out the sunlight.

Yakov rented a place in one of these dreary buildings, an airless, one-bedroom apartment with communal toilets. The Rosens could find no peace there. Everyday new waves of German, Jewish, and Italian immigrants arrived to labor long hours in unsanitary and unsafe sweatshops. The congested and unhygienic environment caused childhood diseases to spread with grim regularity. Elevated trains pulled by stubby locomotives shook whole buildings as they rattled by spewing smoke and cinders. The noise from streets being torn up for the installation of gas mains, street lamps, water mains and sewers made it impossible to carry on a normal conversation. Yakov felt trapped within the maze infested with pickpockets, con men, vagrants, and thieves—where strangers of every race and creed thronged the noisy thoroughfares day and night.

Valinsk now shone in the surreal light of nostalgia, evoking a longing, deep inside the marrow of his bones for things

153

familiar: the distinctive, recognizable faces of his shtetl; the ancient forests of birch, spruce, and oak where he had roamed in search of ripe blackberries bursting with juice, and yellow mushrooms tastier than roasted chicken; the tempting, sweet odor of apples from the winter root cellar; the fresh tingle on his tongue of new snow that covered the humble shtetl in grace. In the sudden spin of remorseless memory he saw Leah's face twisted with rancor, and the reproachful eyes of the congregation as he carried the Torah from the shul. Uncle Hershel had truly loved him as a son, but in the end Aunt Sonia and her daughters had spurned him. His confused heart ached, but he vowed to make a success of his life in America, and always to keep to the teachings of the Torah. In addition, dismal letters from Frieda telling of her struggle to make ends meet, renewed his determination to bring his sister to America as he had promised.

He despised the young ruffians who inhabited the poor neighborhoods of the city where he trundled his cart. They chased him and taunted him, called him a "dirty Jew," tried to yank his beard or knock off his hat. Whenever this happened, the new immigrant told himself, *I'm in America now. I don't have to be afraid*. He would not give in to self-pity, which he viewed as the worst kind of cowardice. He began carrying a heavy walking stick to wield as a weapon. Soon the hooligans learned to watch out for the mighty little peddler with the big stick, who would whack them soundly if they came within range.

Yakov began to hear of opportunities in the South, particularly in Ricksburg, Alabama founded by the Yankees after the Civil War where Northern industrialists had been quick to see that the natural occurrence of coal, iron ore, and limestone in the region created ideal conditions for the production of pig iron, crucial to the manufacture of a variety of implements.

He wrote Chana's cousin, Cecil Kleinas, who had opened a general store there. Kleinas replied that he needed an assistant he could trust, and offered Yakov a job should he decide to leave New York. The peddler quickly accepted despite warnings that he was better off in the city.

"Here in New York they don't arrest us or kill us just because we're Jews, like they did in the Old Country," a *landsman*, or countryman, pointed out.

"So what are you saying?"

"I've heard that the South isn't so good for Jews," the man said rolling his eyes.

"How can you know that? You've never been there," Yakov challenged.

"Do you know Mike Perelman?"

"The one who works at the newspaper stand?"

"Yes, ask him. His sister lives in a place called Alalabamala?"

"*Du bist farmisht*, you're confused. It's Alabama."

Yakov talked to Perelman, who, to his relief, assured him that his sister was doing well in the South.

"How bad can it be?" Yakov asked Chana. "After all, Ricksburg has a small but established Jewish community. And with a job waiting for me I can make a fresh start."

Once again, the couple began to save every cent they could. In the interim, Yakov developed a knack for ferreting out the most lucrative corners for peddling his wares and began to pride himself on being a first-rate salesman. Each morning, no matter the weather, he donned his black coat and broad-brimmed hat, bade good-bye to Chana and Aharon, and pushed his cart for miles across the city. By year's end, he had saved enough to buy train tickets and when he arrived in Ricksburg, rent a room for the first month until he received a steady paycheck from his new job.

The family boarded with Mrs. Nellie Pickens, who let rooms to them in the deteriorating Georgian style mansion her grandfather had built. To prepare meals Chana had to descend a flight of wooden stairs to the basement kitchen where she could draw water from a well over which the house had been erected. Keeping kosher was exceedingly difficult under these conditions. Chana purchased her own pots, pans, dishes and flatware, and bought dairy and vegetable products to avoid non-kosher meat. Mrs. Pickens, a kindly woman, accommodated the Rosens'

155

request to keep and store their utensils completely separate from the others. A committee from the Baptist Church came to welcome the newcomers to their town with a basket of fresh fruit, Mrs. Pickens having forewarned them not to offer them baked goods.

Yakov immediately reported to Kleinas for employment at his general store. Encouraged by the promise of a two percent commission on every sale he made, the new arrival eagerly set to work. To his chagrin, Kleinas would allow him to make only two or three sales before ordering him to the stockroom to unpack merchandise. Stifling his frustration, the apprentice told himself that he had not traveled this far only to end up working for someone else, especially someone who treated him badly. He vowed that with God's help he would open his own bakery just as he had in Valinsk. Closing his eyes he conjured up the sweet, yeasty smell of braided egg bread, dark rye, and chewy bagels. He pictured the elegant red and gold lettering, Rosen's Bakery, painted on the storefront, beckoning customers inside. They would need cash to start their own business, but somehow he knew they would manage to save enough.

Yakov began scouting for a good location with affordable rent for the bakery. The baker had an eye for detail and quality. He quickly settled on the block of two and three story cast-iron Victorian buildings along Second Avenue, between Eighteenth and Nineteenth Street, as the prime location. These distinctive structures, fueled by the industrial boom following the Civil War, mirrored the trend seen in major cities like Chicago.

Still carrying the same wooden stick, just in case of trouble, he studied with approval the fluted columns, handsome molding, arched windows, panels embossed with acanthus leaves, and fanciful balustrades—all made of cast iron. The expansive glass windows that flooded the interior with sunlight astonished and delighted him.

When the Rosens had put aside almost enough for their bakery, Yakov took his wife downtown to show off the location he most coveted. "We'll attract plenty of customers," Yakov predicted. "They already come here to shop at Lowe's

Department Store, Zeeman's Discount Furniture, Henson Jewelers, or to do business at the Stern Brothers' Bank." He pointed out each business with his stick. "There's the barbershop and beauty parlor on the corner. And in the middle of the block, there's the vaudeville theater."

"So, where could we put the bakery?"

"See that the small building between Zeeman's and Lowe's?"

"The one with a big window downstairs and three fancy windows upstairs?"

"Yes, that one. And there's a for-rent sign in the window!"

"Yakov, my palm is itching; that's got to mean we will be counting a lot of money, soon!"

"So, I should rent the place! But there's just one problem. Mr. Billy Tucker owns that property, and he's a known Jew hater."

"I believe it's *bashert* for *us* to own that fine building one day," Chana declared. "If it's meant to be, you'll find a way."

"I agree. But being a Jew counts against me."

"And how!" Chana said rolling her eyes.

"But I am going to approach Tucker hat in hand, anyway. He's a businessman; he won't turn down a good deal—even from a Jew."

It turned out that Tucker had no intention of leasing the space to Yakov, but he wanted to see him squirm and beg. If Tucker hadn't already heard gossip that Rosen was a Jew, Yakov's outmoded formal attire and his thick accent set him apart. "I cannot rent you space in my building, Mr. Jewson," he declared.

"Excuse me, it's Mr. Rosen."

"Rosen, Jewson, you people have ungodly names." Tucker spat a stream of brown tobacco juice into a can. "I can rent you a shotgun house near nigger town."

"Excuse me, what kind of house? Near what town? I don't want to sell guns."

"Hee! Hee! Hee!" The great lump of the bigot's stomach heaved with merriment. "You people're sharp bidness men. Bet

157

you can turn that shotgun into a real nice place." He took a swig of Coke with a handful of peanuts in it, puffed out his lips, and bugged out his eyes. Yakov knew he was being trifled with, but he dared not offend the malicious property-owner if he still hoped to rent in the building. With difficulty he held his temper as he left, saying he needed time to think things over.

Outside, Yakov paced up and down the block. The black hat and woolen suit he wore, even in the heat and high humidity, did little to quell his anger.

Marching back along the street, he paused in front of the small, cramped furniture store and noted for the first time a hand-lettered sign: CLOSING OUT SALE, EVERYTHING MUST GO! He stood on the sidewalk, feeling the hot pavement through his boots, wondering and pondering. Then suddenly a bell jingled and Yakov found himself being propelled inside the store by a tall, thin, ugly cadaver of a man.

"He was a bag of bones, and he looked like he was dying of consumption," Yakov told his wife later. "But to me he was an angel sent from God."

A hand came toward him, "Joe Earl Zeeman's the name." Yakov took the proffered hand, and winced as Zeeman squeezed till his bones cracked.

Zeeman, who had been observing the progress of Kleinas's greenhorn assistant up and down the block and noted his brief encounter at Tucker's establishment, said with a sneer, "You don't need to be doin' business with that man." He steered the would-be baker through a jungle of cheap furniture and seated him in an overstuffed chair. Placing his hands on the chair's arms, Zeeman bent down until his face was level with the top of Yakov's head.

"This store's for rent," he crooned, and Yakov could smell stale tobacco and moonshine on his breath.

He felt his heart racing, his mouth filling with the bile of distaste, but he spoke calmly. "Mr. Zeeman, let's talk business. How much rent you want?"

After a brief discussion they settled on an amount that Yakov could afford. Before the landlord could change his mind, he had signed a lease, and handed over the deposit with an agreement to pay the rest when Zeeman vacated the premises at the end of the month. Then he stepped out of the store with a smile of satisfaction playing at the corners of his mouth.

Once again he found himself on the steamy sidewalk, but the heat no longer bothered him. With a spring in his step, he retraced the route. He could not wait to tell Chana that he had closed a deal on such excellent premises; he knew she would be proud of him.

As he turned the corner Tucker stepped in front of him, blocking his path. "Hey, you two-timing Jew-boy, you cut a deal with Zeeman. Took the business right from under my nose, didn't you?"

"Mister, I don't want no trouble," Rosen had had enough bullying for one day. This time he made no attempt to curb his rage. He lifted his walking stick and swung it a fraction above Tucker's head so rapidly that it whistled through the air. Caught off guard the bully ducked and staggered backwards, compressing his huge paunch with an audible "Oomph!" When he recovered, badly needing to salvage his dignity, he spat a gob of brown tobacco juice onto Yakov's boots. With a bitter taste in his mouth, he watched Tucker swagger away.

The baker had heard it whispered that the Ku Klux Klan had a following around Ricksburg and that Tucker was one of their leaders. A visiting rabbi from Atlanta had confirmed this, warning the Rosens about the KKK. He told them that the Klan had gained strength after Mervyn Newman, a German Jew, had been framed for the rape and murder of a young factory worker named Marjorie McPhee, and lynched by the clan. Yakov was horrified to learn that under the pretext of upholding the morals of the community, the Klan harassed, kidnapped, whipped, and even murdered those who met with its disapproval—especially Negroes, Jews, Catholics, and foreigners. Thinking these gloomy thoughts, he resolved to remain vigilant and to protect himself, his family, and the Rosen Torah from their hatred.

Once in operation Rosen's Bakery was open every day except Saturdays and Sundays. Saturday, the Sabbath was a good day for business and some fellow countrymen kept their stores open, but the heir to the Rosen sacred legacy would not violate any commandment, let alone the commandment to rest on the Sabbath that is a cornerstone of Jewish observance.

Chana found herself working in the bakery just as she had in Valinsk. Still high-spirited, still resentful of her hard lot, she traded petty insults with her husband while they toiled.

"'*Balmalocha*, expert with the golden hands, what's taking you so long to knead the dough?" she chided.

"My dear wife, if your words alone could make the dough rise we wouldn't need yeast," Yakov carped.

"*Oy vay! Zalts in dyne oygen, feffer in dyne noz*," Woe is me! Salt in your eyes, and pepper in your nose! Chana retorted, pushing a stray strand of hair under her cap with the back of her floury hands.

"Always handing out a feast of curses," Yakov tossed back.

"What shall I answer, for you are a man and have studied the Holy Books, while I am merely a woman not wise to the words of the sages," Chana said, with a toss of her head. And so they passed the time, slinging barbs, sharing their frustrations and affection.

After school, Aharon joined his parents in the bakery, helping to clean the ovens, sweep the floor, and wait on customers who liked his sunny personality. While he worked he listened with a mixture of amusement and irritation to his parents' bickering in Yiddish, and began to hone in on their sly sense of humor. In high school, during school holidays, Aharon enjoyed delivering baked goods to neighborhood customers. Three mornings a week he hitched their old horse, Barney, to a wagon loaded with a variety of breads and pastries displayed in large wicker baskets, and drove through the neighborhood where kids waited eagerly to pet the horse or feed him carrots that Aharon provided.

The Rosens' reputation for quality baked goods spread, and in time they saved enough to buy a house in a "nice" neighborhood where other Jewish families resided. The brick and

160

clapboard folk Victorian, with a big front porch, sat on a corner lot. It had two bedrooms and a bathroom upstairs. On the main floor was a parlor with a fireplace; on one side pocket doors lead to a study, on the other, French doors opened to the dining room; beyond that was the kitchen. In the far corner of the property sat a neglected carriage house once used by a local innkeeper.

Finally, Yakov sent for his sister Frieda, lifting a huge burden from his conscience. Hearing of the Rosens' good fortune, those in Valinsk and surrounding shtetls schemed and dreamed of coming to America in the hope that they too would prosper.

By now a fairly sizeable community of Jewish immigrants had settled in Ricksburg, made up of German Jews, who had arrived first and were in the majority, and Litvaks, or Lithuanian Jews who came later. These two communities remained separate from one another. While Germans Jews adapted more easily to local customs, Litvaks with a mind-set shaped by their intense orthodoxy, remained steeped in their shtetl ways.

Aharon was too young to appreciate this lively, stubborn, eccentric community that marched to a code deeply rooted in the old country, yet they paraded through his boyhood. Here, as in Valinsk, they continued to speak Yiddish, lobbing jokes and insults at one another using the same salty vernacular. Everyone knew the eccentricities of those labeled the *alta kocker* (crotchety old man), *baleboosteh* (mistress of the house), *bandit* (pain-in-the-neck), not to mention the *chachem* (clever or learned person), *draykop* (confused person), *farbissener* (sullen person), *ganif* (shady character), *knucker* (big shot), and *macher* (someone with connections). And a true Litvak could easily point out the *meshuggana* (crazy person), *paskudnika* (vulgar person), *shlemiel* (simpleton), *schmendrick* (pipsqueak), *shmo* (unlucky jerk), *shnorrer* (a moocher), *shlimazel* (chronically unlucky person), and of course the *yenta* (the gossip).

They vented their exasperation, their affection, and their bond to one another through a robust and distinctive sense of humor so habitually that Aharon began to join in the fun by imitating them. When he did this, his parents shushed him disapprovingly. The boy could not understand why he was

161

forbidden to emulate their harmless wisecracking. To him Yiddish came to mean these "funny" words with which you could spice up English to achieve comic effects. To his parents, whose ears were attuned to the nuances of the language, their son's distortions were disrespectful.

The German Jews of Ricksburg had already built their own synagogue, but the Litvaks disapproved of their reform services, preferring their own place of worship. So Yakov held regular readings from the Torah at his home. On weekdays the men met in Yakov's study; only the most pious were invited to attend. The Rosens' residence was far from ideal to serve as a shul. However, the carriage house, once cleaned and scrubbed, adequately accommodated families on High Holidays and Saturday morning services. When they all gathered, the women and small children sat behind the obligatory partition praying, kibitzing and shushing their offspring. The splendid Rosen Torah imparted a special solemnity to services, despite the makeshift shul.

At first Aharon was allowed to escape into the backyard to play with the other kids. However, as his Bar Mitzvah approached, under pressure from his family and the expectations of the congregation, he was required to be more serious and had to stay inside to pray. Restless and bored, he observed the men's rapt faces, their bodies swaying to the timeless liturgy. As the prayers flowed on and on, and the layman cantor's voice swelled above all the others, sometimes the melodic, Oriental cadences gripped him. In his imagination the shul seemed to sway to the pulse of the chanting. But too soon after the services, the mysterious and hidden meaning captured inside the music faded, leaving him stranded in a humdrum world.

As much as the Litvaks were grateful for the use of the Rosens' home they needed a permanent place to worship. Soon they began a campaign to raise money to build an Orthodox shul where they could feel they belonged and where the Rosen legacy could be suitably housed. The fund raising progressed slowly and finally stalled, as the group was smaller and less affluent than the Reform Jews. Even though he would not admit it, Yakov was in no hurry to remove the scroll from his abode. He could feel its presence like an inextinguishable flame, and was reluctant to give up the sense of peace it brought him as he struggled to make a place for himself and his family in this foreign town.

As Aharon grew into adolescence he began to question his parents' need to cling to the ways of the past. Their son's defiance threatened to violate the haven they so scrupulously guarded from those like Tucker, who wished them ill. His parents never questioned their heritage, nor did they have the slightest interest in promoting their religion to others; all they wanted was to be left in peace to live in accordance with Torah and its time-honored commandments.

When Aharon challenged his father he became defensive. "You have comforts undreamed of in Valinsk! You did not have to work yourself to the bone to get out of poverty," he lectured.

"I work hard in school and in the bakery. Why won't you allow me to make friends with kids who aren't Jewish?"

"You never suffered from pogroms. I could tell you terrible things," Yakov threatened.

"I know life was hard in the shtetl. But it's different here."

"Don't you understand that these Christians are just being polite? They don't know anything about us. They don't trust us. They don't respect us."

"But Jews do not trust or respect Christians, either!" The boy exclaimed.

"Why should I apologize to anyone for my beliefs or look for their approval? Are you ashamed of who you are?" Yakov said, scowling at his son.

Aharon protested that he just wanted to be like any other American boy. He didn't want to hurt his father by telling him that it was humiliating to hear people call Litvaks "wet behind the ears," "just off the boat," and "greenhorns." Nevertheless, there was something he had to say.

Folding his arms across his chest, the teenager announced with an apologetic grin, "I want to change my name to Aaron. I'm tired of people not spelling or pronouncing my name correctly."

The color drained from Yakov's face, and with a shout of outrage he confronted his son. "You want to be an American just like the others! You, the heir to the Rosen Torah! It shows lack of respect for your heritage, for the Torah, and for your pious grandfather, Aharon Lurie, for whom you were named."

Tears of frustration pooled in the adolescent's eyes.

His father's heart constricted with sorrow. In the bright new promise of America, his son could not see the importance of tradition; his faith was bleaching away like a sepia tint left out in the sun. But how could Aharon comprehend the ways of the shtetl? How could this new generation understand that in Valinsk, where people teetered on the fringes of poverty, the Torah was their enduring hope and refuge, their guide to maintaining their dignity and humanity in a brutal world?

Hearing voices raised, Chana came in from the kitchen with a concerned frown. Her son looked across the room, their eyes met, and she raised her eyebrows. She knew that she could create only a truce in this contest of wills that would flare up again and again. *How can I stop the fighting?* she asked herself. *How can Yakov teach Aharon to follow tradition when he does not value or respect his father's devotion to it?*

Despite his father's disapproval, Aharon, now called Aaron by everyone with the exception of his parents, made a conscious effort to assimilate. In part to win acceptance among his peers, he participated in extramural sports, and the school's concert and marching bands. He wore the knee pants and stylish, flat cap in vogue. His father objected to his attire, fearing it was the first step toward non-observance, to becoming unworthy of the Rosen Torah.

The day the bandmaster chose Aaron to play lead trumpet was a defining moment for the budding young musician. It conferred on him the certain knowledge that he had exceptional talent; it provided him with a shield he could use to resist his father; and the hope that it might one day win his father's support. Aaron understood that this inborn gift was not something he could thrust aside; it was the essence of his very identity.

Aaron began to invite friends home for musical jam sessions, with mixed results. When his American schoolmates stepped into the Rosens' home, he experienced a secret thrill, as if he were committing an act as forbidden as eating pork. At the same time his parents' obvious discomfort embarrassed him. His father never failed to take his son aside and whisper, "Are they Jewish? If they're not, don't allow them to see our Torah."

To avoid making a scene he mumbled, "Sure, Papa. Don't worry my friends are okay," but he could not completely understand his father's paranoia.

Even in the face of his son's youthful rebellion, Yakov believed that in time he would outgrow his foolishness. Yet Aaron's yearning for acceptance as a wholly "normal" American came into direct conflict with the mission to which his father had dedicated his life: the preservation of Orthodox Judaism in this new land.

❦14❧

A Trial by Fire

With one tuchus you can't dance at two weddings.

Old Eastern European Saying

In his junior year of high school, Aaron developed a crush on Alice Bodin who played the flute in the school band. A delicate beauty with milky skin, dark curls, and clear amber eyes revealing just a hint of sadness, her gentle nature made Aaron feel like a knight who could rescue her from the wicked world. He sat directly behind Alice in the band, watching her covertly, feeling the whole range of emotions that a youthful passion brings on: joy, despair, agitation, and excitation. One afternoon, while Yakov and Chana were at the bakery, Aaron found the courage to invite the charming flutist to his home to practice for the upcoming school play.

When she peeked into the study her eyes were instantly drawn to the ornate glass fronted cabinet that housed the scroll. Through the frosted panes she glimpsed the magnificent red silk mantel embroidered with a golden border of twisting grape leaves.

"Aaron, what is that? Can I see it?" she asked, pointing with a trembling finger. He caught her hand, and shook his head.

"What's wrong?"

"It's our family Bible," he answered offhandedly, hoping to avert her interest. When Alice persisted, he explained as simply as he could that it was a handwritten scroll or Torah, containing the first five books of the Bible, and that his great-great grandfather had commissioned it over a hundred years ago.

"That's really wonderful, Aaron. I would like to know more about your religion," she said, with a reassuring smile.

"And I would like to know more about yours," he said, meaning it.

One Sunday Alice invited him to a gathering of young people interested in Unitarianism. Like the Rosens, the Unitarians had no church building, no ordained minister; they met in the homes of the members. Aaron liked their open-mind, nonjudgmental attitude. He reassured himself that he was not turning away from Judaism, simply educating himself about beliefs and customs different from his own. The Bodins who had recently changed from the Southern Baptists to the Unitarian Church, welcomed their daughter's friendship with Aaron.

"Alice says that Aaron is a marvelous musician, but he often plays the class clown!" Mrs. Bodin remarked to her husband.

"No wonder that young man brings Alice out of her shell," Mr. Bodin said.

"I agree he's helping her overcome her shyness. Still, I worry about our daughter." Mr. Bodin noticed an expression of sadness pass across his wife's face, as if her eyes were fixed on a long, dark road, and saw a traveler in terrible danger. When he reached out to comfort her, she smiled tremulously, but the sadness lingered in her eyes.

When Aaron began to be seen around town with Alice, it upset Chana's friends. "How can you allow your son to go with a Christian girl?" they chided.

"Aharon's a good boy," Chana said, bristling at the criticism, yet privately vowing to put a stop to the budding friendship. When her son returned from school she confronted him. "Thank God your father does not know about this!"

When Aaron told Alice that they disapproved of him keeping company with her, she exclaimed, "Why can't your parents accept us going together? We are good friends. We do no harm to anyone."

167

"It's forbidden for me to date a Christian. They're afraid I will abandon my religion," he said sadly. Alice stroked his face gently with the tips of her fingers. "But I'm not going to end our friendship, because of my parents," he declared.

"You mean we should sneak around?" Alice said, frowning.

"No, I'll find a way. In the meantime, can we continue to meet at your house?" he asked, hoping to forestall further gossip, and his parents' ire.

Soon afterward, Aaron received distressing news that Alice had been diagnosed with tuberculosis and sent to a sanitarium on the outskirts of Ricksburg. Without telling his parents, he visited Alice as often as he could get a ride with the Bodins, and wrote long letters between visits. However, he could not hide his fears from his mother for long. One evening, finding himself alone with her, he asked as she sat darning socks, "Isn't it a mitzvah to visit the sick?"

Chana gave a start, and looked up from her darning. "Yes. But who is sick?"

"It's Alice, she has tuberculosis. I've been visiting her in the sanitarium outside town." He turned his face away to hide unshed tears.

Chana reached out and took her son's hand; she could feel him trembling. He was afraid for Alice, with good cause as no certain cure for the disease existed. To comfort him, Chana said, "I'm sure Alice is getting good care at the sanitarium."

"Ma, she's so sick," Aaron whispered miserably.

A chill ran through her. She should discourage Aharon from continuing to see the girl, but she pitied Alice, and she could see her boy's suffering. She recalled Yakov's lovesick eyes following her in Valinsk, and his wonderful romantic letters; she tried to put these thoughts from her mind in order to be firm, but tender emotions overruled her.

Chana had allowed her mind to wander; now her son was gazing at her, waiting for her response. "Aharon, you want to see Alice, so go visit her, but its better that you don't tell your father." She simply hadn't the heart to stop her son from carrying out this mitzvah.

On his visits to the sanitarium, Aaron and Alice sat on the shady porch where rocking chairs were set up to catch the cool breezes wafting over the mountaintop. For a while melancholy enveloped them, then their youthful zest for life took over, and they talked animatedly about their dreams for the future.

One sultry summer afternoon, when not a trace of air moved even on the mountain, Alice confided that she had stumbled upon a collection of letters written by missionaries in China. She read and reread them late at night when she felt most frightened and alone; they helped her to feel at peace as if passing through a dark passage into the light of a divine presence.

"Aaron, can you imagine the missionaries journeying through that strange land? Just picture them living in poor villages surrounded by rice paddies, and acres of crimson poppies. Those beautiful blooms that produced opium broke their hearts, because addicts became lost souls that could not be converted to Christianity."

The lovelorn boy looked over the verdant canopy of trees to the hazy slate-blue hills rolling away in the distance, wishing he could fly away with Alice. In his mind's eye he saw her running through fields of giant red poppies, her arms spread wide, her dark hair streaming behind her. "Aaron, did you hear what I said? Are you daydreaming?"

"Uh, yes, I heard," with a guilty start he noticed that she was perspiring profusely. "Alice, we should go inside, it's too hot out here."

After he had poured lemonade and they had settled in the gloomy sitting room, he resumed, "You were telling me about the missionaries."

"They went to China to serve the poor. They lived like peasants, braided their hair into pigtails like workingmen, ate strange food like fried grasshoppers, and dried grubs. Yet they counted it an honor and privilege to bring Christianity to them, and never said a word about sacrifice." Alice's eyes blazed too brightly in her pale, damp face.

169

Aaron peered at her anxiously.

"Don't you see?" she persisted.

"No. What are you talking about?"

"You know, workers are badly needed to administer shelters for opium addicts, and there just aren't enough female missionaries to take care of women addicts."

"You want to live with opium addicts!" His mouth twisted incredulously.

"Yes. I want to be a missionary!" Tossing her head defiantly, Alice pressed a handkerchief to her mouth to muffle a cough.

"You can't be serious!" he protested. "Besides, your folks wouldn't allow you to go to China."

"We could elope!" Alice challenged him.

Aaron jumped up and made the motions of playing his trumpet while humming Mendelssohn's *Wedding March*.

Despite herself, she burst into laughter.

"But if we elope your parents would blame *me*, not you." It suddenly occurred to Aaron that it would be exciting to live in an exotic culture completely different from his own—without guilt or the stern expectations of his family.

"Seriously, if I became a missionary my parents would be proud of me."

Aaron snorted, "I bet they wouldn't!"

"Wouldn't your parents allow you to become a missionary in the name of Judaism?"

He could not suppress a chuckle, "Jews don't do missionary work."

"Why not?"

"They just don't."

"Ask your rabbi for an explanation," Alice retorted, miffed that he wasn't taking her seriously.

Outside the sanitarium windows glowed like mother-of-pearl in the setting sun. When Alice rose to leave, she crumpled her handkerchief into the palm of her hand, but not before Aaron saw the ominous bloodstain on it.

On his next visit Aaron was better prepared. "Our rabbi says that the idea of getting people to convert is not part of Judaism."

"Is that so?"

"The rabbi says that the Torah is for all humanity, whether Jewish or not. Any human being who faithfully observes the seven laws of Noah written in the Torah will earn a place in heaven."

"Really?"

Handing her a sheet he said, "Yes. Here, I've made a list of the laws for you."

He observed her mouthing the list of prohibitions against: Idolatry, Murder, Theft, Sexual Promiscuity, Blasphemy, Cruelty to Animals—and the establishment of courts of justice. Looking up with a frown, she declared, "Still, missionaries can help to get out the word!"

"I liked what the rabbi said about not needing to convert from one religion to another because they all teach kindness and compassion," he said.

"Well, won't I be showing compassion as a missionary?"

"Yes, but the Torah is for all people. No conversion to Judaism is necessary, and therefore there is no need for missionaries," he insisted.

"But doesn't the Torah say that the Jews are God's chosen people?"

"I asked the rabbi about that, and he said that our God is the God of all people, but the Jews were given the special task of living by His commandments, so it's our responsibility to always be fair and just to others—although few of us can to do this."

Alice's eyes teared. "Dash it, Aaron, you speak like a book! I never thought of it that way." She paused to take a sip of water then said, "Still I feel a strong calling to missionary work."

"Alice I don't approve of forcing religion down people's throats!" He didn't want to upset her, but he could not hide his disapproval.

"Don't you understand? I want to alleviate human suffering!"

"You can do that without becoming a missionary."

Bright spots burned on Alice's cheeks and her lips trembled.

"I'm sorry, but I can't believe your parents would give their approval to do something so . . . so dangerous," he said more gently.

"My parents want me to fulfill my dreams!" Alice turned her head to cough into the handkerchief. Aaron could have kicked himself for distressing someone who might never realize her dreams.

"Mine want me to follow in their footsteps, but I'm not sure that I can." He groped to find words to express his longings and conflicting loyalties. "I want to travel the world! To play my trumpet to my heart's content, but there's no way they'll let me. They want me to have a normal job, a normal life, get married, have children with a good Jewish girl."

"Aaron, you have to do everything in your power to get them to understand! This is America, not Lithuania."

It was one thing for him to be critical of his family, another to hear it from her. Wanting to close the gap that had opened between them, he said, "You're lucky to have trusting parents."

A fit of coughing wracked her frail body, and a nurse quickly came to help her to her room. She never divulged to Aaron the pact she had made with God, promising Him that if she recovered from her illness she would devote the rest of her life to serving the poor.

Alice's health seemed to improve, and for a while there was hope that she might recover. Then towards the end of winter, she weakened and finally succumbed. The realization that Alice's aspirations would never be achieved, wrenched the heart out of Aaron, leaving a dark hole in its place that made him want to crawl away like a sick animal. However, he had sworn to carry out her one last wish, no matter the consequences.

Before she passed away, Alice had specified, in a detailed will, how she wished her funeral to be conducted. Her parents were disconcerted by their daughter's bizarre plans and tried their best to dissuade her. For all their entreaties, Alice remained adamant that she wanted to be put to rest in a way that brought her and others closer to the mystical essence of God. In the end they could not bear to go against their daughter's wishes, and joined Aaron in making a solemn promise to do as she had asked.

Since there was no Unitarian minister in the town, the dying girl chose the Reform rabbi, Daniel Loeb, to preside at her funeral as the Orthodox rabbi would not do so. Even Rabbi Loeb was reluctant to conduct such a funeral, but in the end he agreed out of compassion for the Bodins.

On a bitterly cold February night, exactly at the stroke of midnight, the funeral cortege with a hearse and four horse-drawn carriages in the vanguard, clattered over the icy path toward the Christian cemetery on the wooded outskirts of the town. The carriages pulled up at an open grave illuminated by lanterns mounted on poles. A huge bonfire disseminated its heat to friends and relatives shivering and weeping at her graveside. As Alice's pure white casket was lifted from the hearse, the rabbi intoned the Kaddish prayer for the dead.

When the casket was lowered slowly into the black hole, Aaron looked up to the heavens, his heart leaden with sorrow. There was no moon, only distant, cold white stars to pierce the darkness. Low on the horizon, as if suspended by a mysterious force, he could just make out the Northern Cross centering the universe. The rabbi gave a brief, poignant eulogy, ending with El Malei Rachamim, the prayer asking for her soul to rest in peace.

Alice's parents each tossed a single red rosebud into her grave. Aaron followed suit, then every mourner presented Alice with a rose, covering the white coffin with blood-red blooms. They all stood with heads bowed in silent prayer under the lanterns sputtering in the chill winter wind, until the bonfire burned to embers. Only then did the mourners, frozen by cold and grief, return to the carriages and depart. Aaron alone stayed next to the dying coals to keep watch until dawn.

As he stood swaying in misery, a light flurry of snow began to fall, spreading a frosty mantle over his sweetheart's raw grave. An owl, hunting for prey on silent wings, swooped above his head. Possums, creatures of the night that occupied this melancholy place, awoke to scavenge for food. Heedless of death, driven by instinct, they scurried over tombstones. Where graves were not yet excavated, flowers not yet planted, they froze, sniffing the air for danger, their eyes glowing in the dying lantern light. Aaron wished to join their heedless quest to escape the anguish throbbing inside him like a jagged wound. *Death will come for all of us,* he thought, *no matter what faith we have followed in life.*

Immediately after the funeral a boy in the high school band, whose father worked for the *Ricksburg News*, had described the midnight interment to him in sensational detail. The following morning, Yakov read an account of the strange burial in the local newspaper with mounting outrage. The article named Aaron Rosen as the liaison between the Bodins and the Jewish Reform rabbi.

Yakov berated his son for participating in this outlandish and ungodly burial. Aaron made a valiant attempt to defend himself: Alice, his friend in the band, had requested this memorial service and burial, and he was doing a good deed for the Bodin family by carrying out her last wishes, he explained.

His father wasn't convinced. "With one *tuchus* you can't dance at two weddings," he huffed about backsides. His nostrils were pinched and his breath came in short wheezes.

"We're talking about a funeral, not a wedding," Aaron retorted.

"I'm saying that it's not possible to follow two different religions at the same time," his father snapped back.

"Papa, I get it. But I haven't converted to Christianity just because I helped to carry out my friend's wishes. "

"Enough, I don't want to hear another word!"

The pious Jew saw rebellion growing in his son like a disease. He told his wife, "I don't recognize my son. He doesn't want to go to shul, he doesn't pray, he speaks and dresses like a gentile. He's turning into a *goy* as I am watching." Chana had to agree that their Aharon was being lured away from his family

174

and his religion. She regretted her complicity in her son's friendship with Alice, but it was too late.

Determined to convey his displeasure, Rosen made an appointment with Rabbi Loeb. After preliminary courtesies, the irate father declared, "With due respect, I don't want to talk about distasteful things or put my nose where it's not wanted, but shouldn't we ask ourselves what we can do to help our children grow up to be decent Jews?"

"Mr. Rosen, of course we need to teach our children to be honorable and faithful," the rabbi said in a reassuring tone. "But it is also true that we live in America now."

"It's *because* we live in America that we have to work even harder to instill in our children what it means to be a good Jew," Yakov protested.

The rabbi scrutinized the baker over his gold-rimmed spectacles. "Mr. Rosen, one can be devout without isolating oneself from the world. I said Kaddish at that poor girl's funeral, and what is wrong with that? Kaddish, as you know, represents the golden link between life and death, and shines Divine light on *all* whatever their faith."

Yakov's face flushed with anger. "Rabbi, you can't be proposing we Jews should compromise our religious beliefs to fit in?"

The rabbi said in measured tones, "I respect your orthodox principles, but you have to put the shtetl mentality behind you."

Yakov could no longer control his temper. "So! You approve of letting others corrupt our religion?" He rose from his seat trembling with indignation. "You of all people! A rabbi— even a Reform rabbi—should be an example to others."

Loeb's mouth drew into a thin line. Rosen had insulted him and Reform Judaism. "Mr. Rosen, do not contact me until you are ready to apologize." He took off his glasses, rubbed the bridge of his nose, and motioned for his visitor to leave.

When Yakov's nemesis, Tucker heard about Alice's funeral he saw his chance to get back at Mr. Yakov Rosen. He began by stirring up the latent hostility of his fellow Klansmen toward the Jewish community at large. He spread rumors about the "heathenish manner" in which the Rosen boy and the rabbi had conducted the "good Christian" family's burial. Tucker kept up his malicious ranting until the Klan's anger ignited.

The frightening sound of shattering glass, and the ominous flicker of flames outside the bedroom window, woke Yakov and Chana. The valiant baker grabbed his cane and ran down the hallway, Chana ran to the kitchen to get her cast iron skillet, Aaron seized his baseball bat and sprinted from his bedroom. Brandishing their weapons, the three rushed outside, only to find that the Klansmen had disappeared into the night, leaving a burning cross on the lawn and a brick in the parlor. As Yakov watched in horror at the desecration of the perpetrators' own religious symbol, he was transported forty years back in time to his Uncle Hershel's home in Valinsk . . .

He sat bolt upright in his bed rigid with terror, listening to the crunch of heavy boots on cobblestones and the harsh shouts of soldiers coming closer. There was the nerve-wracking sound of breaking glass. Someone grabbed his hand and yanked him out of bed. He felt his uncle's hot breath in his ear as he whispered: ""Run! Hide!" before he shoved him out the window into the night. The boy's instinct for survival kicked in, and he ran barefooted to the chicken coop. He could hear soldiers smashing down doors and splintering furniture as they ransacked the house. He lay in the mud and excrement, aching with cold and fright, until the bedlam ceased and his uncle came for him . . .

Recalling this night of terror so vividly, a deep weariness set in. "Even in America they hate us," he sighed.

"Better they burn their cross than our Star of David," Chana answered with derision.

Despite the tension Aaron chuckled at his mother's plucky rejoinder. "Ma, you're the best," he said, hugging her.

The father gazed at his son standing tall and proud, ready to take on the world, his shock of black hair wild and disheveled, his eyes dark and smoldering. And he shook his head in wonderment and apprehension. He had come to the New World

176

determined to put down roots, and he had done so in raising his boy in this adopted country. But the strange contradictions of this land were sweeping Aharon away from him. The dread that dwelt within him stirred, exhaled its foul breath, and growled, "The Klan is going to destroy your Torah."

While his neighbors cowered behind closed curtains, a searing rage swept through him, shoving aside fear. He would prevail over these new enemies; he would protect his holy legacy no matter the cost. Before first light, the keeper of the scroll crept out of the house and transported it to a safe place. He would not divulge, even to his wife, where he had hidden it.

The attack by the Klan precipitated a crisis for the worshippers who had been meeting in the Rosens' home. Many blamed Yakov and the building committee for doing a poor job of soliciting funds. Only with a secure building they owned could the Torah be protected from attacks or theft. After heated discussions they made the decision to step up the campaign, and to take out a loan for any short fall if necessary.

The assault of the KKK sent shock waves through the town, as far as Atlanta, and even around the country. Money poured in, and within months, construction of the new shul was underway.

From then on, Yakov became ever more obsessed with the preservation of the scroll. His unwavering conviction that the Rosen Torah belonged not only to his family but also to his people, sustained him; the enormity of his responsibility made him unyielding in his faith.

He kept on lashing out at his son, blaming him for what had happened. "Mr. Popularity! You had to bring strangers into our home? I warned you not to show them the Torah. And that funeral! You knew Mr. Tucker and the Klan were just looking for an excuse to stir up trouble. But no, you wouldn't listen!"

When his son did not respond, he pointed an accusatory finger at him and growled, "It's your godless ways that have caused problems for us. In the Talmud it says that Hashem declared that even if Jews abandon Him, they should continue to follow His laws."

177

"Would you still follow God's laws if you were not certain that He exists?" he retorted, stung by his father's accusations.

"Obey the Torah! Practice and study the laws! Then you will know God exists!" Yakov's hand flew toward his son of its own volition. With a shock he felt a sting on his palm and saw the livid welt forming on his Aharon's face. He hadn't meant to slap him but the damage was done.

From that day on, Yakov demanded that his wayward son follow the observances of an Orthodox Jew. Each morning had to begin with prayers and the donning of *tefillin*, winding the leather straps attached to containers that held excerpts from the Torah printed on parchment, onto his arms and forehead. He also insisted that Aharon observe the Sabbath. "You have to tell your so-called friends that Friday night and Saturday must be reserved for the proper observance of our *Shabbat.*"

"I will attend services, and eat the Friday night meal with my family. But when the dinner is over, I want to go out with my friends." he said in an attempt at compromise.

Yakov drew back his shoulders, pointed his finger at his son, and proclaimed, "Never forget that you will be the next inheritor of the Rosen Torah!"

"How can I forget?"

Yakov swallowed the bile filling his mouth. To him the faithful practice of Judaism was no onerous duty but a daily source of comfort and stability in a turbulent and hostile world.

Chana did not approve of her son's free spiritedness either, yet she recognized that they had pushed Aharon too far, and for the time being, persuaded her husband that it would be wise to allow him a little freedom.

The contesting forces unleashed by Alice's funeral left Aaron emotionally exhausted—his father's orthodoxy versus Rabbi Loeb's reformism, the Baptists against the Unitarians, the KKK against almost everybody. He just wanted to get on with his life. As a release, Aaron spent more and more time practicing his trumpet. Soon he began to show extraordinary musical aptitude, which his mother championed by paying for music lessons.

Despite the tension engendered by his father's oppressive discipline, music was the one passion father and son shared. Yakov had taught himself to play the violin, and in the evening, he spent hours practicing and also listening to Chassidic and Klezmer melodies, Yiddish songs, and Cantorial music. Lacking formal training, he braced the instrument awkwardly against his chest then played with amazing zest. Chana sang folksongs to accompany him. She too, had no training, yet her singing was moving and poignant. These wonderful evenings listening to his mother and father remained with Aaron long after he had left home, reminding him that music has the power to soothe and to uplift, to bring chaotic thoughts and turbulent emotions into harmony.

In his last year of high school, he began to consider music as a career, although he knew this news would unleash an inferno of opposition from his parents. In the solitude of sleepless nights, his resolve only ripened and grew. During his waking hours, he tried to summon the nerve to speak to his father, but could not.

One wintry morning, as he helped his mother make a batch of buttery, yeast dough, he blurted out the truth. He wanted to continue his musical training by studying with a renowned musician in New Orleans. He told her that he had already had lengthy discussions with Mr. Schultz, the band director at his school. She continued kneading the dough as if she had not heard him, but he knew her too well to be deceived. It was the calm before the storm. He bit his lower lip and waited.

"Your Papa will be so sad," she began in a soothing voice.

"And why is that?" he asked, playing along, although his heart was pounding.

"Because he wants you to become a scholar, maybe a lawyer, or even a rabbi, most of all he wants you to be a chazzan."

Aaron shook his head and sighed, "I know, I know. I must never forget that my father will bequeath the Torah to me."

"Don't mock him!" Chana chided. "Besides, you can be a musician without making it your vocation."

179

"No, without my trumpet and its music I don't have a place in the world . . . I mean I feel it deep inside me," he said, grappling for words to convey his passion.

Chana stopped kneading and looked directly at her son. "But how will you explain it to your father! He will feel that you have forsaken him."

"I already asked Mr. Schultz to help me convince Papa, he'll explain everything," Aaron replied, wiping his sweating hands on the apron around his waist.

"Yes, it's better Mr. Schultz should speak to Papa. Then he can decide what is best for you."

"But I've decided that's what I want!"

"No, Aharon. You cannot do this without his blessing."

"Okay, but in the meantime, please prepare Papa."

"Ask Mr. Schultz to stop by the bakery after school."

The bandmaster began by assuring the Rosens that with the right training, Aaron could become an extraordinary musician. "In my opinion, if you're going to be a musician," he said with a wry smile, "you should be a great one. After all, there are better ways to starve."

Aaron thought that his father would never stop questioning the teacher in his search for the flaws in his plans. To his relief, Mr. Schultz remained calm and answered Yakov's questions honestly.

After Schultz left, with the fresh coffee cake Chana had given him, the dispute between father and son continued and did not abate for the rest of the week. Yakov's unrelenting theme was that a musician's life was too uncertain, not entirely respectable, and that he feared his son would lose his Jewish identity if he went to live on his own in New Orleans. Mr. Shultz met with Mr. Rosen several times afterward, but was unable to persuade him to give the budding musician a chance at a successful career.

Aaron moped around the house, stubbornly refusing to give in to his father's wishes. He played on his mother's emotions, knowing that she doted on him. She had encouraged his natural mischievousness since he was a small child, and he had soon learned to run to her for protection. This ingrained

180

habit reasserted itself in the brewing crisis. She was his last hope, if she could not get his father to capitulate, no one could. At first his mother resisted her son's pleas, but his obvious unhappiness was hard to endure. The feud in their household had to be resolved, and Chana was now determined to find a way out of their impasse.

That afternoon, when Aaron was almost through cleaning baking trays caked with cooking oil, she turned to him and declared with a nervous smile, "All right, I'll try to help win Papa over."

A wave of joy broke over him. He wanted to put his head on her shoulder and weep. In a broken voice he mumbled, "Thank you, Ma."

Waving a finger, she admonished, "And you will promise your father to stay in touch with the Jewish community in New Orleans, to observe *Shabbat*, and to attend services regularly."

For a moment the reality of what she had asked him to do frightened him, yet he could not turn down the chance she was offering. He stammered, "Yes, Ma, I promise." It was the only way he could put an end to the turmoil in their home "When will you tell Pa?"

"I'll find the right time," she reassured him. His heart throbbed with love for her, and also with anguish now that she had joined him in battle.

After the Shabbat meal that Friday night, it became clear that Chana was about to put their plan into action. She began by prompting, "Aharon, do you want to tell your father about your promise?"

Before the young man could respond, Yakov interjected, "How many times have I told you that I'm not opposed to your being a musician as a sideline? All I want is for you to have a decent profession, and to be a good Jew. Is that too much to ask of my son?"

Chana quickly intervened. "Please, listen Yakov. Aharon has promised that while he is away from home he will not abandon his *Yiddishkeit*."

His father jerked his head back and stared into his son's eyes. Aaron willed himself not to drop his gaze although his heart was hammering and he could feel himself trembling. Finally, the moment passed and Yakov let his hands fall to his side. "You made this promise?"

Aaron nodded. Only the pallor of his face revealed the tumult inside him.

"Tell your father exactly what you promised to do."

"I promise to join the shul, to observe the Sabbath, and to become part of the Jewish community in New Orleans." A shudder passed through him at the terrifying reality of the pledge he had just made.

Yakov fished for a handkerchief in his pocket, blew his nose, and said, "Well, a fine musician in the family isn't the worst tragedy." Aaron understood that this act of concession was his father's unspoken avowal of love, and it soothed and consoled him.

"But, above all, you must keep your promise to follow the teachings of the Torah."

"I will." Like a puppy wagging its tail, Aaron nodded his head obediently.

"Not so fast young man. You must first agree to this additional condition: I will help with the living expenses for the first year, after that you are on your own. You will have only one year to prove yourself."

"Thank you!" Aaron exclaimed with heartbreaking earnestness. "You have granted me new life!" Grabbing his trumpet he rushed out of the house to share his good news with Mr. Shultz.

❧15❧

Aaron Rosen, the Rebel Musician

The richest inheritance can become a burden.

Talmud

Aaron boarded the night train that passed through Ricksburg on its way to New Orleans feeling jubilant, hardly able to believe his good fortune. Since childhood he had listened to the plaintive whistle of the train, resonating like a trumpet call summoning him to faraway places. Too overwrought to sleep, he stuck his nose against the window and surveyed the darkened countryside slipping by; he could discern no clear demarcation between land and sky, no moon, no stars.

At dawn as the train approached the city, he caught the first glimpse of Lake Pontchartrain silvering in the early light, as the mist's gauzy veil lifted. Enchanted, he watched the sun rise from the lake, crawl over the horizon and seem to follow the train like a great orange balloon. He hummed a droll, silly little Yiddish folksong he had learned at home that he couldn't get out of his head.

Feygele, feygele,
Pi-pi-pi
Vu iz der tate?
Geforn in ru.
Vos t'er brengen?
A fesele bir.
Vu t'men shteln?
Hintern tir.

Ver vet trinken?
Ikh mit dir.

(Tiny bird, tiny bird/ Peep-peep-peep/ Where is your daddy?/ Away on a trip./ What will he bring?/ A mug of beer./ Where will he put it?/ Behind the door./ Who will drink it?/ I with you.)

He disembarked at the terminus amid the jostling of passengers elated that he had arrived in the city of his dreams in the throws of giving birth to a new species of music. A mecca to musicians, it attracted a kaleidoscope of people who mixed as freely as the myriad of insects pollinating a lush garden.

With his precious trumpet clutched under one arm and his suitcase dangling from the other, Aaron stood looking about, waiting for Papa Laine, who, on the recommendation of Mr. Schultz, had agreed to take the novice under his wing. Laine had established the Reliance Brass Band in the 1880s, and was respected both as a pioneer of jazz and nurturer of musical talent.

A man in a smart blue jacket with gold buttons and trim, and a cornet under his arm, raced onto the platform. *Must be Laine,* Aaron said to himself, and ran forward to greet him.

"Sorry I'm late," Laine apologized, shaking hands with Aaron. "Just got finished playing a funeral parade. Are you hungry?" Without waiting for his new apprentice to reply, he went on, "Let's go get a bowl of gumbo at Chez Marie's, and some jambalaya. My, my, I can use some jambalaya."

Aaron, having eaten strictly kosher food all his life, too easily followed his new mentor toward his first nonkosher, or *treif,* meal. Just as his father had feared he took the path of least resistance, to taste the forbidden delights of Creole cuisine. After the repast the pair migrated to several bars and dance clubs, where they sat absorbed in the new sound of dance bands, which softened the loud brasses with the mellow tones of violin, guitar, and string bass.

It was well past midnight by the time they arrived at 32 Royale Street, where Laine had rented a room for his young protégé. "That's your place," the cornetist said, stabbing a lighted cigarette in the direction of a decaying, but still gracious French-style mansion. In the flickering gaslight Aaron saw Laine's nostrils flare as he brought his face close to Aaron's ear and hissed, "Boy, stay away from too much booze, and stay away from gambling." He paused to let his warning sink in. Then, tapping his index finger into Aaron 's forearm to punctuate each word, he cautioned, "And steer clear of prostitutes if you don't want to end up just another stiff floating down the mighty Mississippi."

The night of revelry, the musician's paternal advice, and his physical closeness induced an unexpected feeling of camaraderie, but before Aaron could thank him, Laine melted into the shadows. Alone, Aaron stood on the sidewalk, absorbing the elation of the exciting, risky life opening up to him.

He knew he should find his room and lie down, but despite his fatigue and the booze he had sampled, he was too overwrought to sleep. He paced the sidewalk in front of his new home, still clutching his trumpet and suitcase, admiring its ornate balconies, fanciful wrought-iron balustrades and dormer windows set into rounded gables. The waning moon drifted like a recumbent silver bowl above the city. A breathless hush had descended in this interim between night and dawn, and he shut his eyes, leaned against a lamppost, and felt a drowsy gladness.

The sudden, plaintive notes of a flute broke Aaron's reverie. He roused himself to follow the music into the courtyard. The sound seemed to come from the branches of an old magnolia tree but he could see nothing in the dark tangle of foliage. He walked around the tree, trying not to step on broken pottery, mounds of oyster shells, and discarded household junk littering its base. "Is anyone there?" he called up.

The music ceased, and in its place he heard, "You one of Papa Laine's protégés?"

"Why, yes I am, sir."

A chuckle like oil gurgling from a narrow-throated bottle came down to him, followed by the rustle of someone scrambling through the branches. In the dark, Aaron could just make out a bush of hair surrounding a round head like a coiled aura.

185

"Bo Riddles." A hand thrust out, Aaron shook it.

"Aaron Rosen. Pleasure to meet you, sir."

"You the one rented the room at the top," Bo stated. "I'll take you up."

He followed Bo up a creaking flight of stairs, trying not to stumble over loose treads.

"This will be your home sweet home. But watch out for the landlord; he's a mean one!" Bo said as he bent to open the door with a large iron key.

Inside, Aaron set his belongings down on the small bed and looked around the narrow room he would call home. It smelled of mildew, cigarette smoke, and stale liquor. Wallpaper peeled off the walls, and the floor sagged. He opened the French doors at one end and found himself on a wide balcony of ornate iron grillwork. It looked onto the courtyard overgrown with weeds, strewn with trash, strung with washing lines, all shaded by the beautiful magnolia. *I will sit out here under the stars and play my trumpet*, he thought, and his heart fluttered against his chest like a nightingale about to be released from its cage.

Just before dawn an insistent banging on his door awakened Aaron.

"Who is it?" He mumbled.

"It's your landlord."

The landlord? What would he want so early? He called out groggily, "What's wrong?"

"You need to pay me the rent," said a voice cold and rough as a discarded razor.

Sleepy and naked, he rolled out of bed, fell to the floor with a painful thump, struggled to his feet and grabbed the sheet to cover himself. He opened the door a crack to find the landlord peering at him with dull eyes, sweating and obese, and a mouth twisted into a belligerent sneer. Aaron handed over the first month's rent, and the man went away without a word of welcome or thanks. When he had disappeared down the gloomy stairwell, Aaron stepped out onto the balcony in his improvised toga and looked up at the sky above. It was hazy and leaden, without a moon or stars, impenetrable and stagnant. Feeling lost and unsure, he retreated inside, urinated, and drank a mouthful of warm brown water from the leaking faucet. Soon after, Bo knocked on the door to walk him to the docks, declaring that all musicians had to find a day job while waiting for their musical careers to take off.

By daylight Aaron saw that his lodgings were close to the red-light district. The streets thronged with an astonishing stew of people who like him had come to seek their fortune: French, Creole, Italian, Irish, African, Caribbean, German, Mexican, and American Indian. His heart sank as he saw the kind of longshoreman work Bo was offering. He would toil all day like a slave in Egypt loading heavy bales of cotton onto ships bound for England, and unloading great claws of green bananas from South America. Many of the laborers looked wretched and worn down, others seemed tough and spoiling for a fight.

"How can you stand work like this?" Aaron said, shuffling uncomfortably from foot to foot.

"You get used to it," Bo answered, rolling his eyes.

"I can't do this; it's not fit even for beasts!" From Bo's resentful glare, Aaron knew that he had said the wrong thing.

"I told you, I need the dough, man!" Bo turned on his heels and walked away. Watching him join the dockworkers, the would-be musician sent up a prayer that his stipend from his father along with what he might earn as an apprentice with Laine's band would be sufficient to support him through the coming trial year. He turned on his heels and headed back into the streets.

In New Orleans he soon fell into a routine. At night he played with the Reliance Band, filling in with the easy parts on the trumpet, learning by listening attentively to each musician's special style. He returned to his room well after midnight, tired but burning with the desire to play as thrillingly as the musicians in the band. Clamping a pillow over his ears to shut out the city's late-night din, he tried to sleep, finally sinking from fatigue into uneasy dreams.

At dawn he woke to the cacophony of the city in motion: the clatter of horses' hooves, the rumble of carts and carriages, the whistle of steamboats, the hoot of tugs, the shouts of vendors. Bleary-eyed and half-asleep, he splashed water over his face. Then he made his way to a cafe near the river to sip strong coffee with a hint of bitter chicory and munch on hot beignets powdered with sugar, while monitoring the street life around him.

Revived, he returned to his balcony to practice the trumpet, ignoring the whining mosquitoes and the buzzing flies, intent on developing technical virtuosity with his tongue and fingers to produce spine tingling high notes and somber low notes that would express the joy and pain, fulfillment and frustration, peace and anguish he felt inside. At noon the cry of hawkers selling gumbo and crawfish drew him downstairs for a snack. In the late afternoon he, like many in the city, took a much-needed catnap to rest up for the evening's entertainment.

As night fell, the eager student explored the city, ducking into jazz halls, nightclubs, and dance halls, feeling at once overwhelmed and exhilarated by the life pulsing around him. He paused to watch street musicians and tap dancers, enthralled by their inventiveness and exuberance. The pungent smells of seafood, hot peppers, and fried pastry combined with the heady perfume of magnolias and the odors of sour beer, vomit, perspiration, and urine invaded his senses. Women beckoned from the doors of smoky saloons and the windows of cheap dives; the almost unbearable stirring in his loins emboldened him and he vowed that soon he would take one that he fancied. Reluctantly, he walked on, stepping to the rhythm of plunking banjos and tinkling pianos rising above the scraping of chairs, the chiming of glass and cursing of drunks, dreaming all the while of composing a "street symphony" that would incorporate these discordant sounds.

New Orleans was a Turkish steam bath of sensations that opened his pores and let the music seep in. The place was awash with harmonies of every variety; Italian operas, French music-hall tunes, Creole ditties, minstrel songs, African spirituals, American, Italian, and Cuban beats, the latest hits from New York, and even German polkas and marches. Best of all there was

188

ragtime and blues melding into jazz—New Orleans style jazz in its vibrant and explosive beginnings. Aaron first heard the word "jazz" used in Storyville, the red-light district of the city, as a slang word for "licentious," and indeed the music itself carried the insistent sexual energy and spiritual freedom of the town giving birth to it.

He felt liberated in this multicolored, sensuous world, free of the restrictions that bound him in Ricksburg, the son of Yakov and Chana. He felt no calling to follow their narrow path, the way of his ancestors that had brought so much sorrow; he did not wish to be freighted down with the Rosen legacy. Yet he could not dismiss the pledge he had made to his father.

Upon his departure from Ricksburg, his parents had given him letters of introduction to friends, urging him to contact them. Aaron had been so busy and excited that weeks passed before he called upon them. To keep his promise, and to alleviate his conscience, he first visited David and Miriam Beekman, business acquaintances of the Rosens. They kindly invited him to a Shabbat dinner.

The following Friday, Aaron rode the Street Railway to the Beekmans' grand home on St. Charles, which backed up to shotgun houses and Creole cottages of the African, American, and Irish working class neighborhoods. He arrived late, perspiring and disheveled, explaining that he had had a gig in a funeral parade in the Vieux Carré.

A native of Berlin, Mr. Beekman was the proprietor of a flourishing downtown department store. His wife, Miriam, was fashionable and gregarious, and hailed from Cologne, Germany. In startling contrast to the pious, down-to-earth shtetl Jews so familiar to Aaron, the Beekmans were Reform Jews—evidently not something his father had realized—and they were sophisticated, their imposing home filled with antiques and paintings.

Over dinner, the couple and their equally elegant guests discussed plans for an upcoming fund-raising banquet for widows and orphans sponsored by a Jewish charitable organization. To his amazement the menu was to feature green

189

turtle soup, oysters, and soft shell crabs, all strictly prohibited by kosher dietary laws.

From the conversation around the table, it soon became evident that his hosts and their friends actively participated in the broader social life of New Orleans, and did not center their lives exclusively on the Reform synagogue, Temple Emanu-El. This was Aaron's first direct experience with such a worldly life style, as Orthodox and Reform Jews, both in Ricksburg and New Orleans, rarely socialized, though they lived within a few blocks of one another. While he fantasized about what it would be like to possess the Beekmans' wealth and sophistication, he did not feel comfortable in their world; it was too cliquish, and, in its own way, just as confining as the one to which his parents belonged.

Next, the young musician paid an obligatory visit to Myron and Dell Solomon. The Solomons, a taciturn elderly couple, were Orthodox Jews from Lithuania. They attended the small shul, Kenesseth Israel, in the Crandolet Street neighborhood, the heart of the Jewish district. Like the Rosens, the Solomons owned a bakery on Dryades Street, the commercial center for Eastern European Jews, where kosher butchers, shochets, and delicatessens catered to those who needed kosher products and craved the comforting taste of foods from home. It was all too familiar to Aaron. The Solomons were a painful reminder of the promises he was failing to keep, and he disliked the bouts of guilt these visits brought on. He soon found excuses to decline the Beekmans' and Solomons' invitations to meals or to attend services with them.

He could not resist the lure of his musical pursuits or his fascinating, eclectic mix of new friends. The longer he lived in New Orleans, the stronger and more thrilling its magnetism, and the more distant and alienated he became from life in Ricksburg. Here a budding musician could reinvent himself in any fashion he chose.

On Sundays he began going with his fellow musicians to the open field, known as Congo Square, to see the Africans make music with an uninhibited sensuality he had never known. The drummers clad in colorful caftans, their teeth gleaming like ivory,

190

their ebony skin glistening with sweat, played drum rhythms derived from voodoo and Cuban habanera, unlike any Aaron had heard. His heart leapt with the very first tap-tap-tap of the snare drums, his body pulsed to the bass drum's somber boom-boom-boom. The din resounded in his head and set his hands and feet in motion. The drumming subtly changed as new rhythms began to overlap one another like colored veils, and the brass instruments howled their response. The Africans played on and on; compelling him to keep on dancing, clapping and singing, until he came out of his trance to find himself in the middle of the street in the thick of a crowd. He returned many Sundays to join the revelers in their insatiable appetite for music that transcended all classes and races.

Jazz bands, flourishing like honeysuckle vines, were in constant demand at dance parties, parades, cabarets, sporting events, riverboat excursions, political rallies, and church socials. Even funeral processions had to have their brass band. When Laine asked Aaron to play at the funerals, he was especially thrilled.

Wearing the royal blue uniform and cap with gold trim, Aaron tuned up while the procession gathered and spilled out onto the streets. Bam! Boom! Bam! went the drum. On the slow march to the cemetery the musicians chose subdued, sad songs. On the way back they broke into exuberant marches to celebrate the departed's journey to heaven. At a signal from the grand marshal, the pace quickened and Aaron strutted with the crowds dancing alongside, swirling around him, and abandoning themselves to the music as it rose to a crescendo. When the parade ended, Aaron itched to keep going, even though his feet were tired and his mouth parched.

When Laine, at last, hired him to play for some special events other than funerals, he could not suppress a loud whoop—though Papa Laine cautioned his apprentice that he was not ready to take him on as a full-fledged member of the Reliance Brass Band. Stung by this judgment, Aaron worked harder than ever to improve, gradually displaying the skills honed during the hours of practice on the balcony. Finally, his mentor invited him

191

to join the band at the nightspots and music halls where they were the featured entertainment.

The group included a bass drummer, a clarinetist, a trombone player, Papa on cornet, and Aaron on trumpet. Aaron loved playing jazz New Orleans style, with the musicians weaving separate melodies into a captivating counterpoint—a "hot" sound that allowed for, and demanded embellishment and improvisation. The cornet would begin punching out the melody, passing it from instrument to instrument, with the trombone smearing a countermelody and the clarinet weaving through it all with its delicate filigree.

As the trumpeter's probationary year drew to a close, he became increasingly apprehensive. If Papa Laine did not offer him a place in the band as a fully-fledged member, he would have little means of supporting himself. His situation was dire. He had failed to keep his promises and his parents were certain to cut off his allowance. If that happened, Aaron knew that it would be necessary for him to pursue a profession as his father wished him to do. Yet there was something within him that was stronger than rationality: something that grew and grew and beat for freedom; that made him climb and climb to test his gifts to their utmost limits. For all the force of his father's will, the voices that reached him were those that chimed with his own inner voice, with the musicians who said: *Twenty years from now I want to say I did it. And I would do it again!*

As the last month approached, and the allowance his father had granted him would cease, nightmares invaded Aaron's sleep. He would awake, tangled in damp sheets, to the awful realization that his stay in New Orleans might soon come to end.

When, finally, Laine offered his trumpeter the possibility of going on tour, the blood rushed to his head. Slapping the bandleader on the back, he yelled, "You won't be sorry!"

"Slow down" Laine cautioned, with a twinkle in his eye, "Let's hear what the other musicians have to say."

Harry, the clarinetist, was the first to give Aaron his blessing: "There's no end to this boy's imagination. He can play a

192

chorus eight or ten different ways." With Harry's blessing, Aaron knew for sure that he would be counted in; the rest would follow suit.

The group traveled along the Gulf Coast, up the lazy Mississippi to Memphis, and as far as Chicago. Aaron savored his first taste of life on the road, sending souvenir postcards home to his parents and friends. After six months of touring, he returned to New Orleans, relishing his triumph. That he had succeeded in carving a place for himself as a jazz musician was a heady brew. His newly minted independence opened fresh avenues that he itched to explore. With money jingling in his pocket, Aaron decided to treat himself to a front row seat of a lavish performance at the French Opera House.

↞16↠

Aaron and Marlene

He who has no wife is not a proper man. He lives without joy and blessing.

Talmud

During the opera Aaron's eyes were drawn again and again to a large-boned, handsome woman on stage, with a moon-pale face, a luxuriant tangle of auburn hair, strong patrician nose, distinctive high forehead, and intense blue eyes. The singer had a supporting role in the opera, but Aaron could hear her voice soaring above all the others, and it filled him like pure water gushing from an underground spring into a dry well. The tallest member of the cast, she floated on the hazy penumbra cast by the foot lights, as regally as a ship upon the waves. After the performance he made it his business to find out who she was. Her name was Marlene McCormack, and she hailed from County Cork, Ireland, by way of Boston.

For days he loitered at the back entrance to the opera house, hoping to talk to her. Whenever he caught sight of the captivating Irish singer, some admirer accompanied her. He grew bolder and sent her an invitation to hear him play at the Creole Club. To his delight, she showed up. Several years older than he, at first she treated Aaron as an impressionable youngster who shared her love of music. Once she came to appreciate the depth of his passion for music, they began to attend musical events of every sort. Marlene enjoyed his sunny personality, his nonstop laughter, his irreverent wisecracking.

When Marlene went on tour with the opera company, to her astonishment her would-be suitor got leave from Papa Laine and followed along for a week, snatching time with her between rehearsals and performances. He loved everything about her: the way her arms floated like wings when she danced, the way she drew her breathe in between her strong white teeth when she sang, the way her voice rose and fell with an Irish lilt when she was excited, the way she smiled when she caught his impassioned gaze reading her own desirability and beauty in it. To his misery he had promised to rejoin Laine's Band; after that brief time together he returned to New Orleans, while Marlene continued on.

Three months later, when the tour came to an end, Aaron rushed backstage to declare his undying love for Marlene.

"I admire your musical gifts, and I love your company," Marlene said, her voice husky with tears, "And I will always care for you like a sister cares for a brother." Before he could respond she added, "While on tour I became engaged to Mario Puzzi, a tenor with the opera company."

His humiliation was so abrupt and painful, that he spun around four times tipping over a vase of roses before he found the exit. Then he shoved the door open and rushed off into the wet, foggy night.

Heartsick, Aaron walked the streets for hours. He noticed couples holding hands, leaning into one another with the look of love in their eyes, and he watched them jealously. He drifted around all night, shrouded in the mist rising from the Mississippi, willing himself to put Marlene in the past. He needed to get away. He packed his bags and headed to Los Angeles.

He landed a place with the Sunset Creole Band, in the forefront of jazz music on the West Coast. Although he enjoyed playing with the band, he missed New Orleans. In Los Angeles, jazz was still in its infancy, just entertainment for the few; in New Orleans, it was part of the fabric of everyday life. He yearned to be parading in the streets with Papa Laine, playing at weddings and funerals, weaving the intricate, heart-pounding rhythms that set people jiving. He stuck it out in Los Angeles for a year before returning to New Orleans. There he ran into a friend who told him that Marlene had broken off her engagement and that she was still with the opera company. The jilted suitor did not hesitate; he swung into action. Borrowing an elegant carriage from a wealthy patron of jazz, he rode to the alley behind the opera house at a fast clip. Once there, he was not at all sure what he would do when Marlene emerged. To his joy the instant she spotted him, her deep blue eyes widened, the color rose high on her cheeks, she threw back her head as if she would shout to the moon, and cried, "Aaron! Where on Earth did you get this contraption?"

He jumped out and took her hands in his, kissed them, and drew her up onto the seat. He traced the outline of her regal profile, and let his fingertips linger on her lips before kissing her mouth. They broke apart only when the other performers emerged from the building and gathered around to gape at them.

"Let's go," Marlene whispered.

He pulled on the reins and as the horses trotted away he leaned over and kissed his darling again. When he released her, she said with a glint of tears in her eyes, "My, my Aaron, you've grown up fast on the West Coast!"

Aaron knew then that she no longer regarded him as her little brother. Giddy with happiness, he wanted to hold her full body close, to stroke her shining hair, to feel her sweet breath on his face, to look deep into her beautiful eyes. Marlene put her hand on his arm and squeezed it; a burning thrill rushed through him. Sitting side-by-side on the carriage seat, he had the distinct sensation that they were floating, rocking through a sea of love, suspended in time, soon to be lovers, forever.

From the start, the opera singer had an unerring instinct for tapping into the wellspring of Aaron's musical inspiration. This natural intuition created an almost mystical connection between the two that could not easily be broken. With Marlene's encouragement, Aaron started his own band, which he named the Irish Rose Jazz Opera Band in her honor. Marlene agreed to sing with the band even though women were not well accepted in jazz groups. The range and clarity of her voice were great assets, and in no small measure promoted the band as something special.

When the trumpeter played, his whole appearance was transformed. Marlene recalled how once his loose-limbed, skinny frame had amused her. Without meaning to be cruel, she had dubbed him "Mr. Scarecrow." His limbs seemed too insecurely attached to his body, and his face composed of odds and ends: thick dark hair, deep-set, smoldering black eyes, a nose with a hump in it, jaws that jutted awkwardly. But his body became an instrument of mystical power when he put the trumpet to his lips and drew music directly from his soul. Then she saw the sensuousness of his full lips puckered tightly around the trumpet's mouthpiece, the delicate beauty, yet surprising strength of his long fingers as if threaded with steel wires, dancing over the trumpet's stops. There was a sexual aura to him as he swayed to the music that set her heart racing.

Despite their shared bliss, the shadow of his father's disapproval hovered over them. Without a shred of a doubt to ease him, Aaron knew his parents would be outraged if he married out of the faith, so he told Marlene that it would be best to keep their relationship secret from them for the present. When his lover questioned the need for deception he attempted to downplay it. Whenever he returned to Ricksburg for a few days to observe the Jewish High Holidays, he did not invite Marlene to accompany him. He told her that he saw no reason to cause his parents grief. But in his heart he knew that their secret, like a time bomb ticking, would one day explode in their faces.

In the meantime, the Irish Rose Band was gaining in reputation. Just months after forming the ensemble, they landed a steady gig at the Cafe Souris near the port in the French Market area of the Vieux Carré. Sandwiched between a ship's chandler on the lower floor and the proprietor's residence above, the cafe was a favorite hangout for musicians and jazz aficionados.

One evening after their performance, the pair were unwinding over a glass of cold beer. Harry, the clarinetist from Papa Laine's Band, who often joined them for a jam session, came

197

through the door. For a while they exchanged gossip about the local scene, then Harry asked teasingly when the two of them were planning to get hitched. A lazy grin spread across Aaron's face and he rolled his eyes sheepishly.

Marlene's eyes flashed, and with a forced smile she said, "Harry, me boy, that's a question I've been asking meself." Then she scraped back her chair, and grabbed her shawl and purse. Aaron reached over and grasped her elbow, but she pulled away, and he had to trot after her.

In the carriage, they clopped along in silence while he struggled to find words to explain, yet again, why his parents would vehemently oppose their getting married. In the light of a gas lamp he saw two circles of red burning on her cheeks. To mollify her, he whispered gently in her ear, "In Yiddish, they say if you are lucky enough to find your soul mate then it's *bashert*, it's destined to be. Marlene, you are my bashert."

She shot back, "That's enough of your nonsense for one night."

He pleaded, "How can I convince you of the bitterness and sorrow our marriage would cause my parents."

"Begorrah, they haven't set eyes on the likes of me, so how can they find fault with me?" Marlene retorted, slipping into Irish brogue, a sure sign that she was upset.

"It's not you personally they would dislike, it's who you are. Anyway, who could find fault with you, my beautiful Irish rose."

"That's enough blarney, just give it to me straight?"

Grappling to explain the world according to Yakov and Chana, he chose his words carefully. "With my parents there's no way to leave God out of the reckoning. The Torah forbids a Jew to marry someone who is not of their religion. They are Orthodox Jews who live strictly by the commandments set down in our Torah. And they expect me to do the same."

"You're a grown man, why are you so afraid of them?"

"I admit I'm scared of my Dad," he said gloomily.

"You have the right to make your own choices," she declared hotly.

"My father doesn't see it that way. He accuses me of being a rebel for choosing to become a musician—which in his view is not a respectable way to make a living."

"Ahh, Aaron my darling rebel, surely *you* can stand up to him!"

To mask his embarrassment he blew out his cheeks, and beat his chest.

"Stop playing the fool. Have you honestly tried to talk to your father?"

"It would do as much good as telling him to stop breathing." He put his arm around Marlene's shoulders, and he could feel the tension in her. "Can you try to understand that my father believes that as his son it's my responsibility to carry on the traditions of our people?"

Aaron caught the bewilderment in her eyes.

"It's like . . . well, like I'm the heir apparent of his kingdom. You see I will be the next inheritor of our family Torah. It's over a hundred years old, and my father carried it in his arms from the old country. To him, marrying out of my faith would be the same as shunning my birthright . . . you know like a prince abdicating the throne brings shame and dishonor to his family and his nation."

She threw back her head and laughed. "That's going entirely too far!"

"It's no joke, my father lives and will die by the laws of our religion, of *our* family Torah to which I am the heir. It expressly forbids and does not even recognize marriages between Jews and those of other faiths." His voice was hoarse with emotion. An image of his father rose up in his mind; his face distorted by rage, his mouth twisted in a snarl of pain, a trembling finger condemning him. These memories filled him with guilt and with sorrow.

Taking her hands in his, he pleaded, "Is it so hard to understand? Don't Catholics frown on interfaith marriages?"

"I suppose so," Marlene said, massaging her brow. "When my cousin Mary Catherine married a Protestant, the church required her fiancé, Shamus Murphy, to sign a document

199

pledging that their children would be raised Catholic. That caused a great ruckus within the Murphy family."

"And so we Jews are also against interfaith marriages especially because of the children being lost to our religion."

They were silent for a while. Then Marlene wrapped her shaking arms around Aaron's waist, and whispered, "I'm not sure I want children."

He shut his eyes to let what she had just said sink in. Then he leaned over and kissed her. "I love you, and always will no matter what."

The carriage passed from the shadows into a flare of light from a saloon window, and the Irish singer saw that her lover was close to tears. The bitter, hollow place in her heart expanded with a new tenderness. "It's okay, me boy. I love you too." At that moment the family storms they knew would surely come seemed far away.

Each time Aaron visited Ricksburg, Chana nagged him about getting married. "The Talmud says, 'He who has no wife is not a proper man. He lives without joy and blessing.'"

"Ma, it's not easy to find a woman who would be good enough for your son," he teased.

Chana was not so easily fooled. She noticed the radiance in his eyes, the rosy color in his cheeks, his secret smiles, and suspected that her son was in love. She could only conclude that the woman was not acceptable to the family, which meant she was not Jewish. Still, the good woman decided not to pry, hoping that his love affair would run its course.

Marlene's ability to compromise, absorbed at a tender age, permitted Aaron to keep up the deception. Difficult as it was, she conceded to Aaron's wish for secrecy. Unlike Aaron she had no parental opposition; her parents had died when she was quite young, and an aunt, desperately poor, living on public assistance with a brood of her own, had taken her in. The young orphan had learned how to be accommodating in order to survive. Her savior turned out to be Sister Dolan, the choir mistress of the Catholic Church she attended. The nun recognized the native beauty of Marlene's voice and encouraged her to develop her talent. The young singer had made her way to Boston with nothing but a letter of introduction from the Sister. After a few months in the city, on a dare, she joined an Irish band, and traveled with them to the balmy southern port of New Orleans. There she had the good fortune to be spotted by a noted voice teacher, who saw her potential, and nurtured it.

In their musical world, the couple lived together, made music together, and shared their gifts with the brilliant community of New Orleans jazzmen. In the easygoing, insulated world, they flourished like tropical plants in a hothouse. In a sense they were married to music alone, and neither gave thought to having children. When Marlene discovered to her amazement that she was pregnant, they were shocked and unsettled. Then, as the miracle of it seeped into them, they cried with gratitude.

With a child on the way, Marlene now insisted that they should marry, and Aaron agreed. The conflict with his parents he had dreaded for so long had finally arrived. He tried to stay calm, but the prospect of a terrible row made him feel ill. With the crisis looming, he got up the courage to ask Marlene if she would consider converting to Judaism.

At first she refused to take him seriously, declaring, "You can take the girl out of Ireland, but you can't take the religion out of the girl." When Aaron persisted, she retorted that he was no more a practicing Jew than she was a practicing Catholic. He tried to explain that she should convert if only for the sake of family unity; if she did it would blunt his father's disapproval, and pave the way for the acceptance of their grandchild. She countered that it would be hypocritical to convert without a shred of spiritual commitment. He would just have to face his father like a man. Over the next days they continued this dialogue without coming to a resolution.

Then one evening in the carriage on their way home from a performance, without preamble, Marlene declared that Aaron had finally overcome her resistance. She had made up her mind to go to his "church" the next day, and to convert in order to keep the peace. To her bewilderment, Aaron eyes widened in surprise,

201

then he threw back his head and exclaimed, "Oh, if only it were that easy!"

When she calmed down, he explained that to become a Jewess was a complicated process. First, she would have to be interviewed by a rabbi to prove that she was sincere. Then she would need to study under his supervision for many months. After that she would have to pass a test and undergo a series of conversion rituals.

Now it was her turn to guffaw. She said Aaron had to be touched in the head to think she would go through all that. She didn't want to convince a rabbi of her sincerity, and she had no interest in studying; she had no head for such things. Taking Marlene's hands in his, he said he understood.

Nevertheless, the stress of having to face his father took a toll on them both; spats broke out between them too frequently. They would begin talking about something trivial, which soon devolved into a heated argument. The unacknowledged source of their quarrels was the fear of Yakov Rosen's wrath. Concerned about their emotional stability, Marlene said that even if she didn't convert, she would concede to raising their child as a Jew. However, she warned him that he would have to shoulder that responsibility on his own. Now the wayward son had no choice but to resign himself to the dreaded dispute he had postponed for so long by living a life of subterfuge. It was his fervent hope that in time his father would find a way to accept his wife and child, and the family would settle into a workable, if fragile relationship.

ॐ 17 ॐ

The Power of the Torah

Neither shall you make marriages with them; your daughter you shall not give to his son nor his daughter shall you take for your son, for they will turn away from following me.

Torah

As Marlene's pregnancy moved into its second trimester, Aaron could no longer delay breaking the news to his parents. On his next visit home, he waited until he was alone with his mother in the kitchen where she was most at ease. Perched on a stool, Aaron watched her capable hands chop and slice vegetables for the Sabbath meal. Light from the window showed the stains on the white apron that covered her heavy breasts, the sheen of her hair just beginning to gray twisted into a bun at the nape of her neck, and the fine lines around her eyes and mouth. With a deft movement she cut an onion in half, exposing its fleshy layers. The pungent oils drew moisture from Aaron's eyes, nature's watery defense, not genuine tears of sorrow but false tears revealing those inside him. He drew in a deep breath, and tried to marshal his courage.

With throat closing and heart pounding, Aaron willed himself to tell her that he planned to marry Marlene, that she was pregnant with his child, and that he wanted their acceptance in spite of their religious principles. Unhinged by emotion, he gestured awkwardly, blushed, and stumbled over his words. His mother listened without comment, but he could see the lines deepening around her mouth and her eyes narrowing.

When he had finished, Chana dropped the knife on the chopping board, slumped into a chair, and sat with her head bowed.

Aaron waited in silence.

When she finally looked up there were tears of reproach in her eyes. "He will never forgive you! You broke your promise to him, and to me, to keep your *Yiddishkeit*."

"I'm sorry. Ma, I love Marlene, please help me . . ." he pleaded. "Now that a child's on the way, you have to consider that."

In the heavy silence that followed, the wayward son sat with eyes downcast, listening to his mother's labored breathing.

Finally, Chana asked, "Does that woman you are about to marry have a commitment to keeping a Jewish home?"

"Ma, she has agreed that our child will be raised as a Jew."

"You mean she is not prepared to convert to Judaism?"

"Believe me, we have discussed it."

"What good is discussion without action?"

"Marlene says that she will consider it only if she feels a spiritual calling to do so."

Devastated, Chana took to her bed where she prayed for guidance. She could think of no easy way to tell Yakov that he was about to have a grandchild conceived out of wedlock, by a woman who was not of their faith.

Three more miserable days dragged by, and then it was time for Aaron to return to New Orleans. Chana heaved herself out of bed and readied for the battle between father and son.

With his mother's complicity, Aaron prepared to face his father's wrath. After faltering through the speech he had rehearsed so many times in his head, he saw with a stab of fear his father's face turning to stone. As he gazed pleadingly at him, he noticed that he had grown prematurely old; his red beard was streaked with gray, and deep lines bisected the space between his eyebrows in the manner of someone who had spent a lifetime frowning. Aaron stood in the middle of the parlor, bracing himself for what was to come.

Aiming a trembling finger at his son, Yakov commanded, "I forbid you to marry this woman!"

A tight band constricted Aaron's heart; his father had demanded what he could not, would not do.

"Papa, please listen to me. I promise that I will raise my child as a Jew!"

"How can your child be a Jew when the mother is a gentile?"

"Marlene and I have agreed to raise our child as a Jew," Aaron implored

"Still the child will not be a Jew."

"He can convert to Judaism himself when he is an adult."

"You will bring terrible shame upon me and destroy our family's *yichus*. You will break the Torah's commandments!"

"You can punish me, but I beg you, do not blame my wife or your grandchild. "

"You have no pride in your heritage!"

"If you cannot find it in your heart to forgive me, I understand. I never wanted to hurt you. I'm sorry that I can't devote my life to following Judaism, as you wish me to do."

He saw his mother's mouth tighten into a bitter line, "Yakov, please listen, your son is asking for your forgiveness! "

The silence that followed was like the split second of lightning that precedes an explosion of thunder.

"Go! Get out of my house. Get out of my sight!" Yakov commanded. The defiant son turned and fled upstairs as though a beast, crouching and ravenous, was about to tear him apart.

As he flung his few belongings into a suitcase, Aaron felt like a whipped cur. He castigated himself for his foolishness, for believing that he had the freedom to choose how to live his life without consequences. He had been seduced by the lifestyle of New Orleans, thumbed his nose at tradition, and ignored his religion as perilously as a ship disregarding a lighthouse signal near a rocky coast. He had dared to hope that there existed a remote possibility of winning his father over.

Dragging his feet, he descended the stairs, walked out onto the street and stood, sick at heart, looking back at the familiar childhood home from which he had been banished. A full moon rose above the rooftops, pouring its cold blue light over bare branches and shuttered windowpanes.

Inside the house Yakov sat slumped over the kitchen table, ranting against his son. "If that woman does not convert to Judaism, I'll refuse to acknowledge their union. I'll cut off all contact with them. I'll disown him, strip him of his right to inherit the Rosen Torah." He raged on, "I'll go into mourning, and say the prayer for the dead." Yes, he would sit *shiva* for the prescribed seven days and say the Mourner's Kaddish. His son would be dead to him from that day on. He fumed on and on. His wife's frantic efforts to calm him served only to set off yet one more tirade.

The moment Aaron stepped onto the station platform in New Orleans, Marlene knew by the slouch of his shoulders and the droop of his eyelids that the meeting with his parents had gone badly.

"Aaron? Are you all right?"

"Yes."

"You look bad."

He shrugged. "I'm fine, really. Just a little tired, I guess. A headache."

"Let's take the trolley car home."

As they rocked along, Aaron sat awkwardly stooped with his hands gripping his knees.

Marlene squeezed his arm, gently. "Please tell me what's wrong."

"My father kicked me out. That's what's wrong!"

"Jesus and Mary!"

"Just what I dreaded."

"That's terrible."

"He demands that you convert to Judaism." His voice faltered.

If he thought he would get sympathy from his fiancée, he was wrong. "Your father won't accord me the dignity of meeting me, but he believes he has the right to order me to change my religion!" she retorted, in a loud voice. Several passengers

206

swiveled in their seats to look at her, only to be met by an angry glare.

"True, he doesn't have the right," Aaron agreed miserably.

The rest of the journey was made in silence.

After a warm bath, Marlene's agitation finally subsided enough to console her dejected husband. While they could see no immediate solution to regaining his father's trust, he and Marlene had to believe that Yakov would relent when his grandchild arrived. Taking Marlene in his arms, Aaron declared fervently that they would go down to city hall to be married in a civil ceremony the very next day.

Marlene gave birth to Abraham Shaul Rosen, on June 28, 1914 — the day the Archduke Franz Ferdinand, heir to the throne of the Austro-Hungarian Empire, was assassinated unleashing the ravenous beasts of war. They had chosen the name Abraham in honor of Marlene's father Abracham, the Irish version, and Shaul Rosen, Yakov's father, the newborn's deceased great-grandfather.

On the night of his son's birth, Aaron received a message that his wife was in labor and rushed from the Cafe Souris, to find Marlene, assisted by an experienced midwife, in the last stages of a difficult labor. Marlene squeezed her eyes tightly shut against the unrelenting pain, and cried to God for help. Great throbbing waves threatened to pull her under, snuff out the flame that was her very existence. Finally, mercifully, the new life struggling to be born, with a great howl of protest, smeared with mucus, cradled in the gentle work-worn hands of the midwife, released her body, bruised, ripped, and battered, back to her.

After long, anxious hours, Aaron gazed with love and awe at the tiny, wizened boy, with a delicate fuzz of red hair, and bright, green eyes. When his wife lifted their son's hungry mouth to her breast, Aaron saw that the newborn child bore an unmistakable resemblance to his father. A lump rose in his throat. *Surely my father will accept this child as his grandson and heir, even if he rejects me*, he thought, and a sudden flush of triumph shot through his veins.

Chana wrote poignant letters declaring that she longed to see her grandson, Abraham Shaul, the namesake of Yakov's father. Yet she dared not go against her husband's wishes — that would only make matters worse. She urged her son to understand that his father had disowned him because a devout Jew had no choice but to follow Hashem's divine commandments. It was not in his power to change them to suit himself, even it the consequence meant sundering himself from the son he loved. Still, Chana promised to do what she could to bring about a change of heart, and to come as soon as the time was right.

The months passed without a word or sign from Yakov, when just the smallest gesture would have served as an act of compassion to assuage the rift between father and son. It wounded the new parents deeply that the grandfather refused to acknowledge his only grandson.

Still Aaron swore that no matter how long he had to wait, he could not relinquish the hope that his father would one day forgive him, and embrace his grandson.

✺18✺

Abraham Rosen Coming of Age

"Today I have become a man."

Bar Mitzvah boy

The Rosens were affectionate but inattentive parents; neither could depart for long from the life they had built around jazz. Music defined them; in that they were secure. As long as Aaron held a horn to his lips, he would always find purpose and joie de vivre. New Orleans was in an economic decline and many ambitious players had migrated to greener pastures in Chicago and Los Angeles, but thanks to their loyal fans, Aaron and Marlene were able to keep their band together.

When they were not on tour or playing at local nightspots, they spent long hours at the city's cafes and nightclubs, socializing with the musicians and their followers. The couple worked at night and slept till noon, leaving little time to care for or to play with their child. They engaged a Creole woman, Jeanette Grace, to serve as his nanny. From an early age, Abraham amused himself under her watchful eyes, and explored the city's neighborhoods with her.

The boy and his nanny set out each morning for the French Market near the docks, her ample torso covered with a crisp, white apron, a big basket hooked in the crook of her arm thick as an Andouille sausage. With the boy trotting by her side, Jeanette Grace walked briskly, her buttocks wobbling like two overstuffed pillows.

209

A self-appointed neighborhood gossip, Jeanette Grace stopped at back alleys and kitchen doors to gather the latest rumors and scandals. Abraham liked this routine best in winter. When the sky hung low and gray over the cast iron balconies and cobblestone courtyards, they would be invited into the kitchen for hot milk and marble cake made with cane syrup so sweet it caused his stomach to ache. In summer, while Jeanette Grace chatted with the hired help along the way, he rolled glass marbles, bright as a cat's eyes, along the hot sidewalk until the heady incense of magnolia blossoms and the heat made him woozy and he begged for a glass of cold lemonade.

Once they reached the French Market, his Creole nanny became all business, inspecting the colorful tiers of vegetables and pyramids of fruit with a practiced eye. She haggled expertly with the merchants who respected her acumen. Abraham especially loved the juicy, ripe strawberries and gorged himself until his mouth was stained red and the spaces between his teeth were wedged with tiny seeds. Next they headed for the fish market to pick the freshest seafood from baskets piled high with squirming blue crabs, translucent shrimp, glistening oysters, and pink crawfish. The boy was no trouble to Jeanette Grace, being content to occupy himself observing the life around him, or retreating into an imaginary world.

When he began school, Abraham missed the comforting presence of his nanny. He was shy and physically awkward, and stuttered when he was anxious, which made him a handy target for bullies. As for the schoolwork, he soon became bored with set lessons, advancing so rapidly that his teachers sent him to the library, where he spent many enjoyable hours reading whatever took his fancy.

Aaron and Marlene, while awed by their son's precocious intellect, tried in turn to teach him to play the piano, the violin, and the guitar, with little success. They hired the finest teachers, but still Abraham made modest progress. When he played for them, the look of displeasure in his parents' eyes hurt him deeply. He longed to earn for himself the proud and adoring gaze they so freely bestowed on one another, but he had no inborn bent for playing an instrument.

It soon became apparent that Abraham was more interested in understanding how musical instruments worked. He examined the piano's mechanism, pried up the keys, and plied the piano tuner with questions. To satisfy his curiosity, he disassembled a trumpet and flute, and then to his parents' amazement precisely reassembled them. Nothing was too small or large to engage his curiosity, from mundane kitchen gadgets to the abstract physical laws of the universe. Since they could not make a musician out of him, Aaron and Marlene simply indulged their son's inquisitiveness, allowing him to tinker with whatever he found around the house.

Despite his inability to play, Abraham appreciated music. He loved to hear his dad on the trumpet and listen to his mother singing. It thrilled him to watch as his father raised the horn to his lips and blew the first high, pure notes signaling the other instruments to begin. And when his mother's clear and passionate voice rang out above the music, he pretended that she sang for him alone.

As Abraham grew older, his parents took him on tour with them during school vacations. In the company of adults, the boy soon learned to play poker, to drink a little wine, and to appreciate jazz.

Nearing his tenth birthday, he persuaded his parents into taking him to a benefit concert at which they were featured performers. Keyed up with excitement, he entered the hotel with them and stood uncertainly in the glittering foyer, scrutinizing women in evening gowns and men in tuxedos sipping cocktails amidst potted palms, parading in pairs over the marble floor, or reposing in red velvet chairs. Following in the current of his parents' passage across the lobby, he observed his mother pass her hand through the bend of his father's elbow, then glide toward the ballroom. They were magnificent, he thought, his father in a black tuxedo with long tails and a green velvet waistcoat with matching cravat, his mother sheathed in a silvery satin gown bespangled with emerald sequins.

In the ballroom where the concert was to take place, Abraham hid behind maroon velvet curtains and watched his parents with awe and adoration. After the concert, they drifted off with the musicians, leaving him alone in the darkened ballroom. Eventually he dozed off and dreamed of tossing his father's shining trumpet into the mucky Mississippi River. As it hit the water bubbles began popping from the trumpet's mouth with a rude slurping sound. With a crow of satisfaction, he saw it upend and fill with mud as the river sucked the shining instrument down into its ooze. Then he raced home and set fire to the piano, dancing and clapping round it whooping like a wild Indian as the flames crackled and leapt higher and higher . . .

With a start, the boy felt someone shaking his shoulder. "Abraham, wake up!"

His eyes flew open to see his father standing over him, face flushed, eyes bloodshot, the smell of whiskey and cigarettes on his breath. Abraham stuttered "I didn't do anything wrong. I p-p-promise I didn't," feeling confused and guilty about his dream.

He was aware of his mother's comforting hands on his face and her familiar musky smell like a corona around him. "Poor darling, did we leave you all by your little self? Were you afraid we wouldn't come back for you?"

"C-c-can we go home now?" the boy whispered.

"Sure kid." His father pulled a bill from his wallet and pushed it into his palm.

Abraham crumpled it into his trouser pocket without a word of thanks. With his head down, the unhappy boy shuffled out of the ballroom. When Marlene tried to take his hand, he pulled away.

Chana wrote to Aaron regularly, reminding him of his as yet unfulfilled promise to bring his son up as a Jew. Although too proud to admit it, the musician was waiting for his father to acknowledge the existence of his grandson; a passive aggressive tactic to delay taking action in the hope that in time it would coerce his father into relenting. Their awful confrontation had left him hurt and bitter. Only Yakov's acceptance of Abraham as his own flesh and blood could undo, at least in part, the damage done.

On Abraham's twelfth birthday, with his Bar Mitzvah just a year away, Chana wrote an emotional letter beseeching her son not to postpone his grandson's religious education a day longer. She warned him that if he did not do so he would loose his last chance to get his father to yield.

As an appeasement, or peace offering to his parents, the errant musician joined the Reform synagogue, the one he had visited with the Beekmans when he first arrived in New Orleans. It was an imposing structure with a facade of dark red brick, graceful arches, and a blue Star of David crowning the portico. He knew his father did not approve of Reform Judaism; however, there was no choice. According to Orthodox law, as the offspring of a non-Jewish mother and a Jewish father Abraham was considered a non-Jew; to become a Jew he would have to undergo conversion as an adult. Soon after joining, Aaron approached the synagogue's rabbi to make arrangements for his son's Bar Mitzvah. Since Abraham had not attended the three-year preparation, the rabbi advised him to engage a private tutor.

Marlene made an effort to be accepting of her son's religious instruction. She was not a practicing Catholic anymore than Aaron was an observant Jew; in that way they maintained a truce that lasted for years, yet she retained an emotional attachment to her Church she could not articulate. She avoided discussions about religion, but if pressed Marlene would joke that since her mother had been a woman of great religious conviction she had taken Catholicism in with her mother's milk.

Her husband understood that it was not easy for his wife to honor the promise she had made just over a decade ago to let him raise their son as a Jew. To express his gratitude, he composed a jazzy variation of the Irish ballad, *My Wild Irish Rose*, and dedicated it to her. Marlene loved it, and with her championship, Aaron began working more seriously on musical compositions.

Unknown to him, his wife had plans of her own for their son, which she decided it would not be wise to reveal until after

213

the Bar Mitzvah celebrations. It was her intention to transfer Abraham to a Catholic school starting in the eighth grade, although it violated the agreement she had made to allow their son to be brought up as a Jew. When the time came, she would assure Aaron that she had selected the school because it provided the best academic program in the city. In the interim, she would go along with preparations, leaving to her husband the task of convincing their son that it was necessary.

That conversation between father and son took place in the music room, the indisputable heart of their household, dominated by an upright piano of dark rosewood, with a whimsical crest of interlaced dragons carved on the lid. Aaron's trumpet, in its worn leather case, sat on a high-backed chair, like a pampered and treasured pet. Sheets of music were strewn everywhere, on the mantle, the carpet, on chairs, tables, and in cartons. Gesturing to his son to sit on the black velvet sofa near the French doors looking out onto a shady courtyard, Aaron said without preamble, "Son, it's time we got started preparing you for becoming a Bar Mitzvah. It's time for you to become a man."

"You don't say! But what exactly is that?"

"At thirteen a Jewish boy is accepted as a mature member of the synagogue, responsible for his religious acts. It represents his acceptance as an adult."

"But why do I have to have a Bar Mitzvah?"

"Well, son, I guess we need to follow our family traditions. I had one, and so did your grandfather and great-grandfathers going back for generations. I really want you to do this."

"Okay. So what do I have to do?"

"You will need to learn how to read and write Hebrew, and to chant your portion from the Torah and *Haftarah*, or the Book of Prophets."

"It could be fun to learn a foreign language, sort of like learning the languages of science and math," Abraham replied thoughtfully.

"For a year you'll need to put aside at least two hours, twice a week, after school for tutoring."

214

"That's a lot!"

"I know, but normally it takes three years."

"What is a Torah?"

"The first five books of the Bible. On a boy's Bar Mitzvah he reads and chants in front of the congregation from a Torah, a special hand-written, sacred scroll."

"Hmm, I'm not sure that I want to do that."

"Son, it would mean a lot to me." Then he added, "Think of all the presents you'll get, the great party we will make for you, and how proud we will all be of you!"

"Whoa, Dad! That's nice, but why? You're not religious."

"I made a promise to your grandparents before you were born. Please, do this for me."

"But I've never met them."

'I'm hoping that this special ceremony will change that. You see they are angry with me for not following the laws of our religion. My father won't forgive me for breaking a promise to him . . ." he broke off.

More than his words, the look of pent-up misery on his father's face caused the boy to refrain from prying. He knew that there existed a tremendous animosity between his parents and grandparents, which overshadowed their lives like a monster hiding in its lair. He shied away from it; afraid that his probing would release something dangerous, expose painful and shameful things he did not want to know about.

Wanting to please his father and to ease his unhappiness, maybe even bring his divided family together again, the boy said, with a big grin, "If that's what you wish, it's okay with me."

Young Rosen's guide through the ancient, complex rituals of the Bar Mitzvah was Mr. Barshefsky, an elderly, chain-smoking gentleman, with roots in the yeshivas of Lithuania. Abraham enjoyed the challenge of learning Biblical Hebrew. Without vowels, punctuation, or musical notation, reading the Torah is the equivalent of seeing "hs" in English, and recognizing whether it represents "house," "hose," "his," or "has." The special chanting of the Torah is done to melodies indicated by tropes or symbols, however, these do not appear in the hand-

215

written scroll, only in the printed text. In order to sing in a way that is musically pleasing and correct, Abraham needed to memorize and transfer the symbols appropriately to the Torah.

With his facility for learning, the student quickly retained the ancient Hebrew chants and blessings just sufficient for his Bar Mitzvah; the modern, spoken language was not a requirement. With regret, Mr. Barshefsky recognized Abraham's immense gifts. There was no end to what they could have studied together, no limit to the Yiddishkeit he might have instilled in his pupil — if only they had been granted the time.

The relationship between tutor and boy remained cordial until Abraham began to ask probing, disturbing questions. At the time, he was devouring popular science from books and magazines, which convinced him that many of the stories in the Torah could not be true. If you believed that the Earth and the Universe were created in six days then you had to disregard the scientific observations that the solar system took much longer than that to be "born." If you believed that Adam and Eve were created approximately 6,000 years ago, you had to ignore the fossil record showing that dinosaurs existed millions of years ago and that they predated humans. When he queried Mr. Barshefsky about these apparent contradictions, the tutor became annoyed, dodged the questions, ridiculed him, or feigned amusement. Abraham began to suspect his tutor of intentionally deceiving him.

In the end his teacher lost patience with his pupil's constant grilling, "Look here Mr. Smarty, enough questions! You should be ashamed of yourself. This is a time when a young man assumes the responsibility for following the Torah's commandments, not for doubting them. You seem resentful of this as if it were a heavy yoke on your shoulders when you should be overjoyed to be given the privilege of fulfilling Hashem's commands."

Abraham responded with a stony stare. He had been misunderstood and there was no use trying to defend himself. The boy conceded reluctantly. He wanted to please his father, and to continue to enjoy his unaccustomed attentiveness and praise. Even worse, he felt that if he quit now his grandparents would find out, and that he would be guilty of ruining the chance to heal the hostility between his father and grandfather.

In the meantime, Aaron wrote glowing letters to his mother describing her grandson's excellent progress, hoping that she would pass the information on to Yakov. Chana dared not hand the letters directly to her husband, but left them on the desk in his study, on the night table next to his bed, on the kitchen table praying all the while that he would read them. He steadfastly refused to even glance at anything that came from his son. The poor women's stomach lurched each time she found a letter crumpled in the trash. As the day of the special day drew near, Chana finally summoned the nerve to tell Yakov that his grandson had been preparing for his Bar Mitzvah. She pleaded with him to attend, or at the very least, to send a note or a gift.

In response Yakov folded his arms and shook his head angrily. The years of estrangement had not weakened his resolve. He lived by the word of God, in which a man's duty is to protect and obey His Torah and its sacred commandments or see them perish.

She had feared the worst, yet she could not accept it. Her anger burst forth in a shout of rage. "Enough already!" Your son has kept his promise to provide *your* grandson with a Jewish education and to teach him how to become a true Bar Mitzvah! For the sake of your grandson, it's time to forgive." Her husband's silence, his pitiless wrath served only to fuel her outrage. "All these years I have longed for my grandson and you have forbidden me to go to him," she sobbed. "I can't take it anymore. If you won't go, I will."

Yakov turned to the wall and rocked back and forth, intoning his prayers in a steady drone that barricaded him from the world.

Soon after, Aaron received a shocking letter in which Chana bemoaned Yakov's refusal to attend. Crushing it in his hands, he berated himself for believing that his father would ultimately relent. He recalled the triumph of his own Bar Mitzvah. How flawlessly he had recited portions from the Rosen

Torah in the shul Yakov had helped to establish; the look of approval and pleasure on his parents' faces when the rabbi congratulated them. How he had basked in the light shining from their eyes after the Talmudic discourse he had given on Saturday during the festive lunch following the service. He wanted that for his own son; he had even hoped that Abraham would read from the Rosen Torah; it was his birthright.

After receiving his mother's gloomy letter, the bitterly disillusioned son began to suffer migraine headaches that drained the color from his eyes and caused him to curl up in pain. As he lay in the darkened bedroom, Marlene gently massaged his forehead in a futile attempt to alleviate his suffering.

"I wish I knew what triggers these hellish migraines," Aaron moaned,

"Your father's vengeance!" Marlene hissed.

"What?"

"He carries ancient history around like a ball and chain. It's not right that he keeps punishing you and Abraham. It's high time you let go of him."

"He is my father, no matter what," he whimpered.

"The man is a monster! Does he not have one iota of pity or remorse in him?"

"Marlene, please stop."

"There's no reasoning with you." She dropped her hands heavily to her sides and stood up.

"Maybe you should have converted to Judaism," Aaron lashed out, his chest heaving as if he were about to be sick.

"How dare you blame this on me!" Before he could say another word, she hurried out of the room, closing the door behind her with a thud.

Aaron pulled the blankets over his head, and lay moaning in pain and despair. He had broken the long truce between them regarding religion, now it would be hard to regain her trust.

Abraham was not privy to the quarrel between his parents, but he felt the tension. With a child's perceptiveness he understood that his father wanted to end the estrangement from his grandparents. Was that not the main purpose for his Bar Mitzvah, he wondered miserably, wishing that he had someone in whom to confide.

On Saturday, the day of the ceremony, Abraham stood on the raised platform looking out on the congregation, feeling like an imposter faking his sincerity. He caught the proud gaze of his parents, yet he could see the tension in their faces. His grandmother Chana, who had found the courage to defy her formidable husband, wept as she looked up at him adoringly.

Just two days ago he had seen his grandmother in the flesh for the very first time, stepping onto the station platform assisted by a porter. He hung back, observing her supervising the transfer of luggage onto a cart. She looked dignified in a loose-fitting black dress trimmed with lace, and a hat that partially obscured her face. Before he could react, his father gave him a shove. "There's your grandmother! Go to her."

Embarrassed and unsure, Abraham stuck out his hand and said, "Pleased to meet you, Grandmother."

"Abraham, my darling grandson!" She opened her arms to him. Chana had ached to hold him in her arms, to feel the ties of blood between them. Now the apprehension in his eyes warned her that it would take time to get to know this shy boy. She took the hand he had proffered. He wanted to snatch it from her grasp, to hide from her piercing scrutiny, but he didn't want to be rude.

"So much like your grandfather," she whispered. As she bent to kiss him on the cheek, he felt her trembling.

With a start Abraham realized that his attention had wandered; the rabbi was tapping impatiently a letter on the Torah with the silver pointer to indicate the beginning of the portion he should begin chanting. Feeling all eyes riveted on him, Abraham experienced a moment of panic. The color drained from his face, causing his freckles to show vividly. He opened his mouth to begin and heard himself stuttering out the first syllable; involuntarily his face contorted into a grimace of shame. Taking a deep breath, he willed himself to begin over; to wail out the chants as his father had done before him, and his father's father,

219

back to the first Bar Mitzvah ever celebrated. When the service was over, everyone was crowded around him to offer congratulations.

That evening, the Rosens had invited their friends to a post-celebration dinner at the Belle Tambourine, vaunted as the finest hotel in the Vieux Carré. The train journey and the emotional stress of the occasion had exhausted Chana, and Aaron was concerned that another late night would be too much for her. Chana insisted that she could no more miss her grandson's reception than stop her heart from beating.

A surge of pride caused Aaron to strut as he escorted his mother across the plush carpet of the hotel lobby and into the reception area outside the ballroom. Wearing a black satin dress embroidered with tiny pearls, she looked distinguished, even in old age. Yet this rare moment of pleasure was tarnished by the absence of his father.

The waiters brought around platters of succulent appetizers—crabmeat crepes, oysters on the half shell, and boiled shrimp—and the bartender took orders. Soon after, the doors to the ballroom were opened and the guests took their places at the tables assigned to them. After Aaron's introductory remarks welcoming the guests, the entrée—fillet mignon or salmon—was served. To his dismay, Aaron discovered that the kosher meals he had specially ordered for his mother and Mr. Barshefsky and his wife, had not arrived. He rushed to apologize, and to assure them that their dinners would soon be delivered.

While the guests gorged themselves, Chana sat with her hands in her lap, dabbing at angry tears leaking from the corners of her eyes. The regal grandmother, looked round the room dismayed to see that her son's friends were a rainbow mix of disreputable-looking entertainers; as far as she could tell there were just a mere handful of Jewish guests. There was nothing that Aaron could do to salvage the situation and the misplaced meals, except to continue to apologize profusely. Finally, he gave instructions to one of the kitchen workers to take a taxi to a kosher deli near the Garden District to order takeout food. By the time it arrived, the main entrée had been consumed and Chana and the Barshefskys were too insulted to do anything but pick at the food grudgingly.

When Abraham rose to thank his parents, his grandmother, and his teacher, he felt the same discomforting sense of playing out a charade he had experienced earlier. Everyone applauded, but he was glad when it was over. After the feast, the Irish Rose Band invited the guests to dance and soon they were stomping to the music of the Charleston, the Cakewalk, and the Turkey Trot.

Marlene had organized a grand finale to complete the occasion. At a prearranged signal, the lights were dimmed, and as the band struck up "Happy Birthday," waiters wheeled a huge cake with thirteen glowing candles into the center of the ballroom. Marlene, tipsy by then, foolishly belted out an Irish folksong. She repeated the chorus each time encouraging everyone to join in. Not to be outdone her husband bounded onto the stage and began singing, "When Irish Eyes Are Smiling." The guests all gazed up at the couple looking adoringly at one another. Noticing the candles burning down, Abraham thought, *Even after reading flawlessly from the Torah, which I put up with for the sake of my father, the spotlight is on my parents. At the moment of my triumph, they have forgotten me, again.*

When the applause quieted down, Aaron kissed his wife and returned to his seat next to Chana. The candles on the cake had melted almost to the frosting, and Marlene hastily beckoned Abraham to cut the confection.

It was all too much for Chana: no kosher food, no hora dance, the scarcity of Jewish guests, the inappropriate love songs, and her sorrow for her husband's absence. She could not deny what Yakov had known all along: their son no longer understood what it meant to be a Jew. Overcome by emotion, she picked up her beaded purse, rapped Aaron smartly on the ear, and hobbled out of the ballroom, shaking with rage.

As Aaron followed Chana, Marlene quickly gestured for the band to launch into "When the Saints Come Marching In."

In the lobby he seated his mother in a comfortable chair. "My grandson has no hope of remaining a Jew surrounded by these people," she fumed. "Maybe it's a good thing your father was spared seeing how you live!"

He knew then that it was all over. The slightest hope of reconciliation had vanished. The whole event had been nothing but a sham, and his mother had seen through it.

"Ma, you're exhausted. I'll call a cab to take you to the house. I'll ask Jeanette Grace to go with you and help you get settled for the night," he said brokenly, wishing he could leave with her.

When the last guest had departed, it was Abraham's turn to confront his father. "Dad, this was supposed to be my celebration!" The knot swelling in the boy's throat was choking him. He swallowed hard and forced himself to go on. "You and mother acted like fools. And Grandmother just cried and walked out. My whole family embarrassed me in public!"

"Don't yell at me," his father retorted too loudly. The catering staff, removing the last remnants of the festivities, pretended not to hear the raised voices. Seeing his son's flaming cheeks, and burning eyes, Aaron recanted, "I'm sorry, I didn't plan for this to happen."

"Then why did Grandmother act so angry? Why didn't my grandfather show up?"

"Your grandfather is very devout, and that makes him different from us."

Abraham rolled his eyes to express his indignation.

"What I really mean is that it's his mission to keep the Jewish way of life alive. I mean . . . he believes that it is a *sin* not to pass his religion on to his descendants. Don't you see?"

Abraham shook his head in disbelief.

"You have to understand Judaism is my father's life. He feels that God has commanded him to . . . to punish me for not following tradition by marrying your mother."

"But didn't we follow tradition by having this Bar Mitzvah?"

"Heck, I thought so, even if we just did it for my Papa."

Suddenly the nasty little voice of guilt whispered in Abraham's ear, if you hadn't been such a big doubter, hadn't kept

222

on plaguing Mr. Barshefsky with your questions, this wouldn't have happened.

Marlene, who had been following this exchange, now joined the battle. "How can you call that selfish old man, Papa? The way he has treated you, ignored me, rejected all of us, it's cruel—insane!"

"Please don't get hysterical like my mother."

"I don't blame her! She's had to put up with that man's hatred for all those years."

Abraham cut in, "Does your father really *hate* us?"

"No, I don't think so. I know for sure that he did love me—once."

"Then how could he act like you don't exist?"

"I already told you. He disowned me because of his religious beliefs."

"What do you mean? Does Judaism say you should act as if your child is *dead* just for marrying a non-Jew?" Abraham's lips were trembling.

In a last futile, and inept attempt to defuse his son's anger, he cuffed him lightly on the shoulder and grinned, "Hey kid, I'm not a psychiatrist, or a rabbinical scholar, just a fool musician."

"Don't clown around; I'm not a little kid anymore!"

His son's vehemence shocked Aaron. He wondered desperately what he could say to comfort him. In a sudden spin of memory, that long ago, near-death experience aboard *The Deutschland*, came back to him. He could see his father curled around the Torah like a dead man, hear himself wailing "Papa, Papa, don't leave me!"

Perhaps it would help to tell him about that and about the Rosen Torah. "Uh, maybe it would comfort you to know that our family has a very special heirloom, a treasure . . . I mean a legacy that will be yours one day!" he said, hesitantly.

"What are you talking about?"

Abraham wasn't sure how to begin.

"Dad, you just said something about a special treasure or *legacy* for me," Abraham urged.

223

As quickly as it had come, the impulse to tell his son about the Torah left him. He could never, would never forgive his father for depriving Abraham of his love. For that reason the Rosen Torah no longer existed for him or for his son.

"Dad, say something. Is it a secret?" he persisted.

"Oh, no! It's nothing, really. It'll be best to tell you about it when we've all had time to calm down." Doubt replaced anger on the boy's face. Pretending not to see it, Aaron yawned, stretched his arms above his head to mask his misery and shame. "It has been a long day, young man, you did a fantastic job, thank you! Now it's time to get some sleep."

He reached out to embrace his son, but Abraham pushed him away. "You shouldn't have made me do this," he retorted, silently vowing to erase the whole Bar Mitzvah from his memory and his life.

✆19ᴖ

Little Einstein

The tradition of study, the reverence for ideas, the inculcated passion to analyze and to know has led many Jews to distinguish themselves in literature, philosophy, medicine, law and science.

Leo Rosten

After his Bar Mitzvah Abraham found a way to escape from his callous and embattled family. He set up a home lab in a large storage closet just off the kitchen to experiment with what his mother called "stinks and bangs." When he attempted to duplicate the groundbreaking experiments of his new heroes, pioneering chemists, among them Lavoisier and Davy, he produced clouds of noxious-smelling gas, much to the alarm of his mother and Jeanette Grace.

Awakened one afternoon from her siesta by fumes and explosions, Marlene rushed into her son's lab yelling, "B'gosh, the likes of you would do proud to the wild folks that live in the hills and dales of Derry! You're going to blow us to kingdom come!"

"Don't worry I know what I'm doing," the budding scientist said with a grin.

The nanny stood glaring at her charge with her hands on her ample hips, but secretly she was glad to see Abraham asserting himself.

Aaron sauntered in whistling a tune he had been working on. "It's all right," he said, in support of his son. "He could be getting into worse mischief. As the boy says, he knows what he's doing."

Eventually, the household became inured to the strange odors emanating from Abraham's lab, and Marlene even quit threatening to throw out the collection of chemicals, crystals, rocks, and fossils piling up in his room. Aaron encouraged his son giving him an allowance to buy the materials he needed to carry out experiments, believing that his fascination with chemistry was a passing phase that he could indulge.

Under the tutelage of his science teacher, Mr. Kremer, known affectionately as Mr. K, Abraham's interest in chemistry broadened and deepened to include electricity. He began experimenting with batteries and bulbs; later his curiosity extended to photography, magnetism, and radiology.

His young student admired and respected Mr. K's vast knowledge, and his honesty in admitting that he did not have all the answers to his pupil's precocious questions. The boy identified more with his science teacher than with his own father. His teacher reciprocated by guiding Abraham through the discoveries of great scientists: Galileo, Newton, Darwin, the Curies, Einstein, and Fermi. He encouraged his eager pupil to join the science club where he made friends with Malcolm McCourt, the oldest of nine children.

From a working class family, Malcolm saw his scientific aptitude as a way out of poverty. He was one of the few boys who shared Abraham's burning curiosity, and he often invited his new friend home where they would spend hours cooking up experiments in his improvised lab. Concerned that Abraham was too solitary a boy, Marlene and Jeanette Grace would ply Malcolm with delicious cakes and pies to entice him back.

In his senior year, Mr. Kremer selected his protégé for the prestigious Science Talent Competition. With his mentor's support, Abraham entered and won. Malcolm, who had hoped he would be the chosen one, was disappointed and envious. He turned against his former friend, and to bait him, began calling him "Christ killer" and a "kike" in front of the other boys, instigating others to join in.

It made no sense to Abraham to be branded a Jew by a Catholic, when he was half-Catholic himself. With his red hair and green eyes he didn't think he looked stereotypically Jewish. He couldn't understand the need of his peers to use Judaism against him; why his heritage was important to others when it wasn't of consequence to him. He had put all that out of his mind after the Bar Mitzvah, yet now it was being used to demean him. He tried to ignore their taunting, but the day before school let out for the Christmas vacation, Malcolm began to whip him with a wet towel in the locker room.

"Leave me alone. Ssstop!" To his horror, Abraham heard himself stammering. The next thing he knew, the spiteful young man hit him squarely on the jaw and shoved him into a scalding shower, where the other students joined in the beating. When the bell rang to go to the next class, they left him trembling on the tile floor, wiping tears, snot, and blood from his face. Half-blinded, he groped for his glasses, pushed them onto the bridge of his nose grimacing with pain. Limping over to the mirror he saw that he was bleeding from a gash on his forehead. He craned his neck and saw angry welts rising on his back where he had been flailed with the towels. Hurriedly drying, he dressed and ran to class.

Shame prevented him from telling his parents or teachers about the ugly incident. Knowing he had only a few months before graduation, he kept away from Malcolm and his gang as best he could, but it was humiliating to be ostracized.

At sixteen, aided by a strong recommendation from Mr. K, Abraham was awarded a scholarship to the University of Chicago. His parents were thrilled. To his surprise, they decided to accompany him on the overnight journey aboard the *Panama Limited*, a luxury all-Pullman car. Aaron had been about the same age as his son when he had boarded the train from Ricksburg to New Orleans, trembling with anticipation, to launch his career as a musician. He recalled how he had tilted out the window and waved goodbye to his mother dabbing tears from her eyes, and to his father moving his lips in silent prayer. They had cast a gloom over his adventure with their stern disapproval. He was

227

determined not to send his son off that way.

Now that long-ago trip evoked more recent and even bitterer memories. Just a month before Abraham's departure for Chicago, Chana had sent word that his father had passed away after a long illness. She had not requested his attendance at the funeral, and he knew that it was a last slap in the face from his father. He had silently raged against Yakov's scorn, vowing that he would never treat his own son so cruelly. He did not know, nor did he care to whom Yakov had bequeathed the Rosen Torah, he only knew for certain that he was not to be its next inheritor. The hypnotic, reverberating rumble of the *Panama Limited* evoked a sense of peace that helped to ease these unpleasant thoughts.

The three whiled away the time playing cards, enjoying meals in the dining car, occasionally remarking on something that caught their attention. Night fell, spilling a swath of velvet darkness perforated by yellow points of light from the occasional farmhouse or riverboat. At a rural crossing they saw a rickety farm wagon loaded down with a brood of young children and the family's meager possessions. Aaron shook his head, and with a sweeping gesture pointed to the deluxe polished brass sconces and inlaid mahogany paneling of the dining car.

"Don't let this fool you, Son." His sudden gravity startled Abraham. "I believe there will be hard times ahead, and we will have to scramble to get through them, no matter what President Hoover says to the contrary."

"I hear rumors that these trains already carry more hobos than freight," Marlene sighed. She feared that the privileged life at the university might not teach their son much about how to survive in a harsh world.

By the time they were ready for bed, the train was nearing Memphis, which marked the halfway point of their journey. Abraham excused himself, saying that he was ready to turn in.

He lay in his berth between starched sheets, recalling the events of a day he would remember with pleasure. He was about to fall asleep when a thrill of anticipation akin to fear rushed through him. His eyes flew open; by morning the train would reach its destination, then he would be left to fend for himself in a strange and perhaps hostile city.

The day after his arrival in Chicago, Abraham stood with his fellow freshmen in the grand convocation hall to be welcomed by the president, faculty, and trustees. He had outgrown much of his childhood shyness; still he did not find it easy to make new friends. As luck would have it, a popular athlete, Edwin Norton, was assigned as his lab partner in chemistry. Edwin took an immediate liking to Abraham dubbing him "Little Einstein." The moniker caught on, and the reticent student relished the sense of acceptance it conferred on him.

The athlete invited his new classmate on camping, hiking, and fishing trips. To his surprise Abraham discovered that he found pleasure in the excursions and the easy camaraderie of the students who, because of Edwin, quickly accepted him. The strenuous outdoor activity helped wind down his overactive mind. At night he fell into a restful, and dreamless sleep. A creature of the city, he began to develop a love for the outdoors.

That summer, Edwin landed a job with the Chicago, Burlington, and Quincy Railroad, and encouraged his friend to join him. Known as the "Q" it was one of the pioneer railroads that began its run westward from Chicago to the Mississippi River in 1858. As it expanded, it became the main line for settlers moving west. Edwin and Abraham were assigned to an engineering crew in charge of surveying and mapping the land for the new railroad tracks for the CB&Q's expansion beyond the Mississippi. Each day they tramped for miles through the woods. At night they ate simple meals cooked on a smoky campfire that helped ward off swarms of mosquitoes.

One night Aaron was awakened from a deep sleep by a furtive rustling nearby. He lay on his bedroll, confused and apprehensive, trying to decipher the direction and cause of the noise. As his eyes accommodated to the darkness, he could just make out a herd of white-tailed deer moving in single-file through the clearing. When the last deer had disappeared, he gazed up at the cobalt dome pierced by glittering stars and mused: *There is a vast universe that exists independently of human beings, governed by laws we do not fully understand.* The quest to grasp these mysteries beckoned him as brightly as the stars above. As he dropped back to sleep, an inner peace flowed through him and he knew with certainty that scientific research would be his life's work.

Abraham returned to Chicago in the fall, fit and tanned, and more confident. His professors recognized their student's exceptional potential. When he graduated three years later, *summa cum laude,* with a degree in physics, they encouraged him to study abroad, writing letters of recommendation to the University of Cambridge that helped pave the way for their star pupil.

The interval between graduating and waiting to receive the notification from this prestigious university alternated between happy anticipation and gloomy agitation. When the letter of acceptance came, Abraham read it over and over to allow the glorious words to sink in: "Dear Mr. Rosen: It is our great pleasure to inform you that the Admissions Committee has voted to offer you a place with a full research scholarship in the Department of Physics, at the University of Cambridge." To truly convince himself of his good fortune, he sang the letter to the tune of Beethoven's "Ode to Joy." As his voice soared, his hopes transformed themselves from tremulous dreams into triumphant reality.

He visualized the venerable English institution as a river swollen by the irresistible energy of the greatest intellects of science. Now he would be swept toward new frontiers that would soon revolutionize human understanding.

Before departing, Abraham arranged to spend a few days with his parents in New Orleans to enjoy some quiet family time. He should have known better. They threw a huge surprise party for him at Café Souris, where the musicians, including Papa Laine and the Reliance Brass Band, toasted and roasted him as "The Little Einstein of New Orleans." Then, as the rising sun dimmed the gaslights along the avenue, they carried their hero home in a blissful haze.

❧ 20 ❧

Abraham Abroad

It was the season of Light, it was the season of Darkness, it was the spring of hope, it was the winter of despair, we had everything before us, we had nothing before us.

Charles Dickens, A Tale of Two Cities

Abraham found the trans-Atlantic voyage, from New York to Southampton aboard the *RMS Statendam*, as intoxicating and unsettling as a first romance. The ceaseless heaving and swelling, sinking and rising of the ocean made him dizzy and sick, yet he could not keep his eyes off it, it was so beautiful and so wonderful.

He arrived in Cambridge glad to feel solid ground beneath his feet, and impatient to begin his dream of probing the secrets of the universe. Besides coursework, to his dismay he drew a heavy schedule of menial lab work as the most junior member of the research team. When he requested more responsibility, his colleagues reprimanded him for being uncooperative and arrogant. Communication problems made matters worse, as he found it hard to break through the English reserve. Unable to fully participate in the scientific research, he turned instead to Shakespeare, frequently attending performances of the great bard's plays. He developed the habit, annoying to some, amusing to others, of quoting passages from Shakespeare to express his emotions.

As the months passed, Abraham became more isolated and depressed. That winter, he attended a conference in Stuttgart,

231

Germany, where he was introduced to Professor Karl Staub, a pioneer in nuclear physics. The two immediately sparked one another with ideas and questions. The unhappy American confided that he was disenchanted with Cambridge, and recognizing the young man's brilliance, the professor invited him to study at the University of Stuttgart where he would serve as his mentor. Abraham felt that he had been thrown a lifeline and enthusiastically accepted.

His professors at Cambridge warned him to consider the dangerous and volatile political situation developing in Germany since Hitler had come to power in 1933. Abraham chose to ignore their warnings. As soon as he completed his first year, he left for Stuttgart, where he found lodgings in an attic room near the university.

He enjoyed the lively neighborhood beer halls painted with murals of idyllic pastoral landscapes; their *gemutlichkeit,* or good fellowship, despite his poor German; the hearty beer, wurst, schnitzel, and sauerkraut; and the enthusiastic singing to the accompaniment of live orchestras. In summer, the crowds moved outdoors to the courtyard gardens. Then gangs of Nazi thugs began showing up, belting down beers, shouting out anti-Semitic songs and beating up Jewish students while the management and police stood by and watched. He was so sickened by the brutality that he stopped going.

Professor Staub noticed Abraham's loneliness and invited him to dinner at his home. By then, the young scholar had lost weight and his face had taken on a sickly pallor. When he brought his protégé home, he looked so emaciated that Gertrud Staub, the professor's wife, became alarmed. Taking her husband aside, she inquired, "Can this young man be suffering from tuberculosis?"

"No, my dear, I am certain he is in good health."

"But how can you be so sure?" she protested.

Gertrud insisted that their family doctor examine Abraham. The sympathetic doctor assured them that their young friend was generally healthy, but warned that he showed all the symptoms of depression: loss of appetite, loss of weight, and difficulty sleeping.

"What he needs is a place where he can feel at home," Gertrud prescribed. From that day on, the kindly wife invited her husband's student to drop by whenever he felt like a home-cooked meal. Abraham eagerly complied, in part because she was an excellent cook in the old-fashioned German style. Also the Staub's open-minded, very secular approach felt comfortable to him. But it was the Staub's daughter, Martha, who truly drew Abraham to their home.

Martha, a raven-haired, handsome woman with liquid blue eyes, bore a startling resemblance to his mother Marlene. When the professor's daughter sat down with obvious pleasure to play the piano, he felt completely at home. In her company, the smitten young man became lightheaded, as though he had been too long in the sun or had had too much to drink. Too timid to disclose his feelings, and judging her to be at least five years older, he contented himself with worshipping her from afar.

At first, Martha found this shy, soft-spoken, and awkward young American *lustig*, or amusing, yet his brilliance and his passion were compelling. She sensed a fire burning inside him. Though cautioning herself about their age difference, she lay at night in bed imagining their bodies entwined. She could tell that Abraham felt comfortable with her, that he enjoyed her company, yet he never seemed to notice her as a woman. When she played the piano he would sometimes lean over her, and the gentle brush of fine, red hair that covered his arms, and the salty, male odor of his perspiration made her heart race. She tried to hide the trembling of her fingers by playing faster to keep up with the rhythm of her fluttering heart.

Already twenty-eight, an age considered old for those not yet married, Martha was ripe for love. Then the thought of Wilhelm Schmidt held her back like a leash around her neck. Her lover had gone off to America, promising to send for her once he got settled. He never had. Fear of suffering such anguish again made her uncertain and hesitant. But her desire for Abraham would not abate, until it overwhelmed her pride and uneasiness, and she began to devise ways to be alone with him. That summer she persuaded her father to invite Abraham to join them for their weeklong holiday hiking in the Alps. He gratefully accepted, happy to explore terrain that recalled his enjoyable outdoor adventures with Edwin Norton when a student at the University of Chicago.

Each morning after breakfasting on strudel or rolls and coffee with cream prepared by the chalet-owner's wife, Hilda Schultz, they hiked the mountain trails. To Martha's consternation, however, Professor Staub took advantage of these outings to engage his student in complex scientific discussions. Swinging their alpenstocks briskly, the two would become completely engrossed, and she would cease to exist. She had to content herself with watching Abraham's lean body move easily up the path, gesticulating freely as he made a point. *So American,* Martha thought, *not showing proper deference to his elders.*

A hunger for him settled in her lower belly that needed to be appeased. On the last day of the holiday, Martha decided to alter her destiny. Into a basket she packed a woolen blanket, two towels, a thermos of hot coffee, and bread and cheese she had coaxed from Hilda by promising to play her favorite lieder, by Schubert and Schumann. As usual, the Professor and Abraham were soon engaged in lively conversation. Shivering with anticipation, Martha allowed them about fifteen minutes; then she strode up the path and slipped her hand into the crook of Abraham's elbow.

"I want to show Abraham the waterfall marked here," she said.

The professor scanned the map that his daughter handed him, cleared his throat and said, "*Ach Lebeshein,* it's too steep for your mother!"

"Why don't you walk with Mama? Abraham and I will go on together." With that she steered the man of her desire firmly away.

When Abraham and Martha reached the waterfall, they were both panting. They perched on the rocks where great plumes of water plunged into a deep silver-gray pool fed by the runoff from melting snow.

"Do you like to swim?" Martha said.

"I do."

"Will you swim with me?" Her voice was husky with passion. A pulse throbbed in her throat as she undid the buttons of her blouse with trembling fingers. Then she turned away and pulled down her hiking trousers.

As if gravity itself were tilting him toward her, he heard himself say, "I will swim with you." And when he took off his clothes Martha didn't look away. She laughed and dived into the pool. He cupped his hands over her full breasts and kissed them. The water was numbingly cold, and within minutes they were back on the bank rubbing each other down.

Martha quickly produced a blanket and wrapped it around them. Then, to her surprise and amusement, Abraham paraphrased some lines from Shakespeare's *The Tempest*: "Full many a lady I have eyed with best regard but some defect in her did quarrel with the noblest grace she owed and put it to the foil: but you, O you, so perfect and so peerless, are created of every creature's best!" And so they became lovers.

Adoring Martha lifted the dull sadness that had weighed him down. His released sexual energy shocked him back to life, and boosted his intellectual drive. With Professor Staub as his adviser, Abraham began to prepare a paper that astonished his mentor with its originality and potential significance. Only the escalating Nazi viciousness he had first seen in the beer halls soured Abraham's sweet new life.

Early one morning he received an urgent note from Professor Staub. He rushed to his office to find the normally composed professor pacing the worn rug in front of his desk, a badly crumpled copy of the morning news in one hand and a cigarette in the other. His face was ashen, and he had not shaved. Abraham felt his hands go clammy.

"Abraham, have you read this morning's news?"

"No, I haven't."

The professor took a long drag on his cigarette before crushing it in a glass ashtray filled with butts. "So, you know nothing about the Nuremberg Laws?"

"I have been absorbed in my work," Abraham said apologetically.

"Well then, I'll summarize the disgusting events."

Staub recounted that on September 11, 1935, the Nazis had opened their annual conference in Nuremberg with unusual vitriol. After five days of rabble-rousing propaganda and frenzied torchlight parades, Hitler announced the enactment of the Nuremberg Laws. The first law proclaimed that Jews were forbidden to display the official German flag. The second declared that only persons with pure German blood flowing through their veins could be citizens of the Reich. If a person was the descendant of one or more Jewish grandparents, was a member of the Jewish community, was born of a marriage with a Jew, or was born as the result of extramarital intercourse with a Jew, then that person was a *Mischling*, someone of mixed blood. In addition, even a gentile married to a Jew, could be stripped of all rights as a citizen. The third law prohibited marriage and extramarital sex between Jews and German citizens of pure blood.

When the professor had finished, Abraham remained seated, clenching and unclenching his jaw. As an American and a scientist he could not accept it. "I can't believe it! What on Earth do they mean by using pseudo science in a deceitful attempt to classify people as if they were animals, and going on about pure blood. That's not science, that's bullshit!" In his anger Abraham thumped his fist on the desk.

Staub sat down heavily, rigid as a tin soldier. "Please! Try to calm yourself."

"Herr P-P-Professor, are you t-t-trying to t-t-tell me that I have to leave G-G-G-Germany?" he stuttered.

"No, no! I'm the one who may have to leave." The professor began pacing again. "You see, my grandfather on my father's side was Jewish, and my wife is Jewish, and that makes my daughter, Martha, a Jew."

Abraham, though on the verge of panic, was dismayed to hear himself utter an involuntary nervous snicker.

"Look here, young man this is no laughing matter," Professor Staub objected. "Things will get much worse before they get better!"

"I apologize, Herr Professor," Abraham said, struggling to regain his composure. "You see I am also a half-Jew through my father's family, the Rosens. What do you advise me to do? Do you think it will be okay to stay until the end of the year?"

"If you are prepared to take that chance."

"Thank you. I am learning so much from you. And your family has been so kind to me." He surreptitiously wiped away tears with the back of his hand. "I will always be grateful."

"We will do as much as we can before the ax falls," the professor concluded gloomily.

The irony of being branded as a Jew, again! The fetid spreading of anti-Semitism! All this unlocked remembrances of his Bar Mitzvah party at the Belle Tambourine; about the awful feud between his father and grandfather over his mother being a gentile; and about the "treasure" his father had started to reveal. He suspected it had something to do with his Jewish lineage, and he vowed that when he returned to the States he would pry it out of his father.

As Christmas approached, a profusion of lights bloomed across the city. Despite the pervasive apprehension, as wintry dusk settled, Abraham joined the professor's family, bundled in coats, on their stroll along the main street where art students collected rent money by drawing colored chalk reproductions of the Madonna's of Giogione and Fra Angelico on the sidewalk. At the outdoor cafes filled with shoppers, they treated themselves to hot coffee and rich pastry, but did nothing to stop their feet from freezing in the chill. They did not linger on these outings as they once had; the mounting anti-Semitism made them apprehensive and suspicious of every policeman, every hostile glance.

Just weeks before Abraham's departure, over a dinner of roast pork and sauerkraut, Professor Staub cleared his throat and confessed, "What a fool I was to believe that I was safe from the Nazis! Thank God you are returning to America, Abraham."

"But what will *you* do, Herr Professor?"

"I have to make plans . . . but you understand it will not be so easy." He blew his nose on a crisply laundered handkerchief and took a fresh cigarette from a gold case to signal that he was about to adjourn to his study.

On the last weekend before Abraham was to leave for home, the lovers made plans to secretly spend time together at a remote inn in the mountains. The Staubs knew that their daughter had started a relationship with the young student, but Martha wanted to keep their love life discreet.

Early Friday morning, they took the train from the Stuttgart Hauptbanhof to a village near the Swiss border, then a carriage drawn by two white horses to the inn, nestled on the slopes of an alpine forest. The chalet had no electricity, and flickering candles and huge stone fireplaces radiated the only source of light and heat for the guests. After a simple meal accompanied by good Rhine wine, they retired to their room. In the darkness beyond the window, a curtain of falling snow concealed them from the world as they abandoned themselves to a night of passionate lovemaking.

They departed on Sunday, blissfully secure that the bond between them could never be broken. In Martha, Abraham had at last found someone who understood his lonely alienation, his obsession with science, and could encourage and comfort him. For her part, Martha was ecstatic to have found a man who loved her and would always be loyal to her. She believed that he was destined for greatness, but that he was emotionally fragile and would need her strength and understanding.

The following week, Abraham boarded a train for the port of Hamburg, where he was to sail for New York. As he stood on the platform chatting with the Staubs, who had come to see him off, he had the odd feeling he had been here before. Then he recalled that as a child he had badgered his father—who didn't like to talk about the past—into telling him the story of his journey from Lithuania to America and how he had sailed aboard the *Deutschland* from the port of Hamburg.

History is repeating itself, Abraham thought and he felt hairs on the back of his neck rise. He was escaping the fearsome menace of Nazism, but what would become of the Staubs? When the conductor called out orders to board the train, he saw that Martha was weeping. A painful, heavy sadness settled over him, and he swore, *I'll find a way for us to be together soon.*

❧ 21 ❧

Abraham and Martha

The awful choice between life and death is in your hands.

Talmud

On returning to the States, Abraham accepted a position as a doctoral fellow at the University of California at Berkeley, and was soon engrossed in his research and studies. He corresponded with Martha regularly, keeping alive her hope that he would send for her soon. Her correspondence kept Abraham abreast of events in Stuttgart and reassured him of her continuing affection. Yet with each succeeding letter, he sensed his beloved's growing apprehension. In his correspondence Abraham questioned Martha about the Staubs' plans to immigrate to the United States and offered to do what he could to help. She replied:

Abraham, please understand that many scientists of father's caliber have already left Germany. Even the great Einstein himself has found a place in Princeton. Sorry that I cannot give you details of our arrangements, but I trust that father with the necessary help of his good friends and benefactors will do what he must to protect his family.

Martha's implications were unclear to Abraham. Did she mean the Staubs were already receiving assistance from other friends and benefactors? As a postdoctoral fellow he was under pressure to meet deadlines, so he put the letter aside, fully intending to come back to it by the end of the week. Before he

240

could do so, he received an urgent telegram from the professor himself, imploring for help. He had to leave for the United States immediately, as he had been dismissed from his post under "The Law for the Restoration of the Professional Civil Services." The law stripped the professor, together with a quarter of the physicists of Germany — among them Nobel Prizes laureates — of their livelihood. To survive they had to emigrate.

Sick at heart, in a burst of energy fueled by guilt and fear, Abraham frantically contacted scientific organizations, American philanthropists, and refugee organizations working to get scientists and their families, now in terrible danger, out of Germany. Putting his work on hold, he did everything he could to obtain the Staubs' immigration papers. This was no easy task.

Due to U.S. immigration laws, few Jews were eligible to come to America; the prohibition on immigrants likely to become a public charge created a de facto exclusion for all Jews as they were banned from transferring any wealth out of Nazi territory. To receive clearance, one needed proof of a guaranteed job in America, and that was hard to come by in the chaos preceding the war. This left many trapped in Germany and elsewhere as Nazi power extended. After months of battling red tape, countless phone calls, and interviews with harassed bureaucrats, Abraham was able to obtain all the necessary documents to secure a position for Professor Staub at Berkeley. On December 1, 1937, the family arrived in their new country. They were among the fortunate to escape before the Nazis denied all exit visas.

It was a sunny California afternoon when the train pulled into the Southern Pacific Railroad Station, in Oakland, a handsome 1912 Beaux Arts building with tall, arched windows. Abraham instantly spotted Martha as she stepped onto the platform, blinking uncertainly in the sunshine. She wore her dark hair in thick braids wound tidily around her head and a fur coat much too warm for California. Framed by a dark collar, her face was pale and drawn. Professor Staub and Gertrud trailed uncertainly behind her. The couple had aged visibly since he had last seen them a year ago.

Abraham rushed over and they all hugged tearfully. He slipped the porter a generous tip then led the weary family to his car. He nudged his hand in the crook of Martha's elbow, and she leaned against him; even through the heavy fur coat he could feel her trembling. She looked directly into his eyes as if waiting for a signal, and he felt the heat of awakening desire. The couple was too enthralled to notice the knowing glances being exchanged between the professor and his wife. The obvious love between the young couple, the brilliant sunshine, exotic palm trees, bright flowers, and tranquil, healthy Americans were overwhelmingly heartening after the terrors and deprivations of Germany. The professor and his wife could not stem the tears of gratitude and relief brimming in their eyes.

Abraham had rented an attractive Spanish-style stucco-and-brick house for the Staubs in Berkeley. Thoughtfully, he had stocked their kitchen with fresh produce, and needed staples.

Clasping her hands with joy, Gertrud exclaimed, "I'm so excited and so happy to be here, I can't shut my eyes! I will make a wonderful meal to celebrate." When Abraham and Martha offered to help in the kitchen, she shooed them away.

Out on the terrace, Martha was reluctant to respond to Abraham's questions about their flight from the Nazis. "I don't want to talk about that, for now it's enough that thanks to your efforts, we are here," she said.

The two stood quietly savoring the peaceful view of the Berkeley Hills and the distant blue glint of San Francisco Bay. On the darkening hills, slats of light from half-shuttered windows and glimmering halos from street lamps sketched the contours of the hillsides, seeming to echo the radiant constellations suspended above them.

Abraham put his arms around her, and brushed his lips across the nape of her neck, tender and defenseless as a child's.

"What are we going to do now?" Martha asked, shivering despite the warmth.

"Can we be lovers again?" he whispered.

"I don't know," she said, gently pushing him away and folding her arms across her chest.

"Why not?"

He tried to draw her close, but she warned, "Not here. Not now."

Despite her protest, he twisted Martha against him and kissed her. Excitement surged through him as she opened her mouth, enticing him with her tongue. When they stopped, he saw that she was crying.

"What's wrong?"

"Don't you see everything has changed between us?"

He shook his head.

"In Germany you were a lost child. I was the one who rescued you."

"Rescued me like a child?"

Seeing the hurt in his eyes, she said, "I am the child now, the one who needs to be supported." She wanted to sound brave, but her voice sank to a tremulous whisper.

"Martha, you're safe now. You have nothing to be afraid of."

She wanted to shake him, to plead with him: *We cannot continue to be lovers as we were in Stuttgart. I want more than that. I want marriage and a family,* but pride and uncertainty choked the words in her throat. She could not endure the thought of losing him, nor resist his passion. They became lovers again.

Just weeks after the Staubs' arrival, Martha learnt that she was pregnant. Her first reaction was a frightening sinking sensation like falling into deep, murky water. She had been enjoying her good fortune; now shame overwhelmed her. At the thought of disgracing her parents, of their disapproval, her shoulders sagged and her face burned. She crumpled onto the bed, her arms around her belly, and sobbed silently. When she heard her mother clattering pots in the kitchen, Martha hurriedly dried her tears. In the bathroom, she scrubbed her face and brushed her hair with rough strokes while examining her image in the mirror's silvery depths. Her eyes met their reflection and she counseled herself: *I will not give in to shame, to acting out of a childish concern about how others might judge me; I am not guilty of*

243

any crime. I feared that I would be denied the life-changing experience of motherhood, how could I not be happy now?

She had to tell Abraham that he was about to become a father, and after the initial shock surely he would be pleased and proud to be her husband. She smiled at herself in the mirror glad to see the glow returning to her cheeks. At dinner her bright eyes and lively conversation deceived her parents. How could they guess that her heart was overflowing with a confusing mix of anxiety and joy?

The following day she broke the news to Abraham as gently and as tactfully as she could, saying with a happy lift to her voice, "Don't you think it would be wonderful to have a child of our own?"

He pulled her into his arms and pressed her to him. She kissed his eyelids and the soft spot throbbing in his neck, hoping to hear words of love. Instead he said, "I've never really given it much thought."

Had he rebuffed her or had he missed her cue? "I'm pregnant! What can be more beautiful and more right than creating a new life!"

"What did you say?"

"I'm pregnant."

"Are you sure?"

"Yes!"

"Oh boy! I need time to think . . ."

"There is no time! Your child is already growing inside me! Are you ready to be a father!"

He looked away, shamed by her scorn.

She was weary of being his secret lover. "I'm not one of your experiments gone wrong. It's over between us," she cried. "Please leave!" She strode to the front door and opened it.

"Martha, please, your news shocked me!"

"I'm through playing games with a boy." Before he could say another word, she propelled him out the door and shut and bolted it, leaving him standing on the front porch, feeling like a fool.

He made repeated attempts to see her, but she had given instructions to her parents not to let him in. Nor would she take his calls or read his letters. He sat for hours at his desk staring into space or lying on his bed rerunning their last conversation in his head, feeling like the boy she had called him. He felt a deep love throbbing inside him; he had to make a commitment to marry her, to be a father to their child, or the black shadow of regret would follow him for life.

Four days after their heated confrontation, Abraham waited for Martha near Founder's Rock, a secluded spot on the edge of campus. As she strode up the path with her dachshund, the wind blew her dress against her body and he thought he could just discern the slight swelling of her abdomen. He rushed over to her, took her firmly by the shoulders, and proposed with all the fervor and sincerity she had hoped for. The events of the last few days overcame her — the exhaustion, the humiliation, the disappointment and outrage at having been rejected. She sank against the rock, trembling so violently that her little dog began to yap. Abraham took her hands in his, and gazed imploringly at her.

She exclaimed, "Yes, I will marry you."

They embraced, feeling that they had come home, feeling no longer alone, whispering their love to one another.

After joyfully announcing their betrothal to her parents, and making a long-distance phone call to Abraham's mother and father, over the next few weeks they all excitedly discussed preparations for the wedding.

Charles Lindbergh's solo flight across the Atlantic had inspired a boom in air travel, making it possible for Aaron and Marlene to fly from New Orleans to California for their son's wedding. Three days before the wedding, they boarded a Ford tri-motor plane at dawn. As airplanes were certified to carry passengers only during daylight hours, they were scheduled to spend the night in Albuquerque, New Mexico, before flying on to San Francisco.

On the morning that his parents were due to arrive, Abraham awakened from a bizarre dream, hearing a voice hissing in his ear: *God does not play dice with the universe.* He flung back the sheets, hurling a biography of Einstein that he had been reading, to the floor. With clammy hands, he shrugged on a cotton robe and went into the garden shrouded in early morning fog — the majestic result of cold sea spray colliding with the hot air of the Central Valley.

Although fully awake, the vivid images and the horror of his dream persisted . . . his mother and father, seated side by side inside an airplane, zoom over shifting red dunes and steep blue mesas. Aaron lifts his trumpet to his lips and blows piercingly high notes; great, feathered wings sprout between his shoulder blades and begin flapping to the rhythm of the music. Iridescent bubbles from the trumpet's mouth float through the cabin. To the delight of the passengers, Marlene catches the bubbles in her sensuous mouth and blows them out as miniature red devils rhythmically swishing their long tails to the trumpet's beat . . . now everyone's dancing . . . A tremendous explosion cracks the plane from side to side, spewing bodies and debris into space. *Oh, God! Oh God!* Lit by the fiery tails of meteors, Aaron and Marlene tumble through the void, laughing and clutching one another in ecstasy. From high atop a mesa, Abraham lifts Jeanette Grace's big basket to catch them. *Oh, I can save them if only I can reach high enough!* But they plummet to earth, turn to dust, the sun dies behind the horizon, blackness strangles the stars, their ashes are blown away. The howling of the wind drowns out the awful sound of his keening.

When news of the crash reached them hours later, the groom-to-be had already told Martha of his dreadful premonition.

Abraham struggled to cope with the loss of his parents. It had come too abruptly and much too soon. He walked around in shock, mournfully uttering lines from Shakespeare's *Romeo and Juliet*: "'All things that we ordained festival, / Turn from their office to black funeral; Our instruments to melancholy bells, / Our wedding cheer to a sad burial feast, / Our solemn hymns to sullen dirges change, / Our bridal flowers serve for a buried corse, / And all things change them to the contrary.'"

246

The Staubs thoughtfully made arrangements for the memorial service in the Berkeley Botanical Gardens, in Strawberry Canyon high above the main campus. They hoped that Abraham would be up to giving the eulogy, but he declined saying that he was too distraught to do so. Instead he requested that Magnus Berthe—his close friend who held a position in the Department of Physics—read the tribute he had composed to his parents.

Abraham stood in a daze, holding onto Martha like a man who had recently gone blind, his gaze fixed on the verdant oak covered slopes tumbling down into the creek. At the conclusion Magnus looked directly at the couple and spoke. "Today we have sent your beloved mother and father to their rest. Now our concern must turn towards the living. You, Abraham, and you, Martha," he paused, "are soon to be married. As a community we have an obligation to *comfort* you, to help you overcome your sorrow, and to restore your faith so that you can begin a new life together joyfully."

For a brief, terrifying moment the word "comfort" hung in the air like a message written in invisible ink. Along with the painful sense of loss, of relationships never quite fulfilled, he now recalled the unsolved puzzle of his legacy. The confrontation in the ballroom of the Belle Tambourine after his Bar Mitzvah replayed in his mind:

It should comfort you to know that our family has a special treasure, a wonderful legacy.

What comfort, Dad? What is the treasure? Is it a secret?

Oh, no. It's nothing, really.

He had believed that one day his father would reveal the mystery, but Aaron had taken it to his grave.

For days after the service, he kept thinking about it. Was it just his imagination or had his father meant to tell him something important? A secret is corrosive as water seeping through limestone, and it ate at him. He told himself that he really did not care if his father had kept something from him. Or did he?

Gertrud and Martha took care of all the arrangements for a small, subdued wedding. For the venue they chose the Berkeley

247

Faculty Club, located in the heart of the campus, a charming pink stucco structure with overhanging beams nestled into a grove of redwoods, oaks and maples. The Staubs' friend, Judge Josh Mullins, officiated at the ceremony held on the sloping green fan of lawn known as the Faculty Glade.

Before the couple exchanged vows, the judge paid homage to Aaron and Marlene, drawing a parallel between their mysterious journey into the afterlife, and the wonderful voyage the bride and groom were now embarking upon. The judge's unusual, even bizarre analogy, sent shivers through the guests, and served as a grim reminder of the transitory nature of existence while underscoring the extraordinary love of the two committing themselves to a one another — "'til death do us part." Afterwards, the guests were escorted to the dining room with windows framed by wisteria, and French doors opening onto a terrace overlooking the glade. The newlyweds, completely overwrought by life-altering events of the past weeks, remained clinging to one another until Gertrud came to reassure them, and, once they had regained their composure, usher them inside to celebrate with their guests.

Abraham and Martha rented a house on a quiet street near the Berkeley campus and the Staubs' home. Their son, John Aaron Rosen — named after Martha's maternal grandfather Johannes — was born seven months after the wedding. The new wife and mother combed antique stores for heavy, ornate European furniture to decorate their home in a way pleasing to her, giving pride of place to an old-fashioned grand piano. She would not wear the more casual slacks and blouses coming into vogue, despite Abraham's encouragement, preferring dresses and practical shoes she had always worn. She raised a family of dachshunds as though they were her children, slipping them morsels of food under the table despite Abraham's protests. The new husband indulged his wife's idiosyncrasies, returning to his studies with renewed vigor.

In 1943, when John turned five, Abraham completed his doctorate in theoretical physics and joined the faculty as assistant professor. Soon afterward he was recruited to work on a top-secret project in New Mexico, and was honored and thrilled to meet with Robert Oppenheimer, the project's leader. The eminent scientist never spoke of making a bomb lest the word should slip out in unauthorized places; he called it "the gadget," but Abraham instantly grasped what he meant.

Uncertain if he should commit himself to such a momentous project, before making the decision, Abraham and Martha took a vacation in Yosemite National Park, leaving little John with his grandparents. On long hikes in the mountains, they discussed the pros and cons of joining the mission. Abraham explained that Oppenheimer had indicated they would be handling hazardous material, and that they would attempt to build a weapon to put an end to the war; yet, if they succeeded, it would result in untold devastation. The young scientist desperately wanted to halt the spread of Nazism, and the carnage ravaging the world. Did the end justify the means?

Martha had no doubts. How in good conscience could they stand by while Hitler threatened to overthrow the free world? He agreed with his wife, having experienced the dreadful scourge himself. The Staubs and thousands like them were victims of Adolf Hitler's poisonous actions. Still, he feared that seeking peace with the aid of a dangerous and cruel weapon would come back to trouble those who had created it.

By the time they returned to Berkeley, despite his qualms, Abraham had arrived at the decision to join the project at Los Alamos; it would be their temporary home until this terrible war was over. The chairman of the department had reassured him that he could return to his position on the faculty. With that choice behind him, he was now free to put his extraordinary intellectual powers to use.

✥22✥

Abraham and the Making of the Bomb

"Now I am become Death, the destroyer of worlds."

Hindu scripture

The havoc of war drove the Rosens out of their peaceful home on a dangerous and top-secret mission to an isolated place in the high desert. Despite their apprehensions the long train journey to Los Alamos came as a welcome hiatus between the frantic preparations to close their home and the challenges awaiting them.

As they stood on the platform with little John in tow, impatiently waiting to board the train that would convey them due east to New Mexico, the Staubs and a few friends materialized through the vapor billowing from the train, to bid them farewell. Their goodbyes belied the deep unease lurking behind their cheerful smiles.

Seated in the carriage, familiar sights flashed by: a mushrooming subdivision, a tiny hamlet perched above a ravine, a grassy hillside where placid cows grazed, a lovely meadow bedecked in lupines, poppies, and wild onions, a sturdy timber trestle bridge, the spreading canopy of an apricot orchard, a colorful roadside fruit stand. A slow gathering of sadness descended on Abraham and Martha as these vignettes receded and became fragments of the past. Then they were away from the suburban sprawl, into unfamiliar territory. Snaking through vistas of unpopulated terrain, each milestone marked their forward rush into an unknown and uncertain future. Abraham tried to concentrate on reading scientific papers but was distracted by bittersweet memories of the train journey from New Orleans to Chicago with his parents almost two decades ago, and the excitement that awaited him.

The following morning after a restless sleep, they pulled into Lamy Station, where the project workers were transferred onto buses for the next leg of their trip to Santa Fe, before heading on to Los Alamos. When the Rosens arrived in Santa Fe, little more than a siding in the middle of nowhere, an officer informed them that for security reasons they would not be staying in the town, but at a guest ranch commandeered by the U.S. Army. He introduced them to a young private assigned to drive them to the remote location. Within minutes he loaded their luggage onto a rundown old Dodge sedan—the only car available with wartime shortages—seated Abraham in the front and Martha and John in the rear, and, as the car pulled away in a cloud of dust, cried, "Hold on to your hats, folks!"

John whooped with delight as they bounced along rutted roads following the dizzying switchbacks that skirted the mesa. A recent rainstorm had muddied the track and, to their son's amusement, his parents had to help heave the car out of the mire in several places. On one stretch sharp rocks, washed down from the hillside, ripped a hole in the already badly worn right front tire. They had no choice but to wait in the heat while the officer changed it. By late afternoon, they arrived at the ranch. Martha found a scanty supply of goods in the pantry; canned corned beef, dried fruit, and packets of stale crackers. Fortunately, she had brought along home-baked cookies, assorted nuts, and a large thermos of milk for John hastily purchased in Santa Fe.

After a snack, Abraham and Martha sat on the porch and took stock of their surroundings while John played in the dirt with his toy train. The ranch house was a simple rectangular adobe structure with a long front porch shaded by an overhanging roof. To the east the land rolled away, like a vast rose-and-tan ocean, to the smoky-purple peaks of a distant range. They watched, enchanted as the rays of the setting sun deepened to crimson, burnishing everything to blazing hues of a surrealistic painting—twin turquoise-blue doors, red garlands of chilies hanging from eaves, far-off mauve peaks. Shading her eyes, Martha hungrily drank in this dazzling visual feast.

"Oh, Abraham," she breathed, crossing her arms over her chest, her mouth opening into an O like that of a small child. "Maybe I'm imagining this. Maybe I'm not here at all but in Germany, dreaming all this."

"Then we must both be having the same wonderful fantasy." He pulled his wife to him, comforted as always by the generous curving warmth of her body.

"I wish we could stay here forever," she murmured.

Early the next morning they set off on the last leg of their journey. The travelers marveled at the wild beauty of the countryside. To the west loomed the dark bowl of the Jemez Mountains' caldera. The east slope of the mesa, eroded by the Rio Grande, fell precipitously into the valley intersected by the thin green line of the meandering river. Still farther to the east rose the Sangre de Cristo Mountains, an outstretched claw of the great Rockies. To the south, a deep canyon, carved by a sandy stream fringed by quivering cottonwoods, gashed the land.

As they approached the Los Alamos complex itself, the Rosens saw with a sinking feeling that it was a military installation entirely surrounded by barbed wire. Inside, cheap temporary barracks with coal-burning stoves had been hastily thrown up. There were no sidewalks, so residents would have to pick their way between buildings, through dust or mud. However, they were fortunate to be among the few assigned a residence in one of the original buildings, once part of a school for boys—soon dubbed Bathtub Row, as they were the only apartments in Los Alamos with bathtubs.

Like everyone else, the Rosens had to put up with restrictions for the duration of the project that cut them off from normal life, and from friends and family outside the barbed wire fence. They wore ID badges at all times and their mail was inspected. Tight security was a way of life at Los Alamos, but they understood the absolute imperative to keep the project top secret. While Abraham was elated to be working with his peers,

Martha resigned herself to life behind barbed wire. Fortunately, she felt a kinship with other families at Los Alamos, especially those who were European-born and had fled to America. Although they spoke little about these harrowing experiences, those like herself, who had witnessed the sinister spread of the Third Reich, were bound together by what they had endured, and by the imperative to stop the madness. A disturbing reality haunted them; only fate and an ocean had spared them from death in Hitler's Europe. Friendships with these families helped alleviate the isolation of Los Alamos.

The Rosens especially enjoyed the friendship of Emily and Magnus Berthe—his former colleague on the faculty at Berkeley—who had also been recruited for the project. Their boy Peter was John's age. The two families shared a love of the outdoors and often went on hiking or skiing expeditions in the surrounding mountains.

Just weeks after their arrival, in the fleeting silver light that heralds dawn in the desert, Martha awoke with a sense of happy anticipation. Pulling back the covers and slipping out of bed, she stood listening to Abraham's slow breathing. The bedside clock showed four fifty. Moving to the window, she pushed the curtains aside, and felt the pleasurable brush of cool desert air wash over her. On the ground below, a young Native American woman sat cross-legged, motionless, glowing like honey in the rising sun. Her black hair, parted in the center and plaited into two thick braids, framed her moon-shaped face. Like a reluctant child sent to school for the first time, she sat with the corners of her mouth turned down and her chin tucked in. When Martha called out a greeting, she looked up with a steady, almost defiant expression in her almond-shaped, black eyes. The sight of her, the sheer surprise of her being there, compelled Martha to run downstairs still in her night robe.

Her name was Lola Tuse, she told Martha in halting English, and she was looking for work. Martha immediately alerted the security guards at the front entrance in case Lola had somehow slipped through the checkpoint. The guard reassured her, after thorough questioning, that the girl was the daughter of

253

the mess cook who lived on the base with his family. Martha was drawn to this reticent young woman and did not hesitate to hire her, especially now that a baby—still unbeknownst to Abraham—was on the way. Within days, the new member of the family was holding them spellbound with tales of her people, the Jicarilla.

Martha began taking day-trips to nearby pueblos and ancient cliff dwellings, accompanied by Lola and little John, after first obtaining the necessary security clearance. On their feast days she attended special ceremonial dances. The teachings and religion of the Native Americans, which the Catholic Church had all but erased, fascinated Martha. The earthy artistry of their traditional crafts, spoke to her. The Rosens temporary home soon filled with baskets and pottery collected on her forays. To Abraham's surprise, his unpretentious wife adorned herself with bright, silver and turquoise necklaces, bracelets, and rings.

One day she returned with a new find, a beaded wine bottle. Proudly displaying it to Abraham, she exclaimed that it showed how ingeniously the Jicarilla had preserved their traditional skills. Turning the bottle in his hands to admire the lively colors and intricate patterns, Abraham remarked, "It's very pretty, but still it's just a discarded old wine bottle."

His comment touched a raw nerve. "In case you haven't noticed, Americans have nearly destroyed the traditions of these people, including their traditional art." A melancholy expression came into her eyes, "And Germans are systematically, and brutally erasing everything artistic or cultural they bogusly deem non Aryan."

"And we will defeat their criminal intentions!"

They were silent for a while. Then Martha said, cryptically, "Here's to new wine in old bottles!"

Abraham raised his eyebrows. "What are you hinting at?"

"That despite the war, life goes on."

"And?"

"Abraham, haven't you noticed—I'm pregnant!" she said with a pleased chuckle.

Ten months after their arrival, Clara Rosen, named after Martha's paternal grandmother, first saw the light of a desert dawn. To celebrate the special occasion, the proud father handed out slices of rich fruitcake that Martha had baked in advance, in place of the usual cigars and chocolates unobtainable with wartime restrictions. Unlike John, who was a rambunctious child, Clara was a peaceful little thing. The sight of Lola with Clara became commonplace, the baby's tiny head of fine auburn hair and bright blue-green eyes peeking out of her nanny's papoose brought a smile to everyone's lips.

Abraham adored baby Clara, but as a vital part of the scientific team, he had little time to devote to her. His group had been assigned to work on a trigger device that would bring the plutonium core to the critical point needed to initiate spontaneous fission. For him, as for many of his colleagues, this was the chance of a lifetime to solve theoretical problems that had puzzled the greatest scientists of the age, and, more importantly halt the terrible war; they drove themselves, working long hours in search of the breakthrough. Oppenheimer, as did other top physicists, believed that as early as 1939, German scientists had succeeded in making uranium isotopes, bringing the reality of a German atomic bomb perilously close. They had to succeed or their enemies would prevail; they were convinced that they were in a desperate race with Nazi Germany.

As the project moved toward the climactic test explosion, code named Trinity, everyone could feel the tension rising at Los Alamos. A patch of flat, desolate scrub about sixty miles northwest of Alamogordo, home to thorny yucca, poisonous scorpions, centipedes, rattlesnakes, fire ants, and tarantulas, was chosen as the test site. No one wanted to contemplate the consequences of failure; the scientists kept on working until they dropped from exhaustion.

The night before the scheduled test, Abraham stayed up playing poker with his team. Anxiety rose when around midnight a thunderstorm raged through the area, passing dangerously close to the test tower. Oppenheimer himself became alarmed; if the bomb were detonated in a storm, the wind would carry lethal radioactive material many miles away.

Around three-thirty in the morning when the storm began to subside, Abraham decided to go to the mess hall. As he picked his way between darkened buildings, suddenly a rackety din halted him in his tracks. In moonlight filtering through fleeing storm clouds he saw hundreds of frogs mating in the puddles formed by the downpour. For a moment he stood entranced, spinning around in surprise as someone came up behind him.

"So, the miracle of life goes on!" It was his friend Magnus.

"But will it go on after the bomb?"

"It's too late to worry about that, Abraham. Let's get some breakfast before the big bang."

They joined others for powdered eggs, bitter coffee, and soggy French toast, which did not settle Abraham's already queasy stomach. Around the room, men were playing cards, smoking, reading, chatting, taking out sticks of gum, crumpling the wrappers into balls, tossing them into nearby trash cans, or just staring into space. They snapped to attention when a weather report crackled over the loudspeakers: the storm had passed to the east. Everyone in the room cheered and scrambled for the door. Outside they boarded buses for the short ride to the viewing bunkers.

As instructed, they applied thick layers of suntan lotion and donned dark glasses, shivering in the chill of dawn. As the seconds ticked slowly away, Abraham could feel his pulse racing. Time seemed to drag and expand — July 16, 1945, a day they could never erase. Suddenly, warning rockets flared upwards with a menacing hiss and sirens wailed. The final countdown had begun. Abraham's lips moved, "10-9-8-7 . . ." Intense light hit his eyes, he staggered, bumped his head on something hard, fell heavily to the ground as a wave of heat penetrated his very core. *Oh God! I will be fused into a shard of glass on the desert floor!* He groped blindly for his glasses and pressed them to his eyes. An immense violet pillar of unearthly light boiled upward, setting the universe on fire. A tidal wave of sound roared up the valley toward, through, and beyond him. He put his hands over his ears and groaned as a searing pain scoured the inside of his head.

Crouching, hypnotized, he watched the fire surge higher and higher until it formed an immense mushroom-shaped cloud towering over the landscape. As if from a great distance, he heard cheers and shouts. Half-blinded and deafened, he reached out to shake the hands of those around him, to embrace his colleagues trembling with elation and fear.

Abraham and Martha joined the noisy throng in the main cafeteria where free drinks were dispensed from improvised bars and a wind-up gramophone was belting out current hits. To the surprise of his colleagues, who did not know of his roots in jazz, Abraham danced wildly, surrounded by a cheering, clapping audience.

After the euphoria, the imminent danger of putting such a weapon to use galvanized many of the scientists into action. Like a man clawing for a lifeline, Abraham joined in the campaign to halt the use of the very nuclear bomb they had helped create. He signed a petition urging a demonstration drop somewhere in the Japanese countryside away from the city, as a warning of what was to come and of the awful devastation that would follow a nuclear explosion over a populated area. If that did not convince the Japanese to surrender, then the bomb could be dropped directly on a city. To Abraham's chagrin, this recommendation was strongly resisted by those in power. Oppenheimer himself was a proponent of dropping the bomb on a city, as soon as possible, believing that it would save millions of American soldiers.

Abraham was also a signatory to a petition drafted by Leó Szilárd the Hungarian-born physicist who had helped to launch the A-bomb project, asking the President not to resort to the use of atomic bombs in the present phase of the war. This petition was also sent to Sizlard's colleagues at Oak Ridge and Los Alamos urging the need for scientists to take a moral stand on the use of nuclear weapons.

Their pleas made no difference. Within two weeks of the test near Los Alamos, on August 6, 1945 a nuclear bomb was

257

dropped on Hiroshima, killing thousands of civilians. When news reached Los Alamos the next day, it struck Abraham like a bullet through his heart. Clutching his chest with both hands, he grabbed the back of a chair to keep from sinking to his knees. The phone on his desk rang. He groped for the receiver. "Hello." His voice sounded cracked and foreign to him.

"Abraham, you heard the news?" It was Magnus.

A wave of nausea filled Abraham's mouth with bile. "Yes, it's making me sick. I have to go, " he croaked. Hanging up on his friend, he made his way outside in a daze.

Storm clouds were gathering over the mountains, lightning shimmered, and the wind whirled dust devils high into the air. With a great blast, the rain came down, drenching him before he reached their apartment on Bathtub Row. Turning the key in the lock, he stepped silently into the entry and stood staring into space, unmindful of the puddle spreading on the rug.

Martha emerged from the kitchen wiping her hands on her apron. "Abraham, you're home early. What's wrong?"

"Turn on the radio." His eyes followed her as she walked across the room. With his head bowed he waited for the static to clear, then the President's voice rang out:

Sixteen hours ago an American airplane dropped one bomb on Hiroshima and destroyed its usefulness to the enemy. That bomb had more power than 20,000 tons of TNT. It had more than two thousand times the blastpower of the British "Grand Slam" which is the largest bomb ever yet used in the history of warfare. The Japanese began the war from the air at Pearl Harbor. They have been repaid manyfold. And the end is not yet. With this bomb we have now added a new and revolutionary increase in destruction to supplement the growing power of our armed forces. In their present form these bombs are now in production and even more powerful forms are in development.

"Oh, my God," Martha exclaimed. As she took her husband in her arms, she recalled so many scenes—the cryptic exchanges, the hushed voices, the frantic pace of work, the exhaustion, and the deep mystery surrounding Trinity. She helped her husband remove his sodden clothes, settled him in an armchair, and brought him a whiskey.

"There's blood on my hands, Martha," he said, pushing the drink away.

"Please, swallow this," she pleaded. After he had gulped it down, she called Magnus to come over.

When Martha had settled the men with drinks, his colleague reached forward and patted Abraham's knee, "My friend, you must put things in perspective. This in all probability will force the Japanese to surrender, and put this terrible war to an end."

"We who were *paid* to make weapons of destruction did it willingly, now we have to face other perhaps equally horrible consequences," Abraham observed gloomily.

"You were happy working at Los Alamos. What changed that?"

"We did." He meant "we" the survivors, the guilty ones. "We closed our eyes to the outcome of what we were doing."

"Enough of this polemic, Abraham! We are scientists, not prophets," Magnus snapped.

"He's one of a somewhat rare species, a scientist with a conscience," Martha said softly.

"For most of my life I've tried to ignore the ugly reality around me," Abraham castigated himself.

Not wanting to agitate his friend more than he already had, Magnus went outside to smoke his pipe. When he returned, the couple was sitting by an open window, lost in their private thoughts. The thunderstorm had moved on, leaving only a ragged fringe of tawny clouds over the mountains, and, as the night fell the sky began to blaze with starlight.

Abraham's angry outbursts and self-recriminations were met by the calm, reasonable voices of Magnus and Martha. After

259

midnight, the three dozed off, exhausted by the emotional turmoil. Hours later, it seemed to Martha, she awoke with a start. The lamp had been extinguished. In the faint light of the moon she could make out Magnus's bulky shape in the armchair. Her eyes moved to Abraham's chair. With a sickening lurch of her stomach, she saw that it was empty. In a low, aggrieved voice she did not recognize as her own, she cried out, "Abraham, where are you?"

Awakened by her cries, Magnus groped for the light, and saw that his friend was gone and the door ajar. Then he heard a voice declaiming: "'O horror, horror! Tongue nor heart cannot conceive nor name thee. Awake, awake! Ring the alarum-bell. Murder and treason! Shake off downy sleep, death's counterfeit, and look on death itself! Up, up, and see the great doom's image.'"

Magnus rushed to the open window. "What in the devil is he saying?"

"He has the habit of quoting Shakespeare when he is upset," Martha said with a wan smile. "I think that's *Hamlet*."

They went outside, retrieved Abraham and called the base doctor, who prescribed a sedative. Martha curled next to Abraham after he fell into a fitful sleep. She held him in her arms, comforted by the familiar pulsing of his heart, and the maleness of his shape. Abraham turned toward her, and eased his head into the soft place between her neck and shoulder. They clung to one another, survivors caught between an enormous catastrophe and an awesome triumph.

Three days after Hiroshima, a nuclear bomb was dropped on Nagasaki. Now the dynamic, vital atmosphere at Los Alamos turned to horror, in spite of the fact that the bombings had forced Japan into surrendering. Even John could see it in his father's sagging shoulders that replaced the purposeful stride. Instead of rushing off to the lab, he sat alone in his study, reading heart-rending accounts of the deaths in Japan, and the hideous slaughter of the Holocaust in Europe. He lingered over the dreadful photographs in the newspapers and magazines showing human beings reduced to skeletons imprisoned behind barbed wire, looking at the world with eyes devoid of hope. In shallow graves, naked corpses lay piled and twisted one upon the other, mouths contorted as they inhaled their last noxious breaths.

At this nadir of his life, the hand of providence, in the guise of Mendel Snyder, an older cousin from Atlanta, reached out to Abraham. Mendel had come across an article about the work done by Los Alamos scientists, which mentioned Abraham Rosen. Recognizing him as a relative, Mendel immediately sent a letter of congratulations, and introduced himself as the son of Yakov's sister, Frieda, and therefore first cousin to Abraham's father, Aaron. He wanted to reestablish broken family ties, and invited the Rosens to be his guests.

For security purposes, mail to Los Alamos residents was delivered to a post office box in Santa Fe, New Mexico. When Mendel's letter from Atlanta belatedly reached him, Abraham was not sure how to respond. At first he was suspicious, and reluctant to become involved. Having grown up without the benefit of an extended family, he had no desire to find unsolicited relatives. He knew only too well the power of family to wound one another. His in-laws, the Staubs, were his only family now that his parents were gone; he had grown to adulthood with a sense of himself as a loner, but cherishing his independence.

Martha understood her husband's alienation. Still this was an opportunity to get away from Los Alamos. In a world gone mad, she thought the ties of family offered a lifeline, a way to keep one's sanity. With her assurance that it would be a respite for them all, and that it would be good for John and Clara to get to know their cousins, Abraham accepted the warm invitation.

After receiving permission to leave Los Alamos for a two-week vacation, the Rosens boarded the train for yet another unfamiliar destination. As Abraham dozed to the lonesome cry of its whistle, melancholy reflections surfaced. He had come so far, and achieved so much since his unfortunate Bar Mitzvah. He had sworn to forget it; still the hurt and the guilt festered inside him.

261

Perhaps the Snyders would reveal the mystery his father had taken with him to his death.

❧ 23 ❧

The Fourth Inheritor: Mendel Snyder
Attempts to Right an Injustice

As we discover our identity, our desire for eternity guides our range of vision beyond the span of our own life.

Martin Buber

Mendel Snyder's son, Nathan, met the Rosens at the airport with a hearty "Welcome to Atlanta! Glad to meet y'all. First stop, my father's place on Washington Street." He shook hands with them, and then escorted the family to a yellow DeSoto with fancy exterior chrome, big cone-shaped taillights, and an Indian chief's head on the hood. He opened the car doors smiling, "Make yourselves comfortable," and off they went.

Abraham complimented Nathan on the smoothness of the ride.

"That's the hydromatic transmission they've installed in this model," he said proudly.

Chatting comfortably about the comparative merits of cars built by Chrysler, Ford, Chevrolet, and Studebaker, before wartime restrictions had halted the assembly lines, they glided through hilly woodlands of pine, oak, beech, and hickory on the outskirts of the city. This landscape appeared unfamiliar to Abraham. Growing up in New Orleans, the South was to him the open waters of the Gulf, the great brown, coiling Mississippi River, and the steamy bayous. Then, with a frisson of recognition, the sweet perfume of magnolias and honeysuckle, the cloying humidity, the calming tone of Nathan's southern drawl happily reminded him, *Ah, this is the South of my youth.*

As they neared the Snyders' home, dark cumulonimbus clouds, sprouting great towers and turrets, loomed over them; with a deep rumble the sky opened wide and rain fell in sheets.

"Here we are," Nathan said, turning into the driveway. The headlights flared over azaleas and rhododendrons, festooned with rosy bouquets, drooping under the weight of the rain. A blaze of lightning illuminated a redbrick mansion on a gentle hillside; the next snaked over majestic magnolia and a white columned front porch. For a moment all was dark, then a blue flash lit up a white cupola.

Nathan parked the DeSoto under a porte-cochere, sheltering them from the downpour, where Mendel Snyder waited to greet them. In his seventies, with broad shoulders and a considerable paunch, inquisitive brown eyes framed by wire-rimmed glasses, and a halo of gray hair fringing a shiny pate, he projected the look of a self-made man, a man who had done well for himself and was proud of it. Indeed, he ran the best delicatessen in Atlanta.

"Welcome to our home," Mendel cried, coming forward to shake hands. Then he gestured to the houseboy who hurried forward to collect their bags.

Waiting in the spacious living room was Mendel's wife, Illene, who embraced them warmly. "So good to see you. Come in. Come in! You must be tired after such a long journey. Would you like some tea?" She was a petite woman, elegant in a fragile, doll-like way. She wore a fashionable maroon velvet skirt that fell gracefully to her ankles, and a soft, gray silk blouse with a floppy bow around the collar. Over tea served with peach pie, they made small talk to break the ice. The Rosens were pleasantly surprised that the exchange, between relatives who had just met, was so relaxed.

After refreshments, Illene rang the bell for the maid to clear the table, and then she rose and said, smiling, "I'll show you to your rooms. There's time to bathe and rest. Dinner will be served in an hour." They followed her to their assigned bedrooms, up a curving flight of stairs and down a cool, dim passage with high ceilings.

Seated in a paneled dining room with a white marble fireplace at one end, they partook of a four-course dinner accompanied by a good Cabernet. After the Spartan life at Los Alamos, Abraham couldn't help being impressed. *Ah, wealth! The allure of it! Surely, one of man's greatest temptations,* he mused.

They conversed about how their families were connected to one another, about the Japanese surrender and the future now that the war was over. Later, Mendel, a gracious host and raconteur, entertained them with family stories of the bygone days.

"The early Jewish settlers who came to the South eked out a living as peddlers, you know, pushing a cart, like your grandfather Yakov. Through hard work, in time they became proprietors of their own stores. Yakov and Chana worked themselves to the bone and achieved much. The Rosen Bakery in Ricksburg was known for its quality, and customers came from quite a distance to buy their rye bread, bagels, and pies," he boasted.

"Is the bakery still in existence?" Abraham asked.

"Before your grandfather passed away, a fellow countryman bought the bakery, and even carried on his tradition by using the same recipes. Later, the business was moved from its original location downtown to a shopping center in the suburbs of Ricksburg. The current owner has added a New York-style deli."

"What was my grandfather like as person?" Abraham wanted to know.

"My mother, Frieda, worshiped him. Did you know that Yakov scrimped and saved to bring her to America? He was very stern, but everyone respected him for his piety and his devotion to Judaism. And he is still honored as one of the founding members of the Orthodox shul in Ricksburg."

Honored he may be, but he was a zealot that hurt my father deeply, and tore my family apart, Abraham thought bitterly.

"What was Abraham's father, Aaron, like?" Martha interjected.

"Aaron had a sunny personality. He liked to clown around." Martha saw the broad smile on Mendel's face, but his eyes shone more brightly than they should have.

"My father was a born showman," Abraham agreed. "Some called him a rebel, when he was just a free spirit with a big heart." There was a catch in his voice.

Mendel shook his head and sighed.

They were silent for a time. Then Martha tactfully led them away from this painful subject. "Yakov, Chana and your mother came from Lithuania, didn't they?"

Mendel put his fork down, hooked his fingers together to gather his thoughts. When he looked up there was a gleam in his eye. "I loved mother's yarns about Valinsk, a little village at the edge of a deep, dark forest inhabited by wolves and bears." He turned to smile at John.

John was an energetic, inquisitive, headstrong boy who could not sit still for long. He was also the possessor of an overly active imaginative. Now Mendel's resonant voice, relating tales of long ago and far away, held him spellbound.

"My mother Frieda and her brother Yakov, lived with their righteous Uncle Hershel, his good wife Sonia, and their three beautiful daughters, Miriam, Ida, and Leah, in a little wooden house with a steep roof. Near the entrance to the home there was a trap door into a root cellar where they stored fat potatoes, turnips, beets, carrots, and sweet apples and pears for the winter. Valinsk overflowed with geese, ducks, chickens, goats, cows, horses, and cats. A tall picket fence surrounded the house to keep animals out. My mother had a pet cat named Kippah, because of the black patch on her head that looks like the skullcap I'm wearing. She spoke to Kippah in Yiddish and, being a very intelligent cat, he would answer with a meow or a flick of his tail."

"Did she have a pet dog too?" John asked.

"No, few people kept dogs because they bite and bark too much."

"Maybe it was because they couldn't afford to feed them?" Illene chimed in.

"Well, maybe. But my parents told me they didn't like dogs because they attacked people." Mendel cut into a fried chicken leg, and chewed on a morsel before continuing. "Or maybe it was because they were attacked by "non-Jewish" dogs that they came to dislike them." There was a twinkle in his eye, as he gently poked fun at the world of his forefathers.

Observing that the boy was too young to get his attempt at humor, Mendel hastened to add, "But in the winter *chickens* practically became pets when they were allowed to sleep under the oven. The stove was stoked with wood because there was no electricity in the houses back then. The kitchen was the center of activity. A big pot of soup always simmered on the stove. There was no indoor plumbing, so they had to use an outdoor toilet and fetch water from the well, even in winter when ice and snow covered everything. There wasn't much furniture in the house, but my mother loved the heavy brass Sabbath candlesticks, the silver wine goblets, and the big copper tea urn that held hot water at all times; most precious of all were their holy books. If I close my eyes, I can smell burning wax candles, wood smoke, brewing tea, salted herring, and ripe apples."

"Tell us more about the forest," John pleaded, pushing black-eyed peas around on his plate.

"Ah, the oaks were enormous! Five men holding hands could not circle the trunks! And the trees grew so thick they kept the sun out in the summer, and the snow from falling to the ground in the winter. Thousands of birds lived in the forest! The river was full of fish—huge pike and little garfish. There were wild horses, deer, bears, foxes, hares, squirrels, and wolves. Even the hunters were afraid of those hungry wolves." Mendel's voice fell to a whisper as he reached this part of the tale.

"Tell us about the wolves!" John's eyes were wide with excitement.

"I'm sure Uncle Mendel will tell you all about the wolves, later," Abraham admonished gently. "Right now I want to hear about the people of the shtetl."

"Ah, I could tell stories about the citizens of Valinsk: the humble wagon drivers and coachmen; the hard-working market-people with their whisk brooms, who sold goods of all sorts, everything from sewing needles to earrings, candlesticks to furs and clothing. About the brilliant scholars who read holy books all day long. There were also tailors, watchmakers, bakers, seamstresses, blacksmiths, carpenters, shoemakers, and poor peddlers. Working hours were regulated by daily praying times. The Shabbat brought all business activity to a halt. The routine hustle and bustle of daily life also came to a standstill during the High Holidays, when the shtetl, for all practical purposes, closed down. They formed a closely-knit community and everyone helped those in need."

"Surely there was the usual amount of suffering and conflict?" Abraham inquired.

"Naturally. Not everyone in Valinsk lived in harmony. Most of the disputes arose over religious matters. In fact, from what my mother told me, I got the impression that members of the shul were at each other's throats most of the time. Only in the cemetery did harmony prevail, where everyone bent to the authority of the old sexton of the burial society. He was so feared he was called the Tsar of the Corpses." Mendel paused for the smiles and chuckles to subside before continuing.

"Then there were a few who disgraced themselves by drinking too much, or sleeping with peasant women."

"Remember the children . . ." Illene shushed him with a finger to her lips.

"Or gave in to greed by enriching themselves at the expense of their neighbors. Some boys were born scholars. Others made constant mischief, and although the teacher often hit them with a stick, they learned nothing."

The storyteller swallowed the last drop remaining in his goblet, pushed his empty plate away, and sighed contentedly. He had eaten his fill. "Most were poor. They lived on potatoes and cabbage. They saved the chickens for their eggs, only sacrificing them to make golden, healing chicken soup. There's a saying that if a poor man eats chicken soup, either he or the chicken must be

268

ill," Mendel's said with a wry smile. Then, on a more somber note, he continued, "Shmuel Rosen, our patriarch, was a hard-working, clever business man who become one of the few wealthy men of the shtetl."

As Abraham listened, an uncanny feeling came over him. For the first time in his life, he felt linked to his forefathers, and to a shared heritage. It dawned on him that his life was a small but integral part of a long and complex history with deep ancient roots. Still Mendel's depiction of the shtetl appeared overly romantic, "What about the pogroms?" he asked bluntly.

Martha frowned and made a surreptitious downward motion of her hand. His newly found cousin snorted and rubbed his chin. In the silence that ensued, the distant clatter of utensils being washed in the kitchen replaced the conversation.

Illene broke the lull. "Mendel's mother, Frieda, the family storyteller, avoided talking about the pogroms. Maybe she didn't want to frighten the children, maybe it was too painful, or maybe she just wanted to forget."

Martha nodded. "My family can't talk about the suffering in Germany, either."

"You're right. My father didn't like to talk about growing up in Ricksburg, or about his father." Abraham agreed ruefully.

Their host took a handkerchief out of his pocket, and blew his nose. Then he studied the scientist over the tips of his extended fingers. "Do you want me to continue?"

"Yes, there is so much I don't know about my family."

Regaining his composure, Mendel went on. "The High Holidays were a time for family gatherings. In the years after Yakov disowned Aaron, my mother Frieda, and your grandmother Chana, always wept on these occasions because Aaron, Marlene and you, were not with them."

The sorrow in Mendel's eyes made Abraham wince.

"Much as I respected him, I feel that your grandfather committed a great injustice. Perhaps it is time for me to put things right."

"Mendel, what happened in the past is over. I don't dwell on it," Abraham replied sharply. For years no one had mentioned the falling-out between Aaron and Yakov. He wished now that he hadn't provoked Mendel into bringing it up. As he had feared, too often family gatherings aroused unpleasant emotional undercurrents.

"I understand, Abraham, but perhaps it is possible to right an *injustice* through the teachings of the Torah. We *can* do justice through our Torah." He cocked his head to one side waiting for Abraham's response.

Unsure of what Mendel was alluding to, Abraham observed, "Ah, justice! How sweet it is to bring about justice. Perhaps it is even sweeter than revenge."

Now Mendel and Illene were puzzled. Mendel frowned and opened his mouth to say something, then seemed to think better of it.

"You were saying something about the Torah?" Abraham prompted.

"You've studied it?"

"No, I learned just the portion I needed to know for my Bar Mitzvah, that's all."

"I see," Mendel said, unimpressed.

Abraham leaned forward and inclined his head, a gesture meant to encourage his cousin to continue. Evidently feeling that the moment was not right, Mendel declined to respond.

To break the tension, Illene said, "I'm going to get Frieda's photo album. I think you will find it most interesting."

"So, Frieda came to America a few years after Yakov? Did other relatives join her, or are some still in Lithuania?" Martha inquired.

A grim expression passed across Mendel's face. "Some remained in Valinsk and the surrounding towns, but we haven't heard from them in a long time. Please God they are still alive."

"I'm sorry." *We keep upsetting these good people*, Martha thought, regretting that she had asked. To her relief, Illene retuned with a leather-bound album and began leafing through its pages; many of the images had faded to reddish brown. When she came to the one she was looking for, she showed it to the Rosens.

Martha's eyebrows rose in surprise. "This one looks just like Abraham!"

"That's Abraham's grandfather Yakov," Illene said.

Martha traced the outline of the angular jaw and aquiline nose with the tips of her fingers. "Abraham looks exactly like his grandfather," Martha mused. "May we look through this album with you? We want to learn more about the Rosen family."

"Yes, of course. Let's make ourselves more comfortable on the sofa," Illene said, rising to usher her guests from the dining room to the living room.

As they bent to scrutinize the old family photos — disinterring the human beings buried in the dust of time — intimations of their lives, of their personalities emerged. Illene's quiet commentary knitted the history of the family together for Abraham and Martha. Yet as they closed the album on the last photograph, the ancestors lingered in their minds, disturbing them with unanswered questions.

When everyone had retired for the night, after the children fell asleep in the adjoining bedroom, and the Rosens were ensconced in an enormous antique four-poster bed, Martha replayed the conversation in her head. Unable to get to sleep she whispered, "Abraham, I think when Mendel spoke of wanting to right an injustice through the Torah he was trying to tell you something. What did he mean?"

"How should I know? If he has something on his mind he needs to be more direct. If it's important, I'm sure Mendel will let me know before we leave." Abraham turned onto his side to get into a more comfortable position.

"Maybe," Martha said, wishing that her husband hadn't been quite so brusque with the Snyders.

"Don't worry, the truth, whatever it is, will come out." Yawning, Abraham put his arm around his wife. "Shush, do you hear the cicadas and frogs? Ah, how they bring back childhood memories."

The next two days passed pleasantly with visits to the extended Snyder family and tours around Atlanta, a town with an unfortunate history, having been burnt down by General

271

Sherman's troops during the Civil War. They took in a movie at the Fabulous Fox, one of the most ornate movie palaces in the country, drove by the small apartment where Margaret Mitchell had resided while writing Gone with the Wind, and visited Loew's Grand Theater built in 1893 as DeGive's Grand Opera House, where the great classic American movie, based on Mitchell's novel, premiered.

On Friday, just before sunset, Abraham and John accompanied Mendel to the synagogue to attend the Sabbath service. Martha and little Clara remained at home with the women.

As the light began to ebb into darkness, surrounded by her daughter and granddaughters, Illene placed a kerchief over her head, and bent to light the candles in the tall brass candlesticks standing on the sideboard, and moved her hands over the flame as if drawing their warmth into her. Covering her eyes with her hands she softly intoned the traditional blessing, then greeted her family with a heartfelt, "Shabbat Shalom."

Having heralded the Sabbath bride into the house, her hostess took Martha's arm and, followed by the others, walked out to the front porch to wait for the men. The women had been busy all day, supervising the preparation of traditional foods, setting the table with flowers, fine linen, and the best china. From the flow of their conversation Martha understood that the Snyders' daily lives centered on the synagogue. On Monday nights they met for Talmud study. On Tuesday they attended Hebrew classes. Wednesday evenings they worked with their charities. Some attended the Thursday evening seminar, conducted by a university professor, on Chassidic history and thought. The Sabbath they devoted to worship, and Sundays they held classes for the children.

Despite this closely-knit Orthodox community, Nathan's twin daughters, Sheila and Sherry, grumbled that they had been excluded, because of their family's Lithuanian origins, from "Ballyhoo," the annual courtship weekend bash for college-aged sons and daughters, sponsored by the German-Jewish Reform community.

"So ignore them, and their silly functions, there are plenty of other nice Orthodox boys to date," their grandmother counseled. "Besides, Reform Jews are not observant enough."

"Bubby, Atlanta isn't the shtetl," Sheila retorted.

"We'll miss the most fabulous parties," Sherry added with a grimace.

"*Nu, vos iz neias?*" So, what's news? The grandmother said, with a dismissive shrug.

Martha found herself comparing the Snyders' lives to her own in Stuttgart. The Staub's household had been thoroughly secular; everything had revolved around her father's scientific work, their love of music, and their congenial extended family. How she missed the intricate network she had taken for granted. Her ties of blood had extended all over Germany — aunts, uncles, their husbands and wives, first cousins, second cousins, and even third cousins. Where were they now? Many had disappeared in the gas chambers of Treblinka and Auschwitz. Now they existed only in her nightmares.

She could not yet find a way to speak to these kind Atlanta relatives of the extermination — the pain and sorrow, terror and shame were still too raw. To hide the emotional turmoil she was feeling, Martha looked down at her baby and kissed her forehead. Clara had fallen asleep on her lap, lulled by the warm breeze, the *chirr-chirr* of cicadas, and the murmur of voices. Glad for an excuse to leave, she carried Clara off for a short nap, promising to return in time for dinner.

By the time the men got back from the synagogue, Martha had composed herself and was back on the porch. Mendel introduced two Jewish traveling salesmen he had invited for dinner that he had met at the shul — one worked for a New York coat manufacturer, the other for a shoe company in New Jersey. Showing hospitality, especially on the Sabbath and Holidays, is a mitzvah; besides, Mendel enjoyed inviting strangers.

After everyone had been introduced, Mendel placed his hands on the children's' heads to bless them. Filling an ornate silver goblet to the brim with wine, he held it in his right hand, and recited *Kiddush*, the blessing sanctifying Shabbat, in his best

273

alto. Then he sat, drank deeply, and poured the rest into cups for those around the table to sip. After the ritual hand washing, they resumed their seats. With a flourish Mendel raised the two loaves of braided bread and said the blessing over them, then sliced and dipped the bread into salt, ate a piece and then passed it around. Martha thought: *with the homely aroma of chicken soup floating in from the kitchen, and the candles shining on the sideboard, it's such a warm feeling, as if we are all bound together.*

The repast went on for several hours, interrupted frequently by prayers, the singing of psalms, and lively discussions around Torah-related subjects. Abraham and Martha, unfamiliar with the Sabbath traditions, felt a little awkward; nevertheless they enjoyed the ritual, the songs, and the traditional food. The first course, gefilte fish — fishcakes of minced white pike seasoned with saffron — was served with horseradish from Illene's vegetable garden. Homemade chicken soup with noodles came next, then roast chicken served with potato *kugel*, or pudding. For dessert, there were baked apples, cookies, and an assortment of pies.

Martha thought, *the past is caught in their cooking, just as it is in mine. These women offer food as a way to honor their heritage.*

Satiated, Abraham leaned back and studied the Rosens and Snyders sitting at the big mahogany table, as if he were viewing a painting — excluding the two rather nondescript salesmen from his scrutiny. He visualized himself in a tableau with these people, all caught in the golden glow of candlelight as the night lapped at the windowpanes. Together they created a harmonious, dynamic composition against a shadowy background enlivened by the silky sheen of dark green, blue and purple dresses, the sparkling silverware, the glowing red wine, and the creamy-white camellias in a heavy crystal bowl.

At the head of the table, Mendel and his wife, Illene, presided over them all. From beneath heavy eyebrows, the patriarch surveyed his family with kindly dignity and pride. Illene gazed at them possessively, her drooping eyelids soft as rose petals, her dark lustrous hair shot with gray, and her slim neck showing the first wrinkles of age. Seated to Mendel's right

274

were himself, Martha, Clara next to her, and John next to him. Martha's blue eyes sparkled, the corners of her mouth lifted in a dreamy smile as if she had glimpsed a kindlier world. The auburn ringlets framing Clara's cherubic face bounced as she banged on the tray of her highchair. John tipped his head to one side and looked at his mother with a happy grin as he devoured another cookie from a heaped platter. Seated next to Clara, Bubby Matla, her wrinkled skin as soft as chamois leather, gazed adoringly at the playful child.

To Illene's left the Snyder's son, Nathan, sat between his wife, Debbie, and their twin daughters, Sheila and Sheryl. Nathan, who managed the suburban branch of the Mendel's deli, wore the ragged edge of his receding hairline, the Rorschach blot of the wine colored birthmark on his cheek, the curve of his nose, and the sad droop of his dark walrus mustache like distinctive badges of courage. Debbie bent sideways to listen to her husband's conversation with Abraham, a finger pressed against the curve of her high cheekbones, red lips pursed into a circle; there was something haughty in her expression. Abraham detected a Snyder family trait in the twin girls' smooth olive skin, dark hair and inquisitive eyes. *But the resemblance is subtler than that*, Abraham thought, *it's a complicated network of similarities passed on in the genes*. Greg, the teenage son of Mendel's daughter Barbara, seated next to the twins, half rose from his seat impatient to leave now that the meal was almost over. His lanky black hair, deliberately parted down the middle and slicked back, lent him a somewhat defiant air.

At the opposite end of the table sat Barbara, and her second husband, Frank, both partners in a well-known law firm. Barbara, welcoming and homely as a loaf of bread, murmured something to her husband, who had inclined an ear toward her. Abraham saw himself observing them all with sharp eyes and a brooding expression, his squared jaw thrust forward.

How amazing that I am connected to all of these people. Abraham reflected. They are rooted in Atlanta's Jewish community in a way that makes them secure, perhaps even a little smug. They have no cause to question their identity or their place in society, while mine has

275

always been nebulous. As an adult I made a place for myself as scientist, and that was enough — until the bombs were dropped, until the concentration camps.

Seeing her husband staring off into space, Martha said brightly, "Illene, these dishes are wonderful, delicious!"

"The recipes were handed down from my grandmother, Bubby Kyla Goodman, who grew up in Lithuania. She was a real *baleboosteh*, housewife and hostess par excellence. She immigrated to America with my mother to a small town here in Georgia. There wasn't any money to spare in the household back then. Believe me, it wasn't easy for her to keep a kosher household in a rural community. She had to travel to Atlanta where there was a kosher butcher. She had to bargain for a little bit of fish for a cent less, or haggle with the butcher to throw in a few extra meat bones."

"So your family moved from Lithuania, to Germany, then to the U.S.?" Martha asked.

"Yes, my parents moved to Berlin when I was twelve. So my roots are in Lithuania."

"Ma, please don't bore our guests with your stories of the old days," Barbara pleaded. "Next you'll be teaching them to speak Yiddish the way you tried with us."

"It's sad that the younger generation doesn't want to learn Yiddish," Illene rebuked her daughter. "It is a rich language with wonderful songs and stories."

"John has picked up quite a lot of German from my parents," Martha said, "but I don't suppose he or his sister will speak it fluently."

"Sometimes, just for fun, I imitated my mother's Irish brogue, " Abraham interjected, with a wry smile.

Mendel raised his eyebrows at all the babble. "Abraham, a family is the container of a person's identity and his heritage, just as surely as a jug holds wine," he added pointedly, "I believe that the ties of family should be kept strong."   "But the feud between my father and his father broke those ties! To borrow your metaphor, my grandfather smashed the jug and spilled the family's heritage."

"I'm very sorry for all that. But perhaps there is some way to mend the damage and rekindle ties?"

"It's too late for my father," Abraham replied, failing to keep the rancor from his voice. He felt Martha's hand squeezing his, cautioning him to stop.

At the other end of the table, he caught the tail end of a conversation about Pearl Harbor, then something about President Truman and the surrender of Japan. Then suddenly he became aware that everyone was looking directly at him.

Barbara stood and lifted her wineglass. "A toast to Abraham and the brilliant team of scientists who brought the war to an end!"

"To Abraham!" They all lifted their glasses.

His body stiffened as guilt lapped over him. *Other men were thrown into the killing fields of war while I was tucked away at Los Alamos. These people have no idea of the terrifying reality of nuclear warfare. They damn me with their praise.* He forced a smile, lifted his glass. "Now it's my turn to propose a toast to Mendel and Illene for this wonderful family reunion and, of course, for the excellent food."

"To a wonderful host and hostess!" they all echoed, clinking their glasses.

"I want you to know that Ma insists on hosting Shabbat even though we say it has become too much for her," Barbara remarked.

"When my cook, Pearl, decides to quit, that's when I'll quit," Illene sniffed, bringing a lace handkerchief to her nose. "Pearl grew up on a tenant farm in Georgia, and has worked for our family for many years. She has a way of mixing the southern cooking of her childhood with our kosher traditions, with marvelous results."

"So, Ma, give Pearl a good pension and let her retire," Nathan teased.

"Are you ready to give up Pearl's fried chicken, okra and tomato stew, pecan pies or molasses cookies? Or my brisket?" Illene was proud of her roast beef, having adjusted the traditional recipe to the southern style, by adding chili sauce, grainy

277

mustard, brewed coffee, and red wine. Her grandmother's recipe had been simpler; a slab of meat seasoned with honey and lemon juice, salt and pepper.

Nathan rolled his eyes in mock horror. Everyone laughed—the kind of joking among people who are comfortable with one another's foibles and even poke fun at them. After the laughter had run its course with intermittent good-natured chuckles and dabbing of the eyes, Mendel turned to Abraham and beaming warmly said, "I want you and your family to join us for Rosh Hashanah."

"Thank you. If we can arrange it, that would be swell."

On the last day of their visit, Mendel took Abraham to the synagogue for the morning service, telling him that he wanted to show him something of importance. Afterwards, he led Abraham up the steps to the raised platform, and stood before the polished wooden door of the Holy Ark framed by white marble columns. In the amber glow of the brass lamp hanging above the Ark, Abraham could hear Mendel's rapid breathing as he opened the doors to reveal the sacred Torahs clothed in rich silk and velvet mantels. Then slowly, reverently, his lips moving silently in prayer, he removed one of the Torahs with jingling bells, placed it on the lectern, slipped off its finials, breast plate and red silk mantle then carefully unrolled the scroll.

Abraham peered over at Mendel rocking back and forth on his heels in prayer, jarring loose a sliver of memory like a reflection in a shattered mirror; he had observed the rabbi In New Orleans executing these exact motions as a boy of thirteen. With a shiver he recalled his regrettable Bar Mitzvah.

Mendel turned to Abraham, "This Torah has survived catastrophes: devastating fires, monster storms at sea, and venomous serpents."

Abraham raised his eyebrows in amazement then bent to examine the scroll.

Mendel continued, "It is our family's precious inheritance commissioned by your great-great-great-grandfather Shmuel Rosen, and brought to America by your grandfather Yakov

Rosen. According to our patriarch's wish, this Torah must be passed down from father to son, or failing that, to a nephew."

Abraham shot upright. Could this be the legacy his father had kept from him all those years?

Mendel rubbed his chin ruefully. "Did your father ever mention this Torah to you?"

"No he did not! Why on earth did he find the need to be so secretive about it?"

They stood in the hushed sanctuary, with the Rosen Torah between them, the dust motes dancing in the tunnel of light streaming from the clerestory windows. Finally, Mendel said, "I know what your grandfather did was not right. But it was the result of a long, unhappy history. Yakov had a hard life—maybe that helps to understand why he disowned your father. Do you know that he sat *shiva* for him when he married your non-Jewish mother? That's the traditional period of mourning for the dead."

"What! That's terrible, despicable!"

"Perhaps you are being too harsh."

"No, I don't think I am!"

"Please don't hold a grudge against your grandfather, let him rest in peace, for the sake of your children. For them you should know about the history of this cherished inheritance."

"Mendel, for God's sake, just tell me in plain words exactly what's on your mind."

"Let's go to a place where we can talk in private."

After returning the Torah to the Ark with the proper blessing, they left the synagogue and walked around the corner to the park. On the way, Mendel stopped off at his deli to pick up sandwiches and Cokes. Settling on a park bench they unwrapped the sandwiches, and ate.

"Mendel, in spite of the horrible hurt my father suffered, I absolutely have to question his motives for keeping the Rosen Torah a secret from me."

"Perhaps it was his way of retaliating against his father. Could it be that by refusing to acknowledge its existence he was rejecting his father just as his father had rejected him?"

"Maybe so. But knowing this doesn't take away the pain or the injustice! I don't understand why my grandfather was never able to reconcile with his son or why he refused to acknowledge me, his own grandchild. Surely the years should have abated his anger!"

Breaking a piece of bread into crumbs, Mendel scattered them to the pigeons hovering nearby. "I too, have found Yakov's unforgiving nature hard to bear, but perhaps I have come to some understanding of what motivated him. You see, his obedience to God's commandments never wavered. If you will allow me, I would like to tell you the tale of Tevyah the milkman and his daughter Eve as told by our beloved Yiddish writer Sholom Aleichem, who wrote so movingly of the shtetls in the early years of this century."

Abraham nodded for him to go on.

"First, you must picture your grandfather, Yakov, as Tevyeh and Eve as your father, Aaron."

"Okay."

"Tevyeh is riding home in his rickety cart after delivering the day's milk to his customers. His heart is heavy with grief because Eve, his youngest daughter, has married a gentile against his wishes. Although Tevyeh tries not to think of Eve, he keeps remembering how he used to hold her in his arms and soothe her with lullabies until she fell asleep with her little head resting on his shoulder. And he longs to hold her close once more. All of a sudden his horse comes to a halt, almost tossing him from the cart. Tevyeh looks up and there is Eve standing in the road unharmed as the day she left home. He is about to jump down and throw his arms around her, when he hears a voice warning him, 'Tevyeh remember what she has done!' With a fearful crack of his whip he lashes his horse into action. In desperation, Eve lunges forward and grabs the reins crying, 'Father! Father! Let me die if you won't speak to me!'

"Tevyeh whips the horse again, and as the cart springs forward, he wills himself not to look back, although his heart is breaking. Questions keep repeating themselves in his head. *Is this the way a father should behave? Why did God allow different religions to coexist? Have I taken too much responsibility upon myself when my children disobey God's commandments?*

"He becomes angry with himself because he can't find answers, and to drown out his daughter's voice crying, 'Father! Father! Let me die!' he begins singing the afternoon prayer: 'Blessed are those that dwell in Thy house; they shall praise Thee forever.' But no matter how loudly he sings he can still hear her voice.

"After that he never spoke of Eve to anyone, but sometimes he is overcome by a strange longing to go to her. Then one day he puts on his Sabbath coat and drives over to the train station, goes up to the window and asks for a ticket to Hotzeplotz. That's where his daughter lives with her gentile husband. And the ticket agent replies that he has never heard of such a place. Tevyeh answers 'That's not my fault that you never heard of it.' And he drives back home."

When he had finished, Abraham said, "That's a very painful story, but thanks for trying to help me understand Yakov. But the old beliefs and the fanatic piety he brought with him from the shtetl, that he tried so hard to transplant in America, were doomed to fail. Don't you think?"

"No! Traditions that have survived for so many centuries can't be tossed away so easily," Mendel retorted. "Listen to me Abraham, if I could return to the shtetl what would I find there?

"Probably not a trace of our family."

"Yet, the shtetl lingers in our food, our attitudes, our language, our dreams, our nightmares. Can we ever leave the shtetl behind?" Catching Abraham's bewildered look, he went on, "The deeply ingrained values of *Yiddishkeit*, the Jewish way of life, don't die easily! They've survived for thousands of years."

Abraham wanted to cry out: But my father discarded those traditions—albeit at a heavy price. And I have discarded them too. What good are they if they are the cause of heartbreak? Instead he said, "It's good that you inherited the Torah, and have conscientiously served as its caretaker."

Mendel lifted his Coke, "A toast to the world of your ancestors, of your grandfather Yakov!"

281

Now is the time to speak your mind, Abraham told himself. But what could he say? *No thanks, religion with all the intolerance and prejudice it engenders is not for me* – only to see Mendel deeply hurt? He couldn't insult his kindly relative. He hesitated a moment longer. Then clinked his Coke against Mendel's.

"L'Chayim! To Life! To our traditions!"

"L'Chayim," Abraham echoed half-heartedly.

To Abraham's surprise, now that the roots of his grandfather's vengeance had been exposed, and he had discovered what his father had been hiding from him all those years, he felt an emotional release from the mistaken guilt that had dogged him—like a child who finds that the monster he feared under his bed is simply not lurking there. The responsibility of safeguarding the Rosen Torah that might have fallen to him, had passed on to the Snyders, and that seemed quite fitting.

❦24❧

Mendel Snyder's Dilemmas

Dogs fight over a bone, mourners over a will.

Yiddish folk saying

Back in the mid 1870s, Mendel's father, Sydney Snyder, had first taken his son to Klein's, a few months after his Bar Mitzvah. It was Mendel's first experience dining out.

The deli, located on Broad Street in downtown Atlanta, stood in the center of a busy commercial hub. Just around the corner from the *Atlanta Constitution*, it was a magnet for journalists, who packed into the place at all hours to stuff themselves with hefty servings of New York-style specialties: thick garlicky corned-beef and pastrami sandwiches on rye, fat kosher hot dogs with tangy sauerkraut, fresh chewy bagels with cream cheese topped with smoked salmon, flavorful scarlet borscht and sour cream, steamy matzo ball soup, and chicken noodle soup.

Circulating in the cigarette haze, were a cloying abundance of smells: kosher dills, pickled onions, fresh bread and bagels, with undercurrents of perfume and aftershave, hair pomade, shoe polish, cigars and newsprint. To his embarrassment the boy could hear his stomach rumbling as he inspected succulent bowls of chopped liver, blocks of cheese in bright red skins, and hunks of smoked meat inside the display case.

Sitting at the marble counter, perched on a pivoting bar stool, Mendel drank it all in: the checkerboard black-and-white

283

tiled floors, the bright murals splashed on the walls, the ornate pressed-tin ceiling tiles, and the big fans that spun the fog of cigarette smoke into lazy ribbons. In booths and at tables, men and women talked, and smoked, and laughed as if they were in charge of the world.

Klein took an instant liking to young Mendel and hired him as a part-time busboy that same day. Snyder's secondhand furniture store was not doing well, and the extra money came in handy for the family. He never tired of the gusto with which the diners ate, the hubbub of conversation, and the constant flow of customers. He made it a point to get to know the regulars, to keep their coffee cups filled, and to put extra bowls of pickles and slaw on their tables.

Impressed by Mendel's enthusiasm, Klein promoted him to successively better-paying jobs. He came to rely on his assistant, eventually promoting him to manager. When the old man belatedly decided to retire, Mendel had been working at the deli for over a decade, and hammered out a deal to buy the business.

Mendel was a go-getter who kept his ears open as the journalists heatedly debated the hot issues of the day. Sometimes he learned about breaking stories before they hit the headlines. His instinct kicked in when he overheard the reporters talking in awed voices about John Pemberton's imminent sale, to a local business, of his secret recipe for Brain Tonic, for a whopping $2,300. Rumor had it that the buyer, Asa Candler, was planning to market the tonic as Coca-Cola. Acting on a tip, Mendel was among the first to purchase a block of the company's original stock — and to offer the new soft drink to his customers.

Another bit of news that paid off came during the gubernatorial campaign of 1906, which soon became racist and inflammatory. The deli owner got advance warning that white mobs were about to take to the streets. He had the sense to close and board up his store, immediately. This quick action prevented his place from being vandalized by the rabble that beat and killed blacks in parks, in stores, and even on trolleys. Mendel's business acumen did not go unnoticed by his Uncle Yakov. He began soliciting his nephew for advice on when to buy or sell on the stock market.

In the spring of 1929, Mendel received bad news that his uncle had suffered a stroke, and hastily set out on the arduous trip to Ricksburg.

To his distress, he arrived to find Yakov mute, drooling, and tethered to a wheelchair. When he tried to speak to his nephew, the sounds came out as unintelligible grunts. As the months went by, with little improvement, his family began to suspect that the old man was suffering from dementia. Chana insisted, however, that the intense expression in his eyes, when spoken to, proved that a flame of intelligence still burned within. She swore that she could understand Yakov, and that he had conveyed a message to her: in a reoccurring dream he saw Aharon wearing a prayer shawl and chanting from the Rosen Torah as he swayed back and forth. He longed to embrace his son, yet when he reached out to touch him, he encountered nothing but thin air. As Yakov struggled to convey his disturbing vision to his trembling wife, tears poured from his right eye, while the rest of his face, paralyzed by the stroke, remained immobile.

Mendel promised his distraught aunt he would be back soon, but when he returned to Atlanta, everyone was plunging into the rapidly rising stock market. With a little cash and a lot of credit, anyone could play, and play they did! Mendel was tempted to join in the frenzy, but shrewdly resisted. When the bottom fell out of the market, setting off a worldwide depression, he was one of the few in a position to buy blue-chip stocks for just pennies — Radio Corporation of America, Montgomery Ward, General Electric. That canny move would later earn him a fortune.

Soon after the crash, Mendel received a telegram announcing that Uncle Yakov had passed away. He had been in awe of his uncle, and he made plans to leave immediately. Early the following morning, he and his wife Illene set out for Ricksburg in their Chevrolet. Despite the heat she wore a black

285

crepe-de-chine dress over a full set of undergarments that included a whalebone corset. A wide-brimmed straw hat with a black veil, black gloves, and black high-heeled shoes completed her mourning attire. Mendel wore a dark suit and tie with a black fedora.

Even with the latest improvements installed in the Chevrolet — rubber tires with inflated inner tubes, electric windshield wipers, hydraulic brakes, and a radio — the winding, two-lane highway, still partly unpaved, made for a slow, tiring journey.

It had been a hot and unusually dry summer, turning the countryside from vibrant green to drab shades of brown. Even the wild kudzu vines, snaking up trees and over clay embankments, had withered. The hot current of air flowing through the open windows brought little relief to the couple, but there was nothing to be done but to press on if they were to reach the funeral on time. Mendel permitted only three stops. The first was for fuel from a run-down store with pumps set outside in the dirt, the second to use an outhouse without running water. For the third stop, Mendel pulled off the road and parked under the shade of an oak tree for a picnic of boiled eggs and chicken washed down with a thermos of tea. Within minutes of opening the basket, a few scrawny children working in the cotton fields nearby, gathered to gaze at them with hungry eyes. Illene offered food to the young field hands but they retreated nervously, so she put the full basket on the ground, and ordered Mendel to drive on. They arrived in Ricksburg in the late evening, hungry, soaked in sweat, covered with dust, and worn out.

At Yakov's request, his funeral was to be carried out in the traditional Eastern European manner so that after his body had been washed his soul could enter Gan Eden, or paradise. Accordingly, his corpse was transported to the cemetery building where it had been placed on the *taharah bret,* the board on which bodies are laid for the cleansing, with his feet facing toward the door and candles at either side of his head. After the *tahara,* or cleansing ritual by members of the burial society, his entire body was clothed in white linen and covered with his prayer shawl, from which one of the fringes had been cut. Two pieces of pottery were placed over his eyes, and a forked twig in his hand, so that at the coming of the Messiah his body would be supported as it rose from the dead. While these rites were being carried out, members of the synagogue recited psalms.

Public viewing is discouraged by Jewish tradition, but as a sign of respect to his uncle, Mendel insisted on personally performing *shemirah*, the ritual act of watching over the dead, although his aunt had already arranged for a *shomer*, a watcher, to be present from the moment of her husband's death. The nephew felt it was the right thing for him to do and proceeded to a small antechamber at the burial grounds. The sight of his uncle's corpse encased in shrouds filled Mendel with wonder; it had been transformed into a consecrated object, to be disposed of with reverence, as an ancient Torah scroll is buried once it becomes unreadable. Through the long hours his emotions fluctuated from despair to hope. Would his uncle reach out to him from the next world? Had he written a codicil to his will to forgive his only living son? Would Aaron attend the funeral as a last gesture of respect? Was it conceivable that Yakov had bequeathed the Torah to his grandson as his final act of reconciliation? He prayed that his uncle had executed a last act of forgiveness to make amends for the hurt he had caused. *Death is undefeatable, but our deeds may live on to do harm as well as good,* Mendel mused sitting besides his uncle through the night *saying* Psalms. Then on a somewhat happier note: *only by passing on our genes, and preserving our traditions can we strive to defeat Death; that is the closest we can come to eternity.*

A month after the burial, Mendel scrutinized the old daguerreotype portraits of relatives from the old country on the wall of Yakov's study, as he waited impatiently for the executor of the will. Turning from a photo, Bessie Jaffe, a distant cousin, caught his eye.

"Despite all the hardships of the shtetl, they at least knew who they were," she said, gesturing to the photographs. "They didn't question things like the younger generation does. They

287

lived out their lives according to tradition, guided by the rabbis and the community," she added.

"You're right," Mendel agreed. "The Jews who first came to this country were deeply religious. Now many feel that the Orthodox religion is no longer relevant."

Bessie's son, Stuart, joined in, "Why shouldn't we question things? The ways of the shtetl don't apply in America; here it's a land of opportunity." In a derisive tone he added, "Who would want to live as they did, isolated from the rest of the society?"

The entrance of a lawyer and the president of Yakov's synagogue, delegated as executors, cut the conversation short. Everyone stopped talking and looked expectantly toward them. *Like dogs eyeing a bone,* Mendel thought. The final consequences of what had happened many years ago were about to be revealed.

To Mendel's satisfaction, his uncle had amassed a small fortune. He had left Chana well provided for, and willed the rest of the money to the synagogue, and to a variety of charitable institutions. After the lawyer had read the details of the will, the executor took Mendel aside and handed him an envelope.

Going out into the hall, Mendel slid a letter out with shaking hands. Suddenly his heart missed a beat. *Was it possible that his uncle had chosen him to be the inheritor of the Rosen Torah?*

As he read the first sentence, a wave of vertigo made him squeeze his eyes shut before he could go on.

My Dear Nephew Mendel,

I bequeath to you the precious Rosen family Torah. This Torah, as stipulated by our revered ancestor, Shmuel Rosen, should be handed down from father to son, or to a nephew. Since I no longer have a son I am entrusting it to you. The solemn duty of appointing the next inheritor will one day fall to you. The Torah can never be donated to any shul, although it should be housed there in the Holy Ark, and read from regularly.

It has been on loan to only two Orthodox shuls, the Valinsk Shul, in Lithuania, and Knesseth Emanuel, in Ricksburg, of which I am a founding member. It is my wish that you continue this tradition. Notice that each inheritor has inscribed his name upon the olive wood posts, including Shmuel, our patriarch, and the inheritors, Yitzhak, Hershel, and myself, Yakov Rosen. Please inscribe your name with the others. Do not write with pencil, with ink, with gallnuts, even with blood; instead carve your name so it can never be erased. Honor the Torah as you would your father and mother. It is a great responsibility but also a great blessing to be entrusted with our Torah. May you and future generations abide strictly by Hashem's commandments.

Go in peace,
Uncle Yakov Rosen

The letter was signed and witnessed. A giddy mixture of elation and pride bubbled up inside him. He recalled his cousin, Aaron, reading from this Torah at his Bar Mitzvah. How proud the family had been. He and his cousin had not been close as he was ten years his junior, but Aaron's sunny personality had won him over. No one could have foreseen the shame and sorrow the future would bring. Clasping the letter to him, he did not try to stem the tears rolling down his face. To be *the chosen one* was almost too much to bear. Already he imagined the weight of the Torah as he took it from the Holy Ark and the sound of his voice as he lead the congregation in prayer. Uncle Yakov had bestowed honor and prestige on him greater than money could buy, greater than he deserved.

He felt a tap on the shoulder and turned to see Chana's grief-stricken face. "What does Yakov have to say to you in that letter?" she demanded.

"He bequeaths the Rosen Torah to me," Mendel said, and felt his heart thump against his ribs.

"You cannot accept it! I forbid it!" Chana cried, bursting into tears.

"Aunt Chana, please calm yourself. We must respect Yakov's wishes. It would be a wrong not to do so."

"That Torah is my son's and my grandson's birthright. You have no right to rob them of it," she sobbed.

289

Mendel felt trapped. If he went against his uncle's wishes, he would dishonor the deceased. He knew that in Talmudic law, as in common law, when a man makes a will it is binding on the heirs. If he accepted the Torah, however, his aunt would never forgive him. As for Aaron, he had no idea what he wished for. As far as he knew, his cousin had severed connections with his family many years ago, as witnessed by his absence at the funeral.

"Aunt Chana, please. I am not at fault in this matter."

"If you don't pass the Rosen Torah on to Aharon, let it be on your conscience."

"We are too upset to think clearly or make a proper decision," Mendel said, placing her hands gently on Chana's shoulders.

"There are no decisions to be made. Mendel must give the Torah to Aharon," the grieving widow declared, leaning unsteadily on her cane. When Mendel reached out to support her, she brushed him aside with surprising force.

The return journey to Atlanta was harrowing. The new heir discussed the moral dilemma with his wife, hoping that she would see things more objectively. If he followed his uncle's wishes, Chana would hold a grudge against him for the rest of her life.

"Mendel, to me it's clear that you should keep the Torah, since it was willed to you," Illene reasoned.

"I agree. But I don't want to hurt Chana or my cousin."

"Yakov gave up his son for dead many, many years ago. You can't change that."

"Nevertheless . . ."

"You are being foolish. Aaron didn't come to the funeral. Doesn't that tell you something?"

"Perhaps Yakov left instructions forbidding him to attend."

"He should have come. Even if it meant standing at the grave after everyone left."

So their conversation spun around and around until both were exhausted.

The day after returning home, Mendel sat in his study sipping tea, still trying to resolve his predicament. In an effort to put his conscience to rest, he sought the advice of Rabbi Kraft. The rabbi said on the one hand he should honor his uncle's last will, on the other he could see no harm in renaming his cousin Aaron Rosen, or his cousin's son, Abraham Rosen, as the next heir to the Torah, if he wished to do so, as it had not been explicitly forbidden by Shmuel Rosen. Mendel took this as a moral directive. He lost no time in getting Aaron's address from Chana then composing a letter offering the Rosen Torah to him.

Days passed and Mendel began to doubt that Aaron would reply. He tried to be patient, resolving that if he did not hear from him within two weeks he would assume that his cousin had rejected his offer.

Finally Mendel received a curt reply:

Thanks for offering to pass the Rosen Torah on to me. However, I do not want anything from my father. I do not need any reminders of him. Please keep the Torah. If that is my father's last wish, so be it.

Aaron

He was saddened by his cousin's unresolved bitterness, yet gladdened that the burden of guilt had been lifted from his shoulders. He sent the letter to Chana, hoping to put the matter to rest. He had done what he could. Now he was free to be the proud inheritor to the Rosen Torah. He immediately made arrangements to bring the scroll from Ricksburg directly to his home, first consulting Rabbi Kraft on how best to transport his legacy. The rabbi reassured him that as long as he took care not to damage the Torah, he could transport it himself without defiling it. However, he offered to accompany Mendel to ensure its safety, an offer Mendel gladly accepted.

The return journey from Ricksburg seemed interminable. Nervous and elated, as if bringing home a newborn child, Mendel drove more cautiously than usual. As soon as he reached his residence, he carried the Torah to his study, where Illene and the children, Nathan and Barbara, were waiting eagerly. He placed it carefully on the writing table, and stepped back to let them admire it.

"Oh, it's beautiful," their daughter Barbara said, clapping her hands in delight and leaning in to touch the silver bells on the posts.

"Just touch the Torah with your eyes, dear," Illene reprimanded her gently.

"Can you take off the cover so we can see it?" Nathan asked.

Mendel removed the silk cover, and the shield, then read out the names of the previous inheritors etched on the olive wood posts: "Shmuel Rosen; Yitzhak Rosen, Hershel Rosen, and Yakov Rosen. Proud as she was, there was something in the tenor of Mendel's voice, an undertone of gloating and smug self-satisfaction that Illene did not like.

"Now it is *my* honor to inscribe my name, Mendel Snyder, along with the others." With a flourish he produced a wood carving knife with a sharp tip from his desk drawer. As he started to inscribe his name, his hands shook; he steadied himself and carved his name on the smooth wood with deep, steady strokes. A new emotion leapt up inside him to see his name alive on the Torah post, and to know that his descendants would admire it long after he had departed this mortal toil. He also recognized the feeling of triumphant glee, uncomfortably akin to the shallow greed and pride of a child with a coveted toy, and he silently warned himself against becoming too possessive, too self-important. Up until that moment he had been a moderately observant Jew, not a deeply spiritual one. Now that he had inherited the Torah, he vowed to take his religious obligations more seriously. Then breathing a long sigh, Mendel signaled with his eyes for the rabbi to say a blessing.

"We praise You, Eternal God, Sovereign of the universe: You have called us to Your service by giving us the Torah. You have given us a Torah of truth, implanting within us eternal life."

When the rabbi finished, Mendel placed the Torah in a heavy mahogany cabinet. There was one large compartment with doors above where he would place the Torah, and two open shelves below. The doors gleamed with inlaid designs of walnut, ebony and boxwood. On the shelves volumes of leather bound books displayed religious titles along their spines, like solemn gentleman. With a solid click the new caretaker turned the key in the brass locks, and straightened up with a grunt of satisfaction.

"Dad," asked Nathan, "can I read from this Torah at my Bar Mitzvah?"

Mendel chuckled, and tousled the boy's hair. "Of course son, we expect no less of you." Then, turning to the rabbi he said, "I will make every effort to keep it from harm while in my home. By the end of the month I will make arrangements to transfer it to our shul." To his relief, Rabbi Kraft did not attempt to persuade him to place the Torah in the synagogue immediately. He understood that Snyder wanted time to savor his inheritance.

On a Monday, two weeks after the installation of the Rosen Torah in the Snyder's home, a *minyan* of ten men gathered in the study for the evening service. Before reaching into the cabinet, Mendel drew the heavy green curtains across the windows looking out onto his wife's meticulously tended rose garden. Opening the cabinet door with a smooth turn of his brass key, the heir reached inside. Although his eyes and hands told him that the scroll was not there, he simply could not credit his senses. He frantically searched beneath his desk, behind the loveseat and leather armchair—nothing.

Then he cried out, "Oh, my God, this is not possible!" The outcry drew Illene to the study to find out what had happened. She immediately instigated a thorough search of the house, but the Torah was nowhere to be found.

Mendel blamed himself for the scroll's disappearance. He contacted his friends at the *Atlanta Constitution* and gave them the story in the hope that the publicity might bring in clues leading to the recovery of the lost scroll. He alerted auction houses from coast to coast that specialized in Judaica to be on the lookout for the stolen scroll. He called in the police and filed a report with them. He hired a private detective recommended to him by Rabbi Kraft. The Rosen Torah had to be found, no matter the cost.

❧25❧

The Strange Case of the Torah
and the Seraph Serpents

The Lord sent seraph serpents against the people. They bit the people and many of the Israelites died.

Torah

The morning after the Torah's disappearance, private detective Shelby Bunson bounded up the steps of the Rosen residence to find Mendel waiting anxiously for him on the columned front porch. He stuck out his hand, and said congenially, "Well, ha'you, Mr. Snyder." Mendel shook hands, thanked him for coming at such short notice, and then ushered him into the study.

After examining the cabinet where the scroll had been housed, Bunson seated himself in the chair facing his client's desk, and began his questioning, "Let's start with what we know." He pulled out a black, leather-bound notebook, and licked the tip of an indelible pencil leaving a purple stain on his bottom lip. "You discovered that your Torah had been stolen around six o'clock last night?"

"That's correct."

"Any suspects?"

"It's obvious that no Jewish person—not one in his right mind—would have stolen it," Mendel replied.

Bunson drew a worn cotton handkerchief from his suit pocket, and blew his nose hard. He was a big man, with thinning, tea-colored hair, protruding ears, sagging cheeks, and big, brown, red-rimmed eyes that gave him the mournful but alert expression of a beagle on the hunt. "Mr. Snyder, why would you rule out a Jewish person?"

"Stealing a Torah is like stealing our soul. It would be a sacrilege."

"Well, I'll be darned!"

Mendel raised his eyebrows, and looked sharply at the detective. "You should understand that a Torah is a hand-written scroll containing the first five books of the Bible, in Hebrew. It it is the foundation of our religious teachings. In the broader sense "Torah" means Judaism as a religion, a philosophy, a commitment, and a set of values. A good Jew lives by the Torah and its commandments."

"Hmm," Bunson said thoughtfully. " And the thief has broken the eighth commandment, 'Thou shalt not steal.'"

The bereft inheritor put his palms flat down on the writing desk, leaned forward, and looked directly at Bunson. "My Uncle Yakov conferred a great honor upon me by bequeathing the family Torah to me. You see, the Rosen Torah has passed down to me through three generations." Mendel was about to say, but did not, that his uncle had bestowed it upon him not as a gift but as a sacred trust. In losing the Torah, he had violated that trust.

Bunson observed his client; his fingertips were pressed to his mouth to still the trembling of his lips. Lowering his gaze, he waited for him to recover his composure. When Mendel cleared his throat, the detective raised his pencil ready to continue.

Straightening his shoulders, Mendel went on, "And the craftsmanship of the Torah is exquisite! In 1791, a renowned Jerusalem scholar inscribed every letter of the scroll in Hebrew, using a special quill. The scroll itself is attached to posts of olive wood. On top of each post is a silver finial with bells and a crown set with semiprecious stones. When it is rolled up and stored away, it is covered with a red mantle of precious Damascus silk embroidered with gold thread. Over the mantle, suspended from chains, hangs a solid silver breastplate, engraved with a golden lion of Judah, and a graceful silver *yad*, or pointer, for the reader to use." Mendel paused to allow the detective to finish jotting down his points; he seemed to be scribbling every word into the notebook. "So you see, our Torah can never be replaced. It is our heritage. You can't put a dollar figure on that."

The detective clapped his notebook shut. "Mr. Snyder, I reckon that this Torah is more important to your family than money. Still, can you give me a rough estimate of its value in dollars and cents?"

"I just had our Torah appraised for insurance purposes. It's worth about five thousand dollars."

"Five grand! That's a lot of money, that's more than I make in a year, and besides these are very bad times. Where there's money to be made . . . " detective said, scratching his earlobe with the end of his pencil.

Mendel frowned. He did not like to be reminded of the Great Depression that was spreading through the country, crippling businesses and bouncing people into the streets. "Any other theories?"

Bunson hesitated and lowered his voice in an attempt at delicacy. "Eh, there are people who don't think much of your religion. Have you considered that?"

Mendel felt the hair rising on his scalp. "You mean anti-Semites."

"Yeah, them."

Mendel was silent for a long moment. "But only the immediate family and a handful of close friends from my synagogue knew about the Torah."

"Maybe so, but what about the hired help?"

"They didn't know about the Torah. I kept it locked in that cabinet."

"The cabinet was not jimmied open. Someone had access to the key."

"I kept the key in my desk drawer."

"One of the servants could have seen it. He, or she, might have overheard your prayer services. They might have thought you were doing . . . uh, some kind of blasphemy, you know what I mean?"

"What are you talking about, Bunson?" He rose abruptly and his mouth tightened into a thin line

"You said the Torah was written in Hebrew?"

"Yes, we read from it in Hebrew. So no one here would know the language."

"I'm saying if someone overheard you it could have sounded like devil worship."

"Good God!"

"I'm not saying it happened. But country folk hereabouts are a mite superstitious."

"Stop with the theories and stick with the facts!" Mendel snapped.

"Okay, Mr. Snyder. First, I believe that the theft was an inside job. Nothing else is missing, and there are no signs of a break-in. So, if you don't mind, I'll start by interrogating your staff." Bunson poised his pencil over his notebook, "Their names would be?"

"My wife, Illene, will introduce you to Pearl, our cook; Sadie, our housemaid; and Lester, our gardener. Do whatever is necessary to find the Torah."

"Don't worry, I'll get to the bottom of this."

Mendel drew a gold pocket watch from his vest, and snapped it open. "I need to get to work, please wait here for my wife." He rose abruptly. "Good day, Detective Bunson," he said, extending his hand. "I'm counting on you to bring the Torah home."

Five minutes after Mendel had left, the private investigator followed Illene into the kitchen, where she introduced him to Pearl. Bunson could see from the way the cook bustled around that the kitchen was her domain. She wore a starched white cap and apron that contrasted with her dark skin. Her feet, encased in red felt slippers, were tiny in comparison to her puffy ankles and thick legs. The tiled walls glowed in the reflection of white porcelain sinks, white metal cabinets, and a rack of burnished copperware. The sugary fragrance of freshly

297

baked fruit pies mingled with the sharp odor of disinfectant. Before he could ask the first question, the cook gave him a piece of her mind. She wanted him to know that she was a God-fearing Christian woman who had been Mrs. Snyder's cook since her son Nathan's Bar Mitzvah. She knew how to prepare kosher food, had memorized the recipes for all the traditional dishes. Folding her arms across her heaving chest she glowered at the detective. Clearly, she could feel him judging her, and judged him right back.

Bunson interrogated her briefly, while continuing to scribble. Then tapping his pencil on the table sharply, said, "Thank you, Pearl. I appreciate your help. Now will you please call Sadie?"

Peeved, now that he had cut short the interrogation, the cook sashayed over to the back stairs and called down into the basement. "Sadie, you come up to the kitchen now. Gentleman wants to talk to you!" Pearl heard no reply and called again. She sighed and he heard the uneven slap of her slippers as she disappeared down the basement stairs.

The cook found Sadie studying a page of women's underwear in the new Sears Catalog. "Get upstairs, girl! That policeman wants to talk to you."

Sadie, a light-skinned black girl with a sullen droop to her close-set eyes, did not look up. Everything about her was elongated except her fleshy nose, with its flaring nostrils, and her large, shapely lips.

"Girl, did you hear me? Get upstairs!" Pearl ordered.

Slowly, Sadie rose and climbed the stairs. At the top she halted to survey the strange man.

"How d'yah do. I am Detective Bunson," he said, inclining his head politely. "I just wanted to ask a few questions." He could see the antipathy in Sadie's down turned mouth, and the fear and suspicion in the rapid blinking of her eyelids. After he had questioned the maid, to his chagrin, he could find nothing incriminating in her story.

Next he questioned Lester Dozier, the gardener. The man's pale skin was burnt to leather by the sun. He wore

298

threadbare work jeans, a belt buckle with the Confederate flag, and heavy boots that appeared too large for his feet. "You a detective?" Lester asked.

"Yes, I'm Detective Bunson." He got up and shook Lester's hand. "Please sit down. I just needed to get some information from you."

"Yes sir."

On a hunch, Bunson exclaimed, "My granddaddy served as a proud Southern foot soldier in the War Between the States!"

The gardener snorted, and slapped his knees. "Why, my granddaddy did too! Ma told how he rode with Nathan Bedford Forrest at Shiloh and Chickamauga. He got his thumb shot off," Lester put his palms together and said sanctimoniously, "Our Lord knows best who has strayed from His path, and He knows best who are the guided ones."

Bunson allowed him to continue in this vein for a minute or two, then shot a question at him, "You ever seen Mr. Snyder praying over his scroll?"

"Huh?" Lester's washed-out translucent blue eyes blinked rapidly. "You accusing me of something?"

"No. But I judge you to be a religious man."

"Indeed I am!"

The detective continued to question Lester; he was sure the gardener was hiding something, but he could not find any leads.

Evening service had already begun when Lester pulled onto the strip of blacktop in front of the Church of the Holy Spirit. The church, once a gas station and a country store, now displayed a small, wooden cross on its rooftop. The gardener puffed out his lips in annoyance when he noticed that the spaces in front were all taken, obliging him to park in a patch of tall thistles behind the building.

As he stepped out of his pickup, a rush of wind blew the heat off the asphalt into his face. *Not like heaven,* he thought; *more like the other place.* Purple storm clouds roiled above, building to ominous towers shot through with veins of lightning. Always on

299

the lookout for signs and omens, Lester felt the hairs on his scalp tingle. He shivered despite the oppressive summer heat, feeling the Spirit move through him. The sudden *ba-wang* of thunder started the dogs barking and silenced the bullfrogs and crickets. A fork of lightning split a nearby pine tree in two with a resounding whack, snapping Lester out of his trance. Scooping his prize, wrapped in an old blanket, from the flatbed he ran across the parking lot. Just as he reached the church doors, the wind picked up and a hard splatter of rain stung his face. He bent over to protect his burden and pushed into the church as the full force of the rain struck.

The preacher's voice thundered from the pulpit. "And suddenly there came a sound from heaven as of a rushing mighty wind, and it filled the house where they were sitting. And there appeared unto them cloven tongues like as of fire, and it sat upon each of them. And they were filled with the Holy Ghost, and began to speak with other tongues, as the Spirit gave them utterance."

Brother Billy Crane gestured to the congregants to strike up the music. Guitars, drums, cymbals, tambourines, and singers wailed and thumped. People jerked to the din like puppets, shimmying and shaking in ecstasy. With a down chop of his hand, the preacher signaled for the music to cease. A man in his sixties, Crane had a hard little potbelly that protruded from his otherwise skinny frame. Weathered skin, wide-set blue eyes, and bowed legs gave him the look of a cowboy more than a preacher. He spied the gardener standing in the back under a picture of Jesus, with a large bundle in his arms, and he could tell by the look on Lester's face and the way he held it that he had brought something special.

"Welcome Brother Dozier. Step up to the pulpit. What have you brought here?"

All heads turned as Lester walked down the aisle, smiling, proud to be the center of attention. Gently, he placed the scroll on the lectern, removed the old blanket, then stepped forward and hoisted the Torah aloft for all to admire its rich velvet coat and swinging, tinkling and sparkling ornaments. The congregation exhaled as one. *Ahhh!* Though they had no idea what it was, they knew that the rich-looking object must be something special.

The preacher licked his lips and pressed his thumbs into his temples. "Will you preach tonight, Brother Dozier?"

"I will," Lester said, rocking forward on the balls of his feet and looking over the congregation. He slowly removed the solid breastplate and pointer, and red silk cover. The silver bells on the posts tinkled creating a gentle clamor in the suddenly hushed church. Then he untied the silk strap and undid the scroll rolled around the olive posts, to expose the strange black lettering, and then placed it on the reading table. The fine craftsmanship of the Torah set it apart from its shoddy surroundings, like gold among the dross.

He picked up the elegant silver pointer and ran it under the words from right to left and top to bottom as he had seen his employer doing when he spied on him from the rose garden. "Mmmmm-uh, sheekalahhh, ha kanu, vena heynu," he chanted, rocking backward and forward in an uncanny imitation of Mendel Snyder. An electrifying impulse seemed to pass down the gardener's spine, as he felt the unaccustomed power to hold the congregation under his spell. "Signs and wonders! Healing and prophecy, the casting out of devils and speaking in tongues!" His eyebrows twitched up and down as he spoke. "These are signs of the Holy Spirit speaking through us. I come to you guided by Jesus, bringing this gift to all believers."

"Amen. Thank you, God," the dozen or so men called out, praying that this scroll would connect them with a higher power — provided that they had not sinned against the Lord. Lester darted from behind the pulpit and thumped his feet. "Everything's gonna be all right!" he shouted. A chorus of amens rose from the congregation. The guitar twanged a few chords, the drums and tambourines joined in, everyone rose, and began to clap and stomp, sway and sing.

In the midst of this frenzy, Brother Crane shouted, "No, No-wuh!" He raised his arms high and his eyes rolled upwards. "Everything's NOT gonna be all right. We first got to get right

301

with Jesus." He stepped behind the pulpit and reached for a hinged wooden box. Holding it up to the light, he peered through the screened top. Those close up could hear the rattling. Crane lifted the cage high over his head and danced around the pulpit until perspiration plastered his shirt to his back and rolled down his face. Suddenly he stopped, flipped the lid open, withdrew a venomous yellow canebrake rattlesnake, and passed it to Lester.

The snake began to search the air with its forked tongue then slowly twisted around Lester's arm. Three men danced toward the serpent boxes, caught them just behind their heads, and began removing the snakes. Shouting praises, praying, and dancing with a rattler, the gardener felt himself lifted up in a white blur. He began to feel weak and dizzy, but kept on. Lester's snake rattled a rapid, dry, clicking sound, its hair-raising warning, before rearing up. He staggered back as the sharp teeth pierced his left elbow. The pain was so exquisite that he thought he would die right there. He let go of the viper, dropping it onto the Torah, where it writhed over the soft vellum then slithered to the floor. Brother Crane lunged forward, and managed to grab it and thrust it back into the cage.

Later Lester told his wife, "I never saw the rattler strike, but he hit me hard. It was like a spiked baseball popped me. I was preachin', and dancin', and I lost my grip, I wasn't watchin' it."

Soon after the serpent struck, Nurse June McCoil received an anonymous call for help. When she arrived, she found Lester in Brother Crane's trailer adjacent to the church. Nauseated and slumped over the toilet, his skin gray and clammy, the sick man told the nurse that he wanted to stay where he was and let the Holy Spirit take over. She could see that the venom was well on its way to killing him; his elbow was blue, his pulse rapid, weak and unsteady. He would certainly die if left untreated. The nurse called for an ambulance.

When Lester regained consciousness in the hospital, Brother Crane was praying over him. "Cast the devil out of this sinner! Redeem him!" For the next twenty-four hours he floated in and out of consciousness.

While making a routine call to his client, Mr. Snyder, the detective was told that Dozier had been bitten by a snake while gardening in the backyard of the Snyder's home. "Was anyone with your gardener when the snake bit him?" Bunson inquired.

"No, my wife and I were away at the time."

"Have you spoken to the other hired help? Did they see anything?"

"No one saw it. My wife thought that maybe Lester worked late that day, and they had already left. Do you think something's not kosher?"

"That's what you pay me to find out, Mr. Snyder."

"Well, find out soon because my wife wants me to keep on paying his salary and the hospital bills."

"Mrs. Snyder must think highly of Mr. Dozier."

"My wife loves her rose garden, and it's hard to find a good gardener."

Mrs. Snyder confirmed that he was an excellent gardener. She said that she knew little about his private life other than he was married and had no children. She said that her cook complained that when she gave him lunch in the kitchen, Lester asked too many questions that were none of his business.

Marveling at the Snyder's gullibility, the detective drove to the hospital. There the receptionist informed him that Mr. Dozier was still in the ICU, and could not receive visitors. Gazing at her with his mournful, beagle eyes, Bunson fished out his ID badge and flashed it at her. "Ma'am, I understand that you have to do your duty, but so do I. When do you think Mr. Dozier will be well enough to talk to me?"

"I'm just the receptionist. They don't tell me anything."

"Wait a minute . . ." Bunson started to say, but she had already turned her back to him to pick up the telephone. He would just have to bide his time. He camped in the waiting room until, hours later, Lester was able to sit up and take some nourishment.

He found Dozier slumped in the narrow hospital bed looking ashen. He grudgingly answered the detective's questions, repeatedly declaring that he had been cutting the underbrush in a

303

patch of woods at the back of the Snyders' home when the rattlesnake attacked. He had driven himself to the emergency room and then passed out.

"You're lucky to be alive, buddy. When something like that happens, it must make you want to put things right with the Lord."

The hapless gardener reached for the pitcher on the bedside table, tipped some water into a glass, stirred the ice with his forefinger, and nodded sullenly.

"Do you often work overtime?" the detective pressed on.

"Huh?"

"Mrs. Snyder thought that you worked late the night of the accident — after the other servants left."

Lester stretched his skinny neck like a rooster about to crow. "Yes, our Lord will reward those who work hard. 'Now he that planteth and he that watereth are one: and every man shall receive his own reward according to his own labor.'"

The men stared at each other warily, like wrestlers looking for an opening. Then Bunson quoted him back: "'Let him that stole, steal no more: but rather let him labor, working with his hands the thing which is good, that he may have to give to him that needeth.'"

Lester struggled upright. "You fixin' to accuse me of something?" he hissed, his mouth drawing back to reveal teeth stained with tobacco juice.

"Your fifteen minutes are up, sir," a nurse, pushing a medicine cart said, as she entered the room. He was not going to get anything more out of Lester. The best he could do was to put a tail on him as soon as he was released.

Bunson's suspect proved to be shrewder than he appeared, staying away from the church for two months after his discharge from hospital. *It takes one to know one,* Bunson ruminated, *he's a good ole "dumb southerner" like me. I'll have to find a way to outwit him.*

In the eyes of the congregation, Lester's survival was a sure sign of his redemption — and of the Torah's power. After he had stolen the Torah he did some reading in the bible, and learned that God on Mount Sinai gave the Torah to the prophet Moses. Surely there could be nothing more powerful than that.

Just a few weeks subsequent to Lester's snakebite, Nancy Jill, his wife, became pregnant for the first time after nine years of marriage, and his mother's arthritis stopped hurting. The congregation took note and began treating the gardener with new respect. Once Lester dared to return to the Church of the Holy Spirit, they insisted that he "read" from it in tongues so that the spirit, released by the power of Torah, would move within them. The congregants began testifying that the scroll was helping them to renounce worldly temptations.

Brother Crane began to feel threatened by Dozier's growing prestige within the church, and even more by the theft of the Torah. He had cornered the gardener into confessing that he had "borrowed" it from his wealthy employer—but solely for the deliverance of the people of their church, he had declared with conviction. The preacher understood that he would be named as an accessory to the robbery should the police find out about it, and that filled him with apprehension verging on panic.

He started a campaign to ostracize Lester, declaring that the scroll was the devil's work and that it would lead them into the ways of sinners. Under the preacher's influence several members admitted to subsequently falling away from Jesus through drinking and fornication. They challenged those who believed that Lester's scroll had strengthened them, claiming that since Lester had begun bringing it to church they could not stay out of sin's way.

Rattlesnakes began to appear on the Doziers' porch. Nancy Jill pleaded with her husband to get rid of the Torah. He refused, arguing that they needed to keep it until the baby was born to assure the good health of mother and child. Then, Bryant Punkin, a venerable member of the church, was bitten by a snake and died. The incident was reported in the news, where it caught Detective Bunson's eye:

Rattlesnake Bites Man in Grip of Holy Spirit

After surviving several snakebites without the help of modern medicine, and losing his wife, Vera Punkin, to the venomous bite of a yellow timber rattler, eighty-three-year-old Bryant Punkin died for his faith at a religious revival. Just minutes after the rattler sank its fangs into his left wrist, he succumbed, still rejoicing in God.

Lester Dozier, a neighbor of the Punkins, said, "They were just good, quiet people. They were not unusual except that they kept snakes in boxes in their garage."

According to sign followers, to receive the power of the Holy Ghost one must repent of their sins, stop sinning, and lead a godly life. The snake handlers maintain that by following these three steps the Holy Ghost will empower you to follow the signs. The signs themselves include speaking in tongues, casting out demons, handling serpents, drinking noxious potions and healing the sick. Some stick their fingers into live electrical sockets while engulfed in the power of the spirit. They quote from The Gospel of Mark, "In my name shall they cast out devils. They shall speak with new tongues. They shall take up serpents. And, if they drink any deadly thing, it shall not hurt them. They shall lay hands on the sick, and they shall recover."

Within this Holiness Faith only a few members handle snakes. Mr. Punkin was one of an estimated 100 snake-handlers at some 35 churches scattered throughout Alabama, Georgia, Tennessee, West Virginia, Kentucky and Indiana. The majority of these handlers firmly believe scripture instructs them to handle snakes, drink strychnine and handle fire.

State prosecutors have ruled that in Georgia, the First Amendment, which protects the free practice of religion, is superseded by the potential danger of these practices. Accordingly the state has ruled that snake handling is a felony.

When he had finished the article, the investigator folded the newspaper, chewed on his bottom lip then fished out a cigarette and lit it. He inhaled deeply and contemplated a stain on the ceiling for several moments. "That's it!" he said stubbing his cigarette into an empty coffee mug. "I knew there was something fishy about that Lester character and the story he spun."

Brother Crane also stepped up his crusade against the gardener. At a weekend picnic held in the woods behind the church, he approached Lester as he worked his way through a plate of fried chicken, potato salad, baked beans, and wedges of cornbread.

"You know the devil works in mysterious ways," Crane said, placing his hands on Lester's shoulders and gazing at him beneath hooded eyelids.

The gardener licked his fingers. "He does indeed, Brother."

"Sometimes the devil tempts us with good fortune, but we should resist temptation."

Lester wished Crane would go away and leave him to enjoy the food.

"Resist temptation. Oh, yes!" Nancy Jill echoed, folding her hands over her swollen belly.

"The devil tempts us with material things to fill us with false pride," Crane persisted.

Lester was beginning to get nervous.

"I notice that you have a fine new truck," the preacher remarked, shooting a finger at a shiny flame red Ford glinting in the parking lot.

"Oh yes, that truck comes in mighty handy for hauling garden supplies."

Exasperated by the man's failure to catch on, the preacher said, "Give up the scroll. It is the work of the devil!"

"Huh?" Lester swallowed hard enough to cause his Adam's apple to bob up and down.

"Worshipping the scroll that you took is like worshipping the heathen god Baal. Just like when the people of Israel angered the prophet Moses for believing in false idols."

"You know Lester loves the Holy Spirit," Nancy Jill said.

Lester did not want to cross Crane, but he was not about to give up his stolen prize. "I don't see what you mean," he said, wiping his fingers on a napkin. "You know, I'm not as smart as you, Brother Crane. You know I took it from the home of the rich man where I work—but *only* because I wanted to help our people find salvation. Let me think and pray over what you have revealed to me."

"And I am concerned about *your* salvation and . . ." Crane halted in midsentence, his eyes swiveling to a spot just behind the gardener. Sensing an unfriendly presence, Lester turned to follow Crane's gaze. The hard glitter of sunlight made it difficult to see. Then, just five yards away, where the blackberry bushes tangled at the edge of the woods, Lester saw a gun barrel poke through the leaves. With a yelp he took off running, but Brother Crane, realizing in a flash what was happening, stuck out his foot and sent him sprawling.

Ignoring the sharp blackberry spines, Bunson stepped out of the woods and held the gun on Lester. "You best come in quietly for questioning."

Handcuffing his suspect, he sped to his office just around the corner form the police station and two blocks away from Mendel's Deli. At first Lester played dumb, hanging his head, sticking out his lips, and swearing he hadn't done anything wrong. When the detective read back the conversation between Lester and Crane that he had transcribed in shorthand while hidden in the bushes, the hapless gardener had no choice but to come clean. An outburst of hysterical piety followed. He ranted that he had done it for the glorification of his church, and to become one with the Holy Spirit. Bunson waited for Dozier's tirade to run its course, then charged the man with grand theft, and had him held in the jail pending a hearing before a judge. Next he quickly obtained a warrant to search Dozier's home.

An hour later, in a cloud of dust, the detective parked his old Packard in front of a log house on the outskirts of Atlanta. He turned off the ignition and surveyed the place with a practiced eye. In the shade of a central breezeway that cut through the middle of the house, two mangy-looking dogs lay sleeping. The front porch sagged, and the brick chimneys at each end were crumbling. He got out and walked over to the tool shed on the north side of the house where Dozier said he had hidden the stolen Torah in a large wooden fruit crate, beneath the snake cages.

Bunson played his flashlight over the junk crammed inside the shed. When he was twelve, he had jumped into a ditch to retrieve a ball where a rattlesnake had been sunning itself. Its fangs pierced his right leg just below the knee so that he became deathly ill and had to be hospitalized. Ever since, the detective had a terrible fear of snakes. His pulse raced as the beam of light came to rest on the cages. Gingerly, he picked one up, and an ominous rattling issued from inside. With a yelp he dropped it onto the dirt floor. Fighting the urge to run, he reached for his revolver and picked up a second cage. Cold sweat trickled into his eyes as he peered at the spot where the cages had been — and spied the crate the suspect had described.

At five in the morning, while Mendel dreamed of chanting from his lost Torah, and the sky glowed with the approach of dawn, the phone on his bedside table rang with shrill insistence.

He fumbled for the receiver, placed it next to his ear, and heard, as if from a great distance, Detective Bunson telling him, "Good news, Mr. Snyder! Your Torah has been found. Unharmed. I'm on my way to return it to you."

A feeling of extraordinary happiness, of relief, sluiced away the dread he had lived with for weeks. Mendel leaped out of bed with a shout of elation. It was as though a beloved family member had been restored to them. Illene sat up in bed, her eyes sparkling, anticipating the joyous news before her husband could convey it to her.

Later, gathered in the living room, listening to Bunson's harrowing tale, their joy was tempered by disappointment. They had trusted Lester Dozier, and treated him well, now he turned out to be a thief. They wanted to know what could have possessed the man to commit such a heinous crime.

Bunson lifted one shoulder and shook his head. "In this case we can rule out sex and money, which are the motives of crime more often than not. After all, Dozier made no attempt to sell the Torah. Maybe he was lusting after power and glory, or maybe he was just a religious maniac — a nutcase."

"He was very religious," Illene responded. "He told me that working in my garden made him feel closer to the Lord. But I don't think that makes him crazy."

"My guess is that your gardener stole the Torah because he wanted to look a whole lot bigger in front of his snake-handling church," Bunson said.

"I don't understand what this snake handling is about. It is so far removed from our faith."

"Well, Mrs. Snyder, folks hereabouts grow up with it, and I did a little research beyond what I already knew. Most accounts say that it started in about 1909 in Cleveland, Tennessee. That's where a man named George Hensley was preaching on Mark 16:18 'They shall take up serpents.' At the end of the sermon, he took a big rattlesnake out of a box with his bare hands. He handled it for many minutes, and then challenged his congregation to hold the snake in order to test the strength of their faith."

Illene shuddered. "If Lester does that, then perhaps he is crazy."

"Dozier may have believed the Torah would help him get close to the Holy Spirit. Don't Jews study the Torah as a way to get closer to God? It's possible that's what Dozier believed?"

"The important thing is that you found our Torah," Mendel said, cutting the conversation short. He thanked the detective before dismissing him with a generous sum.

When Mendel returned from the deli that evening he went straight to his study. The image of his Torah with snakes writhing over it dampened his elation. He had heard vague tales of snake handling, but the strangeness, the awful reality of the practice, had never touched his life. With an unpleasant start, he recalled the story of God sending serpents against the Israelites. The thought that there could be some association with Dozier's religion and the Hebrew Bible upset him; Bunson's earlier remarks about the gardener wanting to aggrandize himself were also unpalatable. Thumbing through the Chumash, the printed

310

version of the Torah, searching for passages about snakes, he read aloud, "Make for you a fiery serpent and set it upon a pole, and it shall come to pass that whosoever is bitten, when he looks at it, he shall live."

There were other scriptural references to being bitten as a punishment. "The Lord sent seraph serpents against the people. They bit the people and many of the Israelites died," he muttered, jotting down the passage from the book of Numbers in large, square text as if by writing it out some gem of truth might be revealed to him. He questioned why God had chosen to punish people in this terrible way. Mendel felt all this tearing at his heart. It pained him to think that law and order, decency and reason, did not prevail against madness and treachery—even at the peril of incurring the wrath of God. As if waking from a nightmare, he looked around his study like a stranger in his own house: the loveseat upholstered in green damask, the intricately carved mahogany cabinet, the heavy writing table, the brown leather wing-backed chair, the silk rug. He had spent a lifetime accumulating fine possessions, yet all it amounted to was self-aggrandizement.

That evening after work, Mendel started a letter to Lester Dozier asking—no demanding—an explanation of why he had stolen the Torah. After several false starts he put down his pen and sat staring at his reflection in the dark windowpane, seeing the lines on his face deepen and become stern. There was no point in questioning an ignorant and deceitful man like Lester. Outside, the distant lights of the city winked on the horizon, and he contemplated the evil lurking there. In spite of this, Atlanta, *his* city, had been good to him; it had provided him with a place to succeed and for his family to take root.

When Illene looked in on him, she saw an unaccustomed expression of sadness on his face. What was upsetting him now that the Torah had been found? He replied that the burglary by a snake handler might be God's way of warning him against his own arrogance, his own possessiveness, reminding him to take better care of his legacy. But he *had* taken good care of the Torah, his wife protested. Besides, it had been returned to them,

311

seemingly unharmed. They turned to gaze at the scroll on the table — ancient, sacred, unchanging — in a chaotic, fleeting world. The teachings of the Torah could not protect them from barbarism any more than the study of art or music, history or science; Germans under the Third Reich had proved that. Yet the Torah commanded them to do mitzvot so that justice would prevail. A sense of stability and peace seemed to emanate from the scroll and to hold them in its numinous embrace.

"Enough of trying to play the sage!" Mendel sighed, "All I want is peace of mind. It's time to make some practical decisions. I'll call Rabbi Kraft to arrange for the Torah to be placed in the synagogue." Straightening his shoulders, he reached for the telephone. Besides organizing the transfer, he had many perplexing questions for the rabbi.

The rabbi could barely follow Mendel's complex tale of the lost and found Torah, or address his questions immediately. Only careful inspection would reveal if the thief had defiled the Torah, rendering it non-kosher for use in services. In the interim he granted permission for it to be stored at the synagogue.

Later that day, the rabbi's assistant found a space in the basement of the shul. Rabbi Kraft came to ask for God's blessing on the area so that the Torah would not lie there like an abandoned corpse. Before he left, the assistant locked the door securely. The next day, three authorities carefully examined the Rosen Torah for any signs of damage, especially for dirt marks, faded lettering, torn pages, or deterioration; any of these might render the Torah *pasul*, or unusable for prayer services.

A few days later, the rabbi called with the good news. The experts had declared the Torah intact. However, some letters had turned brownish red, and according to the laws, the ink has to be black like a raven, and others had faded or flaked off. These needed to be repaired, especially since damaged letters can change the whole meaning of a word. The inheritor readily agreed to pay for a qualified scribe to repair the script. In the meanwhile, Illene would put together a committee to plan a special ceremony for the Rosen Torah.

Mendel was about to put down the receiver, when Rabbi Kraft asked, "Would you indulge me in a little *pilpul*, fine analysis, to examine the pros and cons of what the Torah means to our people?"

Mendel agreed, wondering what the rabbi had on his mind.

"Let's begin with the question: Why is the Torah an inheritance, yet not an inheritance?"

Mendel paused to collect his thoughts, and then replied, "God gave the Torah to Moses on Mount Sinai. It says that the Torah and its commandments were given only to Israel or the people of Jacob."

"Excellent. In *Deuteronomy* it is written, 'Moses bound us by the Torah, an *inheritance* for the community of Yakov, or Jacob.'"

"So, how is the Torah *not* an inheritance?"

"Aha! Think about it."

"Okay, God said that those who obeyed His commandments would be blessed and those that broke them would be cursed. Still, I don't see how it's not an inheritance."

"Let me give you a clue. In the Gemara, our rabbinical commentaries, it is said that while a baby is in his mother's womb he knows the entire Torah. However, when he is ready to be born an angel comes and slaps him on his mouth causing him to forget everything. The sages say that it must be that heaven wishes a person to acquire the teachings of the Torah through his own toil, because there is no value to the Torah if it is received purely as a gift."

"In other words," Mendel said thoughtfully, "if we receive an inheritance as a gift with no effort on our part, it will have little meaning?"

" Good. Now, take your thinking one step further. As God's Chosen People we *inherit* the Torah but . . .?" the rabbi prompted.

"But without *studying* it we cannot understand or inherit its *teachings*?"

"Excellent. And I am sure that you will apply that new insight to the Rosen Torah, and share it with your family."

"Of course." Mendel replaced the receiver slowly, uncertain if he had just been dealt a clever sermon or a sly insult.

Three months later Mendel and Illene sent out invitations to the congregation, printed on ivory stock with gold lettering, requesting their presence at a Ceremony of Acceptance. The Committee had previously agreed that Sunday, a day of rest, was a good day because it would draw attendance from university faculty, and interested non-Jews, even the mayor. Nevertheless, Illene preferred Saturday morning, the day of their Sabbath, and her will prevailed.

On the arranged day, they ushered the Torah in like a bride, and beaming like the father of the bride, Mendel carried it down the isle. The rabbi gave a short sermon, which ended with a question: "What is the Torah without children to receive it? What is Judaism without the linking of generations? Our children not only bring us to life: they bring our Judaism to life."

A stab of sadness cut through Mendel, despite his elation and his pride. Unshed tears stung his eyes, and he felt his heart constrict. *Uncle Yakov, are you listening from your grave? You have bestowed honor and prestige on me, greater than I deserve. In doing so you have sundered your son Aharon, and your grandson Abraham, from their family, their religion, and their heritage. Did you bequeath the Torah to me as a way of punishing them? At the end, why did you not reach out from the grave to make peace with them after those long, bitter years?*

✑26✑

The Fifth Inheritor: Abraham in the Land of Israel

The Torah lives — even in a hovel, up to its neck in dirt.

Yiddish folk saying

Two years after Abraham's opportune and enjoyable visit with the Snyders, he received a late night call from Mendel's daughter, Barbara. She said that her father had passed away in his sleep, having suffered no previous illness other than the infirmity of old age. The funeral would be held in two days. As he listened a vision Mendel floated before him like an old sepia photo: inquisitive brown eyes, with a hint of sadness, a halo of silver hair, the upright stance of a man who had done well for himself. Sorrow pressed down on him, and a lump rose in his throat.

"Abraham, are you there?" Barbara asked.

"Yes, I'm here. Please accept my deepest condolences. Thank you for calling." He hung up feeling sad and ill at ease, and something else inexplicable, the premonition that he was about to embark on a strange journey.

Regrettably, the Rosens could not make the flight from California to Atlanta in time for Mendel's burial. A week afterward, as Abraham and Martha were sitting down to dinner, the phone rang. It was the Snyders' lawyer calling to inform him that Mendel had bequeathed the Rosen Torah to him. As he replaced the receiver, he saw Martha gazing at him with concern.

315

He proclaimed with a catch in his voice, "'I have full cause of weeping, but this heart shall break into a hundred thousand flaws. Or ere I'll weep.'"

"Instead of quoting Shakespeare, just tell me what happened."

"The Snyder's lawyer called to say Mendel has chosen me to be the Rosen Torah's next inheritor."

"*Mein Gott!* The Rosen Torah is a magnificent bequest. I assumed that the Torah would pass on to Mendel's son, Nathan."

"I really wasn't looking for this honor. I do know that Mendel very much wanted to right the injustice done to my father by my grandfather. " He rubbed his forehead and frowned.

"Did you make it clear to Mendel that we are not practicing Jews?"

"I thought I did. But something about the way I said it must have been too indirect. You see I didn't want to insult the old man."

"I understand. So, what will you do with this Torah?"

"I have no idea."

"Why don't you call Nathan to reassure yourself that there isn't any bad blood between the two of you? After all, he is the rightful heir. If he wants the Torah, you should offer to relinquish it.

"That's a good idea."

"But be careful how you approach him," his wife cautioned. "You don't want to offend him."

Abraham called immediately. After polite chitchat, he cautiously approached his concern. "Nathan, I want you to know I am deeply honored by your father's bequest of the Torah."

"We are happy for you."

"And I want you to know that I will take good care of it, but I'm not sure I'm the right one."

"I trust you to do what is right."

"It doesn't concern you that I am not a practicing Jew?"

"My father knew that, but still he wanted you to have the Torah."

"Perhaps I don't deserve such an honor."

316

"No?"

Abraham plunged ahead. "To be frank, I never expected your father to leave the family legacy to me. It has come as a complete shock."

"I understand."

"I would like to propose that the Rosen Torah remain in the Snyder family, if they so desire it. I do not see any legal obstacles to my returning it."

"Ah, I see what is bothering you," Nathan said with a dry chuckle. "Well, don't concern yourself about it. My father explained to me before he died why it was important to bequeath the Torah to you. He wanted to get you back on the right path."

Abraham found Nathan's voice annoyingly soothing, as if meant for a child. "I am not sure what you are getting at."

"Abraham, listen to me. Your grandfather disowned your father. That alienated you from your family, your religion, and your people. It is my father's fervent hope that the Rosen Torah will lead you back to your roots and to Judaism. He felt that you are the one most in need of the Torah's benevolent power."

He understood that his cousin spoke out of kindness, but he felt like a charity case. Apparently the Snyders saw him as a lost soul who needed to be brought back into the fold. Mendel had expressed his desire to redress the wrong done by Yakov Rosen, and Nathan had agreed that it was the right, even the righteous thing to do. No, there could be no question of returning the Torah. If he refused the bequest, it would offend them deeply. There was nothing more to say. Abraham ended the conversation with his thanks, but gained no comfort for himself. When he related the conversation and his feelings to Martha she accused him of being overly sensitive, as usual.

A week later, a copy of Mendel's will, with the portions concerning the bequest, arrived. The new heir carefully read the stipulations. First, Mendel requested that he add his name to those inscribed on the Torah's posts. Abraham read the list Mendel had compiled to his wife: "Shmuel, our patriarch, then Yitzhak, Hershel, Yakov, Mendel, and now myself, the fifth inheritor."

317

"You certainly can honor that request," Martha said.

"Another stipulation is that I place it in an Orthodox synagogue, with the ownership to remain in the Rosen family."

"That could be a problem. Why don't you talk this over with my Dad?" she suggested.

The next weekend, they sat on the Staub's terrace at sunset, making desultory conversation, until Gertrud sang out, "Come for dinner!"

At the table, Karl lifted his wineglass to them. "*Herzlichen Gluckwunsch!* Congratulations Abraham! Martha tells me you've inherited a priceless family Torah."

"Thank you."

"You don't seem happy about it."

"To be honest, Karl, I don't feel that I am the most worthy for this particular honor."

"Dad," Martha prompted, "tell Abraham what happened to the Torahs during the war."

"It is difficult to speak of it," Karl said, putting down his glass with a sigh. "Every month we sent packages of food and money to my sister and her family. You see, like me she married a Jew. But by 1939, all mail had ceased coming out of Germany. What little we could gather from the newspapers was a story of growing horror. Finally I received a letter, smuggled out of Germany." Karl pulled a creased envelope from his shirt pocket, "This is from my sister Rosemarie, and relates the terrible fate of her husband's grandfather, Joe Marx." He handed it to Abraham.

Unfolding the letter, he gently smoothed the creases on his knee. It was written in German in a dense, flowing script difficult to read. Slowly he read:

My Dearest Karl,

What anguish preceded Zaida Joe's death! I have described only the bare details. If I allow myself to dwell on his suffering I will break down.

On the Friday before Passover, Zaida got wind that the SS extermination unit would be coming at dawn to ransack our

318

neighborhood. He immediately sent word to the rabbi that before the SS troops came, he would take it upon himself to rescue from the synagogue the Torah his family had donated.

He must have agonized all night trying to think of a way he could do it. Before the first light of dawn, when the curfew was over, he left the house without waking a soul. Then he made his way through the darkened streets to the synagogue. By the light of the oil lamps he went to the ark and removed the Torah. But he never made it to safety. The rabbi himself witnessed the Nazi storm troopers club grandfather to death on the synagogue steps. He saw him fall with the Torah still cradled in his arms.

"Those Nazi bastards!" Abraham hissed. Then he drew a deep breath and tried to put his thoughts in order. Carefully folding the note, he returned it to the professor. "What happened to the Torah?"

The professor clasped his hands to hide their tremor. "I don't know. I've been told that the Nazis shipped all the Torahs they plundered to Prague. As always, they had a sinister master plan. They were going to build a museum of artifacts of the Jewish race, once they had systematically exterminated them!"

Abraham could feel the familiar sadness wrenching him away from the light, a drowning man caught in a black tide. Whatever being a Jew meant, he could not close his eyes to the millions who had perished. By a quirk of fate it had fallen to him to preserve the Rosen Torah for posterity.

"Shakespeare said, 'There's nothing good or bad, but thinking makes it so.' For once The Bard was wrong, dead wrong. What the Nazis did was utterly evil."

"Now you understand how fortunate you are to inherit your family scroll."

"It is a great honor, but also a heavy burden, and I'm uncertain of how I can best carry out that responsibility."

Soon after Abraham's conversation with his father-in-law, Martha listened to a fiery radio speech by David Ben Gurion, the first prime minister of the newly formed state of Israel. He talked passionately about the pressing need of the nascent country to absorb thousands of displaced Jews from Europe as well as the Islamic countries. "Too often in the past we Jews threw up our hands and cried out to God in despair. Now it is time to take fate in our hands, to fight with all our might for a place as a nation and a people."

Ben Gurion went on to say that without American aid, thousands of Jews who had flocked to Israel would be doomed to remain in temporary transit camps. His speech affected Martha; she and her parents could so easily have been displaced persons. She felt that if she made a pilgrimage to the Holy Land, the part of her soul that had been lost when she fled Germany would be restored. Her husband, however, would not easily be swayed by such raw emotion; she had to find a way to convince him that it was important for them to go. After dinner that evening, she began the opening salvo by declaring that it would do him good to get away from work, and it would be an extraordinary experience to witness the birth of a homeland for Jews, to see history in the making.

"That could be interesting, but why do the Jews need a country?" Abraham asked.

"You might as well ask why our family needs a home!" she retorted. "Jews have wandered, like orphans, from nation to nation for two thousand years. And the whole world shut the doors to Jews fleeing the Nazis. We must have a country for our People to be free!"

"Okay, you're right. Jews should have a country they can call their own, especially for the survivors of the Holocaust."

"And don't forget the Jews being oppressed by Communist regimes," Martha added.

"Yet why a tiny strip of the Middle East — without oil, or minerals, and little water — with hostile Arabs as neighbors? Why that piece of land?" Abraham provoked her.

"Abraham, you know very well that Jews believe that God promised that land to them!" she burst out. "They've believed it for millennia. Our leaders searched all over the world for a land where we could settle, that would be our safe haven. One said Palestine, another Argentina, a third Brazil. Some

320

thought Africa would be a suitable place. Yet no nation welcomed us. So if Jews want to live as a nation, there is no other way but to go to the Holy Land of our forefathers, the land of the patriarchs, which is bound to our history."

"Bravo Martha!"

"Enough Abraham! Please, no more discussion, let's just go!"

Seeing his wife's passion and determination, Abraham agreed to the trip. Martha immediately contacted her widowed niece, Cora Goldfarb, the daughter of her father's youngest sister, now living in Jerusalem. She had survived the war by being sent to England as a child on the Kindertransport, a rescue effort by the British Committee for the Jews of Germany that brought thousands of refugee children to Great Britain, between 1938 and 1940.

Martha made arrangements for John and Clara to stay with her parents while they were away. Shortly before the trip, clashes between Arabs and Israelis started escalating, but Cora urged them not to change their plans.

The long flight from California to Israel was tedious. When Cora met the Rosens at the airport, they were exhausted; she drove them to her apartment, where they went straight to bed. The next morning Abraham and Martha were awakened to the nasal chanting of muezzins calling the faithful to prayers. From the band of grainy light filtering under the blinds, he saw that dawn was near. He dozed off, only to be aroused by the call of the muezzin followed by the chiming of church bells. "Don't need an alarm in this place," he grumbled, groping for his slippers.

They found Cora in the kitchen, sipping a demitasse of Turkish coffee and reading the *Jerusalem Post*. "Shalom. I hope you feel more rested," she said. She was a small, energetic woman with long strawberry blonde hair held away from her face by a colorful batik scarf. She seated them comfortably on a tiny balcony overlooking the city and the distant hills, where she brought them a large tray loaded with bagels, boiled eggs, cream cheese, pickled herring, olives, and fruit.

As they partook of the plentiful Israeli breakfast, Cora inquired, "Did you sleep well?"

"We did, thank you, except for the noise of distant thunder," Martha replied.

"That wasn't thunder, it was artillery shelling. There are reports on the radio and in the newspaper of clashes between Egypt and Israel in the Gaza Strip."

"Really! That's alarming," Abraham said, sipping fresh orange juice from a tall glass.

"I'm afraid that Egypt might block Israeli ships from moving through the Suez Canal."

"It's more dangerous than I imagined," Martha said, frowning.

"Yes, but remember that Muslems are not just fighting Jews, they are splintered into factions, and fight each other to the death to defend their own interests."

Cora paused to light a cigarette. "After breakfast you'll come with me to see my school of arts and crafts."

"That's where you work, isn't it?"

"Yes, in the ceramic studios. Can you be ready in about thirty minutes?" They nodded. "And don't forget to wear comfortable shoes. We will be walking."

That brought a smile to Abraham's lips. "That'll be great," he exclaimed, glad that they would be exploring the city on foot.

A colorful ceramic tile painted with the words "Bezalel School of Arts and Crafts" distinguished the place from similar buildings made of golden Jerusalem limestone.

"The school established here, in 1906, is named for the ancient artist Bezalel, who is described in the Bible as having crafted the furnishings of the wilderness tabernacle." Seeing their blank looks, Cora added, "a portable sanctuary that served as the sacred tent where the Israelites worshipped during the forty years they wandered the desert with Moses." Sounding like a tour guide—in fact she conducted tours of the center—Cora continued, "The mission of the school is twofold. First, to create an authentic Israeli style. Second, to provide immigrants with revenue from the production and sale of handicrafts."

Having given her spiel, Cora led them to her studio where they wandered around looking at wall decorations, then came over and watched admiringly as Cora painted colorful glazes onto tiles used as wall decorations and street signs set into the corners of buildings. The artist was so engrossed in her work she seemed not to notice that they were there. After a while she looked up, and seemed startled to see them. "Why don't you two visit the galleries? Be back at my studio at noon; then we'll go for lunch."

As they toured the display areas, exhibiting both traditional and contemporary pieces, Martha darted from object to object while Abraham moved methodically pausing to read the information and to examine each piece. In the first exhibit hall, dedicated to synagogue art, a splendid Torah surrounded by related objects beckoned him to draw nearer. In the adjacent room, silver filigree artifacts for special festivals were displayed. Abraham next admired a Chanukah lamp with appliqués of turquoise, a pair of Sabbath candlesticks ornamented with carnelian, and a whimsical spice container fashioned into a tower. In the third hall, dedicated to copper pieces, there were mezuzah cases, sconces, seder plates and pitchers. These lovely artifacts were exhibited as works of art removed from their religious context. Yet, Abraham reflected, one could not appreciate their true significance without knowing their symbolic meaning. Each one seemed to call out to him: *Remember me as you pass me by!*

Engrossed by the displays, Abraham and Martha had lost track of the time, and had to hurry back to the studio to meet Cora. "We'll go to lunch at Minsky's Deli," she said, placing tiles in the kiln and wiping streaks of paint from her hands. "Their food is good, but not expensive."

After a waiter had seated them at a tiny table on the sidewalk, Cora asked, "What did you think of our art?"

"The pieces were beautiful," Martha said. "You have so much talent in this country!"

"Thank you."

"One thing puzzles me," Abraham said. "I noticed the title of the contemporary exhibit, "Crafting a Jewish Style," but I couldn't discern a unified, distinctive one."

"That's an interesting observation." Just then a waiter came to take their orders.

Martha invited Cora to order for all of them, as she no doubt knew what was best on the local menu. Their hostess selected a typical Israeli lunch of falafel and a finely chopped green salad with yogurt dressing. As the waiter hurried away, Cora continued, "The earlier pieces show a clear Oriental influence while the later ones are influenced by modern Western trends. You see, Jewish artists who immigrated to Palestine following Hitler's rise to power rejected the strong influence of Orientalism. They argued for a new Jewish style that would incorporate the modern European experience of the Diaspora Jew who had never lived in Palestine or modern Israel."

Martha visualized the objects she had just viewed. "Yes, I see how the artists have fused traditional elements into a more contemporary style."

The falafel and salad arrived, and they abandoned the conversation to the enjoyment of eating. Over coffee Cora resumed, "This question of a Jewish style is nagging at you?"

"I guess so," Abraham said.

"Perhaps you are searching for your *own* identity."

"Maybe. I'm only half Jewish, as you know." He was unexpectedly stung by Cora's bluntness. "But it's easy for you to scoff at me; you've never had to question who you are."

The artist narrowed her eyes. "You couldn't be more wrong! Like other German Jews, I believed myself to be assimilated. Until Hitler unleashed his madness on us, we never questioned our acceptance as German citizens. We were completely unprepared for what happened."

"I'm sorry. I wasn't thinking."

"It's okay. Let's stick with art. You are right in seeing that the question of Jewish *cultural identity* is central to these artists. Like us they are searching, too."

"Isn't that a good thing?" Martha asked. "Doesn't that make them eager and open to new techniques and styles?"

"It's a kind of paradox. The search for identity must be based on tradition. It just can't be manufactured out of thin air. Yet, artists don't want to be bogged down by tradition." Cora dropped a sugar cube into her coffee.

"I see," Martha said, furrowing her forehead. "I remember seeing a documentary about a dangerous deep-sea dive to save the rusting hulk of a Civil War battle ship. Why, I ask, would they put men's lives in danger for that?"

"You tell me." Cora challenged.

"I guess they were reclaiming America's history," Martha said tentatively. "And naturally the museum sponsoring the salvage wanted the artifacts for display." Martha brushed a persistent fly from her face. "You see American culture is a mosaic of many different cultures. And like the Israelis, they're looking for their special identity and heritage."

"Very interesting!" Cora stabbed the air with her cigarette for emphasis.

"Speaking of heritage," Martha said turning to her husband, "why don't you tell Cora about the Rosen Torah?" Swiveling her head back to her cousin she added, "Abraham just inherited a wonderful family legacy, a Torah that's over a hundred and fifty years old. I think it's causing him an identity crisis."

"You think so?" Putting on a mock professorial air, Abraham raised his eyebrows.

Cora held up her cup of coffee, toasting him, "Congratulations!"

Abraham wagged his finger at her, as if chiding a small child.

For a moment Cora looked surprised, then chuckled, "I mean congratulations on your *inheritance*, not on having an identity crisis."

"Thank you," he said stiffly.

"So, tell me about the Torah."

"It's a long story, Cora. Maybe we should save it for tonight."

She nodded, and he signaled for the bill.

Abraham looked away, allowing the unfamiliar hubbub of Jerusalem's streets wash over him. He idly observed a Chassid dressed in a fine black coat and broad brimmed hat, followed by a man in ragged clothing carrying a placard proclaiming, "Jesus is our Savior". Close on their heels, a tall, bearded Muslim wearing a white turban and long robe strolled by.

Catching Abraham's bemused gaze, Cora said, "This Land attracts more than its share of the faithful and also the fanatical."

That evening after dinner, she served coffee and cake on the balcony. When everyone had relaxed, she asked Abraham to tell his story. Wiping crumbs from his mouth, he folded his hands on his lap and began.

"Once upon a time, in a distant shtetl far across the ocean, there lived a brave and pious man named Shmuel Rosen, our patriarch, who commissioned a marvelous Torah. His son Yitzhak, the poet and cantor, was the first to inherit it. Next came Hershel the righteous, also a cantor, and following him the devout orphan, Yakov the baker. Yakov and his little sister Frieda were grateful for their kind Uncle Hershel and his good wife Sonia who took them into their home to live with their three lovely daughters." The story that had been coiled inside him since his visit with Mendel unraveled like yarn from a spinning wheel. The women reclined, eyes half closed, carried along by his eloquence.

When Abraham came to the part about his ill-fated Bar Mitzvah in New Orleans, he hesitated. Martha rotated her hand, indicating that she wanted to hear all he had held back for too long.

The storyteller cupped his chin, and fell silent.

"Let me get you something to drink," Cora said, and disappeared into the kitchen to emerge in minutes with three glasses of red wine. Abraham drank the mellow wine, then plunged on, recounting the unfortunate train of events, which

326

had been set in motion long before his birth: how his father had married a gentile woman against his parents' wishes, how his grandfather, Yakov, had sat *shiva* for his son Aaron, how he had disowned him, how he had never forgiven Aaron even after his grandson was born, how he had refused to show up for a special occasion in his own life, his Bar Mitzvah, how his grandmother, Chana, had gone into a rage and left early, all compounded by his own humiliating confrontation with his father after the Bar Mitzvah. His father and grandfather had never reconciled; at the very end Aaron had not even put his father to rest by attending the funeral. Later, the resentment, the hollow disappointment he felt on discovering that his father had withheld telling him about their special family legacy.

By the time the story concluded with Mendel's "gift" of the Rosen Torah, both women were in tears. His bequest had been extraordinarily courageous and benevolent; in order to right an injustice, he had chosen Abraham over Nathan, his own flesh and blood; a decision fraught with the risk of incurring the disapproval of his son and of his wife; of sowing dissention, like bitter weeds, among Mendel's extended family long after he had gone to his grave.

Martha's heart ached, and she wanted to cry out: Why did you keep these things hidden from me, Abraham? Why couldn't you share your pain with me as I shared mine with you?

"To think that the Rosen Torah survived natural catastrophes, bigotry, and greed for so many years, to remind us of who we are!" Cora exclaimed.

"It is amazing." Abraham sighed, "Yet I have mixed feelings about being the keeper of the Torah."

"Do you?"

"As you know, I'm not a practicing Jew. I am not qualified to pass on its teachings or its traditions."

"But Abraham you *are* worthy of the Torah! If you hadn't succeeded in making the atomic bomb the war would have dragged on and thousands more innocent citizens and soldiers would have been killed, along with our people and our heritage."

He found Cora's praise excessive, even misguided. He rose, stretched his arms above his head and leaned over the balcony. As night fell, the Jerusalem hills had turned from hues of olive, fading to browns and then black. Rich cooking smells of garlic and cumin drifted through the air from open windows. A light snapped on in the apartment across the street. Through a slit in the lace curtains he saw a young woman with dark tresses, clad in a yellow robe, dancing with sheer abandon, unspooling her emotions to the music blaring from her radio.

Cora fished out a cigarette and started to light it, then paused. "So, the heart of your story is the irreconcilable rift between your grandfather and his son, which sundered you from your family. And your "godfather," Mendel Snyder, has tried to mend that rift by bequeathing the Rosen Torah to you." Cora's voice had gone low with emotion. She looked away, waved at laughing teenagers passing under the streetlamp below.

"So, what's the moral of my story?" Abraham challenged.

"To answer that I would need to know if you have forgiven, or will ever forgive, your grandfather."

"To be honest, I wish I could say that I have forgiven him but I can't. He hurt my father so deeply that he never revealed the existence of the Rosen Torah to me."

"Forgiveness can release us from the wrongdoings of the past. In order to forgive we have to confront the anger, the shame, and the guilt caused by the harm done to our sense of self worth. If we try to escape the pain, we will be caught in the cycle of revenge and regret forever," Cora said.

Caught off guard by Cora's incisive analysis, he threw up his hands in defeat, but the hurt showed in his eyes.

Impulsively she got up and hugged him, "I'm sorry, I didn't meant to upset you. Thank you for telling your story. You did it so beautifully."

"You did," Martha agreed, but her heart felt heavy. When her husband bent over to whisper his apology for not revealing this traumatic part of his life to her, she touched his lips with trembling fingers.

Noticing the tender exchange between her two guests, Cora quietly began loading plates, cups, and wine glassed onto a tray. As she exited she said with a warm smile, "Tomorrow we will visit my daughter, Tamara, and her family on the kibbutz, Degania. It's on the Sea of Galilee. You'll enjoy the drive out there. Since tomorrow's Friday, we need to get an early start to arrive in time for Shabbat, besides it's not safe driving after dark. Also, on Friday nights the young *kibbutzniks* get together to party, so that will leave us quiet time to relax and to chat." She yawned, "Now we should get some rest."

The Rosens took pleasure in meeting Cora's family, her daughter Tamara her husband Levi, and their two sons Micah and Alon. They saw the grueling work on the collective farm, and the sparse living conditions. Yet the warm, sunny weather eased life, and young people from all over the world lent it an international flavor. The *kibbutzniks* did not feel they were living a life of drudgery; they were committed to serving their country.

After a traditional Shabbat meal, they sat under the cascade of stars, listening to the night sounds. The rustle of wind in the palm trees, the grunts of nocturnal animals and chirr of insects, created a soothing backdrop. Yet there was a menacing undertow to the night.

When Martha voiced these thoughts, Levi nodded. "That's exactly the feeling that comes over me on night-guard. Out there the darkness is filled with splendor and beauty but also with terrible danger. You are alone. You have no idea if an enemy is hiding behind a rock, or if the next step won't be your last."

"To guard all the sleeping souls, exhausted from their day's work and trusting in your watchfulness, takes tremendous courage," Martha said.

"I must do this for my children, no one must take away our birthright."

Her heart went out to Levi. His eyes were fierce with determination, his skin prematurely lined by the sun, and his dark, unruly hair already shot with gray. It was one thing to hear about danger, another to be in its midst. She thought that she could never survive such stress. Yet she respected the bravery and idealism of these men and women serving on the perilous frontline.

In the few remaining days in Israel, the Rosens explored the ancient sites: the gates to the walled Old City, the Western Wall, and the Temple Mount. On the last day they visited the market. As they strolled along browsing for souvenirs, Abraham could not help speculating about the scribe who had so masterfully created their Torah. Might he have lived in one of these ancient dwellings? Mendel had informed him that their scroll was created in Jerusalem in the last decade of the eighteenth century. However, the names of the Torah scribe and the emissary who made the hazardous journey from the shtetl were long forgotten. Martha, who had rambled ahead, beckoned Abraham to a stall where she was bargaining over a silver amulet shaped like a hand, which the shopkeeper assured them would avert evil from befalling them.

On their return flight from Israel, Abraham and Martha attempted to sort out their impressions. It had been an immense pleasure to visit Cora's children and grandchildren on the kibbutz, to see a branch of Martha's family thriving after the Holocaust. For Abraham the trip had given him a keener awareness of his heritage, and his responsibility as the inheritor to find a home for the family Torah.

Soon after their homecoming, by timely coincidence, the Rosens received an invitation to visit the Jewish Museum in Berkeley, nearing completion. The museum's ambitious goal was to build the world's largest archive documenting Jewish life in the western United States. To this end they were acquiring artifacts, and oral history collections of the past 150 years. They were also seeking rare and historic documents, photographs, films, newspapers, and periodicals.

Jacie Selman, the curator, who had heard about the Torah through the Staubs, welcomed the Rosens then showed them the museum's acquisitions to date. Afterwards, she invited them to a nearby coffee shop. Over pastries she asked Abraham to consider donating the Torah to the museum. He had anticipated this, and had a ready response. He could not donate the Torah to the museum as it was a family inheritance, not his to give. However, he would consider loaning it to them.

Over the next few days, Abraham debated, with his wife and his in-laws, the pros and cons of housing the Torah at the museum. He argued that it would provide a safe haven for their legacy, and also an excellent opportunity for others to view it and to learn about its significance. Martha countered that the Torah is the foundation of a *living* religion. While at Los Alamos she had witnessed the Native Americans struggling to preserve their religion and their traditions, although much of it had been lost.

"So what is your point?" Professor Staub challenged.

"If the Rosen Torah were the relic of a dead religion, it would be different; but Judaism has survived for thousands of years. There are detailed rituals about how to dress and undress a Torah, and how it must be read and studied. It should not be viewed as an artifact or an icon in a museum, but should be used and honored as a living presence."

Gertrud turned to her daughter, "By the way, now that Abraham has inherited the Torah, perhaps it would be appropriate to join a shul? It would provide a more fitting place for the scroll and fulfill the wishes of the previous inheritors."

Martha replied sharply, "Well, that's not for me to say, that's up to Abraham."

He sat with his eyes narrowed and his jaw working, thinking over what had been said.

With an impatient toss of her head, Gertrud added, "And what about John and Clara? It's their inheritance too. You need to think about your children."

Abraham felt burdened with a responsibility he had not sought. They were demanding too much of him, they were goading him to join a synagogue, and to forgive his grandfather. These things were not possible. It was all Mendel Snyder's doing; he ought not to have asked this of him. He chided himself for not having been more candid with Mendel. But he was beyond reach. And here he sat, stalled by conflicting emotions, unable to get on with his scientific work. They were all staring at him, expecting him to come to a wise decision.

331

He rose to his feet and declared, "I will place the Torah in the museum." Martha felt at once rebuked and relieved. With a rush of emotion, she noticed how distinguished he looked. The years had chiseled his face into sharp, ascetic angles, and his eyes radiated with intelligence and vitality.

As he shrugged on his jacket, Abraham felt his gloomy indecision fall away like an old scab. Although he was violating stipulations in Mendel's will to place the Torah in a synagogue, he had struck a compromise by providing a place of safety and dignity for it.

Shortly after, the Rosens sent invitations to the Snyders, inviting them as honored guests to the official opening of the Jewish Museum in Berkeley. They declined without explanation. Puzzled and offended, Abraham placed a long-distance call to Nathan Snyder, who told him bluntly that he disapproved of placing the Torah in the museum, and that he should return it to him. The Snyders would house it in the Orthodox synagogue in Atlanta, where it belonged. Abraham reminded him that he *had* already offered to return the Torah, and he had declined. Not wanting to foment ill feelings, Abraham explained that he had already promised the Torah to the museum and could not go back on his word. The exchange left both parties upset, damaging the newly forged relationship between the two families. In time, Abraham hoped that Nathan would come to accept his decision.

The Rosens and the Staubs attended the grand opening. They were pleased and proud to see the Torah prominently displayed in the main exhibit hall. After that, like a top knocking into walls and then spinning away in another direction until it finally came to a halt, Abraham felt a serenity he had not experienced in a long time. He had dispensed his obligation honorably, and could now focus on his work. After the depression and the guilt, he felt charged with renewed energy.

❧ 27 ❧

The Sixth Inheritor: John Rosen, the Dreamer

We are the music-makers,
And we are the dreamers of dreams,
Yet we are the movers and shakers,
Of the world forever, it seems.
"Ode" by Arthur O'Shaughnessy

When the Berkeley Jewish Museum hosted a reception in honor of those who had loaned or donated artifacts, John and his sister Clara accompanied their parents and grandparents, attending as honored guests. John did not know quite what to expect but enjoyed being treated like a VIP. Displayed on a pedestal in a glass case in the center of the hall, the open Rosen Torah and its accessories immediately caught his attention.

Mesmerized by the array of strange objects gleaming inside he fantasized himself as Long John Silver discovering a pirate's treasure—so deep into daydream that when a hand shook his elbow, he jumped. He heard laughter, and looked up to see Jacie Selman, the curator, standing before him in a flowing black silk skirt. Embarrassed, he stammered, "Eh-eh-eh-excuse me, did you say something?"

"You're a fortunate young man to have so wonderful a Torah!" she repeated.

John forced a grin and thanked her, looking around the circle of his family for approval.

Just then a youthful gentleman wearing a white satin skullcap and open-necked dress shirt joined their circle. Miss Selman introduced the Rosens to Rabbi Michael Ziff of the Orthodox synagogue in nearby Palo Alto, and then quickly excused herself. Watching her retreat, her skirt swishing around her high heel shoes, he wished he were older and more grown up.

After quizzing Abraham about the Rosen Torah's history and how he came to be its inheritor, the rabbi looked at John appraisingly. "You know your Torah is not just a mysterious relic from the olden times. Like an ancient map it can guide you to hidden treasures of life."

The boy's eyes widened in surprise, had the rabbi read his thoughts?

"Now what treasures are to be found inside the Torah?"

"I . . . I don't know," he stammered.

"If you take time to *study* the Torah you will discover them," the rabbi said, with a smile. Then he turned to look directly at Abraham and Martha. "Even for non-practicing Jews a limited amount of study together as a family can transmit the meaning and substance of Torah. Don't you agree?"

John could tell from the way his father frowned, and adjusted his glasses on the bridge of his nose that he was displeased.

After Rabbi Ziff left, Martha patted Abraham on the arm. "What have you and Jacie Selman got against the rabbi?"

"Enough to dislike him," Abraham growled, cryptically.

When they returned home, Martha brewed tea and they sat in the kitchen reviewing the reception at the museum. Abraham thought it had been a congenial affair without being too pretentious. Martha agreed. "I am happy that it went off well," she said, "but weren't you a little short with Rabbi Ziff?"

Abraham raised a hand. "No Martha," he said, "it was the rabbi who was rude to me. You see, before coming to California, he held the post of assistant rabbi to the Orthodox synagogue in Atlanta, the one Nathan Snyder belongs to."

Martha raised her eyebrows.

"I am sure he knows that Nathan disapproved of my placing the Torah in the museum. Obviously he's taken the Snyder's side, and is trying to needle me."

"I'm sorry to hear that, I liked Nathan. I hope the rabbi didn't upset Jacie Selman too."

"The rabbi and Nathan have no right to sit in judgment on me! It's just another example of religious intolerance," Abraham protested. He thought of saying more about his dislike of fanatics, and his disappointment in the Snyders, but he wanted to savor the evening.

Martha put down her tea, and sighed. Neither of them spoke — there was nothing more to say just then.

Soon afterward, Martha became active on the Jewish Museum's board of directors, and began attending their lecture series on Jewish culture, which ranged from art and music, to history and ethics. Abraham joined the movement to halt the arms race that had begun with the buildup of the Soviet Union. It concerned him that Eisenhower — like Truman before him — believed that nuclear weapons were the most effective way to protect the nation from the Communist menace. He fired off scathing letters to editors, condemning Eisenhower's plan to be in a position of readiness to attack the Soviet Union with nuclear-armed missiles and bombers.

"Abraham, please don't try to take the world on your shoulders," Martha pleaded.

"I must do my part to halt the madness," he insisted, sounding more sure than he felt. "Though some call doing nothing, "benign neglect" to salvage their conscience, rationalizing that there is little they can do to bring about change. But I have to do something!"

"But if you believe that you are responsible for all the transgressions of the government that represents you, then the moral burden would become too heavy to endure!" Martha protested.

In a twist of irony, the government funded Abraham and his team at the University of Berkeley to work on developing surveillance satellites to verify that countries were not building

335

nuclear arms. He was pleased that he could continue to work against the proliferation of nuclear weapons. Still he complained that science should be used for much more than to police others, declaring to anyone who would listen, "Science should make peaceful contributions to healing, to enriching life, to freeing the spirit."

Martha's eyes flashed, "Abraham, you're getting to be an old bore. I've heard this too many times before."

"Am I?" he said half-teasingly. "My colleagues and students don't think so." The Rosens' home had become a gathering place for scientists, writers, and students concerned about the way in which science and technology impacted society.

"Maybe they really come for my home cooking," Martha joked. Then after a pause, "Anyway, I'm sure that the benefits of the work you are doing for the space industry will far out weigh any negative outcomes."

"When did you become an expert on such matters?"

"Am I not the daughter of an eminent physicist, and the wife of a famous nuclear scientist?" she teased, a smile twitching at the corners of her mouth.

It wasn't long before Abraham found other causes to champion. One evening in the kitchen pouring himself a glass of milk before going to bed after the last guest had departed and the house was quiet, John overheard his parents through the screen door talking out on the patio.

"Abraham don't you think that your involvement in defending unpopular causes is becoming obsessive?" his mother challenged.

"Unlike my ancestors who were powerless to effect change, it is my obligation to do what I can to stop injustice, for in my blood and bones I am one of them," his father replied.

"Which ancestors are you referring to?"

"Those who lived in the shtetls inside the Pale of Settlement, and were powerless pawns of the Russian Empire, and all those who died in the Holocaust," his dad shot back.

In the silence that followed, the shelf clock chimed the hour, and John heard his mother ask, "So, despite your steadfast

336

abandonment of Judaism, your family legacy has altered your perspective after all?"

"I suppose it has."

"For the better," she declared.

"Heir to the Rosen Torah, or not, you know I stand for justice, for behaving as a decent human being, and as such I will continue to fight for the oppressed, for those who have lost control over their fate."

"The Torah teaches that we can create a more just society by remembering the injustice done to us," his mother said.

"Since attending the Jewish Museum's educational programs you have become quite a sage," his father remarked. John heard the scraping of a chair and footsteps coming toward the door into the house. "I should write a letter about the Rosenberg trial to the editor before turning in for the night," he heard his father say.

"What are you going to say?

"That although David Greenglass, a machinist working at Los Alamos, swore he verbally passed on information about the atomic bomb to Julius Rosenberg, the alleged spy for the Soviets, in my opinion Greenglass did not have sufficient scientific understanding to transmit any "secrets" of use to the Russians. I believe that the trail is being provoked by fear and paranoia of the Communist threat now that they have exploded an atomic bomb."

His father's angst made a profound impression on the adolescent. He devoured Isaac Asimov's *I, Robot* and Ray Bradbury's *The Illustrated Man* and *The Martian Chronicles*, gifts from his dad who encouraged him to read science fiction. In his father's opinion it was the only form of literature that thoughtfully explored the ways in which technology and science would one day change society, for better or for worse.

In high school his English teacher, Virginia Hamilton, recognized his writing talent and encouraged him to work for the school newspaper. At first he wrote crude short stories set in the African jungle inhabited by hunters, ivory poachers, and wild animals. On his own initiative he launched a science fiction club and a magazine, *Futurism*, both to entertain sci-fi fans and also to provide an outlet for his own tales.

His parents were intrigued and delighted by their son's facility for spinning yarns. However, after graduating from high school, when John declared that he planned to make a living as a writer instead of attending college, they insisted on discussing other options.

Next day, in the late afternoon, the family hiked into the hills behind the Berkeley campus where they could debate the issues. John set a fast pace up the steep trail, while Abraham and Martha determinedly kept up with him, until finally he called a breathless halt at a huge, flat rock near the top. The three perched there to admire the magnificent view of the entire East Bay. Abraham uncorked a bottle of wine, then, handing a glass to his wife and son, he said, "First, a toast to your graduation and to your transition to adulthood." After they clinked glasses Abraham continued, "John, so long as you enjoy writing strictly as a hobby, it's fine with me. But we want you to go to college and get a degree and a profession. It will be something to fall back on if your writing doesn't work out."

The son gave his father a hard look, and two angry spots burned on his cheeks. The three proceeded to debate the pros and cons of college. Abraham said that he had never questioned the necessity of getting a college education. John countered that one didn't need college to become a successful writer. Martha disagreed saying that writers needed as much education as anyone, if not more. Having reached an impasse, the three sat gazing at the view. Far below them, miniature houses roosted on the steep hills, tiny cars sped over diminutive freeways, and the fiery sun slipped behind the Golden Gate Bridge into the vast Pacific Ocean.

"Dad, writing is a profession—not a *hobby*. It's my passion, just as science is your passion."

"Well, if it's a profession then shouldn't you get a degree in literature," Martha shot back.

338

Abraham looked appraisingly at his son, defiance blazing in his eyes. "Why don't you tell us exactly what plans you have in mind?"

"Plans? You talk about life as if it were a scientific experiment. To me the fun is going with the flow, letting things just happen," he countered.

"Don't attack your father! He wants what's best for you," Martha reprimanded.

"I'll be content to live at home, to work as a newspaper delivery boy, to keep on writing, and publishing *Futurism*, until you kick me out or I make it on my own."

Martha wasn't going to let her son off easily. "I agree with your father that you *should* go to college." Just to play the devils advocate she added, "You could consider going to the yeshiva, instead of a regular college. After all you will be the next inheritor of the Rosen Torah."

Caught off guard, father and son stared at her.

Abraham grimaced as he contemplated what his wife had said; surely she didn't believe John was suited to a religious life? Still, after the trip to Israel she had become fascinated by Jewish history and culture, and then soon after Abraham had loaned the Rosen Torah to the museum she had become active on the museum's board. Or perhaps she was cleverly provoking their son into thinking about the soundness of his scheme?

Abraham looked over at John, who met his gaze. "Son, what do you think of your mother's suggestion?"

"I think that yeshiva is the worst possible choice for me. I've been writing since I was a kid, and that's what I want to keep doing. When I sit down at the typewriter it feels right. Like, you know, it's my purpose in life to tell a story so powerful it will shape the way my readers view the world!"

Abraham recognized his son's passionate nature that mirrored his own. "I won't push you into going to college if the motivation doesn't come from inside."

Startled by his father's unexpected support, he blurted out, "Wow, do you mean it, Dad? I thought you would lay down the law about this."

"You'll need to make enough money to pay for your own expenses. If you don't make headway as a writer, in the first year or so, will you then agree to go to college?"

John nodded enthusiastically. "That's groovy, Dad."

The three descended the track over tall grass meadows backlit in the last rays of the sun, and through a shadowy grove of eucalyptus trees, inhaling their sharp scent in the gloom, each absorbed in their own thoughts.

With this agreement, John easily settled into a routine. He got up at dawn to deliver papers, took a short break for breakfast then worked on his writing until late afternoon. He still found time for surfing and for flirting with girls on the beach. The California sun tanned his skin and bleached highlights into his hair. Surfing broadened his shoulders, hardened his muscles, and lent his hazel eyes the distant squint of a sailor scanning the horizon. He began to resemble the movie heroes he had once fantasized about.

While John reveled in his easy-going life style, a shiver of apprehension shattered the country's short-lived complacency. On October 4, 1957, the Russians succeeded in launching the first man-made satellite, Sputnik, into space. The Rosens drove into the hills, away from the city lights, hoping to catch a glimpse of the little aluminum sphere. It was said to be no larger than a beach ball, yet capable of circling the globe and emitting a steady stream of data to its Soviet masters. They were about to leave when, through their powerful binoculars, Sputnik appeared as a tiny moving dot of light smaller than all but the faintest stars — or did they imagine it? They looked to the heavens and thought it dominated the world; now who could stop the Russians from dropping a nuclear weapon anywhere on the planet?

As a consultant to the American team racing to launch its own satellite ahead of the Soviets, Sputnik represented a personal defeat for Abraham. Over the next few months, he and their regular circle of friends debated what Sputnik would mean to the U.S. in the future.

John was in no mood for his father's gloomy polemics. For him the conquest of space was exciting, and triggered a storm

340

of ideas that he was eager to use in his science fiction writing. He had just read Jack Kerouac's *On the Road,* which whet his craving to roam free, to experience life in the raw. To the young writer, Kerouac seemed to validate his own yearning to break away from society's conventions. It was not long before he acted on this need.

With the money saved from the sale of his short stories he had enough to purchase a second-hand Oldsmobile, which he dubbed the Green Wasp. Brushing aside his parents' concerns, he teamed up with two friends who agreed to share the expenses of a proposed adventure. Brimming with excitement, they spent the following weeks planning a yearlong road trip from California to New York.

One morning before dawn, wearing worn jeans, leather sandals, and dark glasses, John set out on a journey that would change his life.

As Abraham watched the fancy taillights receding down the hill like will-o'-the wisps, he recalled his own odyssey to Cambridge, then on to Stuttgart; his nervous excitement, his soaring hopes, fantastic dreams, and unexpected disappointments. Martha harbored doubts and regrets. When John returned would he have grown away from them? Would the experience mature him or stunt him? And something more nagged at her—a feeling that although they had fostered his independence, perhaps they should have guided him more closely and bound him more firmly to convention and tradition

As the Green Wasp rounded the last bend, its rear lights blinked on and off, its horn honked, and John stuck his hand out the window and waved his last goodbye, before disappearing from view.

∞28∞

John and Helen

Sustain me with raisin cakes,
Refresh me with apples,
Because I am lovesick.

Song of Solomon

Hungry to savor life in all its authentic guises and raw flavors, John and his friends began a frenetic cross-country odyssey in search of adventure. Like their hero Kerouac, they visited black jazz joints and Mexican whorehouses, experimented with drugs, participated in drunken orgies that got them arrested twice. They had close calls with thugs and were once mugged so badly they ended up in an emergency room with deep lacerations and ugly bruises. They slept in sleazy hotel rooms infested with bedbugs and lice, endured hunger and cold, and shared in the misery of the homeless.

A year and two months later, John returned to Berkeley, looking thin and unkempt but otherwise whole. His taking off had worried his parents, but he had been conscientious about staying in touch via long-distance telephone calls and postcards, and that had allayed their anxiety to some extent.

On the journey, John had begun to map out a timeline of themes for a series he planned to call Justice Robots. These would be scientific detective novels set in the future, in which robots help humans solve the dilemmas of space exploration. Reminiscent of his father, his characters would militantly oppose the sinister use of new technology.

342

True to his vision, a year after the road trip, *Marble Egg*, the first of the Justice Robots series was published, and won him recognition as a promising young science fiction writer. His parents now congratulated themselves on permitting their son to pursue his passion despite their misgivings, and decided to throw a party for him.

Martha cooked all her special dishes, filled the house with massive bouquets, and sent invitations to their eclectic mix of friends: pompous academics, long-haired Berkeley professors, noted scientists and writers, fawning science fiction fans, and gorgeous young surfers with their sexy dates. The unlikely mélange gathered at the Rosens' place to drink champagne and consume rich food then drift onto the terrace to dance to a Latin band. By dawn Martha and Abraham had fallen asleep on the couch. John and his current girlfriend made love in the battered Oldsmobile as the rising sun filtered away the night; it was a moment of unfettered happiness for him.

John continued to work on the Justice Robot series, and when he was invited to teach at the prestigious Clarion Science Fiction Writers' Workshop, along with well-known authors he had once worshipped from afar, he knew he had won the acclaim he had dreamed of. There he met Helen Ridgely, a long-legged, long-necked, pale blonde with a sensuous mouth, and pensive, dreamy gray eyes, who wore drab, unfashionable cotton dresses. He was drawn to her reticence, to her startling dissimilarity from the overly confident, self-centered girls in tight fitting jeans, gaudy tops, and chunky jewelry in vogue.

Their mutual interest in science fiction provided a springboard for easy conversation. On the third day of the workshop, after class John invited Helen to a coffee shop where they could relax and talk more intimately. To break down the formality between them, sitting next to her, he wove colorful stories about his cross-country adventures. With her hands folded demurely in her lap, Helen listened intently. His sturdy maleness, his wide chest and shoulders aroused forbidden feelings deep inside her. With his long hair streaked gold by the sun and tied into a ponytail, he could have been mistaken for a hippie; except for the clean blue jeans, dress shirt open at the neck, and tan sport coat that lent him the air of a college professor.

He finally stopped talking, leaned back in his chair and smiled at her. "So, Helen Ridgely, that's my story. What's yours?"

Helen blushed and tucked her hands under her thighs like a child. "There's not much to tell." Her voice sounded more plaintive than she intended, and she could see disappointment in his eyes. "I mean, I might as well be a nun living in a convent!" To her dismay, tears welled in her eyes and her mouth quivered. Then she saw a light spark in his eyes, a tender glance, and his hands reached out to her. She almost flinched as he wiped the tears from her face, but the gentle touch of his fingers sent a thrill down her spine.

As John gained the shy young women's confidence, he began to piece together the story of her life. She grew up as an Army brat whose family never stayed in one place for long. This nomadic life-style taught Helen how to fit in, or at least blend in, despite always being the newcomer. Her mother, Lenora Ridgely, was of Welsh descent and came from a small town in rural North Carolina. The constant moving unnerved her mother, but her religion served as a pillar of stability in their roving existence. The Ridgelys were staunch members of a radical splinter sect, the True Believers—disapproved of by the main branches of the Pentecostal Church—that preached the reality of hellfire and brimstone and the importance of self-denial. They relentlessly hammered its dire messages into their daughter.

On her sixteenth birthday, Helen begged to enter a school where she could devote her life to serving God. At first her father protested, but her mother prevailed. The minister at their church used his influence to secure Helen a place at their religious boarding school, Cedarwood of the True Believers.

There, the regime was even more austere than at home. In order to kill all natural desires, the girls ate stale, sometimes even rancid food. They studied and worshipped behind a walled compound, lived in spartan dorms, fasted at least two days a

344

week and spent long hours kneeling on the cold church floor praying. Helen wore the required uniform at all times: a loose-fitting brown skirt; a coarse, white cotton shirt; a tight, brown headscarf; and black, lace-up shoes. Under the vigilant eyes of Principal Glanton, a formidable middle-aged woman, teachers inflicted punishments with a heavy hand. At night transgressors had to mop and wax floors, peel potatoes, and scour bathrooms. Helen devoted three years of her life to serving the church with every fiber of her being, praying and hungering for salvation.

After graduation, not knowing where to go or what to do, she appealed to Principal Glanton to hire her as a secretary. And so, she worked and prayed for three more years. Yet with the persistence of acidified rainwater seeping into limestone, her faith began to erode, leaving behind a dark maze of underground fractures and caves. The pious young woman could no longer deny that she felt no holier or closer to Jesus, no matter how hard she fasted, prayed, and denied herself physical comforts. Deep inside, a gnawing yearning for something more meaningful ate at her morale.

Her solace at this troubling time was the city library, where she could sometimes slip away from the principal's stern watch to read for an hour or two. Seated at a fluorescent-lit reading table in a remote corner of the third floor, she lost herself in novels that would not be permitted at Cedarwood. In this way Helen vicariously experienced lives rich with sensory pleasures that she believed she would never experience. Clandestinely she began to write short stories that explored the suppressed desires now invading her dreams. It was in this state of crisis that Helen had seen a notice posted on the library's bulletin board about a science fiction writers' workshop. She knew full well that Glanton would not approve, but, in a moment of rebellion, she enrolled.

There she met John Rosen, now sitting close to her with warmth and invitation in his eyes, his arm around her shoulders. It was an exotic, new sensation to feel the breathing of another, an intimate, fragile bond foreshadowing wonderful things to come. All these years, she had thought herself invisible to men;

345

now she was the focus of John's attention. Knowing this filled her with elation and hope, dread and fear. For the first time, Helen experienced the pleasure of being close to someone who accepted her without reservation, who did not interrogate her about the state of her soul. Carefree and easy-going, John was the complete antithesis of her church people; he liberated her. For his part, John was drawn to this naïve and timid woman with a spark he felt sure lay hidden within, just waiting to be ignited.

Although she was terrified of being discovered, Helen sneaked away to meet John after class. The way he seemed completely at ease with himself drew her to him. Independent, yet respectful of his parents, he spoke of his childhood with pleasure and affection. His dreamy nature, his vivid imagination, and his free spirit fascinated her. Yet when he spoke of his journey across America, she feared his wild side, his readiness to experiment and to break rules.

On the second to last night of the workshop, Helen returned to her room at the True Believers center to find the principal waiting for her. Although lying was against everything she had been taught, Helen said that she had gone to the library and to the bookstore to do some research. Glanton continued to interrogate Helen until she confessed that she was attending a writing workshop and, worse yet, one that taught science fiction.

The principal was incensed. "You are playing with fire, with evil," she hissed. "I strongly advise you against going back. Those people can expose you to nothing but filth!" The network of veins on her nose turned to purple with indignation. Helen felt the familiar fear rising inside and lacked the courage to meet the malice in the principal's eyes. It was clear that the woman was enraged not simply by her enrollment in writing classes, but by her implicit bid to break away from the confines of their enclave.

The following evening, as Helen sat brooding in her room, she heard a sharp rap on her door. "If you go tonight, you will be playing with evil!" Glanton's words spat through the keyhole. Helen longed to cry out: *Your religion has not worked for me! I have not found God. I am suffocating. Yet, where can I go? What can I do? If I don't go now, I will never go.* She sat on in miserable silence.

Alone in her room, Helen's face burned with rage. She threw herself onto the bed, dug her fingers into the coarse blanket, and pressed her mouth into the hard pillow to suppress the sobs wracking her body. Her need to get away was now overwhelming. Helen tiptoed downstairs with her heart hammering in her chest. Using her secretary's key she opened the door to the office where she worked, reached for the telephone with clammy hands, and called John.

"Don't worry. I'll come and get you." His voice was low and soothing.

"You don't understand. They'll never forgive me if I leave."

"Everything will be fine. Don't pack. Just take your purse and personal items. I'll meet you at the entrance to Cedarwood."

"I'll be there," Helen whispered. "May God forgive me."

Alerted by John, Abraham and Martha were waiting in the kitchen to welcome and reassure the fugitive. "Enjoy!" Martha said, handing the terrified girl a mug of hot chocolate and a generous slice of apple tart with whipped cream. Having spent years in penance and fasting, Helen was overcome by the tantalizing smells, and the sweet moisture filling her mouth. Even so, an irrational burst of fear made her hands tremble as she reached for the mug.

John saw her distress. "Helen, you are not a slave. Glanton has no power over you. Don't give her authority to tell you how to live your life!" She flashed him a grateful smile, and although her eyes were swollen and red, in the Rosens' kitchen she felt safe. John's parents felt compassion for this tormented young woman. They could not condone the brainwashing and degradation she had to endure. Knowing that she had no place to go, they invited her to stay with them.

Although it took some effort, the next day they persuaded Helen to call the principal to inform her that she had chosen of her own free will to live outside the confines of Cedarwood. Predictably, Glanton continued to intimidate Helen. She sent letters filled with fearsome imagery and threats, in an attempt to persuade her to return. It called upon all of Helen's strength to resist going back to the life that had threatened to destroy her.

After years of living in a structured, protected community, the new independence bewildered and frightened her. She could do whatever she wanted, go wherever she wanted, wear whatever she wanted; and yet the frenetic pace of life "outside" terrified her. At Cedarwood everyone had known who she was; now people she did not know, who did not care about the state of her soul, crowded her. She suffered from recurrent nightmares and panic attacks, that would leave her gasping for breath, choking with fear, her eyes twitching, and her body covered in perspiration. Had it not been for the support of the Rosens, she would have fled back to the shelter of her church, where she knew her place and precisely what was expected of her.

To provide some stability and independence, Abraham helped Helen to be hired as a secretary in the Physics Department at Berkeley, where she amazed everyone with her efficiency and diligence. After work, she came home to the Rosens, ate, talked to John and his parents for a while, slept for an hour or two, then worked on her writing. She found writing cathartic, a way of putting her deepest fears and hopes outside herself. She told John, "Through my stories I want to help people believe in their dreams, find comfort, and bring false gods crashing down."

"False gods? Hey, girl! Be careful not to come across as preachy. Focus on telling a good story," John advised her.

When she was not writing, Helen enjoyed participating in community theater. She had little experience beyond performing in religious plays, yet despite her timidity, she had a natural dramatic flare and stage presence. Slowly she began to enjoy the exhilaration of new pursuits. It had taken months for her to outdistance her fears, but once she had won, she was not bitter about her past. She told John that her insistence on clinging to the church and to Glanton was partly her own fault. She had been too weak to stand on her own.

He conceded that this was true. Still, it did not excuse the sect's horrible abuse. "You are incredibly forgiving. If I had been abused and brainwashed like that, I would be furious and resentful." He saw that he had upset her. Clearly this was not the time to air his views on religion. In his opinion, history clearly demonstrates that governments too closely bound to religion become inhumane and callous, resulting in crusades, inquisitions, and witch hunts. For now, John reveled in Helen's newfound zest for life, her courageous decision in leaving.

With this hard-won confidence, she insisted on moving out of the Rosens' home to rent a room in an old Craftsman bungalow not far from the Berkeley campus. To its detriment, the present owner had subdivided the house into five bedrooms, two downstairs, and three small upstairs rooms, with one bathroom on each floor; the tenants shared a living room and the kitchen on the ground floor. Though it had fallen in status, it retained the unmistakable outlines of its former beauty. To her, the house was gracious and inviting without being stiff or formal. Visitors mounted three steps to a deep porch supported on fieldstone columns and shaded by a gabled overhang with wide eaves, exposed rafters, and decorative brackets. Inside, the dark wood paneling of the living room and a big fireplace surrounded by glazed green tiles, lent a cozy feel to the place. Her little room under the eaves on the second floor, with a dormer window that created an alcove for her bed, was equally snug. She loved the place and dubbed it the Shady Lady. John teased her about being too emotional, about loving the house more than she loved him. She came back with, "Sir, I dub thee Spock," alluding to the *Star Trek* character who struggles to find a balance between his Vulcan logical self and his human emotional self. John had to throw back his head and laugh at her only too apt nickname.

John visited Helen almost everyday, sometimes helping her prepare the vegetarian meals she liked, chopping fresh vegetables into neat cubes for savory soups flavored with fresh herbs. In fine weather, they ate on the front porch, observing the world go by: a college student wearing a bright necklace of love-beads and carrying a heavy backpack covered in stickers, pedaling his bicycle down the road; a long-haired hippie, in a fringed vest, ambling along strumming a folk song on his guitar;

349

and a couple smooching unabashedly in the front seat of a red Ford Mustang parked across the road. In cooler weather they retreated to the kitchen, surrounded by the chatter of the other residents. John came to love the ambience of the Shady Lady, too.

After meals they wrote for a few hours, and read the latest drafts of their stories to one another. Observing John's dedication to his craft, she felt a rush of pride. He didn't write merely because he had talent; he wrote because he was passionate about sharing his vision: to invent new ways to survive, with love and courage, in a world divided by hate and fear. And he wasn't afraid to experiment—as she was—to devise techniques, through trial and error, for telling a story with integrity and authority.

They went for long walks holding hands, or drove with her head on his shoulder down to the bay in his decrepit Olds that he somehow kept in running condition, despite its age. John burned with ardor, but she was not ready for sex. When they kissed too long and too deeply, she drew back, frightened by the kindling of her desire. "John, stop," she would cry. "Don't do this!" Accustomed to young women who were free about sex, he saw the irony of having fallen in love with a prim-and-proper virgin. He nicknamed her Miss Primrose. By refusing to yield to him, she challenged, and aroused him. When his tension grew too intense, in the aura of her muted beauty, he would go surfing in the cold, fast waves to quench his fervor. He bided his time, knowing that if he took gentle but persistent steps, she would eventually open to him.

One evening, engrossed in writing, John stayed later than usual at the Shady Lady. It was past midnight by the time they went downstairs to the kitchen for a late-night snack. Except for one denizen asleep on the couch with an empty beer can clutched in his hand, they were alone. John grilled cheese sandwiches and made cocoa, while Helen washed a stack of greasy dishes left in the sink. He tried to start a conversation but she seemed distant and unresponsive; little percussive notes of metal, glass, and china punctuated the silence growing between them.

"What's bothering you?" John asked at last, placing his hands on her shoulders and turning her to face him.

"I was thinking of my mother," she said. "She would disapprove of the way I live now."

"Hey! What's wrong with being a bad girl, Miss Primrose?" Everything about her aroused him; the flowery scent of shampoo in her hair, the silky hiss of nylons brushing against her thighs, the thought of the moist, rosy crevice between her legs. His hands cupped her face, moved down to touch her breasts; she shuddered, took his hand, and led him outside to the garden.

They lay on the grass, looking up through the filigreed branches of an old almond tree to the sky unfurled above them like a black velvet shawl stitched with silver beads. Without words, he kissed her again and again. She wanted both to hide and reveal herself, to delight him with the fullness of her body. His eyes burned into her, causing her blood to flow sweetly into her thighs and breasts. She thought, *This is the moment I have longed for.*

When a light snapped on in the kitchen, they pulled abruptly apart, still smiling, knowing that they would consummate their love soon. For now, they were content to sit holding hands, watching the starry constellations spinning above them.

Shortly after that, a bedroom downstairs became vacant and John at last moved out of his parents' home to live with Helen. Abraham and Martha were disconcerted by this arrangement, despite the obvious affection between the two. They knew that young people across the country were embracing free love and drugs — and they feared for them.

Just as the Rosens had predicted, the young lovers were being lured into the emerging counterculture. Gradually, the Shady Lady became one of countless communal scenes where people crashed in at any hour. Deep in the midst of the confusing 60s, Helen and John argued about all of it: civil rights, Pop Art, the Beatles, the Peace Corps, the Kennedy brothers, the environment, even Barbie dolls. Later, they debated what the U.S. was doing in Vietnam. Sometimes they disagreed, but more often they found common ground. One issue, the use of drugs, became a source of friction and began to drive them apart. She condemned those who took drugs as weak and foolish, and said that it made no sense to destroy the body and mind for momentary pleasure. He countered that she was blowing things out of proportion, and that she was beginning to sound too self-righteous.

In the mornings, they found people passed out on the floor in the living room, throwing up on the porch, slumped over the kitchen table. The old house, which had smelled of aged waxed wood, sweet over-ripe apples, and a trace of mildew, all masked by a lemony cleanser, now reeked of urine, vomit, and pot.

"The place is like a garbage dump," Helen protested, stepping over yet another body blocking the stairs. She continued to grumble as she cleaned up one more mess in the kitchen.

"Don't lose your cool. It's just one or two kids that can't handle it," John said, attempting to downplay what was obvious around them.

"You are the one who can't handle it." Helen turned away and stared out the window, trying not to succumb to his charm.

"Hey, don't take it so seriously."

Turning her back to him to hide her tears, she began stacking dishes.

"Okay, so I do a little pot, no different from my parent's drinking a glass of wine or a snifter of brandy."

She felt anger blossom inside her like a red flame. "Don't insult me, or your parents. What you're doing is self-destructive."

"How? I'm still the same person. I haven't changed. I'm still your Spock."

"You haven't been writing seriously since you started smoking pot."

"Oh, give me a break. I just had a story published!"

"I think it's time for us to move."

"What? You love the Shady Lady."

"Not the way it is now. Please, John, can't we find another place?" She dabbed at the tears spilling from her eyes with a dishtowel. "I love you, but I can't stay here!"

352

He put his arms around her, "Let's not quarrel."

"I'm sorry, but I meant what I said. I do love this place, but I won't be part of this chaos." John opened his mouth to say something, but Helen raised a hand. "Please, there's no use arguing. I've decided to move out by the end of the month."

To John's humiliation and astonishment, Helen rented a small apartment across town. He was shocked by her strength and her courage to stand by her convictions; he had not believed she would leave him. She had been so needy, so insecure when they first met. He wanted to call her and beg her to return, but he was too hurt and too proud to do it.

⊰ 29 ⊱

Rites of Passage

Storytelling is a holy activity equal to Torah study or prayer.
Chassidic teaching

The decision to break up with John caused Helen deep anguish. She tried to bury her misery in work, but she missed him and was tempted to move back to the Shady Lady. By day she continued to work in the Physics Department. She also enrolled for evening courses at a nearby community college, taking as many drama-related courses as she could. Late at night she fell into bed exhausted, closed her eyes and burrowed beneath the blankets like a mouse hiding from sharp claws, only to lie awake brokenhearted, lonely and afraid. She couldn't stop longing for John, nor rid herself of the sense of being adrift on stormy seas, clinging to the flimsy raft without the strong wind of faith to direct her to shore. In this unhappy frame of mind, Helen discovered that although she had renounced her church and declared herself an agnostic, she needed some spiritual support. When a friend, Lisa Lamont, invited her to attend a meeting at the Center for Spiritual Enlightenment, she accepted.

On Sunday morning Lisa picked her up, and drove through a neighborhood of run-down houses. They parked on a side street and entered the center through a wrought-iron gate set in a high adobe wall. At the far end of a garden, spreading live oaks softened the sharp angles of a contemporary glass and concrete chapel. Not since her defection from the Church had she set foot in a place of worship. A growing tension tightened her jaws and neck, sure signs of a bad headache coming on.

Folks, young and old — in calico Mother Hubbard dresses, blue jeans, miniskirts and boots, and tie-dyed long skirts — chatted, greeted new arrivals, and flitted around on errands to prepare for the service. Inside, beneath glass skylights, the twisted branches of an old oak, growing through the floor, sliced the sunlight into gold ribbons that fell across a long table covered with a white cloth and baskets of braided bread. When the hymn singing began, Helen resisted the urge to join in. Having escaped the fearsome embrace of her True Believers Church, she dreaded being lured into some other creed. She clutched the pew in front of her, managing a nervous smile when anyone caught her eye.

On the drive home, Lisa asked her friend if she had enjoyed the service.

"It was a little confusing to me. Was it a mix of Christianity, Buddhism, and maybe Judaism? They all seemed sincere, yet I didn't feel part of it, " Helen replied.

"Give yourself time before making up your mind."

"I did pick up information about meditation and yoga classes. Maybe I'll give them a try."

"Good for you," Lisa said, patting Helen's hand.

They drove in silence through the quiet Sunday streets. Helen closed her eyes against the brightness outside and let her thoughts wander. What was she searching for? The faith that had sustained her once had turned out to be a poison cup from which she had drunk too deeply. Yet, now that she was free to choose to live as she wished, something was still missing.

"Penny for your thoughts," Lisa said, startling Helen.

"I've never told anyone this, but sometimes when I look around, the visible world seems sort of like a coral reef, you know? As if just below the surface, a rich mystical life is hidden from our eyes."

"You're confused. Maybe meditation *will* help you to sort out your feelings."

Helen felt herself blushing. *Some things should be kept private*, she thought.

Despite her qualms, she signed up for meditation and yoga at the center. To her surprise, she found that her mind easily emptied of thought, allowing her to slip into a relaxed state, and her long, supple limbs were ideally suited to yoga. After the first series of workouts, she began to loosen up; the Hindu discipline was rapidly becoming a passion.

John stayed on at the Shady Lady and drifted back into his carefree life — surfing, romancing girls, smoking marijuana, and writing when an idea took hold. At night he frequented coffee shops that reeked of burning "grass" and pungent incense, lulled by the ballads of folksingers lamenting society's ills. The nightly news gave intimations that President Lyndon Johnson could be escalating the war in Vietnam. The young dreamer, sensing no present danger to himself, coasted pleasantly along.

He wanted and missed Helen, but the thought of her self-righteousness and her preaching kept him from contacting her. John appeared to be enjoying his carefree existence, but he didn't fool his mother. She saw that the separation from Helen had hurt him deeply.

Helen often dropped by to visit the Staubs, as there was an unspoken understanding that she was still part of the family. She saw that Helen was just as lonely and miserable as John. Martha encouraged Helen's friendship knowing that it increased the odds that the two lovers might reunite. However, the bond between the women went deeper than that. Helen needed a caring and levelheaded confidant, and Martha filled that role with instinctive empathy. Martha genuinely enjoyed Helen's company, her relationship with her own daughter having grown distant since her marriage into a wealthy and status-conscious family. Clara had wedded Joseph Labatt, a wealthy, Sephardic businessman from Philadelphia, and now lived with him in Wynnewood on Philadelphia's Main Line, one of the nation's most exclusive WASP addresses.

It pained Martha to see two people with so much love to give separated by misunderstanding and false pride. John needed Helen's steadying influence, and she his exuberant zest for life. She approached the subject with John somewhat obliquely, quoting from the Torah, which says that God made Eve from Adam's rib, and ever since, the divided halves seek and yearn for each other. She noticed her son's irritation; still she threw caution aside and blurted out, "I wish you and Helen would make up. You're good for each other!"

"Please, don't pry Ma," he retorted.

She wanted to say more, but she saw that it wouldn't do any good. So she murmured, "Sorry, I didn't mean to interfere," then despite herself she added, "You are free to make your own mistakes and, hopefully, to learn from them."

John awoke each morning with a vague, aching feeling of loss. When he showered and soaped, the missing sensation of Helen's warm body swept through him. Still he told himself that he enjoyed his independent lifestyle, that he was glad to be part of the youthful rebellion sweeping the nation, and that he loved his current girlfriend, Mary Lomb, a committed activist on the frontline of student protests. Then, a series of crazy and frightening events invaded his halcyon days.

One evening, a girl living at the Shady Lady nearly died of a botched abortion performed by a back alley midwife using a rubber hose. John heard terrible screams and rushed to her room. He was powerless to stanch the gush of blood, or the girl's agonized moaning. He tried to comfort her until the ambulance arrived, but horror and pity caused him to sob like a child. Soon after that he attended a party in San Francisco where he drank LSD dispensed in Kool-Aid. As the drug took hold, sounds were altered into shifting, fantastic shapes and colors. People appeared to be wearing malevolent masks. Terrified that he was going insane, at the same time he felt that he was floating peacefully outside his body observing himself writhing and screaming on the sofa. In the midst of these disturbing experiments, a girl living at the old house died of an overdose of acid. When the paramedics finally arrived, John wanted to tear the death mask off her face as they carried her lifeless body to the ambulance. He could neither accept the abrupt divide between life and death, nor the finality of her demise.

The final blow came just a month afterward, when someone planted a car bomb under an unmarked police car that had been parked nearby and was keeping the Shady Lady under surveillance on suspicion of subversive activities. Fortunately, the crude device failed to explode and no one was hurt. John had no prior knowledge of the plot, but the police arrested him. He was taken in for hours of rough interrogation. The suspect was Mary Lomb, his girlfriend, who had slipped into hiding without a word to anyone.

For hours John sprawled on the bed, immobilized by shame and doubt, searching his memory for clues that should have warned him that Mary was dangerous. She had the bad-girl face of a moll in a gangster movie, but he had found that attractive. He cringed, recalling that after a student rally, she had once fumed, "I have a very hard time with this slogan of non-violence because I don't believe that I am non-violent!" At the time he hadn't thought of this as dangerously irrational, just brushed it aside as overly emotional. He willed himself into believing that she would walk into the room at any moment to declare her innocence; now she existed only on the most-wanted-fugitive posters.

After the botched abortion, the fatal drug scene, and the attempted bombing, a veil of gloom and disillusionment settled over him that he could not shake. He had to face the fact that he needed to change. Sick at heart and frightened, John considered talking to his parents, but he was too ashamed to admit what a fool he had been. He thought of calling his sister, Clara, but he was not close to her. Besides, she would have nothing but disdain for his lifestyle and his friends. He rarely visited her because he had nothing in common with her or the upper crust society she was part of, now that she married into the wealthy Labatt family. In his opinion, the WASP hierarchy ostensibly accepted families like the Labatts because they seemed "less Jewish," being affluent and the descendants of Spanish Jews who had arrived in the area in the 1730s, before the Revolutionary War. Lithuanian Jews like the Rosens, who had come later and in poverty, held far lower rank. However, no matter their wealth or professional status,

Jews were not accepted in their clubs, law firms, or banks. Still, his sister wanted above all to fit in, and she worked hard to erase the slightest trace of her mother's foreign roots and preferred not to talk about her "bohemian" paternal grandparents. She was ever vigilant against making any gesture that was a fraction too broad, any laugh too loud, or an enunciation a little too unusual. To her brother, her efforts failed. He easily recognized the distaste of Clara's friends by their glassy gaze and lowered lids. Clara could not help but see it, too; that they were their "token Jews," and although she held her shame inside, it showed in her eyes. He itched to humiliate her with biting words, to strip away her arrogance and hypocrisy, the charade she insisted on playing, especially for the hurt it caused his parents.

In despair, he turned back to Helen. He admitted that the culture of "free love" and drugs had seduced him, and that he had childishly enjoyed flaunting society's conventions, believing that he was fashioning a more peaceful and compassionate world. Seeing John, usually so cheerful and confident, now sad and remorseful, she longed to take him in her arms and comfort him.

Reaching for his hand, she sympathized, "I'm sorry for your suffering. What do you plan to do now?"

"Win you back, Miss Primrose," he said, with a repentant grin.

"I believe you know how to do that, Spock."

Under Helen's calming influence, he stayed away from his old haunts, moved back in with his parents, and began to write steadily again. Although gratified by the change, she was concerned that he needed something more to refocus his life than she alone could offer. One Sunday morning she suggested that he go with her to the Center for Spiritual Enlightenment.

John's old rebelliousness had not been quenched. "Look, I know some sort of religion is important to you. But, in my opinion, if you lead a productive life, surround yourself with good friends, and with people you love and who return your love, what more do you need?"

"You still deny that you need spiritual guidance?" she challenged him.

"Yes. Suffice it to say, I grew up in a secular household, or, to put it bluntly, without a shred of religion."

"Yet we both have ghosts haunting our past that we need to put to rest. Maybe spirituality might help. Come with me. If you don't like it, I promise I won't ask you again," Helen challenged.

"I don't need mumbo jumbo to feel good about myself."

"Then why did you turn to dope in the first place?" Helen could no longer put aside the nagging worry about John's experimentation with drugs.

"Listen, marijuana was harmless fun."

"That begs the question. Did you take hard drugs?"

"Okay, I admit I was intrigued by the possibility of achieving an altered state of awareness."

"Stop trying to sidestep the subject. Did *you* use drugs?"

"Yes." he said quietly. "And I definitely don't plan to repeat that experiment."

"I believe you," she said with new warmth in her voice.

He wanted to move in with Helen, but she insisted that before that happened, she needed to be sure that this time it would be for keeps. He understood that she meant marriage, but he hesitated to make such a final commitment. The issues separating them so preoccupied John that when his mother called to remind him of his promise to attend the opening of a contemporary art exhibit at the Jewish Museum, he admitted guiltily that he had forgotten about it. Undaunted, she insisted he and Helen join Abraham and herself for the reception, adding that while there, it would be a great opportunity to show Helen their family Torah. With a promise to call Helen and extend the invitation, John replaced the receiver, feeling annoyed; in his opinion his mother was becoming a might too serious about their Torah since they had placed it in the museum.

In the museum's lobby, Jacie Selman greeted the foursome warmly, and invited them to move around the gallery at their own pace to enjoy and absorb the exhibit. A series of paintings by the artist Ben Shahn soon caught Helen's attention. She studied them intensely, reading the explanatory notes carefully. When John came up to her, her eyes were sparkling. "Listen to what this artist says: 'I must paint those things that are meaningful to me. What shall I paint? I shall paint stories that beg to be told.'"

John started to comment, but at that moment Miss Selman joined them.

"You admire Ben Shahn's work?" the curator inquired.

"I do. Especially because his art tells stories that seem to probe our conscience," Helen replied.

"It's important to tell our stories. Did you know that according to Chassidic teaching, storytelling is a holy activity equal to Torah study or prayer?" she asked, turning to John.

After a thoughtful pause, he queried, "A holy activity in the sense that stories explore moral issues, right?"

Ms. Selman nodded. "And, to keep our stories and our traditions alive, we should tell them to our children and our children's children. In that way we can pass on the wisdom they contain."

"John is a terrific writer and storyteller," Helen said proudly.

Abraham and Martha exchanged glances of approval. Martha had come to appreciate Helen's admiration for their son's talent. Still, they made an odd couple, she thought. Helen was introverted, timid, and spiritual. John was gregarious, worldly, confident, and, sometimes reckless. Yet both, in their own way were "seekers of wisdom and truth." Martha thought that they could be happy together.

Helen broke into Martha's private musings, "The stories John writes really challenge us to think about the importance of making ethical choices for the future of all humanity."

John caught a twinkle in the curator's eye that caused him to blush awkwardly. He wondered if she took Helen for nothing more than that of a love-struck girlfriend, or did she know of his success as an author? Perhaps Ms. Selman still remembered him as the daydreaming unsure adolescent he had once been.

"Speaking of passing on traditions, you must see the Rosen Torah after you're through with this exhibit," Ms. Selman said, turning to Helen.

When they entered the gallery with their Torah prominently on display, John couldn't resist a little bragging. "It's unreal to think that my grandfather, five generations removed, commissioned this awesome scroll from a scribe in Jerusalem, and that it has survived to end up here, for thousands to admire."

Helen's eyes were fixed on the venerable work of art, her gaze traveling slowly over the scroll. The high color on her cheeks, the smile hovering around her mouth, and the light in her eyes betrayed her complete awe. When Martha asked if she understood the significance of the Torah, Helen did not respond. The scroll and its accoutrements seeming to float luminously in their glass case held her enthralled: the delicate silver finials with crowns set with lovely stones and miniature bells; the handsome red silk mantle embroidered in gold; the heavy breastplate of solid silver with the lion of Judah raised upon it in gold relief; the perfect lettering.

Turning to her son with eyebrows raised, Martha started to say something, but John put a finger to his lips to hush her. Helen could be extremely moody and distant; he had learned that it was best to leave her to her thoughts at such times. Still, he couldn't help wondering what fascinated her about the Torah. Its antiquity? Its sacred genesis? Its exquisite craftsmanship? The wisdom it contained? That it was their family legacy?

Standing there in the peaceful, airy gallery, with the intricate artifacts and Torah before her, a feeling of calm sweetness overtook Helen, an inner conviction that they were part of a larger design she could not yet fathom. Together the Rosens formed a ring around the Torah, as if encircling an ancient tree to protect and to draw strength from it.

Then, like a swollen river overflowing its banks, the orderly routine of their lives was thrown into complete turmoil. John received notification that he had been drafted into the Army. He had witnessed the brutal deaths of Americans and

Vietnamese graphically on TV, and had participated in the antiwar student protest on campus. It was a war he didn't want any part of. Should he dodge the draft and run off to Canada? Should he go willingly into a deadly conflict that the U.S. had no business being involved in, especially at a time when the fighting in Vietnam was escalating? If he became a draft dodger, would he lose Helen? How could he cut himself off from his parents? His friends? Would he have to live as an expatriate forever? Even the lesser details of fleeing to the north seemed appalling: the long, cold winters away from the surf and the sun, a frigid exile from which he might never return. He needed to talk this over with his parents, with Helen, with close friends.

That evening, they gathered around the Rosens' kitchen table. Everyone looked so grim that John said half-jokingly, "As the first order of business let me say I refuse to be drafted into an army that will chop off my ponytail, and shave my head."

His parents, who had never really approved of the way he wore his hair as a badge of artistic license, smiled weakly.

Getting down to business, John declared, "Evading the draft, in my opinion, is consistent with the very best American traditions of resistance to unjust authority."

"I don't believe in this war. But the thought of you as a draft dodger and a fugitive, is extremely upsetting," Abraham said.

"Sometimes war is necessary, and Judaism teaches the supreme value of life, yet our people are not pacifists. The Torah says that wiping out evil is also part of justice. Still, I agree that I don't want my son in this war," Martha countered.

John tried another argument. "My friend Steve went to Canada not because he is an antiwar radical, but because he is more interested in furthering his education than in fighting."

"So, how does that apply to you?" his mother asked with good reason. "By your own choice, you passed up college some time ago."

They discussed his options at length, without coming to a resolution. While they agreed that John should not go to war, they found no satisfactory alternative.

To quiet his mind, that weekend he went surfing with his buddies at Spanish Bay, just south of Monterey. Conditions were perfect and they rode the waves all morning, ate lunch on the beach, and drank cold beer. Late in the afternoon he again paddled out to the Pacific swells. Alone on his sleek surfboard he floated, arms outstretched waiting for the big wave. Suspended between the shining swells and the wind-swept sky, his mind emptied of all thought. He did not see the peaked fin, the menacing flash of jaws, or the jagged rows of teeth until searing pain burnt through his thigh. His hand shot out, made contact with rough skin, grabbed the slimy cavity that was the beast's gill slit and pulled and pulled and would not let go. Like a trap being pried open, the steel jaws slowly released. The dreadful crushing pressure abated, but not the pain. Blood-red waves smashed over him, blinded him, and threatened to steal his consciousness and his life. He clung to his board long enough for the lifeguards to reach him and pull him to shore, though he did not hear the sirens' scream or the cries of people on the beach.

Miraculously, despite the huge loss of blood from the long deep gash in his thigh that exposed the bone beneath, he survived. The orthopedic surgeon told him the wound, even when healed, could restrict the movement of his leg. He might walk with a limp and run only with difficulty, yet in an ironic twist, this unfortunate handicap exempted him from the draft.

He lay in the hospital trying to make sense of this new reality. He understood now that he was not totally in control of his destiny, that his life would take many unexpected turns. That filled him with a terrible and yet exciting realization that life was too short to waste playing around like a child. Fate had provided him with a chance to start anew, to quit behaving as if he was immortal. The terrifying encounter put his priorities in order: they were and would always be Helen, and his writing. He must take that woman as his wife.

Helen sat by his hospital bed day after day, talking little. Once when he opened his eyes, she was completely immersed in a book. He lifted his head, feeling giddy and faint from painkillers, and could just make out its title, *This is Our Torah*. The wound in his thigh began to throb, but he groaned more in annoyance than pain.

She looked up, startled. "Are you okay?"

"Yeah," he said. When she rose to refill his glass with water, he waved her away. "I see you're reading about the Torah. Does it tell you that growing archaeological evidence from digs in Israel call into question Biblical stories, including the Exodus?"

After a long pause, she said, "I suppose all of the stories in the Torah cannot be proved by scientific evidence. But whether or not it is true in a literal and factual sense is not that important to me." The earlier comfortable silence between them suddenly became strained.

When he was almost well enough to be discharged, he asked his mother to help him choose an engagement ring, stipulating that she must keep it a secret. Martha beamed; she had been hoping for the event, and had already decided to give her maternal grandmother's heirloom ring to her son just for this purpose. John loved it.

After the doctor's late afternoon round the next day, John sat smiling at Helen from his wheelchair. Then he took a deep breath and proposed, "Will you marry me, Helen?"

She tried to speak but was overcome by emotion. He fumbled in his pocket and took out the ring, set with sapphires and diamonds that had belonged to his great-grandmother, Kyla, and placed it on her finger.

She gazed at it, a smile of pure happiness illuminating her face. When she spoke, her voice was low with emotion, "Yes, I will marry you, John." She bent to kiss him. There were unshed tears brimming in Helen's eyes as she walked over to the window to compose her thoughts. She had journeyed so far from her past, had distanced herself from her family; still they were part of her, and she hoped that they would be happy for her now. She loved John and had grown to love his parents who had shown such great compassion for her. Now she could give them her affection without reservation. *For giving and sharing love is what brings joy to life, and makes pain and sorrow bearable*, she thought.

When John returned home they began making plans for a simple wedding.

The night before the marriage, just three months after the shark attack, a storm rode in from the Pacific. Rain came down in torrents through the night. Morning dawned. The rain diminished to a steady drizzle. A pastel carpet of wind-strewn petals festooned the lawn, and fallen tree limbs blocked the roads. Yet no one had the heart to cross Helen who had dreamed of a wedding ceremony on the terrace of a small inn in Carmel. So there they stood, lovers in the mist. The bride wore the palest gold silk with a shimmer of tiny pearls, and held a bouquet of yellow primroses in her trembling hands. The groom in a tux, still the handsome California surfer, but gamy-legged and stiff as a wedding cake ornament. Parents and friends surrounded them. Only the Ridgelys refused to attend a wedding not held in their church, despite Helen's attempts at reconciliation. Eager and nervous, they faced the justice of the peace. Too soon, it seemed, the vows were said and rings exchanged. After all the false starts, they were truly married.

❧ 30 ❧

A Bittersweet Legacy

To remain silent and indifferent is the greatest sin of all.

Elie Wiesel

When John and Helen returned from their honeymoon, they agreed that it was time to make a fresh start. The small farming town of Susmook in the Willamette Valley of Oregon, populated by no more than sixteen thousand souls, and less than two hours drive from the nearest city, Eugene, seemed a perfect match for them. Concerts, art exhibits, speaker's forums, and community theater were offered at the local college about 20 miles south of town. It was close enough for shopping and entertainment, far enough to provide a peaceful setting. The town also boasted a good school system, and public library.

They leased, with an option to purchase, a white clapboard cottage on the edge of town that reminded them of the Shady Lady—with a stretch of the imagination. There was a fireplace in the living room, a finished room in the attic for John's office, a covered front porch with a distant view of the mountains, and Helen's favorite place, a small orchard with mature fruit trees and berry bushes.

In Susmook, the newlyweds settled into a comfortable routine. They got along with their neighbors, who thought of them as the "arty" couple from the city. Away from the distractions of the Bay Area they enjoyed uninterrupted hours of writing, hiking, and even salmon fishing. In fact Helen spent more time editing John's manuscripts than working on her own

367

romantic fantasies. To make up for her lack of progress, she decided to keep a journal. John said it would siphon her creative energy away from her novels; she thought that a journal would provide a kind of sanctuary where she could freely explore her thoughts, hopes and fears, and celebrate their new life together.

When Helen became pregnant, they were delighted. "I can't wait to meet my child," she said. "I feel certain that being a mother is going to be wonderful!" John felt a tender pride as his wife grew large and radiant.

They named their baby boy Abe, after his grandfather Abraham. Helen had chosen the name to honor her father-in-law, and, although the family had explained that naming a child after a living relative is not customary amongst Ashkenazi Jews with roots in the Rhineland and Eastern Europe, the mother prevailed.

Holding her exquisite, fragile, wobbly-headed baby gently against her breasts released a primal maternal instinct that forged a permanent bond between mother and son that could never be sundered. The infant had his mother's sandy-colored hair along with her pensive gray eyes, and soon showed intimations of his father's high energy and adventurous spirit.

When Abe turned three, Helen enrolled him in play school for a few hours each day. She desired more children, but after several miscarriages was diagnosed with endometriosis, an uncontrolled growth of the cells lining the womb, and was advised to have a hysterectomy. John tried to raise Helen's spirits. He encouraged her to take up writing again, but after her continued failure to publish, she did not have the will to go on. She was still eager to help him edit and proofread his stories, although she sometimes found the work tedious. Eventually she took a part-time job teaching drama at the two-year college nearby. Later, she threw her energy into starting a community theater group with special children's performances.

Abraham and Martha came to visit often and little Abe loved playing with his grandparents. For the next two years, their lives in Susmook flowed peacefully along. Then news came that Abraham had been diagnosed with prostate cancer, which shocked them out of their complacency. The doctors said that he would have to undergo radical surgery and chemotherapy. John persuaded his parents to come to Susmook so his dad could recuperate. A week after their arrival, on Wednesday, September 16, 1970, a Palestinian terrorist group called Black September executed eleven Israeli athletes and their coaches attending the Olympics in Munich, while millions of people watched the crisis unfold on television. A melancholy pall hung over the Rosens in the wake of the killings.

The next day, the family picnicked at the park near the town's marina to try to recover their shaken equanimity. They munched on sandwiches, watching small pleasure boats nosing their way out to the river against a stiff wind, and windsurfers skimming across the water like giant dragonflies. The air was warm and fragrant, as if the mountains were a living body exhaling the scent of coniferous trees. When Abe begged his grandfather to tell stories about his childhood, they were grateful for the diversion.

During this recuperative phase, Abraham had begun relating tales about the Rosen family. In the evenings, as dusk fell, they gathered in the rustic den to hear him reminisce; especially about Aaron and Marlene, little Abe's great-grandparents who had died in a plane crash. As Abraham wove his yarns, the boy could see the nanny, Jeanette Grace with her big basket, setting out each morning with grandfather in her wake, and sense the riotous smells, colors, and sounds of the French Market near the docks.

"My parents were in love with music," Abraham was saying. "My father's trumpet and my mother's voice made a perfect combination. Her mezzo-soprano wrapped itself around his brilliant notes, making rhythms that left you breathless."

"A pity they didn't make a recording." John said.

"That's right," Abraham replied, "And unfortunately, I didn't inherit their musical gifts, so I needed to find another talent."

"But you have achieved great things as a scientist!" John said.

"Grandpa, did you make a big bomb that could blow up the world?" Abe asked.

An awkward silence followed the boy's innocent question. "Where did you hear that, son?" said John.

"I heard Aunt Clara telling her friends. She said Grandpa was famous. How did you get famous, Grandpa?"

"You're famous if you have done something important that a lot of people know about. Your Grandpa's work helped to bring the war to an end," John said, tousling the boy's hair.

"Are you famous too, Dad? Lots of people read your stories."

His son's naïve praise caught him off guard. John chuckled and said, "You know I love to make up stories. And I feel very lucky that people enjoy them."

"Abraham, what were your parents really like? I mean, outside of the music?" Helen wanted to know.

"It's impossible to separate them from their music. They were sweet, happy souls. But they didn't have much time for me. I try not to blame or to judge them."

Helen nodded sympathetically. Abraham went on to explain how his father, Aaron, had abandoned his Jewish heritage.

"I understand," Helen said, handing a cookie to Abe, who was becoming restless now that the conversation had taken a serious turn. "My mother cast me off, too. She never forgave me for abandoning *her* church." Every Christmas Mrs. Ridgely sent a card beseeching her daughter to seek salvation in Jesus before it was too late. It left her feeling dispirited and unsettled. "No hurt cuts more deeply than that of being rejected by one's parents," she reflected sadly.

It had grown chilly in the den. John went to the fireplace and held a lighted match to a sheet of newspaper. A flame flickered then flared, its yellow-orange tongue lapping at the brittle paper until the kindling caught fire, sending a golden shower up the chimney.

"John, do you remember our visit to Mendel Snyder in Atlanta?" Abraham asked.

370

"Sure I do."

"There I learned for the first time of the Rosen Torah. My father never told me about it." The sick man shivered and held his hands towards the fire. "I also found out that my grandfather, Yakov, had bequeathed the Torah to his nephew Mendel, not his own son, my father. Mendel offered to return the Torah to my dad, but he rejected it. He said that he didn't want anything to remind him of his father."

"So how did the Torah come back to you?" Helen inquired.

"I inherited the Torah from Mendel. You see Mendel wanted to redress the wrong he felt my grandfather had done to my father."

John glanced over at his wife, and seeing her eyes alight with interest, felt a stab of hostility; should she be prying into family skeletons best left in the closet?

"As you know, it now resides in the Jewish Museum in Berkeley," Abraham went on.

"You saw our Torah before you and John were married," Martha reminded them.

Helen nodded and smiled.

"I want to pass on its custody to you, John," Abraham said.

John had assumed that he would inherit the Torah, but hearing his father say it sounded like a death sentence for Abraham. "It'll be years before that happens," he said with forced cheerfulness.

"John, I need to know that you will take full responsibility for the Torah."

"Yes, I will if you want me to. But you know I'm not any more religious than you. Maybe I'm a poor choice."

"I used that same argument when Mendel bequeathed it to me," Abraham said with a deep sigh. "Nevertheless, for me the Torah has come to stand for more than the perpetuation of a religion, it serves as a reminder of the many tragic periods in human history and urges us to speak out against hatred and

371

bigotry whenever they manifest themselves." His eyes flashed with conviction.

After a pause he repeated, "So, can I count on you to ensure the safety of our inheritance? That will be your solemn obligation, nothing more — unless you wish it."

"Yes, Dad you can count on me, that'll be no problem. Don't worry about it."

"Well, now that that's settled, it's time I told you as much as I know about our Torah and the Rosen family." He adjusted the cushion behind his back, and Martha covered his lap with a blanket. "Mendel told me that it was commissioned in 1790, by our patriarch, one Shmuel Rosen, residing in the village of Valinsk, Lithuania. "

"Yes, you've mentioned Shmuel Rosen, my great-grandfather six generations removed. Can you tell me why he commissioned it?"

"Perhaps we should continue this conversation tomorrow? It's getting late," Martha protested, casting an anxious glance at Helen.

"Okay, nurse," Abraham said, "but let me sit by the fire for a little while." In a few minutes he fell asleep in the chair. Outside, the wind moaned over the shadowy landscape; inside, the fire reflected light onto the windowpanes, as if casting out the darkness.

When John awoke, a slice of moonlight was streaming over his bed through a gap in the curtains. He sat up and heard the eerie sound of a piano played so softly that it was barely audible above his breathing. He could not get back to sleep and, slipping out of the warm sheets, dressed quietly. As he fished his boots from under the bed and groped his way downstairs, Helen stirred inside her pocket of dreams but did not wake.

He found his father in an armchair, eyes shut, fingers tapping lightly, listening to Scott Joplin's ragtime. He looked so frail that John felt his heart grow cold with apprehension, and tears spilled down his face. Sensing someone standing at the door, Abraham opened his eyes and gestured for him to sit in the chair beside him. Seeing his son's anguish, Abraham asked him to put on the recording of Mozart's *Eine Kleine Nachtmusik*. Neither could find the strength to say what was in his heart. Instead, their hands touched. As the embers died in the fireplace and the night turned imperceptibly into dawn, they let the music speak for them. Helen found them asleep, holding hands, with the record spinning on the phonograph, emitting a repetitive scratching sound. She choked back a sob with the awful premonition that father and son had said their intimate farewells.

The following evening was unexpectedly warm, and the family gathered on the porch to enjoy the peaceful lull between the close of day and nightfall. They sat quietly watching the colors of the forest and distant mountains alter under the lowering angle of the sun, from pastel washes of mauve to deeper hues of fuchsia, until the world disappeared. In the darkness Abraham cleared his throat and picked up the conversation where he had left off the night before. "I'll tell what I know about the Rosens who inherited the Torah, but there are large gaps in the family history. What I do know comes from Mendel Snyder, through Mendel's mother Frieda Rosen, the sister of Yakov Rosen. It all started with our patriarch, Shmuel Rosen.

Turning to Abe he began, "Once upon a time, in the faraway land of Lithuania, in the shtetl of Valinsk, on the perimeter of a shadowy forest not far from the Baltic Sea, a man named Shmuel Rosen, a simple tavern keeper, and his third wife Rachel lived with their six daughters, and only son, Yitzhak, the apple of his eye." Abraham began slowly, hesitantly, then like a symphony the pace picked up and swelled to a crescendo.

The warm night, Abraham's meditative tone, the poignant lives of the inheritors and their legacy, all evoked bittersweet reminiscences for Martha of the night in Cora's Jerusalem apartment when, belatedly, secrets of the past had been revealed to her.

By the time Abraham had finished, everyone looked dazed.

"That's an incredible story," Helen said, breaking the awed hush. "Maybe I'm the only one here who believes in miracles, but it is miraculous that the Torah survived."

Abraham shook his head and chuckled.

"What's funny, Dad?" John asked, unsettled by his father's sudden shift of mood.

"Me, of all people, as the family historian!" Abraham laughed, overcome by the irony of his role as custodian of the Rosens' religious birthright. He tried to hold back his sudden mirth, but his low chuckle grew into a belly laugh that sent tears rolling down his checks. His laughter was so startling and infectious that little Abe laughed back at his grandfather in delight, hoping for another funny story. As the last sputters of amusement died down, Helen stood, and took Abe by the hand. "Time for bed," she declared. "Give Grandma and Grandpa a big hug." The child ran forward to embrace his grandparents.

"I hope I wasn't too irreverent," her father-in-law apologized. "I don't know what set me off. But I want you to know that I respect the Torah, and that I take my accountability as its keeper seriously."

Helen patted his arm. "I understand. I'll bring out some snacks when Abe's tucked in for the night."

Sitting in the cool night air, they experienced the release that comes after a good laugh. Soon Helen returned with a pot of freshly brewed tea, and the remains of an apple cake her mother-in-law had baked from apples picked in their orchard. Pale and rigid, Abraham sat with his spine pressed against the pillows on the back of his chair. The family could see that he wasn't feeling well. The thought that the chemotherapy might not have eradicated the cancer quickly dissipated the light-hearted mood.

"Helen, I want you and John to visit our Rosen Torah, again," Abraham said, jabbing a piece of strudel onto his plate.

"John, we're free next week, we should arrange to go," Helen pushed a stray strand of hair away from her face with trembling fingers that betrayed her intense feelings.

"Dad, you were planning to go back to Berkeley next Friday. Why don't we drive back with you? While we're there we can all visit the museum."

Abraham nodded his agreement. The night was quiet, the air laden with the scent of pine and spruce.

For a while they all sat quietly letting the serenity soak in, then Helen spoke directly to her father-in-law, "I would like to study the Torah. It would help me to understand and to appreciate the Rosen legacy, and to prepare little Abe as the next inheritor."

"Thanks, Helen, I think that's a good idea," her father-in-law said.

She shot him an appreciative look.

"However, I should warn you that it takes years to study the Torah. I once made a stab at it. I tried to approach it as a scientist, you know, as a set of logical laws or regulations. It didn't work. I suppose because religion is based on faith, not rationality."

Helen brushed stray crumbs from her lap and sighed. Sensing her disappointment, he hastened to add, "But still I think you should go ahead—don't let me discourage you. As you well know, I devoted my life to science, almost to the exclusion of everything else."

"Thanks, I will find a way to get started," Helen said.

Martha leaned forward, "Abraham, while you didn't succeed in mastering the Torah, don't you agree that it brought you back to your heritage in a meaningful way?"

"You're right, my darling. Until the detonation of the bomb over Japan, our meeting the Snyders, the visit to Israel, and before Mendel bequeathed the Rosen Torah to me, I didn't give a thought—let me be honest—I didn't give a damn about my heritage. Still the Rosen Torah reminded me of my irrevocable connection to my ancestors."

His father's reflections summoned up the conversation he had overheard years ago, hidden in the kitchen, when his father had first acknowledged his feelings about being linked to his ancestors still warring in his blood.

"It seems that the past is like energy that's never lost. You remember the law of the conservation of energy in physics? It states that although energy is never lost, it can change form," the scientist mused.

"Or the past is like a seed floating on the wind until it lands in fertile soil and sprouts in a new place," John added.

"Sometimes with unpredictable results!" Helen interjected. She was wearing her hair in a long braid that swung back and forth as she swiveled her head from Abraham to John.

"More cake anyone?" Martha asked. Everyone motioned a negative. She gathered cups and plates onto a tray then carried them to the kitchen.

There was a pause after she had left, then Abraham spoke, "Since Helen sounded serious about embarking on a study of the Torah, it might be interesting for you to join her, John."

It didn't sound like Abraham to push things, but evidently the illness was affecting him. "Dad, you don't have to study the Torah to qualify as its inheritor," John retorted.

"True, but why don't you think about it?"

Suddenly the son had a sinking feeling that as his father became even more ill, like a man on death row, he was turning to religion as a source of comfort. "You have had a great career. And lived up to the highest ethical standards without steeping yourself in religion," John said, sounding more offended than he had intended.

As if he had read his mind, Abraham quickly replied, "Don't think that I'm undergoing a religious conversion because I am dying. Nevertheless, during my illness I have considered what I want to do with the time left to me." John wished his father would stop speaking as if the end was near, but he was on a roll. "First, I will carry on with my research as long as I have the strength to do it." He rubbed the stubble on his chin thoughtfully, before going on. "Philosophers say that my kind of passion is similar to a religious quest, and perhaps there's some truth to that. But rest assured, my dedication to science is not founded on any religious doctrine. I respect open-minded scientific inquiry, and despise those whose dogma tries to impede it. "

His son felt a renewed rush of love and admiration for his father.

Just then Martha, returned to the veranda, and catching the end of the conversation remarked, "Only the deepest

376

conviction that rational laws govern the universe has enabled men like my husband and my father, and great men like Kepler, Newton, and Einstein to dedicate their lives to uncovering the principles of physics!"

"Please don't put me on a pedestal with those great men!" her husband said with a wry smile.

Furrowing her forehead in concentration Helen asked, "Abraham, don't you think that *both* science and religion should free us to use our abilities in the service of mankind?"

"That's a lofty slogan, Helen. But yes, I do agree! I may not be religious in the traditional sense, but I believe in compassion."

"Not all of us are as fortunate as you to find our life's work so early on," Helen said. "We have to search longer for the greater purpose of our lives." She paused before going on. "For me, religion should *not* be rooted in fear of punishment by an all-powerful God, or on the hope of a reward in Heaven after death. It should be founded on guiding us toward living more loving, and more meaningful lives! This is why I want to study the Torah," she said, her eyes alight with determination, her hands clasped together with excitement.

Abraham thought: How ironic that this woman who came to us like a frightened refugee fleeing from a cruel creed has now become the one who wants to assume the burden of preserving our family's religious heritage.

That night Helen slept restlessly, and in the early hours the pitiful yowling of her cat, Pocahontas, about to give birth, woke her. She slipped downstairs to make a comfortable place for her in the kitchen, and stroked her back, until finally, she delivered a litter of six healthy kittens. Afterward, she could not get back to sleep. To organize her thoughts she pulled out the journal she had been keeping and wrote:

> The discussion this evening about the past, and about heritage, was thought provoking. I wonder — will the legacy of the Torah, which God willing, be passed on to our son Abe, yield sweet or sour fruit?

377

Will it come to bless or to haunt us?

As prearranged, when John's parents returned to Berkley, all five paid a visit to the museum to view their Torah first-hand. Abe, then five years old, was spellbound. In its place of honor inside the glass case, it appeared to him mysterious, unreachable. He wanted to stroke the scarlet mantle with his fingers, to heft the heavy silver and gold ornaments in his hands, to unroll the mysterious half-open scroll. To the boy it was as impressive as a king's treasure—even this small portion displaying the precise brushstrokes of more that a century before. Each black letter, exactly in proportion to the next, composed of bold lines and fine lines; of strokes descending vertically, stepping out diagonally or flowing horizontally, some capped by elegant crowns—all alighting on the parchment like mysterious, unfamiliar bird prints upon snow. Perhaps, someday when he was grown he could write such letters and they would allow him to hold the Rosen Torah.

To Helen the scroll called to her like the Rosetta Stone—deciphering the code to wisdom, magically reaching across time and space to impart its meaning and to tell a people's history. To Abe's consternation his mother began to weep, and he began to sob in sympathy. Recalling his own wonder as a boy when he had first seen the scroll, John understood their emotions. Yet, while he paid respectful homage to the Torah as the repository of their heritage, he questioned the need to follow its doctrines, and doubted that those who did so would necessarily right the evils that have plagued society from the beginning of time.

Soon after their return from Berkeley, Helen learned that an Orthodox Rabbi, Morris Browdy, living in nearby Eugene, currently served neighboring small communities. To satisfy the desire to know more about Judaism, growing insistently inside her, she drove to Eugene to see him.

The rabbi was away, but his young and energetic wife, Trudy Browdy, greeted her warmly. She listened to Helen's story of the Rosen Torah and her wish for her son to take pride in it.

Touched by her sincerity, the rebbetzin immediately agreed to take this stranger on as a pupil. She reassured Helen that her studies would be rewarding; the Torah's code of ethics, its commandments, would guide her life, and she could impart that knowledge to her son to prepare him for his role as steward of the legacy. Just weeks after beginning her studies, in the morning when the house was still quiet, Helen wrote in her journal:

> I awakened early to pure falling, drifting snow as the sun came up behind the mountains. It was so peaceful, so uplifting, so heartening. When I study Torah with Trudy, sometimes the narrow, hollow place inside me fills with warmth. I glimpse a whole world of new truths, but it's difficult to put them in perspective. Christians believe that you must accept Jesus in order to be saved; they deny life in heaven to non-believers. Judaism does not believe in original sin. It affirms the inherent goodness of the world and its people. It asserts that the gates of heaven will be open to all. I cannot help regretting that I spent my youth in vain — yet am I sure I have found the right path?

Over the months of study, the two women developed a warm friendship. Helen gained enough confidence to ask Trudy hard questions. First, did Moses really write the Torah? The rebbetzin explained that Orthodox Jews believe God composed the Torah, and transmitted it at Mount Sinai to Moses, who copied it down word for word. Since every word of the Torah comes from God, they say none of the Torah's laws may be changed or set aside. Trudy, off course, would not elaborate on the views of other Jews such as Conservative, Reform or Reconstructionists. But later, when Helen delved into it, she found that many scholars have came to the conclusion that the Torah is the work of human beings, composed from ancient source documents. These were combined into the form in which we have it today. They assert that the Torah was completed by the 5th century BCE, following the Jews' return to the Land of Israel after having been exiled to Babylonia.

During their time together, the rebbetzin discussed why all the Jewish people so revered the Torah. To begin with, she explained, it preserves the oldest stratum of our history. Reading Torah opens a window into the long-ago world of our forefathers, as if excavating an archeological treasure layer by layer towards our very beginnings. Also the Torah is the foundation of our Jewish traditions and practices, of our holidays, festivals and of our customs, which are an integral part of birth, marriage, death, eating, clothing, and prayer. In addition, she told Helen that the Torah contains compelling universal narratives — the creation story, the tale of Adam and Eve, Noah and the flood, and the Tower of Babel. We come to see and to understand ourselves in the noble and fallible heroes whose lives and deaths are recounted in this scroll.

Cupping her hands together and looking directly into Helen's eyes, she said, "We cherish the Torah as the direct word of God, and our people struggle to understand what God requires of them in this world."

And there were still more questions Helen asked: Why don't you believe in Jesus as the Messiah? Do you believe in heaven and hell? In angels and the devil? What happens to the soul after death? What is the nature of God and the universe?

Over the following months, Helen's mentor patiently explained her understanding of these spiritual matters — not entirely to her pupil's satisfaction but enough to provide a framework on which she could develop her own thinking. One thing became clear; the founding laws of Judaism had not changed in three thousand years, and despite modern variations in custom and observance, for Jews worldwide the Torah remained the fundamental guide.

On the High Holidays, Rosh Hashanah and Yom Kippur, and on festival days, she began to appreciate the significance of this people's legacy and history. On Simchat Torah, as she watched the young boys dancing in shul, arm in arm with the old men like droplets in the vast, timeless ocean of the Torah, she too

380

wanted to dance with abandon; to find a way to pray with her whole body as well as with her mind and heart.

Unexpectedly, Helen's recent immersion in Judaism now provided a different dimension to her experience of yoga so that she began to make unusual associations with the Torah texts and the principles of the Hindu discipline. Standing perfectly balanced on one leg in the yoga tree pose reminded her to root herself in the wisdom of the Torah, the Tree of Life. For her, the yoga postures became the vehicle that freed her internal wisdom — not the external form of the positions, but the way that they seemed to release new thoughts and perceptions. Although it was an unorthodox and whimsical way to absorb Judaism, Helen persevered. She had to find her own path to peace and spirituality.

❧ 31 ❧

The Convert and the Extremists

The stranger who lives with you should be as a citizen among you, and you should love him as yourself; for you were strangers in the Land of Egypt.

Torah

Helen had completed six months of study with Trudy Browdy, when one mellow sunny morning while Abe was at school, on impulse, she and John decided to raid the farmer's market for fresh produce, lunch at the Fish Stew on the town's marina, and run errands.

Parking the car near Fiedler's processing plant, close to the railway siding where tank cars waited to be filled with beet sugar, they headed down Main Street. They strolled by the old-fashioned general store, the Swiss bakery, the redbrick library, the antique store, the white clapboard Presbyterian Church, and the contemporary yellow brick Baptist Church. At the coffee shop on the corner, Helen halted abruptly, and took a deep breath before declaring in a rush, "I'm thinking of converting to Judaism."

"You can't be serious!"

"But I am," she insisted. "Years ago I left my religion. I ran away from it because it was crushing my spirit. Now I'm not running away. I'm running toward something I believe in."

John raised his eyebrows.

"I wish you would come and listen to Trudy. The story of Jewish survival is amazing! Just think, many religions of ancient times have disappeared, but even when Jews were driven out and scattered across the Earth, they held on to theirs, through observance of the Torah's commandments. Judaism has survived for thousands of years — despite horrifying persecution. And even in this century, Hitler's Third Reich tried to exterminate the Jews."

An acquaintance riding by on a bike waved to them. John called out a cheerful hello, but Helen was so lost in thought she didn't notice. When the light changed, he steered her across the intersection as she plunged on, "Did you know that the survival of Judaism is not at all certain now? In the last forty years at least a quarter of American Jews have chosen to become members of other religions. Can you believe that the descendants of European Jews who resisted conversion at the cost of their lives are now voluntary converts?"

Before John could reply, he saw with relief that they had reached the Fish Stew, putting that conversation on hold for the moment.

They enjoyed an unhurried lunch of wild salmon, just hours out of the river, grilled on a wood fire, and coated with melted butter and fresh herbs. John mopped up the last drop of sauce with a hunk of sour dough bread, and grinned contentedly.

Then Helen picked up where they had left off. "Will you support my conversion to Judaism?"

John looked at her determined, unsmiling face, her mouth set in a stubborn line. "Helen, you don't have to convert. You can enjoy yoga and meditation, and study the Torah." He saw that she was hurt, but he wasn't going to be a hypocrite and say he approved. Besides, if she had made up her mind, what he said wouldn't dissuade her.

That evening after Abe had gone to bed, they continued the debate. "I don't want to get into an argument," John said, filling two wine glasses. "But I wish you would rethink this idea of converting. Stop putting your trust in something that is the stuff of legends and folklore, and that you choose to believe has a higher mystical authority." He paused trying to think of a way to protect her from the hurt and disappointment that might lie ahead.

Helen held her goblet up to the light and contemplated the distorted reflection of her face on its surface. Putting the glass down, she leaned forward on her elbows. "I've given it serious thought. Please don't trivialize it. Like your father you have been fortunate to find your passion early in life. I am still searching."

He looked at his wife with bright, observant eyes. From the tilt of her jaw and the hard glint of tears in her eyes he saw her resolve. They could not settle their incongruent views on religion; all they could do was agree to disagree. He shrugged, and said, "Okay, you win."

"I don't want to *win*, John! What I want is your understanding and support." That night she confided in her journal:

> John has conceded to my converting to Judaism. How I wish he were happy and enthusiastic about it. His opinions are so clear-cut there is little room for me to discuss my groping thoughts struggling to free themselves. I am grateful that there are things we do share: our joyous love of nature, our deep distrust of fanatics and extremists and, above all, our abiding love for one another, and for our son.

Trudy explained that there are two ways a person can be a Jew. "You can either be born a Jew or you can convert."

"Our child, Abe, is a Jew because his father is a Jew, isn't he?"

"No. The traditional ruling is that if your mother is Jewish then so are you. It doesn't matter if your father is Jewish or not."

Helen's shoulder's sagged.

"I don't mean to discourage you, but you should understand that Judaism doesn't actively encourage conversion. This is the reason there are no Jewish missionaries."

"Surely they want converts?"

"They want them to be totally committed. If it were easy to convert, people might do it without much thought. And, you see, we Jews have been forced many times to convert away from Judaism; it happened, for example, in Spain during the Inquisition. So we are hesitant about converting others; it's aggressive and disrespectful. "

Helen gave serious consideration to what her teacher had said, but it did not alter her resolve. She took the next step by making an appointment to appear before a rabbi, in this case, Rabbi Browdy, Trudy's husband. Before Helen's interview, Trudy groomed her anxious pupil, reassuring her that things would go favorably.

On the appointed day, the rain came down in drenching torrents on the drive to Eugene, causing Helen to arrive late. She wanted to make a good impression, but her damp, crumpled dress, limp hair, and tardy arrival made her self-conscious and awkward. The rabbi, a balding, middle-aged man in a dark suit, was of medium height and build, but the vigor and enthusiasm he projected gave the impression of a larger person. He asked her to be seated, and without preliminaries inquired, "Mrs. Rosen, why do you want to become a Jew?"

"Why shouldn't I?" she said defensively, immediately wanting to bite her tongue for its impulsiveness.

"There are several reasons. The most obvious being that you will assume a heavy burden. Jews have been oppressed throughout history. And despite our freedoms here in the United States, there is still anti-Semitism."

"I am aware of that. As you know, I've been studying with your wife, and we have discussed this. I truly feel that Judaism is right for me," Helen said, trying to keep her voice from trembling.

"You are not doing this just to please your husband?"

"Not at all. He is not a practicing Jew. I have discussed this with him, and he agrees that I should do what is right for me."

"Maybe his folks want it?"

"I've been married to John for many years, and my in-laws have never raised the issue."

Are you willing to raise your child as Jewish? Are you prepared to learn about the rules for keeping kosher, and to keep a kosher home? Are you willing to attend services at the shul? To keep the Sabbath holy? To observe our holy days? The exchange continued—to Helen a round of implied allegations that she needed to defend, and did. The air seemed to have become thin and her eyes began to tear. She fished in her purse for a tissue, suddenly feeling a desperate need to get away.

"You must establish a daily time for study and adhere to it."

Helen nodded emphatically. "I intend to do that. Actually, I'm doing that already."

"Very good. Since you are a woman, you are not obligated to study theoretical knowledge so much as the practical aspects of the Torah's commandments. In addition, you should study *mussar,* those parts of the Torah that teach us to improve our character."

"Yes, Trudy has explained that, too."

"We will also require you to learn about the history of the Jews," Rabbi Browdy kept on.

"That should be very interesting. I want to understand, to feel and to become part of the Jewish people."

Sitting back in his chair, and cradling his fingers, her interviewer said, "Mrs. Rosen, I admire your sincerity and intelligence, but you weren't raised Jewish. You haven't had time to study and to think seriously about issues of our convoluted heritage, our precarious homeland, or about anti-Semitism. Your identity wasn't built on these things. Defining yourself as a Jew is more than study, it will take years of personal experience, practice and involvement."

Helen's heart sank.

Then the rabbi leaned forward and asked gently, "What has led you to this place in the journey of your life?"

An unreasonable panic gripped her. She put her fingertips to her eyes, and willed herself time to think, to visualize the

Rosen Torah. Seeing her distress, the rabbi poured a glass of cold water for her. She sipped gratefully. Her mind cleared. Now she looked directly at him; he had opened a way through the thicket of thorny questions to the end she sought.

"The first Torah I ever saw was my husband's family legacy, passed down through the descendants of the Rosen family for generations. It was on display in a museum, behind glass. I was awed by its timeless beauty, its meticulous artistry, and drawn to its mystery and the wisdom encoded in its ancient writings," she began. "Later, I learned how the five books were given to Moses during his communion with God on Mt. Sinai. How the path to being a good Jew is not dependent only on what you believe or your faith. The key to becoming a good Jew hinges on your *actions*, by what you do to repair the world and make it a better place."

Rabbi Browdy cleared his throat, and said sincerely, "Mazel Tov! It seems that you are ready to become a Jew."

Helen bounced out of her chair in excitement, but he signaled for her to be seated.

For the first time the rabbi smiled, and she beamed back.

"My wife was impressed with your dedication, now I will become your new teacher. When our studies are complete, you will meet with the Beth Din, a religious court, made up of three male rabbis who will oversee the formal conversion. They will determine the extent of your knowledge and commitment to Judaism and to no other religion. There will be questions, but they are not meant to trap you."

For the first time, Helen was more at ease knowing that the rabbi would serve as her guide through the labyrinth of ritual she would be required to follow if she were to become part of a religion she desired to make her own.

"After that you will go to the mikvah, a pool of pure, running water. There you will remove all clothing, and completely immerse yourself. The submersion is a symbol of the womb, and you will come out of the water "re-born" as a Jew. It is also customary to take a Hebrew name at this time."

"That will be my honor." She could feel the rapid staccato of her heart begin to slow.

"I want you to know that it is a special mitzvah to love and to be kind to converts. It says in the Torah, 'You shall love the convert like yourself, for you were strangers in the land of Egypt.' In other words, you should be especially compassionate to them." As he escorted her to the door, Helen's knees almost gave way with relief.

John tried to accept his wife's decision gracefully, but it wasn't easy. When they had first met, she was struggling to free herself from the bonds of her religious sect; now she seemed to be returning to a new religion with a vengeance, albeit from another direction. To reassure her husband and to keep his interest, Helen shared what she had learned at her sessions with the rabbi. He had explained that when a Christian "leaves" Christianity then he or she is no longer regarded as a Christian. If Jews "leave" Judaism they are still considered to be Jews by other Jews because of their mother or they have converted.

One night after making love, Helen explained that the Torah prescribes that one should engage one's body in consecrated actions. Buddhists and some Christians believe celibacy to be the highest path, and that indulging in sex is giving in to the lower self, she explained. For Jews, it also sanctifies the act within marriage as the most potent way to unite with God. It is a commandment for a husband to satisfy his wife above and beyond the commandment of procreation.

Suppressing a grin, John conceded that there was a positive aspect to studying the Torah. Although John willingly engaged in these philosophical discussions with his wife, he could not overcome his life-long distrust of organized religion. He found himself becoming more and more uneasy with Helen's immersion in her studies. Sensing his discomfort, Helen reminded him that she wasn't being obsessive; she was active in the children's plays at Susmook Community Theater, and taught drama at the community college.

The people of the small town were not overly pushy about wanting the Rosens to attend church, although they extended invitations to do so. The trouble began when the prospective convert tuned into the local television station while baking challah, and saw part of a gospel show happening at the high school.

"We are claiming this place for the Kingdom of God — that Jesus will be exalted over Litton High School!" local evangelist Sylvia Morton declared to kick off the show. The program went on to take student testimonials and ended with a skit depicting a boxing match between Jesus and Satan, with God as referee. Jesus won and stood with hands raised, while the students cheered.

The Rosens had tolerated high school players and coaches praying on the football field, but preaching at the school was too extreme. Helen turned to Trudy for advice. The rabbi's wife counseled her to talk to the superintendent of the school district, Mr. Pushton, and agreed to accompany her. Helen was completely unprepared for what he said once the two women were behind the closed doors of his office.

"Mrs. Rosen, I am concerned for you and your family. I believe all your problems would be over if you would go back to being a Christian. And your husband might consider converting to Christianity, too." His mouth spread into an ingratiating smile.

Trudy squared her shoulders, drew her lips into a tight line, and demanded, "Mr. Pushton, no one has the right to pressure others on what religion to follow, especially a public servant. I think you owe Mrs. Rosen an apology."

The superintendent cleared his throat and held up a palm. "Now, calm down, Mrs. Browdy, "I'm just trying to protect Mrs. Rosen." He forced a grin so wide that they could see the gold fillings in his molars.

"Mrs. Rosen doesn't need protecting, she needs an apology. Right now!" Trudy said, emphasizing every word.

"Well, we can all get along, can't we? I meant no offense." He escorted them out, still protesting that he had not meant to upset them.

When they walked out of the school, Trudy exploded, "That man is a despicable bigot. I'm going to call my husband and see what he thinks we should do next."

After hearing his wife out, Rabbi Browdy said without hesitation, "You need to contact the Anti-Defamation League. The ADL is in the business of reminding school officials of basic rights set out in the Constitution and court rulings that limit the role of religion in public schools. I'll call them first, let them know what's going on, and tell them to expect your call."

To Helen's astonishment the superintendent of their school system, Mr. Pushton, appeared to be open to the involvement of the ADL. She did not know if his new attitude was genuine, or based on fear of a lawsuit, but she was relieved that he was not opposing them. He even sanctioned a countywide training session for principals, taught by the ADL, on the do's and don'ts of schoolhouse religion. He allowed Rabbi Browdy, Trudy, and the Rosens to participate. Helen foolishly believed that the battle was won when Pushton barred revival-like programs in county schools. In a statement to the press, the superintendent was even quoted as saying: "We ought to leave the teaching of religion and the Bible to the parents and to the church." The ADL's spokeswoman concluded that the district's response had been positive.

It was a Pyrrhic victory. Rumors began to circulate that Helen had filed a lawsuit against the school system similar to one in a neighboring county that had resulted in a lengthy and highly publicized court fight over school prayer across the state. People stopped talking to the Rosens, and avoided them on the street. They began to receive harassing calls. One woman accused them of trying to turn the school into "The Jewish League."

When Abraham heard what was happening, he lamented to Martha, "I did what I thought was right. I wanted to bring some order to my corner of the universe while there was still time. But by relating the history of the Rosen Torah and disclosing my intention to bequeath it to John, I unintentionally encouraged Helen to convert to Judaism. I have caused nothing but trouble. I should have kept silent."

"It's ridiculous to blame yourself. The blame rests on those who perpetuate bigotry," Martha said, determined not to show how shocked and panicked she felt.

To Helen's dismay, her children's performances at the Susmook Community Theater were no longer popular. Teachers who had brought hundreds of children to her shows now choose not to attend. Plays had to be cancelled. The season was in ruins. Anna Samson, whose twelve-year-old son, Barry, starred in one of the plays, told a local television interviewer, "Kids don't know about politics. They just can't understand why all of a sudden everyone is rejecting them."

The head of the theater board, Billy Roberts, told Helen in confidence that teachers refused to attend because of her complaints about Christianity in the school. "Most of them said that they had talked to other teachers in their grade and they felt the same way." He added, "I'm sorry, but I would describe it as a boycott."

"What can we do about this?" she said, feeling her tongue thickened with rage.

"I really don't know. Perhaps it will blow over. Right now, low attendance has led to more red ink," Roberts said, shaking his head. He reduced her fee per-show, but the situation did not improve financially. Soon after that they eliminated her position.

Two months later the community college cancelled its drama courses for the following semester, leaving Helen without work. She confronted the president of the college, but he flatly denied that the decision was motivated by revenge. He said that economics, not intolerance, had led to the loss of her job. "We had to close the Drama Department because a cost analysis showed it was losing money," he told her.

John tried to reassure his wife that the worst was over, and for a while things did quiet down. Then Abe, now in first grade, came home with a swastika painted on his backpack; the next day, there were swastikas on his gym socks. Kids began punching him in the halls, throwing spitballs at him, and they refused to sit next to him or to play with him. He became withdrawn and reluctant to go to school. His parents could not bear to see the bewilderment and hurt in their child's eyes. Helen drove down to the school, and making no attempt to conceal her indignation, marched into the office to inform Mr. Graham, the principal, that her child was being harassed, and that it must stop. To his credit, Graham personally informed the students that those caught bullying others would receive severe punishment. As a result, the physical harassment abated. Still, the Rosens knew that their child was being shunned.

John, who had never experienced anti-Semitism, was disgusted. He hated to admit it, but he felt humiliated and frustrated. Optimistic by nature, he fought off the unaccustomed pessimism. "I just can't believe this. I've never, ever had anyone put me down other then the usual kid stuff. This is vicious, sick. I'll call the fathers, the ones I know personally."

He followed through with telephone calls, and although he made every effort to be tactful, many parents took his attempts as a personal insult. "The whole thing's backfired. It's my job to protect my wife and child, and I've failed," John apologized. He took Helen in his arms: "I just want to grab you and Abe, get in the car, and get the heck out of here," he said, trembling with rage. There had been a seismic shift in their lives and in his assessment of himself as the guardian of his family.

Helen always came to him for support; now she was his pillar of strength. "You have not failed us. What kind of a message would we give if we left? I want to teach Abe to stand up for his beliefs and to learn that the United States Constitution stands for all of us."

"But I won't tolerate seeing you and our son get hurt."

Helen chastised him gently. "This is not the time for us to be cowards."

"You're right," he agreed, clenching his jaws. "There are only three months left in the school year, so we can wait it out. In the meantime, I'll have to restrain myself from kicking people in the ass!" Ever the idealist, he had not entirely given up hope that the nasty thing would burn itself out. Like his father, he regretted that the profound influence of the Rosen legacy on his wife had unleashed such bigotry. In his mind he began to hatch a story about the danger of blindly pursuing a spiritual path as a way of working through troubling issues.

The story's protagonist, Chang Min, is a party bureaucrat in Vietnam where communism has triumphed over the world. The Communist Party is run by a dictatorship that keeps the population docile through hallucinogenic drugs, which may also cause genetic mutations. Chang buys an illegal anti-hallucinogen, Realtrope, through an underground movement. Under its influence he meets with the party leaders whom he has followed unwaveringly. The drug enables him to see, with horrifying clarity, the leaders for what they truly are—cruel biological mutants. The supreme leader himself is not human, but an almighty, godlike machine that preys on all living things not obedient to his will. The story ends with Chang mortally wounded. As his life ebbs away he says, "It seems that illusions are more bearable than reality."

At the time, it seemed a good idea to knit the evils of blind faith, Communism, mind-altering drugs, and bigotry into one story. When it was published under the title *Merciful Hallucinations*, it succeeded in offending many different factions. John Rosen fans defended him, holding that he had written— with integrity, insight, and humility—about the awful reality of an ideology or religion carried to extreme, which results in its followers cruelly and maliciously persecuting those who do not believe as they do.

Initially, the overt attack on the Rosens seemed to abate, still some children continued to ostracize their son. Helen no longer felt safe shopping, after a woman actually spat on her. The horrible nightmares she had suffered in the months after leaving the True Believers Church, returned in full force.

"I cannot stand by and watch my family being humiliated and intimidated. We have to go!" John insisted in a tone that brooked no argument.

Helen told her friends, her voice quivering with emotion, "Your support has helped my family get through this terrible time. And I still want to believe that good and decent people will defeat bigotry." She could not go on for the tears.

When the story of proselytizing in public schools and the harassment of the Rosens hit the national news, Helen appeared

393

on TV saying, "Narrow-minded and mean-spirited people have forced my family to leave this town."

In a statement to the press, the Anti-Defamation League pointed out that what happened to the Rosen family was not that unheard of in rural areas with few Jewish residents, although it was particularly disappointing that this happened in Oregon with its history of tolerance. ADL Regional Director Jay Sher, was quoted saying, "There's a calculated strategy in some of these isolated places to integrate specific religious doctrine into a school environment." He continued, "Our Founding Fathers clearly understood the importance of separation of church and state."

That night Helen conceded, "It's time for us to leave. I do not like feeling like a coward, and I hate to leave Trudy and Rabbi Browdy, and the few friends I've made. But for Abe's sake we must go."

❧ 32 ❧

John and Helen on the Farm

All things grow with time – except grief.

Yiddish Proverb

John and Helen began combing the classifieds and contacting realtors in search of a place that they could call home. They both wanted a sanctuary in the country, surrounded by acres of land where they could live in harmony with nature. Ever since reading Rachel Carson's *Silent Spring*, the Rosens had hoped to live in a way that would do less harm to the environment. Carson, a marine biologist, had written that DDT, sprayed on roadsides to control weeds, worked its way up the food chain, affecting birds and fish, and ultimately humans. With the passionate conviction of crusaders, the Rosens were enthusiastic about starting an "experimental farm," or ecological demonstration project. When John heard about a farm for sale near the town of Nonana, about two hours north of Susmook, with a river running through it and a view of the mountains, the family immediately arranged to inspect the property.

On the drive out it rained heavily; when they arrived at the turn off to the rocky county road, a watery sun emerged. Three-fourths of a mile up, they came to a driveway leading up to the farmhouse. On a slight rise they could see it, looking sad and discarded as a dried gourd. The gate was open and they couldn't spot any cars, so John drove slowly up to the house. As they approached they saw weeds had split the porch, a mud dauber wasp's nest hung from the eaves, and a broken rope swing

395

dangled from a birch tree, the earth below it ground as soft and fine as sifted flour by children's feet. They parked, then sat staring in disbelief at the lovely backdrop of three conical mountains and the glint of the pure river meandering through the property. With their hearts racing they jumped out of the car to explore.

They wandered through the empty barn, where the faint smell of horse manure still lingered, then trudged up the hill to a little cemetery with hundred-year-old graves on a hilltop. In a clearing, ringed by a stand of pines, they stumbled on a spring hidden under a canopy of wild blackberries, and drank its delicious, icy water. Helen imagined gathering fresh eggs, and digging new potatoes out of the dirt. Abe declared that he wanted a pony. John said it was the perfect property for them — but the farmhouse was in such bad shape that it would need to be torn down and another built in its place.

Helen bit her bottom lip apprehensively before asking, "Won't the expense be too much for us?"

John waved his hands dismissively, and assured her that his novels were selling well now and they should be able to handle the expenses. If they tackled some of the work themselves, they would save enough money to stay within budget and build the house of their dreams. Helen let out a whoop of joy and pronounced that she wanted the Shady Lady to be the inspiration and the name for their new farmhouse; it should have the same deep front porch shaded by wide eaves, decorative brackets, and three gables; inside, there would be a big den and a fireplace surrounded by hand-made tiles. John declared that the homestead should be anchored into the hillside and built with natural materials to harmonize with the land and do minimal damage to the environment. Abe wanted his room to have a view of the mountains. On the drive back to Susmook, John, Helen and Abe were jubilant, bubbling over with schemes.

Construction of the new Shady Lady dragged on through the winter as Helen and John worked inside the freezing shell of the house, wearing boots and down coats until the cold drove them to the car, where they cranked up the heat. When summer arrived, the house still lacked some of the wood flooring and a bathtub, but they had electricity and running water provided by gravity from the nearby spring.

After the move to Nonana, Helen had come up with the idea of homeschooling Abe. She told John that she didn't want to expose their son to the cruelty of those who did not respect differences, or to the physical and emotional abuse of bullies. In addition, it was evident that he was a bright child who could advance more rapidly than in a traditional classroom setting. Instruction at home would leave time for Abe to learn how to care for living things, for baking, gardening, playing, and reading, and to be together as a family. If she was honest with herself there was more to it than that. Having been victimized as a child, she understood that words with which a child's mind and heart are poisoned — through sheer malice or blind fanaticism — remain branded in their memory, and in time will burn a hole in their soul.

After she had laid out all her reasons to John for homeschooling, she was shocked when he exploded, "Do you want our boy to become a hermit? Do you want to have no time to yourself? It will take a major commitment of your time, and a chunk of money to buy all the books and resources."

"You are making enough from royalties, and I do have the time. If we have to make sacrifices, then we have to. We need to do what's best for our son."

"I am sure there could be a lot of red tape to this."

They argued back and forth until John agreed to try it.

Abe was happy with homeschooling especially since he did not have to spend time commuting, or doing tedious homework. After working on his lessons in the morning, he helped his mother in the kitchen, or his father with his latest experimental projects, read novels and comic books, or roamed the farm and the woods. Although Abe entertained himself for hours, John wanted his son to socialize with his peers, so he enrolled him in soccer, baseball, swimming, music and art classes offered in Nonana.

Over the months that seamlessly rolled on, the Rosens adjusted cheerfully to an unfamiliar and physically arduous routine at the Shady Lady. The farm chores were endless, but the beauty and peace of the place were a balm to their troubled past. Dragged from military base to base, Helen now cherished the stable home that would become her protective shell. Her one source of regret was that she could no longer study Torah with Rabbi Browdy and Trudy. She missed their friendship and guidance and vowed to search for someone to replace them, soon.

John devised a strategy to launch his ecological project. His first goal was to improve the energy efficiency of their home. To this end he built inexpensive solar collectors, made from recycled beer cans, to provide hot water and to heat the house in winter from an underground storage tank. The solar device spoiled the graceful roofline of the house; nevertheless, John declared it an efficient solution. Next he constructed a small reservoir to catch and recycle rainwater for their vegetable and flower gardens. With the aid of a neighbor, he created a "wind machine" that worked on a vertical axis and automatically adjusted itself to the direction of the wind, providing maximum power to be used to light their home and to operate their appliances. It worked well but sometimes made a strange moaning sound that upset Helen's acquired brood of stray cats.

Helen and Abe helped John erect stone terraces at the back of the house and fill them with homemade compost. The vegetables they planted there produced bumper crops that were the envy of their neighbors. Buoyed by this success, John built a greenhouse onto the back porch for growing vegetables in the winter. Not all his experiments turned out well; attempting to convert chicken droppings into methane turned into a smelly, foul disaster.

All along John kept on writing. Early in the morning he would be at his old portable typewriter tapping out a rapid, machine-gun rhythm. In the afternoon he worked on his projects and chores around the farm. At night, around the dinner table, he would read passages from manuscript pages stacked by his plate.

When Helen made suggestions, he eschewed them, as men are wont to do, but occasionally he would scribble notations on the margins for later consideration.

His critics deemed that he had not produced one great masterpiece, but praised him for his steady stream of well-crafted stories. They paid tribute to his work saying that he challenged his readers to think about the impact of man on the environment and the hold of big government on society. They commended his scientific accuracy and in-depth research that set high standards for other science fiction writers. John did not pay attention to them, but Helen read all his reviews — although the unfavorable ones upset her — only reading aloud the ones that praised his work.

A few critics detected religious themes in John's novels, which surprised them both. One analysis declared: "Rosen's stories, which are psychodramas, are pervaded by a sense of the sacred because his heroes, after undergoing many arduous trials, reach a superior, more ethical state of consciousness."

In a radio interview John declared, "I am a philosopher who uses story-telling to formulate my perceptions of the "truth," and of our struggle to understand it. My readers say that my tales about the irrational nature of man help them to better understand themselves and the issues that trouble them."   When the interviewer persisted on probing the author about his religious views, he responded, "I explore what we humans must do to make life civil, and to tolerate our differences. In this connection I explore what the Bible says as well as what it does not say on very salient questions, such as whether it promotes tolerance, or sanctions it. For example, homosexual acts between men are called abominations and are a crime subject to the death penalty. And there is nothing in the Bible *specifically* forbidding rape, slavery, or genocide."

Toward the end of December, when Abe was away visiting his grandparents in Berkeley, the homesteaders found themselves alone on the farm. As Helen rose to clear the dishes after dinner, John caught her hand and said, "Leave the washing up. Come sit by me." He put on a recording by Simon and

Garfunkel, "Bridge Over Troubled Water," and uncorked a bottle of white wine from a local winery. Outside a chill wind blew off the mountains, and the moon in its last quarter hovered like a silver tiara over snowy peaks.

Helen moved close to John on the couch, unbraided her hair and let her shoes fall onto the floor. "I'm so glad we moved here. I feel at peace in this place." After a pause she confessed, "But I feel guilty about dropping my Torah studies."

They had been so busy, John had not given much thought to it; still, if he were frank with himself, deep down he had hoped that Helen would set that part of her life aside. Nevertheless, out of consideration he asked, "Do you want to look for someone around here who might help you with your studies?"

"After all that has happened, I'm not sure what I want."

John cocked one eyebrow, and waited for her to continue.

"To be honest, I don't seem to miss studying with the rabbi as much as I miss Trudy's friendship."

"I understand. We don't get much company out here."

"And I miss the yoga, too. John, I'm thinking of offering classes. We could clear a space in the barn. Now that you have one part of it heated, it would be perfect."

"If you can get a group to come out here, why not? We'll give it a new coat of red paint, and repair the shingles."

"Great!" Helen said, still not smiling.

"So why the unhappy face?"

"Tell the truth; do you think less of me for not going through with my conversion? I have a tendency to believe passionately in something for a time, then find I cannot follow through."

He could tell by the droop of his wife's shoulders that she was upset, even ashamed of failing to keep her pledge. He was used to Helen's self-criticism and her moral debates, but the self-abasement in her tone worried him. To reassure her, he said, "Of course not. You already know what I think—there's no need to affiliate with any particular religious organization to do good in this world."

"Still, I let myself down."

400

"Look, if you feel that strongly, in place of an Orthodox conversion you might consider Reform Judaism, which has less strict requirements."

She appreciated his advice, and his avowal that he didn't think her weak or indecisive. Yet she still felt unmoored.

"I'm aware that there are other denominations of Judaism that are much less stringent in their observance," she replied defensively. Then taking a deep breath, she said, "Even if I don't convert, I am determined to teach Abe about Judaism. Knowing about his heritage will help our son to understand himself and to be proud of who he is. If he ever becomes the target of anti-Semitism again, he won't be so humiliated and confused . . ." Helen broke off, finding it hard to put her emotions into words.

"All right, Miss Primrose, I'll go along with the program as long as our son's religious instruction does not cause him to become intolerant of others with differing beliefs." He slipped his hand around her waist and pulled her to him. The last plaintive bars of "Bridge Over Troubled Water," and its powerful lyrics rang in her ears echoing John's love for her, soothing her disappointment in herself.

Soon after, Helen met Emily Brown, a retired schoolteacher and a volunteer at the public library where she read stories to the children. The women were drawn to each other by a shared love of reading and storytelling. Over coffee at the old-fashioned bakery on Main Street, where customers could see stacked bags of flour and sugar, and smell bread and pies baking, Emily told Helen that she had lived in Nonana all her life. She and her husband, Lou, had raised four children, now grown, and had just become grandparents of twin boys. They were active in the church and ran a Bible study camp for kids in the summer. After her traumatic experiences in Susmook and at Cedarwood of the True Believers, Helen was leery of Emily. She began to thaw when Emily leaned forward and confided in a stage whisper, "Since I retired, I need to keep active. I don't want to become mentally and physically lazy as one of my Potbellied Pig pets in need of a shot of vitamins. When I saw you, I thought, 'There's someone different, someone that will get my juices flowing!'"

Helen was so taken aback that all she managed to say was, "Potbellied Pigs, huh?"

Emily chuckled, "I've been a pig person ever since I got my first breeding pair twelve years ago, Yogi and Berra. Lou and I produce piggies for adoption, but only as many as we can place with responsible, caring people. They make great pets because they are so affectionate and they love companionship. Many pig owners allow their pets to share their beds. We do it every so often, and let me tell you, a porcine sleeping partner is warm and cuddly on a cold winter night."

Seeing the twinkle in her eyes, Helen quipped, "As long as a piggy pet doesn't hog the bed."

Her new acquaintance roared with laughter. Before they parted, she invited Helen to join the book discussion group that met monthly. Helen doubted that she would have much in common with small-town ladies still she agreed to attend.

On the night of the meeting, Helen arrived at the Brown's house and was warmly introduced to the group. When her hostess mentioned her interests in the Torah, drama, and yoga that Helen had shared with her, she felt herself flinching and wished she hadn't let her guard down so soon. *They're going to think you're a dangerous nut, or a lost soul,* she thought. To her surprise the women found her interests fascinating. They admitted that they needed to exercise and wanted to try yoga under her tutelage.

"It'll be my pleasure. Why don't we meet at my home?" she said, delighted at the chance to make friends.

As she got to know these women, she found them generous, opened-minded, and admired the way they found time for charitable work. She felt ashamed of having prejudged them so quickly.

First, Sissy Crim—the mother of six, who somehow made time to work for Habitat for Humanity—showed up on Helen's doorstep with a welcome basket and two freshly baked loaves of pumpkin bread. Then, after a storm blew shingles off the Shady Lady's roof, Grace Tolbert and her husband Ted, the pastor of one of the local churches, pitched in to help repair the damage.

402

Meanwhile, Judith Benson, who worked part-time as secretary of her church, kept Helen current with the local gossip, but never in a mean-spirited way. And Abe and her son Stan, about the same age, become happy playmates.

Having moved around too frequently to make deep friendships, Helen now found herself building a circle of close friends. "I envy the way these women wear their convictions and their religion so gracefully and so tolerantly. I was afraid they wouldn't approve of me — of us," she told John.

"They are good people, good Christians. They are as tolerant and as civic minded as the people I knew in Berkeley."

"More than that — they've become my best friends." Helen experienced a rush of emotion that overflowed into a big hug for her husband.

That Christmas, Judith invited the Rosens to help decorate their tree. The two boys merrily strung popcorn and cranberry garlands while sampling gingerbread men and candy canes meant to ornament the tree. On the way home Abe asked his mother if they could put up a Christmas tree, too. Helen could see nothing wrong in celebrating Christmas marked by smiling Santas, sleigh bells, Bing Crosby, festive parties, delicious dinners, and gifts for everyone; she had always loved these things about Christmas. But despite its secularization, Christmas, she understood, is not religiously neutral. It is still Christian, even though its trappings often overwhelm the religious message. Her son had presented her with a dilemma: whether to go with the alluring flow of Christmas or stand aside as a Jew.

Helen discussed her dilemma with John. "Can't you be both Jewish and Christian?" she asked, half in jest. "Can't you celebrate both Chanukah and Christmas? Why does it have to be one or the other?"

He replied that some did put up trees they called Chanukah bushes, but that seemed a mite hypocritical to him.

To console herself Helen wrote in her journal:

Christmas has left me feeling sad, out of place. The Torah says that peace comes to those who are just, kind, and honest. Christians say the same about those who take Jesus into their hearts. Muslims speak similarly about those who follow the teachings of the Prophet, Mohammed. I think if you want to test this, look at the followers of any faith. If they are just and loving to others, their claims that their belief makes them so are true. If they are hateful then their claims that their God brings peace and love, are false. Faith, prayer, and ritual alone, are not enough. The broad heritage of Torah is justice and righteousness. Abraham is a good man despite his lack of faith; still he isn't always at peace with himself. John is a compassionate human being and content with his lot, although he, too, isn't religious. How can I find serenity?

In the end, despite John's skepticism, she lit the Chunukah candles, and put up a tree for Christmas—a small tabletop version—to please Abe, she said.

The weeks following Christmas went by in the familiar round of tasks and activities, clouded by apprehension over Abraham's deteriorating health. Eighteen months after the move to the farm, they received the call they had been dreading. Their beloved Abraham had passed away in his sleep.

John had loved and respected him as a father and as a compassionate human being. His grief left him feeling dizzy and so overwhelmed he was unable to drive, and asked Helen to take the wheel. They arrived in Berkeley late that night to find Martha waiting up for them. She had endured Abraham's illness stoically. Now they held her close and wept inconsolably together. *Better to let the grief out,* John thought, *than to hold it inside where the pain will become unbearable.*

As promised, Abraham had bequeathed the Torah to John; his decision that the Rosen legacy should remain in the

Jewish Museum, at least for the foreseeable future, had been made prior to his father's demise. It had not been arbitrary, or based solely on personal convenience. John had talked it over with his family. Abraham had agreed with him, Martha gave her approval — especially since she was still active on the museum's board, and saw that by showcasing the Torah in the educational outreach program, they were reaching a broader population. Helen, the one dissenting voice, thought that her husband's decision bordered on indifference knowing that a kosher Torah should be used in religious services. John understood that others might judge him to be shirking his responsibility, but he was doing nothing disrespectful. When Abe became the next inheritor, he would be free to decide what to do with his legacy.

As if to make amends for her husband, Helen began to study Torah with Abe in earnest, doing her best to remember what she had been taught and to do some studying on her own. He enjoyed this special time with his mother, but not the long hours of study. When he complained, she reminded him that the teachings and commandments of the Torah had been studied continually for 3,000 years, and scholars were still interpreting and debating its meaning.

Around this time a recurring nightmare began to invade Abe's sleep with lurid images . . . Decked out in a silly yellow clown's costume and red jester's hat with tinkling silver bells, he parades the Rosen Torah around the Jewish museum; torn and stained parchment signs with red arrows guide him through dark hallways filled with phantom music. A crush of warm bodies buoys him along. *Oh! Oh no!* The crowd begins pressing forward, surging toward him, reaching out to touch the scroll with sharp-clawed hands. He screams and wraps his arms tightly around the Torah to protect it. A blast of wind snares him upward, carries him aloft until the pleading upturned faces with lolling tongues, and grabbing, begging hands with gnarled fingers, recede into confetti dots. He holds onto the scroll for dear life as they soar and swoop over fog-shrouded oceans, forests, and mountains . . . now he hovers above the Shady Lady, with his mother below him crying in the wilderness, "Keep flying with the Torah, Abe!"

When he reaches out to touch her, she ignites into a burning pillar of salt. *Ohhh, ohh . . .*

Shaking himself awake after each dream, Abe kicked off his blankets and padded to his parent's bedroom, where he would stand gazing at his mother curled like a fetus next to his father, until his heart quit pounding. He would return to his bed and pull the covers over his head, swearing to put more effort into his Torah studies.

The Rosens were content and at ease on the farm until their tranquility was irretrievably shattered. Then in her early forties, Helen was diagnosed with cancer. She underwent chemotherapy that left her debilitated and weak. Her friends from the book club and yoga class—Emily, Sissy, Grace, and Judith—drove out to the Rosen farm to help with the housework, and to keep her company when she felt up to it.

Helen hated the enforced inactivity and began sorting through stacks of family photographs. Her sister had sent a box of Ridgely family albums after her mother had been sent to a facility for those suffering from Alzheimer's disease. One photo that drew her attention showed her as a teenager, all legs and teeth, next to a spray of white lilies for the church altar. Now, more than thirty years later, observing this younger version of herself, she was reminded of the unhappy girl who had once inhabited her body. She had been full of passion, but thwarted by sudden, uncontrollable mood shifts from rage to sadness to euphoria, uncertain, yet longing with all her heart to be a good Christian—to feel Jesus moving in her. She was no surer of her beliefs now than she had been then, but she needed to believe, now more than ever, that there was a loving God who watched over her, and that there was an afterlife for her soul.

When John emerged from their bedroom that day, he resolved to carry out a special mission for his suffering wife. She had requested that he bring the Rosen Torah from the museum to the Shady Lady. It tortured John to see Helen under extreme duress. In his despair and anguish he was willing to do whatever he could to ease his beloved's pain and fear—even if it went against his own sensibilities. Yet when he contemplated the incredible odyssey of the family Torah freighted with history and culture, he was plagued with doubt. It had journeyed across continents, and over the ocean to its present home in Berkeley. Should he now risk removing it from its place of safe repose? This Torah that had been witness to the rites of passage of generations of Rosens, their births and Bar Mitzvahs, their marriages and funerals. Nevertheless, if it would serve to comfort his wife and erase the terrifying look of hurt and fear from her eyes, he would do whatever she asked.

There would be no difficulty in honoring her request since it belonged to him and was simply on loan to the museum. In a state of quiet despair, he made plans to take possession of the scroll and bring it to Helen.

John's call to Jacie Selman came as a shock, and she almost blurted out, *Do you think that an isolated farmhouse is an appropriate place for the Torah?* But it was a tactless thing to say given the circumstances. Still, she regretted the museum's loss. For a while she considered calling Martha to dissuade her son, but that would only increase the stress the family was under.

Helen had made a further request, that John locate someone with whom she could study Torah. Although he had serious reservations, on his wife's behalf he contacted the Sontags, a family of Chabad-Lubavitch Chassidic Jews, who had moved to a nearby community from Crown Heights, New York. He had heard of this ultra-orthodox group and wondered what defined them. Did they do nothing but pray? Wear strange garb, long beards, big hats, and hair curls in place of sideburns? Pay no heed to the rest of the world? He needed to do some research.

The Chabad, John discovered, would welcome the Rosens. Non-Orthodox Jews, who had grown up without any real exposure to "authentic" Judaism, even those seeking alternative paths in eastern religions, knew the organization for its openness. In addition, he found that Chabad's mission, at which they had been highly successful, is to educate and encourage every Jew to do *mitzvot*, even if not fully committed to living strictly according to the Torah. With this reassuring information, John made an appointment to meet Bella Sontag who indicated an interest in working with Helen.

At the first meeting John was surprised that Bella and her daughter, Gena, the oldest of a brood of nine, did not fit his preconceptions. In place of the antiquated garb he had anticipated, the women dressed in contemporary, if modest, clothing, and they were outgoing, rather than reserved. Yet as they talked, John could not rid himself of the feeling that in blindly following custom, ritual, and law, they were more devout than wise, and that they were judging him. Bella and Gena agreed to come out to the farm once a week to study Torah with Helen, saying they considered it an honor.

When the Sontags drove up to the farm the following week, John welcomed them warmly, then escorted them to the barn where he had housed the Rosen scroll. In the center of a cleared space he had scrubbed clean, stood the reading table with a lid that opened to a spacious compartment that he had built from recycled cedar. Taking the Torah from its safe storage, he placed it on the table, removed its adornments and chiming bells, then, half opening it, he gestured for the Sontags to come forward. Mother and daughter stood rooted to the spot, and then backed away, eyes wide, lips parting and closing soundlessly. Mistaking their reaction for awe at the magnificence and antiquity of the Torah, with a forward motion of his hand John again invited them to examine the scroll.

"You have brought this precious sefer Torah *here!*" Bella cried, finding her voice at last.

"Yes, it belongs to our family."

"Don't you don't know that for communal prayers the Torah can be read only in the presence of a *minyan* of ten men?" Bella said, her voice rising,

"And that it should be housed in a Holy Ark, not here in a barn?" her daughter interjected.

Angered by their accusatory tone, John was tempted to dismiss them; for Helen's sake he controlled himself. Apparently he had broken with tradition in a way that was disgraceful; now he would have to reassure them that he meant no disrespect.

Choosing his words carefully, he said, "I didn't mean to offend you. Please accept my apologies."

Bella closed her eyes and inclined her head.

"Will you still agree to study Torah with Helen?" John asked.

"Of course. We can study from the *Chumashes* we brought with us, the printed version of the Torah."

"Thank you. I'll take you to Helen. She is waiting for you in the house, but please don't upset her."

After the unpleasant scene, his feelings towards the Sontags verged on hostility, but for his wife's sake he tolerated them. Still, he felt that he was complicit in perpetuating a falsehood: that the Torah would somehow snatch his wife from death's jaws or pave her way to heaven. He could not speak his mind for fear of hurting Helen, but it all seemed surreal to him.

In the days of illness that followed, Helen's journal entries reflected her continuing search for guidance:

> In my former existence as a Christian fundamentalist, I searched the Bible as I once scoured pots, scrubbed floors, washed linens, and pulled weeds, for hour upon hour each day till my skin turned raw, and my soul was seared, hoping to feel God in my life. Now, when I study the Torah with Bella and Gena, like a nomad dying of thirst I crawl toward an oasis. Sometimes peace wraps around my body, desiccated to a thorny root, despite the pain that is tearing me away from this world. Just to know that the Torah is near, radiating its divine presence, comforts me.

Despite heroic treatments, Helen's illness did not relinquish its grip. Through the pain, Helen continued to reflect on her life as it drew to a close:

> I see my life branching above me like a mysterious tree, each bough laden with a different fruit. Some I

409

chose to pick, and others I rejected. Some were ripe and sweet, others hard and sour, still others, like forbidden desires, beckoned to me. Yet I'm not afraid. Judaism does not believe one can be condemned to *Gehenom* forever—a sort of Hell without Satan. It is the place where all human souls, after departing their bodies, stay for a time to purify themselves before reuniting with the Almighty in heaven. If, in God's judgment, a person has to enter *Gehenom*, the maximum amount of time spent there would be one year.

Helen succumbed after a two-year battle, leaving John and Abe utterly bereft.

John tried to escape into the fantasy world of his stories, but failed. It was as if he had suffered a stroke that blocked the flow of words from his brain to his hands. Anxiety attacks caused his heart to thump wildly in his chest, sweat to exude from his pores, and his mind to race erratically, rendering him completely unable to write. A year after Helen's death, on the day that they would have celebrated their eighteenth wedding anniversary, the widower still battled bouts of anguish and depression. As he sat in his study attempting to work on a novel dedicated to Helen, he imagined that he was talking to her. "The thing is a maze of subplots that even an Einstein wouldn't understand," he complained.

"You never liked editing," she said.

"And I don't like it any better now," he growled.

It was always exciting for him to begin something rather than to end it. He never tired of snaring the words darting in and out of the depths of his brain like iridescent fish. For him, starting a novel was similar to embarking on a journey to an unexplored kingdom. You never knew what you might find there, but once you had reached your destination you had no desire to retrace the path. He desperately needed Helen's help; she had shaped his words more than he had realized.

Hunger and the dimming light of the setting sun broke his reverie. He rose and went to the kitchen where he assembled an avocado and bean sprout sandwich and heated a bowl of vegetable soup; out of habit and respect for Helen's memory, he kept mostly to a vegetarian diet. He moved over to the bookshelf, set the food down on the coffee table then pulled out an album. Flipping through it, he willed himself not to succumb to melancholy. The photos brought back memories caught like tiny, bright sea creatures in the tide pools of his mind. In one, Helen sat on a log looking directly at him, self-conscious but self-possessed, as if prescient of the image's power. In another, she hiked up a mountain trail, her hair caught in a tortoise-shell clip and piled nonchalantly atop her head, looking back at him with a jaunty grin. Each picture visually froze a precious moment in time; then, as he turned the pages, the series evoked the passing of time itself, unfolding the story of their continuing love and happiness he sorely needed to remember in his mourning. He pulled out another album, then another. Photos at every stage of their lives were a testament to their wonderful years together. Yet gnawing grief paralyzed him. Since her death he could not find his way back to the world.

He went out on the porch and threw the remains of his lunch into the yard for the noisy, greedy gaggle of geese and brood of chickens. The world, once lightened by Helen's blithe spirit, seemed an eternity spinning inside a black hole, a daily grind of meaningless tasks.

He found the brutal loneliness of night the hardest to endure. As if echoing his sorrow, a screech owl's mournful whistle followed by its muted tremolo, pierced the night and his lonely heart. Weather permitting, he often slept on an old cot he dragged out to the porch; he could not bear to go inside, where everything reminded him of her absence. But this time, the cold drove him indoors.

He lay on the sofa and let his mind fill with visions of strange worlds he had created in his novels until he drifted off . . .

A bolt of lightning zaps through him, smashing him into atomic particles wheeling in eternal, infinite space. What is that? Who is that? Slowly it coalesces into a whole. It's Miss Primrose!

"Mr. Spock, it's time for the yoga classes to begin," he hears her voice ringing out from the void.

He woke, his face wet with tears, still half-believing that she was there in the dark room, feeling the warm pressure of her body against him. As he threw off the blankets, the cold air made his skin prickle. In the bathroom he snapped on the light; there was no underwear drip-drying there, just the lingering scent exhaled from her homemade potpourri of dried petals and herbs.

Sometime in the night a plan hatched in his brain, and he arose that morning with an energizing sense of purpose. First, he called Emily to get her agreement to teach a yoga class. Then he found Helen's address book and, after breakfast began calling her friends. He simply said, "I want Helen's yoga class to resume. I hope you can come this Thursday at seven." Her friends seemed genuinely pleased to hear from him and promised to be there. He also called Bella and her daughter Gena Sontag, inviting them to arrive after the class, to participate in a memorial ceremony. Later that day, on the drive back from Abe's friend's house, John shared his plans with his son and was delighted by his enthusiastic response. "Dad, after the yoga I should read a portion from the Torah. As soon as I get home I'll find the right passage."

Late Thursday afternoon, Emily's battered green Volkswagen bus pulled into the driveway in front of the red barn bearing all nine members of Helen's yoga group. They hugged John and Abe, leaving no time for awkwardness, lit incense candles, and spread their mats in the area cleared for yoga. Emily, who had assisted Helen with the classes, instructed them to lie down on their mat to begin breathing exercises. Emily's gentle voice moved them through the positions like currents of air that bends tree limbs without breaking them. As they posed like a tree, she repeated Helen's words, "Consider how Etz Chayim, Hebrew for the Tree of Life, draws you to your source, to your roots."

412

The intense hues of the setting sun filtered through the big dusty windows, casting a diffuse glow over the exercisers moving like slow dancers in a trance. As the session progressed, John had a strange, floating illusion that the barn appeared to be turning, on an imaginary fulcrum, with the sun's movement westward.

When the class drew to a close, Emily instructed them to return to the sitting position. John had momentarily fallen into the gentle cocoon of slumber, and arose serene. As he ran the tips of his fingers over his eyes to brush away the drowsiness, he saw Gena and her mother Bella emerging from the shadows into the ring of light spilling over the circle of Helen's friends. Mustering a smile he gestured for the two women to be seated, yet as he did so he felt that they were intruders come to disturb his hard-won tranquility.

Unlocking the cabinet, he carefully placed the Rosen Torah on the reading table covered with a white linen cloth but did not unroll it. Everyone's attention was riveted on him, except for the Sontags; Bella gasped then exchanged glances with her daughter, who silently shook her head in response.

Abe started with Genesis. "The universe was emptiness and void, and from it God fashioned the world. And after that, God breathed life into a pile of clay and created Adam. But Adam was alone, so God caused him to fall into a deep sleep and took a rib from him. And he created a helpmate for Adam from his rib, called Eve, the mother of us all." When he had finished, Abe smiled tremulously and said, "That story has special meaning for me because it symbolizes the special union my father and mother shared for so many years."

Afterward, John set out slices of his homemade bread, a platter of fruit, and herb tea, and they all related what Helen had meant to them. John spoke of his love for his wife. "With her I felt alive. Colors seemed more vibrant, food tasted more delicious, and life was more joyful."

Then it was Emily's turn, "She had a talent for connecting with people, and of making them feel treasured. Her gift to all of us was the gift of true friendship." As each one related their bond

413

with Helen, their remembrances helped John and Abe to begin letting go of their sorrow; to start the healing that flowed from the love and affection Helen had given to them. John's grief was still there, but it no longer felt lodged inside every cell of his being.

The Sontags lingered after the group had left. "It was a very special mitzvah to memorialize your dear wife, Helen." Bella's voice was low and raspy, her eyes smoldering and dark.

"Thank you." A smile lit John's face.

"But I have to be honest with you. You *misused* the Torah."

A frown replaced John's smile. He stood with his hands clenched by his sides, struggling to control himself. "Mrs. Sontag, my only intention was to honor my wife."

"My mother's upset," Gena, interjected quietly. "She doesn't mean to insult you. However, we believe that it would be appropriate for someone more suitable, someone more qualified to take care of the Torah."

"What are you getting at?"

"Gena is saying that my husband and I would be willing to take custody of the Torah until Abe is old enough to decide where he wants to place it," Bella declared.

"No! Never!" John's refusal ricocheted off the loft. If he allowed them to make off with his inheritance how would he retain control of its destiny? The Sontags were honorable if overly zealous, but might it not be tempting to take possession of this extraordinary Torah? And what if the Sontags left the area and some other rabbi took control of it? What if it fell into unscrupulous hands? He could imagine countless scenarios in which the scroll could be lost to the Rosens forever. He had made a promise to his father to protect and honor it, and he would do it.

Bella clasped her hands together in supplication. "We have no intention of keeping your Torah, we . . ."

"Please leave before I say something I will regret," John cut her short. Then he turned on his heels and strode into the night

414

✺ 33 ✺

The Seventh Inheritor: Abe Rosen, the Would-Be Rabbi

A goat has a long beard but that doesn't make him a rabbi.
                                                    Yiddish folk saying

When Helen had first been diagnosed with cancer, the idyllic period of Abe's childhood on the farm ended. The battle robbed Helen of the strength to continue homeschooling him. Reluctantly, John had enrolled his son at the Junior High in Nonana, despite misgivings that he would find difficulty in adjusting to public school. One troubling issue was that Abe refused to cut off his ponytail or put away his outmoded tie-dyed T-shirts. John told himself that his son simply didn't need to blend in. After all, he and Helen were unconventional, and perhaps the boy did not feel undue peer pressure to conform.

As the days dragged by, Helen could tell from the way her son slouched when he came home from school, the downcast look on his face, his unaccustomed aloofness, the way he picked at his food, that he was unhappy. When she questioned him, he said that some of his classmates called him weird.

In an attempt to comfort him, his mother had reached over and squeezed her son's shoulder. "Abe, they don't know how to deal with people that are different from them, they're just trying to get a rise out of you. If you ignore them they'll quit bothering you." She then went on to suggest that he dress more like his peers, and offered to take him shopping.

415

Straightening his shoulders, Abe said with a show of bravado, "I'm not a little kid anymore. I can handle it."

He chose not to reveal that because he was quiet and gentle, with his mother's soulful gray eyes fringed by long lashes, and her full red lips, they taunted him with "gay boy." They threw spitballs and pencils at him, elbowed him in the corridor, knocked his books to the floor, and bullied him in countless ways whenever they got the chance. Worse, a boy in a higher grade told Abe that he was gay himself, and invited him to a movie. Abe began to wonder if there was something wrong with him. The bullying, especially the mistaken belief that he was gay, were hateful and humiliating. He longed to rest his head on his mother's shoulders and cry, but he was too embarrassed to do so. Instead, he folded his anger and shame inward, where it continued to fester; burying his misery caused more harm than the actual abuse the kids heaped upon him.

After his mother died what remained of the adolescent's confidence evaporated. Normally an early riser, he began to oversleep and was often late for school. He ate little and lost weight. His lanky frame appeared to be all bones that stuck out awkwardly as he walked. At home he retreated to the sanctuary of the barn where his mother had spent so many peaceful hours doing yoga, or reading the Chumash with him. His grandmother Martha could not reconcile this morose, withdrawn teenager with the curious and lively boy he had once been.

Sequestered in his grief and his fantasy world, John offered little comfort to his son. In his misery, he turned to his mother and pleaded with her to come to live on the farm. It would be a hardship to pull up roots, and to isolate herself from her friends and the community she had grown to love, still now that Abraham was gone she was lonely. Seeing her son and grandson so forlorn broke Martha's heart and filled her with anxiety. Without mulling over her decision, she resolved to come to their rescue. But before she could put her house on the market, she had to dispose of the accumulations of a lifetime.

Two weeks later, John and Abe arrived in the Ford pickup and hauled off what Martha had, with regret, set aside for disposal, before returning to help transport her possessions to the farm. She had also lovingly packed her Native American pottery collection, and arranged for the piano, which needed special care, to be delivered by a trucking company specializing in such transportation.

With Martha to comfort them and to run the household, the cloud of despair hanging over the Shady Lady began to lift. By day she filled the house with the savory smells of her cooking, and at night, with the soothing harmonies of her piano. However, the grandmother's attempts to impose her Teutonic sense of order met with marginal success. When she cooked meals that tasted best eaten hot, they did not come to the table when she called. Martha scolded her son and grandson, but they were not accustomed to eating on schedule; Helen had been an indifferent housekeeper who followed her whims. Having watched her mother grow bent by long hours at the stove and ironing board, she had made a vow not to become a slave to these "instruments of torture."

John spent long hours writing and working on his latest projects, but neglected to clean out plugged gutters, to grout loose tiles, or replace broken screens. Abe piled his games, books, and records that had fallen out of favor, in great heaps as if it was all discarded loot. Martha endured their slovenly ways, as they were clearly in better spirits and more productive, though her patience was sorely tested. John found a mainstream publisher for his novel *The Zen Seeker*—a huge coup, as these publishing houses usually rejected science fiction genre. He lovingly dedicated this newest work to Helen. Life had also improved for Abe since making new friends in the chess and computer clubs, and he maintained good grades without having to study much.

Computers soon became the most avid shared interest between father and son. John had initially launched Abe into the arena of computers, after hearing about two young men, Steve Jobs and Steve Wozniak, who had produced a personal computer in a garage. He bought one from a company called Apple as soon as it hit the stores and set it up in his study so that he and Abe could work side by side. Martha was heartened to see how the

417

hobby brought them together after being isolated by grief for so long. Programming the computer to do anything, from the most mundane task of crunching numbers to the exotic process of creating graphics challenged and wholly absorbed them.

As Abe advanced rapidly from basic programming to more complicated languages, his father became aware of his extraordinary problem solving skills. Intrigued by the challenge, the boy often worked late into the night, and Martha found herself chiding him to get a proper amount of sleep.

Abe had discovered another passion, one that he chose not to share with his family. Whenever he could, he slipped into the barn. When his grandmother queried him about spending so much time there, he shrugged and said he was just reading. Martha wasn't fooled; she knew that there was more to it than that. She couldn't miss the preoccupied look in his eyes, or the funny smile playing at the corners of his mouth when he emerged from his hideaway. Although she disliked spying on her grandson his behavior worried her. One evening she crept into the barn and stood quietly observing him. He was reading the Chumash in a kind of trance and did not look up. After a while she tiptoed away. She did not want to be accused of snooping, so she waited and hoped that Abe would confide in her or his father when the time was right.

Her observations could not reveal that, for Abe, studying the Torah somehow triggered images of his mother so intense that he relived the times he had spent with her in this pursuit. Not knowing how to explain this mystical experience he did not confide in his father or his grandmother for fear they might think he was going crazy; more than that, he couldn't endure anyone interfering with his contact with his mother.

Martha became even more alarmed when Abe asked her if she had seen his mother's address book, saying that he wanted to call Bella Sontag. When Abe put down the phone following a lengthy conversation with the rebbetzin, he seemed excited but did not volunteer any information. That evening sitting round the kitchen table, he picked at the savory roast beef and mashed potatoes his grandmother had prepared; even his favorite dessert, fruit tart, failed to tempt him. After clearing the dishes, Abe returned to the table where his father sat engrossed in reading a submission for a science fiction magazine. When he finally looked up and reached for his mug of coffee, he saw that his son was staring at him.

"Something on your mind?" John said with a smile.

"Have you decided what to do with the Rosen Torah?" he blurted, the blood rushing to his face.

'What do you mean?"

"You've not honored it as it deserves to be honored," the adolescent rushed on.

"Whoa! Slow down."

But Abe kept on going, "You should have given the Torah to Bella and Gena when they begged for it. They were so good to Mom."

Choking back the resentment flaring inside him, John said, "Look Abe, we talked about this before. Giving custody of the Rosen Torah to anyone but a member of the family would be risky. Just take a moment to think about it."

Abe glared at him.

"Lately I've been thinking that I need to follow my father's example and loan it back to the museum."

"But it should be used in religious services!"

John grimaced, then said quietly, "One can forge an intimate relationship with religion or choose to sit it out. I chose to sit it out. When you inherit the Torah, you can decide what is best."

"I don't care about your views on religion. All I know is I want to study with the Sontags." He took a deep breath then plunged on. "I want you to loan the Torah to Rabbi Sontag's shul!"

"No, it's not that simple. As I've pointed out, if the Sontags take possession of the Torah, we could easily lose track of it. I'm not saying anyone would deliberately steal it, but you never know what could happen."

"Maybe, but that's what I feel is the right thing to do," Abe shaded his eyes with his hands to hide his angry tears. They were both silent for a while.

When John spoke, his tone was resigned. "Alright, if it's what you want, I will have a lawyer draw up legal papers to ensure that the Sontags understand that our Torah is only on loan, that it belongs to the Rosen family, and that no decision concerning it can be made without my consent."

"Thanks Dad, " he said, hugging his father, "I'll call the Sontags to give them the great news!"

John remained sitting at the kitchen table, feeling strangely at peace, experiencing a glimpse of life in which there was no disharmony, no sorrow, no loss, no death.

In the intervening years Abe continued to study with the Sontags, Chabad-Lubavitchers, and joined their synagogue. In high school he went beyond the rudiments to become proficient enough to read with fluency from the Torah itself. Standing on the *bima* chanting from his scroll gave him a special feeling of accomplishment, and sometimes he felt his mother's presence watching over him, taking pride in him as he reached toward manhood.

In a strained and difficult conversation with his father and grandmother, Abe told them that he had decided to convert to Orthodox Judaism. Both expressed their doubts about his readiness for such a significant decision. John said he should not rush into it—he needed to be sure it would be a lifelong commitment. Martha agreed that it would be better to wait until after college to decide. Stubborn as he was, Abe went ahead with his formal conversion.

When Abe graduated from high school, John and Martha should have been prepared for his announcement: He planned to enroll at Yeshiva University in New York, and eventually go on to the Rabbinical Seminary.

When his father found his voice, he said bluntly, "There are so many other possibilities! Why this?"

"This is my calling."

"Why, when you would make a brilliant software engineer?"

"Please don't oppose my choice just because you don't hold with religion!"

The two sat facing each other, sparring partners in an unequal match.

"Abe, even if we should agree to your plan, do you have the credentials to get into a yeshiva?"

"According to the Sontags I do. I've studied with them for almost five years, and been through a *halachic* conversion, or an Orthodox conversion. And Rabbi Sontag has written a letter of recommendation for me."

"Have you researched this yeshiva you plan to attend?" John pressed.

"Yes, Yeshiva University in New York offers a dual educational program, so I can combine liberal arts and sciences with the study of the Torah and Jewish history."

"But have you thought about whether you are suited to the profession? A rabbi, as any religious leader, should be someone who can listen to everyone's troubles. Son, you have a brilliant mind, but you're impatient with people."

"I'll learn how in rabbinical school," he said, with a dismissive shrug.

"'I doubt it, seminaries tend to be very academic places."

"I agree with your father," Martha interjected. " I think you may be making a mistake, one that you'll regret. I don't believe you will be happy in New York, it's so different from our life here."

"It's time I got away. I need to experience something other than small-town America. You grew up in the Bay Area, and even took that trip across the country. Dad, I've lived in the backwoods all my life."

"The backwoods, huh?" John grimaced. "Anyway, you don't need to go to New York for adventure, you could go to a big-city college here in California. You can decide about rabbinical school later."

Abe pleaded, "Dad, I've given this a lot of thought. Try to respect my wishes. One reason I am preparing for the rabbinate is to show respect to the Rosen Torah in the proper manner."

"But you can do that without becoming a rabbi." Abe silently cursed the day he had invited the Sontags into their lives.

Martha said solemnly, "You know we only want you to be happy. But does it make sense to choose a career in order to right what you perceive as a wrong?"

John nodded his agreement. "Don't you want to be a part of the technological revolution that's coming?"

"I can pursue that later," the aspiring rabbi said defiantly.

"Not if you want to be one of the pioneers."

"I've already discussed all this with Rabbi Sontag. He has recommended me for a scholarship, so my tuition should be covered. There is no need to cross-examine me. My mother's hands have reached out from the grave. She wants me to do this," he said with conviction.

John knew then that he had lost the battle. If he objected to his son go to yeshiva, he would be blamed for everything that went wrong in the future.

Forcing a smile, he said, "So, do rabbis make a good living? After all, one has to be practical."

Abe ignored the question. "Granddad Abraham would have understood, even if you two don't really get it."

John felt judged, and found wanting; he knew that Abe had never approved of his views on religion, and by association, his seeming indifference to the Rosen Torah. He wished miserably that Helen's quest for peace, for a spiritual path, hadn't come to haunt their son. He wished that his legacy hadn't asserted its sway over Abe, but he had no power to change the past, no power over what Shmuel Rosen, the family patriarch, had set in motion almost two centuries ago.

Life in New York proved to be a daily struggle for the freshman from Oregon. From the first day in yeshiva he felt alienated from the students and teachers. He didn't fully understand them and they didn't understand him. Coming from the West Coast, they did not take him seriously; some thought less of him for it, others openly dubbed him "The Cowboy Yid." They were unlike the Sontags, and even more different from the mainstream liberal Jews he had known out west. These New Yorkers were sure of themselves to the point of being self-righteous. They had lived their entire lives in Jewish enclaves, and had been sent to youth groups or summer camps where they easily absorbed the traditions of their forefathers, while he had lived on a farm away from any sizeable Jewish community. Nevertheless, he was determined to save face and complete the first year before rethinking his plans.

To exacerbate his misery, he received news that his beloved grandmother had passed away. Soon after he had left for yeshiva, she had suffered a stroke that left her partially paralyzed. His father had refused to place her in an "assisted living facility," nursing his mother tenderly to the end. Abe immediately flew back for the funeral, returning unsettled and restless with a lonely, empty space inside him.

In a course on the History of the Jews, taught by Professor Nathan Silverstein, he found some small relief. The professor was knowledgeable, articulate, with a sly sense of humor. When he invited Abe to join a group of elderly Holocaust survivors on a trip to Lithuania, he grabbed at the chance, grateful that he would not have to ask his father for money, as his grandmother had left him a small lump sum. He was curious to see for himself what kind of place had shaped his ancestors, in particular his grandfather Yakov, three times removed, who seemed to have inflicted so much pain upon the family. He wanted to experience first-hand how the culture of the shtetl could bind a man like Yakov to his religious traditions so irrevocably that, no matter the cost, it could never loosen its grasp on him.

Their travel itinerary, organized around the requests of the group, included visits to the shtetls within a radius of about fifty miles of Vilna, the capital. A hotel in that city was to serve as headquarters. On the long flight over, Abe had time to review what he had learned in Professor Silverstein's class.

Over the centuries, Swedes, Poles, Russians, and Germans had battled for control of Lithuania. The Jews were first invited to settle there by Grand Duke Vytautas in 1410. At one time they had grown to about a third of the population of Vilna, living on the eastern fringe of the baroque Old Town. Between World Wars I and II, under Lithuanian rule, Jewish culture flourished, and Vilna became one of the most important centers of Judaism in Eastern Europe. This "golden age" ended with the German occupation of Lithuania on June 24, 1941. Orchestrated by the Germans, an organized massacre of the Jewish population ensued. Those who survived the initial killings were herded into ghettos, and once trapped inside, were easily rounded up, shot, and thrown into mass graves. The few that escaped fled into the forests. The German occupation that had lasted from 1941 to 1944 decimated their Jewish population, and devastated the country as a whole.

When the Soviets took control of Lithuania after World War II, Joseph Stalin launched anti-semitic purges. A second wave of mass executions and deportations annihilated almost all of the surviving Jews. Abe's guidebook described Vilna, including Old Town, as the most architecturally beautiful of the Baltic capitals — sadly, the city had only one surviving synagogue.

That was the extent of his knowledge of Lithuania, and it scarcely prepared him for what he was about to encounter.

On the first day, at the request of Irwin Aronoff, a retired physician, the group headed for a farm near the village of Troki, where he hoped to find a woman he had known only by the name of Anna. As a girl, she had carried scraps of food to him as he hid in a pigsty on her family's farm. He told them that Anna would now be in her mid-fifties, but he felt certain that he would recognize her even after all these years.

The search began with a bus ride through the countryside. It lumbered and sputtered over narrow roads running between fields of rye and flax. Horses still plowed the land; people still drew water from wells; daffodils and dandelions as big as roses sprouted in the yards. Through the grimy bus window Abe observed dilapidated wooden houses; scrawny chickens scratching in the dirt; women wearing faded cotton dresses, long aprons, and kerchiefs folded around their heads, their skin prematurely dried and wrinkled like plums left out in the sun. Some waved and smiled as they went by, showing missing teeth or teeth capped with gold. Others cast suspicious sideways glances from their bent-over stance in the fields. In contrast to the magnificent forests of the Pacific Northwest, and the robust, confident Americans, the land and people seemed depleted, exhausted.

Since their route skirted Valinsk, the Rosens' ancestral shtetl, Abe requested they make a quick stop there. It was even smaller than he had imagined, with modest wooden houses, and, on the square, only vacant or rundown stores. The big cobblestones and the well Abe had seen in photographs had been replaced by drab concrete. To his dismay, the wooden shul had been converted into shabby apartments. Not a trace or a remembrance of the Rosen family appeared to have survived in this poor place. Yet as he stood looking around like a lost boy, he imagined that along the old road running through the square and the shtetl, Jews had once vied for business, walked to the synagogue, clopped out of town on horseback, and even traveled off to America. Along this humble street, engraved with memories, Jews were carried to the cemetery where defaced gravestones now guarded the bones of his forebears. And down this road doomed Jews had been herded to their mass graves.

With these melancholy thoughts running through his head, Abe boarded the bus for Troki. When they arrived at the town, a villager directed them to four separate houses where women named Anna now lived. The first Anna, blind and partially deaf, was too old. The second was a girl in her teens. The third, a Ukrainian, had only recently settled in the village. Somewhat disheartened, the group drove down a muddy farm road for about a mile until they came to a steep-roofed, weathered country house with an attached barn. A boy, playing with a puppy, stopped to gape at the odd-looking strangers who had suddenly appeared at his gate. Irwin called to him in Lithuanian. In response the boy dropped the squirming puppy, ran helter-skelter up the path lined with apple trees, and called loudly through the front door.

A woman as plain and wholesome as wheat bread appeared in the doorway, peering at the strangers, wiping her hands on a clean white apron tied around her ample waist. Irwin walked up the path toward her, searching the details of her face. It was rosy and weathered as a prune and her fair hair was tucked under a blue kerchief. Then Irwin threw his hands triumphantly into the air, and cried out: "Anna!"

For a moment the farmwoman was too startled to respond; then a shudder of recognition passed through her like a gust of wind, lifting her shoulders, shaking the kerchief from her head, and forcing a high-pitched cry from her lips. She ran along the corridor of trees, through shafts of yellow sunlight alternating with deep purple shadows, into his embrace. Abe stood in the high grass observing them, touched by their joy. He couldn't understand what they were saying, but it was plain that the special bond forged between them in that terrible time had endured.

In bed that night, as Abe reflected on what he had witnessed, he could not sleep imagining the terror that Irwin had lived through, hiding like a hunted animal from those who would murder him. He had survived for months, fearing that at any moment he would be discovered and put to death like a cockroach underfoot. Such an experience could destroy one's sanity; yet Irwin had survived as a rational and compassionate human being.

The next day, as requested by Saul Klein, a successful realtor, the group set out for the Rudniki Forest to search for the makeshift grave of Saul's brother. Saul and his brother had joined a unit of Russian partisans. During the war, they had trained them in guerrilla warfare, supplying them with weapons and explosives. In the fall of 1943, he and his brother were dispatched on a mission to blow up a railroad. As they made their way through the forest, a German unit ambushed them. Saul managed to escape, fleeing amid flying bullets. He did not know what had befallen his brother, and for months clung to the hope that he had been taken prisoner.

Later, a farmer who witnessed the ambush informed Saul that the Germans had shot his brother and left him to rot in the woods. After they departed, the farmer had buried him in a shallow grave. Although half a century had passed since that fatal day, Saul's yearning to put the past to rest had never abated. By dogged persistence, he had succeeded in finding the peasant who claimed to have buried his brother, and convinced him to help locate the grave. Everyone in the bus knew the story, and Abe could tell from the mournful faces and hushed silence that they all felt compassion for his suffering.

The old farmer led them to the place where he remembered burying the fallen guerrilla. By the time they reached it—a shallow depression marked by a black boulder covered with lichen—they were worn-out and miserable, scratching at insect bites and dripping with perspiration.

Saul did not fall to his knees weeping and wailing, as they had anticipated, but remained rigid, white-faced, and mute. The forlorn travelers stood with him in the gloom, surrounded by a silence so profound they could hear the icy blood of death pulsing through their bodies. Suddenly Saul turned on his heel to face them. "This is not where my brother lies," he growled. "It's not the right place."

His wife reached for his hand, "How do you know this, Saul?"

Abe thought, *the human mind, overwhelmed by suffering and evil, often denies a reality too painful to support. Perhaps it is easier for him to cling to the belief that his brother miraculously escaped.*

On the last night, after a meager meal of boiled potatoes and coarse brown bread, Abe went up to his room and slid between rough, cold sheets. The place smelled of stale cigarette smoke, and cheap carbolic soap. He was too disturbed by the events of the past few days to rest. Against all logic, guilt overwhelmed him for not having endured the pain inflicted upon the survivors. He was merely an observer, not a victim, a voyeur who had no right to intrude on their suffering.

He tried to make sense of the malice he had witnessed, but he could not. He felt angry, alienated. For no other reason

427

than that they were Jews, men had slaughtered their fellow human beings in cold blood, and he could not accept this. *How had God allowed this to happen? Perhaps He is just our creation,* Abe thought.

He castigated himself, the next inheritor of the Rosen Torah, for being weak; he had arrogantly coerced his father to remove the Torah from the barn and place it in the care of the Chassidim. Now his faith had been tested and it had failed him. He lived in his head, and was not drawn to people, nor was his conviction profound enough. The Lithuanian experience finally convinced him that he was not cut out for the life of a rabbi.

He quit the yeshiva. After that he felt emptied of everything but skepticism. "The Cowboy Yid," he said to his reflection in the bathroom mirror, pleased that the label no longer embarrassed him, "will be rolling back west to spend a few weeks with his father talking over the old dream of becoming a computer engineer." He lifted the razor and began shaving off the straggly, dirty-blond beard he had tried growing.

When he returned to Oregon, he had a new appreciation for America. Nowhere in Lithuania had he found the comforts of home, the hot showers, and the abundant variety of food he had taken for granted; the freedom to chose his beliefs and his path in life as he saw fit. Home again, he reveled in the spacious beauty of his native mountains and forests reaching up toward the sky, the unfettered liberty to roam the land, and the certainty of being welcomed. However, he was profoundly saddened that his beloved grandmother was not there to welcome him.

John was overjoyed to have Abe back on the farm. He had been so alone since his mother passed away. He assured his son that if he chose a career in computer science he would be more than willing to support his studies. Privately, he congratulated himself on being the one who started Abe down a path that now seemed so fitting; he did not gloat that he had been right about the yeshiva as well. He hoped that after having tried the restrictive garb of Orthodoxy, his son would feel free to partake of whatever the world had to offer.

One evening, however, when Abe ended the conversation by slapping his thighs and declaring, "I've got to get my hands on a big pile of venture capital," John could not resist an obvious jab, "Oh, so the wayward rabbi is becoming a capitalist!"

"And my father the utopian dreamer is helping me to become just that!" Abe quipped.

When summer was over, Abe enrolled at Berkeley, his grandfather's alma mater. There, computing rapidly became his life's work. In his senior year, he began to search for a way to start up his own company and spent hours discussing possibilities with his father. His eyes sparkling with enthusiasm, he expounded on his ideas for developing systems to network computers within companies and to the outside world so that software and data could be easily shared and updated.

The yeshiva was now a foolish dream never to be realized; the burgeoning computer sciences beckoned him like a marvelous space ship that would rocket him to new frontiers.

❧ 34 ❧

Abe and Shelley

Train up a child in the way he should go: and when he is old, he will not depart from it.

Proverbs

In his four years at college, Abe dated girls only casually. Then, the year before graduating, he met Shelley Fox. The way he stared at her, as if she were the most beautiful girl in the world, broadcast to everyone that he was in love. Abe, normally reserved and cautious, asked her for a date the first time they met. She accepted.

They made an odd couple. Abe had his mother's pale complexion, long, lanky limbs, dark blond hair, and meditative gray eyes. Shelley was petite and graceful, with smooth olive skin, a heart-shaped face, sparkling brown eyes, a full-smiling mouth, and a mass of unruly dark hair that fell to her shoulders. She was high-spirited, gregarious, and easy-going; Abe was introverted and obsessed with his work. Her bubbly, outgoing personality delighted and entertained Abe. His ambition attracted her, and she tolerated his edginess as the touch of arrogance that came with a brilliant mind. He nicknamed her "Foxy." In retaliation, she affectionately dubbed him "Cyborg."

Shelley's traditional Jewish upbringing differed sharply from Abe's unconventional childhood. He confided that his father openly declared himself to be an atheist, while his mother had been raised in the True Believers Church. Later he turned to Judaism for spiritual succor, and had converted to Orthodox

Judaism, but had now fallen away from being strictly observant. He stopped short of telling her that he had once studied to become a rabbi.

Before Shelley, Abe had been leery of falling in love; yet her lack of inhibition swept him off his feet. Soon after they met, she invited him to have sex without a trace of embarrassment. That she found him extremely attractive acted as its own aphrodisiac and seemed to dissolve the old hurts of classmates in Nonana who had taunted him. She soothed the old wound they had inflicted on him by attempting to label him gay.

After dating for a year, they began to get more serious. Shelley said that she thought it was time for him to meet her folks, George and Esther Fox. She primed him for the visit, telling him that her parents had emigrated from Israel to the United States when she was a four-year-old. They had successfully adjusted to mainstream America without losing their identity as Jews or their memory of the trauma of war.

They arrived at the Fox home in Oakland on a foggy Sunday morning. The house was a typical 1970s split-level. As she rang the bell, Shelley sang out, "It's me, Mom," and Abe saw her reach out to touch the *mezuzah* on the doorframe lightly with her fingertips and move them to her mouth to kiss.

A well-groomed woman in her early sixties, with salt and pepper hair clawed back into a bun, opened the door and greeted them with a smile. "Come in. Come in," Mrs. Fox said, taking Abe's arm and leading him into the den. "I've been looking forward to meeting you." Seating him on the couch next to her, she began to fire personal questions with an obvious subtext. That made him uncomfortable knowing she was prying into whether his family was prestigious enough for theirs.

"Is your family from around here?" Abe thought, what she is really getting at is, *I know most of the Jewish families in the area. Why haven't I met your parents?*

"Where do they attend Temple?" *Are they observant Jews?*

"Do your folks belong to a country club?" *Do they circulate in the right social circles?*"

To conceal his awkwardness, he smiled and replied as briefly as he could without seeming to be rude. Shelley saw that Abe was ill at ease.

When they first met, she had noticed his defensiveness about being Jewish. When she had questioned him about it, he retorted, "If you had suffered anti-Semitism directed at you *personally*, you might be sensitive too."

"My grandfather and father are both survivors of the Holocaust, being taunted by a few bullies shouldn't be compared to what Holocaust survivors suffered." Shelley had shot back. "Believe me, what happened to my family has affected my life. But I won't give in to fear or paranoia, because if I do, then the forces of evil will have won." Shelley's quiet rejoinder had shamed him at the time.

Recalling this past conversation, Shelley now came to rescue him from her mother's probing. "Mom, please. Why do you think that if someone is Jewish, they must know every Jew in the Bay Area?"

Embarrassed that his discomfort was so obvious, Abe tried to cover it up. "Oh, feel free to ask questions, Mrs. Fox."

The mother knew her daughter well, and hastily shifted gears. "Please help yourself," she said, offering her guest a tray of homemade cookies. "Would you like some coffee to go with these?"

"That would be great," he said.

Knowing that her daughter didn't like coffee, she added, "I'll bring you a Coke, Shelley," and disappeared into the kitchen.

Abe looked around the room. It was redolent of nostalgia for Israel. A display cabinet housed an elegant brass menorah and memorabilia: a delicate woodcut of Jerusalem, seen through stone arches; a miniature Chagall poster of vivid floating images; heavy silver candlesticks. The coffee table, with a colorful mosaic of entwined branches and flying birds, supported a neat stack of Israeli art books. Everything was pleasing to the eye, coordinated and in its place—except for one item, a black shadow box. Mounted inside the frame, like an awful accusation, were torn and faded items: a ragged strip of silk from a prayer shawl, two

432

crumpled badges with the yellow Star of David, and a yellowed official Auschwitz postcard. The front bore the original Hitler stamp cancelled at the Auschwitz 2 post office on February 2, 1942. In spidery lettering, the inmate had signed his name: Walter Fox, prisoner tattoo number 1124; date of birth, February 12, 1908; block number, 13; and the camp postal address, Auschwitz O/S Postamt 2. Abe surmised that Walter Fox was Shelley's grandfather, and that the two yellow stars belong to him and to her father, George Fox. Those relics were grim witnesses to past misdeeds, specters of the Holocaust that still haunted the world. Goose pimples prickled the back of Abe's neck. How could the Foxes find the courage to reveal, to even advertise their terrible past? Not until his own trip to Lithuania had that tragic history come back to haunt him with so great a vengeance.

Mrs. Fox returned bearing a tray loaded with poppy seed cake and butter cookies, a pot of coffee, and a Coke. As she put the tray down on a low table Mrs. Fox noticed Abe examining the shadow box.

"You know I was born in Israel. My husband George is from Warsaw, and a survivor of the concentration camps, he immigrated to Israel after the war. Some years after we married, we came to America." At Abe's questioning gaze, she waved her hand and smiled. "It's a long, complicated story, so I'll save it for another time." She poured a cup of coffee and handed it to him.

"My grandmother, Martha Staub, was from Stuttgart, Germany, Abe said. "My great-great-grandparents on the Rosens' side hailed from Lithuania." This seemed incomplete and he blurted, "And then there's some Welsh-Pentecostal, and even Irish-Catholic blood in me." The shadow box had disturbed his equanimity, now he quickly wished he could retract the addendum. Until that moment he could have sworn that questions of identity and religious affiliation were no longer important to him. Suddenly, he felt exposed, naked, an oddity that fit in nowhere.

He could tell that he had surprised Mrs. Fox. "Oh, how interesting," she said, smoothing her skirt and rearranging the pillows on the couch.

433

"This is delicious," he said.

But Mrs. Fox wasn't to be distracted. She leaned toward him and said quietly, "No matter how tangled your family tree I feel deep inside me that you have a Jewish *neshama*, a Jewish soul."

"I . . . I once attended a yeshiva and planned to become a rabbi," he confessed, brushing crumbs from his mouth.

"Aha! I see there's more to you than meets the eye, young man!"

Shelley winced noticeably, tilted her head back for the last drop of Coke, and remarked, "Some rebbetizin I would make!"

The three sat in awkward silence, listening to the growling of a lawnmower outside, not sure who should speak next. They were relieved when Mr. Fox came in with a broad smile on his face and his hand extended, "Hi, I'm George, glad to meet Shelley's young man, at last."

The conversation turned to computers, the one area where Abe felt safe with strangers. He had a knack for explaining technology to those who weren't technical, and a charismatic way of transmitting his excitement. Soon he had the Foxes asking questions, impressed by his vision of a future in which computer technology would become an ever-more powerful tool of mass communication.

As he got to know Shelley's family, Abe envied and admired how comfortable they were with their American-Jewish identity. Yet why had the Foxes chosen to openly display Holocaust items that other survivors would find so painful? The question gnawed at him, causing him to raise the subject with Shelley once or twice although she avoided answering him, saying he should ask her father.

One evening, Shelley, who was at home "babysitting" her parents' cocker spaniel, Goldie, while they were out of town, invited him over for the weekend. After dinner, they sprawled on the sofa, their heads propped against soft pillows, drinking what was left of the wine. From where he was lounging on the sofa, Abe had a clear view of the shadow box with the dreadful Auschwitz postcard.

Before he could stop himself, he exclaimed, "I just can't understand why your father displays those terrible reminders."

Shelley sat up with a jerk, and he could see from the flare of her nostrils that he had angered her.

"Sorry, Foxy." He repeated the apology then tried to pull her close.

When she spoke, she did not look at him. "Okay, Cyborg, if you insist on me spelling it out, I will. After years of suffering in silence, my father came to the decision that he would not hide his past as if he were ashamed of it. Instead, he said that he would exhibit these shameful mementos as badges of honor and as symbols of his triumphant survival. So it's all out there for you to see — and to judge."

Chastened, Abe dropped his head.

"It's okay," she said, "I get defensive when people question me about my Dad's experiences. But I am learning to deal with it. Confronting the past has helped him to move on with his life. And it has helped his family as well." She met his gaze. "Don't you know that keeping the past hidden does more harm than good?"

After making love, they dozed off with their arms around each other, satiated with pleasure. In the early hours of the morning, Shelley woke, propped herself on an elbow, and gazed down at her sweetheart. Gently she ran her fingertips along the line of hair that ran from his chest to his pubis.

He opened his eyes and lay still, admiring her. *She is more curvaceous than she appears when clothed. Her breasts are more generous, her hips more flared,* he thought, and a sharp spasm of desire and jealousy pierced his chest. "When you make love to me," he whispered, "Do you think of your other lovers?"

She tossed her head back. "Chill out, Abe!"

She saw that his eyes had darkened and narrowed, and the corners of his lips had pulled downward. "Sorry, I didn't mean to pry. I guess I just want there to be no secrets between us."

A few weeks later the Fox family invited Abe to celebrate Passover with them. They had asked not only family, but also

435

strangers, which he knew is a mitzvah according to the Torah. Like Jewish homes in the neighborhood and around the world, the table was set with a sparkling white tablecloth, the best china and silverware, a pair of antique brass candlesticks, three matzahs covered with an embroidered cloth, and a silver Kiddush cup filled with wine over which the prayers are recited before the start of the meal. A *Seder* plate with symbolic foods—a boiled egg, a shank bone, greens, a vegetable dipped in salt, bitter herbs (horseradish), and sweet apples mixed with wine, nuts, and cinnamon—graced the head of the table. In the center, stood the silver goblet for Elijah the prophet, who would travel from home to home, to share a drop of wine celebrating joy and freedom.

Reading from the special book known as the Haggadah, George Fox presided, a soft cushion at his back to indicate that he was a free man not a slave. However, Esther Fox kept the event moving by fretting over her husband's frequent digressions to comment or even to make a joke.

"George, please don't prolong things, the children are becoming restless, and the food is getting cold and dry." In between the special rituals of the Seder, she moved back and forth between the kitchen and the dining room, checking on the dishes she would lovingly serve.

The rituals symbolized the freeing of the slaves from bondage in Egypt—which shaped the people into a community ready to receive God's Torah. These included reciting the blessings over wine, washing hands, dipping vegetables in salt water in remembrance of the tears shed by Jewish slaves, breaking the middle matzah in commemoration of the unleavened bread the Hebrews baked in haste before they fled, eating the paste of apples and wine to represent the mortar and bricks of their hard labor.

Children played an important role, the youngest asking the four age-old questions which lead to the story being told as answers. Beaming with the excitement of showing off to all of the company, and prompted in a loud whisper by her older brother, Esther Fox's great niece, seven-year-old Robyn, asked the four questions concerning why this night is different from all other

436

nights: Why do we eat matzah instead of bread? Why do we eat only bitter herbs? Why do we dip the herbs twice? Why do we eat in a reclining position on this night?

Everyone took turns reading a portion from their Haggadahs, recounting anew the ancient Israelites' harrowing exodus from Egypt over 3,000 years ago, as if they themselves had lived the experience. They dipped their little finger in wine as they retold how God sent ten dreadful plagues to force Pharaoh to yield: blood, frogs, lice, flies, pestilence, boils, hail, locusts, darkness, and the most fearsome of all, the deaths of the firstborn — but the angel of death passed over the Jewish homes.

When the children rushed from the table to find the *Afikomen*, a hidden piece of matzah, a rowdy search ensued until Robyn emerged, flushed and triumphant, to claim her prize. Mr. Fox's face broke into a grin as he pulled foil-wrapped chocolates from his pocket with a flourish.

Stimulated by the feast and the four cups of wine they had just consumed, everyone joined in the singing of traditional songs. They concluded the Seder by shouting out loud, "Next year in Jerusalem!"

For Abe, growing up without extended kin, where people created their lives and identity independent of family, the sense of ritual, and of identifying with and connecting to the past had been absent. He was touched by the warm, liminal space engendered by these ancient traditions. Mrs. Fox insisted that he take home leftovers, and when Abe kissed Shelley goodnight knowing that they were both part of a culture that went back to ancient times, he felt joined to her in a special way

Shelley and Abe decided to get married eight weeks after his graduation. Mrs. Fox suggested a traditional wedding. Her daughter enthusiastically agreed — with the caveat that she adapt some rituals to modern times.

"A Jewish wedding is rooted in tradition, why would you want to change anything?" Mrs. Fox objected.

"Ma, back in the days of the shtetl when Jews lived in close-knit communities a wedding was done strictly according to ritual. Today it's different; we live in a changing world!"

437

"But shouldn't we still value our customs?" Mrs. Fox challenged.

"Yes, we should, but what keeps them alive is their relevance to us."

On the day of the wedding, before the ceremony under the *chuppah*, the bride and the groom and their entourages gathered in separate rooms, in the synagogue complex. After a little schnapps and merriment, Abe, wearing a dark suit and a pale blue silk vest Shelley had made for him, signed a Ketubah, or marriage contract, and witnessed by two of their friends. Afterward, the groom and his father, father-in-law, relatives and friends, went in procession to veil the bride, an ancient custom called Bedekin. In a small reception room seated on a throne-like chair — flanked by her mother — Shelley looked radiant. She wore a vintage white satin sheath dress with a beaded bodice, trimmed with the palest blue lace around the hem, and matching white high-heeled satin shoes she had unearthed at a second hand store; an old lace veil framed her jet-black tresses and teasing eyes that seemed all the darker against the whiteness of her dress. Abe gazed at her as if he didn't dare to touch her. She smiled at him as he reached for the veil with trembling fingers and dropped it over her face, signaling his commitment to clothe and to protect her — reminiscent of Rebecca covering her face before marrying Isaac.

Shelley had planned her own special touches for the guests; a Klezmer band, dressed in colorful garb, stood on the steps outside the shul to greet them with joyful music, and then to escort them inside. The ceremony in the sanctuary took place under a *chuppah* of intricate handmade lace fashioned from the tablecloth Shelley's maternal grandmother had bequeathed her. The ceremony unfolded according to the time-honored customs: blessings over wine; placing of the ring on his bride's right index finger, a solid gold band with no holes to represent an everlasting bond, as the Talmud states that this finger is closer to the heart. Abe was surprised to find himself so tranquil at his juncture, listening and answering to the vows with solemn joy as he slipped the ring on her finger. Then the rabbi read the marriage contract to the bride, and sang the Seven Blessings over a second cup of wine.

Everyone shouted "Mazel Tov!" when Abe brought his shoe down on a glass to shatter it—symbolic of the spiritual exile of the Jews after the destruction of their Holy Temple in Jerusalem; also a reminder that relationships are as fragile as glass and must always be treated with care, love and respect.

Afterwards they all proceeded to the reception hall to dance the hora, the exuberant traditional folk dance. Circles of men and separate circles of women, danced around the couple of honor lofted high on chairs in the center, who laughed out loud with happiness. When the guests were too tired to continue, they seated themselves for the feast. Family and friends good-naturedly roasted and toasted the bride and groom. After dinner, Abe rose to thank everyone for celebrating with them and to say how much he loved his bride. Not to be denied, Shelley stood and made a short but witty speech about how opposites, like "Foxy" and "Cyborg" attract one another. After that it was time to recite the blessing "Birkat Hamazon," Grace After Meals. Then the klezmer band and guests got into full swing, the party animals staying until the musicians packed up at midnight.

John Rosen, as father of the groom, had arrived for the wedding festivities feeling apprehensive. He found formal weddings too often pretentious and cold. In this marriage, however, the genuine affection of the families toward Abe and Shelley made the unfolding of rites meaningful and beautiful. It accomplished what a formal ceremony is meant to do— crystallize the pure essence of a culture, to be passed down to future generations. To his surprise he had thoroughly enjoyed the celebration.

Two years after the marriage, their daughter Neta Helen Rosen arrived; red, and blotchy, with a tiny scrunched up face, and miniature fists clenched as if sparring at life for having rushed her into the world so rudely.

Shelley could not have been happier, although she had only an inkling of how demanding a child could be. Abe was tender to his baby daughter but he left early for work and came

439

home late. Shelley began to complain that he was obsessed with his career, that he was always too exhausted to do things with his family. She said that she didn't want much from him, just a little appreciation and attention. Abe protested that he understood, and promised to spend more time with them. Despite his intentions to spend more time with his wife and diuaghter, ambition crowded them out. To build his own company, Interweb, he put in brutally long hours and expected his employees to do the same. He could be inspiring, even considerate, but too often he was intimidating and insensitive in his drive for perfection. Abe begged Shelley to be patient, saying that in time he would realize his vision to expand Interweb's services from university departments and libraries to businesses and even to individual customers so that people could easily share data electronically.

Their marriage faltered on with Shelley's outbursts becoming more strident. He accused her of not supporting him at a time critical to putting Interweb on a solid footing; she accused him of neglecting his family. Their differences, which initially had seemed complementary, now became barriers. The long slow process of disengagement began; the creeping arguments that become ever more frequent, ever more bitter. Although they went to marriage counseling, after six years they parted. Abe felt a sense of relief at extricating himself from a marriage that caused so much stress and made him feel bad about himself, but he had to acknowledge that he had failed his wife, and especially his daughter.

The months immediately following their separation and subsequent divorce did not seem real to Abe. He kept busy at work, well into the night. When he came home to the apartment he had rented, he would lie on the bed half-asleep, fantasizing that Shelley was with him and they were still in love. In the few hours before daybreak he would drop into a shallow sleep interrupted too soon by the morning sun prying his eyelids open. Restless and alone, he would whisper to himself, *I am happy to be alive*, but he was not. To get away from the ache in his heart, he would stand in the shower for a long time. Then he would leave early for work, not even stopping to brew a cup of coffee. Driving to his office, unsolicited, the image of Neta with headphones clamped to her ears rose behind his eyes, dreamily singing, "Don't worry, be happy." A smile pulled at the corner of his mouth; despite his misery he couldn't help feeling lucky to have such a pretty, lively daughter. He vowed that he would be a better father to her.

After the divorce, Neta, now turning six, lived with her mother and spent part of the summer on Grandpa John's farm, as Shelley's relationship with her father-in-law remained cordial. Neta took delight in rambling through the old house, soothed by the sunlight glowing on the dark wainscoting, the big tiled fireplace, the shelves crammed with books, the view of the wildflower garden and orchard, and the meandering river, and far off mountains through the windows. On rainy days she snuggled on her bed under the gables to read or play imaginary games. On sunny days she tagged after her grandpa, asking questions and chatting incessantly, helping to weed the garden, feed the animals, and tinker with his projects. In the evenings, she and grandpa settled on the deep front porch enclosed by square fieldstone supports while he regaled her with stories of "the olden days."

The growing affection between the grandfather and grandchild spilled over into the relationship between father and son. The e-mails between John and Abe became subtly more affectionate, reflecting the new warmth between them. Then without warning, Abe received a call that his father had suffered a massive heart attack and was in intensive care in a Eugene hospital. He drove the seemingly endless miles between the Bay Area and Eugene at a reckless speed, but his Dad died before he could make it to his beside.

With his father gone, Abe felt a terrible emptiness in his life and the pressing need to say Kaddish for him, to send his father on his journey now that he no longer resided with him in the physical world. It was his way of paying homage to him even though his father had not believed in prayers. He had always known that he would inherit the family legacy, and he was proud to be its caretaker, but now the responsibility seemed greater than he had anticipated with all the other pressing demands on his time. The Torah still resided at the Chassidic shul, and would remain there until he had time to think about what was best.

His business, now in a "browser war" with Sentella, a company using its dominant position to control the Internet's standards and protocols, required all his attention. Just weeks after John's funeral, the founder of Sentella was to testify before a Senate Judiciary Committee on its allegedly anticompetitive practices toward Interweb and others. The outcome of that hearing was critical to the survival of Abe's company, and he was working around the clock with a team of lawyers to combat his rival. In the midst of this battle Abe received a distraught call from Shelley—Neta had broken her arm at gymnastics in a fall from a balance beam.

He rushed to the hospital in time to see his daughter, looking white and fragile, her pupils constricted with pain, being wheeled into surgery. He sat with Shelley in the hospital waiting room, mute with worry. Yanked out of the hectic pace of work, Abe recalled with a stab of guilt that he had not seen his daughter for several weeks. He reached over and tried to take Shelley's hand, but she pulled away. "I suppose you've been too busy worrying about exercising your stock options to see your daughter."

It shouldn't have hurt that his ex-wife disapproved, and yet it did. With great effort he swallowed his pride and said, "Listen, I feel bad for not visiting our daughter more often." Avoiding her accusatory stare, he said, "I swear I will devote at least one day a week to Neta—no excuses." If he expected her to be appeased, she was not.

"One day won't do it. I need you to take care of Neta for about ten days." She was about to begin a new job, and needed him to baby-sit their daughter for the coming week now that she had broken her arm.

His mouth fell open, and he closed it with some effort. "It's not going to be easy getting away from work. There are things going on. The Company's survival is on the line!"

Shelley rolled her eyes again, a warning sign he knew well.

"Okay. Okay," he conceded. She had neatly cornered him and she knew it.

The day before Neta was to be released from the hospital, Abe decided that he needed to clear his head, feeling tired and jittery, and fair or not, Shelley's criticism had unsettled him. He left work early to drive home and pick up his new hi-tech bike then cycle out to an idyllic place he knew well. Within an hour he had left the monotonous sprawl of the suburbs behind. Once free of the traffic, he pedaled furiously, pumping as hard as he could. The steady swish of rubber rolling over asphalt, the cool breeze on his face, emptied his mind of thought. His muscles were quivering with fatigue by the time he caught the first glimmer of water and turned onto a dirt trail. He padlocked his bike to a sturdy sapling, and walked beneath redwood trees so tall and dense he felt himself to be swimming in a watery green light. Emerging from the redwood forest he followed a track to a little stony beach at the waters edge.

Leaning against a rocky outcropping he breathed deeply absorbing the serenity. Before him a small lake, cupped by wooded hills, fanned out in a perfect crescent. He stooped over and saw his reflection trembling in the water. *I am a man looking at myself, watching myself, searching for myself.* When his breathing slowed, he opened his backpack, and pulled out bottled water and a granola bar. While he ate his mind kept plunging into the deep well of memory. He visualized his mother sitting motionless in the lotus position; eyes closed, face calm, a shaft of sunlight finding her through the dusty barn windows. He saw his father in his poster-lined study, absorbed in his fantasy. A pair of dreamers, both had created their own worlds far from the mainstream. He yearned now to feel his mother's embrace, to be in the company of his father once more. He had purposefully distanced himself from their dreams, choosing a different path, joining the rat race in pursuit of his vision. Now he wished himself back on the farm. His parents were gone, and his beloved grandmother; he couldn't look to them for answers. He needed to turn to the future, yet the past seemed to stick to his heels. Remembrances of his family, so in harmony with this elemental scene, floated in the pristine air, whispering a promise of revelation to guide his actions.

Willing his mind to empty he gazed over the motionless water and woods; in a blink the scene that had seemed as eternal as a diamond, changed. A sudden gust of wind ruffled the lake scattering silver threads of light over the waves then rushed through the trees, shaking the leaves into quivering green fans. Two blue herons standing in shallow water quietly watching for the gleam of fish flapped upwards in alarm, circled the shore, then veered back to their wading point. A redheaded woodpecker clinging to a dead limb at the top of a tree, drummed into the bark with a sharp *rat-tat-tat*. Lines from Walt Whitman's poetry came to him: *To me the converging objects of the universe perpetually flow / All are written to me / and I must get what the writing means.*

The revelation he awaited never came; reality flooded back into his meditative space. He was divorced, struggling to cope with the expectations of a daughter and an ex-wife, embroiled in a legal battle to save his business. He had no grip on the question of the Rosen Torah: *What does it mean to me? What should I do with it? Will it be simpler if I just leave it with the Chabad-Lubavitchers?*

And there was an added complication: coincidentally, just weeks after John's heart attack, Rabbi Sontag had asked Abe, now the seventh inheritor, for permission to remove the Torah from the Lubavicher shul, and place it in the Chabad House Jewish Student Center, at the University of Oregon. *What should he do about that?* With a wave of remorse he recalled that he had accused his father of dishonoring the Torah. He had gone so far as to consider becoming a rabbi to make himself its worthy heir. But the trip to Lithuania had changed him. Surely if his faith had been strong he would not have questioned these things. Since then his connection to the Torah had become tenuous, distant; now he had to reevaluate his responsibility to it.

444

And so his thoughts wheeled round and round as he watched an eagle, airborne on magnificent wings, soar in circles high above. He had a sudden urge to camp on the shore for the night, but he had promised his daughter that he would visit her in the hospital to read her favorite bedtime stories. *Neta is only eight, and she needs her father. She needs me. Enough philosophizing,* he thought. He left the place in frustration, unable to come to a resolution.

Abe put on a cheerful smile as he entered his daughter's hospital room and leaned over to kiss her. He couldn't help noticing how closely she resembled her mother: the same olive skin, heart-shaped face, sparkling brown eyes, full mouth and unruly black hair.

"How's Daddy's girl?"

"Did you bring me a surprise like you promised?"

Abe felt the happy mask on his face crumble. "Yes, sweetie pie. I'm going to bring in your surprise. But first you have to close your eyes."

He lurched out of the room before his daughter could reply, remembering the gift shop in the lobby. Jabbing the elevator's down button impatiently, he pulled a fifty-dollar bill from his wallet, and was just considering taking the stairs two at a time when the doors slid open. In the shop he grabbed the biggest teddy bear, pressed the bill into the startled cashier's hand and rushed back. The look on his daughter's face when he handed her the stuffed animal was worth it. As he hugged Neta, he admitted that he had been as self-centered as Shelley had claimed, and silently renewed his vow to be a better father.

At that moment Abe experienced a belated epiphany: The Rosen legacy would create a new and special bond between himself and his neglected daughter. He would transport the Torah from the Lubavitcher shul, and house it in the Foxes' synagogue, Congregation Beth Jacob. Then he would study its teachings with Neta, as he had once studied them with his mother. He would also attend services with her. Each time the Rosen scroll was removed from the ark, each time it was held up to the congregation, each time it was placed on the bima and read from would serve as a reminder to Neta of her long and prestigious heritage. This spark of inspiration soon dimmed at the thought of having to face the Sontags. In the years since his defection from the yeshiva he had seen little of them, except for the occasional visit on the High Holy Days of Rosh Hashanah and Yom Kippur.

According to the legal agreement first drawn up by John, the Sontags had to consult him before making any decision concerning the Torah. Abe was still procrastinating over their request to place the Rosen Torah in the Chabad Student Center, where it would be a draw for young people. If he now turned down their appeal, those affiliated with the Center would feel that he had deprived them of the Torah. He hoped that if he explained his motive it would help to blunt their disapproval.

He called on Rabbi Sontag to forewarn him of his plans to move the Torah. Drawing his brows into a deep frown, the rabbi replied that it would be a great loss to Chabad. However, if Abe commissioned a new hand-written scroll for them, it would certainly help to rectify the situation. Before Abe could think of a reply to this outrageous request, the rabbi offered to appoint a scribe from the Holy Land to write a new Torah dedicated to the students at the university. Taken completely by surprise, Abe said he would need some time to think it over.

Looking directly at him, the rabbi said that they were considering him for the Thomas. B. Tenenbaum Award — named after a generous benefactor — and given to those who support the mission of Chabad to promote Judaism. Abe cringed inwardly; he wasn't a shining example of religious virtue, and it irked him to be bribed with an award he didn't deserve.

As if he could divine what Abe was thinking, the rabbi said to himself, *He won't be getting the "Torah scholar" and certainly no award for being pious, so what's wrong with receiving an honor for making a generous and significant gift to us?* Aloud he said, "It would be a great mitzvah to do this for us, Abe. And it would honor your family."

446

"Thank you rabbi, but I don't need a prize to do what is right. It's the memory of my late mother that should be honored. The gift of a Torah should be given in her name. As you and your family know, she was the one who led me back to Judaism."

The rabbi's breath caught in his throat as a wave of sympathy washed over him. Chastened at not having thought of paying tribute to Helen Rosen himself, he opened his mouth to say something to remedy his lack of tact but Abe, quickly ended the conversation by saying that he would consider his proposal but could make no promises.

Over the next few days he weighed his options. If he refused to commission a Torah, how could he keep to the moral high ground? The solution came from an unexpected source. George Fox had been in the process of transporting a Holocaust Torah to their synagogue in Oakland. The scroll was one of thousands saved from destruction at the hands of the Nazis during WW II and repaired by Westminster Synagogue in London. Now that Abe had made up his mind to house the Rosen Torah at their synagogue, Mr. Fox offered to donate his Holocaust scroll to the Chabad Center, thus freeing Abe from the obligation to commission a new Torah. Abe promptly agreed to the proposal with the proviso that he reimburse Mr. Fox for expenses and, most importantly, dedicate the Holocaust Torah as a gift in memory of his mother, Helen Rosen, which pleased Rabbi Sontag very much. This new twist allowed Abe to achieve his purpose, and to honor his mother in a way she would have found meaningful and loving.

Once the Rosen Torah had been installed at the Foxes' synagogue with all the proper ceremony, Abe began by teaching Neta how to read and write the Hebrew alphabet. At first he was impatient, having no realistic expectation of how rapidly an eight-year-old could learn. The first lessons were a disaster, and ended with Neta complaining that they were boring. Fortunately, a friend suggested that he make their sessions more fun by transforming the 22 letters of the Hebrew alphabet into people or objects associated with their shapes. Soon Abe had his daughter playing enthusiastically along with him. She wrote poems about the letters — the first of many she would compose over the years. From then on he kept devising interesting new ways to teach Neta.

After the first year, Abe found a more advanced program where instructors encouraged parents and children to study together on Sundays. His ex-wife couldn't legitimately object to this arrangement; secretly, however, Shelley was envious of the close new relationship between father and daughter. To counteract it, Shelley made a point of going with Neta to services, and to classes to prepare her for her Bat Mitzvah. Almost overnight, both parents began promoting a strong religious education. Still, God remained a source of puzzlement to the child. Abe had talked to her about her grandmother, Helen, and how she had studied the Torah in her search for a spiritual life. Neta wished she could have known her; she would have been the one who would have understood her.

When Neta turned eleven, the parents began to arrange for an extravagant Bat Mitzvah party. On the brink of becoming a woman, the preteen still looked like a child, her dark hair still fell to her waist, and her lips still formed a childish bow, but her boyish stride, the aggressive tilt of her jaw, and her level gaze, gave intimations of what she was yet to become.

When a year later, the special day of her Bat Mitzvah at last arrived, Neta chanted her portion from the venerable Rosen Torah forgetting about the congregation gazing up at her, praying with a wonderful sense of fulfillment. The Torah sang to her, she sang to it, and somehow its commandments seemed to reach across countless generations filling her with awe. There was such a haunting quality to Neta's chanting — as if she were listening for something beyond their hearing — that when she had concluded, gasps of admiration echoed around the sanctuary. For a moment she stood with her head bowed. When she looked up, her eyes shone, and an enigmatic smile played around her mouth.

Both parents felt more than rewarded for their efforts. The rabbi himself congratulated them, quoting, *Train up a child in the way she should go: and when she is old, she will not depart from it.* The compliant Bat Mitzvah girl left them unprepared for the rebellious teenager she was about to become.

On her fourteenth birthday, at the start of a new millennium, Neta sat at her dresser and examined herself in the mirror that had witnessed her transformation from a child to a young woman. She turned her face to one side then the other, sighing unhappily. The childish softness had given way to more angular features, in her opinion her chin jutted out too far, her nose was too long, her lips were too big, and her skin too dark. There and then she decided to change her look. She cut her hair and colored it green with Kool Aid, pulled it into two ponytails held in place by big, yellow plastic sunflowers, applied chalk-white face powder, scarlet lipstick, and black mascara. Without consulting either parent, she pierced her ears, nostrils, and navel and embellished them all with silver rings. She put on a scanty tank top that revealed her bare midriff, and short shorts that exposed the tops of her thighs. When Abe saw the transformation he literally gasped, then ordered his daughter to get rid of the outrageous attire.

He received only a dismissive shrug. "Dad, get real!"

"Don't play those games with me, young lady. I've provided you with everything, including a sound religious education. You know the difference between right and wrong, so why flaunt yourself like this."

"Okay, list three things you want me to change."

"You're in no position to bargain with me! Wash that garbage off your face, shampoo your hair, remove those rings, and change into regular clothing."

His daughter conceded this particular battle, but soon found that a better strategy was to play on his feelings of guilt. She accused her father of caring more about his work than about her, and there was just enough truth in this accusation to get results. At sixteen, when Abe offered to get her a reliable used car, she talked him into buying a new one. She argued that if he drove a Jaguar and Shelley a Mercedes, she should not have to endure secondhand wheels. Abe reluctantly agreed, with the proviso that she paid the hefty insurance premium out of her

449

own allowance; as she couldn't afford it, her ruse misfired. Neta protested that he was too strict, but she respected him for not giving in to her completely. The subject of dating created an even greater tension between them. Whenever her father inquired about boyfriends, she accused him of prying. Abe defended himself by declaring only half-teasingly that he wanted to make sure that the boys his daughter dated were good enough for his princess.

The tactic Neta deployed to manipulate her mother was to claim neglect. She accused Shelley of spending all her time being a do-gooder in public. "When I need you, you're too busy grandstanding for feminist causes. Is spending time with me too dull and boring?" Again, the nubbin of truth in this charge gave it potency.

In the years after the divorce, Shelley had worked her way up the corporate ladder to become a regional sales manager for a TV company's local affiliate. While she enjoyed the work, Shelley was furious when she discovered that her base salary was less than a man's salary with the same position in the company. She joined the National Organization for Women, worked hard in their local chapter, and gathered the information and resources she needed to prod her boss into a substantial raise.

When Neta scoffed at her mother's feminist zeal, she had replied. "If believing that both male and female workers should be treated with equal respect and given equal pay for equal work, makes me a feminist, then that's what I am."

The daughter wasn't prepared to concede anything to her mother, even if she was right.

"It's because women fought against chauvinist pigs that you have choices, young lady!" Shelley declared to drive her point home.

Neta shrugged and blew a strand of hair from her forehead but kept up the silent treatment.

"Also, can you tell me that a woman's reproductive rights are not worth fighting for?" Shelley pressed on, "You mean they shouldn't have the right to decide about contraception, or abortion?"

Neta tugged at a stray strand of hair. She was thinking of taking birth control pills so she could have sex—if she found some guy she liked. Still she did not condescend to reply.

Thoroughly frustrated, her mother forged ahead. "What about the way feminists have helped women take official positions in the synagogue formerly open only to men?"

Neta could keep silent no longer. "Don't have a cow, Mom! You know I've been working with the Jewish Youth Association so women can participate in everything, including reading the Torah. Not like the Ultra-Orthodox who separate women behind a barrier so they don't even have the chance to see the Torah, never mind read from it."

Now it was Shelley who saw an opening. "Orthodox women wouldn't approve of what your youth group is doing."

"Why would we willingly want to take second place to men?"

Shelley chortled in triumph. "So, you admit you're a feminist!"

Cornered, Neta came back with a non sequitur. "Don't worry, Mom, I'm not interested in men, anyway." To cover her embarrassment, she turned to a lie. "I just wish those boys would stop bugging me for dates." Actually, no one had asked her out. She marched out before Shelley could question her about those boys.

✥ 35 ✥

The Eighth Inheritor: Neta Rosen, the Aspiring Filmmaker

Do not judge your fellow human until you have managed to put yourself in his shoes.

Mishnah

In the slow alchemy of her summer before college, Neta began the process of transforming herself from an awkward, rebellious girl into a determined young woman. She lived in three parallel worlds: working at a local TV station where she had wrangled a job, socializing with friends who would soon be off to distant colleges, and retreating to the Shady Lady to commune with herself and the amazing spirit of her grandfather. Toward the end of summer, Shelley interrupted her daughter's pleasant state of suspended animation with a call from Japan where she was on a business trip.

Awakening her from a deep sleep, well after midnight, her mother announced that she was getting married to Hiroshi Hosada, the man she had been working with to market American television shows to Japan.

"Listen, I've got the most exciting plans for our wedding," Shelley rushed on. "Hiroshi and I want to be married in a Shinto shrine on top of a mountain near his family home. I'll fly back, and then we can travel together to Japan for the wedding. We want you to be there with us. It'll be a very special experience for you!"

Groaning as she ended the call, Neta marched into the kitchen and made a mug of hot chocolate. Turning on the TV, she plopped down on the couch, spilling the hot liquid onto her thighs in her agitation. She needed to talk to someone; without considering the ungodly hour, she called her father.

When Abe answered, she blurted out, "Oh my God, you won't believe what an insane thing Mom's going to do!"

"Let me guess," Abe said, sounding alert despite the hour. "She's found an alternative spiritual community we've never heard of?"

"Close. My mother is marrying some Japanese guy—I think he's a Buddhist. Anyway, they plan to get married in a Shinto temple on top of a mountain."

"Huh?"

"I tried to talk her out of it, but you know she doesn't listen."

"I guess she's become a JuBu." With sharp stab of regret, he thought back to the traditional wedding he and Shelley had shared with such hope and joy.

"A what?" his daughter insisted.

"Your mother's a JuBu. She maintains the religious practices and beliefs of Judaism, somehow coupling it with Buddhism and other Eastern religions."

"That's so weird!"

"Yeah, but we can't stop her from doing it or from getting married to anyone in any way she pleases, can we?"

"But she wants me to go with her to Japan."

"You don't have to go. But it could be interesting. Maybe it will inspire your poetry, and you could get great footage with that high definition video camera I gave you on your birthday." Ever since Abe had given Neta her first camcorder for her Bat Mitzvah, she had been making amateur movies. In high school she had even begun to flirt with the idea of a career as a filmmaker.

Barely a month after that telephone conversation, Neta and Shelley boarded the plane for Tokyo. Buckled in her seat, Neta's thoughts wavered between excitement and agitation.

453

Would the Shinto wedding, arranged with such haste, be creepy or exotic? Disrespect her family heritage, or recognize it in some way? Would she feel embarrassed or comfortable with her new Japanese family? Would Hiroshi be strange or normal, unfriendly or welcoming? By the time they touched down at the Narita International Airport, they had passed through nine time zones and gained a day, leaving Neta disoriented and sleep deprived.

As they exited customs, a barrel-chested man, ironed into an impeccable blue business suit, matching dress shirt and red silk tie, stepped forward and bowed. Shelley returned the bow, and introduced her daughter and her fiancé to one another. Then she impetuously hugged and kissed him.

Quickly disengaging himself, Hiroshi turned to his soon-to-be stepdaughter with a close-lipped smile. "Ah, so pleased to meet the beautiful daughter," he said, bowing formally again.

"Congratulations," Neta said with such faked congeniality that a bubble of saliva flew from her lips to Hiroshi's left cheekbone. Too polite to acknowledge this accident, he continued to bow and smile, later surreptitiously wiping his cheek with a spotless white handkerchief. Escorting them out of the terminal, he explained in good but heavily accented English that he had arranged for the two of them to spend the night in Tokyo at a five-star-hotel.

Morning came too soon, and Neta awoke to the unaccustomed smells of Japan—incense and steamed rice—still groggy and disoriented, not ready to make the journey Hiroshi had planned to Takamatsu, on the island of Shikoku, to meet his parents, the Hosadas.

Late that night, after a trip by bullet train and motor coach over the huge bridge to the island, Neta settled herself cross-legged on the woven straw tatami mat in the guest bedroom of the Hosada home. Yawning deeply, she opened her journal, and made her first entry:

August 3, 2010, Tokyo to Takamatsu

We arrived to find Hiroshi's parents waiting for us at Takamatsu station in their gleaming Honda hybrid. I don't get Hiroshi's parents, they bow and smile, but I sense their cold disapproval. Their house is wedged into a narrow alley of homes that are cloned from the exact same template. Inside, we sipped green tea from transparent porcelain bowls delicate as eggshells. Outside, an exquisite courtyard beckons:

Silver water spilling into a stone bowl
Scarlet maple leaves floating on the surface.
Yellow-as-egg-yolk ginkgo leaves
drifting down on emerald moss.
Letting myself fall, hover, glide
Living only for the present
Not caring about the heartless transience of life,
yet craving something more.

She woke the next morning to the indistinct burble of a foreign language. She felt more rested, yet the odd sense of detachment lingered. Before leaving the elder Hosadas, they made offerings of water, rice, salt, and wine and, on this special occasion, money to their *kami*, or household gods, to secure favor for the betrothed couple. After this Shinto ritual, the three climbed into the Honda, and waved goodbye to the parents, who had protested that they were too frail to undertake the long and arduous journey to a far off mountaintop.

Neta stayed aloof, doggedly nursing her resentment. Shelley took every opportunity to poke her daughter with her elbow and whisper threats and supplications to be friendly and to enjoy the trip. Despite Neta's determination to give her mother a hard time, the sunny day was so cheerful that she began to admire the vistas opening before her. Taking out her journal and squinting in the bright morning sun that fell across the page, she wrote:

455

August 4, 2010, Takamatsu City

The kamidana, or household shrine, stands like a miniature pagoda on a shelf inside the Hosada home. Paper lamps bathe the shrine in a gentle halo of light. Maybe it's disrespectful, but I couldn't help making some vague association between the Holy Ark bathed in the light of the eternal lamp. The Rosen Torah is a world away, yet I am tied to it by an umbilical cord.

Biting the end of her pen, she paused to gather her first impression of Japan into a poem.

Ripe persimmons
dangling from the trees
orange globes of autumn

Rice fields
swaying in the breeze
delicate rows of onion grass

Stone houses,
rising up the hillsides
gray steps into the sky

Slow streams
coursing through the valley
long green snakes

Rice stacks
drying in the fields
pyramids of golden straw

Rounded hillocks
reclining by the brook

breasts of Venus De Milo

Many people
scuttling to work on the bullet train
packed canned fish

Japan.

Around noon, they stopped at a roadside stall and dined on meaty udon noodles in a tasty broth, served in elegant lacquered bowls, along with steamed vegetables and green tea. Since meeting Hiroshi, Neta had kept up the silent treatment but he remained calm and smiling, seemingly immune to her sullen behavior. After the satisfying meal she relaxed and allowed her curiosity to take over.

"Is it customary for Japanese to get married at a shrine?" she inquired.

Hiroshi bowed slightly. "Hai! In Japan we celebrate weddings with a Shinto ceremony. The Shinto priest, or Kannushi, calls to our Japanese Gods to bring good luck. The couple take their vows by drinking sake three times."

"Is there someone who started Shinto? You know, like Moses, or Jesus, Buddha or Confucius?"

"Shinto is about the gods in nature, and how human beings are part of nature, there is no one sacred book, and no one prophet or god who has power over all. It's a very old belief and we do not know how it got started."

"You two sit and talk. I'm going to buy some postcards," Shelley said. Neta wasn't fooled by her mother's obvious ploy to leave her alone with Hiroshi.

She wanted to say that Shinto was a pagan religion, but with her mother gone she felt obliged to keep polite conversation going. "What does the bride wear?"

"She wears a white kimono with her hair done in the Japanese old style. You know, an up hair style, with beautiful ornaments and combs." He fluttered his hands above his head in imitation. "You can see traditional brides in Ukiyo-e paintings."

457

"Ukiyo-e paintings?"

"*Hai*. It means, floating world. Artist's intention is to remind us that life passes by quickly, so life is precious. Ukiyo-e are very beautiful. They show human feelings. You understand?"

"I think so." She took a sip of tea, and suddenly a thought popped into her head; she needed to ask her mother's fiancé, *Geez! Can't you include something of our traditions in your ceremony?* She hesitated, perhaps it was wrong of her, even rebellious, to insert Judaism into Shinto rituals. But surely her mother understood that this alien, pagan ceremony would be painful to her daughter. Was it too much too ask that she remember and honor her Jewish heritage?

Neta took another sip of tea. Opposite her she saw Hiroshi glance at his wristwatch. *He does not want me here. He has no interest in me. In his eyes I am the troublesome daughter,* she thought. He looked at his watch, again. *I am boring him. Well, then, here goes . . .*

"I have a request to make. I would like you to include the breaking of the glass ceremony that is an important part of our Jewish traditional wedding." She saw a fleeting grimace pass over his impassive face, but rushed on, "You see, this ancient custom reminds our people that even during a time of joy we should remember the tragic destruction of our Temple in Jerusalem. It also reminds us that life is short."

Hiroshi looked directly at her; she had finally caught his full attention.

At that moment her mother returned and noticed the strange smile on her daughter's face. "What's making you grin like the Cheshire cat?"

"That's for me to know and you to find out, Mom."

Back in the car, Neta settled back to watch the scenery float by. When they pulled into the parking bay in front of the *ryokan*, a Japanese combination of spa and guesthouse, the nearby mountaintops blazed in the sun's last fiery light. After checking in, Hiroshi suggested that they enjoy a traditional Japanese bath. Slipping on the *yukata*, a cotton kimono, and slippers provided by the inn, Neta went down to the bathhouse. She didn't know what protocol to follow, so taking her cue from the women she sponged and rinsed herself down thoroughly at the washing sinks, before wading into a deep, hot bath fed by a natural underground spring. She left feeling cleansed and relaxed, and despite the shared facility, it had somehow been a private experience.

Afterwards she joined Shelley and Hiroshi in the dining room, where, seated at low tables, they were served steamed rice, soup, seafood, and pickled vegetables, all in covered lacquerware bowls. Lifting one bowl then another, Neta gingerly, and with difficulty tried scooping morsels into her mouth with the chopsticks. The three ate in polite silence broken only by Shelley's intermittent chatter.

"Do you know that traditional Japanese pilgrims walk a route of about 1400 kilometers to travel the circuit of eighty-eight temples on this island? Can you imagine?" Shelley jabbed her chopsticks into what looked like octopus. As she lifted the piece toward her mouth, the sticks slipped and it squirted sideways onto the table.

"*Hai*, the Japanese have been doing pilgrimages for over a thousand years," Hiroshi added. Handling his chopsticks with effortless grace he appeared not to notice Shelley's awkwardness.

Neta giggled as her mother attempted to retrieve the octopus. "Gross, Mom. You're never going to make it as a geisha girl." She glanced sideways at Hiroshi and caught his look of disapproval, and was pleased she had gotten a reaction from him.

"Well," she said stridently, "do they have geisha girls in modern-day Japan?"

His eye's widened at her implied insult. He put down his chopsticks.

Shelley shook her head disapprovingly.

"Sorry, folks, I'm losing it." she apologized. "I need to get some shut-eye." Neta got up, bowed, and said, "*Ohayo gozaimasu*," inadvertently using the Japanese for good morning, instead of good night. Hiroshi rose, and to convey his disapproval gave a bow that was little more than a nod, while her mother glared at her as she walked out.

Neta chastised herself on her way to the room. *Okay, so my remark about geishas was rude! At least I didn't say my great grandfather invented the atomic bomb we dropped on his country.*

Back in her room she stretched out on her tatami mat and tried to relax. She admitted to herself that she was enjoying some parts of this trip, but the basic quarrel with her mother continued in her head. *Why did you bully me into coming to Japan? Why are your family and your tradition, your Jewishness, suddenly so unimportant to you? Why did you choose to marry someone so alien? I resent your new husband not being Jewish. Here we are paying respect to their Japanese ancestors, and turning our backs on our own.* She lay rigid, now forgetting the beauty of the countryside; the exquisite landscapes of Japan seemed less real than her anger.

Early the next morning, bleary-eyed from a fitful sleep, Neta shuffled to the balcony where she could view the sweep of the village down to the bay, and breathe the heady moisture-laden fragrance of mountain air. Despite the threat of rain, Shelley had insisted that they proceed to Kotohiragu Shrine, popularly called Kompari-san, where the priest would perform the marriage ceremony.

After careful consideration, Shelley had selected a stylish yellow-silk pants suit for herself, and had insisted that her daughter wear a matching blue one. The groom wore a dark sport coat with a white dress shirt open at the neck; once they reached the shrine he would put on a blue silk tie. For comfort, they all wore sneakers and carried more formal shoes, rain jackets and umbrellas. Neta brought along her video camera to record the wedding for absent family and friends.

Despite her grievances, Neta could feel her excitement rising as the little wedding party started the long climb to the top. Looming out of the mist were pagoda-like shrines and twisted pines encrusted with moss. The mist turned to drizzle, pooling in the hollows worn into the stone steps by legions of disciples. Resolute as ants, pilgrims in white cotton jackets and white hats

460

ascended to the Shrine dedicated to the god of the sea. Then the rain pelted down, and they ran for shelter under the eaves of a small pagoda. The pilgrims disappeared beneath black umbrellas, bobbing upward like a forest of marching mushrooms. A strange thought popped into her head: the world's great religions, like mushrooms, were born out of decay or corruption. Since her conversation at the roadside inn where they had lunched, she hadn't found the right moment to follow up on her request. *It's now or never she thought.* Fishing out a glass wrapped in paper towels, she said to her mother, "I've brought this for the breaking of the glass ceremony. I already asked Hiroshi about it."

He gave her a blank look, but her mother came to rigid attention. She knew her daughter well; she wasn't just asserting her will but being willful. If Hiroshi refused Neta's request she would spoil the happy occasion with her sullenness, yet if she conceded to her daughter, her fiancé might be offended. Still, if she encouraged Hiroshi to go along with her daughter, it could create a more harmonious atmosphere between all of them.

Reaching out, she took Hiroshi's hand in hers and said plaintively, "If it's possible, I would like that."

Neta held her breath, and when Hiroshi said, "Perhaps it can be arranged, but first I will need to consult with the Shinto priest waiting for us," she exhaled, and smiled for the first time.

They pressed on as soon as the rain let up, determined to reach the inner shrine at the top, before the next downpour. Two more steep flights brought them to the summit, gulping for air.

Neta heard her mother exclaim, "This is so beautiful! Thank you for bringing us here."

Hiroshi bowed and took Shelley's hand. His eyes were unnaturally bright in his smooth-as-ivory face. Seeing their happiness, Neta wanted to weep. Hope and hopelessness vied within her—the hope that someday she might find someone who looked at her that way, and despair at the odds against it.

They proceeded under the big red gate of Gonin-byasho, or Five People. Hiroshi dipped a bamboo ladle into a stone water basin, washed his hands, and bowed his head in prayer before entering the shrine. Shelley and Neta did likewise. Inside the shadows of the temple the spicy-sweet fragrance of sandalwood and incense perfumed the air. They gathered on a raised platform where the couple held a lengthy, whispered conference with the priest about the Jewish wedding ritual of breaking a glass.

At the commencement ceremony began, Neta started the video and caught the fleeting ritual electronically. Later, she recorded her feelings in her journal:

> I observed their wedding through the eye of my camera, but remained aloof, a voyeur. The Shinto priest performed the purification ceremony in his long red robe, shiny black hat, and lacquered clogs. Like a bad omen I sensed my grandparents' disapproving spirits hovering nearby. Their blood, dark with the tragic past, ran icily through my veins. I shivered and dug my fingernails into my palms. And a poem came to me:
>
> Poor forebears robbed of your sacred traditions,
> do not despair
> Generations to come will mingle
> their lifeblood without fear
> Banding people together
> in a shining multicolored coalition.
>
> With a stroke of my poem I attempted to persuade my ancestors to be more tolerant, but I'm hypocritical. The truth is, I do not want to abandon my heritage. So I made a solemn vow to be married by a rabbi in a traditional Jewish wedding, when and if the right one comes along. As these thoughts ran through my mind, Shelley and Hiroshi recited their vows, sipped sake three times, and placed rings on one another's fingers. Then Hiroshi stamped his foot down on the glass, and over the muffled shattering, I shouted, "Mazel Tov!" The priest chimed right in with a "Mazel Tov." I swear,

I nearly laughed out loud in surprise. What a rush! Then in a heartbeat it was over. They are husband and wife, bound together by a "purification" ritual administered by a strange priest and presided over by alien gods. Still, thanks to me, we included just a little of our own traditions—even if it was out of place.

When the nuptials were over, the three began the long descent down the mountain each captured by their own thoughts and emotions. At the ryokan, they bathed to ease their aching muscles, then gathered in Neta's room to view the unedited video of their marriage ceremony that Neta wanted them to have as a gift.

After the screen went blank, and Shelley exclaimed, "Wow! I love it!" Neta realized that she had been holding her breath.

"Your video is as beautiful and as sensitive as an Ukiyo-e painting, I will treasure it," Hiroshi said, bowing deeply.

Tears sprang to Neta's eyes; all she could manage was a strangled thank you. Now, still high on the mountain air, her emotions raw, she found herself deeply moved by his affirmation of her talent. Yet the extreme close-up shots of the faces—the priest's too solemn weary countenance, her mother's too wide-open smiling mouth and scarlet lips, Hiroshi's too shrewd almond eyes and tiny ears—she had intended to be more mocking than approving. Had she unintentionally paid homage to the spiritual symbolism of the ceremony? Had it touched her in some way despite her disapproval? Or had Hiroshi and Shelley simply projected their own feelings into it?

After the married couple left, Neta closed her eyes, but the extraordinary events of the past few days kept replaying in her head. Hours later a violent storm woke her from a restless doze to a strange high-pitched vibration. She lay listening to the wind shrieking. Neta snapped on the lamp, took a deep breath, then rushed to the bathroom wincing as her bare feet touched the cold tiles. As she lay back on the mat, she heard her mother's muffled voice calling her.

She opened the door and saw the newlyweds bundled in their yakutas standing in a shaft of light projected from a wall sconce. "The storm woke us. We wanted to make sure you were okay, it sounds like a cyclone is brewing."

"No, I'm not okay. Oh, I wish I hadn't come on this trip," Neta whined. The resentment she had been nursing boiling to the surface.

There was a visible struggle on Shelley's face. "What's upset you, sweetheart?"

"Oh, don't be so damned insensitive."

"About what?"

Neta had baited the hook, and her mother had swallowed it. "Since we arrived in Japan have you shown any respect for our family's traditions? Have you given any thought to how bad it makes me feel to see you married into another religion? You taught me the importance of our heritage. You even studied the Torah with me! But now you've turned away from it."

They glared at each other; then Shelley blinked and opened her arms wide. "Oh, sweetheart, you're just frightened and overwhelmed. I haven't converted to another religion. I'm still a Jew and will always be! We even included the breaking of the glass!" She leaned forward and whispered into her daughter's ear, "When we return to America we will have a second wedding with a traditional Jewish ceremony. Now give your mother a big hug."

Neta wanted to fall into her mother's arms, but anger and skepticism held her back. "I'm not a child," she said loudly, feeling the needles pricking her eyes.

"Then don't behave like one."

Just then a man poked his head into the corridor, looked at them with raised eyebrows, and said something in Japanese. Embarrassed, Hiroshi tightened the belt of his yakuta around his waist, bowed, and said something in an apologetic tone. Taking Shelley's elbow, he steered her to their room next door. As Hiroshi fumbled at the lock she heard her mother say, "Please don't take offense. My daughter's just very tired and overexcited."

"She is young, and the young must have their say," she heard him murmur.

How could he understand when he knows nothing about Judaism, or about my family? Neta thought.

Although the anger inside her had been released by the emotional outburst, she slept poorly. At daybreak she slipped outside, camera in hand, and strolled down the hill to the bay. The cyclone had passed on, leaving clouds, white and plump as chrysanthemums, hovering low over jade water; exotic remnants of its power. People began drifting by, but no one acknowledged her presence, not even the scruffy dogs. She wanted to be greeted and to return the greeting, to feel connected to the world around her. She had to suppress the urge to dance and shout, to make faces just to attract attention. To divert this crazy impulse, Neta began recording the place and its people. Behind the lens, the feeling of being invisible, of being nothing but a disembodied eye, continued to dog her as it had for the entire trip.

The next day she returned to Tokyo to board a plane for the long flight to New Orleans. After blowing up at her mother and insulting Hiroshi, Neta was relieved to be leaving the honeymooners to their peculiar bliss. It was time to begin college, to embark upon her future. It was time to find out who she was, on her own.

ঔ 36 ঙ

The Torah Continues its Odyssey

The Torah wants to circle the bima, and since it cannot do this, a Jew becomes its "feet," transporting the Torah around the reading table, just as feet transport the head.

Rabbi Yosef Yitzchak of Chabad-Lubavitch

Neta had chosen Tulane University, in New Orleans on the opposite side of the country, partly because she longed to get away from home. Another advantage was Tulane's location in the South, which would provide the opportunity to explore her Southern roots. There, her great-great grandfather, Aaron the jazz musician and black sheep of the family, had played an authentic part in the local music scene, and in the evolution of jazz. His father, Yakov the baker, had emigrated from Valinsk, Lithuania and settled in nearby Ricksburg, Alabama. Members of the Snyder family still lived in not-too-far-away Atlanta, Georgia; she hoped to visit them and to absorb something of their experiences; to learn more about this branch of the Rosen family.

It had not been easy to persuade her parents, after the devastation of New Orleans by Hurricane Katrina, that she had made a good choice. They toured the campus to see for themselves that the university, located uptown, had been spared major damage. The French Quarter and trendy shopping malls, places where the students liked to flock, were reopened for business. In addition, much of the city's basic character and infrastructure had been restored, although, regrettably, many lower lying and poorer neighborhoods had not. Most important,

466

a full offering of classes had resumed. There was also a thriving Hillel, the campus organization for Jewish students.

Arriving in New Orleans directly from Japan, Neta could not have felt more disoriented. The afternoon sun blazed down from a brassy sky and the humidity smacked her like a wet mop. She wanted a cold shower to wash away the discomfort and the grime of travel and the confusion of her last few days. The campus, abuzz with fresh-looking, excited students, made her acutely aware of the sorry state she was in, and rekindled the feeling of alienation that had dogged her in Japan. She stood on the edge of the quadrangle, suitcase in hand, watching students surge about, hooting at one another like kids at play. After getting directions to her residence, she trudged across campus to a new concrete structure, said to be hurricane proof, which was to be her home.

Over the ensuing weeks, Neta acted like one who has no time to waste. First she registered for required classes toward a degree in film and cinema studies, focusing on the history, development, theory, and criticism of the film and video arts, and the basic principles of moviemaking and production. Then she joined several organizations and threw herself into extramural activities. These included Hillel and the campus newspaper. Purposefully, step-by-step, she began to build a network of people and accomplishments that would win her the approval she hungrily sought.

She volunteered to serve on the Hillel Student Board, where she participated in planning Shabbat services, dinners, holiday celebrations, and special events. She was especially drawn to working with the Jewish Women's Collective that invited speakers to discuss topics focused on feminism and Judaism. Like a dog digging for hidden bones, the deeper she dug the more empowered she felt.

On the student newspaper she was assigned to work under the assistant editor of the reviews section, a junior named Jay Lockhart. She impressed Jay with her willingness to do mundane as well as more complex tasks and to complete them before deadline. When she asked for more challenging work,

467

however, he became evasive, saying that when something came along he would let her know. Neta quickly saw that she could do a better job than Jay, but she hid her frustration as she waited for her chance.

It came when Jay's father took ill and he had to leave suddenly. The ambitious freshman immediately volunteered to take over his assignments, which very much pleased the editor. She did an excellent piece reviewing a play on gay issues in such an engagingly in-your-face way that when Jay returned two weeks later, the outpouring of student responses, positive and negative, made it impossible to remove her. Without a shot being fired, she had seized the best assignments while he was now given lesser projects. Jay knew that Neta had cleverly manipulated the situation to her advantage, but there was little he could do. Besides, she was not willing to back down to soothe his ego, feeling that she had the greater talent and worked harder.

Jay had not let go easily. During one argument he called her a "scheming bitch." Her heart pounding, she retorted, "Trashing me isn't going to help you get ahead. You need to improve your writing skills." Then, with a forced smile, she added, "I'll be happy to help edit your work." Her rival turned white with rage, and for a moment she thought he was going to strike her. Instead, he resigned from the paper, and Neta gained a reputation as someone not to be trifled with.

In the first week of December, Abe scheduled a visit to his daughter, timing it so that it wouldn't interfere with her studying for the-end-of semester exams. Neta noticed how gaunt and tired he looked beneath his suntan and expensive clothing. She knew that her father's business ventures had come perilously close to failing; he had succeeded in rescuing them and even assembling a business empire. His success had come at a high cost. He remained single, and his relationships with women did not last. Neta was appalled by the way he lived alone in a crumbling, sparsely furnished mansion in Palo Alto, California that he hadn't troubled to restore.

She proudly introduced him to her friends on the campus, and then they attended Hillel services conducted by Rabbi Yossi Feinbaum. The rabbi greeted Abe warmly and conveyed in glowing terms how impressed he was with his daughter's energy and commitment. He made a special point of telling Abe that Hillel had no Torah of its own, that he had to borrow one to carry back and forth. Abe guessed that his daughter had been bragging about the Rosen Torah, and its connection to her family in the South. However, he decided not to take the bait.

Just before his return to California, the rabbi paid him a visit. This time he did not mince words; he asked Abe as the inheritor, if he would consider housing their family Torah at Hillel. "We feel that the Torah would be given special homage here and would be used weekly," he reassured Abe.

"Rabbi Feinbaum, our Torah is over two hundred years old, an irreplaceable inheritance. I don't think that college students are the most reliable stewards. And New Orleans is prone to hurricanes."

The rabbi nodded to show that he understood. When he closed his eyes he could still see the Torah scrolls recovered from Congregation Knesseth Israel, the Orthodox synagogue, two days after Hurricane Katrina. When the rescue workers brought them out in a boat, the scrolls were blackened and soaked in toxic water.

"Mr. Rosen, we learned our lesson after Katrina. Believe me, I would take every precaution to ensure that your Torah is safe even in the face of another hurricane. I will make it my personal responsibility to see that it is handled with care and with reverence."

"One other consideration— for most of its history our Torah has resided in Orthodox synagogues."

"You have a point, but times have changed. Think how it would inspire our students, in particular the women, to have a Torah, especially such a wonderful Torah as yours."

"Let me think this over," he told the rabbi.

That evening Abe invited his daughter out for dinner in the French Quarter. Until that night, he had been too busy and too preoccupied, and Neta had been too young for him to talk at length about his early life and its difficulties: his harassment as a little kid in Susmook, his mother's free-spirited practice of Judaism, her insistence on religious tolerance that had brought on a wave of anti-Semitism, his humiliation in middle school when he dressed like a hippie, his being branded gay, his grief at his mother's untimely death, his misery at Yeshiva University, his loss of faith after the visit to Lithuania. Now he felt the urge to explain those formative years to his daughter; despite his success he was lonely and needed to reach out to someone who loved him. As he talked, he released emotions bottled deep inside him for years. She listened to his extraordinary extended confession and understood for the first time all the despair and rage her father had experienced, and how it had all served a purpose — toughening him to surmount obstacles. After hearing his tale, Neta looked at her father with different eyes. He had suffered more than she could have guessed. Beneath the driving ambition, he had hidden his tender heart from the world.

She leaned over and kissed him on the forehead, "Thank you for sharing your story with me Dad. I will treasure it forever." She was gratified that he had allowed her to see his fundamental and caring self — not just the brilliant entrepreneur driven to succeed — and moved by his courage to expose his deepest emotions. Yet there was one thing he had not revealed that would play havoc with their relationship: the scar left by mistakenly being branded as gay.

"Thank you for accepting your old dad, warts and all." Abe said, massaging his temples, before going on. "Do you know why I placed the Torah in Congregation Beth Jacob after your mother and I divorced?"

Neta leaned forward to catch every word.

"You see, although I personally lost faith in a benevolent God who watches over each one of us individually, I wanted you to have a strong sense of belonging to a family and a tradition. The Rosen Torah is your link to me, to our lineage, our history, and our people."

"Dad, you know sometimes I pretended not to care, just to get back at you. But having this special heritage has been so important to me."

He turned away, but not before his daughter saw the tears gleaming in his eyes.

The one sour note in their evening came when Abe, yet again, asked his daughter if she had a boyfriend, and she snapped at him in real anger. The source of her resentment was as much her own confusion as her wish for privacy. Neta had dated a few men, but their advances always turned her off. She kept hoping that someone would fulfill her desire for an intimate relationship, but so far it hadn't happened, and she didn't know the reason why.

Seeing the hurt on her father's face, she added, "You know I hate it when you pry into my love life. Besides, what with classes, the newspaper, and Hillel, I haven't got much time to play. I've become a workaholic like you!"

Love tinged with regret spilled inside him. "Neta, I want only the best for you!"

After their intimate conversation Abe flew home feeling more relaxed and happier than he had in a long time. Nevertheless, he was keenly aware that the unresolved issue of their scroll could disrupt the new rapport between them. Before leaving for the airport, Neta had made a point of letting him know how much the loan would mean to her and to the students, adding that it would boost attendance at services, and he would be doing a great mitzvah.

There was no doubt in Abe's mind, however, that their legacy was safer at the Foxes' synagogue. When he sent Neta an e-mail listing his concerns, she replied that Hillel would benefit far more from the presence of their wonderful Torah than her grandparents' congregation, which already possessed other beautiful scrolls. In her opinion he was being overly possessive. The e-mails went back and forth, and with each one she became more adamant. Abe wasn't easily swayed knowing that his headstrong daughter was manipulating him despite his serious qualms.

After weeks of "negotiation" Neta resorted to the one tactic that upset him most; she deliberately ignored him, refusing to answer his e-mails, phone calls, or text messages. Finally he left a voice message saying that he had reconsidered, and had made the decision to transfer the Rosen Torah to Hillel.

Abe's electronic ring tone, *tum, tum, de, dee,* went off in the midst of a business meeting.

"Hi, it's me, Dad. Do you really mean it?"

"Sure, I do."

"Wow, that's great! When will you bring the Torah to us?"

"I'll try to reschedule my meetings. I have to be at the big electronics show in Las Vegas, and then head to Tokyo." The dozen employees around the conference table sat at attention waiting for their boss's instruction.

"Dad, stop making excuses."

"I'm not. Will you check with Rabbi Feinbaum if the end of this month would be okay?" Then before she could respond he added, "Wait, cancel that. I think it would be better if I talked to him first."

"But I . . ."

The connection was lost. For once, the minor glitches of the wireless age had worked to his advantage.

Abe had intended to inform Rabbi Milton Adler at the Foxes' synagogue of his plan to remove the Rosen Torah. Before he could find the time to do so, he received a distressing call from the rabbi. With mounting pain he listened to the shocking news. There had been a theft at the synagogue; all seven Torahs residing in the Holy Ark, including Abe's, had been stripped of their silver ornamentation — finials, breastplates, and pointers.

To comfort him, the rabbi reflected, "It is possibly one of the ironies of spiritual life that our most sacred artifact is constructed, not from rare metals or precious stones, but from the commonest of materials. Your scroll is unharmed. Although robbed of all its accessories it is as holy as before."

The rabbi's words afforded Abe meager solace. His deep-seated emotional attachment to this most cherished heirloom, and

472

his responsibility to preserve it made the loss much worse than the robbery of any material object.

The larceny heightened Abe's concern about transferring the Rosen Torah. He called Neta with the bad news only to hear her lament, "Dad, I can't believe this happened! Our Torah won't be the same without its beautiful adornments."

"If you feel that way, perhaps I shouldn't bring it to Tulane."

"Don't you dare go back on your promise," his daughter quickly retorted.

Abe accompanied the unadorned Torah on its flight across the country to his daughter's school. The journey turned into an unanticipated adventure. A sefer Torah must travel as hand luggage to prevent damage and to show proper respect, and this caused problems with airline security. As he approached the checkpoint holding the Torah wrapped in a tallis, the guards suspected him of being a terrorist with a double-barreled gun! Abe and the Torah were immediately taken aside for a body scan. As the mechanism scrutinized him, he tensed up, then thought: *what am I afraid of? It's just x-ray images. I don't have anything to hide, so what's the problem? I'd rather they take extra precautions than be blown out of the sky by terrorists.* Then he thought wryly, *Maybe they can develop a scan that looks at a person's thoughts. Now that would really be interesting.*

When the Torah itself was x-rayed, Abe implored them to be careful. After a lengthy interrogation, he was finally cleared to board the plane. Humbled but relieved, he placed the Torah on the seat next to him — for which he had been required to purchase a second ticket — and breathed a sigh of reprieve.

The plane banked steeply, and they were soon up through the clouds where the sun shot shafts of sunlight through the fisheye cabin windows, then leveled off heading east. Surrounded by the steady drone of the engines, Abe reflected on the marvelous odyssey of his Torah: from Jerusalem where it was created, to a shtetl in Lithuania on the back of a donkey; from Lithuania across the Atlantic to New York City aboard a steamship; from New York to Alabama on a train; from Alabama to Georgia via automobile, and from the Deep South to the West Coast aboard an airplane. Now it was returning to the South, winging its way high above the Rocky Mountains, to New Orleans.

As its most recent inheritor, he had made a series of decisions altering its destiny: moving it from the Shady Lady's barn to the Sontags' shul, then to the Foxes' synagogue, Congregation Beth Jacob, in Oakland. Now it was on a yet another voyage. By relinquishing the Rosen legacy to his daughter and Rabbi Feinbaum he hoped that he was not abdicating his own responsibility; but Neta revered their Torah in a way he never could. Would this be the scroll's final destination? Was it destined to keep following its inheritors on their disparate journeys? Could their scroll survive the vicissitudes of fate? Before he could entertain further reflections, Abe nodded off.

Before Saturday evening service prior to sundown, Rabbi Feinbaum and a procession of students, led by Neta, carried the Torah across campus to the sanctuary at Hillel House. When everyone was seated in the sanctuary, the rabbi gestured for Abe to place the scroll on the reading table.

Turning to the students he made a short but heartfelt dedication. "We thank the Rosens for this sefer Torah that now comes to light up our lives. We consider it a sacred treasure. We pray that we may be worthy of the long history that this scroll represents. May each of us deepen our commitment to a life of Torah, living lives that bring honor to the Jewish people and advance the cause of peace and justice in the world."

The girls began to weep quietly. A pretty girl with intelligent brown eyes sobbed out loud. Neta introduced her friend, "Dad, I want you to meet Greta Benjamin. She's from the Chabad synagogue in Newark, New Jersey. She's in her sophomore year and plans to major in architecture."

"Pleased to meet you," the young woman said, dabbing at her tears. Unaccustomed to such public emotion, Abe felt awkward.

"What's upset you, Greta?" Neta asked gently.

"Can I please touch the edge of the Torah with my *siddur*?"

"Sure," Abe said, smiling.

"My family is ultra-Orthodox. I was never allowed to touch a Torah . . . except when I was a small child with my father in the men's section." Her voice choked up with emotion.

Abe wondered how on earth this timid young woman had persuaded her ultra-Orthodox parents to allow her to attend a college so far from her home.

Neta reached over and quietly, without drama, put her arms around Greta.

"Sorry to make so much fuss," Greta apologized.

Seeing the students gather strength from the Rosen Torah evoked such poignant recollections of his mother during her last illness that Abe almost broke down himself. The Torah's current sanctuary would have shocked his ancestors; certainly they would have disapproved. But, Abe thought, *it is inspiring these young women, and this is in keeping with the times.*

As if reading his thoughts the rabbi said, "In Orthodox synagogues woman still sit behind a divider, which separates them from the men and prevents them from getting near the Torah. But don't you think it's good that women's prayer and study groups are now established, and women are reading the Torah at their services?"

The girls hugged Abe and thanked him for sharing his precious inheritance with them. He observed how much his daughter enjoyed being the center of attention. It concerned him that despite being bright and competent, Neta was still insecure, always seeking the limelight; he hoped she would outgrow it.

At the conclusion of the Sabbath dinner, Rabbi Feinbaum asked everyone to stand as he proposed a toast to Abe and his daughter. "Once again I would like to thank the Rosens. Be assured that with us the Torah will be honored and kept safe. With us it will continue to change lives and deepen the meaning of modern Judaism. L'Chaim."

"L'Chaim!" they chorused, clinking their glasses.

Before Abe's departure on Sunday the rabbi called. "I just wanted to thank you for bringing your scroll to us. You have done a wonderful mitzvah. If you would like, there is one more mitzvah you can perform."

"What might that be?"

"You may have noticed the ink has become flaky or faded in several places. You know that it doesn't permeate the parchment; it sits on top. If a piece of ink breaks off, it can change the meaning of the word. Also, every Jew is commanded to write a Torah. This mitzvah can be achieved by filling in a single letter outlined by a Torah scribe."

"Yes, I know," Abe said.

"Torahs should be koshered regularly to keep them in good repair. With your permission and the help of a scribe, we will take off and redo however many letters we need to. Every Hillel student will have the opportunity and honor of fulfilling this mitzvah by inking in letters outlined by the scribe," the rabbi explained.

"Go ahead and arrange it. I will pay the cost," he said, well satisfied that his mission had been accomplished without a hitch.

❧ 37 ❧

Neta's Grand Vision

Neta knew immediately that her documentary would center on the Rosen Torah, connecting the past, present, and future like a golden chain.

Neta Rosen

Soon after the scroll arrived at Tulane, Neta began to work in earnest on a project for her movie-making class titled *Searching for Family Roots,* pouring all her energy and her aspirations into it.

On the flight back from Japan, she had mulled over Hiroshi's compliment on the beauty and integrity of her video. The trip had an unintended consequence; it fueled her desire to become a professional filmmaker, making it stronger and more real. She dared to believe that this project would be the start of her career; that one day she would make socially conscious documentaries that would cause people to laugh and to cry, to change something inside them, forever. More than that, if she were honest with herself, she wanted to be acclaimed and courted by an adoring public.

Her instructor at the university, Professor Berger, required students to pair up for these assignments, and Greta, with whom Neta had developed a close friendship, seemed a natural choice. The professor advised the students not to start shooting until they had laid down a strong story line. Neta knew immediately that the theme would center on the Rosen Torah, connecting the past, present, and future like a golden chain.

Exactly how she would dramatize this concept with moving images remained unclear, indistinct, a mirage. Yet Shmuel Rosen, their larger-than-life patriarch, whose vision had touched the lives of his progeny, rooted itself in her mind.

In the evenings, Neta met Greta at the Pickle Barrel, their favorite kosher deli, to brainstorm.

"The calligraphy of the Rosen Torah is so fabulous, so eloquent. I want to show it in the movie. Before I knew how to read Hebrew, the letters looked like flickering flames to me. When we went to synagogue I gazed at them in the prayer book, absolutely enchanted. Some burned high, and some low. Other looked like sparks, and others like full flames. They seemed to fly off the pages right into my heart, igniting it with whispered secrets," Neta enthused.

"The Hebrew letters remind me of the Chinese characters that I drew in a calligraphy class I took last summer," her partner reflected solemnly.

"How so?"

"Our instructor taught us that to form perfect characters our *chi* must flow from our minds and hearts into our hands, through the brush, and into each stroke."

"Wow, that's incredible!" Their sandwiches arrived, handed off by a waitress hurrying between tables. "And another thing that's incredible is how the Rosen Torah has survived for so many generations."

Greta nodded enthusiastically. "All these thoughts are awesome, but how can we project them in a movie?"

"I want to bring out the long, unceasing flow of time, the contrast of darkness and light, pain and pleasure, and good and evil that is a part of every family's history," Neta mused. "I know that's kind of abstract, but I really want to show how good does, somehow, prevail over evil and indifference."

"Mmm, that's deep. We really do have a challenge. I don't think you'll be allowed to make a video of the Torah, that's our first problem."

"It's not going to be easy, that's for sure. Last week, when I was talking to Rabbi Feinbaum about fund raising for Hillel, I kind of hinted at the idea of capturing our Rosen Torah on video for Professor Berger's project."

"So, what did he say?"

"He got very nervous and upset, and went on about his great responsibility for keeping the scroll safe."

"I hope you didn't arouse his suspicions?"

"No, I agreed with him. Then I dropped the subject. But I'll have to think of a way."

"Be careful, Neta. This could get you in big trouble."

"Don't worry, I'll have everything under control."

"Okay. But how will you represent your ancestors? Do you know much about them?"

"Not that much. But my dad has stacks of family photo albums I could use, and my cousins in Atlanta also have documents and photos." Greta's questioning made Neta uneasy because she knew only fragments of her history.

There was a lull in their chatter as they turned over ideas in their heads. Greta's eyes were alight with excitement, and Neta realized how much she enjoyed sharing this adventure with her. At that moment Neta felt her booted foot gripped between Greta's old sneakers. She did not pull away, although she saw the blush on Greta's face spreading down her neck.

"We have to find a way to bring my family to life!" Now it was Neta who reached out, taking Greta's hand in hers. "I'm not aiming for realism. I want to evoke the spiritual essence of the Rosens and their Torah." She took a deep breath like a swimmer coming up for air. "I'm not sure how, but I know I can do it. I want to link the past to the present. I mean the *spiritual* link between the past and the present. In our family that link is our scroll." She paused, "And Greta, I'm so glad that you are my partner in putting it all together."

"Wow, it's like you really have a mission to create this!" Greta pressed Neta's hand to her lips and kissed it.

That night the aspiring filmmaker dreamed she was swimming in a deep, green lake . . .

She dives underwater and, looking up, sees Greta's naked body cutting through the gloom as gracefully as a mermaid.

Overcome by desire, she rises to the surface just as Greta emerges, iridescent water streaming from her skin and beading on the mound of her pubic hair.

She awoke alive with excitement and confusion, awash with dream-spun desire. She had loved the touch of Greta's lips and desired more. Something she had been denying was pushing its way to the surface, but she wasn't ready to talk to anyone about it—especially to Greta.

Despite her bravado, Neta could not come up with a satisfying approach to their documentary, no matter how many ideas she turned over in her mind, and worst yet, the deadline for completion of the project was nearing. Then, at a flea market near the Old Quarter, it came to her. While browsing through dusty sheets of music she was reminded of her great-great-grandfather Aaron, the jazz musician. She turned the pages this way and that to catch the light. As she did so, she could not help noticing the similarity of the notes dancing on the page to the calligraphy of the Torah. They appeared to march, to run, and even to flutter as if in a breeze, creating works of deep resonance. She now had her vision.

The movie would unfold as a montage, building layer upon layer to give depth and emotion to it. In the background she would show the Torah continuously unfurling to the accompaniment of music, while in the foreground superimposed on the scroll would appear her ancestors, each one in the appropriate setting. Shmuel in a Lithuanian shtetl, Yakov at Castle Clinton, Aaron in New Orleans, Abraham at Los Alamos, and so on, to the present time; connecting each and every ancestor to her, and to each other. For their history was integrally interwoven with their prized Torah, and through it to all of humanity—even to eternity.

Over the next seventy-two hours, driven by a frenzy of inspiration, Neta wrote out the script. She told Greta, "It feels like I have been waiting my whole life to make this. I'm so fired up I can't sleep."

On Friday night before sunset, the Hillel students ushered in the Sabbath with the lighting of candles. As the sun slipped into the Mississippi, gilding the muddy water with liquid fire, she prayed that her scheme would work without a hitch—and her grand vision would be realized.

To execute her plan she hid in the women's restroom, leaving the door slightly ajar, until the lights went off and she heard a sharp click as the rabbi locked the front door behind him. Trembling with fear and excitement she made her way to the sanctuary by the eerie, milky moonlight filtering through the high windows. Gradually her eyes adjusted to the gloom and as if watching an old-fashioned Polaroid picture developing, objects in the sanctuary emerged first in broad outline and then in detail. Her heart hammered against her chest, her mouth was dry and bitter tasting, but she steeled herself to do the deed. She told herself, *No one will ever discover what I am about to do. I will return the Torah long before its absence is noticed.* Murmuring a prayer, she lifted her legacy from the ark, and swiftly carried it down the aisle.

Locking the door but unable to deadbolt it without a key, she ran to where Greta was waiting in the car with its engine running. Placing the Torah on the back seat, and covering it with a blanket, she ordered her accomplice to get going. The moon, high in the heavens, followed them like a malevolent half-shut eye. When they reached home, they pulled on surgical gloves and carefully unrolled the scroll onto a silk prayer shawl spread over the newly scrubbed kitchen table.

"Perfect!" Neta exclaimed, standing back to admire her tableau. The lights Greta had set up for the shoot gave off so much heat that her hands inside surgical gloves were wet with perspiration.

"Maybe we should dim the lights," Greta said, biting her lower lip nervously.

"Okay. Douse one of them, but bring the other one a little closer."

"I'm worried that . . ."

"Keep your cool!" Neta cut her short. "I told you, I'm on fire, I've waited all my life for this! The Rosen scroll has survived for over two hundred years, it'll survive this." She pressed the

481

Record button then slowly began scanning from right to left, starting at the top, to simulate eyes reading a page of Hebrew. For the next thirty minutes or so, with the lights blazing, Greta unrolled the scroll section by section, while Neta recorded sufficient footage to edit and assemble the documentary.

When they paused for a break, she told Greta, "I want the last sequence to be a close-up of the scroll being rolled onto the posts. Ready?"

Greta began to roll up the scroll, but as she did so, her dark and distorted shadow fell over it. Neta moved the light closer and adjusted the angle. Under the intense heat, the silk shawl began to smoulder. Before the petrified girls could react, orange sparks leaped from the shawl toward the open scroll, setting the parchment on fire. Lunging forward with a shriek, Neta grabbed a blanket to smother the flames.

The following Friday night, Neta gathered with the students to welcome in the Sabbath at Hillel House, as usual, but nothing felt ordinary to her. Neta's hands still throbbed from burns she had sustained in the accident. She could feel her heart racing and hear herself hyperventilating. When Rabbi Feinbaum opened the ark to remove the Rosen Torah, his face went rigid, and his tongue seemed stapled to the roof of his mouth. *That explains the unlocked deadbolt*, the rabbi thought, feeling sick with dread.

As if from a great distance she heard Rabbi Feinbaum wailing, "The Rosen Torah has been stolen!"

She froze, rooted to the spot, head bowed, hands clenched against the pit of her stomach, her shoulders shaking with silent sobs. The rest of that awful night passed in a blur of giving statements to the police, fruitless searches and phone calls. Neta first made an anguished call to her father and told him that the Torah had been stolen, and then tried to reach her mother in Japan with Hiroshi, but she didn't answer so she hung up.

The next day, sick with apprehension and lack of sleep, she and Greta sat in the cafeteria picking at their food. When Neta's cell phone rang she wondered anxiously who could be calling to probe her.

"I want to know what's going on at Tulane," her mother demanded without preamble.

The blood drained from her head and her limbs grew heavy. "I . . . I thought you and Hiroshi were at the shrine . . . at a retreat in Japan," Neta said weakly.

Shelley replied that as soon as she had heard the bad news from Abe, she had called. Neta pressed her hand to her chest as if she could stop her heart's hard thumping, and said in a flat tone, "Greta and I have done nothing wrong."

There was a pregnant silence in which she had ample time to visualize the puzzled look on her mother's face before she asked, "What has Greta got to do with the disappearance of the Torah?"

To throw her mother off guard, Neta started to say something deliberately sassy — something to the effect that her mother was more concerned with the whereabouts of an ancient artifact than with the wellbeing of her living, breathing daughter. Before she could, her mother cut her short.

"I'm booking a flight as soon as I get off the phone. I'll be in New Orleans tomorrow. I'll take a taxi to Tulane. I should be there by late afternoon. We can talk then." Then she hung up.

Out of the corner of her eye Neta saw that her collaborator, who had been listening intently, was waiting to hear what had transpired. She flipped her cell phone off, leaned over and said in a hoarse whisper, "Promise me, when my mother arrives tomorrow you mustn't tell her, or anyone else a thing. We will, when the time is right. Trust me."

"I promise," Greta whispered unhappily.

Shelley arrived the next morning, the smell of incense and sandalwood still on her skin, a paler, calmer version of herself from days spent at the shrine.

Neta had a late class to attend, leaving Shelley to wait until dinnertime to talk with her daughter. They met at a place Neta had chosen, near campus that served pizza and beer. When they arrived, it was crowded with students dressed in deceivingly expensive "shabby chic" garb — chattering, laughing, flirting, guzzling down food and drink — and launched on the outward-bound adventure of their lives. Over pizza with anchovies that Neta loved, Shelley inquired about her courses, her professors, and her friends, but it was hard to talk over the noise. Like a tigress watching her cub, Shelley observed her daughter; she looked pale and overwrought, but there was a spark in her eyes, a quiver in her voice she hadn't noticed before.

Only when they were walking back to the dorm, did Shelley approach the disappearance of the Torah. Neta protested, "Please back off, Ma. I'm completely clueless about what happened. I'm still in a state of shock about it. I've told the police everything, and the rabbi nearly drove me crazy with his questions!"

"Is there something you haven't told them that you can tell me?"

"No! Right now I'd do anything, anything in my power to restore . . . I mean, to get our Torah back, don't you know that?" she protested.

Night obscured the expression on her daughter's face; still Shelley caught the glisten of tears. Were they tears of grief or tears of regret? An uneasy feeling crept over Shelley that Neta could be hiding something, but she knew her daughter could turn against her if she continued to probe.

"Patience is one of the attributes of God listed in the Torah. Buddhists also teach the virtue of patience. I'm sure that we will find the Torah if we keep on searching for it," Shelley remarked cryptically.

Suspicious of her mother's uncharacteristic composure, Neta grudgingly attributed it to Hiroshi's calming influence; whatever had caused it, she was relieved to have abated her mother for the time being. They parted with a tacit truce between them, aware that an altercation could still be brewing.

Back in California, Abe had been plunged into sorrow by the disturbing news. He recalled the bizarre history of the scroll that had vanished many years ago under the guardianship of Mendel Snyder. Indeed, the "legend" of the Rosen Torah and the snake handlers had become an inspiring tale of survival woven into the Rosen family history. Now, as the seventh inheritor, he had failed in his duty. He had been remiss, negligent, and careless, he castigated himself. On his watch the scroll had been robbed of its comely adornments, and had vanished altogether like the lost Ark of the Covenant—the sacred Torah container that accompanied the Israelites during their forty years of wandering in the desert. Simply disappeared, shrouded in mystery.

He booked the first available flight to New Orleans where he began an obsessive hunt, rummaging through musty antique stores and out-of-the-way flea markets. He returned to California after a week of fruitless searching, but not before hiring a private investigator. Abe understood that the detective's chances for success were hampered by the lack of identifying marks, as each Torah tends to be an exact copy of the original and cannot be defaced with markings of any sort. And something else nagged at Abe. Although he did not hold his daughter responsible for the loss of their irreplaceable legacy, he had a strange, uneasy hunch that, in a way that he could not fathom, her driving hunger to outshine others may have led to this disaster.

For weeks after the disappearance, rumors and wild speculation continued to circulate. Many thought it had been a prank played by one of the sororities or fraternities too ignorant to understand the harm they were causing, and that the Torah would be returned. The possibility of anti-Semitic elements on campus even surfaced, although no one could single out any person or group as the guilty party. Weeks passed into months, without a trace or a clue. The crime remained unsolved. The scroll had vanished.

The harm Neta had done changed the direction of her life. From that moment on, she wrestled with a predicament to which she could find no easy answer. Should she confess to what she had done and face the awful consequences? Should she keep the Torah hidden to conceal the damage she had done to it? Should she risk taking it to a scribe to see if it could be repaired? If she did that she would be in danger of exposing herself as the perpetrator. Or should she hope for an appropriate moment to declare the truth? Driven by fear and shame, she could not bring

485

herself to tell the truth; the longer she kept her secret, the harder it became to admit her culpability.

"You're playing a dangerous game," Greta warned her, but as an accomplice to the crime she was just as guilty; and she was falling in love with Neta.

"Instead of covering myself in glory, I got an 'F' for not turning in the project," Neta groaned.

"For once, can't you just forget about schemes to promote yourself!"

Greta's recriminations made her feel weak, stupid and cowardly. She could never undo the damage she had done; she was unforgivable. Yet she vowed to find a way to redeem herself, no matter the sacrifice.

❧ 38 ❧

Secrets Revealed and Concealed

The wholest heart is the one that has been broken.

Torah Sages

Soon after the disaster — like co-conspirators in a crime of passion — they became lovers. It had been a stormy night with the wind pushing moisture-laden clouds from the Gulf up the mouth of the Mississippi, to dump torrents of rain on the city. Neta and Greta had stayed late to clean up after the Shabbat dinner at Hillel. When the electricity suddenly went off they waited for a while to see if it would come on again, when it didn't, holding hands they slipped out of the kitchen into the dark pantry at the end of the hallway.

In the small room smelling of mildew and stale crackers, Neta put her hands into the small of Greta's back, leaned into her as if they were going to dance, and kissed her mouth. Greta did not resist. Neta closed her eyes and traced the outline of her spine gently with the tips of her fingers, and kissed her, again. The skin on Greta's back was so warm, so silky-smooth, her breath so sweet smelling. A surge of excitement rushed through her; she felt as free and as wild as the storm howling overhead.

Suddenly the lights buzzed on and Greta reared back with a strangled cry. She put her hand over Greta's mouth to silence her, and they both froze. They heard someone ask who had screamed, and another student reply that they needed to head for the dorm now that the squall had let up. Hardly daring to breathe, the two women hid until they heard the front door shut and footsteps retreating outside. Hysterical with relief and aroused sensations, they quickly departed. On the walk across campus back to their rooms they were too unnerved to speak. In the hallway outside Neta's room, Greta started sobbing, "I'm sorry, I'm sorry."

Neta grabbed her by the shoulders and gasped, " No, I'm not sorry, I love you. I love you."

The next morning, Neta felt transformed into a strange, new person, euphoric but also edgy and guilty. When she entered the noisy cafeteria for breakfast, Greta was already there, waving to her from a corner table; she had to restrain herself from rushing over and kissing her beautiful mouth.

Over the following three years at Tulane, the pair struggled to come to terms with their relationship. Were they giving in to the *yetzer hara* or evil inclination? Or was it about commitment and connection? About "falling in love?" Or just something one can and should "get over?" The questions kept coming like a swarm of locusts. Why did God make them lesbians? Is it possible to be lesbian and an observant Jew? How does being lesbian reconcile with the teachings of the Torah? They could not find easy or satisfying answers to any of these questions. Eventually they found the courage to attend meetings of a gay and lesbian student alliance. There they could talk more openly, and they decided to confide in Sophie Glick, a young reform rabbi who encouraged her congregation to respect and accept all Jews regardless of sexual orientation.

The rabbi reassured them that being different from the norm did not lower one's level of *tzelem Elokim*, of being created in God's image. Still, she acknowledged the need for continuing dialog regarding the religious status of monogamous relationships between gay men, and between lesbians, and the need for special commitment ceremonies. Rabbi Glick helped them to get past the anxiety and shame that they could be mentally ill, even evil. Unfortunately, talking was not enough because they still feared, with good reason, that they could lose the support and respect of their friends, teachers, and especially of their parents.

There would always be doubts and questions, but they felt that they could no more escape love's inexorable force than the diaphanous jellyfish could resist the ocean's current, or a strong swimmer the rip tides. Secure in that knowledge and their love, shortly before Neta was to graduate with a bachelor of film and cinema studies, and Greta with a bachelor of architecture, they made plans for a formal commitment despite the vehement opposition of religious conservatives, and the fear of their parents' disapproval.

The young women knew that could no longer continue to hide the truth. They had to summon the courage to break the news to their parents.

To Neta's immense relief, Shelley accepted their relationship with surprising equanimity, saying that she had been anticipating the announcement for a long time, and that she wished them the best of luck. Neta, who had prepared herself for a heated, even gut-wrenching debate, felt a new tenderness toward her mother. Later, she confided in Greta that she had been skeptical of her mother's marriage to Hiroshi; but since their union she seemed more at peace with herself, maybe the calming influence of Shinto-Buddhism had helped too.

Things had not gone so easily for Greta. When she told her mother, an Orthodox Jew, her face emptied of all expression as if she had just received news that her daughter had died in a tragic accident. Greta sat in the silent living room searching her mother's stony face for the slightest sign of acceptance. When she could no longer stand the tension, she rose and put her arms around her mother. Pushing her daughter away, she slumped over and buried her face in her hands, her shoulders heaving with silent sobs. Then after a few minutes she straightened up, wiped her face with a wad of tissues, and looked up at Greta with so much distaste that her skin crawled.

Resentment drove her to cry out, "Ma, why can't you be happy for me?"

"Oh, Greta, what do you expect from me, when what you are doing is wrong."

"Before you condemn me, I want you to think about what my rabbi, Rabbi Glick said. She says that the Torah does not express any opinion on why God created me this way, but I am as beloved in His eyes as any other Jew, and I am as responsible as any other Jew for observing the mitzvot."

"I beg you not to tell your father," her mother implored.

As Greta turned to gather up her things with shaking hands, she imagined Neta applauding, as she exclaimed, "Get over it Ma! We climbed over the walls of the shtetl mentality when we came to America!"

Neta's "coming out" to her father had gone just as badly as Greta's. In retrospect she understood that it had been foolish to break the news without preparation; that she had allowed herself to be lulled by her mother's acceptance when she should have heeded her lover's cautionary tale.

In New Orleans on a business trip, without prior notice Abe had stopped by to see his daughter at the place she now shared with Greta. In her excitement, and believing that by this time her relationship with Greta was as obvious to him as it had been to Shelley, she had impetuously announced, "Dad, Greta and I have decided to get hitched!" From his stunned expression, she saw that he had denied what was before his eyes, had paid no heed to what was going on in her real life.

As twilight dimmed the room, Abe sat in shocked silence, listening to the rain hissing and spattering on the steamy tin roof, staring at the raindrops' shadows skittering down the wall like tears. The headlights of a streetcar clattering along the tracks briefly fanned the room, illuminating his errant daughter sitting bolt upright at the opposite end of a curved sofa.

Suddenly a low growl rolled from Abe's throat, and he hissed, "That's disgusting! Filthy! How could you pervert someone as decent as Greta!"

Neta's head snapped back. She staggered to the bathroom and slammed the door shut.

Shocked by his upwelling of homophobia, and completely sickened by the whole situation, Abe sat frozen on the couch. Then willing himself to his feet, he followed Neta. Pressing against the bathroom door he could hear water running, and the cold fear that gripped him made him choke out an apology, "Come out, please. I'm sorry, I'm sorry. I apologize." When there was no answer, he pleaded, "Please, can't we talk? I'm afraid this is going to lead to something we might regret."

"Get out of my house!"

"Please, I'm so sorry."

"I swear I'll never talk to you again!" He remained standing there abjectly, until she had abruptly emerged from the bathroom and stormed out of the house.

That night Abe walked for miles along the uneven sidewalks of the city, trying to put his thoughts in order. He ignored the drifting homeless who accosted him, and the stray dogs with yellow teeth that sniffed his shoes. Lost in the depths of misery, he was oblivious to the half moon, suspended above the church spire on Jackson Square, following him like a malevolent spy satellite. He wasn't aware of the lovers seated on fluted wrought-iron benches, or the pungent odors of buttery popcorn, spicy hotdogs, and fertile river mud. Try as he might, he couldn't explain his sudden rage. He knew it was wrong, even crazy, but there was something in him that had wanted to humiliate Neta in the same way *he* had been when his classmates had falsely branded him a homosexual. Then he rebuked himself for allowing something that had happened so long ago to still exert control over his behavior. Finally, too worn out to take another step, he took a room in a motel a few blocks from the French Quarter.

He turned on the TV with the volume high and tried to make his mind go blank. But the images would not stop: Neta's look of triumph when she heedlessly announced her plans to marry, the hate that contorted her face when he accused her of perverting Greta, the hot flush of shame he felt at his loss of control, the sharp click of the bathroom door locked against him, the spurt of water like blood from an opened artery, the fury in his daughter's voice.

He should have known that there was something more than friendship between Neta and Greta. He should have taken note of her defensiveness whenever the subject of boyfriends had come up. By refusing to see what was before his eyes he had avoided the pain of acknowledging that his daughter was a lesbian. Abe resolved to do whatever possible to heal the breach he had caused. But first he needed to sleep. He curled up on the bed like a man punched in the solar plexus, and dreamed of the Rosen Torah . . .

He was the auctioneer standing on a stage, looking down at a crowd, seated, row upon row, in cheap folding chairs, bid paddles cocked at the ready. Pointing to the Torah with a flourish he declared, "This next lot is a magnificent handwritten scroll, not just any Torah but the Rosen family Torah. So how can we assess its worth?" Uncurling the fingers of his right hand one at a time, he went on, "Those in the business use five key indicators: size, condition, rarity, authenticity, and provenance." He paused to raise the tension in the audience and caught the eye of a man with a mustache that ran like a neat tassel precisely from the outer edge of each nostril to the corner of his upper lip. His limp black hair was slicked and parted exactly to one side. His expression was as stiff and arrogant as a Nazi officer posing for a portrait.

"First, the size of this wonderful Torah is perfect, not too big, not too small. As for its condition, although ink has flaked off a few of the letters, these can easily be repaired. This rare Torah has survived for over two hundred years. Even more remarkable, it has remained in the same family. There is not a shadow of doubt about its authenticity. As for its provenance, that is the most extraordinary thing of all. We know that a renowned Torah scribe created it in Jerusalem, in 1791. And what is more, we have not only the record of ownership but its own history as well as the history of its inheritors!"

Abe's voice caught in his raw throat. A sadness swept over him as he looked down at the room filled with stony-faced strangers—flea market hagglers, garage sale bargain hunters—intent on buying the Torah for the lowest possible price. His eyes locked with those of the man with the black mustache seated to the side of him. There was something unpleasantly familiar about him. Abe knew that he could place the man if he had just a moment to think, but he had to get on with the auction.

"Consider the magnificent craftsmanship that went into the making of this Torah. Look at the exquisite lettering, the gorgeous silk mantle, intricate embroidery, and the outstanding silverwork! These qualities are there for all of you to behold and marvel at. But it's not possible to put a value on the sacred scroll because how can one put a price on a revered heritage?" A sigh rippled round the room. "Yet here is a once-in-a-lifetime opportunity for you to acquire this treasure. So who will start the bidding at twenty-five thousand? It's disgracefully far below the actual monetary value, but those are my instructions."

No one bid.

"Twenty-five thousand . . ."

No one bid.

"I repeat, twenty-five thousand!"

This time two paddles went up almost simultaneously. The first bidder was the man with the mustache, the other a woman with a halo of dark hair, whose face remained hidden behind her paddle.

"Twenty-five thousand to the gentleman," he said, thinking that the man's paddle had gone up first. "Who will make it thirty-five thousand?" After a few more bids, only the two original bidders remained. Abe skillfully played them up to seventy thousand.

"Seventy thousand. I repeat, seventy thousand. No one?" Pounding the gavel he declared, "Sold to gentleman for seventy thousand."

Then the woman dropped her paddle, and with a sickening lurch of his stomach Abe saw that it was Neta.

She screamed, "*Filthy traitor*, may you burn in hell for selling our Torah to that devil, Adolph Hitler!"

People rose from their seats with angry howls and came toward the podium, ready to tear him apart . . .

Abe awoke with his heart pounding, sick beyond measure at what had transpired between himself and his daughter.

For four long years, he tried to make contact with Neta. Then he attempted to reach his daughter through Greta, but she ostracized him too. In time Neta relented and began to reply to his e-mails and cards sent on birthdays and Rosh Hashanah, but still she steadfastly refused to meet with him. She demanded his unconditional acceptance of her as a gay woman. It never came. While he apologized for insulting her, he fell short of endorsing her life style.

In those years, Neta took on a new persona. She insisted on being called Nat and began to model herself on the Jewish-Mexican artist Frida Kahlo, the strong-willed, tormented painter of the early twentieth century. Like Kahlo, she enjoyed using her sharp humor to deflate her critics and amuse her supporters. Neta even resembled Kahlo, with her smooth olive skin, long black tresses, prominent red lips, the faintest hint of a mustache, and eyebrows that met above her nose. Kahlo's tortured canvases, with their colorful creatures and stark images of suffering, even came to influence her filmmaking.

She became particularly fascinated with one painting, *My Grandparents, My Parents, and I,* which relates to Kahlo's hybrid identity as the offspring of a multicultural and interracial marriage, and alludes to her German-Jewish and Hispanic roots. Like Khalo, Neta never lost pride in her Jewish heritage—the heritage that her parents had instilled deep within, and was inextricably tied to the Rosen Torah; the Torah she should have protected as if it were her child. As a consequence, she lived with a guilty secret she could not find the courage to divulge, or a way to atone for.

Then everything changed when Neta gave birth to a son, Samuel John Rosen, conceived by artificial insemination, and named after Shmuel Rosen, the family patriarch, and his grandfather eight times removed. Only then did she allow her father back into her life. The anger she had nursed was at last defeated by her desire to encourage a loving bond between his grandfather and her child. And she wanted to make reparation for what she had done in order to earn her father's forgiveness. Once she found a way to confess, she wanted him to be proud of her despite her desecration of the Torah. It wasn't just Neta who sought absolution. Abe too, desired forgiveness. Both needed to expunge their guilt: Abe for having caused the estrangement between them and for too easily relinquishing the care of the Torah to Hillel; and Neta for the fateful accident that had befallen the scroll and for hiding and lying about what she had done.

To begin the healing process she sent Abe an invitation to Samuel's *bris*, or circumcision ceremony, along with a poem she composed.

> Let me not to the bond between grandfather and
> grandchild
> Admit impediments. Love is not love
> Which dies when it confronts hateful intolerance,
> O no! It is an ever-fixed mark
> That looks on tempests and is never shaken;
> It is the star to every newborn child,
> Whose worth's unknown, although his radiance
> be cherished.
> If this be error and upon me proved,
> I never writ, nor no woman ever loved.
>
> With apologies to William Shakespeare.

To a fatherless boy, Abe became more than a doting grandfather; he became a hero.

✥39✥

Neta's Quest

A firstborn male child who opens the mother's womb, meaning that he is the first child born to his mother, gets "redeemed" from the priesthood through the Pidyon Haben ceremony.

Torah

The evening of Samuel Rosen's Bar Mitzvah, while he and his grandfather were getting ready for the guests to arrive, Neta stood staring out of the hotel window, reliving the event that had been a turning point in her life. On that dreadful night, she had despoiled the Rosen Torah with her dubious scheme. This act remained a secret from the world, but it ate at her heart like a parasite — until the birth of her son.

His emergence in the world resurrected the vision that had lain dormant within, as a seed germinates after a hoar frost. To hold Samuel in her arms and look into his delicate newborn face was a confirmation that life did triumph over death. With the babe nursing at her breast, Neta had a sudden and, to her, marvelous realization: she could redeem in some way what she had done by resuming the filmmaking project she had abandoned in her freshman year.

When Neta first conceived of the documentary, she had been a manipulative and egotistical student, lured by fame and glory. Later, she had convinced herself that although the Rosen Torah was desecrated, its digitized facsimile would remain as a legacy for future generations. Shmuel Rosen, the family patriarch, had wished for his Torah to be preserved forever; and in a way he could never have imagined, she had done just that. Still, she could not rid herself of guilt. It clung to her like a malicious shadow that seemed to vanish, only to reappear in her nightmares, goading her to fulfill a new vision.

Gradually, she came to understand that the scroll was not an inheritance but a heritage. For while an inheritance — money, land, jewels, artifacts — may be spent or given away by an heir in any way he or she pleases, a heritage like the Rosen Torah must remain in the family to be preserved and transmitted from generation to generation so that it is never forgotten. The significance of the Torah was not its physical manifestation, but its teachings. And the central core of these teachings dies if it is not transmitted to ensuing generations. By resurrecting this project she would make atonement for what she had done through the creation of a valuable new legacy. As first conceived, she would tell the stories of her ancestors. New generations would come to understand who they were and where they had come from; knowing that would shape a strong and proud identity and give purpose and meaning to their lives.

With the rebirth of her endeavor, Neta had found a worthy mission in life. Her son, and the making of the documentary kept her going and gave her heart. For her there was a special catharsis in being a mother, and in creating *Tree of Life*; after much soul searching she had chosen the title to evoke the liturgy proclaiming the Torah as the tree of eternal life.

Shooting footage, composing the sequence, selecting the music, making the whole come together as a vibrant reality, demanded all of her energy and talent. She gave years of her life to researching the past, to disinterring its secrets, and to capturing scenes of her family's history on location.

She was determined to visit Lithuania first, even though her father cautioned her that only a small number of Jews still lived there, and she would find little of interest. Neta disagreed. She argued that after gaining independence in 1991, the Lithuanian government had guaranteed equal rights to national

497

minorities, the Jews included, and, since then, the remnants of their cultural life were being resurrected from the ruins.

Abe had dismissed her optimism. In his opinion, although there now existed a Jewish museum, and even Jewish studies taught at the university in Vilna, this could not bring the singular culture of the shtetl back to life. He said that he doubted she would find a flourishing Jewish community as nearly all of the surviving Jews had gone to America or Israel. Still, obstinate as always, Neta convinced her father to finance the trip. She undertook the journey, certain that if she walked the same roads and breathed the same air, she might come closer to understanding her ancestors and her heritage.

On the first day in Vilna, the capital of the Republic of Lithuania, impatient to explore her ancestral shtetl, she rented a car with a driver to take her to Valinsk, about fifty miles away. When a run-down vehicle leaking oil, pulled up in front of the hotel, she voiced her doubts about its reliability to her guide, Gitanas Mesowitz, who worked for a travel agency specializing in Jewish heritage tours. A big man with a white goatee, dark bags under his pale blue eyes, and a booming voice, offset by a broad smile, Gitanas reassured her that he had brought along a good supply of motor oil. Despite her qualms, Neta was pleased to find her guide pleasant and knowledgeable; he told her that his paternal grandmother, who spoke Yiddish, had raised him.

With her state-of-art camcorder in hand, she determinedly captured everything she saw, asking her guide to make stops along the route to capture the forests and fields, farms and villages. She strolled through Valinsk filming the modest wooden houses. A few old shops remained on the square with no trace of the former Jewish owners. Since her father had visited this place almost two decades ago, the old wooden shul that had been converted into apartments had been demolished; no structure stood in its place, only a plaque commemorating the Jews who had perished in the Holocaust.

When Abe was there he had not visited the old Jewish cemetery. At her insistence, Gitanas agreed to guide her up the steep path overgrown with brambles leading to it. The burial ground was a desolate place. Snow, mud and weeds covered neglected tombstones, many of which had toppled, or been vandalized. Yet Neta, like shtetl Jews before her, saw her pedigree preserved in the old gravestones with rubbed-out stars of David, sinking into the wild grass that covered the graves interring the bones of her forebears, to rise when the Messiah comes.

She began by scouring the mud off the monuments with a stick and washing them with water from puddles of melted snow so that the Hebrew inscriptions could be seen. Then she squatted and reverently traced the worn letters with the tips of her fingers. After cleaning several stones and videoing them, one headstone, half-leaning to the side seemed to be calling to her. She bent low, and washed the mud away, trying to decipher the inscription almost erased by the hand of time. Then with bated breath, whispering the words she could make out she read, with the assistance Gitanas:

Here lies Yitzhak Rosen. Pious and loved by all he observed the Torah. Born 10 Cheshvan 5529. Died . . .

Unfortunately, the rest of the inscription was no longer legible. In shock, she remained kneeling, trembling, sending up a silent prayer for her dear ancestor and the other souls resting there. It was a crisp October day, the sky was a rare sapphire blue, and Neta was filled with awe that she, of all the inheritors, had found this hallowed place. When Gitanas touched her on the shoulder and offered her hot tea from a thermos, she burst into tears. After she regained her composure she captured the remarkable find with the unyielding and faithful eye of her camera.

The next day, she explored Vilnius' old churches, the opera house, government buildings, and monuments to Vytautis the Great. More absorbing to her were the museums; one honored "the Righteous Gentiles," the Lithuanians who had that helped Jews in their dire need. A second museum exhibited relics of the old synagogue: parts of sefer Torahs, mantles, pointers, the front door of a shul, a Holy Ark and a wonderful tapestry depicting the story of Queen Esther. The third, a Holocaust Museum, offered a harrowing experience. She dutifully recorded all these images for *Tree of Life*.

Afterwards, she walked the cramped and narrow streets where the Jewish ghetto once existed, seeing the remains of the yeshiva and an old shul with the Star of David still visible on the worn bricks. Before the war, there were approximately 240,000 Jews in Lithuania; some 220,000 were murdered. It was too much to bear, and she leaned against the wall and mourned inwardly.

The following morning, shaking off her grim mood, she contacted the handful of Jews in the city for video interviews. Over hot lemon tea and tomato sandwiches on rough rye, they tried to make conversation despite the language barrier, gesturing and grimacing at each other with little rapport, except for the guide who translated their sentiments. Abe had been right about that part. It was all very sad, and left her haunted by the feeling that the true reality of the place was the Jewish souls who had once lived and breathed there, who persisted solely in the collective memories of those, like her, who had roots in Lithuania.

Before her departure, she went to the nearby town of Pakroi, where records were kept for the district. She was elated to obtain copies of birth, marriage and death certificates of the Rosen family, invaluable to her research.

However, there, in a moment of candor, one city official confided, "There are very few Jews here. Those that remain are supported by charitable donations from America."

Back in the States, she continued her pilgrimages to retrace ancestral roots and to accumulate footage for the documentary, sometimes taking Samuel along, visiting what was left of her extended family, their homes and businesses and searching for records. Once, he accompanied his mother on a visit to the Jewish Museum in Berkeley. It intrigued him to learn about the magnificent scroll that had once held pride of place in the museum and of its odyssey — only to vanish without a trace. When he questioned her about its mysterious disappearance

500

while housed at Tulane, she had replied, "Oh God, Samuel, that happened so long ago."

"If someone hid it, do you think I might be the one to find it? " he had enquired eagerly.

"No, never . . . well, I shouldn't say never. Maybe you'll find it one day," she replied with a small confessional cringe.

For Neta, the Shady Lady was the most heartrending rediscovery. Abe had rented out the farm to tenants who lived in the small log cabin on the property adjacent to the main house, and acted as caretakers. As she opened drawers in the old house, familiar objects from summers spent with Grandpa John sprang out at her like scenes from a children's popup book. She held each object, embedded with powerful shards of memory, cradled in the palm of her hands. There were dried seedpods she had collected from his vegetable garden, a bright feather headdress she had made for him, and half-melted pink candles from a birthday cake celebrating her tenth birthday. Springs and gears rattled inside broken clocks, and maps opened to lace where bookworms had chewed through them. She tried to clean a porcelain doll in a yellow silk kimono she had played with, but her delicate painted features wiped away leaving streaks of black and red where her eyes and mouth had been.

She wandered the farm looking for the remnants of her grandfather's brave experiments. Thanks to Abe, who visited from time to time, the solar panels and windmills still functioned. Waves of nostalgia pulsed through Neta as she filmed the old house in its magnificent setting.

Sometimes Samuel also accompanied her to the movie studio, where he would sit ignored but taking in everything. Neta had hired just a handful of actors and actresses to double up in a number of roles, and it amazed him how they transformed themselves from gum-chewing, donut-eating, coffee-drinking everyday people into exotic characters of foreign lands and multiple languages, moving mysteriously amid the confusion of lights, cameras, stage sets, and crew members. He was also astounded to see how fragments of reality could be reconstructed in plaster — or even in cyberspace — and appear so true on video.

In spite of Neta's progress, how to transform sorrow and despair for what had happened in Lithuania and to the Rosen Torah, into optimism still eluded her. In the end, somehow a renewed sense of hope had lifted up on its swelling tide, and she had reworked her documentary to reflect that feeling.

What she learned on that journey enriched her, humbled her, and showed her the way to make the documentary uplifting. The seven previous heirs to the Torah had wrestled with the inescapable force of their heritage, with how to reconcile a life of freedom and choice with the restrictions and responsibilities as inheritors. Each one had approached the burden of their inheritance in his own way. Some had treated it with awe and reverence, with unwavering faith and filial piety, with humility and complete obedience to tradition. Others had come to the Torah with baser motives: self-glorification, overweening pride, and burning ambition. Those with no faith to guide them viewed their legacy with puzzlement and cynicism. Yet all came to understand it as a solemn trust. As inheritors, they were irrevocably linked to their ancestors and to their traditions; trustees of their history; witnesses to the tragic fate of their people and to their miraculous survival. They were, lest others forget, standard-bearers for future generations. The Torah was their touchstone, reminding them who they were and where they had come from, charging them to do mitzvot to help ensure that evil would not triumph over virtue, and to do *tikkun olum*, or to heal the world to make it a better place for all.

Obsessively seeking her own redemption in making the film, Neta was too absorbed to acknowledge that she was neglecting the relationship between herself and Greta. To compound their difficulties, Greta had transformed herself from a timid, uncertain student into a confident woman passionate about her religion and her work as an architect, but still wrestled with her own guilt for concealing the truth about what had happened to the Torah. Deep down, she resented Neta for persuading her to act as her accomplice. The ugly secret infected their love for one another.

After Samuel's birth, they often argued over how to raise him. Greta loved the child and wanted to help with his upbringing. That became yet another source of conflict. When Greta took it upon herself to improve the boy's religious education, he would often slip away to play ball rather than go to the synagogue with her. Over Greta's protests, Neta allowed him to play sports on Saturdays. With each passing year Neta became more Reform, less strictly observant, while Greta became more Orthodox, more devout.

There were other problems. Neta complained that Greta was spending too much time away from home. When she was not helping out at the synagogue, she served on numerous committees and boards for Jewish charities. Also there had been much for her to accomplish in her chosen profession. In the years following Hurricane Katrina, the city's public buildings had to be rebuilt, and the National Historic Districts saved from bulldozers of shrewd developers and careless clean-up crews. Fortunately, the community had rallied to the cause, under the aegis of Architecture for Humanity. Joining with other architects, Greta had eagerly offered her services pro bono. She loved being part of a team that improved the wellbeing of people by designing a school, a hospital, a museum; restoring an historic area; or inspiring generations to come with a monumental civic structure.

Often the architect returned home late at night. When Neta came home from her travels or work, to fill the empty hours, she invited her friends to the house or went carousing with them. Samuel learned early that there were separate worlds, one included just himself and his mother, another the network of people in filmmaking—from which he was largely excluded— and a third, himself and Greta. The two women frequently bounced the boy between them.

In elementary school, Samuel's peers taunted him because his parents were lesbians. On the threshold of puberty he became acutely sensitive to their heckling, and turned moody and rebellious, lashing out at his mother Neta, the source of his shame. These attacks outraged Neta. She solicited the help of his teacher and the principal, who agreed that it would be appropriate to talk to the children about respecting differences. That helped keep her son's tormentors at bay for a while. As Neta continued to breathe life into her video, it became her most fervent hope that it would inspire and encourage her son to stand proud and strong against enemies like them.

Fortunately, Samuel found a way to deflect the bullying himself. He was naturally athletic and played football, basketball, and baseball—as early as his age allowed. If he wasn't yet eligible, he hung around until the coach gave permission for him to serve as ball boy. Still, he felt cheated of a father.

The week before his twelfth birthday, Samuel and his mother were driving home from a football practice—at the time he was on a team, not playing, just practicing and waiting for one of the older or stronger boys to sustain an injury. Abruptly he turned off the radio and informed her that he wanted tickets for the New Orleans Saints game for his birthday, not the movie and popcorn she had promised.

When she kept on driving as if she hadn't heard, he yelled, "I wish I had a dad! He would get me tickets for the game."

She accelerated through a yellow light, and said through clenched teeth, "I can't stand your whining, Samuel. I'm the one who brought you into this world. I'm the one that has loved and cared for you." She sounded out of control, and it scared him. He should have known better than to taunt his mother; she had just had another quarrel with Greta, and was as bad-tempered as a wet cat.

Staring straight ahead, not turning to look at him, she went into a kind of monologue, talking more to herself about how much his birth had meant to her. At ten, he couldn't empathize with what she was telling him, and he didn't want to hear that she had pinned so much hope on him. When they pulled into the driveway in front of the house, she turned to look at him as if coming out of a trance. As Samuel jerked the car door open, her chin went up. "If those tickets mean that much to you I'll find some, even if I have to buy them from a scalper!"

Neta made good on her promise, and he thoroughly enjoyed the Saints game, still he let her know that he resented not having a father to go with him, or to cheer him on when he played on a team.

As his Bar Mitzvah approached, more than ever, Samuel missed not having a dad by his side like the other boys. He wanted a father to celebrate the small triumphs as well as the big ones with him, to comfort him, in whom he could confide his dreams and sorrows—even a loving mother like Neta and an adoring grandfather like Abe couldn't compensate for that loss.

❦ 40 ❧

The Ninth Inheritor: Samuel Rosen
and the Tree of Life

The word for "tree" in Hebrew, etz, is composed of two letters: ayin, or eye and tzadik, or righteous one. Just as the Torah is the "tree of eternal life," so does the righteous one, when connected with the "eye" of the Torah, become a tree of eternal life.

Rabbi Yitzhak Ginsburgh

The special guests invited to the premier of the *Tree of Life* at Samuel's Bar Mitzvah, sat hushed with anticipation as the room darkened and the opening scenes rolled . . .

Before their eyes the Rosen Torah unfurls across the screen like an old-fashioned black-and-white hypnotist's spiral, pulling the viewer ever deeper into the past. The syncopated beat of George Gershwin's *Rhapsody in Blue*, an exciting blend of classical, jazz, and pop music, offsets the flowing images perfectly. The scene dissolves to the fallen headstone of Yitzhak Rosen's grave superimposed on the Torah, while voices recite Kaddish, the prayer for the dead. They continue to pray as the voiceover of Neta tells us that her ancestors were from Valinsk, once a vibrant shtetl. Not one Jew lives in Valinsk today, she says.

The cemetery fades as the old shtetl marketplace comes back to life with a rush of activity. Merchants call from booths, cows moo, horses neigh, donkeys bray, while klezmer music plays in the background as if by a troupe of tipsy rascals. The commotion of market day ends as daylight fades, and we follow the Valinskers back to their homes as night comes on.

The black screen transitions to a new day dawning over Valinsk, surrounded by a sinister pine forest, crowned by the wooden synagogue on the hill, its three-tiered roof dusted with snow. The Bar Mitzvah guests follow fathers to work, children to school. They meet those who make shoes, bake the bread, carry the water, and heal the sick, the rich merchants and the poor coachmen. They see the children bent over their studies, young boys at *cheder*, the older ones at yeshiva, and the teachers who taught them. They tell us of their belief, so strong that to study or to teach Torah is a reward and a duty of the heart.

The working day in the shtetl dissolves to the present time; the narrow streets where the Jewish neighborhood of Valinsk once existed, the remains of the market square, the memorial plaque presiding over a plot of weeds where the shul once stood. In rapid succession a montage of emblematic images surges into view: A man on a donkey rides past the ancient walls of Jerusalem. Men, women, and children flee angry flames consuming their shetsl, and lapping like demons at their heels, to plunge into the icy river. To the accompaniment of Leonard Bernstein's *Kaddish*, smoke and flames churn high into the sky above the Valinsk wooden shul, casting a giant pall over the shtetl. The steamship *Deutschland* flounders through killer waves. Yakov cleaves to his beloved Torah as a storm rages at sea. Men in hooded white robes, silhouetted against a fiery cross, are reflected in the wild eyes of Yakov, Chana, and Aaron. Aaron, the maverick jazz musician, blows his horn like the Archangel Gabriel at the Gates of Heaven. Rattlesnakes, venom dripping from their fangs, writhe over the opened Rosen Torah, then, slowly, fades to black.

With blasts of the shofar, succeeding inheritors emerge from the darkness, silhouetted against a crystalline blue sky: Abraham, the philosopher-scientist with the symbol of the atom encircling his head, and a dove with an olive branch in his hands; John, the storyteller and ecologist, in a field of windmills, dreaming with his eyes wide open; and Abe, the business tycoon reflected in a computer monitor as a rabbi.

Orchestrating all of the action is a big bear of a man with bushy eyebrows, luxuriant black beard, and the glittering eyes of a fighting cock. He appears and reappears: serving drinks in his tavern; reflected in the windows of the synagogue with the Torah cradled in his arms, its dainty bells quivering before the mesmerized congregation; dancing to the music of Aaron's trumpet; crouching with Abraham on the desert floor as the universe explodes in a firestorm.

"Look!" Samuel shouts, "Is that our patriarch, Shmuel Rosen?"

After the premier of *Tree of Life*, things changed between Neta and her family; they honored her as their family historian and praised her as an artist. Most significant to her was Abe's forgiveness. That her father had generously helped bankroll her documentary meant more to her than anything; it meant that he endorsed and valued her efforts and her talent. As for Samuel, he was too young to fully understand the significance of that night or to appreciate the awesome legacy his mother had created for him. Learning about his heritage in such a dramatic way helped him to embark on the complex process of shaping his own identity. Still he could not yet grasp that her magnum opus would alter the trajectory of his life.

❦ 41 ❧

Samuel in the Shadow of the Tree

A falsehood, in one sense, a dead thing; but too often it moves about and pushes the living out of their seats.
Samuel Taylor Coleridge, Aids to Reflection

After Samuel's Bar Mitzvah, in comparison to his difficulties in elementary school years, middle and high school proved to be a happier period for him, marred only by the growing estrangement between his mother and Greta. Fortunately, his natural aptitude for athletics and a gift for mathematics paved the way for befriending both the jocks and the nerds. Over time, Samuel cleverly evolved a profitable way to combine these two disparate talents.

His transition to college was a painless, even enjoyable experience; there, students did not know or care about his unusual family. Back in high school he started betting small amounts on sports teams, but continuously lost money. Then, in college, he began toying around with a betting system that did not rely on polls or gut reactions, but on statistics. He applied classroom mathematics to create algorithms that calculated the spread between football and basketball teams and won so frequently that his friends started asking for his picks.

At first, his method drew fire from diehard sports fans because it ignored the conventional wisdom; sometimes, for example, his system denied the advantage to the favored team. But he tested his algorithms rigorously, back-testing them against results from the past twenty-five seasons. For more recent games, he ran the data through a particular point in the season to see how well his spread predicted the winners of the following week's game. His results were more accurate than the experts' predictions, and he became known among the college's gamblers as "the go-to guy."

As graduation approached, Samuel began playing with the idea of turning his hobby into a business. His scheme, to develop a clientele by selling information about his picks through an Internet service, seemed feasible. Neta was enthusiastic about Samuel's venture as a short-term money-spinner and promised to use her network of connections to help launch it. Nevertheless, she urged him to continue on, and get a Masters in computer science for longer-term security, and for experience, to take a job with Abe's company, Interweb. As much as he admired his grandfather, Samuel did not want to be a slave to work, and he wanted to succeed on his own merit. Without making a commitment, he told Neta that he would think about it.

Then, just months before graduation, his beloved Grandfather Abe was fatally injured when a car traveling in the opposite direction skidded around a hairpin bend and ploughed into his bike. He left a small fortune to Samuel that released him from the necessity of having to work. His grandfather's traumatic demise deprived Samuel of his best friend and his hero. A succession of disturbing emotions — disbelief, shock, anger, sadness — robbed him of sleep and invaded his dreams with visions of his grandfather calling out to him for help. To escape his grief and to honor his grandfather's memory in a unique way, Samuel chose to travel to exotic places — to backpack, hike, sail, river raft, ski, hang glide, and surf — to live the life his grandfather hadn't found time for.

His mother tried to dissuade him from taking "the lazy way out," but he ignored it. On the day Samuel completed the final requirements for his undergraduate degree, he embarked upon the great adventure he had mapped out in his head, skipping the graduation ceremony, as he simply hadn't the heart for celebrating so soon after his grandpa's funeral.

He had been living "the good life" for almost a year, when he received shocking news that his mother, Neta, had been found lifeless in bed. Neta's death overwhelmed him with grief and with guilt. He blamed himself for being too self-involved with his own pleasure to see the depth of his mother's pain. The autopsy report concluded that the cause of death was an overdose of sleeping pills.

Neta's use of sedatives could be understood. Edgy, sharp, and ambitious, she drove herself hard, and was never satisfied with her achievements. When the relationship between her and Greta began to disintegrate, they had sought marriage counseling but that only staved off the inevitable. Neta had been a passionate woman, and after Greta left, she had two disastrous love affairs that ended with both women dumping her for other lovers. When Abe was killed, it sent Neta spiraling into deep depression. And after she read her father's will, stating that he bequeathed the Rosen Torah to her—in the happy event that it should ever be found—Neta shaved her head. Samuel did not know that her father's sudden death left behind unresolved issues that only served to prolong her grief. She had sworn to herself that one day she would find complete release from guilt by revealing the whole truth to him about the Rosen Torah; his untimely end destroyed that last hope.

Samuel had been about to leave for an appointment with the waves of Boca de Pascuales in Mexico, when Neta's friend called to break the tragic news about his mother. It shocked him back to reality, exploded over him with more force than even those waves could have delivered. He flew back to New Orleans on the first flight available, promising his girlfriend, Melinda Vascon, whom he had only recently met, to return as soon as he could; the two had entered that stage of infatuation where even a brief separation seemed too long.

Melinda's brother, Daniel, had introduced her to Samuel. The young men had first become acquainted while surfing, and had immediately taken a liking to one another; it was hard to resist Daniel. With burning black eyes, and an unusually deep voice, he was upbeat and affable, an inveterate teller of corny jokes who groaned along with his listeners at the punch lines. They had been riding the waves together for several weeks, when Daniel mentioned that he would not be surfing the following weekend, as he would be celebrating the Passover Seder with his family. Samuel had responded that he was Jewish, too, and the young surfer spontaneously invited him to join the Vascon family for the Seder at Esperanza, their vacation home in the countryside.

Samuel's new friend had picked him up at the hotel in a sleek yellow energy efficient automobile. Hopping into the passenger seat, he had adjusted it precisely to his liking with a touch screen. The car's electric motor ran on hydrogen that had already been topped off, automatically, from an appliance in Daniel's garage. Set into its dash was the equivalent of a wireless laptop computer that connected the vehicle to global positioning satellites, telephone networks and the Internet.

Daniel had driven with the same devil-may-care skill he displayed in the surf: speeding down boulevards lined with angular skyscrapers that overshadowed the remnants of majestic old palaces; flying by "green" high-rise housing that integrated walls of vegetation into the architecture itself; detouring around rutted roads skirting slums. Even in the twenty-first century, hunger and poverty lurked behind wealth and breath-taking technological innovation. Finally, they had turned onto a country road that led to Esperanza. They parked in the driveway where Daniel beckoned him across a sunlit courtyard cloistered behind high adobe walls ablaze with tropical vines, and through carved wooden doors into the cool foyer, decorated with paintings and ceramic plates. The foyer opened onto a living room with a wood-beamed ceiling where Joaquin and Alicia Vascon and the rest of the extended family were gathered.

Instantly Samuel noticed Daniel's sister, Melinda, surrounded by laughing children acting out some sort of charade. He was startled to see that she was dressed in a traditional Mexican costume eerily similar to the one his mother had worn at the height of her Frida Kahlo phase. The soft fabric of her white cotton blouse embroidered with diamonds of maroon, black, and gold, and loosely drapped matching long black skirt concealed yet enhanced the curves of her body. His eyes lingered on her face, without makeup, yet exotically alluring. Her dark, passionate eyes gazed directly and appraisingly back at him. Her straight, stern eyebrows belied the humorous twist of her mouth.

After introductions all round, the Vascons ushered him into a spacious dining room. To accommodate everyone, chairs were crowded around a long table draped with a hand-embroidered tablecloth. With a wave of nostalgia for the many Seders he had celebrated with his family, Samuel's eyes swept over the glowing candles, the wine glasses, the Seder plate, and the covered plate of three matzahs — everything in its place, just as he remembered it.

The time-honored ceremony unfolded as it had through the centuries. Glasses of wine were filled, parsley and boiled eggs were dipped in salt water, matzah was broken, and the moving story of the Exodus recounted. Samuel kept stealing glances at Melinda, and whenever her expressive eyes met his, she smiled.

Only after they had read it all, sung it all, drank the wine as instructed, and were, finally, rewarded with a scrumptious dinner, did the company drift away. It was past eleven o'clock when the parents excused themselves. For the next hour Samuel chatted with brother and sister in the cool shadows of the flagstone patio. Melinda was charming and gracious but she did not seem overly interested in him. Why should she be? He was just a rich American with nothing more purposeful to do than indulge his whims. Seduced by her charms, Samuel became frantic to show her that he had some worth, so he told her and Daniel about the sports' betting system he had developed, and about his plans to turn it into a successful business. While Daniel was intrigued, he could tell that he still scored zero with Melinda.

However, when the talk turned to the Vascon's business, Mexico City Salsa, producing a variety of gourmet foods, he saw a better chance. Neta had been an indifferent cook, and Samuel had long ago decided to learn something about cooking for himself. When Melinda discovered his interest, which was genuine enough, she invited him to come to their test kitchens.

513

On his tour of the family business, Samuel was impressed by the freshness of the ingredients, and the subtle way they blended the flavors to give traditional recipes a new twist. Their mutual interest in food preparation had opened the door for Samuel, at last.

So it was that as his romance blossomed, he had received the sudden, awful news from home. He left Melinda with a leaden heart to attend to his mother's funeral. He promised her that he would be back soon—as soon as he could say a proper farewell to his mother. When the plane touched down at New Orleans airport, Samuel could feel his mother's chimera hovering out there, waiting for him.

A robot controlled by him, carted his duffle bag out to the nearby RUFS, or Rapid Urban Flexible Station. There he boarded a train of individual electric vehicles hooked together that traveled along an automated guideway built in the center of existing highways. At the station nearest to his mother's neighborhood, he swiped his credit card to decouple and to rent the vehicle for two weeks, and then drove to the house. On the ride home, a terrible loneliness descended on him. He missed his mother's high energy, her mischievous smile, even the level gaze that froze him in his tracks and the sharp tongue that reprimanded him for his lack of ambition. His eyes smarted with unshed tears and acrimonious regrets.

By the time he reached the house and plugged in the car to charge its batteries overnight, it was late, and he fell asleep on the couch still in his travel gear. He woke feeling sad and lost. He tried to make himself believe that there was nothing he could have done to prevent what had happened, but horror and despair, like a black hole sucking the life out of him, left him drained of energy. He could not accept that his mother's life had been snuffed out so foolishly, so capriciously.

To chase away the gnawing emptiness, Samuel opened the shutters and in the cheerless predawn light saw the miniature Torah Scroll in its blue velvet cover displayed on a shelf. He recalled with a sudden burst of happiness that his grandfather had presented it to him on his Bar Mitzvah. Then uninvited, a dream-vision of the magnificent Rosen Torah his grandfather had once described to him, rose in his mind's eye; sadly, his bright bubble of pleasure deflated leaving him discouraged and melancholy. Where was the family legacy now? He should have been its ninth inheritor but its mysterious disappearance had sundered that link binding him to his ancestors. He had seen only its likeness in *Tree of Life*. He would never touch his prayer shawl to it or read from it. He swallowed hard to hold back the cry rising in his throat.

Samuel brewed a pot of strong black coffee and searched the refrigerator for edible leftovers. Standing over the kitchen sink, he slapped a dollop of cream cheese onto a stale bagel and watched the sullen dawn break. After one bite he wasn't hungry. The thought that he had to rummage through his mother's private things made him queasy. He longed to hold Melinda close, to look into her eyes and tell her how it had been between his mother and him, about their love-hate dance, which had ended so cruelly. He had never found it easy to express his emotions or to feel close to others; she would help him put into words what he was feeling. He'd had relationships with other women, but Melinda possessed the gift of empathy and she gave it freely.

Despite the early hour, he called Melinda on his mobile phone, to tell her that he needed her, and to beg her to fly north immediately. He gazed at her picture on the monitor, tousled and sleepy-eyed, and longed to kiss her.

At the funeral, Shelley, his ex-mother in law, her hair streaked white and her eyes shielded by dark glasses, clutched her husband's arm with gnarled fingers. The wailing of the wind, mixed with the sound of her jagged weeping, gouged Abe's ears. Greta, his second mother, her face leaden with sorrow, eyes reddened and magnified behind thick lenses, stood at the graveside gazing at him with compassion. She reached for his hand to comfort him, and said brokenly, "I should have been there for Neta when she needed me."

He felt her grief, and wanted to cry out, "We are both to blame!"

Afterwards, the mourners came to the house, swollen-eyed and wrung out. They all gathered in the living room like survivors of a train wreck. Some were old friends he had known since childhood. Neta's more recent friends he did not recognize, having been away at college or traveling abroad. He felt as if their accusing eyes were boring into him even as they tried to comfort him with whispered condolences. He was relieved to see them go before Melinda arrived late that night.

With Melinda by his side, he found the courage to sort through Neta's things. Still he couldn't shake the feeling of being an intruder. There are some people so vivid in life that they seem not to disappear when they die. His mother's presence hovered over the house like a waking dream.

Melinda suggested that they began with Neta's clothes, hanging like shrouds in the closet. Her distinctive fragrance of almonds still lingered there, evoking sharp sad reminiscences: of slipping into her bed as a child, feeling her warmth as he nestled against her, listening raptly to her tall stories. Among his mother's jewelry he found something that puzzled him, a biometric smart card key. He put it aside and made a mental note to find out more about it.

He had never given much thought to what a pack rat his mother had been. Melinda arranged to donate most of her belongings to charitable organizations and left Samuel to decide which items he wanted to keep. There was not much of great monetary worth except for her small collection of Judaica, including enamel and pewter mezuzahs, copper and silver menorahs, and dreidels, of ivory and silver, and his favorite one, the garishly glazed clay spinning top he had made in first grade, and had played with during the festival of Chanukah.

When he found a DVD of the *Tree of Life*, he held it between finger and thumb and squeezed his eyes shut as if he were holding a loaded gun, then he dropped it into a drawer and told Melinda that they would view it later that night; silently he wondered if he could bear to see it just then. But the title had caught Melinda's attention. With a rush of excitement, she commented on its rich symbolism.

516

"The Torah is called the Tree of Life, and is associated with the Garden of Eden and the fall of Adam and Eve. Remember, God forbade Adam and Eve to eat from the Tree of Knowledge of Good and Evil? When they broke this commandment, God banished them from the Garden where the Tree of Life—bestowing immortality on them—also grew. God restored the possibility of eternal life by giving the Torah to the Jewish people—and from them to all humanity." Clasping her hands together she added, "And did you know that the tree is also central to Kabbalah, the mystic study of the Torah?"

Samuel saw that she found all this intriguing and wanted to talk about it, but he just needed to finish the task they had started. To Melinda's disappointment he insisted that they first tackle the stacks of documents his mother had collected while researching the Rosen family history.

There were photocopies from the shtetl of Pakroi, including birth, marriage, and death certificates of the Rosen family going back more than two hundred years. Also copies of Yakov's immigration records from Castle Clinton. Pages copied from city directories listing the addresses of the family in Ricksburg and Atlanta. Articles clipped from the old local newspaper about Yakov and Chana's bakery when they first opened, and ads for Mendel Snyder's deli praising the mouth-watering corned beef and pastrami sandwiches. Rave reviews of Aaron and Marlene's jazz performances, and intriguing photos of their appearances at concerts. Articles that explained and extolled Abraham's work at Los Alamos. Helen's scrapbooks filled with the most favorable critiques of John's science-fiction novels, and interesting articles about their experimental farm, disturbing clippings from the *Susmook News* covering the religious extremists confrontation with the Rosens, and also her fascinating personal journal. There were newspaper and magazine features chronicling the rocky, but spectacular rise of Abe's business ventures. Invitations, one from the Jewish Museum to a lecture honoring Abraham Rosen, another to the opening of an exhibit highlighting the Rosen Torah. And family photographs—lots of them.

The photo Samuel liked best shows the family gathered on the porch of the Shady Lady. Abraham, his great-great-grandfather, sits in a rocking chair with a multi-colored Native American blanket over his knees, looking worn and shriveled as if he is already fading from the world. John, his great-grandfather, leans casually over the porch railings, a faint, almost sardonic smile playing around his mouth. Helen, his great-grandmother, looks toward the mountains, her arms hugging her knees, her eyes dreamy. Abe, his grandfather, then just a boy, sits perched on the bottom step, head half-turned to look back at Helen. Martha, his great-great-grandmother the self-effacing, ministering angel, is not in the picture, probably because she took the photo.

The one Samuel liked least was taken at his Bar Mitzvah. He is standing on the steps of the synagogue looking straight at the camera, his chin jutting out, trying to strike a confident pose. Abe and Shelley stand behind him, Neta and Greta on either side; all beam into the camera. In reality, the setup was a sham. He had been an indifferent Hebrew student and was uncomfortable about having to read from the Torah before the whole congregation. His two mothers had just had one of their bitter quarrels, and the relationship between his grandparents, although long divorced, was still strained, often verging on hostility. In retrospect Samuel understood the picture as a projection of not what they were but what they longed to be—the perfect family. It made him wonder how many other cheerful family photographs are also hypocritical deceptions.

Looking at that image of Abe, he found himself telling Melinda how his free-spirited great-grandparents, John and Helen, had raised Grandpa Abe so unconventionally. He tried to evoke the way the Shady Lady always smelled of wood smoke and cedar, ripe apples, rosemary, mint, and thyme; how the old house creaked like a sailing ship when the wind blew hard; and how the vistas of the snow-capped mountains and dark forests appeared like a delicate watercolor from its deep front porch; how the mountain peaks floated, stratum upon gauzy stratum, in the morning mist.

Most poignant of all to him was Helen's journal. Samuel remembered his mother's cry of surprise when, years ago, she had found it stuck away in a dresser at the Shady Lady. He could still picture Neta leafing through it, pausing to read an entry, looking up with a quizzical expression, and then dipping into another segment like a swimmer testing the water with a toe. He didn't want to snoop, but curiosity got the better of him, and he began browsing through the diary that Helen had kept on and off through the 1970s. His great-grandmother's writings provided much to deliberate, especially her sincere, if thorny path toward Judaism, and her reverence for Torah as a source of wisdom, of hope, and of continuity.

The next day, in the back of an armoire filled with linens and quilts, he discovered a black and gold lacquered box with handwritten letters inside. He started to read the letter on top but an unpleasant presentiment seemed to pull his hand away like a counterweight, causing him to hesitate and glance up.

Through the French doors to the veranda he could see Melinda setting the table for lunch. He watched her arrange red and yellow flowers in a jar, then step back and tilt her head to one side to admire them. She made a small adjustment to the display, then with a deft flick of her wrists she lifted her long hair and twisted it into a knot at the nape of her neck, plucked a yellow daisy from the vase and tucked it behind one ear. Samuel's eyes lingered on her face, lit by dark, expressive eyes. He liked the way her bright, summery cotton dress with a scooped neckline and full skirt accentuated her figure. As if sensing his gaze, she turned toward him, squared her shoulders and lifted her chin, and called, "Lunch is ready."

Seeing him picking at his food, his charming companion tried to cheer him up, but he just stared into the distance and grew gloomier and a little drunk. When Melinda asked what was troubling him, he broke down and admitted that he was nervous about the letters he found. He fervently hoped that they might provide a clue to the identity of his biological father that had been bothering him for a long time.

Her eyes widened then slowly warmed with sympathy as shock turned to concern. "I'm so sorry for your suffering, she whispered. " Samuel's hand came forward, and their fingers laced together.

"It's what fate decreed for me," he sighed. "Still I want to believe that my mother left behind some clue in those handwritten pages that will help connect me with my father, although I'm almost afraid to find out," he admitted.

"Why Samuel?"

"Listen, I didn't consent to being conceived by a donor's sperm! It's hypocritical of my biological parents, and the medical professionals who aided them, to have assumed that my ancestral roots would not matter to the "products" of their cryobanks." He continued more calmly, "If you think about it, my mother's longing to bond with a child is what brought her to the bank in the first place, so why wouldn't a child yearn for the same close relationship? I guess it's not so much that my mother and the donor were coldhearted as that they didn't consider what their offspring might feel growing up. They brought me into the world in a way that deprived me of my right to know where I came from. The donor was guaranteed anonymity and released from any responsibility. No one involved thought about the consequences of their actions." A fleeting smile softened the harshness of what he had just said. He pressed her hand to his cheek then gently moved his lips to the center of her palm and kissed it.

Having attempted to unburden himself, Samuel returned to his mother's correspondence, nervously smoothing the crease lines with the tip of his thumb as he read each one. He had become so accustomed to sending and receiving information via the Internet as e-mail—sterile artifacts of cyberspace—that her handwritten papers seemed too intimate, a violation of her privacy. Worse yet, many were love letters not only from Greta but also from her other lovers that his mother wouldn't have wanted inspected by others. He read them anyway, rationalizing that when someone dies leaving unanswered questions, we deserve any clues the person might have left behind; perhaps they would provide closure, and in so doing allow the living to find peace.

To his utter disappointment, when he had read the last letter he found that they yielded nothing; nothing to show or tell; no father to adore. They failed to provide answers to his questions: Why had she swallowed too many pills? Why had she refused to yield even one little hint about his real father, the sperm donor? Why had she become so obsessed with the genealogy of the Rosen family and the making of *Tree of Life*? He wished that he was drunk enough to dull the pain that throbbed within. It hurt to think that he might never know the identity of his father. And it hurt to imagine what his mother had become after she and Greta separated. *There are secrets and lies that should be buried with the bones of the dead*, he thought.

"I'm going to burn these," he said, sweeping the letters angrily off the desk, sending them fluttering to the floor like shriveled winter leaves.

Melinda pleaded, "Don't be so angry."

"Why shouldn't I be?" he retorted.

"No matter what mistakes your mother made, she loved you. And you should be proud of her achievements. You should be proud of your Rosen ancestors."

"I suppose so," he said, sounding like a sullen child. "But thinking about them makes me ashamed of how little I've done with my life. And God knows who the unknown branch of my family could be—maybe the dregs of humanity. But what if I never find out?" Only to Melinda could he dare to reveal his deepest fears that he might have too much to live up to—and far too little.

She frowned. "Don't you see, our identity is molded by things we have no control over: our genes, our heritage, our childhood upbringing—even our indoctrination." Groping for the right words, she went on, "Sometimes the actions of those we love most leave scars." Melinda's eyes sought his, but he looked away. "Samuel, let the good and honorable things your mother did sustain you. Don't hold grudges against her. Let them go! "

"Ha, just like that," he said, snapping his fingers.

521

An angry light came into Melinda's eyes. "Don't expect sympathy from me if you just want to wallow in self-centered misery."

They glared at one another for a moment, but his anger was quickly overwhelmed by his desire for her.

Waving his hand as if to dismiss negative thoughts, he said, "Let's go down to the French Quarter for a good meal. We've been at this for hours and it's making us crazy." He pulled her so close that he could see the golden flecks in her dark irises, the delicate texture of her skin, her feathery eyelashes. He stood very still, enjoying the feel of her supple body beneath the fabric of her dress.

When they returned to the house, he was feeling saner; ready to view the video he hadn't seen since his Bar Mitzvah. First, he had to reconnect the old DVD player he found behind the flat-panel TV. He inserted the silver disk, then turned off the lights. "I hope this thing still works," he mumbled. When the title frame appeared on the screen he shouted, "Here we go!" and anchored himself on the sofa next to Melinda, like a man about to ride the rapids.

Every scene in *Tree of Life* is steeped in history, and pulsates with vitality. Like Neta's heroine, the tormented Kahlo, his mother juxtaposes images of pain and cruelty, compassion and beauty. She had generated timeless, ancient scenes with her contemporary video footage, studio shoots, and breath-taking computer-generated simulations. After all these years, he was moved to tears, and unexpectedly, with a new respect for his mother. Perhaps it was the antidote for how alone and alienated he felt, the son of a Jewish lesbian, and a father he would never know.

Wrung out from the emotions of the day, they turned in for the night, but he couldn't rest. Moving images flared like firecrackers in his head: a burly, squint-eyed man on the back of a donkey with the Torah strapped to its flanks; a scribe bent over a table, delicately dipping a pure white goose-feather quill into jet-black ink, inscribing flowing letters onto white parchment; the people of Valinsk hovering in the dark, listening to Yitzhak, the sublime poet-cantor, sing. The inheritors of the Torah collide with history. They are the heroes of Neta's video, still somehow she conveyed their flaws — arrogance, excessive ambition, fanaticism and cynicism.

And Neta honored the wives and daughters, too, revealing their energy and sensuality in the way they walk, the light in their eyes, the smile that plays at the corner of their mouths. He, the ninth inheritor, does not appear until the end, shown in a montage, as a baby, then a child, and finally a preadolescent. Samuel could see his resemblance to his grandfather, Abe, in the serious, intense expression in his gray eyes. And he liked to think there was something of his great-grandfather John in him, too. Like him, he was tan and athletic, but there was something different, something hard to define. Maybe it was the upward slant of his eyes, his high cheekbones, and stubbornly straight, raven-black hair.

Neta's powerful vision jolted loose memories he had suppressed for so long. Maybe he had wanted to forget the miserable confusion at his Bar Mitzvah during the premier of *Tree of Life*. For when the credits start to roll at the end, small flames begin lapping toward the Torah, and before the viewers' horrified eyes it is shrouded in smoke! In the last seconds before the screen goes blank, the fragile tip of a sapling thrusts from the flames, growing deep roots and spreading branches until they touch the sky; the thicker limbs have numbers engraved on them, the younger ones are thin and supple without scars. Children hold hands and dance around its giant trunk in the dappled sunlight.

With a stab of pain Samuel jerked upright in bed, now clearly remembering the outburst following the last sequence. When the lights went up, his mother had turned to see Abe slumped over, his whole body shaking uncontrollably and his eyes scrunched in his face like a crushed tin can. And he had cried out, "My God, did you destroy our Torah?"

Samuel recalled seeing his mother's face go waxen, and her hands fly to her mouth. "Dad, please stop!" He visualized her reaching for Abe with open arms, his grandfather pushing her away, her arms dropping to her sides, the expression on her face hardening—a subtle shift that only a child distrustful of his mother's changing moods would notice.

She had swallowed hard before retorting, "Don't you see? I've restored our family history!"

"But we just saw the Rosen Torah burning!"

He could picture his mother looking around the room at the audience she had assembled there. Then her chin came up. "Before the Torah disappeared . . . while I was still in college, I ordered . . . I mean I commissioned a calligrapher to make a facsimile of passages that did not contain God's name. I recorded only those copies burning."

His grandfather remained mute and bowed, and would not respond.

In desperation she cried, "Dad, I swear that's what you just saw!"

Then he had witnessed his grandfather fall into his mother's arms, allowing himself to be wrapped in her embrace. And the family wept and applauded together in an outburst of sheer relief and genuine admiration. He was the only one who had remained seated, gripping the arms of a chair like a spectator at a car collision. He recalled Greta standing apart, a hand at her throat and her upper lip curled in dismay.

Samuel lay in the darkened room with the past exploding in his head, doubts and questions boring into his skull, grasping for some shred of understanding, some scrap of comfort. Melinda said that the good and honorable things his mother had done would sustain him. He had to believe that. But what would Melinda say if she knew that his mother might have desecrated the family Torah, and then lied about it? Would she judge her a fraud and a coward?

❧42❧

The Past Is Prologue

And by that destiny to perform an act
Whereof what's past is prologue, what to come
In yours and my discharge.

William Shakespeare

It took Samuel days to think rationally about what should be done with the family records, photographs and the entire video footage his mother had garnered so painstakingly. Then he had made a call to the Jewish Museum in Berkeley, and talked at length to Bea Lebow, the present curator, who knew of the Rosens and their venerable scroll that had once been prominently exhibited in the museum.

Flipping his cell phone shut he turned to face Melinda who stood waiting to hear what had transpired.

"Was that the curator? What did she say?"

"Bea Lebow seems genuinely interested in seeing my mother's collection. We've made an appointment to meet the day after tomorrow. I'll book tickets to fly out to San Francisco."

"Good. I'll get Neta's stuff packed for the trip."

When Samuel and Melinda arrived carrying two large boxes, the curator said she would need time to look through the materials and asked that they return after lunch. The two whiled away the time walking the campus redolent with tantalizing echoes of his great-great grandparents Abraham and Martha who had been married there in the Faculty Glade on the Berkeley

Campus. After lunch, they returned, feeling a little apprehensive, to hear Bea's verdict.

The curator said that in her judgment there was no question that Neta's materials were significant contributions to historical research. As for *Tree of Life*, in her opinion it was an artistic tour de force, especially in the way Neta had stitched together, from photos and documents, a marvelous quilt of her family's history once torn apart by time. Her eyes flashed with enthusiasm as she went on to say that it underscores the strength of heritage. She respected Neta's integrity for showing the struggle of succeeding generations to hold on to their traditions in a chaotic, hostile, and changing world; and the courage of the inheritors to do right, despite their all too human flaws. She requested that Samuel donate everything to the museum. When Bea got through with singing her paean, Samuel sat in a daze. Finally, he turned to Melinda.

"Samuel, it would be the proper thing to do," Melinda said smiling broadly.

"Yes, I agree," Samuel replied, smiling back.

The next day, the curator called to thank him for the donation, and to let him know about the Wooden Synagogue Project with plans to create a full-scale replica of the only synagogue that once stood in Valinsk. Samuel was incredulous, the very place of worship that had housed the Rosen Torah would be rebuilt right here in Berkeley! Intrigued but skeptical Samuel agreed to meet with Paul Freer, the project director and architectural historian on the faculty of Berkeley.

Early the following day, Samuel shook hands with Freer in his cluttered office. "Ah, so you are the wonderful fruit of your dear mother's Tree of Life," he smiled. Then turning to Melinda he said, "And, no doubt, you are Mr. Rosen's exquisite lady who has tasted this sweet fruit."

His sly sense of humor appealed to them, and they both grinned.

Freer wore faded blue jeans and worn leather sandals, wire-rimmed glasses rested on his patrician nose. He was soft-spoken, graying at the temples, with shrewd blue-gray eyes.

Clearing the papers and books overflowing onto the chairs so they could be seated, he began by explaining his mission to build the shul both as a structure of worship and as a history museum. Fortunately, with the encouragement of a generous donor, the committee was now ready to launch a fund-raising drive.

Pointing to a yellowed old sketch of the Valinsk shul hanging on the wall, he explained that records recovered after World War II showed that it had been constructed in 1760, and rebuilt after the great fire of 1828. The shul had been the spiritual and social center of Jewish life — until the Jews of Valinsk were rounded up and murdered in 1941. Only a commemorative plaque now remained in the shtetl where it had stood. Once there had been many such shuls in Lithuania, Latvia, the Ukraine, Russia, and Poland; sadly, nearly all of them had been destroyed or abandoned after the war.

For centuries prior to the Holocaust, the Jews had built wooden synagogues from the plentiful timber of surrounding forests. These marvels of indigenous craftsmanship and artistic expression were burned, along with ancient manuscripts and religious and cultural artifacts, in Hitler's campaign to obliterate Jewish life and culture. For decades the world believed that these edifices had been lost.

"Then, a team from Hebrew University in Israel discovered two deteriorating shuls in Lithuania. Freer's voice lifted with exticement. "From those structures, along with old drawings, photographs and plans recovered from museums and archives in Lithuania, experts have created working drawings for the construction of the replica." Freer rummaged through a roll of blueprints, then spread the one of the Valinsk Synagogue on his desk for them to examine. The historian continued talking as Samuel and Melinda pored over it.

"Before building the actual structure, a small-scale model of the Valinsk Shul had to be created. To do this we needed to recruit a team of volunteers. To our relief, a mixed group of students, professionals, and artisans signed up for a series of workshops put together by our multidisciplinary team at Berkeley. We commissioned master carpenters to demonstrate

527

the log hewing and timber joinery used in the original wooden synagogues. With the skills in hand, we built a model to serve as a reference for the real shul that will be built once the funds are in hand."

To keep the experience authentic, Freer went on, he and his team had trekked into a nearby forest to cut down four white pines with axes. They hand-carried the logs from the forest to the work site. This backbreaking chore had given him a renewed respect for the old-world craftsmen. Freer actually grimaced as he recalled the experience.

"Does your back hurt?" Melinda asked, solicitous as ever.

"What?"

"I mean from chopping and hauling the timber."

He chuckled, "I did wrench my back and it still gives me problems. Serves me right for thinking I was tough enough or young enough to do manual labor. Anyway, you should see the finished wooden replica."

They strolled the few blocks to the Architecture and Engineering Building where the replica sat on a table display in the lobby. Samuel and Melinda walked slowly around the four-by-four-foot structure topped by the three-tiered dome, expressing their approval and delight at each new discovery. Two sides showed the exterior details of the synagogue, while two sides were exposed to reveal the interior. Freer described each step of its construction in measured academic tones but they could see the passion and pride shining in his eyes.

The team had painstakingly carved each piece for the multi-layered roofs, galleries, windows, balconies, stairs, and doors. To complete the model they had whittled the interior logs for the walls of the main prayer hall and its adjoining entry room, meeting rooms, and women's gallery. When all the components were finished, the team connected them with lap joints and double dovetails in the original way.

"Wow! It's humbling to think that my family prayed there!" Samuel exclaimed.

"Your model is exquisite!" Melinda said.

Freer beamed his pleasure. At that moment, a small group of chattering high school students visiting with their teacher pushed their way into the lobby and paused to view the model while throwing out random comments.

"Hey, this is cool, man."

"Says here that it's the Wooden Shul of Valinsk, originally built in 1760."

"Shul? What's that?"

"A place where Jews worship, you know like a synagogue," a boy in a baseball cap explained.

Freer turned to the students and quietly challenged them, "What story does it tell? Why should you care about it?" He paused as if hoping for an answer. When no one volunteered he said, gesturing to the replica, "It's not a great monument of stone and bronze, it is a humble wooden structure. Yet it is a lasting tribute to a people and to their story. You see, all the Jews who prayed there and lived in that town — men, women, and children — were murdered and thrown in pits after being forced to dig their own mass grave. Why? Because they were Jews. The Nazis and their collaborators decided to exterminate them, and afterwards stole everything they had owned."

"Like they killed Anne Frank and her family," a girl with lively almond-shaped eyes responded.

"That's right." Gathering momentum, the historian went on, "This shul's message is not only about the past; it is a powerful reminder to all of us about how to behave in the future. It calls on us to never repeat the evils of the years gone by; it urges us to acknowledge that whatever our race, heritage, or religion, we belong to the same human species. Recognizing our common bond of humanness brings us all closer to understanding that we are all capable of wrong doing, of cruelty and violence," he swept his hand in an arc to indicate all of them. "But we are also capable of love and compassion, of hope and joy. The terrible and tragic story should inspire you; should give you strength and courage to fight injustice, to promote tolerance, to strive for peace!"

Freer stood there, his eyes now dark as gathering storm clouds, a quizzical half-smile creasing the comers of his mouth and eyes. Quiet. Silence. Then one student tossed his cap in the air and cheered, "Oh yes!" and the others followed suit, clapping and whistling their approval.

Melinda heard Samuel exhale as if he had been holding his breath. When she turned, she saw a new light in his appealingly unusual eyes; tan and muscular, he didn't look much older than the students. At a loss for words, he stuck out his hand and Freer clasped it firmly. Then Melinda stepped forward and kissed Freer, eliciting more cheering.

Pleased and touched by the outpouring of emotion, Freer invited Samuel and Melinda to join him at a nearby coffee shop. The cafe overlooking Sproul Plaza, the hub of the university's activities and, over the years, had been the staging ground for student protests. They found a corner table and ordered coffee and bagels.

Spreading cheese onto his bagel the historian commented wryly, "For many of the great-great grandsons of the shtetls of Eastern Europe, all that remains of their culture are traditional foods like this, a few funny Yiddish words, and family gatherings for the High Holidays."

Samuel nodded. "I guess it's inevitable."

"But is it a good thing?" Freer asked.

"Of course not," Melinda replied, "Because then you might as well say we should forget our past."

Freer smiled warmly at her.

Samuel wanted to know what needed to be done next. The project director repeated that a fund drive was underway.

Samuel replied, "As much as I admire the craftsmanship that has gone into making the model, and how it can serve as a reminder and an inspiration, still I have to question if it is worth spending so much money to rebuild the synagogue, in California, in the 21st century, when there are so many other pressing needs." He saw Melinda raise her eyebrows, and he added, "Like helping to decrease poverty and all the misery that goes along with it, like hunger, disease, malnutrition, and war."

The architect cleared his throat. "For decades, the descendants of the men, women, and children murdered in the shtetl of Valinsk and throughout Lithuania have dreamed of resurrecting the shul to honor their memory. By restoring it to the world, they will assert the survival of their faith, and the triumph of love and compassion over hatred and brutality." His tone had slipped, once again, from being objective and academic to emotional and personal.

Melinda responded enthusiastically, "I'm deeply moved by the determination of your volunteers and the congregation in Berkeley to spearhead the project. It will certainly honor our ancestors. And, as you already so eloquently explained to the students, it will also be a powerful reminder of what happened to them."

It was past noon, and the throng of students had thinned. Freer pushed back his chair, thanked them for their interest, and then reiterated that they needed additional financial support if it were to ever become a reality. Samuel shook hands with him, and said that he would give it serious consideration.

As Samuel and Melinda boarded the plane back to New Orleans they experienced a shared sense of closure, of accomplishment at finding a safe haven for Neta's documents and for the *Tree of Life*.

They arrived home around midnight. Despite the late hour Samuel could not get to sleep. He lay outside on a wicker chaise, wishing that the sad, disturbing events of the past weeks were just a bad dream, wishing that he could return to the carefree life he had been living. At the same time, a feeling of shame at the selfish, shallow Samuel, hell bent on satisfying his desires instead of caring about others, crept over him. He thought about his mother, and the years she had dedicated to the documentary. Then the words she had whispered at his Bar Mitzvah, drifted back to him. She had prayed for her redemption and for peace. The uneasy thought that she had meant redemption for the disappearance of the Rosen Torah, insinuated itself like a roach scurrying out from under his bed. He told himself that he still didn't know with absolute certainty if she had done anything wrong. But what if she had? He gazed up at the moonless sky where the stars bravely glimmered.

He could dimly distinguish the rooflines of the houses along the street, yet clearly sensed the presence of the silent occupants hidden inside, adrift in the subconscious depths of their most intimate dreams. Decades before, Katrina, the terrible hurricane, had almost washed New Orleans away. He had seen the bleak photographs of shattered houses surrounded by wreckage—it amazed him how courageously, determinedly, people had rebuilt on the ruins. He thought of the how the shtetls of Lithuania had been wiped out, too. Maybe, in his small way, he could do something.

He turned, went inside and wrote out a check for a generous donation to help reconstruct the shul. It felt right that he should help to recreate the synagogue that his ancestors had prayed in, and which had housed their family Torah nine generations ago.

When the first diffuse light of dawn crept over the city, he brewed coffee and woke Melinda. They sipped the aromatic beverage on the veranda, and talked about all that had happened over the last few days. He felt more at peace then he had in a long time. It was time to close up Neta's home; all that remained were a few bills to be paid. Among them he found an unpaid rental bill for an extra large safety deposit box located in the main branch of high security city bank, Bank Hibernia. Remembering the smart card key he had found hidden with his mother's jewelry, he called the bank for verification that Neta had indeed rented a box there.

He spent most of the day filling out the necessary documentation to satisfy bank officials that he was the rightful inheritor of the contents of his mother's saftey deposit box. In addition, they needed to run a biometric scan that would permit them to create his card ID and allow him access to the vault and the box using iris scanners. It was just one more chore to complete, Samuel told himself; but once again he sensed that something unresolved, something secretive, enigmatic and disturbing was waiting to be exposed.

The day before returning to Mexico, Samuel rode the light rail to the downtown bank. Stepping into the lobby, he stated his business to a muscle-bound guard who greeted him politely from behind a desk. "Your elevator is right there, sir," he said, "The iris scanner will ID you to open the door."

As he boarded, he sensed the guard watching him with cold eyes until the doors shut smoothly and the elevator descended beneath the bank. The doors opened to reveal an elderly official wearing a pressed slate-gray suit, waiting to escort him. Samuel followed him down a narrow metal-clad passageway until they came to a steel door. "Here is your private viewing room," the man said, "To open it, I will insert my card first, then please insert yours."

He ushered Samuel into a room with oriental carpets and plush chairs. On a tray in the center of a table there were crystal glasses and a bottle of Perrier water.

"Shall I run through the process of accessing your safe?" the official asked. Indicating a conveyor belt that was outside the room in a curving sweep similar to a baggage claim, he explained, "You insert your card into the electronic device above the conveyor. After the computer verifies your ID, enter your account number. Your safe will be retrieved robotically from the vault for you to inspect. When you have finished, making sure it is closed securely, put it back on the conveyor, and then reinsert your key to reverse the process. If you need further assistance at any time, press the call button on the wall next to the door. Everything is automated to protect your privacy. I will leave you now. Take all the time you need to review the contents of your safe. "

When the safe arrived Samuel carried the heavy container into the room, unlocked it, squeezed his eyes shut for a moment, then peered inside. With unsteady hands he withdrew a battered leather case, placed it on the table and pressed back the old-fashioned locks, and opened it. Beckoning like an archeologist's treasure, he saw a red silk mantle covering what appeared to be a scroll, and wooden posts with names inscribed on them. As he tugged off the cover and opened it, a faint but unmistakable odor emanated from the scorched pages that lay before him. He recoiled as if someone had prodded him with a live wire. His thoughts were reeling.

The scarlet mantle, the ancestral names, and the burnt scroll were undeniable evidence that his mother had done something very wrong. Samuel tugged the mantel back on the scroll, shut the case hastily, and returned the safe with its contents to the conveyor. Mumbling a few words to the official outside the room, he stumbled his way out of the bank.

The bright sunlight blinded him but he kept moving, as if trying to outrun the thoughts that droned like hornets in his brain. His mother had told an outright lie about the fate of the Rosen Torah, worse she had covered up what she had done for all these years. Why?

To tell the truth meant condemning herself in her father's eyes; to be absolved she had to lie. Did his mother's blood turn to ice as her courage ebbed away at the premier showing of *Tree of Life*? Had she sought to atone for what she had done by creating it? Had that expunged her guilt? Horns honked as he rushed blindly across the road, pursued by the phantoms of his past.

ৰ৫43৯৯

Samuel and Melinda Live to Tell the Tale

What is hateful to yourself do not to your fellow man. That is the whole of the Torah and the remainder is but commentary.

Hillel

When Samuel and Melinda returned to Mexico, he was emotionally drained, no longer in the mood for surfing or traveling. She knew that he had been badly shaken, that he needed to come to terms with what he had found. Yet when she approached him, he wouldn't talk about it, dismissing her angrily, declaring that what his mother had hidden in the vault could remain there forever as far as he was concerned. Melinda would have liked to let the matter rest, but she understood that he needed to make peace with himself and his mother. She would have to exercise patience; gently engage him in the contrapuntal rhythm of advance and retreat; dance the tango of love until she won his trust. He longed to confide in her but he was ashamed of his mother's deception, he was violated by her lies, dishonored by her deeds, and resentful of the burden she had placed on him.

Seeing Melinda's concern and Samuel's grief, Joaquin and Alicia Vascon, tried to comfort him by including him in their family circle. The Vascons' ancestors, like many Mexican Jews, had fled to the Nueva Espagna in the 1500s, seeking a haven from the terrors of the Spanish Inquisition. They were descendants of "conversos," Sephardic Jews who practiced their religion in secret after they were forced to convert to Catholicism.

In Mexico City, the focal point of Jewish life centered around the Jewish Community Center, which included a place of worship, a theater and art gallery, a private school that offered religious and secular education, a library, and a health club. Referred to as "The Club," these facilities, inside a walled compound open only to members, minimized chances of inter-marriage that Orthodox families feared.

To divert Samuel from brooding, Melinda roped him into volunteering for The Family Table, sponsored by the community center, to provide groceries for families that could not afford basic necessities. Once a month donations were brought to the center where volunteers, many of them children, sorted and packed food and toiletries. Melinda's spontaneity converted what might have been a chore into fun, by inventing games that got them laughing and the work completed in no time.

Samuel admired the way she fit so graciously into her role as part of a tiny ethnic minority. As he got to know Melinda more intimately, she confided that she often felt inhibited by Orthodox Judaism. As a teenager, she rebelled against the many demands and restrictions made upon her: the fear of letting a scrap of meat touch a smear of butter; the limits imposed on fully engaging in religious rituals as a woman; the ban on dating or even socializing with non-Jewish men. To her frustration, her father refused to discuss religious matters, declaring, "If you believe that I have robbed you of your freedom and put you in bondage by raising you Orthodox, then there is no point in arguing with you."

In her late teens, a Reform rabbi from the United States came to Mexico City to establish a new congregation. Melinda saw a way to become more comfortable with her role as a Jewish woman, and began attending the services of the new rabbi. Daniel supported her, but her father was outraged by what he saw as a defection from the faith of his people and a personal insult to him. His daughter tried to reason with him, pointing out that Reform Jews are as proud as Orthodox Jews of their heritage embodied in the Torah; however, they believed that the Torah was inspired by men rather than given directly to them by God.

536

To Mr. Vascon, that was heresy, and he forbade his daughter to have anything more to do with the Reform movement.

Samuel could picture her trying to stare her father down, wanting to scrub the arrogance from his blazing eyes and the scorn from his curling lips. With the only weapon she had—a sharp tongue—Melinda declared, "If Judaism is not capable of evolution—of reform—it will not survive!"

If not for Daniel's intercession, the relationship between father and daughter surely would have deteriorated to the breaking point. In the end, Mr. Vascon reluctantly conceded to Melinda participating in Reform services as long as she also continued to attend the family's Orthodox synagogue.

When Samuel came into their lives, Daniel was about to launch a bold enterprise to expand the family business with a new venture, PeaceCuisine. His timing could not have been more favorable as Mexico City Salsa was booming in the wake of outbreaks of E. coli and mad cow disease that had scared many into becoming vegetarians.

Daniel had come up with a catchy business slogan for PeaceCuisine, "Promote Peace with Salsa." His deceptively simple idea was that business ventures become catalysts for peace when trading partners must overcome their countries' animosities in order for their businesses to prosper.

Predictably, Joaquin Vascon was skeptical. "How on earth can salsa promote world peace, especially in a region like the crazy Middle East?" Turning his palms upward in a gesture of frustration, he added, "Even though some resemblance of democracy has come to the Palestinians, even though they have finally won a state, and most Palestinians seem to have given up on their ambition to drive the Jews into the sea—despite all these things, there still remain splinter groups of fanatics who reject the whole deal and continue their war of terror."

"Don't you see we can promote peace by supporting Middle Eastern enterprises, especially between Israel and the Palestinian state, by buying and importing their products,"

"Exactly what are you proposing?"

"Look, lasting peace has to be founded on a stable economy. If an Israeli businessman buys his olives from Palestine farmers, to produce a vegetable spread, why would the two want to start a war that would harm them financially? We will help get the joint venture going by providing the know-how and capital to set up the facility in Israel, and to market and distribute the product world-wide." Daniel plowed ahead in the face of his father's doubtful frown. "Dad, thanks to your hard work and business acumen, Mexico City Salsa now has the expertise and resources to help with marketing, investment, and product development. What better way to use our distribution network in the food industry, with over 500 sales outlets in Mexico, Canada, and the U.S., to promote business *and* peace?"

Joaquin's eyes narrowed. Was his son using flattery to sell him a bad idea?

Daniel said, with a grin he said, "To launch PeaceCuisine I've already contacted a reputable businessman in Israel about producing delicious spreads made from ancient varieties, known as "Holy Land" olives, grown in Palestine's West Bank and Gaza for millennia, and the marvelous sun-dried tomatoes grown in Israel."

Joaquin had to smile back. "What can I say? Just slow down."

Daniel had a vision, and didn't give up easily. In time he persuaded Samuel and a handful of other investors to provide the capital needed to launch his grand scheme. Samuel knew that it was a risky venture, but this was a low point in his life. His mother's death following so closely in the wake of his grandfather's accident, and the discovery of the desecrated Torah had rendered him shocked and depressed. He needed to find something he could do that wasn't self-centered. To promote the business in the Middle East, Daniel and Melinda were planning to embark on a goodwill tour. When they invited him to join them, he quickly agreed.

As soon as the threesome arrived in Israel they rented an extremely energy-efficient, fuel-cell minibus, which after years of research and development was being mass-produced in Israel. It was the perfect vehicle for traveling through Israel and the Palestinian state. Everywhere they went they handed out sample products made in the new Israeli test kitchen, and gathered valuable business contacts in the food industry. Samuel felt happier than he had in a long time.

Two weeks into their tour, while driving through the Israeli coastal town of Kfar Saba, about 20 miles north of Tel Aviv, Daniel was gloating about their success and said that one day all the ideologies that divide people would fade away and all the religions would unite as one. Samuel scoffed at him, saying he couldn't see an end to religious animosities in their lifetime, declaring, "In Belfast, Beirut, Bombay, Belgrade, Baghdad, Bethlehem, and Jerusalem, fanatic priests, tribal mullahs, and messianic rabbis will continue to incite suspicion and hatred, provoking others to kill in the name of their god and their creed."

Melinda said she wasn't sure she wanted Judaism to be fused into other religions. She believed that religious tolerance is not the blurring of distinctions, but the conscious decision to live in peace with others, to cease persecuting others even when they believe that *their* religion is the one and only Truth, in the same way you believe yours to be. What's more, she said, she refused to accept that comparative stability in the Middle East in the last few years was just a mirage. Her eyes alight with conviction, she declared it a marvelous reality. That was the last conversation they ever had with Daniel.

On impulse, the threesome decided to go to the Arim shopping center in Kfar Saba. The place was crowded, and they were strolling around, window-shopping, when the world was ripped from under them. Samuel could never erase the terrifying reality of being lifted into the air and thrown to the ground like a clod of dirt. Glass and metal shattered all around him, and over the wounded and dying.

For a moment after the blast the bizarre sensation that there were two Samuels, one lying on the ground, the other crawling through the rubble, paralyzed him. Slowly, painfully, the real Samuel began to inch forward on hands and knees over splinters of glass, pools of fresh blood, and mangled limbs torn from bodies. A strangled moan rose from his throat when he found Melinda, one eye hanging from its socket by a bloody thread, sprawled on top of Daniel who stared up at the sky with eyes as cold as marbles and limbs twisted beneath him like snapped twigs. He kept on crawling until he found an emergency worker to come to their aid.

Daniel was killed outright; Melinda lost an eye; Samuel was physically unscathed. They flew Daniel back to Mexico City to be buried in the family cemetery. After his funeral, Melinda, always a tower of strength, fell apart. It was the first time she needed Samuel more than he needed her.

They talked for hours, even though reliving the trauma of the suicide bombing brought on anxiety attacks. Both were forced to acknowledge the overwhelming power of centuries of hatred. They had traveled abroad to build peace without armies or guns, yet they were punished as brutally as if they were accountable for every Palestinian who had ever been killed. They had killed no one, yet, they were heirs to the bloodstained past that had inflicted its wrath upon them.

Melinda opened up to Samuel. She needed someone to hear her, to hold her close, and to share her grief. She had to believe that God had not abandoned her, but she couldn't face her sense of overwhelming guilt. Why had she survived when Daniel had not? Samuel said that their heritage had come back to haunt them; they had become survivors like the multitudes of Jews before them. As survivors they should find a way to turn evil into good. All this agonizing, this baring of souls, didn't answer the question: what to do with the rest of their lives?

❦44❧

Reclaiming a Legacy

And Isaac brought her into the tent of Sarah his mother; he married Rebecca, she became his wife and he loved her; and thus was Isaac consoled after his mother.

Genesis

Like the walking wounded, Samuel and Melinda kept busy. From the Vascons' condominium in Mexico City, where he had been invited to stay, they made excursions into the countryside to explore the open-air markets for ingredients for City Salsa's test kitchens, and also as representatives of the Science and Agriculture Department, to collect seeds for research. Melinda explained with passion in her voice, "Maintaining the many native varieties that can evolve and adapt to changing conditions improves the chances that no single strain of plant will be wiped out by pests, microbial infestation, unpredictable natural catastrophes such as fire, floods and hurricanes, or even by disasters caused by humans like environmental pollution." The indigenous farmers, who sold their produce at the markets, were vital to the worldwide organization to promote global biodiversity.

At the market, with Melinda's encouragement, Samuel learned how to crush herbs between his fingers, bring the leaves to his nose and put a pinch on his tongue to test their flavor and potency. She encouraged him to sample everything: barbequed meat cooked with *piohito*, a sharp-tasting spice; chicken grilled in peppery *yerba santa* leaves; salsa and tacos seasoned with parsley-

541

like *apapalo*; yellow soups spiced with *pitiona* or Mexican oregano; and an astonishing variety of beans—fried, boiled, and stewed. As a true native, Melinda chatted with the Zapotec farmers and their wives, complimenting them on their cooking; as a result they were often invited to visit a farm and share a family meal. Afterward they left with their pockets and bags bulging with aromatic plants, and native seeds, their heads alive with recipes, and their stomachs full. Satiated and tired, they drove in companionable silence, but as night fell, the specter of death returned to haunt them. To keep their sorrow at bay, they turned the radio up to dance music.

One evening, as the sunset bloomed like a bouquet of red flowers against the darkening sky, Melinda said, choking back tears, "It's a year since we lost Daniel, but the terrible pain is still there."

"Do you remember the advice you gave me after my mother's funeral?" Samuel asked.

Melinda didn't respond.

"You told me that I shouldn't allow the past to destroy me. You said let the good and honorable things my mother accomplished guide and sustain me."

"Since then a lot has happened. I've learned that it's hard to put the past to rest."

"It is. But we have to find the courage to go on."

"How?"

"Let's keep building on Daniel's accomplishments," Samuel said.

"I am trying to. But still I can't forget or forgive the evil done to us."

"You have to confront your demons. That's the only way to get free of them."

Suddenly Melinda was angry, "I'm flattered that you remembered my advice, but I haven't seen you put it into practice."

"What do you mean?" he protested. "I've donated *Tree of Life*, and the Rosen archives to the museum, and I've made a generous donation to the Wooden Synagogue Project."

542

"True. But that's not all you need to do. You've left a lot unsaid, and a lot undone." She turned to him and studied his appealing unusual face, his thick ponytail, and his muscular torso under the faded T-shirt. "You want me to confront my demons, yet you refuse to confront your own. You won't let go of your resentment against not knowing who your father is, and you won't deal with what you found inside the bank vault."

Samuel's body stiffened, and he drummed his fingertips on the steering wheel. She saw that he was retreating from her as he always did when these subjects came up.

When they reached the outskirts of the city, pointing to an overlook ahead, Melinda demanded, "Pull over here. I've got something to show you!" He came to a stop, and she jumped out, ran to the front of the car, and motioned for him to follow with the flashlight in her hand.

In the beam of the headlights, he saw with a stab of compassion the beads of perspiration on her upper lip, the blaze in her gold-flecked right eye, the dead stare of the glass eye in her left socket. As he got out she began to beat her fists on his chest. Her cheeks were flaming, and tears streamed down her face.

"Melinda! Melinda! Please, calm down," he pleaded, grasping her hands. Breathing hard, she wrenched herself free and shone the flashlight on an enormous wild fig tree growing at the bottom of a slope, near a barbed-wire fence.

"It's the place where Daniel loved to picnic on our way to the markets," she said.

As Melinda slid down the hill, he scrambled after her. At the tree she took the flashlight and played the beam over its venerable trunk, revealing deep scars, one at the foot of the tree, the other at chest height. Where the fig tree had grown into the fence, its living tissue had fused, like molten glass, over the barbed wire. Tenderly placing her right foot against the lower scar and her right hand over the upper scar, Melinda whispered. "See how this tree has healed itself. How it has surmounted the obstacle blocking its growth, how its roots are strong and deep enabling it to stand through raging storms."

Samuel leaned forward and ran his hands over the scar where the damaged bark had mended. Caught in the undertow of her insinuations but unable to pull away, he listened to her voice coming out of the darkness.

"You can heal yourself if you will just *talk* about what happened. You can't brood over it forever, Samuel."

In the play of the flashlight she caught his eyelids twitching and his jaw clenching with tension. Then he pulled her down beside him under the tree. They sat there listening to the wind raking through the leaves, the stealthy sounds of nocturnal animals rustling in the weeds, the electric shrill of cicadas. He bent to brush his lips over her disfigured eyelid and inhale her heady, melancholy fragrance of jasmine, tears and sweat. When he broke the silence, his voice was so low that she had to strain forward to hear what he had to say. "Ms. Vascon, you may have already guessed what I saw in the vault?"

Melinda caressed his cheek with the tips of her fingers. "I don't want to guess anymore. I'm tired of having your secret occupying my dreams."

He took both her hands in his, and felt a nervous surge in the pit of his stomach. "The Rosen Torah is in that vault."

"God, I knew it! Even though it was supposed to have been stolen years ago. Oh, how wonderful!" Melinda breathed. Then a frown appeared between her eyes. "But why did your mother *hide* it for so long?"

"It was damaged in a fire." His voice sounded rough and unsteady.

"Oh, I'm so sorry! How did it happen?"

"I'm not sure."

There was a charged silence before she replied, "However it happened, yours is not the only Torah that has been damaged. Perhaps it can be repaired. Is there something you are not telling me?"

He shook his head. But there was one secret he just couldn't bring himself to tell her—yet. His mother had lied; there could be no doubt about it now. She had somehow set the Rosen Torah on fire. To cover up what she had done, she hid it, then

544

years later swore, in front of the whole family, that she had burned only a copy of it. *A lie breeds other lies, and secrets breed lies, too*, he thought miserably.

"We should consult our family rabbi." Melinda said quietly. "He can tell us if your Torah can be repaired; if not, he'll advise us on the proper way to proceed."

They rose and at that moment the moon floated out from behind the clouds and bathed Melinda in its blue light. She stood in her characteristic pose; feet planted apart, chin thrust forward, and fists on her hips.

Samuel twisted his mouth into a smile, and said, "So, what are we waiting for? Let's go see the rabbi."

Disarmed, she laughed. "Okay, Señor, I'll call him tomorrow."

As they drove into the city to the Vascon's condominium, lightning slithered across the night sky. The wind picked up, driving the good fresh smell of approaching rain into their faces. Then, the feelings trapped inside Samuel for so long broke loose. He told Melinda how he had finally pieced together the events leading to his mother's desecration of the Torah. He acknowledged his indignation and his shame for what she had done, and his rage at her concealing the deed from him for all these years. He admitted his resentment at her leaving him to clean up the mess. She must have known that he couldn't leave the disgraceful family secret hidden forever.

She sat silently absorbing Samuel's outburst. "You shouldn't punish yourself for what your mother did. Doesn't the Torah say that an individual should be responsible for his own wrongdoing, not for that of someone else?"

"I'm not a scholar," he said gruffly, and they retired to their separate rooms with a brief kiss.

That night at the condo, Melinda and Samuel dreamed similar, interconnected dreams. He dreamed they were in an open-air market swarming with people . . .

The two of them are making tortillas: shaping the dough into little balls, rolling it, slapping it between their palms, flattening it into thin yellow moons. The rolling pin sings, *I love you, I love you.* They stand side by side, their hips barely touching, swaying to the ancient rhythm of tortilla making, happy together, baking them on a hot clay griddle balanced on three stones above a wood fire. It begins to rain out of a sunlit sky. Glowing droplets stream down to earth, with a flourish, he plucks them out of the air and turns them to amber. When his hands are filled with the beads, he tosses them onto the smoking grill.

Melinda yells, "Ay, Caramba!" and tries to scoop them from the griddle; before she can, they begin popping like kernels of corn, giving off a wonderful, sweet smell, releasing ancient insects trapped inside.

Reborn, they spiral upward, while he crows, "See the miracle I have performed!"

He woke from the dream with a start, warm tears on his cheeks, yet aware of the joy and anticipation growing inside him. Unlatching the door, he stepped out onto the shadowy moonlit balcony, stood listening to the primordial song of rain falling on rooftops and trees, and then tapped on Melinda's door.

Melinda awoke to find herself twisted in the sheets, teetering on the edge of her bed. She heard a gentle tapping on the door of the shared balcony, and a voice whispering, "Are you awake?"

Wrapping the hand-woven shawl her grandmother had bequeathed her around her shoulders, she went out onto the balcony, still haunted by her dream. Hastily, before it withered away, she tried to put the images into words for Daniel:

It is early morning. There is dew on the ground. We are in the market making tortillas . . . There's the smell of wet, ground corn, and beads of grease sizzling under the golden tortillas. Oh, oh, what are these things? Manna in the desert? No, no! They're tiny grubs, pure white and inky black, swarming over the tortillas. Sensing my presence they lift their heads, survey me with huge compound eyes. I demand, *Speak worms!*

"The Torah is written, '*eish shahor al gabei eish lavan,*'" black fire on white fire, they chant. Half in fear and half in anger I frantically brush them from the tortillas. Searing pain burns through me. I moan, wanting to sleep forever; instead the flames transform into Hebrew letters that circle rhythmically around me, and the urge to dance overcomes the pain. I cry out, "Samuel, let's dance with them!"

Her dream, symbolizing rebirth and renewal, so strangely parallel to Samuel's, wove a powerful connection between the two of them. They huddled close, two survivors adrift on a raft of dreams, feeling something precious and sweet ebbing away with the first rays of the sun splintering through the Poinciana tree's blood-red blossoms. In the soft, shifting light, the dewdrops clinging to Melinda's hair glowed like an amber halo around her face. How they yearned to remain suspended in this peace forever! Too soon it would be time to return to the harsh demands of reality.

Two days later, Rabbi Lerner ushered the two survivors into his study, offered them mugs of frothy mocha, and gestured for them to be seated on comfortable, high-backed chairs. Samuel took in the posters of Jerusalem and Masada, the desk cluttered with papers and a map of the State of Israel. Breathing deeply he inhaled the earthy smells of the Mexico he had come to love: the rich aroma of freshly brewed coffee with a dash of chocolate and cinnamon, and the musky fragrance of tropical flowers. He half-listened as the rabbi and Melinda exchanged news of their respective families, until she remarked, "It's only months since Daniel left us, Rabbi."

"Thank God you and Samuel have survived to carry on his good work. Remember, do not devote your lives to mourning the dead, put your efforts toward the betterment of the world in this life."

Struggling to regain her composure, Melinda nodded then went on, "Rabbi Lerner, as I mentioned to you, we came to inquire about how to handle a damaged Torah."

Before the meeting, Samuel had requested that she not talk about the Rosen Torah specifically. When Melinda questioned his need for secrecy, he said that he did not want the rabbi's opinion to be clouded by his personal pain. She was skeptical, but to appease him, she agreed to keep it out of the discussion. As a result, the rabbi hoped that perhaps Samuel

547

Rosen or the Vascons might be planning to donate a Holocaust Torah to his synagogue in honor of Daniel.

"Do you possess a Torah, or are you planning to acquire one?" Lerner now inquired. The exchange of anxious glances between the couple was not lost on him.

"We came for advice, not to discuss anything personal," Samuel replied somewhat brusquely.

Seeing that he had touched on a delicate subject, the rabbi began talking in generalities. "You understand, of course, that a Torah scroll is not simply a mass produced book like a printed Bible. It is a sacred handwritten document." He paused, his clever black eyes taking in Melinda's hands clasped tightly around the mug to steady their tremor.

Under his penetrating gaze Samuel shifted in his seat and said, as calmly as he could, "Please go on," omitting to tell that prior to this meeting he had browsed the Internet using key words, such as "damaged torahs," to search for preparatory information—in this technological age information was easy and cheap to come by; wisdom hard to find.

The rabbi continued, "During World War II, the Nazis confiscated thousands of Jewish artifacts, including Torahs, and shipped them to a collection center in Prague. Also, in a desperate attempt to save their scrolls, Jews all over Europe hid them in caves and attics—wherever possible. By the end of World War II, entire families had been wiped out; but many scrolls were found and later transported to London; those from Prague also went to London." Melinda's good eye was fixed on the rabbi's face.

The rabbi kept talking, "The entire third floor of the Reform Westminster Synagogue in London has been set aside for the Holocaust Project that undertakes the process of sorting, cataloging, and repairing scrolls. Some Holocaust Torahs were mildewed. Some were charred by fire. Some were stained with blood. Others had handwritten notes hidden inside them with desperate pleas from the last Jew to touch them. Knowing that they themselves could perish, they hoped their final words would survive them and bear testimony to the world."

Samuel looked down at his hands and frowned. The rabbi was feeding them heartbreaking tales, when all he wanted was a way out of his own dilemma.

"To date, over a thousand of them are on permanent loan to synagogues around the world."

"What if the Torah is not a Holocaust Torah, but an ancient family Torah that has been badly damaged, how should one proceed then?" Samuel persisted.

"Then you should commission a sofer to examine the scroll to see if it can be repaired." The rabbi was becoming more curious, but still exercising patience. "I can recommend an excellent one, if you wish."

"Thank you." Samuel said, feeling the first glimmer of hope flickering inside him. If the Torah could be restored, there could be atonement—not for him, he had done no wrong—but for his mother.

"What if the damaged Torah cannot be repaired adequately for use in a synagogue?" Samuel had to know.

Inclining his head and giving a slight smile, he said, "Whatever is on your mind, you should know that it is an ancient and honored tradition to commission a new Torah scroll in memory of a dear one. The chanting from the Torah confers great blessings on the departed soul in whose honor it has been written."

"But, still what do you do with the permanently damaged one?" Samuel insisted.

"It must not be discarded, no matter how severe the damage, because it is the most sacred object for Jews." Pointing his index finger and waving it for emphasis, he admonished, "In Judaism, a Torah is like a human being. It can never be thrown away or cremated."

"In that case, what should be done with it?" Melinda asked nervously. She wondered if the rabbi had guessed that they were talking about a particular Torah.

"Every unusable Hebrew text that contains biblical references or references to God must be set aside or archived to await the natural process of disintegration. Since ancient times, they have been removed to caves or tombs, to *genizas,* or secret depositories like the one in the Ben Ezra Synagogue in Old Cairo, Egypt. It is even possible that the Dead Sea Scrolls were put aside in this manner. Communities have also buried the unwanted texts in the ground." He swirled the remains of his mocha in the mug before taking a sip. "So you see, Torahs must be reverently buried, as are prayer books, prayer shawls, and other holy objects."

"Surely there is another way?" Although Melinda meant to sound calm there was a pleading tone to her voice.

"Yes, there is. Damaged Torahs are often used for commemorative displays."

She touched Samuel's arm, "Did you hear that?"

"Are these Torahs on display in museums or synagogues?" he asked.

"I have seen them displayed in both places."

The rabbi absorbed the look that passed between the couple.

"I see. But what happened to those who perpetrated the despicable crime against the Torahs? What happens if. . . " Samuel's voice drifted, letting the question trail away. He was thinking of the Nazis who had fled Germany, and had never been punished for their crimes. And he thought of his own mother, and rushed on, "Rabbi, what happens if someone damages a Torah by accident?"

"If the Torah scroll is accidentally dropped, the entire congregation present at the time fasts on a chosen day and gives to charity."

It wasn't the response Samuel was seeking. "I mean how should the person who caused the accident make reparation for what he or she has done?"

"Exactly what sort of accident are you talking about?" He waited for the troubled young man to explain himself, but he just sat there frowning. With a sigh the rabbi went on, "I can see that you are both upset. Please remember that the fate of the Holocaust Torahs, terrible as it is, is a story of hope and of survival against all odds."

550

"Thank you," Melinda said quietly. "We will carry that in our hearts."

"I'm afraid I might not have provided the answers you were hoping for, but I am always available if you need me."

"Thank you," Samuel echoed, getting up to shake his hand.

Glancing at the clock on the wall, Melinda exclaimed, "Ay! It's almost noon. We need to let you get on with your work."

As they were leaving, the rabbi made one last attempt to learn their secret. "My dear mother used to say, the truth hurts. And while the truth can indeed be painful, one should never be deceitful."

Samuel could not hide his guilty start, but then he saw from the rabbi's expression that he had intended no malice. "Don't worry, we will do the right thing."

They emerged from the gloom of the study into the heat and glare of the midday sun, where everything quivered as in a mirage. Samuel kissed Melinda lightly on the cheek, "Thanks. I'm really sorry to put you through so much on account of my family," he said.

"There's no need to apologize. Getting involved with your family and its history has released something inside of me I didn't know was there. I don't fully understand it yet, but I feel there's a new and wonderful life ahead of me. I felt it in my dream."

Taking his arm, Melinda steered him across the street to the tortilleria, where they joined the line waiting to buy tortillas hot off the griddle. Melinda pulled the customary dishtowel from her shopping bag and wrapped the steaming flat breads in it. Then they hurried home before they cooled.

The Vascon's household at Esperanza had its particular rhythms centered on shared meals, reinforcing the bonds of family; the palpable love between them eased Samuel's distress. Every afternoon they gathered in the dining room for *comida*. Hot tortillas in napkin-lined baskets were circulated amid noisy chatter. Then came the soup, brimming with dumplings, vegetables, and slices of boiled egg. Next came roasted chicken with vegetables and refried beans. Baked caramel custard and tropical fruit ended the repast. Afterwards the Vascons retired to their rooms, and closed the shutters against the sun for their long siesta. While the servants cleared the table, Melinda and Samuel stepped out in to the courtyard for some privacy.

They seated themselves in the shade of the arbor overhung with blazing Poinciana trees and magenta bougainvillea, scarlet hibiscus blooming in clay pots, and yellow allamanda vines tumbling over the garden walls.

"Comida, as always, was fantastic!" Samuel said, rubbing his stomach and wishing that he could remain forever in this peaceful garden with lovely Melinda sitting so close he could feel her warmth.

"It used to be filled with laughter," Melinda sighed. "Losing Daniel has subdued us."

He leaned in to take her in his arms, but he felt her tense.

"We need to talk," she said, dropping her chin into her hands and her elbows on her knees, and fixing him with a melancholy gaze.

"I'd rather take a little siesta. Like him." He pointed to the gardener with two dogs spread-eagled at his heels, dozing in the shade.

"Not now," she said, shaking her head. "We need to discuss what the rabbi told us."

"He is a wise man and a scholar. I'm just a humble beach bum. Why would I presume to question him?"

"Samuel, did the rabbi help you to make a decision?"

"Okay. First, my mother did not throw the Torah out. She put it in a safe place. And that was the right thing to do."

Melinda nodded yes.

"I know that doesn't exonerate her completely."

"But what's still eating you?"

"Listen, I just couldn't talk about my mother's misdeed . . . I mean, I couldn't admit she was *lying*. I felt I would be betraying her," he faltered.

"Her *lying?*" Melinda questioned.

He needed to disclose what had happened at his Bar Mitzvah in order for her to understand the magnitude of Neta's deception. Taking a deep breath, he recounted how his mother had denied that the last sequence of *Tree of Life* actually showed the Rosen Torah on fire. That she had covered up what she had done by lying to Abe and the entire family that it was only a facsimile they saw burning.

Melinda took his hand in hers and pressed it to her heart. "Now, finally, I understand why you have been so angry."

"It's more than that. I always admired my mother for her outspoken candor, and her courage. When I found out that she didn't have the integrity or guts to tell the truth, I felt cheated."

"Maybe she wasn't just trying to protect herself, maybe she was very afraid that the truth would cause unnecessary pain to her father, and maybe she was frightened that it would damage the precious relationship between you and your grandfather."

He nodded. "Thank you for understanding. Still, I will never truly know exactly how she came to set the Torah on fire, or why she kept that lie going. But I believe that *Tree of Life* was her way of atoning for what she had done."

"It touches my heart that you are now trying to put your mother's actions in the best light!"

"The way I see it, she was a tormented soul. She knew her actions hurt others, and that's why she was driven to do something about it. She gave twelve years of her life to creating *Tree of Life*. It was her mission, the purpose of her life. "

"I feel compassion for her suffering."

They sat watching a line of ants marching over the stones, a butterfly flitting through the flowers, the shifting shadows in the fountain, and the gardener's dogs' hind legs twitching in their dreams.

Suddenly Samuel felt happy. He jumped up and pulled her into his arms, "You're too serious, my little rabbi," He said twirling her around, and breaking into a song he had heard on the radio over and over again.

I was traveling down Mexico Way
It was a Jewish holiday
I stepped into a temple to pray
What I saw took my breath away.
There on the bima was a vision so pure
My heart tilted like a mezuzah on a door
Then an old man sitting next to me
Tugged at my tallis, and he said to me:
Don't fall in love with a Mexican rabbi
She'll break your heart in two,
Like a matzo tortilla crushed under a shoe.

"Be quiet, you'll wake everyone from their siesta!" Melinda said, giggling.

"I knew from the moment I saw you, that there was a love story in the air," he declared, bending over to kiss her.

"Yes, it was *bashert*, it was our destiny to come together!" Then on a more somber note she said, "And yet, we chose to go to the Middle East of our own free will and as a result Daniel was killed. Was that fate, too?"

She plucked a big, green, oval-shaped bug off her shoe, and holding it lightly between her thumb and forefinger, brought it to his nose to smell the faint sweetish odor it had released. "This poor insect just happened to be crawling over my foot. Should I kill it or release it?"

"Your choice."

Melinda opened her fingers, freeing the insect onto a leaf then watched it hesitate before flying off. "What comforts me is that the Rosen Torah has survived, even though it was damaged. I know that it's hard to make sense of all that has happened. But you and I are survivors too. And we must choose a way to do the right thing, to make good come out of this."

Suddenly he was too weary to wrestle with the future so soon after grappling with the past. The temperature in the garden had risen; the heat and the cloying odor of tropical flora added to his lethargy.

His Melinda wasn't about to let things rest. "Have you heard about Yakov Bunka, the last Jew of Plunge, Lithuania? When the Nazis came, Bunka fled to Siberia, where he found work on a collective farm before joining the Russian army. Of the seventy-two Plunge Jews who did this, forty-two died in combat, including Bunka's father and brother. Bunka took a bullet in his neck, but he survived! Since then he has dedicated his life to fulfilling a promise he made to himself in 1941: to immortalize the memory of the lost Jews of Plunge. Bunka has carved dozens of memorial sculptures, and, so far, he has erected ten of them on the sites where mass murders took place." She paused to lift her long hair and twist it into a knot at the nape of her neck.

With a rush of excitement, Samuel exclaimed, "Bunka's story has given me an inspiration. The central theme of the exhibit we are planning for the Berkeley Jewish Museum should be woven around the meaning of survival and the purpose of our existence as survivors."

"That's great!"

"And I hope that we can restore the Rosen Torah, and then loan it for use in the replica of the Valinsk Synagogue — when it is finally built. If it cannot be properly repaired then we can display it there as a memorial."

Melinda nodded enthusiastically.

"And to ensure our legacy's future, I will stipulate that it must remain in custody of the Rosen family. And I want it to be dedicated to my family, to my mother, and to Daniel, to commemorate and to honor them."

"Perfect!" Clasping her hands over her heart, Melinda said, "And I want to step up our efforts to ensure that PeaceCuisine is a lasting legacy for Daniel," Melinda's voice was choked with emotion.

"I will help you," he said, kissing her tenderly. The burden of feeling like a hapless victim that had masked her radiance was, at last, replaced by happy anticipation of things to come.

❦45❧

Embracing Life

Imagine all the people living life in peace. You may say I'm a dreamer, but I'm not the only one. I hope someday you'll join us, and the world will live as one.

"Imagine" by John Lennon

Samuel and Melinda huddled in the secluded courtyard discussing profound moral questions, and whispering what was in their hearts. He confessed that he was beginning to make peace with his mother for choosing to give birth to him from an unknown donor.

Then Melinda made an astonishing revelation. Over the last few months she had been thinking about becoming a rabbi herself. She confided that at first the thought frightened her because she had once railed against the confines imposed on an Orthodox woman. Gradually, however, she had come to understand that just as there are pious guardians of the past, there are pious agents of change who introduce new practices that will preserve Judaism as a living, evolving tradition, and attract young people to the faith who might otherwise have turned away. Once she overcame her doubt, she realized that the rabbinate was a perfect fit for her—indeed, it was her calling in life. She was drawn to the study of the Torah, felt true compassion for those in need, and had a practical bent for finding solutions to their problems.

Samuel was shocked and more than a little bewildered by her sudden disclosure. While he could not visualize life without this beautiful, passionate woman, he feared that he could not live up to what would be expected of him as the spouse of a rabbi. Melinda reassured him that she loved him for who he was, and that she wanted him to be her partner in life.

She would need to enroll in a rabbinical seminary for four to five years, and had decided on the Hebrew Union College - Jewish Institute of Religion, either in New York or Los Angeles, leading to ordination as a Reform Rabbi. She had even considered going to Germany, the birthplace of Reform Judaism, to study at the Abraham Geiger College at the University of Potsdam.

Wherever Melinda went, Samuel made a vow to go with her and to support her every step of the way. Although they had chosen divergent paths they both pledged themselves to doing what they could to bring harmony to the world.

Samuel and Melinda flew back to New Orleans from Mexico City to remove the damaged Rosen Torah from the vault where it had been hidden for so long. He had arranged to bring the scroll to Rabbi Steven Jaffee, a scribe in Los Angeles, though not without misgivings. He knew in advance that repairing, or koshering a Torah scroll that has been rendered ritually unusable is expensive and time-consuming, and that his might be beyond repair, but he was determined to do it.

He was surprised that a man, who writes with a feather and spends his time thinking about things that seem to have no connection with modern life, wore a suit like any other businessman. They shook hands and he asked Samuel to place the Torah on the table under a skylight. To his enormous relief the scribe did not cross-examine him about how the Torah had been set on fire.

Drawing on white gloves, he explained, "This is to prevent the oils on my hands from getting onto the parchment." Then he undressed the scroll, removing the red mantel and the cord that bound it.

Pointing to the sturdy olivewood posts Samuel pointed out, "You will notice that each inheritor has inscribed his signature on these."

The sofer read aloud the name of the patriarch, Shmuel Rosen, and of all the previous inheritors: "Yitzhak, Hershel, Yakov, Mendel, Abraham, John, Abe." Then carefully unrolling the scroll he inspected it section by section, probing the damaged parts gently with sensitive fingers. When he touched the burnt portions Samuel heard him inhale sharply. Melinda reached over and squeezed Samuel's arm to steady him.

After he had scrutinized the entire scroll, the scribe turned to them and pronounced, "I can restore the Torah, despite the severe damage. I can remove the burnt parchment, and insert new pages with the appropriate text."

"So, when you have completed the work, can we use the Rosen Torah for services?"

The rabbi wrinkled his nose. "No. In my opinion even if my repairs can make it kosher, it's too fragile to take the risk of damaging the original pages."

Samuel felt sick with disappointment. He thought of his mother, his grandfather, and Daniel, and of the desecrated Torah, and once again, he had to accept that life was precarious—a random mix of joy and grief, hope and despair.

"How long will it take to do the repairs?" he asked.

"I can't be exact," the scribe said, rubbing his hand over the back of his neck. "You see, I get strength and energy by working in the ancient way. I mix my own ink, make my own quills from turkey or goose feathers, and prepare the parchment made from a calf killed for food."

"That's wonderful," Melinda said.

"A sefer Torah usually contains 248 columns, and one rectangle of parchment yields space for three or four columns. Thus a Torah may require about 80 skins in all. It can take a full day just to do one column or about one third of a page." He frowned, "I don't like to put an exact time on my work."

"Please, take all the time you need." Samuel said.

"Now, rabbi, to continue the tradition of the inheritors I would like to inscribe my mother's name, and my name on the wooden rollers of our legacy."

The rabbi selected a fine engraving pen from the armamentarium on his desk and handed it to Samuel. Brandishing the pen, Samuel proclaimed, "It is now my honor to inscribe our names." With careful precision he wrote his mother's name, Neta Rosen, honoring her as the eighth inheritor. Then he etched his name beneath it, validating himself as the ninth inheritor. As he did so, he comforted himself with the thought that although the Rosen Torah had not survived wholly intact, its teachings would endure. He had finally come to understand and to accept that the past should not imprison the mind with old grudges, it should become a force to inspire future generations; that Judaism is based on *tikkun olam,* to repair the world. He had, at last, set in motion what his mother should have done many years ago.

As he embraced Melinda, he experienced a catharsis, a marvelous feeling of freedom, of being released, like a trapped animal, from long-repressed, painful emotions.

In working with PeaceCuisine, Samuel discovered that, like his grandfather Abe, he had a flair for business. The Vascons recognized this, and asked that he take over the management of Mexico City Salsa when Joaquin retired, but that, no doubt, would be several years away as Joaquin showed no inclination to slow down. Best of all, there were plans for marrying Melinda, in Mexico City, in six months.

Samuel had other hopes as well; he planned to restore the Shady Lady as a working experimental farm. He had revisited the old homestead, shortly after his grandfather, Abe, died, and it pained him to see it falling into decay. Even the towering blue spruce his great-grandfather, John, planted had been reduced to a blackened stump by a bolt of lightning. He wanted Melinda to feel a strong connection to his family and to the homestead the Rosens had loved. The old place would be a gathering spot for the many children the hoped to have—God willing—and for generations of Rosens to come.

It grieved him that the descendants of their patriarch would no longer be accorded the honor of reading from their Torah. After surviving a long and turbulent history, it would finally be laid to rest in the Wooden Synagogue when the structure was completed—a marvelous facsimile of the one that had been the first home of the Rosen Torah. Shmuel Rosen had wished for his legacy to be a living inheritance for his progeny, not exhibited as a memorial. Still, when the Rosen Torah is displayed for all to see, he will have fulfilled his obligation to keep its teachings alive for the family and to rouse new generations. With this realization he was suddenly filled with hope, knowing that their saga flowed on, and that the Torah stood as a beacon against the treacherous currents of time.

About The Author

Claire Klein Datnow was born and raised in Johannesburg, South Africa. Her family originated from Linkuva, Lithuania. In 1965, she immigrated with her husband Dr. Boris Datnow, to the United States. Her first published work appeared in the Johannesburg daily newspaper, promoting the cause of game preservation. Claire has received numerous scholarships and grants including a Beeson Samford University Writing Project fellowship, and a Fulbright Memorial Fund Teacher Scholarship to travel to Japan. She has published numerous works of fiction and nonfiction. She taught creative writing to gifted and talented students. The impact of historical events on her life and the lives of her family inspired her deep interest in history and led to a M.A. in Public History. She and her family live in Birmingham, Alabama, in the foothills of the Appalachian Mountains. For more information, visit www.mediamint.net.